PRAISE FOR ROBERT LUDLUM'S
BLOCKBUSTER THRILLER
THE BOURNE SUPREMACY

"Prime Ludlum. . . . No quiche and white wine here, just USDA Grade A prime—blood rare. . . . When it comes to robust, two-fisted novels of grandiose dimensions, relentless action and grinding violence, Mr. Ludlum is the undisputed champ. . . . *The Bourne Supremacy* is high–voltage entertainment and, quite honestly, impossible to put down."

—*The Washington Times Magazine*

"Another certain bestseller."

—*Booklist*

"Ludlum's latest has a bestseller quality that many imitate and few master. . . . Legions of Ludlum's fans will send it soaring up the bestseller list."

—*Library Journal*

"A fast-paced, action-crammed thriller."

—*Philadelphia Daily News*

"Welcome back, Robert Ludlum. And welcome back, Jason Bourne. . . . The wait by Ludlum fans was worthwhile. . . . The action, in true Ludlum style, is fast, exciting and, at times, a bit bloody. . . . He doesn't disappoint his readers in *The Bourne Supremacy*."

—*The Pittsburgh Press*

Inside the Kowloon cabaret, head boys and waiters were mollifying the patrons, patting shoulders and clearing away the debris. Suddenly, the manager's eyes were drawn to a clump of white fabric on the floor across the room. White cloth, pure white—the priest's? The *door!* The *laoban!* The *conference!* The obese manager raced to the discarded caftan. Tiny specks and thin streaks of shiny blood soiled the cloth.

"*Go hai matyeh?*" The question was asked by the manager's brother.

"*Come!*" ordered the manager, heading for the door.

"The police! objected the brother. "One of us should speak to them."

"It may be that we can do *nothing* but give them our heads! *Quickly!*"

Inside the dimly lit corridor the proof was there. The guard lay in a river of his own blood. Within the conference room itself, the proof was complete. Five bloodied corpses.

The manager approached a body and stared at the face. "We are dead," he whispered. "Kowloon is dead, Hong Kong is dead. All is dead."

"*What?*"

"This man is the Vice-Premier of the People's Republic, successor to the Chairman himself."

"Here! *Look!*" The manager's brother lunged toward the body of the dead *laoban*. Alongside the bleeding corpse was a black bandanna. It was lying flat, the fabric discolored by blotches of red. The brother picked it up and gasped at the writing in the circle of blood underneath: JASON BOURNE.

The manager sprang across the floor. "Great Christian Jesus!" he uttered, his whole body trembling. "He's come back. The assassin has come back to Asia! *Jason Bourne!* He's come *back!*"

THE BOURNE SUPREMACY

Robert Ludlum

BANTAM BOOKS
NEW YORK • TORONTO • LONDON • SYDNEY • AUCKLAND

THE BOURNE SUPREMACY
A Bantam Book / published by arrangement with the author

Bantam edition / March 1987

Grateful acknowledgment is made to Edwin H. Morris & Company for permission to
reprint an excerpt from "Mister Sandman," by Pat Ballard. Copyright 1954 by
Edwin H. Morris & Company, a Division of MPL Communications, Inc. © Renewed
1982 by Edwin H. Morris & Company, a Division of MPL Communications, Inc.
International Copyright secured. All rights reserved. Used by permission.

ISBN 0-553-26322-6

Published simultaneously in the United States and Canada

Bantam Books are published by Bantam Books, a division of Bantam Doubleday Dell
Publishing Group, Inc. Its trademark, consisting of the words "Bantam Books" and the
portrayal of a rooster, is Registered in U.S. Patent and Trademark Office and in other
countries. Marca Registrada. Bantam Books, 666 Fifth Avenue, New York, New York
10103.

PRINTED IN THE UNITED STATES OF AMERICA

RAD   23   22   21   20   19   18   17

For Shannon Paige Ludlum

Welcome, my dear

Have a great life

1

Kowloon. The teeming final extension of China that is no part of the north except in spirit—but the spirit runs deep and descends into the caverns of men's souls without regard for the harsh, irrelevant practicalities of political borders. The land and the water are one, and it is the will of the spirit that determines how man will use the land and the water—again without regard for such abstractions as useless freedom or escapable confinement. The concern is only with empty stomachs, with women's stomachs, children's stomachs. Survival. There is nothing else. All the rest is dung to be spread over the infertile fields.

It was sundown, and both in Kowloon and across Victoria Harbor on the island of Hong Kong an unseen blanket was gradually being lowered over the territory's daylight chaos. The screeching *Aiyas!* of the street merchants were muted with the shadows, and quiet negotiations in the upper regions of the cold, majestic structures of glass and steel that marked the colony's skyline were ending with nods and shrugs and brief smiles of silent accommodation. Night was coming, proclaimed by a blinding orange sun piercing an immense, jagged, fragmented wall of clouds in the west—sharply defined shafts of uncompromising energy about to plunge over the horizon, unwilling to let this part of the world forget the light.

Soon darkness would spread across the sky, but not below. Below, the blazing lights of human invention would garishly illuminate the earth—this part of the earth where the land and the water are anxious avenues of access and conflict. And with the never-ending, everstrident nocturnal carnival, other games would begin, games the human race should have abandoned with the first light of Creation. But there was no human life then

1

—so who recorded it? Who knew? Who cared? Death was not a commodity.

A small motorboat, its powerful engine belying its shabby exterior, sped through the Lamma Channel, heading around the coastline toward the harbor. To a disinterested observer it was merely one more *xiao wanju,* a legacy to a first son from a once unworthy fisherman who had struck minor riches—a crazy night of mah-jongg, hashish from the Triangle, smuggled jewels out of Macao—who cared how? The son could cast his nets or run his merchandise more efficiently by using a fast pro-peller rather than the slow sail of a junk or the sluggish engine of a sampan. Even the Chinese border guards and the marine patrols on and off the shores of the Shenzen Wan did not fire on such insignificant transgressors; they were unimportant, and who knew what families beyond the New Territories on the Mainland might benefit? It could be one of their own. The sweet herbs from the hills still brought full stomachs—perhaps filling one of their own. Who cared? Let them come. Let them go.

The small craft with its Bimini canvas enveloping both sides of the forward cockpit cut its speed and cautiously zigzagged through the scattered flotilla of junks and sampans returning to their crowded berths in Aberdeen. One after another the boat people shrieked angry curses at the intruder, at its impudent engine and its more impudent wake. Then each became strangely silent as the rude interloper passed; something under the canvas quieted their sudden bursts of fury.

The boat raced into the harbor's corridor, a dark, wa-tery path now bordered by the blazing lights of the island of Hong Kong on the right, Kowloon on the left. Three minutes later the outboard motor audibly sank into its lowest register as the hull swerved slowly past two filthy barges docked at the godown, and slid into an empty space on the west side of the Tsim Sha Tsui, Kowloon's crowded, dollar-conscious waterfront. The strident hordes of merchants, setting up their nightly tourist traps on the wharf, paid no attention; it was merely one more *jigi* coming in from the catch. Who cared?

Then, like the boat people out in the channel, the stalls on the waterfront nearest the insignificant intruder began to quiet down. Excited voices were silenced amid screeching commands and countercommands as eyes were drawn to a figure climbing up the black, oil-soaked ladder to the pier.

He was a holy man. His shrouded figure was draped in a pure white caftan that accentuated his tall slender body —very tall for a *Zhongguo ren*, nearly six feet in height, perhaps. Little could be seen of his face, however, as the cloth was loose and the breezes kept pressing the white fabric across his dark features, drawing out the whiteness of his eyes—determined eyes, zealous eyes. This was no ordinary priest, anyone could see that. He was a *heshang*, a chosen one selected by elders steeped in wisdom who could perceive the inner spiritual knowledge of a young monk destined for higher things. And it did not hurt that such a monk was tall and slender and had eyes of fire. Such holy men drew attention to themselves, to their personages—to their eyes—and generous contributions followed, both in fear and in awe; mostly fear. Perhaps this *heshang* came from one of the mystic sects that wandered through the hills and forests of the Guangze, or from a religious brotherhood in the mountains of far-off Qing Gaoyuan—descendants, it was said, of a people in the distant Himalayas—they were always quite ostentatious and generally to be feared the most, for few understood their obscure teachings. Teachings that were couched in gentleness, but with subtle hints of indescribable agony should their lessons go unheeded. There was too much agony on the land and the water—who needed more? So give to the spirits, to the eyes of fire. Perhaps it would be recorded. Somewhere.

The white-robed figure walked slowly through the parting crowds on the wharf, past the congested Star Ferry pier, and disappeared into the growing pandemonium of the Tsim Sha Tsui. The moment had passed; the stalls returned to their hysteria.

The priest headed east on Salisbury Road until he reached the Peninsula Hotel, whose subdued elegance was losing the battle with its surroundings. He then turned north into Nathan Road, to the base of the glittering Golden Mile, that strip of strips where opposing multitudes shrieked for attention. Both natives and tourists alike took notice of the stately holy man as he passed crowded storefronts and alleys bulging with merchandise, three-story discos and topless cafés where huge, amateurish billboards hawked Oriental charms above stalls offering the steamed delicacies of the noonday *dim sum.* He walked for nearly ten minutes through the garish carnival, now and then acknowledging glances with a slight bow of his head, and twice shaking it while issuing commands to the same short, muscular *Zhongguo ren,* who alternately followed him, then passed him with quick, dancelike steps, turning to search the intense eyes for a sign.

The sign came—two abrupt nods—as the priest turned and walked through the beaded entrance of a raucous cabaret. The *Zhongguo ren* remained outside, his hand unobtrusively under his loose tunic, his own eyes darting about the crazy street, a thoroughfare he could not understand. It was *insane!* Outrageous! But he was the *tudi;* he would protect the holy man with his life, no matter the assault on his own sensibilities.

Inside the cabaret the heavy layers of smoke were slashed by roving colored lights, most whirling in circles and directed toward a platform stage where a rock group ululated in deafening frenzy, a frantic admixture of punk and Far East. Shiny black, tight-fitting, ill-fitting trousers quivered maniacally on spindly legs below black leather jackets over soiled white silk shirts open to the waist, while each head was shaved around its skull at the temple line, each face grotesque, heavily made up to accentuate its essentially passive Oriental character. And as if to emphasize the conflict between East and West, the jarring music would occasionally, startlingly, come to a stop, as the plaintive strains of a simple Chinese melody emerged from a single instrument, while the figures remained rigid under the swirling bombardment of the spotlights.

The priest stood still for a moment surveying the huge crowded room. A number of customers in varying stages of drunkenness looked up at him from the tables. Several rolled coins in his direction before they turned away, while a few got out of their chairs, dropped Hong Kong dollars beside their drinks, and headed for the door. The *heshang* was having an effect, but not the effect desired by the obese, tuxedoed man who approached him.

"May I be of assistance, Holy One?" asked the cabaret's manager.

The priest leaned forward and spoke into the man's ear, whispering a name. The manager's eyes widened, then he bowed and gestured toward a small table by the wall. The priest nodded back in appreciation and walked behind the man to his chair as adjacent customers took uncomfortable notice.

The manager leaned down and spoke with a reverence he did not feel. "Would you care for refreshment, Holy One?"

"Goat's milk, if it is by chance available. If not, plain water will be more than sufficient. And I thank you."

"It is the privilege of the establishment," said the tuxedoed man, bowing and moving away, trying to place the slow, softly spoken dialect he could not recognize. It did not matter. This tall, white-robed priest had business with the *laoban,* and that was all that mattered. He had actually used the *laoban's* name, a name seldom spoken in the Golden Mile, and on this particular evening the powerful taipan was on the premises—in a room he would not publicly acknowledge knowing. But it was not the province of the manager to tell the *laoban* that the priest had arrived; the berobed one had made that clear. All was privacy this night, he had insisted. When the august taipan wished to see him, a man would come out to find him. So be it; it was the way of the secretive *laoban,* one of the wealthiest and most illustrious taipans in Hong Kong.

"Send a kitchen stick down the street for some fuckfuck mother goat's milk," said the manager harshly to a head boy on the floor. "And tell him to be damn-damn quick. The existence of his stinking offspring will depend upon it."

The holy man sat passively at the table, his zealous eyes now gentler, observing the foolish activity, apparently neither condemning nor accepting but merely taking it all in with the compassion of a father watching errant children.

Abruptly through the whirling lights there was an intrusion. Several tables away a bright camper's match was struck and quickly extinguished. Then another, and finally a third, this last held under a long black cigarette. The brief series of flashes drew the attention of the priest. He moved his shrouded head slowly toward the flame and the lone, unshaven, coarsely dressed Chinese drawing in the smoke. Their eyes met; the holy man's nod was almost imperceptible, barely a motion, and was acknowledged by an equally obscure movement as the match went out.

Seconds later the crudely dressed smoker's table was suddenly in flames. Fire shot up from the surface, spreading quickly to all the articles of paper on the surface—napkins, menus, *dim sum* baskets, isolated eruptions of potential disaster. The disheveled Chinese screamed and, with a shattering crash, overturned the table as waiters raced, shrieking, toward the flames. Customers on all sides leaped from their chairs as the fire on the floor—narrow strands of pulsing blue flame—inexplicably spread in rivulets around excited, stamping feet. The pandemonium grew as people rapidly slapped out the small fires with tablecloths and aprons. The manager and his head boys gestured wildly, shouting that all was under control; the danger had passed. The rock group played with even greater intensity, attempting to draw the crowd back into its frenzied orbit and away from the area of diminishing panic.

Suddenly, there was a greater disturbance, a more violent eruption. Two head boys had collided with the shabbily dressed *Zhongguo ren* whose carelessness and outsized matches had caused the conflagration. He responded with rapid *Wing Chun* chops—rigid hands crashing into shoulder blades and throats—as his feet hammered up into abdomens, sending the two *shi-ji* reeling back into the surrounding customers. The physical abuse compounded the panic, the chaos. The heavyset manager, now roaring, intervened and he, too, fell away, stunned by a well-placed kick to his rib cage. The unshaven *Zhongguo ren* then picked up a chair and hurled it at the screaming figures near the fallen man as three other waiters rushed into the melee in defense of their *Zongguan*. Men and women who only seconds ago were merely screaming now began thrashing their arms about, pummeling anyone and everyone near them. The rock group gyrated to its outer limits, frantic dissonance worthy of the scene. The riot had taken hold, and the burly peasant glanced across the room at the single table next to the wall. The priest was gone.

The unshaven *Zhongguo ren* picked up a second chair and smashed it down across a nearby table, splintering the wooden frame and swinging a broken leg into the crowd. Only moments to go, but those moments were everything.

The priest stepped through the door far back in the wall near the entrance of the cabaret. He closed it quickly, adjusting his eyes to the dim light of the long, narrow hallway. His right arm was stiff beneath the folds of his white caftan, his left diagonally across his waist, also under the sheer white fabric. Down the corridor, no more than twenty-five feet away a startled man sprang from the wall, his right hand plunging beneath his jacket to yank a large, heavy-caliber revolver from an unseen shoulder holster. The holy man nodded slowly, impassively, repeatedly, as he moved forward with graceful steps appropriate to a religious procession.

"Amita-fo, Amita-fo," he said softly, over and over again as he approached the man. "Everything is peaceful, all is in peace, the spirits will it."

"Jou matyeh?" The guard was beside a door; he shoved the ugly weapon forward and continued in a guttural Cantonese bred in the northern settlements. "Are you lost, priest? What are you doing here? Get out! This is no place for you!"

"Amita-fo, Amita-fo . . ."

"Get *out! Now!"*

The guard had no chance. Swiftly the priest pulled a razor-thin, double-edged knife from the folds at his waist. He slashed the man's wrist, half severing the hand with the gun from the guard's arm, then arced the blade surgically across the man's throat; air and blood erupted as the head snapped back in a mass of shining red; he fell to the floor, a corpse.

Without hesitation, the killer-priest slid the blemished knife into the cloth of his caftan where it held, and from under the right side of his robe he withdrew a thin-framed Uzi machine gun, its curved magazine holding more ammunition than he would need. He raised his foot and crashed it into the door with the strength of a mountain cat, racing inside to find what he knew he would find.

Five men—*Zhongguo ren*—were sitting around a table with pots of tea and short glasses of potent whisky near each; there were no written papers anywhere in sight, no notes or memoranda, only ears and watchful eyes. And as each pair of eyes looked up in shock the faces were contorted with panic. Two well-dressed negotiators plunged their hands inside their well-tailored jackets while they spun out of the chairs; another lunged under the table as the remaining two sprang up screaming and raced futilely into silk-covered walls, spinning around in desperation, seeking pardons yet knowing none would be forthcoming. A shattering fusillade of bullets ripped into the *Zhongguo ren*. Blood gushed from fatal wounds as skulls were pierced and eyes were punctured, mouths torn apart, bright red in muted screams of death. The walls and the floor and the polished table glistened sickeningly with the bloody evidence of death. Everywhere. It was over.

The killer surveyed his work. Satisfied, he knelt down by a large, stagnant pool of blood and moved his index finger through it. He then pulled out a square of dark cloth from his left sleeve and spread it over his handiwork. He rose to his feet and rushed out of the room, unbuttoning the white caftan as he ran down the dim hallway; the robe was open by the time he reached the door to the cabaret. He removed the razorlike knife from the cloth and shoved it into a scabbard on his belt. Then, holding the folds of cloth together, his hood in place, the lethal weapon secure at his side, he pulled the door back and walked inside, into the brawling chaos that showed no sign of lessening. But then why should it be different? He had left it barely thirty seconds ago and his man was well trained.

"*Faai-di!*" The shout came from the burly, unshaven peasant from Canton; he was ten feet away, overturning another table and striking a match, dropping it on the floor. "The police will be here any moment! The bartender just reached a phone, I saw him!"

The killer-priest ripped the caftan away from his body and the hood from his head. In the wild revolving lights his face looked as macabre as any in the frenzied rock group. Heavy makeup outlined his eyes, white lines defining the shape of each, and his face was an unnatural brown. "Go in front of me!" he commanded the peasant. He dropped his costume and the Uzi on the floor next to the door while removing a pair of thin surgical gloves; he shoved them into his flannel trousers.

For a cabaret in the Golden Mile to summon the police was not a decision easily arrived at. There were heavy fines for poor management, stiff penalties for endangering tourists. The police knew these risks and responded quickly when they were taken. The killer ran behind the peasant from Canton who joined the panicked crowd at the entrance screaming to get out. The coarsely dressed brawler was a bull; bodies in front of him fell away under the force of his blows. Guard and killer burst through the door and into the street, where another crowd had gathered shrieking questions and epithets and cries of bad joss—misfortune for the establishment. They threaded their way through the excited onlookers and were joined by the short, muscular Chinese who had waited outside. He grabbed the arm of his defrocked charge and pulled his priest into the narrowest of alleys, where he took out two towels from under his tunic. One was soft and dry, the other encased in plastic—it was warm and wet and perfumed.

The assassin gripped the wet towel and began rubbing it over his face, sinking it around and into the sockets of his eyes and across the exposed flesh of his neck. He reversed the cloth and repeated the process with even greater pressure, scrubbing his temples and his hairline until his white skin was apparent. He then dried himself with the second towel, smoothed his dark hair, and straightened the regimental tie that fell on the cream-colored shirt under his dark blue blazer. *"Jau!"* he ordered his two companions. They ran and disappeared in the crowds.

And a lone, well-dressed Occidental walked out into the strip of Oriental pleasures.

Inside the cabaret the excited manager was berating the bartender who had called the *jing cha;* the fines would be on his fuck-fuck head! For the riot had inexplicably subsided, leaving the customers bewildered. Head boys and waiters were mollifying the patrons, patting shoulders and clearing away the debris, while straightening tables and producing new chairs and dispensing free glasses of whisky. The rock group concentrated on the current favorites, and as swiftly as the order of the evening had been disrupted it was restored. With luck, thought the tuxedoed manager, the explanation that an impetuous bartender had mistaken a belligerent drunk for something far more serious would be acceptable to the police.

Suddenly, all thoughts of fines and official harassment were swept away as his eyes were drawn to a clump of white fabric on the floor across the room—in front of the door to the inner offices. White cloth, pure white—the priest? The *door!* The *laoban!* The *conference!* His breath short, his face drenched with sweat, the obese manager raced between the tables to the discarded caftan. He knelt down, his eyes wide, his breathing now suspended, as he saw the dark barrel of a strange weapon protruding from beneath the folds of white. And what made him choke on his barely formed terror was the sight of tiny specks and thin streaks of shiny, undried blood soiling the cloth.

"Go hai matyeh?" The question was asked by a second man in a tuxedo, but without the status conferred by a cummerbund—in truth the manager's brother and first assistant. "Oh, damn the Christian *Jesus!*" he swore under his breath as his brother gathered up the odd-looking gun in the spotted caftan.

"Come!" ordered the manager, getting to his feet and heading for the door.

"The police!" objected the brother. "One of us should speak to them, calm them, do what we can."

"It may be that we can do *nothing* but give them our heads! *Quickly!*"

Inside the dimly lit corridor the proof was there. The slain guard lay in a river of his own blood, his weapon gripped by a hand barely attached to his wrist. Within the conference room itself, the proof was complete. Five bloodied corpses were in spastic disarray, one specifically, shockingly, the focus of the manager's horrified interest. He approached the body and the punctured skull. With his handkerchief he wiped away the blood and stared at the face.

"We are dead," he whispered. "Kowloon is dead, Hong Kong dead. All is dead."

"*What?*"

"This man is the Vice-Premier of the People's Republic, successor to the Chairman himself."

"Here! *Look!*" The first-assistant brother lunged toward the body of the dead *laoban*. Alongside the riddled, bleeding corpse was a black bandanna. It was lying flat, the fabric with the curlicues of white discolored by blotches of red. The brother picked it up and gasped at the writing in the circle of blood underneath: *JASON BOURNE.*

The manager sprang across the floor. "Great Christian Jesus!" he uttered, his whole body trembling. "He's come back. The assassin has come back to Asia! *Jason Bourne! He's come back!*"

2

The sun fell behind the Sangre de Cristo Mountains in central Colorado as the Cobra helicopter roared out of the blazing light—a giant fluttering silhouette—and stuttered its way down toward the threshold on the edge of the timberline. The concrete landing pad was several hundred feet from a large rectangular house of heavy wood and thick beveled glass. Aside from generators and camouflaged communications disks, no other structures were in sight. Tall trees formed a dense wall, concealing the house from all outsiders. The pilots of these highly maneuverable aircraft were recruited from the senior officer corps of the Cheyenne complex in Colorado Springs. None was lower than a full colonel and each had been cleared by the National Security Council in Washington. They never spoke about their trips to the mountain retreat; the destination was always obscured on flight plans. Headings were issued by radio when the choppers were airborne. The location was not on any public map and its communications were beyond the scrutiny of allies and enemies alike. The security was total; it had to be. This was a place for strategists whose work was so sensitive and frequently entailed such delicate global implications that the planners could not be seen together outside government buildings or in the buildings themselves, and certainly never inside adjacent offices known to have connecting doors. There were hostile, inquisitive eyes everywhere—allies and enemies alike—who knew of the work these men did, and if they were observed together, alarms would surely go out. The enemy was vigilant and allies jealously guarded their own intelligence fiefdoms.

The doors of the Cobra opened. A frame of steel steps snapped to the ground as an obviously bewildered man climbed down into the floodlights. He was escorted by a major general in uniform. The civilian was slender, middle-aged, and of medium height, and was dressed in a pin-striped suit, white shirt and paisley tie. Even under the harsh, decelerating wash of the rotor blades his careful grooming remained intact, as though it were important to him and not to be abused. He followed the officer and together they walked up a concrete path to a door at the side of the house. The door opened as both men approached. However, only the civilian went inside; the general nodded, giving one of those informal salutes veteran soldiers reserve for the nonmilitary and officers of their own rank.

"Nice to have met you, Mr. McAllister," said the general. "Someone else will take you back."

"You're not coming in?" asked the civilian.

"I've never *been* in," replied the officer, smiling. "I just make sure it's you, and get you from Point B to Point C."

"Sounds like a waste of rank, General."

"It probably isn't," observed the soldier without further comment. "But then I have other duties. Goodbye."

McAllister walked inside, into a long paneled corridor, his escort now a pleasant-faced, well-dressed husky man who had all the outward signs of Internal Security about him—physically quick and capable, and anonymous in a crowd.

"Did you have a pleasant flight, sir?" asked the younger man.

"Does anybody, in one of those things?"

The guard laughed. "This way, sir."

They went down the corridor, passing several doors along both walls, until they reached the end where there was a pair of larger double doors with two red lights in the upper left and right corners. They were cameras on separate circuits. Edward McAllister had not seen devices like those since he left Hong Kong two years ago, and then only because he had been briefly assigned to British Intelligence MI6, Special Branch, for consultations. To him the British had seemed paranoid where security was concerned. He had never understood those people, especially after they awarded him a citation for doing minimal work for them in affairs they should have been on top of to begin with. The guard rapped on the door; there was a quiet click and he opened the right panel.

"Your other guest, sir," said the husky man.

"Thank you so *very* much," replied a voice. The astonished McAllister instantly recognized it from scores of radio and television newscasts over the years, its inflections learned in an expensive prep school and several prestigious universities, with a postgraduate career in the British Isles. There was, however, no time to adjust. The gray-haired, impeccably dressed man with a lined, elongated face that bespoke his seventy-plus years got up from a large desk and walked gingerly across the room, his hand extended. "Mr. Undersecretary, how good of you to come. May I introduce myself. I'm Raymond Havilland."

"I'm certainly aware of who you are, Mr. Ambassador. It's a privilege, sir."

"Ambassador without portfolio, McAllister, which means there's very little privilege left. But there's still work."

"I can't imagine any President of the United States within the past twenty years surviving without you."

"Some muddled through, Mr. Undersecretary, but with your experience at State, I suspect you know that better than I do." The diplomat turned his head. "I'd like you to meet John Reilly. Jack's one of those highly knowledgeable associates we're never supposed to know about over at the National Security Council. He's not so terrifying, is he?"

"I hope not," said McAllister, crossing to shake hands with Reilly, who had gotten up from one of the two leather chairs facing the desk. "Nice to meet you, Mr. Reilly."

"Mr. Undersecretary," said the somewhat obese man with red hair that matched a freckled forehead. The eyes behind the steel-rimmed glasses did not convey geniality; they were sharp and cold.

"Mr. Reilly is here," continued Havilland, crossing behind the desk and indicating the vacant chair on the right for McAllister, "to make sure I stay in line. As I understand it, that means there are some things I can say, others I can't say, and certain things that only *he* can say." The ambassador sat down. "If that appears enigmatic to you, Mr. Undersecretary, I'm afraid it's all I can offer you at this juncture."

"Everything that's happened during the past five hours since I was ordered to Andrews Air Force Base has been an enigma, Ambassador Havilland. I have no idea why I was brought here."

"Then let me tell you in general terms," said the diplomat, glancing at Reilly and leaning forward on the desk. "You are in a position to be of extraordinary service to your country—and to interests far beyond this country—exceeding anything you may have considered during your long and distinguished career."

McAllister studied the ambassador's austere face, uncertain how to reply. "My career at the Department of State has been fulfilling, and, I trust, professional, but it can hardly be called distinguished in the broadest sense. Quite frankly, the opportunities never presented themselves."

"One has presented itself to you now," interrupted Havilland. "And you are uniquely qualified to carry it out."

"In what way? Why?"

"The Far East," said the diplomat with an odd inflection in his voice, as though the reply might itself be a question. "You've been with the State Department for over twenty years since you received your doctorate in

Far Eastern Studies at Harvard. You've served your government commendably with many years of outstanding foreign service in Asia, and since your return from your last post your judgments have proved to be extremely valuable in formulating policy in that troubled part of the world. You're considered a brilliant analyst."

"I appreciate what you say, but there were others in Asia. Many others who attained equal and higher ratings than I did."

"Accidents of events and posting, Mr. Undersecretary. Let's be frank, you've done well."

"But what separates me from the others? Why am I more qualified for this opportunity than they?"

"Because no one else compares with you as a specialist in the internal affairs of the People's Republic of China —I believe you played a pivotal role in the trade conferences between Washington and Peking. Also, none of the others spent seven years in Hong Kong." Here Raymond Havilland paused, then added, "Finally, no one else in our Asian posts was ever assigned to or accepted by the British government's MI-Six, Special Branch, in the territory."

"I see," said McAllister, recognizing that the last qualification, which seemed the least important to him, had a certain significance for the diplomat. "My work in Intelligence was minimal, Mr. Ambassador. The Special Branch's acceptance of me was based more on its own— disinformation, I think is the word, than any unique talents of mine. Those people simply believed the wrong sets of facts and the sums didn't total. It didn't take long to find the 'correct figures,' as I remember they put it."

"They *trusted* you, McAllister. They still trust you."

"I assume that trust is intrinsic to this opportunity, whatever it is?"

"Very much so. It's vital."

"Then may I hear what the opportunity is?"

"You may." Havilland looked over at the third participant, the man from the National Security Council. "If you care to," he added.

"My turn," said Reilly, not unpleasantly. He shifted his heavy torso in the chair and gazed at McAllister, with eyes still rigid but without the coldness they had displayed previously, as though he was now asking for understanding. "At the moment our voices are being taped—it's your constitutional right to know that—but it's a two-sided right. You must swear to absolute secrecy concerning the information imparted to you here, not only in the interests of national security but in the further and conceivably greater interests of specific world conditions. I know that sounds like a come-on to whet your appetite, but it's not meant to be. We're deadly serious. Will you agree to the condition? You can be prosecuted in a closed trial under the national security nondisclosure statutes if you violate the oath."

"How can I agree to a condition like that when I have no idea what the information is?"

"Because I can give you a quick overview and it'll be enough for you to say yes or no. If it's no, you'll be escorted out of here and flown back to Washington. No one will be the loser."

"Go ahead."

"All right." Reilly spoke calmly. "You'll be discussing certain events that took place in the past—not ancient history, but not current by any means. The actions themselves were disavowed—buried, to be more accurate. Does that sound familiar, Mr. Undersecretary?"

"I'm from the State Department. We bury the past when it serves no purpose to reveal it. Circumstances change; judgments made in good faith yesterday are often a problem tomorrow. We can't control these changes any more than the Soviets or the Chinese can."

"Well put!" said Havilland.

"Not yet it isn't," objected Reilly, raising a palm to the ambassador. "The undersecretary is evidently an experienced diplomat. He didn't say yes and he didn't say no." The man from the NSC again looked at McAllister; the eyes behind the steel-rimmed glasses were once again sharp and cold. "What is it, Mr. Undersecretary? You want to sign on, or do you want to leave?"

"One part of me wants to get up and leave as quickly as I can," said McAllister, looking alternately at both men. "The other part says 'Stay.'" He paused, his gaze settling on Reilly, and added, "Whether you intended it or not, my appetite is whetted."

"It's a hell of a price to pay for being hungry," replied the Irishman.

"It's more than that." The undersecretary of State spoke softly. "I'm a professional, and if I am the man you want, I really don't have a choice, do I?"

"I'm afraid I'll have to hear the words," said Reilly. "Do you want me to repeat them?"

"It won't be necessary." McAllister frowned in thought, then spoke. "I, Edward Newington McAllister, fully understand that whatever is said during this conference—" He stopped and looked at Reilly. "I assume you'll fill in the particulars, such as time and location and those present?"

"Date, place, hour and minute of entry and identifications—it's all been done and logged."

"Thank you. I'll want a copy before I leave."

"Of course." Without raising his voice, Reilly looked straight ahead and quietly issued an order. "Please note. Have a copy of this tape available for the subject upon his departure. Also equipment for him to verify its contents on the premises. I'll initial the copy. . . . Go ahead, Mr. McAllister."

"I appreciate that. . . . With regard to whatever is said at this conference, I accept the condition of nondisclosure. I will speak to no one about any aspect of the discussion unless instructed to do so personally by Ambassador Havilland. I further understand that I may be prosecuted at a closed trial should I violate this agreement. However, should such a trial ever take place, I reserve the right to confront my accusers, not their affidavits or depositions. I add this, for I cannot conceive of any circumstances where I would or could violate the oath I've just taken."

"There *are* circumstances, you know," said Reilly gently.

"Not in my book."

"Extreme physical abuse, chemicals, being tricked by men and women far more experienced than you. There are ways, Mr. Undersecretary."

"I repeat. Should a case ever be brought against me— and such things have happened to others—I reserve the right to face any and all accusers."

"That's good enough for us." Again Reilly looked straight ahead and spoke. "Terminate this tape and pull the plugs. Confirm."

"Confirmed," said a voice eerily from a speaker somewhere overhead. *"You are now . . . out."*

"Proceed, Mr. Ambassador," said the red-haired man.
"I'll interrupt only when I feel it's necessary."

"I'm sure you will, Jack." Havilland turned to McAllister. "I take back my previous statement; he really *is* a
terror. After forty-odd years of service, I'm told by a
redheaded whippersnapper who should go on a diet
when to shut up."

The three men smiled; the aging diplomat knew the
moment and the method to reduce tension. Reilly shook
his head and genially spread his hands. "I would never
do that, sir. Certainly, I hope not so obviously."

"What say, McAllister? Let's defect to Moscow and say
he was the recruiter. The Russkies would probably give
us both dachas and he'd be in Leavenworth."

"You'd get the dacha, Mr. Ambassador. I'd share a flat
with twelve Siberians. No thank you, sir. He's not interrupting me."

"Very good. I'm surprised none of those well-inten-
tioned meddlers in the Oval Office ever tapped you for
his staff, or at least sent you to the UN."

"They didn't know I existed."

"That status will change," said Havilland, abruptly serious. He paused, staring at the undersecretary, then lowered his voice. "Have you ever heard the name Jason
Bourne?"

"How could anyone posted in Asia not have heard it?"
answered McAllister. "Thirty-five to forty murders, the
assassin for hire who eluded every trap ever set for him.
A pathological killer whose only morality was the price of
the kill. They say he was an American—*is* an American;
I don't know, he faded from sight—and that he was a
defrocked priest and an importer who'd stolen millions
and a deserter from the French Foreign Legion and God
knows how many other stories. The only thing I *do* know
is that he was never caught, and our failure to catch him
was a burden on our diplomacy throughout the Far
East."

"Was there any pattern to his victims?"

"None. They were random, across the board. Two
bankers here, three attachés there—meaning CIA; a minister of state from Delhi, an industrialist from Singapore,

and numerous—far too numerous—politicians, generally decent men. Their cars were bombed in the streets,
their flats blown up. Then there were unfaithful husbands and wives and lovers of various persuasions in
various scandals; he offered final solutions for bruised
egos. There was no one he wouldn't kill, no method too
brutal or demeaning for him. . . . No, there wasn't a
pattern, just money. The highest bidder. He was a monster—*is* a monster, if he's still alive."

Once more Havilland leaned forward, his eyes steady
on the undersecretary of State. "You say he faded from
sight. Just like that? You never picked up anything, any
rumors or backstairs gossip from our Asian embassies or
consulates?"

"There was talk, yes, but none of it was ever confirmed.
The story I heard most often came from the Macao police, where Bourne was last known to be. They said he
wasn't dead, or retired, but instead had gone to Europe
looking for wealthier clients. If it's true, it might be only
half the story. The police also claimed informants told
them that several contracts had gone sour for Bourne,
that in one instance he killed the wrong man, a leading
figure in the Malaysian underworld, and in another, it was
said he raped a client's wife. Perhaps the circle was closing in on him—and perhaps not."

"What do you mean?"

"Most of us bought the first half of the story, not the
second. Bourne wouldn't kill the wrong man, especially
someone like that; he didn't make those kinds of mistakes. And if he raped a client's wife—which is doubtful
—he would have done so out of hatred or revenge. He
would have forced a bound husband to watch and then
killed them both. No, most of us subscribed to the first
story. He went to Europe, where there were bigger fish
to fry—and murder."

"You were meant to accept that version," said Havilland, leaning back in his chair.

"I beg your pardon?"

"The only man Jason Bourne ever killed in post-Viet-
nam Asia was an enraged conduit who tried to kill
him."

Stunned, McAllister stared at the diplomat. "I don't
understand."

"The Jason Bourne you've just described never existed. He was a myth."

"You can't be serious."

"Never more so. Those were turbulent times in the Far East. The drug networks operating out of the Golden Triangle were fighting a disorganized, unpublicized war. Consuls, vice-consuls, police, politicians, criminal gangs, border patrols—the highest and the lowest social orders —all were affected. Money in unimaginable amounts was the mother's milk of corruption. Whenever and wherever a well-publicized killing took place—regardless of the circumstances or those accused—Bourne was on the scene and took credit for the kill."

"He *was* the killer," insisted a confused McAllister. "There were the signs, *his* signs. Everyone knew it!"

"Everyone *assumed* it, Mr. Undersecretary. A mocking telephone call to the police, a small article of clothing sent in the mails, a black bandanna found in the bushes a day later. They were all part of the strategy."

"The strategy? What are you talking about?"

"Jason Bourne—the original Jason Bourne—was a convicted murderer, a fugitive whose life ended with a bullet in his head in a place called Tam Quan during the last months of the Vietnam war. It was a jungle execution. The man was a traitor. His corpse was left to rot—he simply disappeared. Several years later, the man who executed him took on his identity for one of our projects, a project that nearly succeeded, *should* have succeeded, but went off the wire."

"Off the what?"

"Out of control. That man—that very brave man—who went underground for us, using the name Jason Bourne for three years, was injured, and the result of those injuries was amnesia. He lost his memory; he neither knew who he was nor who he was meant to be."

"Good *Lord* . . ."

"He was between a rock and a hard place. With the help of an alcoholic doctor on a Mediterranean island he tried to trace his life, his identity, and here, I'm afraid, he failed. *He* failed but the woman who befriended him did not fail; she's now his wife. Her instincts were accurate; she knew he wasn't a killer. She purposely forced him to examine his words, his abilities, ultimately to make the contacts that would lead him back to us. But we, with the most sophisticated Intelligence apparatus in the world, did not listen to the human quotient. We set a trap to kill him—"

"I must interrupt, Mr. Ambassador," said Reilly.

"Why?" asked Havilland. "It's what we did and we're not on tape."

"An individual made the determination, not the United States government. That should be clear, sir."

"All right," agreed the diplomat, nodding. "His name was Conklin, but it's irrelevant, Jack. Government personnel went along. It happened."

"Government personnel were also instrumental in saving his life."

"Somewhat after the fact," muttered Havilland.

"But *why?*" asked McAllister; he now leaned forward, mesmerized by the bizarre story. "He was one of us. Why would anyone want to kill him?"

"His loss of memory was taken for something else. It was erroneously believed that he had turned, that he had killed three of his controls and disappeared with a great deal of money—government funds totaling over five million dollars."

"Five *million . . . ?*" Astonished, the undersecretary of State slowly sank back into the chair. "Funds of that magnitude were available to him *personally?*"

"Yes," said the ambassador. "They, too, were part of the strategy, part of the project."

"I assume this is where silence is necessary. The project, I mean."

"It's imperative," answered Reilly. "Not because of the project—in spite of what happened we make no apology for that operation—but because of the man we recruited to become Jason Bourne and where he came from."

"That's cryptic."

"It'll become clear."

"The project, please."

Reilly looked at Raymond Havilland; the diplomat nodded and spoke. "We created a killer to draw out and trap the most deadly assassin in Europe."

"*Carlos?*"

"You're quick, Mr. Undersecretary."

"Who else *was* there? In Asia, Bourne and the Jackal were constantly being compared."

"Those comparisons were encouraged," said Havilland. "Often magnified and spread by the strategists of the project, a group known as Treadstone Seventy-one. The name was derived from a sterile house on New York's Seventy-first Street where the resurrected Jason Bourne was trained. It was the command post and a name you should be aware of."

"I see," said McAllister pensively. "Then those comparisons, growing as they did with Bourne's reputation, served as a challenge to Carlos. That's when Bourne moved to Europe—to bring the challenge directly to the Jackal. To force him to come out and confront his challenger."

"*Very* quick, Mr. Undersecretary. In a nutshell, that was the strategy."

"It's extraordinary. Brilliant, actually, and one doesn't have to be an expert to see that. God knows I'm not."

"You may become one—"

"And you say this man who became Bourne, the mythical assassin, spent three years playing the role and then was injured—"

"Shot," interrupted Havilland. "Membranes of his skull were blown away."

"And he lost his *memory?*"

"Totally."

"My God!"

"Yet despite everything that happened to him, and with the woman's help—she was an economist for the Canadian government, incidentally—he came within moments of pulling the whole damn thing off. A remarkable story, isn't it?"

"It's incredible. But what kind of man would do this, *could* do it?"

The redheaded John Reilly coughed softly; the ambassador deferred with a glance. "We're now reaching ground zero," said the watchguard, again shifting his bulk to look at McAllister. "If you've got any doubts I can still let you go."

"I try not to repeat myself. You have your tape."

"It's your appetite."

"I suppose that's another way you people have of saying there might not even be a trial."

"I'd never say that."

McAllister swallowed, his eyes meeting the calm gaze of the man from the NSC. He turned to Havilland. "Please go on, Mr. Ambassador. Who is this man? Where *did* he come from?"

"His name is David Webb. He's currently an associate professor of Oriental Studies at a small university in Maine and married to the Canadian woman who literally guided him out of his labyrinth. Without her he would have been killed—but then without *him* she would have ended up a corpse in Zurich."

"Remarkable," said McAllister, barely audible.

"The point is, she's his second wife. His first marriage ended in a tragic act of wanton slaughter—that's when his story began for us. A number of years ago Webb was a young foreign service officer stationed in Phnom Penh, a brilliant Far East scholar, fluent in several Oriental languages, and married to a girl from Thailand he'd met in graduate school. They lived in a house on a riverbank and had two children. It was an ideal life for such a man. It combined the expertise Washington needed in the area with the opportunity to live in his own museum. Then the Vietnam action escalated and one morning a lone jet fighter—no one really knows from which side, but no one ever told Webb that—swooped down at low altitude and strafed his wife and children while they were playing in the water. Their bodies were riddled. They floated into the riverbank as Webb was trying to reach them; he gathered them in his arms, screaming helplessly at the disappearing plane above."

"How *horrible*," whispered McAllister.

"At that moment, Webb turned. He became someone he never was, never dreamed he could be. He became a guerrilla fighter known as Delta."

"Delta?" said the undersecretary of State. "A guerrilla . . . ? I'm afraid I don't understand."

"There's no way you could." Havilland looked over at Reilly, then back at McAllister. "As Jack made clear a moment ago, we're now at ground zero. Webb fled to Saigon consumed with rage, and, ironically, through the efforts of the CIA officer named Conklin, who years later tried to kill him, he joined a clandestine operations outfit called Medusa. No names were ever used by the people in Medusa, just the Greek letters of the alphabet—Webb became Delta One."

"Medusa? I've never heard of it."

"Ground zero," said Reilly. "The Medusa file is still classified, but we've permitted limited declassification in this instance. The Medusa units were a collection of internationals who knew the Vietnam territories, north and south. Frankly, most of them were criminals—smugglers of narcotics, gold, guns, jewels, all kinds of contraband. Also convicted murderers, fugitives who'd been sentenced to death in absentia . . . and a smattering of colonials whose businesses were confiscated—again by both sides. They banked on us—Big Uncle—to take care of all their problems if they infiltrated hostile areas, killing suspected Viet Cong collaborators and village chiefs thought to be leaning toward Charlie, as well as expediting prisoner-of-war escapes where they could. They were assassination teams—death squads, if you will—and that says it as well as it can be said, but of course we'll never say it. Mistakes were made, millions stolen, and the majority of those personnel wouldn't be allowed in any civilized army, Webb among them."

"With his background, his academic credentials, he willingly became part of such a group?"

"He had an overpowering motive," said Havilland. "As far as he was concerned, that plane in Phnom Penh was North Vietnamese."

"Some said he was a madman," continued Reilly. "Others claimed he was an extraordinary tactician, the supreme guerrilla who understood the Oriental mind and led the most aggressive teams in Medusa, feared as much by Command Saigon as he was by the enemy. He was uncontrollable; the only rules he followed were his own. It was as if he had mounted his own personal hunt, tracking down the man who had flown that plane and destroyed his life. It became his war, his rage; the more violent it became, the more satisfying it was for him—or perhaps closer to his own death wish."

"Death . . . ?" The undersecretary of State left the word hanging.

"It was the prevalent theory at the time," interrupted the ambassador.

"The war ended," said Reilly, "as disastrously for Webb—or Delta—as it did for the rest of us. Perhaps worse; there was nothing left for him. No more purpose, nothing to strike out at, to kill. Until we approached him and gave him a reason to go on living. Or perhaps a reason to go on trying to die."

"By becoming Bourne and going after Carlos the Jackal," completed McAllister.

"Yes," agreed the Intelligence officer. A brief silence ensued.

"We need him back," said Havilland. The soft-spoken words fell like an ax on hard wood.

"Carlos has surfaced?"

The diplomat shook his head. "Not Europe. We need him back in Asia and we can't waste a minute."

"Someone else? Another . . . target?" McAllister swallowed involuntarily. "Have you spoken to him?"

"We can't approach him. Not directly."

"Why not?"

"He wouldn't let us through the door. He doesn't trust anything or anyone out of Washington, and it's difficult to fault him for that. For days, for weeks, he cried out for help and we didn't listen. Instead, we tried to kill him."

"Again I must object," broke in Reilly. "It wasn't us. It was an individual operating on erroneous information. And the government currently spends in excess of four hundred thousand dollars a year in a protection program for Webb."

"Which he scoffs at. He believes it's no more than a backup trap for Carlos in the event the Jackal unearths him. He's convinced you don't give a damn about him, and I'm not sure he's far off the mark. He *saw* Carlos and the fact that the face has not yet come back into focus for him isn't something Carlos knows. The Jackal has every reason to go after Webb. And if he does, you'll have your second chance."

"The *chances* of Carlos finding him are so remote as to be practically nil. The Treadstone records are buried, and even if they weren't, they don't contain any current information as to where Webb is or what he does."

"Come, Mr. Reilly," said Havilland testily. "Only his background and qualifications. How difficult would it be? He's got academia written all over him."

"I'm not opposing you, Mr. Ambassador," replied a somewhat subdued Reilly. "I just want everything clear. Let's be frank, Webb has to be handled very delicately. He's recovered a large portion of his memory but certainly not all of it. However, he's recalled enough about Medusa to be a considerable threat to the country's interests."

"In what way?" asked McAllister. "Perhaps it wasn't the best and it probably wasn't the worst, but basically it was a military strategy in time of war."

"A strategy that was unsanctioned, unlogged and unacknowledged. There's no official slate."

"How is that possible? It was *funded,* and when funds are expended—"

"Don't read me the book," interrupted the obese Intelligence officer. "We're not on tape, but I've got yours."

"Is that your answer?"

"No, this is: there's no statute of limitation on war crimes and murder, Mr. Undersecretary, and murder and other violent crimes were committed against our own forces, as well as Allied personnel. In the main they were committed by killers and thieves in the process of stealing, looting, raping, and killing. Most of them were pathological criminals. As effective as the Medusa was in many ways, it was a tragic mistake, born of anger and frustration in a no-win situation. What possible good would it do to open all the old wounds? Quite apart from the claims against us, we would become a pariah in the eyes of much of the civilized world."

"As I mentioned," said McAllister softly, reluctantly. "At State we don't believe in opening wounds." He turned to the ambassador. "I'm beginning to understand. You want me to reach this David Webb and persuade him to return to Asia. For another project, another target—although I've never used the word in that context in my life before this evening. And I assume it's because there are distinct parallels in our early careers—we're Asia men. We presumably have insights where the Far East is concerned, and you think he'll listen to me."

"Essentially, yes."

"Yet you say he won't touch us. That's where my understanding fades. How can I do it?"

"We'll do it together. As he once made the rules for himself, we'll make them now. It's imperative."

"Because of a man you want killed?"

" 'Neutralized' will suffice. It has to be done."

"And Webb can do it?"

"No. *Jason Bourne* can. We sent him out alone for three years under extraordinary stress—suddenly his memory was taken from him and he was hunted like an animal. Still he retained the ability to infiltrate and kill. I'm being blunt."

"I understand that. Since we're not on tape—and on the chance that we still are—" The undersecretary glanced disapprovingly at Reilly, who shook his head and shrugged. "May I be permitted to know who the target is?"

"You may, and I want you to commit this name to memory, Mr. Undersecretary. He's a Chinese minister of state, Sheng Chou Yang."

McAllister flushed angrily. "I don't *have* to commit it, and I think you *know* that. He was a fixture in the PRC's economics group and we were both assigned to the trade conferences in Peking in the late seventies. I read up on him, analyzed him. Sheng was my counterpart and I could do no less—a fact I suspect you also know."

"Oh?" The gray-haired ambassador arched his dark eyebrows, and dismissed the rebuke. "And what did your reading tell you? What did you learn about him?"

"He was considered very bright, very ambitious—but then his rise in Peking's hierarchy tells us that. He was spotted by scouts sent out from the Central Committee some years ago at the Fudan University in Shanghai. Initially because he took to the English language so well and had a firm, even sophisticated, grasp of Western economics."

"What else?"

"He was considered promising material, and after in-depth indoctrination was sent to the London School of Economics for graduate study. It took."

"How do you mean?"

"Sheng's an avowed Marxist where the centralized state is concerned, but he has a healthy respect for capitalistic profits."

"I see," said Havilland. "Then he accepts the failure of the Soviet system?"

"He's ascribed that failure to the Russian penchant for corruption and mindless conformity in the higher ranks, and alcohol in the lower ones. To his credit he's stamped out a fair share of those abuses in the industrial centers."

"Sounds like he was trained at IBM, doesn't it?"

"He's been responsible for many of the PRC's new trade policies. He's made China a lot of money." Again the undersecretary of State leaned forward in his chair, his eyes intense, his expression bewildered—stunned was perhaps more accurate. "My *God,* why would *anyone* in the West want Sheng *dead? It's absurd!* He's our economic ally, a politically stabilizing factor in the largest nation on earth that's ideologically opposed to us! Through him and men like him we've reached accommodations. Without him, whatever the course, there's the risk of disaster. I'm a professional China analyst, Mr. Ambassador, and, I repeat, what you suggest is absurd. A man of your accomplishments should recognize that before any of us."

The aging diplomat looked hard at his accuser, and when he spoke he did so slowly, choosing his words carefully. "A few moments ago we were at ground zero. A former foreign service officer named David Webb became Jason Bourne for a purpose. Conversely, Sheng Chou Yang is not the man you know, not the man you studied as your counterpart. He *became* that man for a purpose."

"What are you talking about?" shot back McAllister defensively. "Everything I've said about him is on record —*records,* official—most top secret and eyes-only."

"*Eyes-*only?" the former ambassador asked wearily. "*Ears-*only, tongues-only—wagging as busily as tails wag tigers. Because an official stamp is placed on recorded observations observed by men who have no idea where those records came from—they are there, and that's enough. No, Mr. Undersecretary, it's not enough, it never is."

"You obviously have other information I don't have,"

said the State Department man coldly. "If it *is* information and not disinformation. The man I described—the man I knew—is Sheng Chou Yang."

"Just as the David Webb we described to you was Jason Bourne? . . . No, please, don't be angry, I'm not playing games. It's important that you understand. Sheng is not the man you knew. He never was."

"Then whom *did* I know? Who *was* the man at those conferences?"

"He's a traitor, Mr. Undersecretary. Sheng Chou Yang is a traitor to his country, and when his treachery is exposed—as it surely will be—Peking will hold the Free World responsible. The consequences of that inevitable error are unthinkable. However, there's no doubt as to his purpose."

"*Sheng* . . . a *traitor?* I don't *believe* you! He's worshipped in Peking! One day he'll be chairman!"

"Then China will be ruled by a Nationalist zealot whose ideological roots are in Taiwan."

"You're crazy—you're absolutely *crazy!* Wait a minute, you said he had a purpose—'no doubt as to his purpose,' you said."

"He and his people intend to take over Hong Kong. He's mounting a hidden economic blitzkrieg, putting all trade, all of the territory's financial institutions under the control of a 'neutral' commission, a clearinghouse approved by Peking—which means approved by him. The instrument of record will be the British treaty that expires in 1997, his commission a supposedly reasonable prelude to annexation and control. It will happen when the road is clear for Sheng, when there are no more obstacles in his path. When his word is the only word that counts in economic matters. It could be in a month, or two months. Or next week."

"You think Peking has *agreed* to this?" protested McAllister. "You're wrong! It's—it's just *crazy!* The People's Republic will never substantively *touch* Hong Kong! It brokers sixty percent of its entire economy through the territory. The China Accords guarantee fifty years of a Free Economic Zone status and Sheng is a signator, the most vital one!"

"But Sheng is not Sheng—not as you know him."

"Then who the hell *is* he?"

"Prepare yourself, Mr. Undersecretary. Sheng Chou Yang is the first son of a Shanghai industrialist who made his fortune in the corrupt world of the old China, Chiang Kai-shek's Kuomintang. When it was obvious that Mao's revolution would succeed, the family fled, as so many of the landlords and the warlords did, with whatever they could transfer. The old man is now one of the most powerful taipans in Hong Kong—but which one we don't know. The colony will become his and the family's mandate, courtesy of a minister in Peking, his most treasured son. It's the ultimate irony, the patriarch's final vengeance—Hong Kong will be controlled by the very men who corrupted Nationalist China. For years they bled their country without conscience, profiting from the labors of a starving, disenfranchised people, paving the way for Mao's revolution. And if that sounds like Communist bilge, I'm afraid for the most part it's embarrassingly accurate. Now a handful of zealots, boardroom thugs led by a maniac, want back what no international court in history would ever grant them." Havilland paused, then spat out the single word *"Maniacs!"*

"But if you don't know who this taipan is, how do you know it's true, *any* of it?"

"The sources are maximum-classified," interrupted Reilly, "but they've been confirmed. The story was first picked up in Taiwan. Our original informer was a member of the Nationalist cabinet who thought it was a disastrous course that could only lead to a bloodbath for the entire Far East. He pleaded with us to stop it. He was found dead the next morning, three bullets in his head and his throat cut—in Chinese that means a dead traitor. Since then five other people have been murdered, their bodies similarly mutilated. It's true. The conspiracy is alive and well and coming from Hong Kong."

"It's *insane!*"

"More to the point," said Havilland, "it will never work. If it had a prayer, we might look the other way and even say Godspeed, but it can't. It'll blow apart, as Lin Biao's conspiracy against Mao Zedong blew apart in '72, and when it does, Peking will blame American and Taiwanese money in complicity with the British—as well as the silent acquiescence of the world's leading financial institutions. Eight years of economic progress will be shot to hell because a group of fanatics want vengeance. In your words, Mr. Undersecretary, the People's Republic is a suspicious turbulent nation—and if I may add a few of my own from those accomplishments you ascribe to me—a government quick to become paranoid, obsessed with betrayal both from within and without. China will believe that the world is out to isolate her economically, choke her off from world markets, and bring her to her knees while the Russians grin across the northern borders. She will strike fast and furiously, impound everything, absorb everything. Her troops will occupy Kowloon, the island, and all of the burgeoning New Territories. Investments in the trillions will be lost. Without the colony's expertise trade will be stymied, a labor force in the millions will be in chaos—hunger and disease will be rampant. The Far East will be in flames, and the result could touch off a war none of us wants to think about."

"Jesus Christ," McAllister whispered. "It can't happen."

"No, it can't," agreed the diplomat.

"But why *Webb?*"

"Not Webb," corrected Havilland. "Jason Bourne."

"All right! Why Bourne?"

"Because word out of Kowloon is that he's already there."

"What?"

"And we know he's not."

"What did you say?"

"He's struck. He's killed. He's back in Asia."

"Webb?"

"No, Bourne. The myth."

"You're not making one *goddamned* bit of sense!"

"I can assure you Sheng Chou Yang is making a lot of sense."

"How?"

"He's brought him back. Jason Bourne's skills are once more for hire, and, as always, his client is beyond unearthing—in the present case the most unlikely client imaginable. A leading spokesman for the People's Republic who must eliminate his opposition both in Hong Kong and in Peking. During the past six months a number of powerful voices in Peking's Central Committee have been strangely silent. According to official government announcements, several died, and considering their ages it's understandable. Two others were supposedly killed in accidents—one in a plane crash, one by, of all things, a cerebral hemorrhage while hiking in the Shaoguan mountains—if it's not true, at least it's imaginative. Then another was 'removed'—a euphemism for disgrace. Lastly, and most extraordinary, the PRC's Vice-Premier was murdered in Kowloon when no one in Peking knew he was there. It was a gruesome episode, five men massacred in the Tsim Sha Tsui with the killer leaving his calling card. The name Jason Bourne was etched in blood on the floor. An impostor's ego demanded that he be given credit for his kills."

McAllister blinked repeatedly, his eyes darting aimlessly. "This is all so far beyond me," he said helplessly. Then, becoming the professional once again, he looked steadily at Havilland. "Is there linkage?" he asked.

The diplomat nodded. "Our Intelligence reports are specific. All of these men opposed Sheng's policies—some openly, some guardedly. The Vice-Premier, an old revolutionary and veteran of Mao's Long March, was especially vocal. He couldn't stand the upstart Sheng. Yet what was he doing secretly in Kowloon in the company of bankers? Peking can't answer, so 'face' mercifully required that the killing never happened. With his cremation he became a nonperson."

"And with the killer's 'calling card'—the name written in blood—the second linkage is to Sheng," said the undersecretary of State, his voice close to trembling, as he nervously massaged his forehead. "Why would he do it? Leave his *name*, I mean!"

"He's in business and it was a spectacular kill. Now do you begin to understand?"

"I'm not sure what you mean."

"For us this new Bourne is our direct route to Sheng Chou Yang. He's our trap. An impostor is posing as the myth, but if the original myth tracks down and takes out the impostor, he's in the position to reach Sheng. It's really very simple. The Jason Bourne *we* created will replace this new killer using his name. Once in place, *our* Jason Bourne sends out an urgent alarm—something drastic has happened that threatens Sheng's entire strategy—and Sheng has to respond. He can't afford not to, for his security must be absolute, his hands clean. He'll be forced to show himself, if only to kill his hired gun, to remove any association. When he does, this time we won't fail."

"It's a circle," said McAllister, his words barely above a whisper, as he stared at the diplomat. "And from everything you've told me, Webb won't walk near it, much less into it."

"Then we must provide him with an overpowering reason to do so," said Havilland softly. "In my profession —frankly, it was always my profession—we look for patterns, patterns that will trigger a man." Frowning, his eyes hollow and empty, the aging ambassador leaned back in his chair; certainly he was not at peace with himself. "Sometimes they are ugly realizations—repugnant, actually—but one must weigh the greater good, the greater benefits. For everyone."

"That doesn't tell me anything."

"David Webb became Jason Bourne for essentially one reason—the same reason that propelled him into the Medusa. A wife was taken from him; his children and the mother of his children were killed."

"Oh, my *God* . . ."

"This is where I leave," said Reilly, getting out of his chair.

3

Marie! Oh, Christ, Marie, it happened again! A floodgate opened and I couldn't handle it. I tried to, my darling, I tried so hard but I got totaled—I got washed away and I was drowning! I know what you'll say if I tell you, which is why I won't tell you even though I know you'll see it in my eyes, hear it in my voice— somehow, as only you know how. You'll say I should have come home to you, to talk to you, be with you, and we could work it out together. Together! My God! How much can you take? How unfair can I be, how long can it go on this way? I love you so much, in so many ways, that there are times I have to do it myself. If only to let you off the goddamned hook for a while, to let you breathe for a while without having your nerves scraped to their roots while you take care of me. But, you see, my love, I can do it! I did it tonight and I'm all right. I've calmed down now, I'm all right now. And now I'll come home to you better than I was. I have to, because without you there isn't anything left.

His face drenched with sweat, his track suit clinging to his body, David Webb ran breathlessly across the cold grass of the dark field, past the bleachers, and up the cement path toward the university gym. The autumn sun had disappeared behind the stone buildings of the campus, its glow firing the early evening sky as it hovered over the distant Maine woods. The autumn chill was penetrating; he shivered. It was not what his doctors had had in mind.

Regardless, he had followed medical advice; it had been one of those days. The government doctors had told him that if there were times—and there *would* be times—when sudden, disturbing images or fragments of memory broke into his mind, the best way to handle them was with strenuous exercise. His EKG charts indicated a healthy heart, his lungs were decent, though he was foolish enough to smoke, and since his body could take the punishment, it was the best way to relieve his mind. What he needed during such times was equanimity.

"What's wrong with a few drinks and cigarettes?" he had said to the doctors, stating his genuine preference. "The heart beats faster, the body doesn't suffer, and the mind is certainly far more relieved."

"They're depressants" had been the reply from the only man he listened to. "Artificial stimulants that lead only to further depression and increased anxiety. Run, or swim, or make love to your wife—or anybody else, for that matter. Don't be a goddamned fool and come back here a basket case. . . . Forget about you, think of *me.* I worked too hard on you, you ingrate. Get out of here, Webb. Take up your life—what you can remember of it —and enjoy. You've got it better than most people, and don't you forget that, or I'll cancel our controlled monthly blowouts at the saloons of our choosing and you can go to hell. And hell for you notwithstanding, I'd miss them. . . . Go, David. It's time for you to go."

Morris Panov was the only person besides Marie who could reach him. It was ironic, in a way, for initially Mo had not been one of the government doctors; the psychiatrist had neither sought nor been offered security clearance to hear the classified details of David Webb's background where the lie of Jason Bourne was buried. Nevertheless, Panov had forcefully inserted himself, threatening all manner of embarrassing disclosures if he was not given clearance and a voice in the subsequent therapy. His reasoning was simple, for when David had come within moments of being blown off the face of the earth by misinformed men who were convinced he had to die, that misinformation had been unwittingly furnished by Panov and the way it had happened infuriated him. He had been approached in panic by someone not given to panic, and asked "hypothetical" questions pertaining to a possibly deranged deep-cover agent in a potentially explosive situation. His answers were restrained and equivocal; he could not and would not diagnose a patient he had never seen—but yes, this was possible and that not unheard of, but, of course, nothing could be considered remotely material without physical and psychiatric examination. The key word was *nothing;* he should have *said* nothing! he later claimed. For his words in the ears of amateurs had sealed the order for Webb's execution —"Jason Bourne's" death sentence—an act that was aborted only at the last instant through David's own doing, while the squad of executioners were still in their unseen positions.

Not only had Morris Panov come on board at the Walter Reed Hospital and later at the Virginia medical complex, but he literally ran the show—Webb's show. *The son of a bitch has amnesia, you goddamned fools! He's been trying to tell you that for weeks in perfectly lucid English—I suspect too lucid for your convoluted mentality.*

They had worked together for months, as patient and doctor—and finally as friends. It helped that Marie adored Mo—good Lord, she needed an ally! The burden David had been to his wife was beyond telling, from those first days in Switzerland when she began to understand the pain within the man who had taken her captive, to the moment when she made the commitment—violently against his wishes—to help him, never believing what he himself believed, telling him over and over again that he was not the killer he thought he was, not the assassin others called him. Her belief became an anchor in his own crashing seas, her love the core of his emerging sanity. Without Marie he was a loveless, discarded dead man, and without Mo Panov he was little more than a vegetable. But with both of them behind him, he was brushing away the swirling clouds and finding the sun again.

Which was why he had opted for an hour of running around the deserted, cold track rather than heading home after his late-afternoon seminar. His weekly seminars often continued far beyond the hour when they were scheduled to end, so Marie never planned dinner, knowing they would go out to eat, their two unobtrusive guards somewhere in the darkness behind them—as one was walking across the barely visible field behind him now, the other no doubt inside the gym. *Insanity!* Or was it?

What had driven him to Panov's "strenuous exercise" was an image that had suddenly appeared in his mind while he had been grading papers several hours ago in his office. It was a face—a face he knew and remembered, and loved very much. A boy's face that aged in front of his inner screen, coming to full portrait in uniform, blurred, imperfect, but a part of him. As silent tears rolled down his cheeks he knew it was the dead brother they had told him about, the prisoner of war he had rescued in the jungles of Tam Quan years ago amid shattering explosions and a traitor he had executed by the name of Jason Bourne. He could not handle the violent, fragmented pictures; he had barely gotten through the shortened seminar, pleading a severe headache. He had to relieve the pressures, accept or reject the peeling layers of memory with the help of reason, which told him to go to the gym and run against the wind, any strong wind. He could not burden Marie every time a floodgate burst; he loved her too much for that. When he could handle it himself, he had to. It was his contract with himself.

He opened the heavy door, briefly wondering why every gymnasium entrance was designed with the weight of a portcullis. He went inside and walked across the stone floor through an archway and down a white-walled corridor until he reached the door of the faculty locker room. He was thankful that the room was empty; he was in no frame of mind to respond to small talk, and if required to do so, he would undoubtedly appear sullen, if not strange. He could also do without the stares he would probably provoke. He was too close to the edge; he had to pull back gradually, slowly, first within himself, then with Marie. Christ, when would it all *stop?* How much could he ask of her? But then he never had to ask —she gave without being asked.

Webb reached the row of lockers. His own was toward the end. He walked between the long wooden bench and the connecting metal cabinets when his eyes were suddenly riveted on an object up ahead. He rushed forward; a folded note had been taped to his locker. He ripped it off and opened it: *Your wife phoned. She wants you to call her as soon as you can. Says it's urgent. Ralph.*

The gym custodian might have had the brains to go outside and shout to him! thought David angrily as he spun the combination and opened the locker. After rummaging through his limp trousers for change, he ran to a pay telephone on the wall; he inserted a coin, disturbed that his hand trembled. Then he knew why. Marie never used the word "urgent." She avoided such words.

"Hello?"

"What is it?"

"I thought you might be there," said his wife. "Mo's panacea, the one he guarantees will cure you if it doesn't give you cardiac arrest."

"What *is* it?"

"David, come home. There's someone here you must see. Quickly, darling."

Undersecretary of State Edward McAllister kept his own introduction to a minimum, but by including certain facts let Webb know he was not from the lower ranks of the Department. On the other hand, he did not embellish his importance; he was the secure bureaucrat, confident that whatever expertise he possessed could weather changes in administrations.

"If you'd like, Mr. Webb, our business can wait until you get into something more comfortable."

David was still in his sweat-stained shorts and T-shirt,

having grabbed his clothes from the locker and raced to his car from the gym. "I don't think so," he said. "I don't think your business can wait—not where you come from, Mr. McAllister."

"Sit down, David." Marie St. Jacques Webb walked into the living room, two towels in her hands. "You, too, Mr. McAllister." She handed Webb a towel as both men sat down facing each other in front of an unlit fireplace. Marie moved behind her husband and began blotting his neck and shoulders with the second towel, the light of a table lamp heightening the reddish tint of her auburn hair, her lovely features in shadows, her eyes on the man from the State Department. "Please, go ahead," she continued. "As we've agreed, I'm cleared by the government for anything you might say."

"Was there a *question?*" asked David, glancing up at her and then at the visitor, making no attempt to disguise his hostility.

"None whatsoever," replied McAllister, smiling wanly yet sincerely. "No one who's read of your wife's contributions would dare exclude her. Where others failed she succeeded."

"That says it," agreed Webb. "Without saying anything, of course."

"Hey, come on, David, loosen up."

"Sorry. She's right." Webb tried to smile; the attempt was not successful. "I'm prejudging, and I shouldn't do that, should I?"

"I'd say you have every right to," said the undersecretary. "I know I would, if I were you. In spite of the fact that our backgrounds are very much alike—I was posted in the Far East for a number of years—no one would have considered me for the assignment you undertook. What you went through is light years beyond me."

"Beyond me, too. Obviously."

"Not from where I stand. The failure wasn't yours, God knows."

"Now you're being kind. No offense, but too much kindness—from where you stand—makes me nervous."

"Then let's get to the business at hand, all right?"

"Please."

"And I hope you haven't prejudged me too harshly.

I'm not your enemy, Mr. Webb. I want to be your friend. I can press buttons that can help you, protect you."

"From what?"

"From something nobody ever expected."

"Let's hear it."

"As of thirty minutes from now your security will be doubled," said McAllister, his eyes locked with David's. "That's my decision, and I'll quadruple it if I think it's necessary. Every arrival on this campus will be scrutinized, the grounds checked hourly. The rotating guards will no longer be part of the scenery, keeping you merely in sight, but in effect will be very much in sight themselves. Very obvious, and, I hope, threatening."

"Jesus!" Webb sprang forward in the chair. "It's *Carlos!*"

"We don't think so," said the man from State, shaking his head. "We can't rule Carlos out, but it's too remote, too unlikely."

"Oh?" David nodded. "It must be. If it *was* the Jackal, your men would be all over the place and *out* of sight. You'd let him come after me and take him, and if I'm killed, the cost is acceptable."

"Not to me. You don't have to believe that, but I mean it."

"Thank you, but then what are we talking about?"

"Your file was broken—that is, the Treadstone file was invaded."

"Invaded? Unauthorized disclosure?"

"Not at first. There was authorization, all right, because there was a crisis—and in a sense we had no choice. Then everything went off the wire and now we're concerned. For you."

"Back up, please. Who got the file?"

"A man on the inside, high inside. His credentials were the best, no one could question them."

"Who was he?"

"A British MI-Six operating out of Hong Kong, a man the CIA has relied on for years. He flew into Washington, and went directly to his primary liaison at the Agency, asking to be given everything there was on Jason Bourne. He claimed there was a crisis in the territory that was a direct result of the Treadstone project. He also made it clear that if sensitive information was to be exchanged between British and American Intelligence—*continued* to be exchanged—he thought it best that his request be granted forthwith."

"He had to give a damn good reason."

"He did." McAllister paused nervously, blinking his eyes and rubbing his forehead with extended fingers.

"Well?"

"Jason Bourne is back," said McAllister quietly. "He's killed again. In Kowloon."

Marie gasped; she clutched her husband's right shoulder, her large brown eyes angry, frightened. She stared in silence at the man from State. Webb did not move. Instead he studied McAllister, as a man might watch a cobra.

"What the *hell* are you talking about?" he whispered, then raised his voice. "Jason Bourne—*that* Jason Bourne—doesn't exist anymore. He never *did!*"

"You know that and we know that, but in Asia his legend is very much alive. You created it, Mr. Webb—brilliantly, in my judgment."

"I'm not interested in your judgment, Mr. McAllister," said David, removing his wife's hand and getting out of the chair. "What's this MI-Six agent working on? How old is he? What's his stability factor, his record? You must have run an up-to-date trace on him."

"Of course we did and there was nothing irregular. London confirmed his outstanding service record, his current status, as well as the information he brought us. As chief of post for MI-Six, he was called in by the Kowloon–Hong Kong police because of the potentially explosive nature of events. The Foreign Office itself stood behind him."

"Wrong!" shouted Webb, shaking his head, then lowered his voice. "He was turned, Mr. McAllister! Someone offered him a small fortune to get that file. He used the only lie that would work and all of you swallowed it!"

"I'm afraid it's not a lie—not as he knew it. He believed the evidence, and London believes it. *A* Jason Bourne is back in Asia."

"And what if I told you it wouldn't be the first time central control was fed a lie so an overworked, over-*risked, underpaid* man can turn! All the years, all the dangers, and nothing to show for it. He decides on one opportunity that gives him an annuity for life. In this case that *file!*"

"If that is the case, it won't do him much good. He's dead."

"He's what . . . ?"

"He was shot to death two nights ago in Kowloon, in his office, an hour after he'd flown into Hong Kong."

"Goddamn it, it doesn't *happen!*" cried David, bewildered. "A man who turns backs himself up. He builds a case against his benefactor before the act, letting him know it'll get to the right people if anything ugly happens. It's his insurance, his *only* insurance."

"He was clean," insisted the State Department man.

"Or stupid," rejoined Webb.

"No one thinks that."

"What *do* they think?"

"That he was pursuing an extraordinary development, one that could erupt into widespread violence throughout the underworlds of Hong Kong and Macao. Organized crime becomes suddenly very disorganized, not unlike the tong wars of the twenties and thirties. The killings pile up. Rival gangs instigate riots; waterfronts become battlegrounds; warehouses, even cargo ships are blown up for revenge, or to wipe out competitors. Sometimes all it takes is several powerful warring factions— and a Jason Bourne in the background."

"But since there is no Jason Bourne, it's *police* work! Not MI-Six."

"Mr. McAllister just said the man was called *in* by the Hong Kong police," broke in Marie, looking hard at the undersecretary of State. "MI-Six obviously agreed with the decision. Why was that?"

"It's the wrong ballpark!" David was adamant, his breath short.

"Jason Bourne wasn't the creation of the police authorities," said Marie, going to her husband's side. "He was created by U.S. Intelligence by way of the State Department. But I suspect MI-Six inserted itself for a far more pressing reason than to find a killer posing as Jason Bourne. Am I right, Mr. McAllister?"

"You're right, Mrs. Webb. *Far* more. In our discussions these last two days, several members of our section thought you'd understand more clearly than we did. Let's call it an economic problem that could lead to serious political turmoil, not only in Hong Kong but throughout the world. You were a highly regarded economist for the Canadian government. You advised Canadian ambassadors and delegations all over the world."

"Would you both mind explaining to the man who balances the checkbook around here?"

"These aren't the times to permit disruptions in Hong Kong's marketplace, Mr. Webb, even—perhaps especially—its illegal marketplace. Disruptions accompanied by violence give the impression of government instability, if not far deeper instability. This isn't the time to give the expansionists in Red China any more ammunition than they have already."

"Come again, please?"

"The treaty of 1997," answered Marie quietly. "The lease runs out in barely a decade, which is why the new Accords were negotiated with Peking. Still, everybody's nervous, everything's shaky and no one had better rock the boat. Calm stability is the name of the game."

David looked at her, then back at McAllister. He nodded his head. "I see. I've read the papers and the magazines . . . but it's just not a subject that I know a hell of a lot about."

"My husband's interests lie elsewhere," explained Marie to McAllister. "In the study of people, their civilizations."

"All right," Webb agreed. "*So?*"

"Mine are with money and the constant exchange of money—the expansion of it, the markets and their fluctuations—the stability, or the lack of it. And if Hong Kong is nothing else, it's money. That's more or less its only commodity; it has little other reason for being. Its industries would die without it; without priming, the pump runs dry."

"And if you take away the stability you have chaos," added McAllister. "It's the excuse for the old warlords in China. The People's Republic marches in to contain the chaos, suppress the agitators, and suddenly there's nothing left but an awkward giant fumbling with the entire colony as well as the New Territories. The cooler heads in Beijing are ignored in favor of more aggressive elements who want to save face through military control. Banks collapse, Far East trade is stymied. Chaos."

"The PRC would *do* that?"

"Hong Kong, Kowloon, Macao and all the territories are part of their 'great nation under heaven'—even the China Accords make that clear. It's one entity, and the Oriental won't tolerate a disobedient child, you know that."

"Are you telling me that one man pretending to be Jason Bourne can do this—can bring about this kind of crisis? I don't *believe* you!"

"It's an extreme scenario, but yes, it could happen. You see, the myth rides with him, that's the hypnotic factor. Multiple killings are ascribed to him, if only to distance the real killers from the scenes—conspirators from the politically fanatic right and left using Bourne's lethal image as their own. When you think about it, it's precisely the way the myth itself was created, wasn't it? Whenever anyone of importance anywhere in the South China area was assassinated, you, as Jason Bourne, made sure the kill was credited to you. At the end of two years you were notorious, yet in fact you killed only one man, a drunken informer in Macao who tried to garrote you."

"I don't remember that," said David.

The man from State nodded sympathetically. "Yes, I was told. But don't you see, if the men killed are perceived as political and powerful figures—let's say the Crown governor, or a PRC negotiator, or anyone like that is assassinated, the whole colony is in an uproar." McAllister paused, shaking his head in weary dismissal. "However, this is our concern, not yours, and I can tell you we have the best men in the Intelligence community working on it. Your concern is yourself, Mr. Webb. And right now, as a matter of conscience, it's mine. You have to be protected."

"That file," said Marie coldly, "should never have been given to *anyone.*"

"We had no choice. We work closely with the British; we had to prove that Treadstone was over, finished. That your husband was thousands of miles away from Hong Kong."

"You told them where he *was?*" shouted Webb's wife. "How *dare* you?"

"We had no choice," repeated McAllister, again rubbing his forehead. "We have to cooperate when certain crises arise. Surely you can understand that."

"What I can't understand is why there ever *was* a file on my husband!" said Marie, furious. "It was deep, *deep cover!*"

"Congressional funding of Intelligence operations demanded it. It's the law."

"Get off it!" said David angrily. "Since you're so up on me, you know where I come from. Tell me, where are all those records on Medusa?"

"I can't answer that," replied McAllister.

"You just did," said Webb.

"Dr. Panov pleaded with you people to destroy *all* the Treadstone records," insisted Marie. "Or at the very least to use false names, but you wouldn't even do that. What kind of men are you?"

"*I* would have agreed to *both!*" said McAllister with sudden, surprising force. "I'm sorry, Mrs. Webb. Forgive me. It was before my time. . . . Like you, I'm offended. You may be right, perhaps there never should have been a file. There are ways—"

"Bullshit," broke in David, his voice hollow. "It's part of another strategy, another trap. You want Carlos, and you don't care how you get him."

"*I* care, Mr. Webb, and you don't have to believe that, either. What's the Jackal to *me*—or the Far East Section? He's a *European* problem."

"Are you telling me I spent three years of my life hunting a man who didn't *mean* a goddamned thing?"

"No, of course not. Times change, perspectives change. It's all so futile sometimes."

"Jesus *Christ!*"

"Loosen up, David," said Marie, her attention briefly on the man from State, who sat pale in his chair, his hands gripping the arms. "Let's all loosen up." Then she held her husband's eyes with her own. "Something happened this afternoon, didn't it?"

"I'll tell you later."

"Of course." Marie looked at McAllister as David returned to the chair, his face lined and tired, older than it had been only minutes ago. "Everything you've told us is leading up to something, isn't it?" she said to the man from State. "There's something else you want us to know, isn't there?"

"Yes, and it's not easy for me. Please bear in mind that I've only recently been assigned, with full clearance, to Mr. Webb's classified dossier."

"Including his wife and children in Cambodia?"

"Yes."

"Then say what you have to say, please."

McAllister once again extended his thin fingers and nervously massaged his forehead. "From what we've learned—what London confirmed five hours ago—it's possible that your husband is a target. A man wants him killed."

"But not Carlos, *not* the Jackal," said Webb, sitting forward.

"No. At least we can't see a connection."

"What *do* you see?" asked Marie, sitting on the arm of David's chair. "What have you learned?"

"The MI-Six officer in Kowloon had a great many sensitive papers in his office, any number of which would have brought high prices in Hong Kong. However, only the Treadstone file—the file on Jason Bourne—was taken. That was the confirmation London gave us. It's as though a signal was sent: He's the man we want, only Jason Bourne."

"But *why?*" cried Marie, her hand gripping David's wrist.

"Because someone was killed," answered Webb quietly. "And someone else wants the account settled."

"That's what we've been working on," agreed McAllister, nodding. "We've made some progress."

"Who was killed?" asked the former Jason Bourne.

"Before I answer, you should know that all we've got is what our people in Hong Kong could dig up by themselves. By and large it's speculation; there's no proof."

"What do you mean 'by themselves'? Where the hell were the British? You *gave* them the Treadstone file!"

"Because they gave us proof that a man has killed in the name of Treadstone's creation, *our* creation—*you.* They weren't about to identify MI-Six's sources any more than we would turn over our contacts to them. Our people have worked around the clock, probing every possibility, trying to find out who the dead Sixer's main sources were on the assumption that one of them was responsible for his death. They ran down a rumor in Macao—only, it turned out to be more than a rumor."

"I repeat," said Webb, "who was killed?"

"A woman," answered the man from State. "The wife of a Hong Kong banker named Yao Ming, a taipan whose bank is only a fraction of his wealth. His holdings are so extensive he's been re-welcomed in Beijing as an investor and consultant. He's influential, powerful, beyond reach."

"Circumstances?"

"Ugly but not unusual. His wife was a minor actress who appeared in a number of films for the Shaw brothers, and quite a bit younger than her husband. She was also about as faithful as a mink in season, if you'll excuse—"

"Please," said Marie, "go on."

"Nevertheless, he looked the other way; she was his young, beautiful trophy. She was also part of the colony's jet set, which has its share of unsavory characters. One weekend it's gambling for extraordinary stakes in Macao, next the races in Singapore, or flying over to the Pescadores for the pistol games in backwater opium houses, betting thousands on who will be killed as men face one another across tables, spinning chambers and aiming at each other. And, of course, there's a widespread use of drugs. Her last lover was a distributor. His suppliers were in Guangzhou, his routes up the Deep Bay waterways east of the Lok Ma Chau border."

"According to reports, it's a wide avenue with lots of traffic," interrupted Webb. "Why did your people concentrate on him—on his operation?"

"Because his operation, as you so aptly term it, was rapidly becoming the only one in town, or on that avenue. He was systematically cutting out his competitors, bribing the Chinese marine patrols to sink their boats and dispose of the crews. Apparently they were effective; a great many bodies riddled with bullets ended up floating onto the mud flats and into the riverbanks. The factions were at war and the distributor—the young wife's lover—was marked for execution."

"Under the circumstances, he had to have been aware

of the possibility. He must have surrounded himself with a dozen bodyguards.''

"Right again. And that kind of security calls for the talents of a legend. His enemies hired that legend.''

"Bourne," whispered David, shaking his head and closing his eyes.

"Yes,'' concurred McAllister. "Two weeks ago the drug dealer and Yao Ming's wife were shot in their bed at the Lisboa Hotel in Macao. It wasn't a pleasant kill; their bodies were barely recognizable. The weapon was an Uzi machine gun. The incident was covered up; the police and government officials were bribed with a great deal of money—a taipan's money.''

"And let me guess,'' said Webb in a monotone. "The Uzi. It was the same weapon used in a previous killing credited to this Bourne.''

"That specific weapon was left outside a conference room in a cabaret in Kowloon's Tsim Sha Tsui. There were five corpses in that room, three of the victims among the colony's wealthier businessmen. The British won't elaborate; they merely showed us several very graphic photographs.''

"This taipan, Yao Ming,'' said David. "The actress's husband. He's the connection your people found, isn't he?''

"They learned that he was one of MI-Six's sources. His connections in Beijing made him an important contributor to Intelligence. He was invaluable.''

"Then, of course, his wife was killed, his beloved young wife—''

"I'd say his beloved trophy,'' interrupted McAllister. "His *trophy* was taken.''

"All right,'' said Webb. "The trophy is far more important than the wife.''

"I've spent years in the Far East. There's a phrase for it—in Mandarin, I think, but I can't remember how it goes.''

"Ren you jiaqian," said David. "The price of a man's image, as it were.''

"Yes, I guess that's it.''

"It'll do. So the man from MI-Six is approached by his distraught contact, the taipan, and told to get the file on this Jason Bourne, the assassin who killed his wife—his trophy—or in short words, there might be no more information coming from his sources in Beijing to British Intelligence."

"That's the way our people read it. And for his trouble the Sixer is killed because Yao Ming can't afford to have the slightest association with Bourne. The taipan has to remain unreachable, untouchable. He wants his revenge, but not with any possibility of exposure."

"What do the British say?" asked Marie.

"In no uncertain terms to stay away from the entire situation. London was blunt. We made a mess of Treadstone, and they don't want our ineptitude in Hong Kong during these sensitive times."

"Have they confronted Yao Ming?" Webb watched the undersecretary closely.

"When I brought up the name, they said it was out of the question. In truth, they were startled, but that didn't change their stand. If anything, they were angrier."

"Untouchable," said David.

"They probably want to continue using him."

"In spite of what he *did?*" Marie broke in. "What he *may* have done, and what he might do to my *husband!*"

"It's a different world," said McAllister softly.

"You cooperated with them—"

"We had to," interrupted the man from State.

"Then insist they cooperate with you. *Demand* it!"

"Then they could demand other things from us. We can't do that."

"*Liars!*" Marie turned her head in disgust.

"I haven't lied to you, Mrs. Webb."

"Why don't I trust you, Mr. McAllister?" asked David.

"Probably because you can't trust your government, Mr. Webb, and you have very little reason to. I can only tell you that I'm a man of conscience. You can accept that or not—accept *me* or not—but in the meantime I'll make sure you're safe."

"You look at me so strangely—why is that?"

"I've never been in this position, that's why."

The chimes of the doorbell rang, and Marie, shaking her head to their sound, rose and walked rapidly across the room and into the foyer. She opened the door. For a moment she stopped breathing, and stared helplessly.

Two men stood side by side, both holding up black plastic identification cases, each with a glistening silver badge attached to the top, each embossed eagle reflecting the light of the carriage lamps on the porch. Beyond, at the curb, was a second dark sedan; inside could be seen the silhouettes of other men, and the glow of a lighted cigarette—other men, other guards. She wanted to scream, but she did not.

Edward McAllister climbed into the passenger seat of his own State Department car and looked through the closed window at the figure standing in the doorway. The former Jason Bourne stood motionless, his eyes fixed rigidly on his departing visitor.

"Let's get out of here," said McAllister to the driver, a man about his own age and balding, with tortoiseshell glasses.

The car started forward, the driver cautious on the strange, narrow, tree-lined street a block from the rocky beach in the small Maine town. For several minutes neither man spoke; finally the driver asked, "How did everything go?"

"Go?" replied the man from State. "As the ambassador might say, 'All the pieces are in place.' The foundation's there, the logic there; the missionary work is done."

"I'm glad to hear it."

"Are you? Then I'm glad too." McAllister raised his trembling right hand; his thin fingers massaging his right temple. "No, I'm *not!*" he said suddenly. "I'm goddamned sick!"

"I'm sorry—"

"And speaking of missionary work, I *am* a *Christian*. I mean I *believe*—nothing so chic as being zealous, or born again, or teaching Sunday school, or prostrating myself in the aisle, but I *do* believe. My wife and I go to the Episcopal church at least twice a month, my two sons are acolytes. I'm generous because I *want* to be. Can you understand that?"

"Sure. I don't have quite those feelings, but I understand."

"But I just walked out of that man's *house!*"

"Hey, easy. What's the matter?"

McAllister stared straight ahead, the oncoming headlights creating shadows rushing across his face. "May
God have mercy on my soul," he whispered.

4

Screams suddenly filled the darkness, an approaching,
growing cacophony of roaring voices. Then surging bodies were all around them, racing ahead, shouting, faces
contorted in frenzy. Webb fell to his knees, covering his
face and neck with both hands as best he could, swinging
his shoulders violently back and forth, creating a shifting
target within the circle of attack. His dark clothes were a
plus in the shadows but would be no help if an indiscriminate burst of gunfire erupted, taking at least one of the
guards with him. Yet bullets were not always a killer's
choice. There were darts—lethal missiles of poison delivered by air-compressed weapons, puncturing exposed
flesh, bringing death in a matter of minutes. Or seconds.

A hand gripped his shoulder! He spun around, arcing
his arm up, dislodging the hand as he sidestepped to his
left, crouching like an animal.

"You okay, Professor?" asked the guard on his right,
grinning in the wash of his flashlight.

"What? What *happened?*"

"Isn't it great!" cried the guard on his left, approaching, as David got to his feet.

"What?"

"Kids with that kind of spirit. It really makes you feel
good to see it!"

It was over. The campus quad was silent again, and in
the distance between the stone buildings that fronted the
playing fields and the college stadium, the pulsing flames
of a bonfire could be seen through the empty bleachers.
A football rally was reaching its climax, and his guards
were laughing.

"How about you, Professor?" continued the man on his left. "Do you feel better about things now, what with us here and all?"

It was over. The self-inflicted madness was over. Or was it? Why was his chest pounding so? Why was he so bewildered, so frightened? Something was wrong.

"Why does this whole parade bother me?" said David over morning coffee in the breakfast alcove of their old rented Victorian house.

"You miss your walks on the beach," said Marie, ladling her husband's single poached egg over the single slice of toast. "Eat that before you have a cigarette."

"No, really. It bothers me. For the past week I've been a duck in a superficially protected gallery. It occurred to me yesterday afternoon."

"What do you mean?" Marie poured out the water and placed the pan in the kitchen sink, her eyes on Webb. "Six men are around you, four on your 'flanks,' as you said, and two peering into everything in front of you and behind you."

"A parade."

"Why do you call it that?"

"I don't know. Everyone in his place, marching to a drumbeat. I don't know."

"But you feel something?"

"I guess so."

"Tell me. Those feelings of yours once saved my life on the Guisan Quai in Zurich. I'd like to hear it—well, maybe I wouldn't, but I damn well better."

Webb broke the yolk of his egg on the toast. "Do you know how easy it would be for someone—someone who looked young enough to be a student—to walk by me on a path and shoot an air dart into me? He could cover the sound with a cough, or a laugh, and I'd have a hundred c.c.'s of strychnine in my blood."

"You know far more about that sort of thing than I do."

"Of course. Because that's the way I'd do it."

"*No.* That's the way Jason Bourne might do it. Not *you.*"

"All right, I'm projecting. It doesn't invalidate the thought."

"What happened yesterday afternoon?"

Webb toyed with the egg and toast on his plate. "The seminar ran late as usual. It was getting dark, and my guards fell in and we walked across the quad toward the parking lot. There was a football rally—our insignificant team against another insignificant team, but very large for us. The crowd passed the four of us—kids racing to a bonfire behind the bleachers, screaming and shouting and singing fight songs, working themselves up. And I thought to myself, this is *it*. This is when it's going to happen if it *is* going to happen. Believe me, for those few moments I *was* Bourne. I crouched and sidestepped and watched everyone I could see—I was close to panic."

"And?" said Marie, disturbed by her husband's abrupt silence.

"My so-called guards were looking around and laughing, the two in front having a ball, enjoying the whole thing."

"That disturbed you?"

"Instinctively. I was a vulnerable target in the center of an excited crowd. My nerves told me that; my mind didn't have to."

"Who's talking now?"

"I'm not sure. I just know that during those few moments nothing made sense to me. Then, only seconds later, as if to pinpoint the feelings I hadn't verbalized, the man behind me on my left came up and said something like 'Isn't it great to see kids with that kind of spirit? Makes you feel good, doesn't it?' . . . I mumbled something inane, and then he said—and these are his exact words—'How about you, Professor? Do you feel better about things now, what with us here and all?' " David looked up at his wife. "Did *I* feel better . . . *now? Me.*"

"He knew what their job was," interrupted Marie. "To protect you. I'm sure he meant if you felt safer."

"Did he? Do they? That crowd of screaming kids, the dim light, the shadowy bodies, obscure faces . . . and he's joining in and laughing—they're *all* laughing. Are they really here to protect me?"

"What else?"

"I don't know. Maybe I've simply been where they haven't. Maybe I'm just thinking too much, thinking about McAllister and those eyes of his. Except for the blinking they belonged to a dead fish. You could read into them anything you wanted to—depending upon how you felt."

"What he told you was a shock," said Marie, leaning against the sink, her arms folded across her breasts, watching her husband closely. "It had to have had a terrible effect on you. It certainly did on me."

"That's probably it," agreed Webb, nodding. "It's ironic, but as much as there are so many things I want to remember, there's an awful lot I'd like to forget."

"Why don't you call McAllister and tell him what you feel, what you think? You've got a direct line to him, both at his office and his home. Mo Panov would tell you to do that."

"Yes, Mo would." David ate his egg halfheartedly. " 'If there's a way to get rid of a specific anxiety, do it as fast as you can,' that's what he'd say."

"Then do it."

Webb smiled, about as enthusiastically as he ate his egg. "Maybe I will, maybe I won't. I'd rather not announce a latent, or passive, or recurrent paranoia, or whatever the hell they call it. Mo would fly up here and beat my brains out."

"If he doesn't, I might."

"*Ni shi nuhaizi,*" said David, using the paper napkin, as he got out of his chair and went to her.

"And what does that mean, my inscrutable husband and number eighty-seven lover?"

"Bitch goddess. It means, freely translated, that you are a little girl—and not so little—and I can still take you three out of five on the bed where there are other things to do with you instead of beating you up."

"All that in such a short phrase?"

"We don't waste words, we paint pictures. . . . I've got to leave. The class this morning deals with Siam's Rama the Second, and his claims on the Malay states in the early nineteenth century. It's a pain in the ass but important. What's worse is there's an exchange student from Moulmein, Burma, who I think knows more than I do."

"Siam?" asked Marie, holding him. "That's Thailand."

"Yes. It's Thailand now."

"Your wife, your children? Does it hurt, David?"

He looked at her, loving her so. "I can't be that hurt where I can't see that clearly. Sometimes I hope I never do."

"I don't think that way at all. I want you to see them and hear them and feel them. And to know that I love them too."

"Oh, *Christ!*" He held her, their bodies together in a warmth that was theirs alone.

The line was busy for the second time, so Webb replaced the phone and returned to W. F. Vella's *Siam under Rama III* to see if the Burmese exchange student had been right about Rama II's conflict with the sultan of Kedah over the disposition of the island of Penang. It was confrontation time in the rarefied groves of academe; the Moulmein pagodas of Kipling's poetry had been replaced by a smart-ass postgraduate student who had no respect for his betters—Kipling would understand that, and torpedo it.

There was a brief knock on his office door, which opened before David could ask the caller in. It was one of his guards, the man who had spoken to him yesterday afternoon during the pre-game rally—among the crowds, amid the noise, in the middle of his fears.

"Hello there, Professor?"

"Hello. It's Jim, isn't it?"

"No, Johnny. It doesn't matter; you're not expected to get our names straight."

"Is anything the matter?"

"Just the opposite, sir. I dropped in to say good-bye— for all of us, the whole contingent. Everything's clean and you're back to normal. We've been ordered to report to B-One-L."

"To what?"

"Sounds kind of silly, doesn't it? Instead of saying 'Come on back to headquarters,' they call it B-One-L, as if anyone couldn't figure it out."

"*I* can't figure it out."

"Base-One-Langley. We're CIA, all six of us, but I guess you know that."

"You're leaving? *All* of you?"

"That's about it."

"But I thought . . . I thought there was a crisis *here.*"

"Everything's clean."

"I haven't heard from anybody. I haven't heard from *McAllister.*"

"Sorry, don't know him. We just have our orders."

"You can't simply come in here and say you're *leaving* without some explanation! I was told I was a target! That a man in Hong Kong wanted me *killed!*"

"Well, I don't know whether you were told that, or whether you told yourself that, but I do know we've got an A-one legitimate problem in Newport News. We have to get briefed and get on it."

"A-one legitimate . . .? What about *me?*"

"Get a lot of rest, Professor. We were told you need it." The man from the CIA abruptly turned, went through the door, and closed it.

Well, I don't know whether you were told that, or whether you told yourself that. . . . How about you, Professor? Do you feel better about things now, what with us here and all?

Parade? . . . *Charade!*

Where was McAllister's number? Where *was* it? Goddamnit, he had two copies, one at home and one in his desk drawer—no, his wallet! He found it, his whole body trembling in fear and in anger as he dialed.

"Mr. McAllister's office," said a female voice.

"I thought this was his private line. That's what I was told!"

"Mr. McAllister is away from Washington, sir. In these cases we're instructed to pick up and log the calls."

"Log the *calls?* Where *is* he?"

"I don't know, sir. I'm from the secretarial pool. He phones in every other day or so. Who shall I say called?"

"That's not good enough! My name is Webb. Jason Webb . . . *No, David* Webb! I have to talk to him right away! *Immediately!*"

"I'll connect you with the department handling his urgent calls. . . ."

Webb slammed down the phone. He had the number for McAllister's home; he dialed it.

"Hello?" The voice of another woman.

"Mr. McAllister, please."

"I'm afraid he's not here. If you care to leave your name and a number, I'll give it to him."

"When?"

"Well, he should be calling tomorrow or the next day. He always does."

"You've got to give me the number where he is *now*, Mrs. McAllister!—I assume this is Mrs. McAllister."

"I should hope so. Eighteen years' worth. Who are you?"

"Webb. *David* Webb."

"Oh, of course! Edward rarely discusses business—and he certainly didn't in your case—but he did tell me what terribly nice people you and your lovely wife are. As a matter of fact, our older boy, who's in prep school, is, naturally, *very* interested in the university where you teach. Now, in the last year or so his marks dropped just a touch, and his SAT's weren't the highest, but he has such a wonderful, enthusiastic outlook on life, I'm sure he'd be an asset. . . ."

"Mrs. McAllister!" broke in Webb. "I have to reach your husband! *Now!*"

"Oh, I'm terribly sorry, but I don't think that's possible. He's in the Far East, and, of course, I don't have a number where I can reach him there. In emergencies we always call the State Department."

David hung up the phone. He had to alert—*phone*—Marie. The line had to be free by now; it had been busy for nearly an hour, and there was no one his wife could talk with on the telephone for an hour, not even her father, her mother, or her two brothers in Canada. There was great affection between them all, but she was the ranch-Ontario maverick. She was not the Francophile her father was, not a homebody like her mother, and although she adored her brothers, not the rustic, plain-spoken *lassos* they were. She had found another life in the stratified layers of higher economics, with a doctorate, and gainful employment with the Canadian government. And, at last, she had married an American.

Quel dommage.

The line was *still* busy! *Goddamnit,* Marie!

Then Webb froze, his whole body for an instant a block of searing hot ice. He could barely move, but he did move, and then he raced out of his small office and down the corridor with such speed that he pummeled three students and a colleague out of his path, sending two into walls, the others buckling under him; he was a man suddenly possessed.

Reaching his house, he slammed on the brakes; the car screeched to a stop as he leaped out of the seat and ran up the path to the door. He stopped, staring, his breath suddenly no longer in him. The door was open and on the angled, indented panel was a hand print stamped in red—*blood*.

Webb ran inside, throwing everything out of his way. Furniture crashed and lamps were smashed as he searched the ground floor. Then he went upstairs, his hands two thin slabs of granite, his every nerve primed for a sound, a weight, his killer instinct as clear as the red stains he had seen below on the outside door. For these moments he knew and accepted the fact that he was the assassin—the lethal animal—that Jason Bourne had been. If his wife was above, he would kill whoever tried to harm her—or who had harmed her already.

Prone on the floor, he pushed the door of their bedroom open.

The explosion blew apart the upper hallway wall. He rolled under the blast to the opposite side; he had no weapon, but he had a cigarette lighter. He reached into his trousers pockets for the scribbled notes all teachers gather, bunched them together, spun to his left and snapped the lighter; the flame was immediate. He threw the fired wad far into the bedroom as he pressed his back against the wall and rose from the floor, his head whipping toward the other two closed doors on the narrow second floor. Suddenly he lashed out with his feet, one crash after another, as he lunged back onto the floor and rolled into the shadows.

Nothing. The two rooms were empty. If there was an enemy he was in the bedroom. But by now the bedspread was on fire. The flames were gradually leaping toward the ceiling. Only seconds now.

Now!

He plunged into the room, and grabbing the flaming bedspread he swung it in a circle as he crouched and rolled on the floor until the spread was ashes, all the while expecting an ice-cold hit in his shoulder or his arm, but knowing he could overcome it and take his enemy. *Jesus!* He *was* Jason Bourne again!

There was nothing. His Marie was not there; there was nothing but a primitive string device that had triggered a shotgun, angled for a certain kill when he pushed the door open. He stamped out the flames, lurched for a table lamp and turned it on.

Marie! *Marie!*

Then he saw it. A note lying on the pillow on her side of the bed: *"A wife for a wife, Jason Bourne. She is wounded but not dead, as mine is dead. You know where to find me, and her, if you are circumspect and fortunate. Perhaps we can do business, for I have enemies, too. If not, what is the death of one more daughter?"*

Webb screamed, falling onto the pillows, trying to mute the outrage and the horror that came from his throat, pushing back the pain that swept through his temples. Then he turned over and stared at the ceiling, a terrible, brute passivity coming over him. Things unremembered suddenly came back to him—things he had never revealed even to Morris Panov. Of bodies collapsing under his knife, falling under his gun—these were not imagined killings, they were real. They had made him what he was not, but they had done the job too well. He had become the image, the man that was not supposed to be. He'd *had* to. He'd had to *survive*—without knowing who he was.

And now he knew the two men within him that made up his whole being. He would always remember the one because it was the man he wanted to be, but for the time being he had to be the other—the man he despised.

Jason Bourne rose from the bed and went to the walkin closet where there was a locked drawer, the third in his built-in bureau. He reached up and pulled the tape from a key attached to the closeted ceiling. He inserted it in the lock and opened the drawer. Inside were two dismantled automatics, four strings of thin wire attached to spools that he could conceal in his palms, three valid passports in three different names, and six *plastique* explosive charges that could blow apart whole rooms. He would use one or all. David Webb would find his wife. Or Jason Bourne would become the terrorist no one ever dreamed of in his wildest nightmares. He did not care—too much had been taken from him. He would endure no more.

Bourne cracked the various parts in place and snapped

the magazine of the second automatic. Both were ready. He was ready. He went back to the bed and lay down, staring again at the ceiling. The logistics would fall into place, he knew that. Then the hunt would begin. He would find her—dead or alive—and if she was dead, he would kill, kill and *kill again!*

Whoever it was would never get away from him. Not from Jason Bourne.

5

Barely in control of himself, he knew that calm was out of the question. His hand gripped the automatic while his mind cracked with surreal, rapid bursts of gunfire as one option after another slammed into his head. Above all, he could not stay still; he had to keep in motion. He had to get up and *move!*

The State Department. The men at State he had known during his last months in the remote, classified Virginia medical complex—those insistent, obsessed men who questioned him relentlessly, showing him photographs by the dozens until Mo Panov would order them to stop. He had learned their names and written them down, thinking that one day he might want to know who they were—no reason other than visceral distrust; such men had tried to kill him only months before. Yet he had never asked for their names, nor were they offered, except as Harry, Bill, or Sam, presumably on the theory that actual identities would simply add to his confusion. Instead, he had unobtrusively read their identification tags and, after they left, wrote the names down and placed the pieces of paper with his personal belongings in the bureau drawer. When Marie came to see him, which was every day, he gave her those names and told her to hide them in the house—hide them well.

Later, Marie admitted that although she had done as he instructed, she thought his suspicions were excessive, a case of overkill. But then one morning, only minutes after a heated session with the men from Washington, David pleaded with her to leave the medical complex immediately, run to the car, drive to the bank where they had a safety deposit box, and do the following: Insert a short strand of her hair in the bottom left border of the deposit box, lock it, get out of the bank, and return two hours later to see if it was still there.

It was not. She had securely fixed the strand of hair in place; it could not have fallen away unless the deposit box had been opened. She found it on the tiled floor of the bank vault.

"How did you *know?*" she had asked him.

"One of my friendly interrogators got hot and tried to provoke me. Mo was out of the room for a couple of minutes and he damn near accused me of faking, of hiding things. I knew you were coming, and so I played it out. I wanted to see for myself how far they would go— how far they *could* go."

Nothing had been sacred then, and nothing was sacred now. It was all too symmetrical. The guards had been pulled, his own reactions condescendingly questioned, as if he were the one who had asked for the additional protection and not on the insistence of one Edward McAllister. Then within hours Marie was taken, according to a scenario that had been detailed far too accurately by a nervous man with dead eyes. And now this same McAllister was suddenly fifteen thousand miles away from his own, self-determined ground zero. Had the undersecretary turned? Had he been bought in Hong Kong? Had he betrayed Washington as well as the man he had sworn to protect? What was *happening?* Whatever it was, among the unholy secrets was code name Medusa. It had never been mentioned during the questioning, never referred to. Its absence was startling. It was as if the unacknowledged battalion of psychotics and killers had never existed; its history had been wiped off the books. But that history could be reinstated. This was where he would start.

Webb walked rapidly out of the bedroom and down the steps to his study, once a small library off the hallway in the old Victorian house. He sat at his desk, opened the bottom drawer, and removed several notebooks and various papers. He then inserted a brass letter opener and pried up the false bottom; lying on the second layer of wood were other papers. They were a vague, mostly bewildering assortment of fragmented recollections, images that had come to him at odd hours of the day and night. There were torn scraps and pages from small notebooks and scissored pieces of stationery on which he had jotted down the pictures and words that exploded in his head. It was a mass of painful evocations, many so tortured that he could not share them with Marie, fearing the hurt would be too great, the revelations of Jason Bourne too brutal for his wife to confront. And among these secrets were the names of the experts in clandestine operations who had come down to question him so intensely in Virginia.

David's eyes suddenly focused on the ugly heavy-caliber weapon on the edge of the desk. Without realizing it, he had gripped it in his hand and carried it down from the bedroom; he stared at it for a moment, then picked up the phone. It was the beginning of the most agonizing, infuriating hour of his life, as each moment Marie drifted farther away.

The first two calls were taken by wives or lovers; the men he was trying to reach were suddenly not there when he identified himself. He was still out of sanction! They would not touch him without authorization and that authorization was being withheld. *Christ,* he should have known!

"Hello?"

"Is this the Lanier residence?"

"Yes, it is."

"William Lanier, please. Tell him it's urgent, a Sixteen Hundred alert. My name is Thompson, State Department."

"Just one minute," said the woman, concerned.

"*Who* is this?" asked a man's voice.

"It's David Webb. You remember Jason Bourne, don't you?"

"*Webb?*" A pause followed, filled with Lanier's breathing. "Why did you say your name was Thompson? That it was a White House alert?"

"I had an idea you might not talk to me. Among the things I remember is that you don't make contact with certain people without authorization. They're out of bounds. You simply report the contact attempt."

"Then I assume you also remember that it's highly irregular to call someone like me on a domestic phone."

"*Domestic* phone? Does the domestic prohibitive now include where you live?"

"You know what I'm talking about."

"I said it was an emergency."

"It can't have anything to do with me," protested Lanier. "You're a dead file in my office—"

"Color me deep-dead?" interrupted David.

"I didn't say that," shot back the man from covert operations. "All I meant was that you're not on my schedule and it's policy not to interfere with others."

"What others?" asked Webb sharply.

"How the hell do I know?"

"Are you telling me that you're not interested in what I have to tell you?"

"Whether I'm interested or not hasn't anything to do with it. You're not on any list of mine, and that's all I have to know. If you have something to say, call your authorized contact."

"I tried to. His wife said he was in the Far East."

"Try his office. Someone there will process you."

"I know that, and I don't care to be *processed*. I want to talk to someone I know, and I know you, Bill. Remember? It was 'Bill' in Virginia, that's what you told me to call you. You were interested to hell and back in what I had to say then."

"That was then, not now. Look, Webb, I can't help you because I can't advise you. No matter what you tell me, I can't respond. I'm not current on your status—I haven't been for almost a year. Your contact is— He can be reached. Call State back. I'm hanging up."

"Medusa," whispered David. "Did you hear me, Lanier? *Medusa!*"

"Medusa what? Are you trying to tell me something?"

"I'll blow it all apart, do you read me? I'll expose the whole obscene mess unless I get some *answers!*"

"Why don't you get yourself processed instead?" said the man from covert operations coldly. "Or check yourself into a hospital." There was an abrupt click, and David, perspiring, hung up the phone.

Lanier did *not* know about Medusa. If he had known, he would have stayed on the phone, learning whatever he could, for Medusa crossed the lines of "policy" and being "current." But Lanier was one of the younger interrogators, no more than thirty-three or thirty-four; he was very bright, but not a long-term veteran. Someone a few years older would probably have been given clearance, told about the renegade battalion that was still held in deep cover. Webb looked at the names on his list and at the corresponding telephone numbers. He picked up the phone.

"Hello?" A male voice.

"Is this Samuel Teasdale?"

"Yeah, that's right. Who are you?"

"I'm glad you answered the phone and not your wife."

"The wife's standard where possible," said Teasdale, suddenly cautious. "Mine's no longer available. She's sailing somewhere in the Caribbean with someone I never knew about. Now that you know my life's story, who the hell are you?"

"Jason Bourne, remember?"

"Webb?"

"I vaguely remember that name," said David.

"Why are you calling me?"

"You were friendly. Down in Virginia you told me to call you Sam."

"Okay, okay, David, you're right. I told you to call me Sam—that's what I am to my friends, Sam. . . ." Teasdale was bewildered, upset, searching for words. "But that was almost a year ago, Davey, and you know the rules. You're given a person to talk to, either on the scene or over at State. That's the one you should reach—that's the person who's up to date on everything."

"Aren't you up to date, Sam?"

"Not about you, no. I remember the directive; it was dropped on our desks a couple of weeks after you left Virginia. All inquiries regarding 'said subject, et cetera' were to be bumped up to Section whatever-the-hell-it-was, 'said subject' having full access and in direct touch with deputies on the scene and in the Department."

"The deputies—if that's what they were—were pulled out, and my direct-access contact has disappeared."

"Come on," objected Teasdale quietly, suspiciously. "That's crazy. It couldn't happen."

"It *happened!*" yelled Webb. "My *wife* happened!"

"What about your wife? What are you talking about?"

"She's *gone,* you bastard—all of you, *bastards!* You *let* it happen!" Webb grabbed his wrist, gripping it with all his strength to stop the trembling. "I want answers, Sam. I want to know who cleared the way, who *turned?* I've got an idea who it is, but I need answers to nail him—nail *all* of you, if I have to."

"Hold it right there!" broke in Teasdale angrily. "If you're trying to compromise me, you're doing a rotten fucking job of it! This boy's not for neutering, *wacko.* Go sing to your head doctors, not to me! I don't have to talk to you, all I have to do is report the fact that you called me, which I'll do the second I cut you loose. I'll also add that I got hit with a bucket of wacko-time bullshit! Take care of that head of yours—!"

"Medusa!" cried Webb. "No one wants to talk about code name Medusa, do they? Even today it's way down deep in the vaults, isn't it?"

There was no click on the line this time. Teasdale did not hang up. Instead, he spoke flatly, no comment in his voice. "Rumors," he said. "Like Hoover's raw files—raw meat—good for stories over a few belts, but not worth a hell of a lot."

"I'm not a rumor, Sam. I live, I breathe, I go to the toilet and I sweat—like I'm sweating now. That's not a rumor."

"You've had your problems, Davey."

"I was there! I fought with Medusa! Some people said I was the best, *or* the worst. It's why I was chosen, why I became Jason Bourne."

"I wouldn't know about that. We never discussed it, so I wouldn't know. Did we ever discuss it, Davey?"

"Stop using that goddamned name. I'm not *Davey.*"

"We were 'Sam' and 'Davey' in Virginia, don't you remember?"

"That doesn't matter! We all played games. Morris Panov was our referee, until one day you decided to get rough."

"I apologized," said Teasdale gently. "We all have bad days. I told you about my wife."

"I'm not interested in *your* wife! I'm interested in *mine!* And I'll rip open Medusa unless I get some answers, some *help!*"

"I'm sure you can get whatever help you think you need if you'll just call your contact at State."

"He's not there! He's *gone!*"

"Then ask for his backup. You'll be processed."

"Processed? Jesus, what are you, a *robot?"*

"Just a man trying to do his job, Mr. Webb, and I'm afraid I can't do anything more for you. Good night." The click came and Teasdale was off the phone.

There was another man, thought David at fever pitch as he stared at the list, squinting as the sweat filled his eye sockets. An easygoing man, less abrasive than the others, a Southerner, whose slow drawl was either a cover for a quick mind or the halting resistance to a job in which he felt himself uncomfortable. There was no time for invention.

"Is this the Babcock residence?"

"Surely is," replied a woman's voice imbued with magnolia. "Not our home, of course, as I always point out, but we surely do reside here."

"May I speak with Harry Babcock, please?"

"May *Ah* ask who's callin', please? He may be out in the garden with the kids, but on the other hand he may have taken them over to the park. It's so well lit these days— not like before—and you just don't fear for your life as long as you stay . . ."

A cover for quick minds, both Mr. and Mrs. Harry Babcock.

"My name is Reardon, State Department. There's an urgent message for Mr. Babcock. My instructions are to reach him as soon as possible. It's an emergency."

There was the bouncing echo of a phone being covered, muffled sounds beyond. Harry Babcock got on the line, his speech slow and deliberate.

"I don't know a Mr. Reardon, Mr. Reardon. All *mah* relays come from a particular switchboard that identifies itself. Are you a switchboard, sir?"

"Well, *I* don't know if I've ever heard of someone coming in from a garden, or from across the street in a park so quickly, Mr. Babcock."

"Remarkable, isn't it? I should be runnin' in the Olympics, perhaps. However, I do know your voice. I just can't place the name."

"How about Jason Bourne?"

The pause was brief—*a very quick mind.* "Now, that name goes back quite a while, doesn't it? Just about a year, I'd say. It *is* you, isn't it, David." There was no question implied.

"Yes, Harry. I've got to talk to you."

"No, David, you should speak with others, not me."

"Are you telling me I'm cut off?"

"Good heavens, that's so abrupt, so discourteous. I'd be more than *delighted* to hear how you and the lovely Mrs. Webb are doing in your new life. Massachusetts, isn't it?"

"Maine."

"Of course. Forgive me. Is everything well? As I'm sure you realize, my colleagues and I are involved with so many problems we haven't been able to stay in touch with your file."

"Someone else said you couldn't get your hands on it."

"*Ah* don't think anybody tried to."

"I want to talk, Babcock," said David harshly.

"I don't," replied Harry Babcock flatly, his voice nearly glacial. "I follow regulations, and to be frank, you *are* cut off from men like me. I don't question why—things change, they always change."

"Medusa!" said David. "We won't talk about me, let's talk about *Medusa!*"

The pause was longer than before. And when Babcock spoke, his words were frozen. "This phone is sterile, Webb, so I'll say what I want to say. You were nearly taken out a year ago, and it would have been a mistake. We would have sincerely mourned you. But if you break the threads, there'll be no mournin' tomorrow. Except, of course, your wife."

"You *son of a bitch!* She's *gone!* She was *taken!* You bastards let it *happen!*"

"I don't know what you're talking about."

"My *guards!* They were pulled, every goddamned one of them, and she was *taken!* I want answers, Babcock, or I blow everything apart! Now, you do exactly as I tell you to do, or there'll be mournings you never *dreamed* of—*all* of you, *your* wives, orphaned children—try everything on for size! I'm Jason Bourne, remember!"

"You're a maniac, *that's* what I remember. With threats like those we'll send a team to find you. *Medusa* style. Try *that* on for size, boy!"

Suddenly a furious hum broke into the line; it was deafening, high-pitched, causing David to thrust the phone away from his ear. And then the calm voice of an operator was heard: "We are breaking in for an emergency. Go ahead, Colorado."

Webb slowly brought the phone back to his ear.

"Is this Jason Bourne?" asked a man in a mid-Atlantic accent, the voice refined, aristocratic.

"I'm David Webb."

"Of course you are. But you are also Jason Bourne."

"Was," said David, mesmerized by something he could not define.

"The conflicting lines of identity get blurred, Mr. Webb. Especially for one who has been through so much."

"Who the hell *are* you?"

"A friend, be assured of that. And a friend cautions one he calls a friend. You've made outrageous accusations against some of our country's most dedicated servants, men who will never be permitted an unaccountable five million dollars—to this day unaccounted for."

"Do you want to search me?"

"No more than I'd care to trace the labyrinthine ways your most accomplished wife buried the funds in a dozen European—"

"She's *gone!* Did your dedicated men tell you *that?"*

"You were described as being overwrought—'raving' was the word that was used—and making astonishing accusations relative to your wife, yes."

"Relative to— *Goddamn* you, she was taken from our house! Someone's holding her because they want *me!"*

"Are you sure?"

"Ask that dead fish McAllister. It's his scenario, right down to the note. And suddenly he's on the other side of the world!"

"A note?" asked the cultured voice.

"Very clear. Very specific. It's McAllister's story, and he let it *happen! You* let it happen!"

"Perhaps you should examine the note further."

"Why?"

"No matter. It may all become clearer to you with help —psychiatric help."

"*What?*"

"We want to do all we can for you, believe that. You've given so much—more than any man should—and your extraordinary contribution cannot be disregarded even if it comes to a court of law. We placed you in the situation and we will stand by you—even if it means bending the laws, coercing the courts."

"What are you *talking* about?" screamed David.

"A respected army doctor tragically killed his wife several years ago, it was in all the papers. The stress became too much. The stresses on you were tenfold."

"I don't *believe* this!"

"Let's put it another way, Mr. Bourne."

"I'm not *Bourne!*"

"All right, Mr. Webb, I'll be frank with you."

"*That's* a step up!"

"You're not a well man. You've gone through eight months of psychiatric therapy—there's still a great deal of your own life you can't remember; you didn't even know your name. It's all in the medical records, meticulous records that make clear the advanced state of your mental illness, your compulsion for violence and your obsessive rejection of your own identity. In your torment you fantasize, you pretend to be people you are not; you seem to have a compulsion to be someone other than yourself."

"That's crazy and you know it! *Lies!*"

" 'Crazy' is a harsh word, Mr. Webb, and the lies are not mine. However, it's my job to protect our government from vilification, unfounded accusations that could severely damage the country."

"Such *as?*"

"Your secondary fantasy concerning an unknown organization you call Medusa. Now, I'm sure your wife will come back to you—if she can, Mr. Webb. But if you persist with this fantasy, with this figment of your tortured mind that you call Medusa, we'll label you a paranoid schizophrenic, a pathological liar prone to uncontrollable violence and self-deception. If such a man

claims his wife is missing, who knows where that pathological trip could lead? Do I make myself clear?"

David closed his eyes, the sweat rolling down his face.
"Crystal clear," he said quietly, hanging up the phone.

Paranoid . . . pathological. *Bastards!* He opened his
eyes wanting to spend his rage by hurling himself against
something, anything! Then he stopped and stood motionless as another thought struck him, the *obvious*
thought. Morris Panov! Mo Panov would label the three
monsters for what he knew they were. Incompetents and
liars, manipulators and self-serving protectors of corrupt
bureaucracies—and conceivably worse, *far* worse. He
reached for the phone and, trembling, dialed the number
that so often in the past had brought forth a calming,
rational voice that provided a sense of worth when Webb
felt there was very little of value left in him.

"David, how good to hear from you," said Panov with
genuine warmth.

"I'm afraid it's not, Mo. It's the worst call I've ever
made to you."

"Come on, David, that's pretty dramatic. We've been
through a lot—"

"Listen to me!" yelled Webb. "She's *gone!* They've *taken*
her!" The words poured forth, sequences lacking order,
the times confused.

"Stop it, David!" commanded Panov. "Go back. I want
to hear it from the beginning. When this man came to see
you—after your . . . the memories of your brother."

"What man?"

"From the State Department."

"Yes! All right, yes. McAllister, that was his name."

"Go from there. Names, titles, positions. And spell out
the name of that banker in Hong Kong. And for Christ's
sake, slow *down!*"

Webb again grabbed his wrist as he gripped the phone.
He started again, imposing a false control on his speech;
it became strident, tight, involuntarily gathering speed.
Finally he managed to get everything out, everything he
could recall, knowing in horror that he had not remembered everything. Unknown blank spaces filled him with
pain. They were coming back, the terrible blank spaces.
He had said all he could say for the moment; there was
nothing left.

"David," began Mo Panov firmly. "I want you to do something for me. *Now.*"

"What?"

"It may sound foolish to you, even a little bit crazy, but I suggest you go down the street to the beach and take a walk along the shore. A half hour, forty-five minutes, that's all. Listen to the surf and the waves crashing against the rocks."

"You can't be *serious!*" protested Webb.

"I'm very serious," insisted Mo. "Remember we agreed once that there were times when people should put their heads on hold—God knows, I do it more than a reasonably respected psychiatrist should. Things can overwhelm us, and before we can get our act together we have to get rid of part of the confusion. Do as I ask, David. I'll get back to you as soon as I can, no more than an hour, I'd guess. And I want you calmer than you are now."

It *was* crazy, but as with so much of what Panov quietly, often casually, suggested, there was truth in his words. Webb walked along the cold, rocky beach, never for an instant forgetting what had happened, but whether it was the change of scene, or the wind, or the incessant, repetitive sounds of the pounding ocean, he found himself breathing more steadily—every bit as deeply, as tremulously, as before, but without the higher registers of hysteria. He looked at his watch, at the luminous dial aided by the moonlight. He had walked back and forth for thirty-two minutes; it was all the indulgence he could bear. He climbed the path through the dune of wild grass to the street and headed for the house, his pace quickening with every step.

He sat in his chair at the desk, his eyes rigid on the phone. It rang; he picked it up before the bell had stopped. *"Mo?"*

"Yes."

"It was damned cold out there. Thank you."

"Thank *you.*"

"What have you learned?"

And then the extension of the nightmare began.

"How long has Marie been gone, David?"

"I don't know. An hour, two hours, maybe more. What's that got to do with anything?"

"Could she be shopping? Or did you two have a fight and perhaps she wanted to be by herself for a while? We agreed that things are sometimes very difficult for her—you made the point yourself."

"What the *hell* are you talking about? There's a note spelling it out! Blood, a *hand print!*"

"Yes, you mentioned them before, but they're so incriminating. Why would anyone do that?"

"How do *I* know! It was *done—they* were done. It's all *here!*"

"Did you call the police?"

"Christ, *no!* It's not for the police! It's for us, for *me!* Can't you *understand* that? . . . What did you find out? Why are you *talking* like this?"

"Because I have to. In all the sessions, in all the months we talked we never said anything but the truth to each other because the truth is what you have to know."

"Mo! For God's sake, it's *Marie!"*

"Please, David, let me finish. If they're lying—and they've lied before—I'll know it and I'll expose them. I couldn't do anything less. But I'm going to tell you exactly what they told me, what the number two man in the Far East Section made specifically clear, and what the chief of security for the State Department read to me, as the events were officially logged."

"Officially logged . . . ?"

"Yes. He said *you* called security control a little over a week ago, and according to the log, you were in a highly agitated state—"

"I called *them?"*

"That's right, that's what he said. According to the logs, you claimed you had received threats; your speech was 'incoherent'—that was the word they used—and you demanded additional security immediately. Because of the classified flag on your file, the request was bounced upstairs and the upper levels said, 'Give him what he wants. Cool him.' "

"I can't *believe* this!"

"It's only the middle, David. Hear me out, because I'm listening to you."

"Okay. Go on."

"That's it. Easy. Stay cool—no, strike that word 'cool.' "

"Please do."

"Once the patrols were in place—again according to the logs—you called twice more complaining that your guards weren't doing their job. You said they were drinking in their cars in front of your house, that they laughed at you when they accompanied you on the campus, that they—and here I quote—'They're making a mockery of what they're supposed to be doing.' I underlined that phrase."

"A *'mockery'* . . . ?"

"Easy, David. Here's the end of it, the end of the logs. You made a last call stating emphatically that you wanted everyone taken away—that your guards were your enemy, *they* were the men who wanted to kill you. In essence, you had transformed those who were trying to protect you into enemies who would attack you."

"And I'm sure that fits snugly into one of those bullshit psychiatric conclusions that had me converting—or perverting—my anxieties into paranoia."

"Very snugly," said Panov. "Too snugly."

"What did the number two in Far East tell you?"

Panov was silent for a moment. "It's not what you want to hear, David, but he was adamant. They never heard of a banker or any influential taipan named Yao Ming. He said the way things were in Hong Kong these days, if there was such a person he'd have the dossier memorized."

"Does he think I made it all *up?* The name, the wife, the drug connection, the places, the circumstances—the British reaction! For Christ's sake, I couldn't invent those things if I *wanted* to!"

"It'd be a stretch for you," agreed the psychiatrist softly. "Then everything I've just told you you're hearing for the first time and none of it makes sense. It's not the way you recall things."

"Mo, it's all a lie! I never called State. McAllister came to the house and told us both everything I've told you, including the Yao Ming story! And now she's *gone,* and I've been given a lead to follow. *Why?* For *Christ*'s sake, what are they *doing* to us?"

"I asked about McAllister," said Panov, his tone suddenly angry. "The Far East deputy checked with State posting and called me back. They say McAllister flew into

Hong Kong two weeks ago, that according to his very precise calendar he couldn't have been at your house in Maine."

"He was *here!*"

"I think I believe you."

"What does that mean?"

"Among other things, I can hear the truth in your voice, sometimes when you can't. Also that phrase 'making a mockery' of something isn't generally in the vocabulary of a psychotic in a highly agitated state—certainly not in yours at your wildest."

"I'm not with you."

"Someone saw where you worked and what you did for a living and thought he'd add a little upgraded verbiage. Local color, in your case." Then Panov exploded. "My God, what are they *doing?*"

"Locking me into a starting gate," said Webb softly. "They're forcing me to go after whatever it is they want."

"Sons of *bitches!*"

"It's called recruitment." David stared at the wall. "Stay away, Mo, there's nothing you can do. They've got all their pieces in place. I'm recruited." He hung up.

Dazed, Webb walked out of his small office and stood in the Victorian hallway surveying the upturned furniture and the broken lamps, china and glass strewn across the floor of the living room beyond. Then words spoken by Panov earlier in the terrible conversation came to him: "They're so incriminating."

Only vaguely realizing where his steps were taking him, he approached the front door and opened it. He forced himself to look at the hand print in the center of the upper panel, the dried blood dull and dark in the light of the carriage lamps. Then he drew closer and examined it.

It was the imprint of a hand but not a hand print. There was the outline of a hand—the impression, the palm and the extended fingers—but no breaks in the bloody form, no creases or indentations that a bleeding hand pressed against hard wood would reveal, no identifying marks, no isolated parts of the flesh held in place so as to stamp its own particular characteristics. It was like a flat, colored shadow from a piece of stained glass, no planes other than the single impression. A glove? A rubber glove?

David drew his eyes away, and slowly turned to the staircase in the middle of the hallway, his thoughts haltingly centering on other words spoken by another man. A strange man with a mesmerizing voice.

Perhaps you should examine the note further. . . . It may all become clearer to you with help—psychiatric help.

Webb suddenly screamed, the terror within him growing, as he ran to the staircase and raced up the steps to the bedroom, where he stared at the typewritten note on the bed. He picked it up with sickening fear and carried it to his wife's dressing table. He turned on the lamp and studied the print under the light.

If the heart within him could have burst, it would have blown apart. Instead, Jason Bourne coldly examined the note before him.

The slightly bent, irregular *r*'s were there, as well as the *d*'s, the upper staffs incomplete, breaking off at the halfway mark.

Bastards!

The note had been written on his own typewriter. Recruitment.

6

He sat on the rocks above the beach, knowing he had to think clearly. He had to define what was before him and what was expected of him and then how to outthink whoever was manipulating him. Above all, he knew he could not give in to panic, even the perception of panic—a panicked man was dangerous, a risk to be eliminated. If he went over the edge, he would only ensure the death of Marie and himself; it was that simple. Everything was so delicate—violently delicate.

David Webb was out of the question. Jason Bourne had to assume control. Jesus! It was *crazy!* Mo Panov had told him to walk on the beach—as Webb—and now he had to sit there as Bourne, thinking things out as Bourne would think them out—he had to deny one part of himself and accept the opposite.

Strangely, it was not impossible, nor even intolerable, for Marie was out there. His love, his only love— *Don't think that way.* Jason Bourne spoke: She is a valuable possession taken from you! Get her *back.* David Webb spoke: *No,* not a possession, my life!

Jason Bourne: *Then break all the rules! Find her! Bring her back to you!*

David Webb: *I don't know how. Help me!*

Use me! Use what you've learned from me. You've got the tools, you've had them for years. You were the best in Medusa. Above all, there was control. You preached that, you lived that. And you stayed alive.

Control.

Such a simple word. Such an incredible demand.

Webb climbed off the rocks and once again went up the path through the wild grass to the street, and started back toward the old Victorian house, loathing its sudden, frightening, unfair emptiness. As he walked a name flashed across his thoughts; then it returned and remained fixed. Slowly the face belonging to that name came into focus—very slowly, for the man aroused hatred in David that was no less acute for the sadness he also evoked.

Alexander Conklin had tried to kill him—twice—and each time he had nearly succeeded. And Alex Conklin— according to his deposition, as well as his own numerous psychiatric sessions with Mo Panov and what vague memories David could provide—had been a close friend of Foreign Service Officer Webb and his Thai wife and their children in Cambodia a lifetime ago. When death had struck from the skies, filling the river with circles of blood, David had fled blindly to Saigon, his rage uncontrollable, and it was his friend in the Central Intelligence Agency, Alex Conklin, who found a place for him in the illegitimate battalion they called Medusa.

If you can survive the jungle training, you'll be a man they want. But watch them—every goddamned one of them, every goddamned minute. They'll cut your arm off for a watch. Those were the words Webb recalled, and he specifically recalled that they had been spoken by the voice of Alexander Conklin.

He had survived the brutal training and become Delta. No other name, just a progression in the alphabet. Delta One. Then after the war, Delta became Cain. *Cain is for Delta and Carlos is for Cain. That was the challenge hurled at Carlos the assassin. Created by Treadstone 71, a killer named Cain would catch the Jackal.*

It was as Cain, a name the underworld of Europe knew in reality was Asia's Jason Bourne, that Webb had been betrayed by Conklin. A simple act of faith on Alex's part could have made all the difference, but Alex could not find it within himself to provide it; his own bitterness precluded that particular charity. He believed the worst of his former friend because his own sense of martyrdom made him want to believe it. It raised his own broken self-esteem, convincing him that he was better than his former friend. In his work with Medusa, Conklin's foot had been shattered by a land mine, and his brilliant career as a field strategist was cut short. A crippled man could not stay in the field where a growing reputation might take him up the ladders scaled by such men as Allen Dulles and James Angleton, and Conklin did not possess the skills for the bureaucratic infighting demanded at Langley. He withered, a once extraordinary tactician left to watch inferior talents pass him by, his expertise sought only in secrecy, the head of Medusa always in the background, dangerous, someone to be kept at arm's length.

Two years of imposed castration, until a man known as the Monk—a Rasputin of covert operations—sought him out because one David Webb had been selected for an extraordinary assignment and Conklin had known Webb for years. Treadstone 71 was created, Jason Bourne became its product and Carlos the Jackal its target. And for thirty-two months Conklin monitored this most secret of classified operations, until the scenario fell apart with Jason Bourne's disappearance and the withdrawal of over five million dollars from Treadstone's Zurich account.

With no evidence to the contrary, Conklin presumed the worst. The legendary Bourne had turned; life in the nether world had become too much for him and the temptation to come in from the cold with over five million dollars had been too alluring to resist. Especially for one known as the chameleon, a multilingual deep-cover specialist who could change appearances and life-styles with so little effort that he could literally vanish. A trap for an assassin had been baited and then the bait had vanished, revealing a scheming thief. For the crippled Alexander Conklin this was not only the act of a traitor but intolerable treachery. Considering everything that had been done to *him*, his foot now no more than a painfully awkward dead weight surgically encased in stolen flesh, a once brilliant career a shambles, his personal life filled with a loneliness that only a total commitment to the Agency could bring about—a devotion not reciprocated—what right had anyone *else* to turn? What other man had given what he had given?

So his once close friend, David Webb, became the enemy, Jason Bourne. Not merely the enemy, but an obsession. He had helped create the myth; he would destroy it. His first attempt was with two hired killers on the outskirts of Paris.

David shuddered at the memory, still seeing a defeated Conklin limp away, his crippled figure in Webb's gunsight.

The second try was blurred for David. Perhaps he would never recall it completely. It had taken place at the Treadstone sterile house on New York's Seventy-first Street, an ingenious trap mounted by Conklin, which was aborted by Webb's hysterical efforts to survive and, oddly enough, the presence of Carlos the Jackal.

Later, when the truth was known, that the "traitor" had no treason in him, but instead a mental aberration called amnesia, Conklin fell apart. During David's agonizing months of convalescence in Virginia, Alex tried repeatedly to see his once close friend, to explain, to tell his part of the bloody story—to apologize with every fiber of his being.

David, however, had no forgiveness in his soul.

"If he walks through that door, I'll kill him" had been his words.

That would change now, thought Webb, as he quickened his pace down the street toward the house. Whatever Conklin's faults and duplicities, few men in the Intelligence community had the insights and the sources he had developed over a lifetime of commitment. David had not thought about Alex in months; he thought about

him now, suddenly remembering the last time his name
came up in conversation. Mo Panov had rendered his
verdict. "I can't help him because he doesn't want to be
helped. He'll carry his last bottle of sour mash up to that
great big black operations room in the sky bombed out
of his mercifully dead skull. If he lasts to his retirement
at the end of the year, I'll be astonished. On the other
hand, if he stays pickled they may put him in a strait-
jacket, and that'll keep him out of traffic. I swear I don't
know how he gets to work every day. That pension is one
hell of a survival therapy—better than anything Freud
ever left us." Panov had spoken those words more than
five months ago. Conklin was still in place.

*I'm sorry, Mo. His survival one way or the other doesn't con-
cern me. So far as I'm concerned, his status is dead.*

It was not dead now, thought David, as he ran up the
steps of the oversized Victorian porch. Alex Conklin was
very much alive, whether drunk or not, and even if he was
preserved in bourbon, he had his sources, those contacts
he had cultivated during a lifetime of devotion to the
shadow world that ultimately rejected him. Within that
world debts were owed, and they were paid out of fear.

Alexander Conklin. Number one on Jason Bourne's hit list.

He opened the door and once again stood in the hallway, but his eyes did not see the wreckage. Instead, the
logician in him ordered him to go back into his study and
begin the procedures; there was nothing but confusion
without imposed order, and confusion led to questions—
he could not afford them. Everything had to be precise
within the reality he was creating so as to divert the curious from the reality that was.

He sat down at the desk and tried to focus his thoughts.
There was the ever-present spiral notebook from the
College Shop in front of him. He opened the thick cover
to the first lined page and reached for a pencil. . . . He
could not pick it up! His hand shook so much that his
whole body trembled. He held his breath and made a fist,
clenching it until his fingernails cut into flesh. He closed
his eyes, then opened them, forcing his hand to return to
the pencil, commanding it to do its job. Slowly, awkwardly, his fingers gripped the thin, yellow shaft and
moved the pencil into position. The words were barely
legible, but they were there.

The university—phone president and dean of studies. Family crisis, not Canada—can be traced. Invent—a brother in Europe, perhaps. Yes, Europe. Leave of absence—brief leave of absence. Right away. Will stay in touch.

House—call rental agent, same story. Ask Jack to check periodically. He has key. Turn thermostat to 60°.

Mail—fill out form at Post Office. Hold all mail.

Newspapers—cancel.

The little things, the goddamned *little* things—the unimportant daily trivia became so terribly important and had to be taken care of so that there would be no sign whatsoever of an abrupt departure without a planned return. That was vital; he had to remember it with every word he spoke. Questions had to be kept to a minimum, the inevitable speculations reduced to manageable proportions, which meant he had to confront the obvious conclusion that his recent bodyguards somehow led to his leave of absence. To defuse the connection, the most plausible way was to emphasize the short duration of that absence and to face the issue with a straightforward dismissal, such as "Incidentally, if you're wondering whether this has anything to do with my concern for personal safety, well, don't. That's a closed book; it didn't have much merit anyway." He would know better how to respond while talking to both the university's president and the dean; their own reactions would guide him. If anything could guide him. If he was capable of thinking! Don't slide back—keep going. Move that pencil! Fill out the page with things to do—then another page, and *another!* Passports, initials on wallets or billfolds or shirts to correspond with the names being used; airline reservations—connecting flights, no direct routes — Oh, *God!* To *where?* Marie! Where *are* you?

Stop it! Control yourself. You are capable, you *must* be capable. You have no choice, so be what you once were. Feel ice. Be ice.

Without warning, the shell he was building around himself was shattered by the earsplitting sound of the telephone inches from his hand on the desk. He looked at it, swallowing, wondering if he was capable of sounding remotely normal. It rang again, a terrible insistence in its ring. *You have no choice.*

He picked it up, gripping the receiver with such force

that his knuckles turned white. He managed to get out the single word "Yes?"

"This is the mobile-air operator, satellite transmission—"

"Who? What did you say?"

"I have a midflight radio call for a Mr. Webb. Are you Mr. Webb, sir?"

"Yes."

And then the world he knew blew up in a thousand jagged mirrors, each an image of screaming torment.

"David!"

"Marie?"

"Don't panic, darling! Do you hear me, *don't panic!"* Her voice came through the static; she was trying not to shout but could not help herself.

"Are you all right? The note said you were hurt—wounded!"

"I'm all right. A few scratches, that's all."

"Where *are* you?"

"Over the ocean, I'm sure they'll tell you that much. I don't know; I was sedated."

"Oh, *Jesus!* I can't stand it! They took you away!"

"Pull yourself together, David. I know what this is doing to you, but *they don't.* Do you understand what I'm saying? They *don't!"*

She was sending him a coded message; it was not hard to decipher. *He had to be the man he hated. He had to be Jason Bourne, and the assassin was alive and well and residing in the body of David Webb.*

"All right. Yes, all right. I've been going out of my mind!"

"Your voice is being amplified—"

"Naturally."

"They're letting me speak to you so you'll know I'm alive."

"Have they *hurt* you?"

"Not intentionally."

"What the hell are 'scratches'?"

"I struggled. I fought. And I was brought up on a ranch."

"Oh, my *God*—"

"David, *please!* Don't let them do this to you!"

"To me? It's *you!"*

"I *know*, darling. I think they're testing you, can you understand that?"

Again the message. Be Jason Bourne for both their sakes—for both their lives. "All right. Yes, all right." He lessened the intensity of his voice, trying to control himself. "When did it happen?" he asked.

"This morning, about an hour after you left."

"This *morning*? Christ, all *day!* How?"

"They came to the door. Two men—"

"*Who?*"

"I'm permitted to say they're from the Far East. Actually, I don't know any more than that. They asked me to accompany them and I refused. I ran into the kitchen and saw a knife. I stabbed one of them in the hand."

"The hand print on the door . . ."

"I don't understand."

"It doesn't matter."

"A man wants to talk to you, David. Listen to him, but not in anger—not in a rage—can you *understand* that?"

"All right. Yes, all right. I understand."

The man's voice came on the line. It was hesitant but precise, almost British in its delivery, someone who had been taught English by an Englishman, or by someone who had lived in the U.K. Nevertheless, it was identifiably Oriental; the accent was southern China, the pitch, the short vowels and sharp consonants sounding Cantonese.

"We do not care to harm your wife, Mr. Webb, but if it is necessary, it will be unavoidable."

"I wouldn't, if I were you," said David coldly.

"Jason Bourne speaks?"

"He speaks."

"The acknowledgment is the first step in our understanding."

"What understanding?"

"You took something of great value from a man."

"You've taken something of great value from me."

"She is alive."

"She'd better stay that way."

"Another is dead. You killed her."

"Are you sure about that?" *Bourne would not agree readily unless it served his purpose to do so.*

"We are very sure."

"What's your proof?"

"You were seen. A tall man who stayed in the shadows and raced through the hotel corridors and across fire escapes with the movements of a mountain cat."

"Then I wasn't really *seen*, was I? Nor could I have been. I was thousands of miles away." *Bourne would always give himself an option.*

"In these times of fast aircraft, what is distance?" The Oriental paused, then added sharply, "You canceled your duties for a period of five days two and a half weeks ago."

"And if I told you I attended a symposium on the Sung and Yuan dynasties down in Boston—which was very much in line with my duties—"

"I am startled," interrupted the man courteously, "that Jason Bourne would employ such a lamentably feeble excuse."

He had not wanted to go to Boston. That symposium was light years away from his lectures, but he had been officially asked to attend. The request came from Washington, from the Cultural Exchange Program and filtered through the university's Department of Oriental Studies. Christ! Every pawn was in place!

"Excuse for what?"

"For being where he was not. Large crowds mingling among the exhibits, certain people paid to swear you were there."

"That's ridiculous, not to say patently amateurish. I don't pay."

"*You* were paid."

"I was? How?"

"Through the same bank you used before. In Zurich. The Gemeinschaft in Zurich—on the Bahnhofstrasse, of course."

"Odd I haven't received a statement," said David, listening carefully.

"When you were Jason Bourne in Europe, you never needed one, for yours was a three-zero account—the most secret, which is very secret indeed in Switzerland. However, we found a draft transfer made out to the Gemeinschaft among the papers of a man—a dead man, of course."

"Of course. But not the man I supposedly killed."

"Certainly not. But one who ordered that man killed, along with a treasured prize of my employer."

"A prize is a trophy, isn't it?"

"Both are won, Mr. Bourne. Enough. You are you. Get to the Regent Hotel in Kowloon. Register under any name you wish, but ask for Suite six-nine-zero—say you believe arrangements were made to reserve it."

"How convenient. My own rooms."

"It will save time."

"It'll also take me time to make arrangements here."

"We are certain you will not raise alarms and will move as rapidly as you can. Be there by the end of the week."

"Count on both. Put my wife back on the line."

"I regret I cannot do that."

"For Christ's sake, you can hear everything we say!"

"You will speak with her in Kowloon."

There was an echoing click, and he could hear nothing on the line but static. He replaced the phone, his grip so intense a cramp had formed between his thumb and forefinger. He managed to remove his clenched hand and shook it violently. He was grateful that the pain allowed him to reenter reality more gradually. He grabbed his right hand with his left, held it steady, and pressed his left thumb into the cramp, and as he watched his fingers spread free he knew what he had to do—do without wasting an hour on the all-important unimportant trivia. He had to reach Conklin in Washington, the gutter rat who had tried to kill him in broad daylight on New York's Seventy-first Street. Alex, drunk or sober, made no distinction between the hours of day and night, nor did the operations he knew so well, for there was no night and day where his work was concerned. There was only the flat light of fluorescent tubes in offices that never closed. If he had to, he would press Alexander Conklin until the blood rolled out of the gutter rat's eyes; he would learn what he had to know, knowing that Conklin could get the information.

Webb rose unsteadily from the chair, walked out of his study and into the kitchen, where he poured himself a drink, grateful again that although his hand still trembled, it did so less than before.

He could delegate certain things. Jason Bourne never

delegated anything, but he was still David Webb and there were several people on campus he could trust—certainly not with the truth but with a useful lie. By the time he returned to his study and the telephone he had chosen his conduit. *Conduit,* for God's sake! A word from the past he thought he had been free to forget. But the young man would do what he asked; the graduate student's master's thesis would ultimately be graded by his adviser, one David Webb. *Use the advantage, whether it's total darkness or blinding sunlight, but use it to frighten or use it with compassion, whatever worked.*

"Hello, James? It's David Webb."

"Hi, Mr. Webb. Where'd I screw up?"

"You haven't, Jim. Things have screwed up for me and I could use a little extracurricular help. Would you be interested? It'll take a little time."

"This weekend? The game?"

"No, just tomorrow morning. Maybe an hour or so, if that. Then a little bonus in terms of your curriculum vitae, if that doesn't sound too horseshit."

"Name it."

"Well, confidentially—and I'd appreciate the confidentiality—I have to be away for a week, perhaps two, and I'm about to call the powers that be and suggest that you sit in for me. It's no problem for you; it's the Manchu overthrow and the Sino-Russian agreements that sound very familiar today."

"1900 to around 1912," said the master's candidate with confidence.

"You can refine it, and don't overlook the Japanese and Port Arthur and old Teddy Roosevelt. Line it up and draw parallels; that's what I've been doing."

"Can do. *Will* do. I'll hit the sources. What about tomorrow?"

"I have to leave tonight, Jim; my wife's already on her way. Have you got a pencil?"

"Yes, sir."

"You know what they say about piling up newspapers and the mail, so I want you to call the newspaper delivery and go down to the post office and tell them both to hold everything—sign whatever you have to sign. Then call the Scully Agency here in town and speak to Jack or Adele and tell them to . . ."

The master's candidate was recruited. The next call was far easier than David expected, as the president of the university was at a dinner party in his honor at the president's residence and was far more interested in his upcoming speech than in an obscure—if unusual—associate-professor's leave of absence. "Please reach the dean of studies, Mr.—Wedd. I'm raising money, damn it."

The dean of studies was not so easily handled. "David, has this anything to do with those people who were walking around with you last week? I mean, after all, old boy, I'm one of the few people here who know that you were involved with some very hush-hush things in Washington."

"Nothing whatsoever, Doug. That was nonsense from the beginning; this isn't. My brother was seriously injured, his car completely totaled. I've got to get over to Paris for a few days, maybe a week, that's all."

"I was in Paris two years ago. The drivers are absolute maniacs."

"No worse than Boston, Doug, and a hell of a lot better than Cairo."

"Well, I suppose I can make arrangements. A week isn't that long, and Johnson was out for nearly a month with pneumonia—"

"I've already made arrangements—with your approval, of course. Jim Crowther, a master's candidate, will fill in for me. It's material he knows and he'll do a good job."

"Oh, yes, Crowther, a bright young man, in spite of his beard. Never did trust beards, but then I was here in the sixties."

"Try growing one. It may set you free."

"I'll let that go by. Are you *sure* this hasn't anything to do with those people from the State Department? I really must have the facts, David. What's your brother's name? What Paris hospital is he in?"

"I don't know the hospital, but Marie probably does; she left this morning. Good-bye, Doug. I'll call you tomorrow or the next day. I have to get down to Logan Airport in Boston."

"David?"

"Yes?"

"Why do I feel you're not being entirely truthful with me?"

Webb remembered. "Because I've never been in this position before," he said. "Asking a favor from a friend because of someone I'd rather not think about."

David hung up the phone.

The flight from Boston to Washington was maddening because of a fossilized professor of pedantry—David never did get the course—who had the seat next to his. The man's voice was as irritatingly authentic as the ponderous tones of the accomplished actor on television who assumed the role of the learned elder of a brokerage house and insisted, "They *earn* it!" The phrase kept repeating itself over and over again in Webb's mind regardless of what the professor said, and he kept saying a great deal. It was only when they landed at National Airport that the pedant admitted the truth. "I've been a bore, but do forgive me. I'm terrified of flying, so I just keep chattering. Silly, isn't it?"

"Not at all, but why didn't you say so? It's hardly a crime."

"Fear of peer pressure, or scoffing condemnation, I imagine."

"I'll remember that the next time I'm sitting next to someone like you." Webb smiled briefly. "Maybe I could help."

"That's kind of you. And very honest. Thank you. Thank you so much."

"You're welcome."

David retrieved his suitcase from the luggage belt and went outside for a taxi, annoyed that the cabs were not taking single fares but insisting on two or more passengers going in the same direction. His backseat companion was a woman, an attractive woman who used body language in concert with imploring eyes. It made no sense to him, so he made no sense of her, but thanked her for dropping him off first.

He registered at the Jefferson Hotel on Sixteenth Street under a false name invented at the moment. The hotel, however, was carefully chosen; it was a block and a half from Conklin's apartment, the same apartment the CIA officer had lived in for nearly twenty years when he

was not in the field. It was an address David made sure
to get before he left Virginia—again instinct, visceral distrust. He had a telephone number as well, but knew it was
useless; he could not phone Conklin. The once deep-
cover strategist would mount defenses, more mental than
physical, and Webb wanted to confront an unprepared
man. There would be no warning, only a presence demanding a debt that was owed and must now be paid.

David glanced at his watch; it was ten minutes to midnight, as good a time as any and better than most. He
washed, changed his shirt, and finally dug out one of the
two dismantled guns from his suitcase, removing it from
the thick, foil-lined bag. He snapped the parts in place,
tested the firing mechanism, and shoved the clip into the
receiving chamber. He held the weapon out and studied
his hand, satisfied that there was no tremor. It felt clean
and unremarkable. Eight hours ago he would not have
believed he could hold a gun in his hand for fear he might
fire it. That was eight hours ago, not now. Now it was
comfortable, a part of him, an extension of Jason Bourne.

He left the Jefferson and walked down Sixteenth
Street, turning right at the corner and noting the descending numbers of the old apartments—very old apartments, reminding him of the brownstones on the Upper
East Side of New York. There was a curious logic in the
observation, considering Conklin's role in the Treadstone project, he thought. Treadstone 71's sterile house
in Manhattan had been a brownstone, an odd, bulging
structure with upper windows of tinted blue glass. He
could see it so clearly, hear the voices so clearly, without
really understanding—the incubating factory for Jason
Bourne.

Do it again!
Who is the face?
What's his background? His method of kill?
Wrong! You're wrong! Do it again!
Who's this? What's the connection to Carlos?
Damn it, think! There can be no mistakes!

A brownstone. Where his other self was created, the
man he needed so much now.

There it was, Conklin's apartment. He was on the second floor, facing front. The lights were on; Alex was
home and awake. Webb crossed the street, aware that a

misty drizzle had suddenly filled the air, diffusing the glare of the streetlamps, halos beneath the orbs of rippled glass. He walked up the steps and opened the door to the short foyer; he stepped inside and studied the names under the mailboxes of the six flats. Each had a webbed circle under the name into which a caller announced himself.

There was no time for complicated invention. If Panov's verdict was accurate, his voice would be sufficient. He pressed Conklin's button and waited for a response; it came after the better part of a minute.

"Yes? Who's there?"

"Harry Babcock *heah,*" said David, the accent exaggerated. "I've got to see you, Alex."

"Harry? What the hell . . . ? Sure, sure, come on up!" The buzzer droned, broke off once—a finger momentarily displaced.

David went inside and ran up the narrow staircase to the second floor, hoping to be outside Conklin's door when he opened it. He arrived less than a second before Alex, who, with his eyes only partially focused, pulled back the door and began to scream. Webb lunged, clamping his hand across Conklin's face, twisting the CIA man around in a hammerlock, and kicking the door shut.

He had not physically attacked a person for as long as he could remember with any accuracy. It should have been strange, even awkward, but it was neither. It was perfectly natural. *Oh, Christ!*

"I'm going to take my hand away, Alex, but if you raise your voice it goes back. And you won't survive if it does, is that clear?" David removed his hand, yanking Conklin's head back as he did so.

"You're one hell of a surprise," said the CIA man, coughing, and lurching into a limp as he was released. "You also call for a drink."

"I gather it's a pretty steady diet."

"We are what we are," answered Conklin, awkwardly reaching down for an empty glass on the coffee table in front of a large, well-worn couch. He carried it over to a copper-plated dry bar against the wall where identical bottles of bourbon stood in a single row. There were no mixers, no water, just an ice bucket; it was not a bar for guests. It was for the host in residence, its gleaming metal proclaiming it to be an extravagance the resident permitted himself. The rest of the living room was not in its class. Somehow that copper bar was a statement.

"To what," continued Conklin, pouring himself a drink, "do I owe this dubious pleasure? You refused to see me in Virginia—said you'd kill me, and that's a fact. That's what you said. You'd kill me if I walked through the door, you said that."

"You're drunk."

"Probably. But then I usually am around this time. Do you want to start out with a lecture? It won't do a hell of a lot of good, but give it the old college try if you want to."

"You're sick."

"No, I'm drunk, that's what you said. Am I repeating myself?"

"Ad nauseam."

"Sorry about that." Conklin replaced the bottle, took several swallows from his glass and looked at Webb. "I didn't walk through your door, you came through mine, but I suppose that's immaterial. Did you come here to finally carry out your threat, to fulfill the prophecy, to put past wrongs to rights or whatever you call it? That rather obvious flat bulge under your jacket I doubt is a pint of whisky."

"I have no overriding urge to see you dead any longer, but yes, I may kill you. You could provoke that urge very easily."

"Fascinating. How could I do that?"

"By not providing me with what I need—and you *can* provide it."

"You must know something I don't."

"I know you've got twenty years in gray to black operations and that you wrote the book on most of them."

"History," muttered the CIA man, drinking.

"It's revivable. Unlike mine, your memory's intact. Mine's limited, but not yours. I need information, I need answers."

"To what? For what?"

"They took my wife away," said David simply, ice in that simplicity. "They took Marie away from me."

Conklin's eyes blinked through his fixed stare. "Say that again. I don't think I heard you right."

"You heard! And you *bastards* are somewhere deep down in the rotten scenario!"

"Not *me!* I wouldn't—I *couldn't!* What the hell are you saying? Marie's *gone?*"

"She's in a plane over the Pacific. I'm to follow. I'm to fly to Kowloon."

"You're crazy! You're out of your mind!"

"You listen to me, Alex. You listen carefully to everything I tell you. . . ." Again the words poured forth, but now with a control he had not been able to summon with Morris Panov. Conklin drunk had sharper perceptions than most sober men in the Intelligence community, and he had to understand. Webb could not allow any lapses in the narrative; it had to be clear from the beginning—from that moment when he spoke to Marie over the gymnasium phone and heard her say, "David, come home. There's someone here you must see. Quickly, darling."

As he talked, Conklin limped unsteadily across the room to the couch and sat down, his eyes never once leaving Webb's face. When David had finished describing the hotel around the corner, Alex shook his head and reached for his drink.

"It's eerie," he said after a period of silence, of intense concentration fighting the clouds of alcohol, and put the glass down. "It's as though a strategy was mounted and went off the wire."

"Off the wire?"

"Out of control."

"*How?*"

"I don't know," went on the former tactician, weaving slightly, trying not to slur his words. "You're given a script that may or may not be accurate, then the targets change—your wife for you—and it's played out. You react predictably, but when you mention Medusa, you're told in no uncertain terms that you'll be burned if you persist."

"That's predictable."

"It's no way to prime a subject. Suddenly your wife's on a back burner, and Medusa's the overriding danger. Someone miscalculated. Something's off a wire, something happened."

"You've got what's left of tonight and tomorrow to get

me some answers. I'm on the seven P.M. flight to Hong Kong."

Conklin sat forward, shaking his head slowly and, with his right hand trembling, again reached for his bourbon. "You're in the wrong part of town," he said, swallowing. "I thought you knew; you made a tight little allusion to the sauce. I'm useless to you. I'm off limits, a basket case. No one tells me anything, and why should they? I'm a relic, Webb. Nobody wants to have a goddamned thing to do with me. I'm washed out and up and one more step I'll be beyond-salvage—which I believe is a phrase locked in that crazy head of yours."

"Yes, it is. 'Kill him. He knows too much.' "

"Maybe you want to put me there, is that it? Feed him, wake up the sleeping Medusa, and make sure he gets it from his own. That would balance."

"You put *me* there," said David, taking the gun out of the holster under his jacket.

"Yes, I did," agreed Conklin, nodding his head, and gazing at the weapon. "Because I knew *Delta,* and as far as I was concerned, anything was possible—I'd seen you in the field. My God, you blew a man's head off—one of your *own* men—in Tam Quan because you believed—you didn't know, you *believed*—he was radioing a platoon on the Ho Chi Minh! No charges, no defense, just another swift execution in the jungle. It turned out you were right, but you might have been *wrong!* You could have brought him in; we might have learned things, but no, not Delta! He made up his own rules. *Sure,* you could have turned in Zurich!"

"I don't have the specifics about Tam Quan, but others did," said David in quiet anger. "I had to get nine men out of there—there wasn't room for a tenth who could have slowed us down or bolted, giving away our position."

"*Good! Your* rules. You're inventive, so find a parallel here and for Christ's sake pull the trigger like you did with him—our bona fide Jason Bourne! I told you in Paris to do it!" Breathing hard, Conklin paused and leveled his bloodshot eyes at Webb; he spoke in a plaintive whisper. "I told you then and I tell you now. Put me out of it. I don't have the guts to."

"We were *friends,* Alex!" shouted David. "You came to

our house! You ate with us and played with the kids! You swam with them in the river. . . ." *Oh my God! It was all coming back. The images, the faces . . . Oh, Christ, the faces . . . The bodies floating in circles of water and blood . . . Control yourself! Reject them! Reject! Only now. Now!*

"That was in another country, David. And besides—I don't think you want me to complete the line."

" 'Besides the wench is dead.' No, I'd prefer you didn't repeat the line."

"No matter what," said Conklin hoarsely, swallowing most of his whisky. "We were both erudite, weren't we? . . . I can't help you."

"Yes, you can. You *will*."

"Get off it, soldier. There's no way."

"Debts are owed you. Call them in. I'm calling yours."

"Sorry. You can pull that trigger anytime you want, but if you don't, I'm not putting myself beyond-salvage or blowing everything that's coming to me—legitimately coming to me. If I'm allowed to go to pasture, I intend to graze well. They took enough. I want some back." The CIA officer got up from the couch and awkwardly walked across the room toward the copper bar. His limp was more pronounced than Webb remembered it, his right foot no more serviceable than an encased stump dragged at an angle across the floor, the effort painfully obvious.

"The leg's worse, isn't it?" asked David curtly.

"I'll live with it."

"You'll die with it too," said Webb, raising his automatic. "Because I can't live without my wife and you don't give a goddamn. Do you know what that makes you, Alex? After everything you did to us, all the lies, the traps, the scum you used to nail us with—"

"*You!*" interrupted Conklin, filling his glass, and staring at the gun. "Not her."

"Kill one of us, you kill us both, but you wouldn't understand that."

"I never had the luxury."

"Your lousy self-pity wouldn't let you! You just want to wallow in it all by yourself and let the booze do the thinking. 'There but for a fucking land mine goes the Director, or the Monk or the Gray Fox—the Angleton of the eighties.' You're pathetic. You've got your life, your mind—

"Jesus, take them away! *Shoot!* Pull the goddamn trigger but leave me *something!*" Conklin suddenly swallowed his entire drink; an extended, rolling, retching cough followed. After the spasm, he looked at David, his eyes watery, the red veins pronounced. "You think I wouldn't try to help if I could, you son of a bitch?" he whispered huskily. "You think I like all that *'thinking'* I indulge myself in? You're the one who's dense, the one who's stubborn, David. You don't understand, do you?" The CIA man held the glass in front of him with two fingers and let it drop to the hardwood floor; it shattered, fragments flying in all directions. Then he spoke, his voice a high-pitched singsong, as below the rheumy eyes a sad smile crept across his lips. "I can't stand another *failure,* old friend. And I'd fail, believe me. I'd kill you both and I just don't think I could live with that."

Webb lowered the gun. "Not with what you've got in your head, not with what you've learned. Anyway, I'll take my chances; my options are limited, and I choose you. To be honest, I don't know anyone else. Also, I've several ideas, maybe even a plan, but it's got to be set up at high speed."

"Oh?" Conklin held on to the bar to steady himself.

"May I make some coffee, Alex?"

7

Black coffee had a sobering effect on Conklin but nowhere near the effect of David's confidence in him. The former Jason Bourne respected the talents of his past, most deadly enemy and let him know it. They talked until four o'clock in the morning, refining the blurred outlines of a strategy, basing it on reality but carrying it much further. And as the alcohol diminished, Conklin began to function. He began to give shape to what David had formulated only vaguely. He perceived the basic soundness of Webb's approach and found the words.

"You're describing a spreading crisis-situation mounted in the fact of Marie's abduction, then sending it off the wire with lies. But as you said, it's got to be set off at high speed, hitting them hard and fast, with no letup."

"Use the complete truth first," interrupted Webb, speaking rapidly. "I broke in here threatening to kill you. I made accusations based on everything that's happened —from McAllister's scenario to Babcock's statement that they'd send out an execution team to find me . . . to that Anglicized voice of dry ice who told me to cease and desist with Medusa or they'd call me insane and put me back in a mental stockade. None of it can be denied. It *did* happen and I'm threatening to expose everything, including Medusa."

"Then we spiral off into the big lie," said Conklin, pouring more coffee. "A breakaway so out of sight that it throws everything and everybody into a corkscrew turn."

"Such as?"

"I don't know yet. We'll have to think about it. It's got to be something totally unexpected, something that will unbalance the strategists, whoever they are—because every instinct tells me that somewhere they lost control. If I'm right, one of them will have to make contact."

"Then get out your notebooks," insisted David. "Start going back and reach five or six people who are logical contenders."

"That could take hours, even days," objected the CIA officer. "The barricades are up and I'd have to get around them. We don't have the time—*you* don't have the time."

"There has to be time! Start *moving.*"

"There's a better way," countered Alex. "Panov gave it to you."

"Mo?"

"Yes. The logs at State, the official logs."

"The *logs* . . . ?" Webb had momentarily forgotten; Conklin had not. "In what way?"

"It's where they started to build the new file on you. I'll reach Internal Security with another version, at least a variation that will call for answers from someone—if I'm right, if it's gone off the wire. Those logs are only an instrument, they record, they don't confirm accuracy. But the security personnel responsible for them will send up rockets if they think the system's been tampered with. They'll do our work for us. . . . Still, we need the lie."

"Alex," said David, leaning forward in his chair opposite the long, worn couch. "A few moments ago you used the term 'breakaway'—"

"It simply means a disruption in the scenario, a break in the pattern."

"I know what it means, but how about using it here literally. Not breakaway, but 'broke *away*.' They're calling me pathological, a schizophrenic—that means I fantasize, I sometimes tell the truth and sometimes not, and I'm not supposed to be able to tell the difference."

"It's what they're saying," agreed Conklin. "Some of them may even believe it. So?"

"Why don't we take this way up, really out of sight? We'll say that Marie *broke away*. She reached me and I'm on my way to meet her."

Alex frowned, then gradually widened his eyes, the creases disappearing. "It's perfect," he said quietly. "My God, it's *perfect!* The confusion will spread like a brushfire. In any operation this deep only two or three men know all the details. The others are kept in the dark. *Jesus*, can you imagine? An officially sanctioned kidnapping! A few at the core might actually panic and collide with each other trying to save their asses. *Very* good, Mr. Bourne."

Oddly enough, Webb did not resent the remark, he merely accepted it without thinking. "Listen," he said, getting to his feet. "We're both exhausted. We know where we're heading, so let's get a couple of hours' sleep and go over everything in the morning. You and I learned years ago the difference between a scratch of sleep and none at all."

"Are you going back to the hotel?" asked Conklin.

"No way," replied David, looking down at the pale, drawn face of the CIA man. "Just get me a blanket. I'm staying right here in front of the bar."

"You also should have learned when not to worry about some things," said Alex, rising from the couch and limping toward a closet near the small foyer. "If this is going to be my last hurrah—one way or another—I'll give it my best. It might even sort things out for me." Conklin turned, having taken a blanket and a pillow from the closet shelf. "I guess you could call it some kind of weird precognition, but do you know what I did last night after work?"

"Sure, I do. Among other clues there's a broken glass on the floor."

"No, I mean before that."

"What?"

"I stopped off at the supermarket and bought a ton of food. Steak, eggs, milk—even that glue they call oatmeal. I mean, I never do that."

"You were ready for a ton of food. It happens."

"When it does, I go to a restaurant."

"What's your point?"

"You sleep; the couch is big enough. I'm going to eat. I want to think some more. I'm going to cook a steak, maybe some eggs, too."

"You need sleep."

"Two, two and a half hours'll be fine. Then I'll probably have some of that goddamned oatmeal."

Alexander Conklin walked down the corridor of the State Department's fourth floor, his limp lessened through sheer determination, the pain greater because of it. He knew what was happening to him: there was a job facing him that he wanted very much to do well— even brilliantly, if that term had any relevance for him any longer. Alex realized that months of abusing the blood and the body could not be overcome in a matter of hours, but something within him could be summoned. It was a sense of authority, laced with righteous anger. *Jesus,* the irony! A year ago he had wanted to destroy the man they called Jason Bourne; now it was a sudden, growing obsession to help David Webb—because he had wrongfully tried to kill Jason Bourne. It could place him beyond-salvage, he understood that, but it was right that the risk was his. Perhaps conscience did not always produce cowards. Sometimes it made a man feel better about himself.

And look better, he considered. He had forced himself to walk many more blocks than he should have, letting the cold autumn wind in the streets bring a color to his face that had not been there in years. Combined with a clean shave and a pressed pin-striped suit he had not worn in months, he bore little resemblance to the man Webb found last night. The rest was performance, he knew that, too, as he approached the sacrosanct double doors of the State Department's Chief of Internal Security.

Little time was spent on formalities, even less on informal conversation. At Conklin's request—read Agency demand—an aide left the room, and he faced the rugged former brigadier general from the Army's G-2 who now headed State's Internal Security. Alex intended to take command with his first words.

"I'm not here on an interagency diplomatic mission, General—it *is* General, isn't it?"

"I'm still called that, yes."

"So I don't give a damn about being diplomatic, do you understand me?"

"I'm beginning not to like you, I understand that."

"*That,*" said Conklin, "is the least of my concerns. What does concern me, however, is a man named David Webb."

"What about him?"

"*Him?* The fact that you recognize the name so readily isn't very reassuring. What's going *on, General?*"

"Do you want a megaphone, spook?" said the ex-soldier curtly.

"I want answers, *Corporal*—that's what you and this office are to us."

"Back off, Conklin! When you called me with your so-called emergency and switchboard verification, I did a little verifying myself. That big reputation of yours is a little wobbly these days, and I use the term on good advice. You're a lush, spook, and no secret's been made about it. So you've got less than a minute to say what you want to say before I throw you out. Take your choice—the elevator or the window."

Alex had calculated the probability that his drinking would be telegraphed. He stared at the chief of Internal Security and spoke evenly, even sympathetically. "General, I will answer that accusation with one sentence, and if it ever reaches anyone else, I'll know where it came from and so will the Agency." Conklin paused, his eyes

clear and penetrating. "Our profiles are often what we
want them to be for reasons we can't talk about. I'm sure
you understand what I mean."

The State Department man received Alex's gaze with
a reluctantly sympathetic one of his own. "Oh, *Christ,*" he
said softly. "We used to give dishonorables to men we
were sending out in Berlin."

"Often at our suggestion," agreed Conklin, nodding.
"And it's all we'll say on the subject."

"Okay, okay. I was out of line, but I can tell you the
profile's working. I was told by one of your deputy directors that I'd pass out at your breath with you halfway
across the room."

"I don't even want to know who he is, General, because
I might laugh in his face. As it happens, I don't drink."
Alex had a childhood compulsion to cross his fingers
somewhere out of sight, or his legs, or his toes, but no
method came to him. "Let's get back to David Webb," he
added sharply, no quarter in his voice.

"What's your beef?"

"My *beef?* My goddamned *life,* soldier. Something's
going on and I want to know what it is! That son of a bitch
broke into my apartment last night and threatened to *kill*
me. He made some pretty wild accusations naming men
on your payroll like Harry Babcock and Samuel Teasdale
and William Lanier. We checked; they're in your covert
division and still practicing. What the hell did they *do?*
One made it plain you'd send out an *execution* team after
him! What kind of language is *that?* Another told him to
go back to a hospital—he's been in *two* hospitals *and* our
combined, very private clinic in Virginia—we *all* put him
there—and he's got a clean bill! He's also got some secrets in his head none of us wants out. But that man is
ready to explode because of something you idiots did, or
let happen, or closed your fucking eyes to! He claims to
have *proof* that you walked back into his life and turned
it around, that you set him up and took a hell of a lot
more than a pound of flesh!"

"*What* proof?" asked the stunned general.

"He spoke to his wife," said Conklin in a sudden
monotone.

"So?"

"She was taken from their home by two men who

sedated her and put her on a private jet. She was flown
to the West Coast."

"You mean she was *kidnapped?*"

"You've got it. And what should make you swallow
hard is that she overheard the two of them talking to the
pilot, and gathered that the whole dirty business had
something to do with the State Department—for reasons
unknown—but the name *McAllister* was mentioned. For
your enlightenment he's one of your undersecretaries
from the Far East Section."

"This is *nuts!*"

"I'll tell you what's more than nuts—mine and yours
in a crushed salad. She got away during a refueling stop
in San Francisco. That's when she reached Webb back in
Maine. He's on his way to meet her—God knows where
—but you'd better have some solid answers, unless you
can establish the fact that he's a lunatic who may have
killed his wife—which I hope you can—and that there was
no abduction—which I sincerely hope there wasn't."

"He's *certifiable!*" cried the chief of State's Internal Security. "I *read* those logs! I had to—someone else called
about this Webb last night. Don't ask me who, I can't tell
you."

"What the *hell* is going on?" demanded Conklin, leaning across the desk, his hands on the edge, as much for
support as for effect.

"He's *paranoid,* what can I say? He makes things up and
believes them!"

"That's not what the government doctors determined," said Conklin icily. "I happen to know something
about that."

"I *don't,* damn it!"

"You probably never will," agreed Alex. "But as a
surviving member of the Treadstone operation, you
reach someone who can say the right words to me and
put my mind at ease. Somebody over here has opened up
a can of worms we intend to keep a tight lid on." Conklin
took out a small notebook and a ballpoint pen; he wrote
down a number, tore off the page and dropped it on the
desk. "That's a sterile phone; a trace would only give you
a false address," he continued, his eyes hard, his voice
firm, the slight tremble even ominous. "It's to be used
between three and four this afternoon, no other time.

Have someone reach me then. I don't care who it is or
how you do it. Maybe you'll have to call one of your
celebrated policy conferences, but I want answers—*we*
want answers!"

"You could be all wet, you know!"

"I hope I am. But if I'm not, you people over here are
going to get strung up—*hard*—because you've crossed
over into off-limits territory."

David was grateful that there were so many things to do,
for without them he might plummet into a mental limbo
and become paralyzed by the strain of knowing both too
much and too little. After Conklin left for Langley, he had
returned to the hotel and started his inevitable list. Lists
calmed him; they were preliminaries to necessary activity
and forced him to concentrate on specific items rather
than on the reasons for selecting them. Brooding over
the reasons would cripple his mind as severely as a land
mine had crippled Conklin's right foot. He could not
think about Alex either—there were too many possibilities and impossibilities. Nor could he phone his once and
former enemy. Conklin was thorough; he *was* the best.
The ex-strategist projected each action and its subsequent reaction, and his first determination was that
within minutes after he telephoned the State Department's chief of Internal Security, other telephones would
be used, and two specific phones undoubtedly tapped.
Both his. In his apartment and at Langley. Therefore, to
avoid any interruptions or interceptions he did not intend to return to his office. He would meet David at the
airport later, thirty minutes before Webb's flight to Hong
Kong.

"You think you got here without someone following
you?" he had said to Webb. "I'm not certain of that.
They're programming you, and when someone punches
a keyboard he keeps his eye on the constant number."

"Will you please speak English? Or Mandarin? I can
handle those but not that horseshit."

"They could have a microphone under your bed. I
trust you're not a closet something-or-other."

There would be no contact until they met at the lounge
at Dulles Airport, which was why David now stood at a

cashier's counter in a luggage store on Wyoming Avenue. He was buying an outsized flight bag to replace his suitcase; he had discarded much of his clothing. *Things*—precautions—were coming back to him, among them the unwarranted risk of waiting in an airport's luggage area, and since he wanted the greater anonymity of economy class, a carryon two-suiter might be disallowed. He would buy whatever he needed wherever he was, and that meant he had to have a great deal of money for any number of contingencies. This fact determined his next stop, a bank on Fourteenth Street.

A year ago while the government probers were examining what was left of his memory, Marie had quietly, rapidly withdrawn the funds David had left in Zurich's Gemeinschaft Bank as well as those he had transferred to Paris as Jason Bourne. She had wired the money to the Cayman Islands, where she knew a Canadian banker, and established an appropriately confidential account. Considering what Washington had done to her husband—the damage to his mind, the physical suffering and near loss of life because men refused to hear his cries for help—she was letting the government off lightly. If David had decided to sue, and in spite of everything, it was not out of the question, any astute attorney would go into court seeking damages upwards of $10 million, not roughly five-plus.

She had speculated aloud about her thoughts regarding legal redress with an extremely nervous deputy director of the Central Intelligence Agency. She did not discuss the missing funds other than to say that with her financial training she was appalled to learn that so little protection had been given the American taxpayers' hard-earned dollars. She had delivered this criticism in a shocked if gentle voice, but her eyes were saying something else. The lady was a highly intelligent, highly motivated tiger, and her message got through. So wiser and more cautious men saw the logic of her speculations and let the matter drop. The funds were buried under top-secret, eyes-only contingency appropriations.

Whenever additional money was needed—a trip, a car, the house—Marie or David would call their banker in the Caymans and he would credit the funds by wire to any of five dozen reciprocating banks in Europe, the United States, the Pacific Islands, and the Far East, exclusive of the Philippines.

From a pay phone on Wyoming Avenue, Webb placed a collect call, mildly astonishing his friendly banker by the amount of money he needed immediately, and the funds he wanted available in Hong Kong. The collect call came to less than eight dollars, the money to over half a million dollars.

"I assume that my dear friend, the wise and glorious Marie, approves, David?"

"She told me to call you. She said she can't be bothered with trifles."

"How like her! The banks you will use are . . ."

Webb walked through the thick glass doors of the bank on Fourteenth Street, spent twenty irritating minutes with a vice president who tried too hard to be an instant chum, and walked out with $50,000, forty in $500 bills, the rest a mix.

He then hailed a cab and was driven to an apartment in D.C. North West, where a man he had known in his days as Jason Bourne lived, a man who had done extraordinary work for the State Department's Treadstone 71. The man was a silver-haired black who had been a taxi driver until one day a passenger left a Hasselblad camera in his car and never put in a claim. That was years ago, and for several years the cabbie had experimented, and had found his true vocation. Quite simply, he was a genius at "alteration"—his specialty being passports and driver's licenses with photographs and ID cards for those who had come in conflict with the law, in the main with felony arrests. David had not remembered the man, but under Panov's hypnosis he had said the name—improbably, the name was Cactus—and Mo had brought the photographer to Virginia to help jar a part of Webb's memory. There had been warmth and concern in the old black man's eyes on his first visit, and although it was an inconvenience, he had requested permission from Panov to visit David once a week.

"Why, Cactus?"

"He's troubled, sir. I saw that through the lens a couple of years ago. There's somethin' missin' in him, but for all that he's a good man. I can talk to him. I like him, sir."

"Come whenever you like, Cactus, and please cancel that 'sir' stuff. Reserve the privilege for me . . . sir."

"My, how times change. I call one of my grandchildren a good nigger, he wants to stomp on my head."

"He should . . . *sir.*"

Webb got out of the taxi, asking the driver to wait, but he refused. David left a minimum tip and walked up the overgrown flagstone path to the old house. In some ways it reminded him of the house in Maine, too large, too fragile and too much in need of repair. He and Marie had decided to buy on the beach as soon as a year was up; it was unseemly for a newly appointed associate professor to move into the high-rent district upon arrival. He rang the bell.

The door opened, and Cactus, squinting under a green eye shade, greeted him as casually as if they had seen each other several days ago.

"You got hubcaps on your car, David?"

"No car and no taxi; it wouldn't stay."

"Must'a' heard all those unfounded rumors circulated by the fascist press. Me. I got three machine guns in the windows. Come on in, I've *missed* you. Why didn't you call this old boy?"

"Your number's not listed, Cactus."

"Must'a' been an oversight."

They chatted for several minutes in Cactus's kitchen, long enough for the photographer-specialist to realize Webb was in a hurry. The old man led David into his studio, placed Webb's three passports under an angled lamp for close inspection and instructed his client to sit in front of an open-lense camera.

"We'll make the hair light ash, but not as blond as you were after Paris. That ash tone varies with the lighting and we can use the same picture on each of these li'l dears with considerable differences—still retaining the face. Leave the eyebrows alone, I'll mess with them here."

"What about the eyes?" asked David.

"No time for those fancy contacts they got you before, but we can handle it. They're regular glasses with just the right tinted prisms in the right places. You got blue eyes or brown eyes or Spanish-armada black, if you want 'em."

"Get all three," said Webb.

"They're expensive, David, and cash only."

"I've got it on me."

"Don't let it get around."

"Now, the hair. Who?"

"Down the street. An associate of mine who had her own beauty shop until the gendarmes checked the upstairs rooms. She does fine work. Come on, I'll take you over."

An hour later Webb ducked out from under a hair dryer in the small well-lighted cubicle and surveyed the results in the large mirror. The beautician-owner of the odd salon, a short black lady with neat gray hair and an appraiser's eye, stood alongside him.

"It's you, but it ain't you," she said, first nodding her head, then shaking it. "A fine job, I've got to say it."

It was, thought David, looking at himself. His dark hair not only was far, far lighter, but matched the skin tones of his face. Too, the hair itself seemed lighter in texture, a groomed but a much more casual look—windblown, as the advertisements phrased it. The man he was staring at was both himself and someone else who bore a striking resemblance—but not him.

"I agree," said Webb. "It's *very* good. How much?"

"Three hundred dollars," replied the woman simply. "Of course, that includes five packets of custom-made rinse powder with instructions, and the tightest lips in Washington. The first will hold you for a couple of months, the second for the rest of your life."

"You're all heart." David reached into his pocket for his leather money clip, counted out the bills and gave them to her. "Cactus said you'd call him when we were finished."

"No need to; he's got his timing down. He's in the parlor."

"The parlor?"

"Oh, I guess it's a hallway with a settee and a floor lamp, but I do so like to call it a parlor. Sounds nice, don't it?"

The photo session went swiftly, interrupted by Cactus's reshaping his eyebrows with a toothbrush and a spray for the three separate shots, and changing shirts and jackets—Cactus had a wardrobe worthy of a costume supply house—and finally wearing two pairs of glasses, tortoiseshell and steel-rimmed, which altered his hazel eyes respectively to blue and brown for two of the passports. The specialist then surgically proceeded to insert the photos in place, and under a large, powerful magnifying glass skillfully stamped out the original State Department perforations with a tool of his own design. When he finished, he handed the three passports to David for his approval.

"Ain't no customs jockey gonna' pick on them," said Cactus confidently.

"They look more authentic than they did before."

"I cleaned 'em up, which is to say I gave 'em a few creases and some aging."

"It's terrific work, old friend—older than I can remember, I know that. What do I owe you?"

"Oh, hell, I don't know. It was such a little job and it's been such a big year what with all the hasslin' goin' on—"

"How *much*, Cactus?"

"What's comfortable? I don't figure you're on Uncle's payroll."

"I'm doing very nicely, thanks."

"Five hundred's fine."

"Call me a cab, will you?"

"Takes too long, and that's if you can get one out here. My grandson's waiting for you; he'll drive you wherever you want to go. He's like me, he don't ask questions. And you're in a hurry, David, I can sense that. Come on, I'll see you to the door."

"Thanks. I'll leave the cash here on the counter."

"Fine."

Removing the money from his pocket, his back to Cactus, Webb counted out six $500 bills and left them in the darkest area of the studio counter. At $1,000 apiece the passports were a gift, but to leave more might offend his old friend.

He returned to the hotel, getting out of the car several blocks away in the middle of a busy intersection so that Cactus's grandson could not be compromised where an address was concerned. The young man, as it happened, was a senior at American University, and although he obviously adored his grandfather, he was just as obviously apprehensive about being any part of the old man's endeavors.

"I'll get out here," said David in the stalled traffic.

"Thanks," responded the young black, his voice pleasantly calm, his intelligent eyes showing relief. "I appreciate it."

Webb looked at him. "Why did you do it? I mean, for someone who's going to be a lawyer, I'd think your antenna would work overtime around Cactus."

"It does, constantly. But he's a great old guy who's done a lot for me. Also, he said something to me. He said it would be a privilege for me to meet you, that maybe years from now he'd tell me who the stranger was in my car."

"I hope I can come back a lot sooner and tell you myself. I'm no privilege, but there's a story to tell that could end up in the law books. Good-bye."

Back in his hotel room, David faced a final list that needed no items written out; he knew them. He had to select the few clothes he would take in the large flight bag and get rid of the rest of his possessions, including the two weapons he had brought down from Maine in his outrage. It was one thing to dismantle and wrap in foil the parts of a gun to be placed in a suitcase, and quite another to carry weapons through a security gate. They would be picked up; he would be picked up. He had to wipe them clean, destroy the firing pins and trigger housings and drop them into a sewer. He would buy a weapon in Hong Kong; it was not a difficult purchase.

There was a last thing he had to do, and it was difficult and painful. He had to force himself to sit down and rethink everything that had been said by Edward McAllister that early evening in Maine—everything they all had said, in particular Marie's words. Something was buried somewhere in that highly charged hour of revelation and confrontation, and David knew he had missed it—*was* missing it.

He looked at his watch. It was 3:37; the day was passing quickly, nervously. *He had to hold on!* Oh, God, *Marie! Where are you?*

Conklin put down his glass of flat ginger ale on the scratched, soiled bar of the seedy establishment on Ninth Street. He was a regular patron for the simple reason that no one in his professional circle—and what was left of his social one—would ever walk through the filthy glass doors. There was a certain freedom in that knowledge, and the other patrons accepted him, the "gimp" who always took off his tie the moment he entered, limping his way to a stool by the pinball machine at the end of the bar. And whenever he did, the rocks-glass filled with bourbon was waiting for him. Also, the owner-bartender had no objections to Alex receiving calls at the still-standing antiquated booth against the wall. It was his "sterile phone," and it was ringing now.

Conklin trudged across the floor, entered the old booth, and closed the door. He picked up the phone. "Yes?" he said.

"Is this Treadstone?" asked an odd-sounding male voice.

"I was there. Were you?"

"No, I wasn't, but I'm cleared for the file, for the whole mess."

The *voice!* thought Alex. How had Webb described it? Anglicized? Mid-Atlantic, refined, certainly not ordinary. It was the same man. The gnomes had been working; they had made progress. Someone was afraid.

"Then I'm sure your memory corresponds with everything I've written down because I *was* there and I *have* written it down—written it all down. Facts, names, events, substantiations, backups . . . everything, including the story Webb told me last night."

"Then I can assume that if anything ugly happened, your voluminous reportage will find its way to a Senate subcommittee or a pack of congressional watchdogs. Am I right?"

"I'm glad we understand each other."

"It wouldn't do any good," said the man condescendingly.

"If anything ugly happened, I wouldn't care, would I?"

"You're about to retire. You drink a great deal."

"I didn't always. There's usually a reason for both of those things for a man of my age and competence. Could they be admittedly tied into a certain file?"

"Forget it. Let's talk."

"Not before you say something a little closer. Treadstone was bandied about here and there; it's not that substantive."

"All right. Medusa."

"Stronger," said Alex. "But not strong enough."

"Very well. The creation of Jason Bourne. The Monk."

"Warmer."

"Missing funds—unaccounted for and never recovered—estimated to be around five million dollars. Zurich, Paris, and points west."

"There were rumors. I need a capstone."

"I'll give it to you. The execution of Jason Bourne. The date was May twenty-third in Tam Quan . . . and the same day in New York years later. On Seventy-first Street. Treadstone Seventy-one."

Conklin closed his eyes and breathed deeply, feeling the hollowness in his throat. "All right," he said quietly. "You're in the circle."

"I can't give you my name."

"What are you going to give me?"

"Two words: Back off."

"You think I'll accept that?"

"You have to," said the voice, his words precise. "Bourne is needed where he's going."

"*Bourne?*" Alex stared at the phone.

"Yes, Jason Bourne. He can't be recruited in any normal way, we both know that."

"So you steal his *wife* from him? Goddamned *animals!*"

"She won't be harmed."

"You can't guarantee that! You don't have the controls. You've got to be using second and third parties right now, and if I know my business—and I *do*—they're probably paid blinds so you can't be traced; you don't even know who they are. . . . My *God,* you wouldn't have called me if you *did!* If you could reach them and get the verifications you want, you wouldn't be talking to me!"

The cultured voice paused. "Then we both lied, didn't we, Mr. Conklin? There was no escape on the woman's part, no call to Webb. Nothing. You went fishing, and so did I, and we both came up with nothing."

"You're a barracuda, Mr. No-name."

"You've been where I am, Mr. Conklin. Right down to David Webb. . . . Now, what can *you* tell *me?*"

Alex again felt the hollowness in his throat, now joined with a sharp pain in his chest. "You've lost them, haven't you?" he whispered. "You've lost *her.*"

"Forty-eight hours isn't permanent," said the voice guardedly.

"But you've been trying like hell to make contact!" accused Conklin. "You've called in your conduits, the people who hired the blinds, and suddenly they're not there—you can't find them. *Jesus*, you *have* lost control! It *did* go off the wire! Someone walked in on your strategy and you have no idea who it is. He played your scenario and took it away from you!"

"Our safeguards are spread out," objected the man without the conviction he had displayed during the past moments. "The best men in the field are working every district."

"Including *McAllister*? In Kowloon? Hong Kong?"

"You know that?"

"I know."

"McAllister's a damn fool, but he's good at what he does. And, yes, he's there. We're not panicked. We'll recover."

"Recover *what?*" asked Alex, filled with anger. "The merchandise? Your strategy's aborted! Someone else is in charge. Why would he give you back the merchandise? You've killed Webb's wife, Mr. No-name! What the *hell* did you think you were *doing?*"

"We just wanted to get him over there," replied the voice defensively. "Explain things, show him. We *need* him." Then the man resumed his calm delivery. "And for all we know, everything's still *on* the wire. Communications are notoriously bad in that part of the world."

"The *ex-culpa* for everything in this business."

"In most businesses, Mr. Conklin. . . . How do you read it? Now I'm the one who's asking—very sincerely. You have a certain reputation."

"*Had*, No-name."

"Reputations can't be taken away or contradicted, only added to, positively or negatively, of course."

"You're a fount of unwarranted information, you know that?"

"I'm also right. It's said you were one of the best. How *do* you read it?"

Alex shook his head in the booth; the air was close, the noise outside his "sterile" phone growing louder in the seedy bar on Ninth Street. "What I said before. Someone found out what you people were planning—mounting for Webb—and decided to take over."

"For God's sake, *why?*"

"Because whoever it is wants Jason Bourne more than you do," Alex said and hung up.

It was 6:28 when Conklin walked into the lounge at Dulles Airport. He had waited in a taxi down the street from Webb's hotel and had followed David, giving the driver precise instructions. He had been right, but there was no point in burdening Webb with the knowledge. Two gray Plymouths had picked up David's cab and alternately exchanged positions during the surveillance. So be it. One Alexander Conklin might be hanged and then again, he might not. People at State were behaving stupidly, he had thought as he wrote down the license numbers. He spotted Webb in a darkened back booth.

"It is you, isn't it?" said Alex, dragging his dead foot into the banquette. "Do blonds really have more fun?"

"It worked in Paris. What did you find?"

"I found slugs under rocks who can't find their way up out of the ground. But then they wouldn't know what to do with the sunlight, would they?"

"Sunlight's illuminating; you're not. Cut the crap, Alex. I have to get to the gate in a few minutes."

"In short words, they worked out a strategy to get you over to Kowloon. It was based on a previous experience—"

"You can skip that," said David. *"Why?"*

"The man said they needed you. Not you—Webb, they needed Bourne."

"Because they say Bourne's already there. I told you what McAllister said. Did he go into it?"

"No, he wasn't going to give me that much, but maybe I can use it to press them. However, he told me something else, David, and you have to know it. They can't find their conduits, so they don't know who the blinds are or what's happening. They think it's temporary, but they've lost Marie. Somebody else wants you out there and he's taken over."

Webb brought his hand to his forehead, his eyes closed, and suddenly, in silence, the tears fell down his cheeks. "I'm *back*, Alex. Back into so much I can't remember. I love her so, I *need* her so!"

"Cut it *out!*" ordered Conklin. "You made it clear to me last night that I still had a mind, if not much of a body. You have *both*. Make them *sweat!*"

"How?"

"Be what they want you to be—be the chameleon! *Be* Jason Bourne."

"It's been so long. . . ."

"You can still do it. Play the scenario they've given you."

"I don't have any choice, do I?"

Over the loudspeakers came the last call for Flight 26 to Hong Kong.

The gray-haired Havilland replaced the phone in its cradle, leaned back in his chair and looked across the room at McAllister. The undersecretary of State was standing next to a huge revolving globe of the world that was perched on an ornamental tripod in front of a bookcase. His index finger was on the southernmost part of China, but his eyes were on the ambassador.

"It's done," said the diplomat. "He's on the plane to Kowloon."

"It's God-awful," replied McAllister.

"I'm sure it appears that way to you, but before you render judgment, weigh the advantages. We're free now. We are no longer responsible for the events that take place. They are being manipulated by an unknown party."

"Which is *us!* I repeat, it's God-awful!"

"Has your God considered the consequences if we fail?"

"We're given free will. Only our ethics restrict us."

"A banality, Mr. Undersecretary. There's the greater good."

"There's also a human being, a man we're manipulating, driving him back into his nightmares. Do we have that right?"

"We have no choice. He can do what no one else can do—if we give him a reason to do it."

McAllister spun the globe; it whirled around as he

walked toward the desk. "Perhaps I shouldn't say it, but I will," he said, standing in front of Raymond Havilland. "I think you're the most immoral man I've ever met."

"Appearances, Mr. Undersecretary. I have one saving grace which supersedes all the sins I have committed. I will go to any lengths, indulge in all venalities, to stop this planet from blowing itself up. And that includes the life of one David Webb—known where I want him as Jason Bourne."

8

The mists rose like layers of diaphanous scarves above Victoria Harbor as the huge jet circled for the final approach into Kai-tak Airport. The early morning haze was dense, the promise of a humid day in the colony. Below on the water the junks and the sampans bobbed beside the outlying freighters, the squat barges, the chugging multitiered ferries, and the occasional marine patrols that swept through the harbor. As the plane descended into the Kowloon airport, the serried ranks of skyscrapers on the island of Hong Kong took on the appearance of alabaster giants, reaching up through the mists and reflecting the first penetrating light of the morning sun.

Webb studied the scene below, both as a man under a horrible strain and as one consumed by an eerily detached curiosity. Down there somewhere in the seething, vastly overpopulated territory was Marie—that was uppermost in his thoughts and the most agonizing to think about. Yet another part of him was like a scientist filled with a cold anxiety as he peered into the clouded lens of a microscope trying to discern what his eye and his mind could understand. The familiar and the unfamiliar were joined, and the result was bewilderment and fear. During Panov's sessions in Virginia, David had read and reread hundreds of travel folders and illustrated brochures describing all the places the mythical Jason Bourne was known to have been; it was a continuous, often painful exercise in self-probing. Fragments would come to him in flashes of recognition; many were all too brief and confusing, others prolonged, his sudden memories astonishingly accurate, the descriptions his own, not those of travel agents' manuals. As he looked down now, he saw much that he knew he knew but could not specifically remember. So he looked away and concentrated on the day ahead.

He had wired the Regent Hotel in Kowloon from Dulles Airport requesting a room for a week in the name of one *Howard Cruett,* the identity on Cactus's refined, blue-eyed passport. He had added: "I believe arrangements were made for our firm with respect to Suite six-nine-zero, if it is available. Arrival day is firm, flight is not."

The suite would be available. What he had to find out was who had made it available. It was the first step toward Marie. And either before or after or during the process there were items to purchase—some would be simple to buy, others not, but even finding the more inaccessible would not be impossible. This was Hong Kong, the colony of survival and the tools of survival. It was also the one civilized place on earth where religions flourished but the only commonly acknowledged god of believers and nonbelievers alike was money. As Marie had put it: "It has no other reason for being."

The tepid morning reeked with the odors of a crowded, rushing humanity, the smells strangely not unpleasant. Curbsides were being hosed ferociously, steam rising from pavements drying in the sun, and the fragrance of herbs boiling in oil wafted through the narrow streets from carts and concessions screeching for attention. The noises accumulated; they became a series of constant crescendos demanding acceptance and a sale or at least a negotiation. Hong Kong was the essence of survival; one worked furiously or one did not survive. Adam Smith was outdone and outdated; he could never have conceived of such a world. It mocked the disciplines he projected for a free economy; it was madness. It was Hong Kong.

David held up his hand for a taxi, knowing that he had done so before, knowing the exit doors he had headed for after the prolonged drudgery of customs, knowing he knew the streets through which the driver took him—not really remembering, but somehow knowing. It was both comforting and profoundly terrifying. He knew and he did not know. He was a marionette being manipulated on the stage of his own sideshow, and he did not know who was the puppet or who the puppeteer.

"It was an error," said David to the clerk behind the oval marble counter in the center of the Regent's lobby. "I don't want a suite. I'd prefer something smaller; a single or a double room will do."

"But the arrangements have been made, Mr. Cruett," replied the bewildered clerk, using the name on Webb's false passport.

"Who made them?"

The youthful Oriental peered down at a signature on the computer printout reservation. "It was authorized by the assistant manager, Mr. Liang."

"Then in courtesy I should speak with Mr. Liang, shouldn't I?"

"I'm afraid it will be necessary. I'm not sure there's anything else available."

"I understand. I'll find another hotel."

"You are considered a most important guest, sir. I will go back and speak with Mr. Liang."

Webb nodded, as the clerk, reservation in hand, ducked under the counter on the far left and walked rapidly across the crowded floor to a door behind the concierge's desk. David looked around at the opulent lobby, which in a sense started outside in the immense circular courtyard with its tall, gushing fountains, and extended through the bank of elegant glass doors and across the marble floor to a semicircle of enormously high tinted windows that looked out over Victoria Harbor. The ever-moving tableau beyond was a hypnotic addition to the *mise en scène* of the open curving lounge in front of the wall of soft-colored glass. There were dozens of small tables and leather settees, mostly occupied, with uniformed waiters and waitresses scurrying about. It was an arena from which tourists and negotiators alike could view the panorama of the harbor's commerce, played out in front of the rising skyline of the island of Hong Kong in the distance. The watery view outside was familiar to Webb, but nothing else. He had never been inside the extravagant hotel before; at least nothing of what he saw aroused any flashes of recognition.

Suddenly his eyes were drawn to the sight of the clerk rushing across the lobby several steps ahead of a middle-aged Oriental, obviously the Regent's assistant manager, Mr. Liang. Again the younger man ducked under the counter and quickly resumed his position in front of David, his accommodating eyes as wide as they could be in anticipation. Seconds later the hotel executive approached, bowing slightly from the waist, as befitted his professional station.

"This is Mr. Liang, sir," announced the clerk.

"May I be of service?" said the assistant manager. "And may I say it is a pleasure to welcome you as our guest?"

Webb smiled and shook his head politely. "It may have to be another time, I'm afraid."

"You are displeased with the accommodations, Mr. Cruett?"

"Not at all, I'd probably like them very much. But, as I told your young man, I prefer smaller quarters, a single or even a double room, but not a suite. However, I understand there may not be anything available."

"Your wire specifically mentioned Suite six-ninety, sir."

"I realize that and I apologize. It was the work of an overzealous sales representative." Webb frowned in a friendly, quizzical manner and asked courteously, "Incidentally, who did make those arrangements? I certainly didn't."

"Your representative, perhaps," offered Liang, his eyes noncommittal.

"In sales? He wouldn't have the authority. No, he said it was one of the companies over here. We can't accept, of course, but I'd like to know who made such a generous offer. Surely, Mr. Liang, since you personally authorized the reservation, you can tell me."

The noncommittal eyes became more distant, then blinked; it was enough for David, but the charade had to be played out. "I believe one of our staff—our very large staff—came to me with the request, sir. There are so many reservations, we are so busy, I really can't recall."

"Certainly there are billing instructions."

"We have many honored clients whose word on a telephone is sufficient."

"Hong Kong has changed."

"And always changing, Mr. Cruett. It is possible your host wishes to tell you himself. It would not be proper to intrude on such wishes."

"Your sense of trust is admirable."

"Backed by a billing code in the cashier's computer, naturally." Liang attempted a smile; it was false.

"Well, since you have nothing else, I'll strike out on my own. I have friends at the Pen across the street," said Webb, referring to the revered Peninsula Hotel.

"That will not be necessary. Further arrangements can be made."

"But your clerk said—"

"He is not the assistant manager of the Regent, sir." Liang briefly glared at the young man behind the counter.

"My screen shows nothing to be available," protested the clerk in defense.

"Be quiet!" Liang instantly smiled, as falsely as before, aware that he had undoubtedly lost the charade with his command. "He is so young—they are all so young and inexperienced—but very intelligent, very willing. . . . We keep several rooms in reserve for misunderstood occasions." Again he looked at the clerk and spoke harshly while smiling. *"Ting, ruan-ji!"* He continued rapidly in Chinese, every word understood by an expressionless Webb. "Listen to me, you boneless chicken! Do not offer information in my presence unless I ask you! You will be spit from the garbage shoot if you do it again. Now assign this fool Room two-zero-two. It is listed as Hold; remove the listing and proceed." The assistant manager, his waxen smile even more pronounced turned back to David. "It is a very pleasant room with a splendid view of the harbor, Mr. Cruett."

The charade was over, and the winner minimized his victory with persuasive appreciation. "I'm most grateful," said David, his eyes boring into those of the suddenly insecure Liang. "It will save me the trouble of phoning all over the city telling people where I'm staying." He stopped, his right hand partially raised, a man about to continue. David Webb was acting on one of several instincts, instincts developed by Jason Bourne. He knew it was the moment to instill fear. "When you say a room with a splendid view, I assume you mean *'you hao jingse de fang jian.'* Am I right? Or is my Chinese too foolish?"

The hotel man stared at the American. "I could not have phrased it better," he said softly. "The clerk will see to everything. Enjoy your stay with us, Mr. Cruett."

"Enjoyment must be measured by accomplishment, Mr. Liang. That's either a very old or very new Chinese proverb, I don't know which."

"I suspect it's new, Mr. Cruett. It's too active for passive reflection, which is the soul of Confucius, as I'm sure you do know."

"Isn't that accomplishment?"

"You are too swift for me, sir." Liang bowed. "If there's anything you need, don't hesitate to reach me."

"I hardly think that will be necessary, but thank you. Frankly, it was a long and dreadful flight, so I'll ask the switchboard to hold all calls until dinnertime."

"Oh?" Liang's insecurity became something far more pronounced; he was a man afraid. "But surely if an emergency arises—"

"There's nothing that can't wait. And since I'm not in Suite six-ninety, the hotel can simply say I'm expected later. That's plausible, isn't it? I'm terribly tired. Thank you, Mr. Liang."

"Thank *you*, Mr. Cruett." The assistant manager bowed again, searching Webb's eyes for a last sign. He found none and turned quickly, nervously, and headed back to his office.

Do the unexpected. Confuse the enemy, throw him off-balance. —Jason Bourne. Or was it Alexander Conklin?

"It is a *most* desirable room, sir!" exclaimed the relieved clerk. "You will be *most* pleased."

"Mr. Liang is very accommodating," said David. "I should show my appreciation, as, indeed, I will, for your help." Webb took out his leather money clip and unobtrusively removed an American $20 bill. He extended a handshake, the bill concealed. "When does Mr. Liang leave for the day?"

The bewildered but overjoyed young man glanced to his right and left, speaking as he did so in disjointed phrases. "Yes! You are most kind, sir. It is not necessary, sir, but thank you, sir. Mr. Liang leaves his office every afternoon at five o'clock. I, too, leave at that hour. I would stay, of course, if our management requested, for I try very hard to do the best I can for the honor of the hotel."

"I'm sure you do," said Webb. "And most capably. My key, please. My luggage will arrive later due to a switch in flights."

"Of course, sir!"

David sat in the chair by the tinted window looking across the harbor at the island of Hong Kong. Names came to him accompanied by images—Causeway Bay, Wanchai, Repulse Bay, Aberdeen, the Mandarin, and finally, so clear in the distance, Victoria Peak with its awesome view of the entire colony. Then he saw in his mind's eye the masses of humanity meshing through the jammed, colorful, frequently filthy streets, and the crowded hotel lobbies and lounges with their softly lit chandeliers of gold filigree where the well-dressed remnants of the empire reluctantly mingled with the emerging Chinese entrepreneurs—the old crown and the new money had to find accommodation. . . . Alleyways. . . . For some reason thronged and run-down alleyways came into focus. Figures raced through the narrow thoroughfares, crashing into cages of small screeching birds and writhing snakes of various sizes—wares of peddlers on the lowest rungs of the territory's ladder of commerce. Men and women of all ages, from children to ancients, were dressed in rags, and pungent, heavy smoke curled slowly upward, filling the space between the decaying buildings, diffusing the light, heightening the gloom of the dark stone walls blackened by use and misuse. He saw it all and it all had meaning for him, but he did not understand. Specifics eluded him; he had no points of reference and it was maddening.

Marie was out there! He had to find her! He sprang up from the chair in frustration, wanting to pound his head to clear the confusion, but he knew it would not help—nothing helped, except time, and he could not stand the strain of time. He had to find her, hold her, protect her, as she had once protected him by believing in him when he had not believed in himself. He passed the mirror above the bureau and looked at his haggard, pale face. One thing was clear. He had to plan and act quickly, but not as the man he saw in the glass. He had to bring into play everything he had learned and forgotten as Jason Bourne. From somewhere within him he had to summon the elusive past and trust unremembered instincts.

He had taken the first step; the connection was solid, he knew that. One way or another, Liang would provide him with something, probably the lowest level of information, but it would be a beginning—a name, a place, or a drop, an initial contact that would lead to another and still another. What he had to do was to move quickly with whatever he was given, not giving his enemy time to maneuver, backing whomever he reached into positions of deliver-and-survive or be-silent-and-die—and mean it. But to accomplish anything he had to be prepared. Items had to be purchased, and a tour of the colony arranged. He wanted an hour or so of observing from the backseat of an automobile, dredging up whatever he could from his damaged memory.

He picked up a large red-leather hotel directory, sat on the edge of the bed and opened it, thumbing through the pages rapidly. *The New World Shopping Centre, a magnificent 5 storeyed open complex bringing under one roof the finest goods from the 4 corners of the earth . . .* Hyperbole notwithstanding, the "complex" was adjacent to the hotel; it would do for his purposes. *Limousines available. From our fleet of Daimler motor cars arrangements can be made by the hour or the day for business or sightseeing. Please contact the Concierge. Dial 62.* Limousines also meant experienced chauffeurs knowledgeable in the ways of the confusing streets, back streets, roads, and traffic patterns of Hong Kong, Kowloon, and the New Territories, and knowledgeable in other ways, too. Such men knew the ins and outs and lower depths of the cities they served. Unless he was mistaken, and instinct told him he was not, an additional need would be covered. He had to have a gun. Finally, there was a bank in Hong Kong's Central District that had certain arrangements with a sister institution thousands of miles away in the Cayman Islands. He had to walk into that bank, sign whatever was required of him, and walk out with more money than any sane man would carry on his person in Hong Kong—or anywhere else, for that matter. He would find someplace to conceal it but not in a bank where business hours restricted its availability. Jason Bourne knew: Promise a man his life and he will usually cooperate; promise him his life and a great deal of money and the cumulative effect will lead to total submission.

David reached for the message pad and pencil next to the phone on the bedside table; he started another list. The little things loomed larger with every hour that passed, and he did not have that many hours left. It was almost eleven o'clock. The harbor now glistened in the near-noon sun. He had so many things to do before 4:30, when he intended to station himself unobtrusively somewhere near the employees' exit, or down inside the hotel garage, or wherever he learned he could follow and trap the waxen-faced Liang, his first connection.

Three minutes later his list was complete. He tore off the page, got up from the bed and reached for his jacket on the desk chair. Suddenly the telephone rang, piercing the quiet of the hotel room. He had to close his eyes, clenching every muscle in his arms and stomach so as not to leap for it, hoping beyond hope for the sound of Marie's voice, even as a captive. He must not pick up the phone. *Instinct. Jason Bourne.* He had no controls. If he answered the phone, *he* would be the one controlled. He let it ring as he walked in anguish across the room and went out the door.

It was ten minutes past noon when he returned carrying a number of thin plastic bags from various stores in the Shopping Centre. He dropped them on the bed and began removing his purchases. Among the articles were a dark, lightweight raincoat and a dark canvas hat, a pair of gray tennis sneakers, black trousers and a sweater, also black; these were the clothes he would wear at night. Then there were other items: a spool of 75-pound-test fishing line with two palm-sized eyehooks through which a three-foot section of line would be looped and secured at both ends, a 20-ounce paperweight in the shape of a miniature brass barbell, one ice pick, and a sheathed, highly sharpened, double-edged hunting knife with a narrow 4-inch blade. These were the silent weapons he would carry both night and day. One more item remained to be found; he would find it.

As he examined his purchases, his concentration narrowing down to the eyehooks and the fishing line, he became aware of a tiny, subtle blinking of light. Start, stop . . . start, stop. It was annoying because he could not find the source, and, as happened so often, he had to wonder if there actually was a source or whether the intrusion was simply an aberration of his mind. Then his eyes were drawn to the bedside table; sunlight streamed in the harbor windows, washing over the telephone, but the pulsating light was there in the lower left-hand corner of the instrument—barely visible, but there. It was the message signal, a small red dot that shone for a second, went dark for a second, and then resumed its signaling at those intervals. A *message* was not a call, he reflected. He went to the table, studied the instructions on the plastic card, and picked up the phone; he pressed the appropriate button.

"Yes, Mr. Cruett?" said the operator at her computerized switchboard.

"There's a message for me?" he asked.

"Yes, sir. Mr. Liang has been trying to reach you—"

"I thought my instructions were clear," interrupted Webb. "There were to be no calls until I told the switchboard otherwise."

"Yes, sir, but Mr. Liang is the assistant manager—the senior manager when his superior is not here, which is the case this morning . . . this afternoon. He tells us it is most urgent. He has been calling you every few minutes for the past hour. I am ringing him now, sir."

David hung up the phone. He was not ready for Liang, or more properly put, Liang was not yet ready for him—at least, not the way David wanted him. Liang was stretched, possibly on the edge of panic, for he was the first and lowliest contact and he had failed to place the subject where he was meant to be—in a wired suite where the enemy could overhear every word. But the edge of panic was not good enough. David wanted Liang over the edge. The quickest way to provoke that state was to permit no contact, no discussion, no exculpating explanations aimed at enlisting the subject to get the offender off the hook.

Webb grabbed the clothes off the bed and put them into two bureau drawers along with the things he had taken out of his flight bag; he stuffed the eyehooks and the fishing line between the layers of fabric. He then placed the paperweight on top of a room service menu on the desk and shoved the hunting knife into his jacket pocket. He looked down at the ice pick and was suddenly struck by a thought again born of a strange instinct: a man consumed with anxiety would overreact when stunned by the unexpected sight of something terrifying. The grim image would shock him, deepening his fears. David pulled out a handkerchief from his breast pocket, reached down for the ice pick and wiped the handle clean. Gripping the lethal instrument in the cloth, he walked rapidly to the small foyer, estimated the eye level, and plunged the pick into the white wall opposite the door. The telephone rang, then rang again steadily, as if in a frenzy. Webb let himself out and ran down the hallway toward the bank of elevators; he slipped into the next angled corridor and watched.

He had not miscalculated. The gleaming metal panels slid apart and Liang raced out of the middle elevator into Webb's hallway. David spun around the corner and dashed to the elevators, then rapidly, quietly, walked to the corner of his own corridor. He could see the nervous Liang ringing his bell repeatedly, finally knocking on the door with increasing persistence.

Another elevator opened and two couples emerged, laughing. One of the men looked quizzically at Webb, then shrugged as the party turned left. David returned his attention to Liang. The assistant manager was now frantic, ringing the bell and pounding the door. Then he stopped and put his ear to the wood; satisfied, he reached into his pocket and withdrew a ring of keys. Webb snapped his head back out of sight as the assistant manager turned to look up and down the corridor while inserting a key. David did not have to see; he wanted only to hear.

He had not long to wait. A suppressed, guttural shriek

was followed by the loud crash of the door. The ice pick had had its effect. Webb ran back to his sanctuary beyond the last elevator, again inching his body to the edge of the wall; he watched. Liang was visibly shaken, breathing erratically, deeply, as he repeatedly pressed his finger against the elevator button. Finally a bell pinged, and the metal panels of the second elevator opened. The assistant manager rushed inside.

David had no specific plan, but he knew vaguely what he had to do, for there was no other way of doing it. He walked down the corridor rapidly past the elevators, and ran the remaining distance to his room. He let himself inside and picked up the bedside telephone, pressing the digits he had committed to memory.

"Concierge's desk," said a pleasant voice which did not sound Oriental; it was probably Indian.

"Am I speaking to the concierge?" asked Webb.

"You are, sir."

"Not one of his assistants?"

"I'm afraid not. Is there a specific assistant you wished to speak with? Someone resolving a problem, perhaps?"

"No, I want to talk to you," said David quietly. "I have a situation that must be handled in the strictest confidence. May I count on yours? I can be generous."

"You are a guest in the hotel?"

"I am a guest."

"And there is nothing untoward involved, of course. Nothing that would damage the establishment."

"Only enhance its reputation for aiding cautious businessmen who wish to bring trade to the territory. A great deal of trade."

"I am at your service, sir."

It was arranged that a Daimler limousine with the most experienced driver available would pick him up in ten minutes at the ramped courtyard drive on Salisbury Road. The concierge would be standing by the car and for his confidence would receive $200 American, roughly $1,500 Hong Kong. There would be no individual's name assigned to the rental—which was to be paid in cash for twenty-four hours—only the name of a firm picked at random. And "Mr. Cruett," escorted by a floor boy, could use a service elevator to the Regent's lower level, where there was an exit that led to the New World Centre with its direct access to the pickup on Salisbury Road.

The amenities and the cash disposed of, David climbed into the backseat of the Daimler, and confronted the lined, tired face of a uniformed middle-aged driver whose weary expression was only partially leavened by a strained attempt to be pleasant.

"Welcome, sir! My name is Pak-fei, and I shall endeavor to be of excellent service to you! You tell me where, and I take you. I know everything!"

"I was counting on that," said Webb softly.

"I beg your words, sir?"

"*Wo bushi luke,*" said David, stating that he was not a tourist. "But as I haven't been here in years," he continued in Chinese, "I want to reacquaint myself. How about the normal, boring tour of the island and then a quick trip through Kowloon? I have to be back in a couple of hours or so. . . . And from here on, let's speak English."

"*Ahh!* Your Chinese is very good—very high class, but I understand everything you say. Yet only two *zhong-tou—*"

"Hours," interrupted Webb. "We're speaking English, remember, and I don't want to be misunderstood. But these two hours and your tip, and the remaining twenty-two hours and *that* tip, will depend on how well we get along, won't it?"

"Yes, *yes!*" cried Pak-fei, the driver, as he gunned the Daimler's motor and authoritatively careened out into the intolerable traffic of Salisbury Road. "I shall endeavor to provide *very* excellent service!"

He did, and the names and images that had come to David in the hotel room were reinforced by their actual counterparts. He knew the streets of the Central District, recognized the Mandarin hotel, and the Hong Kong Club, and Chater Square with the colony's Supreme Court opposite the banking giants of Hong Kong. He had walked through the crowded pedestrian lanes to the wild confusion that was the Star Ferry, the island's continuous link to Kowloon. Queen's Road, Hillier, Possession Street . . . the garish Wanchai—it all came back to him, in the sense that he had been there, been to those places, knew them, knew the streets, even the shortcuts to take going from one place to another. He recognized the winding road to Aberdeen, anticipated the sight of the gaudy floating restaurants and, beyond, the unbelievable congestion of junks and sampans of the boat people, a massive, floating community of the perpetually dispossessed; he could even hear the clatter and slaps and shrieks of the mah-jongg players, hotly contesting their bets under the dim glow of swaying lanterns at night. He had met men and women—contacts and conduits, he reflected—on the beaches of Shek O and Big Wave, and he had swum in the crowded waters of Repulse Bay, with its huge ersatz statuary and the decaying elegance of the old Colonial Hotel. He had seen it all, he knew it all, yet he could relate it all to nothing.

He looked at his watch; they had been driving for nearly two hours. There was a last stop to make on the island, and then he would put Pak-fei to the test. "Head back to Chater Square," he said. "I have business at one of the banks. You can wait for me."

Money was not only a social and industrial lubricant; in large enough amounts it was a passport to maneuverability. Without it, men running were stymied, their options limited, and those in pursuit frequently frustrated by lacking the means to sustain the hunt. And the greater the amount, the more facile its release; witness the struggle of the man whose resources permit him to apply for no more than a $500 loan as compared with the relative ease another has with a line of credit of $500,000. So it was for David at the bank in Chater Square. Accommodation was swift and professional; an attaché case was provided without comment for the transport of the funds, and the offer of a guard to accompany him to his hotel was made should he feel more comfortable with one. He declined, signed the release papers and no further questions were asked. He returned to the car in the busy street.

He leaned forward, resting his left hand on the soft fabric of the front seat inches from the driver's head. He held an American $100 bill between his thumb and index finger. "Pak-fei," he said, "I need a gun."

Slowly the driver's head turned. He gazed at the bill, then turned further to look at Webb. Gone was the forced ebullience, the overweening desire to please. Instead, the expression on his lined face was passive, his sloped eyes distant. "Kowloon," he answered. "In the Mongkok." He took the hundred dollars.

9

The Daimler limousine crawled through the congested street in Mongkok, an urban mass that had the unenviable distinction of being the most densely populated city district in the history of mankind. Populated, it must be recorded, almost exclusively by Chinese. A Western face was so much a rarity that it drew curious glances, at once hostile and amused. No white man or woman was ever encouraged to go to Mongkok after dark; no Oriental Cotton Club existed here. It was not a matter of racism but the recognition of reality. There was too little space for their own—and they guarded their own as all Chinese had done from the earliest dynasties. The family was all, it was everything, and too many families lived not so much in squalor but within the confines of a single room with a single bed and mats on coarse, clean floors. Everywhere the multitude of small balconies attested to the demands of cleanliness, as no one ever appeared on them except to hang continuous lines of laundry. The tiers of these open balconies filled the sides of adjacent apartment houses and seemed to be in constant agitation as the breezes blew against the immense walls of fabric, causing garments of all descriptions to dance in place by the tens of thousands, further proof of the extraordinary numbers that inhabited the area.

Nor was the Mongkok poor. Lavishly manufactured color was everywhere, with bright red the predominant magnet. Enormous and elaborate signs could be seen wherever the eye roamed above the crowds; advertisements that successively rose three stories high lined the streets and the alleyways, the Chinese characters emphatic in their attempts to seduce consumers. There was money in Mongkok, quiet money, as well as hysterical money, but not always legitimate money. What there was not was excess space, and what there was of it belonged to their own, not outsiders, unless an outsider—brought in by one of their own—also brought in money to feed the insatiable machine that produced a vast array of worldly goods, and some not so much worldly as otherworldly. It was a question of knowing where to look and having the price. Pak-fei, the driver, knew where to look, and Jason Bourne had the price.

"I will stop and make a phone call," said Pak-fei, pulling behind a double-parked truck. "I will lock you in and be quick."

"Is that necessary?" asked Webb.

"It is your briefcase, sir, not mine."

Good Lord, thought David, he was a *fool!* He had not considered the attaché case. He was carrying over $300,-000 into the heart of Mongkok as if it were his lunch. He gripped the handle, pulling the case to his lap, and checked the hasps; they were secure, but if both buttons were jolted even slightly, the lid would snap up. He yelled at the driver, who had climbed out of the car. "Get me some *tape!* Adhesive tape!"

It was too late. The sounds of the street were deafening, the crowds nothing less than a weaving human blanket, and they were everywhere. And suddenly a hundred pairs of eyes peered in from all sides as contorted faces pressed against the glass—on all sides—and Webb was the core of a newly erupted street volcano. He could hear the questioning shrieks of *Bin go ah?* and *Chong man tui,* roughly the English equivalent of "Who is it?" and "A mouth that's full," or as combined, "Who's the big shot?" He felt like a caged animal being studied by a horde of beasts of another species, perhaps vicious. He held on to the case, staring straight ahead, and as two hands started clawing at the slight space in the upper window on his right, he reached slowly down into his pocket for the hunting knife. The fingers broke through.

"Jau!" screamed Pak-fei, thrashing his way through the crowd. "This is a most important taipan and the police up the street will pour boiling oil on your genitals if you disturb him! Get away, *away!"* He unlocked the door,

jumped in behind the wheel, and yanked the door shut amid furious curses. He started the engine, gunned it, then pressed his hand on the powerful horn and held it there, raising the cacophony to unbearable proportions, as the sea of bodies, slowly, reluctantly parted. The Daimler lurched in fits and starts down the narrow street.

"Where are we going?" shouted Webb. "I thought we were there!"

"The merchant you will deal with has moved his place of business, sir, which is good, for this is not a savory district of the Mongkok."

"You should have called first. That wasn't very pleasant back there."

"If I may correct the impression of imperfect service, sir," said Pak-fei, glancing at David in the rearview mirror. "We now know that you are not being followed. As a consequence *I* am not being followed to where I drive you."

"What are you talking about?"

"You go with your hands free into a large bank on Chater Square and you come out with your hands not free. You carry a briefcase."

"So?" Webb watched the driver's eyes as they kept darting up at him.

"No guard accompanied you, and there are bad people who watch for such men as yourself—often signals are sent from other bad people inside. These are uncertain times, so it was better to be certain in this instance."

"And you're certain . . . now."

"Oh, yes, sir!" Pak-fei smiled. "An automobile following us on a back street in the Mongkok is easily seen."

"So there was no phone call."

"Oh, indeed there *was,* sir. One must always call first. But it was *very* quick, and I then walked back on the pavement, without my cap, of course, for many meters. There were no angry men in automobiles, and none climbed out to run in the street. I will now take you to the merchant much relieved."

"I'm relieved, too," said David, wondering why Jason Bourne had temporarily deserted him. "And I didn't even know I should have been worried. Not about being followed."

The dense crowds of the Mongkok thinned out as the

buildings became lower and Webb could see the waters of Victoria Harbor behind high, chain link fences. Beyond the forbidding barricades were clusters of warehouses fronting piers where merchant ships were docked and heavy machinery crawled and groaned, lifting huge boxcars into holds. Pak-fei turned into the entrance of an isolated one-story warehouse; it appeared deserted, asphalt everywhere and only two cars in sight. The gate was closed; a guard walked out of a small, glass-enclosed office toward the Daimler, a clipboard in his hand.

"You won't find my name on a list," said Pak-fei in Chinese and with singular authority as the guard approached. "Inform Mr. Wu Song that Regent Number Five is here and brings him a taipan as worthy as himself. He expects us." The guard nodded, squinting in the afternoon sunlight to catch a glimpse of the important passenger. *"Aiya!"* screamed Pak-fei at the man's impertinence. Then he turned and looked at Webb. "You must not misunderstand, sir," he said as the guard ran back to his telephone. "My use of the name of my fine hotel has nothing to do with my fine hotel. In truth, if Mr. Liang, or anyone else, knew I mentioned its name in such business as this, I would be relieved of my job. It is merely that I was born on the fifth day of the fifth month in the year of our Christian Lord, 1935."

"I'll never tell," said David, smiling to himself, thinking that Jason Bourne had not deserted him after all. The myth that he once had been knew the avenues that led to the right contacts—knew them blindly—and that man was there inside David Webb.

The curtained whitewashed room of the warehouse, lined with locked, horizontal display cases, was not unlike a museum displaying such artifacts from past civilizations as primitive tools, fossilized insects, mystic carvings of religions past. The difference here was in the objects. These were exploding weapons that ran the gamut, from the lowest-caliber handguns and rifles to the most sophisticated weapons of modern warfare—thousand-round automatic machine guns with spiraling clips on near-weightless frames to laser-guided rockets to be fired from the shoulder, an arsenal for terrorists. Two men in business suits stood guard, one outside the entrance to the room, the other inside. As was to be expected, the former bowed his apology and moved an electronic scanner up and down the clothes of Webb and his driver. Then the man reached for the attaché case. David pulled it away, shaking his head and gesturing at the wandlike scanner. The guard had waved it over the surface of the case, checking his dials as he did so.

"Private papers," Webb said in Chinese to the startled guard as he walked into the room.

It took David nearly a full minute to absorb what he saw, to shake off his disbelief. He looked at the bold—emblazoned—No Smoking signs in English, French, and Chinese that were all over the walls and wondered why they were there. Nothing was exposed. He walked over the small-arms display and examined the wares. He clutched the attaché case in his hand as though it were a lifeline to sanity in a world gone mad with instruments of violence.

"Huanying!" cried a voice, followed by the appearance of a youngish-looking man. He came out of a paneled door in one of those tight-fitting European suits that exaggerate the shoulders and hug the waist, the rear panels of the jacket flowing like a peacock's tail—the product of designers determined to be chic at the price of neutering the male image.

"This is Mr. Wu Song, sir," said Pak-fei, bowing first to the merchant and then to Webb. "It is not necessary for you to give your name, sir."

"Bu!" spat out the young merchant, pointing at David's attaché case. *"Bu jing ya!"*

"Your client, Mr. Song, speaks fluent Chinese." The driver turned to David. "As you heard, sir, Mr. Song objects to the presence of your briefcase."

"It doesn't leave my hand," said Webb.

"Then there can be no serious discussion of business," rejoined Wu Song in flawless English.

"Why not? Your man checked it. There are no weapons inside, and even if there were and I tried to open it, I have an idea I'd be on the floor before the lid was up."

"Plastic?" asked Wu Song. "Plastic microphones leading to recording devices where the metal content is so low as to be dismissed even by sophisticated machinery?"

"You're paranoid."

"As they say in your country, it goes with the territory."

"Your idiom's as good as your English."

"Columbia University, '73."

"Did you major in armaments?"

"No, marketing."

"*Aiya!*" shrieked Pak-fei, but he was too late. The rapid colloquy had covered the movement of the guards; they had walked across the room, at the last instant lunging at Webb and the driver.

Jason Bourne spun around, dislodging his attacker's arm from his shoulder, clamping it under his own and, twisting it, forced the man down and smashed the attaché case into the Oriental's face. *The moves were coming back to him. The violence was returning as it had to a bewildered amnesiac on a fishing boat beyond the shoals of a Mediterranean island. So much forgotten, so much unexplained, but remembered.* The man fell to the floor, stunned, as his partner turned in fury to Webb after pummeling Pak-fei, the driver, to the ground. He rushed forward, his hands held up in a diagonal thrust, his wide chest and shoulders the base of his dual battering rams. David dropped the attaché case, lurched to his right, then spun again, again to his right, his left foot lashing up from the floor, catching the Chinese in the groin with such force that the man doubled over, screaming. Webb instantly kicked out with his right foot, his toe digging into the attacker's throat directly under his jaw; the man rolled on the floor, gasping for air, one hand on his groin, the other gripping his neck. The first guard started to rise; Bourne stepped forward and smashed his knee into the man's chest, sending him halfway across the room where he fell unconscious beneath a display case.

The young arms merchant was stunned. He was witnessing the unthinkable, expecting any moment that what he saw would be reversed, his guards the victors. Then suddenly, emphatically, he knew it was not going to happen; he ran in panic to the paneled door, reaching it as Webb reached him. David gripped the padded shoulders, spinning the merchant back across the floor. Wu Song tripped over his twisting feet and fell; he held up his hands, pleading. "No, please! *Stop!* I cannot *stand* physical confrontation! Take what you will!"

"You can't stand *what?*"

"You heard me, I get *ill!*"

"What the hell do you think all *this* is about?" yelled David, sweeping his arm around the room.

"I service a demand, that is all. Take whatever you want, but don't touch me. *Please!*"

Disgusted, Webb crossed to the fallen driver, who was getting to his knees, blood trickling from the corner of his mouth. "What I take I pay for," he said to the arms merchant as he grabbed the driver's arm and helped him to his feet. "Are you all right?"

"You ask for great trouble, sir," replied Pak-fei, his hands trembling, fear in his eyes.

"It had nothing to do with you. Wu Song knows that, don't you, Wu?"

"I brought you here!" insisted the driver.

"To make a purchase," added David quickly. "So let's get it over with. But first tie up those two goons. Use the curtains. Rip them down."

Pak-fei looked imploringly at the young merchant.

"Great Christian *Jesus,* do as he *says!*" yelled Wu Song. "He will strike me! Take the curtains! Tie them, you *imbecile!*"

Three minutes later Webb held in his hand an odd-looking gun, bulky but not large. It was an advanced weapon; the perforated cylinder that was the silencer was pneumatically snapped on, reducing the decibel count of a gunshot to a loud spit—but no more than a spit—the accuracy unaffected at close range. It held nine rounds, clips released and inserted at the base of the handle in a matter of seconds; there were three in reserve—thirty-six shells with the firepower of a .357 Magnum available instantly in a gun half the size and weight of a Colt .45.

"Remarkable," said Webb, glancing at the bound guards and a quaking Pak-fei. "Who designed it?" *So much expertise was coming back to him. So much recognition. From where?*

"As an American, it may offend you," answered Wu Song, "but he is a man in Bristol, Connecticut, who realized that the company he works for—designs for—would never recompense him adequately for his invention.

Through intermediaries he went on the closed international market and sold to the highest bidder."

"You?"

"I do not invest. I market."

"That's right, I forgot. You service a demand."

"Precisely."

"Whom do you pay?"

"A numbered account in Singapore, I know nothing else. I'm protected, of course. Everything's on consignment."

"I see. How much for this?"

"Take it. My gift to you."

"You smell. I don't take gifts from people who smell. How much?"

Wu Song swallowed. "The list price is eight hundred American dollars."

Webb reached into his left pocket and pulled out the denominations he had placed there. He counted out eight $100 bills and gave them to the arms merchant. "Paid in full," he said.

"Paid," agreed the Chinese.

"Tie him up," said David, turning to the apprehensive Pak-fei. "No, don't worry about it. Tie him up!"

"Do as he says, you *idiot!*"

"Then take the three of them outside. Along the side of the building by the car. And stay out of sight of the gate."

"*Quickly!*" yelled Song. "He is angry!"

"You can count on it," agreed Webb.

Four minutes later the two guards and Wu Song walked awkwardly through the outside door into the blazing afternoon sunlight, made harsher by the dancing reflections off the waters of Victoria Harbor. Their knees and arms were tied in the ripped cloth of the curtains, so their movements were hesitant and uncertain. Silence was guaranteed by wads of fabric in the mouths of the guards. No such precautions were needed for the young merchant; he was petrified.

Alone, David put his retrieved attaché case on the floor and walked rapidly around the room studying the displays in the cases until he found what he wanted. He smashed the glass with the handle of his gun, and picked around the shards for the weapons he would use—weapons coveted by terrorists everywhere—timer grenades, each with the impact of a 20-pound bomb. *How did he know? Where did the knowledge come from?*

He removed six grenades and checked each battery charge. *How could he do that? How did he know where to look, what to press? No matter. He knew.* He looked at his watch.

He set the timers of each and ran along the display cases, crashing the handle of his weapon into the glass tops and dropping into each a grenade. He had one left and two cases to go; he looked up at the trilingual No Smoking signs and made another decision. He ran to the paneled door, opened it, and saw what he thought he might see. He threw in the final grenade.

Webb checked his watch, picked up the attaché case and went outside, making a point of being very much in control. He approached the Daimler at the side of the warehouse where Pak-fei seemed to be apologizing to his prisoners, perspiring as he did so. The driver was being alternately berated and consoled by Wu Song, who wanted nothing more than to be spared any further violence.

"Take them over to the breakwater," ordered David, pointing to the stone wall that rose above the waters of the harbor.

Wu Song stared at Webb. "Who *are* you?" he asked. *The moment had come. It was now.*

Webb again looked at his watch as he walked over to the arms merchant. He gripped Wu Song's elbow and shoved the frightened Chinese farther along the side of the building where soft-spoken words would not be overheard by the others. "My name is Jason Bourne," said David simply.

"Jason Bou—!" The Oriental gasped, reacting as though a stiletto had punctured his throat, his own eyes witnessing the final, violent act of his own death.

"And if you have any ideas about restoring a bruised ego by punishing someone—say, my driver—get rid of them. I'll know where to find you." Webb paused for a single beat, then continued. "You're a privileged man, Wu, but with that privilege goes a responsibility. For certain reasons you may be questioned, and I don't expect you to lie—I doubt that you're very good at lying anyway—so we met, I'll accept that. I even stole from you, if you like. But if you give an accurate description of me, you'd better be on the other side of the world—and dead. It would be less painful for you."

The Columbia graduate froze, his lower lip trembling as he stared at Webb. David returned the look in silence, nodding his head once. He released Wu Song's arm and walked back to Pak-fei and the two bound guards, leaving the panicked merchant to his racing thoughts.

"Do as I told you, Pak-fei," he said, once more looking at his watch. "Get them over to the wall and tell them to lie down. Explain that I'm covering them with my gun, and will be covering them until we drive through the gate. I think their employer will attest to the fact that I'm a reasonably proficient marksman."

The driver reluctantly barked the orders in Chinese, bowing to the arms merchant, as Wu Song started ahead of the others, awkwardly maneuvering himself toward the breakwater some seventy-odd yards away. Webb looked inside the Daimler.

"Throw me the keys!" he shouted to Pak-fei. "And hurry up!"

David snatched the keys from the air and climbed into the driver's seat. He started the engine, slipped the Daimler into gear, and followed the odd-looking parade across the asphalt directly behind the warehouse.

Wu Song and his two guards lay prostrate on the ground. Webb leaped out of the car, the motor running, and raced around the trunk to the other side, his newly purchased weapon in his hand, the silencer affixed. "Get in and drive!" he shouted to Pak-fei. *"Quickly!"*

The driver jumped in, bewildered. David fired three shots—spits that blew up the asphalt several feet in front of each captive's face. It was enough; all three rolled in panic into the wall. Webb got into the front seat of the car. "Let's go!" he said, for a final time looking at his watch, his gun out the window aimed in the vicinity of the three prostrate figures. *"Now!"*

The gate swung back for the august taipan in the august limousine. The Daimler raced through and turned right into the speeding traffic on the dual-lane highway to Mongkok.

"Slow down!" ordered David. "Pull over to the side, on the dirt."

"These drivers are madmen, sir. They speed because they know that in minutes they will barely move. It will be difficult to get back on the road."

"Somehow I don't think so."

It happened. The explosions came one after another—three, four, five . . . *six.* The isolated one-story warehouse blew to the skies, flames and deep black smoke filling the air above the land and the harbor, causing automobiles and trucks and buses to come to screeching stops on the highway.

"*You?*" shrieked Pak-fei, his mouth gaping, his bulging eyes on Webb.

"I was there."

"*We* were there, sir! I am dead! *Aiya!*"

"No, Pak-fei, you're not," said David. "You're protected, take my word for that. You'll never hear from Mr. Wu Song again. I suspect he'll be on the other side of the world, probably in Iran, teaching marketing to the mullahs. I don't know who else would accept him."

"But why? *How,* sir?"

"He's finished. He dealt in what's called 'consignments,' which means he pays as his merchandise is sold. Are you following me?"

"I think so, sir."

"He has no more merchandise, but it wasn't sold. It just went away."

"Sir?"

"He kept wired rolls of dynamite and cases of explosive plastic in the back room. They were too primitive to put in the display cases. Also too bulky."

"*Sir?*"

"I couldn't have a cigarette. . . . Weave around the traffic, Pak-fei. I have to get back to Kowloon."

As they entered the Tsim Sha Tsui, the movements of Pak-fei's constantly turning head intruded on Webb's thoughts. The driver kept looking at him. "What is it?" he asked.

"I am not certain, sir. I am frightened, of course."

"You didn't believe what I told you? That you've got nothing to be afraid of?"

"That is not it, sir. I think I must believe you, for I saw what you did, and I saw Wu Song's face when you spoke with him. I think it is you I am frightened of, but I also think this may be wrong, for you did protect me. It was in Wu Song's eyes. I cannot explain."

"Don't bother," said David, reaching into his pocket for money. "Are you married, Pak-fei? Or have a girlfriend, or a boyfriend? It doesn't matter."

"Married, sir. I have two grown children who have not-bad jobs. They contribute; my joss is good."

"Now it'll be better. Go home and pick up your wife—and children, if you like—and drive, Pak-fei. Drive up into the New Territories for many miles. Stop and have a fine meal in Tuen Mun or Yuen Long and then drive some more. Let them enjoy this fine automobile."

"Sir?"

"A *xiao xin*," went on Webb, the money in his hand. "What we call in English a little white lie that doesn't hurt anybody. You see, I want the mileage on this car to approximate where you've driven me today—and tonight."

"Where is that?"

"You drove Mr. Cruett first up to Lo Wu and then across the base of the mountain range to Lok Ma Chau."

"Those are checkpoints into the People's Republic."

"Yes, they are," agreed David, removing two $100 bills, and then a third. "Do you think you can remember that and make the mileage right?"

"Most certainly, sir."

"And do you think," added Webb, his finger on a fourth $100 bill, "that you could say I left the car at Lok Ma Chau and wandered up in the hills for an hour or so."

"Ten hours, if you like, sir. I need no sleep."

"One hour is fine." David held out the $400 in front of the driver's startled eyes. "And I'll know if you don't live up to our agreement."

"You have no concerns, sir!" cried Pak-fei, one hand on the wheel, the other grasping the bills. "I shall pick up my wife, my children, her parents, and my own as well. This animal I drive is big enough for twelve. I thank you, sir! I thank you!"

"Drop me off around ten streets from Salisbury Road and get out of the area. I don't want this car seen in Kowloon."

"No, sir, it is not possible. We will be in Lo Wu, in Lok Ma Chau!"

"As far as tomorrow morning goes, say whatever you

like. I won't be here, I'm leaving tonight. You won't see me again."

"Yes, sir."

"Our contract's concluded, Pak-fei," said Jason Bourne, his thoughts returning to a strategy that became clearer with each move he made. And each move brought him closer to Marie. All was colder now. There was a certain freedom in being what he was not.

Play the scenario as it was given to you. . . . Be everywhere at once. Make them sweat.

At 5:02 an obviously disturbed Liang walked rapidly out the glass doors of the Regent. He looked anxiously around at the arriving and departing guests, then turned to his left and hurried down the pavement toward the ramp leading to the street. David watched him through the spraying fountains on the opposite side of the courtyard. Using the fountains as his cover, Webb ran across the busy area, dodging cars and taxis; he reached the ramp and followed Liang down toward Salisbury Road.

He stopped midway to the street and turned, angling his body and his face to the left. The assistant manager had come to an abrupt halt, his body lurching forward, as an anxious person in a hurry will do when he has suddenly remembered something or changes his mind. It had to be the latter, thought David, as he cautiously shifted his head and saw Liang rushing across the entrance drive toward the crowded pavement of the New World Shopping Centre. Webb knew he would lose him in the crowds if he did not hurry, so he held up both hands, stopping the traffic, and raced diagonally down the ramp as horns bellowed and angry shrieks came from drivers. He reached the pavement, sweating, anxious. He could not see Liang! Where was he? The sea of Oriental faces became a blur, so much the same, yet not the same. Where *was* he? David rushed ahead, muttering excuses as he collided with bodies and startled faces; he saw him! He was sure it was Liang—but *not* sure, not really. He had seen a dark-suited figure turn into the entrance of the harbor walkway, a long stretch of concrete above the water where people fished and strolled and performed their *tai chi* exercises in the early mornings. Yet he had seen only the back of a man; if it was not Liang he would leave the street and lose him completely. *Instinct. Not yours but Bourne's—the eyes of Jason Bourne.*

Webb broke into a run, heading for the arched entrance of the walkway. The skyline of Hong Kong sparkled in the sunlit distance, the traffic in the harbor bobbing furiously, winding up the day's labors on the water. He slowed down as he passed under the arch; there was no way back to Salisbury Road but through the entrance. The walkway was a dead-end intrusion on the waterfront, and that raised a question, as well as supplying an answer to another. Why had Liang—if it was Liang—boxed himself into a dead end? What drew him to it? A contact, a drop, a relay? Whatever it was, it meant that the Chinese had not considered the possibility that he was being followed; that was the immediate answer David needed. It told him what he had to know. His prey was in panic; the unexpected could only propel him into further panic.

Jason Bourne's eyes had not lied. It *was* Liang, but the first question remained unanswered, even compounded by what Webb saw. Of the thousands upon thousands of public telephones in Kowloon—tucked away in crowded arcades and in recessed corners of darkened lobbies—Liang had chosen to use a pay phone on the inner wall of the walkway. It was exposed, in the open, in the center of a wide thoroughfare that was in itself a dead end. It made no sense; even the rankest amateur had basic protective instincts. When in panic he sought cover.

Liang reached into his pocket for change, and suddenly, as if commanded by an inner voice, David knew that he could not permit that call to be made. When it was made, *he* had to make it. It was part of his strategy, a part that would bring him closer to Marie! The control had to be in *his* hands, not others'!

He began running, heading straight toward the white plastic shell of the pay phone, wanting to shout but knowing he had to get closer to be heard over the sounds of the windblown waterfront. The assistant manager had just finished dialing. Somewhere a telephone was ringing.

"*Liang!*" roared Webb. "Get off that phone! If you want to live, hang up and get *out* of there!"

The Chinese spun around, his face a rigid mask of terror. "*You!*" he shouted hysterically, pressing his body back into the shell of white plastic. "No . . . *no!* Not now! Not *here!*"

Gunfire suddenly filled the winds off the water, staccato bursts that joined the myriad sounds of the harbor. Pandemonium swept over the walkway, as people screamed and shrieked, dropping to the ground or racing in all directions away from the terror of instant death.

10

"Aiya!" roared Liang, diving to the side of the telephone shell as bullets ripped into the wall of the walkway and cracked in the air overhead. Webb lunged toward the Chinese, crawling beside the hotel man, his hunting knife out of its scabbard. "Do *not!* What are you *doing?"* Liang screamed as David, lying sideways, gripped him by the front of his shirt and shoved the blade up into the manager's chin, breaking the skin, drawing blood. *"Ahhee!"* The hysterical cry was lost in the pandemonium of the walkway.

"Give me the number! *Now!"*

"Don't do this to me! I swear to you I did not know it was a *trap!"*

"It's not a trap for me, Liang," said Webb breathlessly, the sweat rolling down his face. "It's for you!"

"Me? You're mad! Why *me?"*

"Because they know I'm here now, and you've seen me, you've talked to me. You made your phone call and they can't afford you any longer."

"But *why?"*

"You were given a telephone number. You did your job and they can't allow any traces."

"That explains *nothing!"*

"Maybe my name will. It's Jason Bourne."

"Oh, my *God* . . . !" whispered Liang, his face pale and lips parted, as he stared at David.

"You're a trace," said Webb. "You're dead."

"No, *no!*" The Chinese shook his head. "It can't *be!* I don't *know* anyone, only the number! It is a deserted office in the New World Centre, a temporary telephone installed. *Please!* The number is three-four, four, zero, one! Do not *kill* me, Mr. Bourne! For the love of our Christian God, do not *do* it!"

"If I thought the trap was for me, there'd be blood all over your throat, not your chin. . . . Three-four, four, zero, one?"

"Yes, exactly!"

The gunfire stopped as suddenly and as startlingly as it had begun.

"The New World Centre's right above us, isn't it? One of those windows up there."

"Exactly!" Liang shuddered, unable to take his eyes off David's face. Then he shut them tight, tears dripping beneath his lids as he shook his head violently. "I have never *seen* you! I swear on the cross of holy Jesus!"

"Sometimes I wonder if I'm in Hong Kong or the Vatican." Webb raised his head and looked around. All along the walkway terrified people were hesitantly beginning to rise. Mothers clutched children; men held women, and men, women, and children got to their knees, then their feet, and suddenly formed a mass stampede toward the Salisbury arch. "You were told to make your call from here, weren't you?" said David rapidly, turning to the frightened hotel man.

"Yes, sir."

"*Why?* Did they give you a reason?"

"Yes, sir."

"For Christ's sake, open your eyes!"

"Yes, sir." Liang did so, looking away as he spoke. "They said they did not trust the guest who asked for Suite six-nine-zero. He was a man who might force another to convey lies. Therefore they wanted to observe me when I spoke to them. . . . Mr. Bourne—*no,* I did not *say* that! Mr. *Cruett*— I tried all day to reach you, Mr. *Cruett!* I wanted you to know I was being pressed repeatedly, Mr. *Cruett.* They kept phoning me, wanting to know when I would place my call to them—from *here.* I kept saying you had not arrived! What else could I *do?* By trying to reach you so constantly, you can see I was trying to warn you, sir! It is obvious, is it *not?*"

"What's obvious is that you're a damn fool."

"I am not equipped for this work."

"Why did you do it?"

"Money, sir! I was with Chiang, with the Kuomintang. I have a wife and five children—two sons and three daughters. I have to get out! They search backgrounds; they give us incontestable labels with no appeals. I am a learned man, sir! Fudan University, second in my class— I owned my own hotel in Shanghai. But all that is meaningless now. When Beijing takes over, I am dead, my family is dead. And now you say I am dead as of this moment. What am I to *do?*"

"Peking—Beijing—won't touch the colony, they won't change anything," said David, remembering the words Marie had said to him that terrible evening after McAllister had left their house. "Unless the crazies take over."

"They are *all* crazy, sir. Believe nothing else. You don't *know* them!"

"Maybe not. But I know a few of you. And, frankly, I'd rather not."

" 'Let who is without sin among you cast the first stone,' sir."

"Stones, but not bags of silver from Chiang's corruption, right?"

"Sir?"

"What are your three daughters' names? *Quickly!*"

"They are . . . they are . . . Wang . . . Wang Sho—"

"Forget it!" yelled David, glancing down at the Salisbury arch. *"Ni bushi ren!* You're not a man, you're a *pig!* Stay well, Liang of the Kuomintang. Stay well as long as they let you. Frankly, I couldn't care less."

Webb got to his feet, prepared to throw himself down again at the first irregular flash of light from a window above on his left. The eyes of Jason Bourne were accurate: there was nothing. David joined the stampede at the arch and slithered his way through the crowds to Salisbury Road.

He placed the call from a phone in a congested, noisy arcade off Nathan Road. He put his index finger in his right ear to hear more clearly.

"Wei?" said a male voice.

"It's Bourne, and I'll speak English. Where is my wife?"

"*Wode tian ah!* It is said you speak our language in numerous dialects."

"It's been a long time and I want everything clearly understood. I asked you about my *wife!*"

"Liang *gave* you this number?"

"He didn't have a choice."

"He is also dead."

"I don't care what you do, but if I were you, I'd have second thoughts about killing him."

"Why? He is lower than a worm."

"Because you picked a damn fool—worse, an hysterical one. He talked to too many people. A switchboard operator told me he was calling me every few minutes—"

"Calling *you?*"

"I flew in this morning. Where is my *wife*—"

"Liang the *liar!*"

"You didn't expect me to stay in that suite, did you? I had him switch me to another room. We were seen talking together—arguing—with half a dozen clerks watching us. You kill him, there'll be more rumors than any of us want. The police will be looking for a rich American who disappeared."

"His trousers are soiled," said the Chinese. "Perhaps it is enough."

"It's enough. Now, what about my *wife!*"

"I heard you. I am not privileged with such information."

"Then put on someone who is. *Now!*"

"You will meet with others more knowledgeable."

"*When?*"

"We will get back to you. What room are you in?"

"I'll call *you.* You've got fifteen minutes."

"You are giving *me* orders?"

"I know where you are, which window, which office—you're sloppy with your rifle. You should have corked the barrel; sunlight reflects off metal, that's basic. In thirty seconds I'll be a hundred feet from your door, but you won't know where I am and you can't leave that phone."

"I don't believe you!"

"Try me. You're not watching *me* now, I'm watching

you. You've got fifteen minutes, and when I call you back I want to talk to my wife."

"She's not here!"

"If I thought she were, you'd be dead, your head knifed from the rest of you and thrown out the window to join the other garbage in the harbor. If you think I'm exaggerating, check around. Ask people who've dealt with me. Ask your taipan, the Yao Ming who doesn't exist."

"I cannot make your wife *appear*, Jason Bourne!" shouted the frightened minion.

"Get me a number where I can reach her. Either I hear her voice—*talking* to me—or there's nothing. Except for your headless corpse and a black bandanna across your bleeding neck. *Fifteen minutes!*"

David hung up the phone and wiped the sweat from his face. He had done it. The mind and the words were Jason Bourne's—he had gone back in only vaguely remembered time and instinctively knew what to do, what to say, what to threaten. There was a lesson somewhere. Appearance far outdistanced reality. Or was there a reality within him crying to come out, wanting control, telling David Webb to trust the man inside him?

He left the oppressively crowded arcade and turned right on the equally congested pavement. The Golden Mile of the Tsim Sha Tsui was preparing for its nightly games, and so would he. He could return to the hotel now; the assistant manager would be miles away, conceivably booking a flight to Taiwan, if there was any truth at all in his hysterical statements. Webb would use the freight elevator to reach his room in case others were awaiting him in the lobby, although he doubted it. The shooting gallery that was a deserted office in the New World Centre was not a command post, and the marksman was not a commander but a relay, now frightened for his life.

With each step David took down Nathan Road, the shorter his breath became, the louder his chest pounded. Twelve minutes from now he would hear Marie's voice. Oh God, he *wanted* to hear it so! He *had* to! It was all that would keep him sane, all that mattered.

"Your fifteen minutes are over," said Webb, sitting on the edge of the bed, trying to control his heartbeat, wondering if the rapid echo could be heard as he heard it, hoping it caused no tremor in his voice.

"Call five-two, six, five, three."

"Five?" David recognized the exchange. "She's over in Hong Kong, not Kowloon."

"She will be moved immediately."

"I'll call you back after I've spoken to her."

"There is no need, Jason Bourne. Knowledgeable men are there and they will speak with you. My business is finished and you have never seen me."

"I don't have to see you. A photograph will be taken when you leave that office, but you won't know from where or by whom. You'll probably see a number of people—in the hallway, or in an elevator or the lobby—but you won't know which one has a camera with a lens that looks like a button on his jacket, or an emblem on her purse. Stay well, minion. Think nice thoughts."

Webb depressed the telephone bar, disconnecting the line; he waited three seconds, released it, heard the dial tone, and touched the buttons. He could hear the ring. *Christ,* he couldn't *stand* it!

"Wei?"

"This is Bourne. Put my wife on the line."

"As you wish."

"David?"

"Are you all *right?"* shouted Webb on the edge of hysteria.

"Yes, just tired, that's all, my darling. Are *you* all right—"

"Have they hurt you—have they *touched* you?"

"No, David, they've been quite kind, actually. But you know how tired I get sometimes. Remember that week in Zurich when you wanted to see the Fraumünster and the museums and go out sailing on the Limmat, and I said I just wasn't up to it?"

There'd been no week in Zurich. Only the nightmare of a single night when both of them nearly lost their lives. He running the gauntlet of his would-be executioners in the Steppdeckstrasse, she nearly raped, sentenced to death on a deserted riverfront in the Guisan Quai. What was she trying to tell him?

"Yes, I remember."

"So you mustn't worry about me, darling. Thank *God* you're here! We'll be together soon, they've promised me that. It'll be like Paris, David. Remember Paris, when I thought I'd lost you? But you came to me and we both knew where to go. That lovely street with the dark green trees and the—"

"That will be all, Mrs. Webb," broke in a male voice. "Or should I say Mrs. Bourne," the man added, speaking directly into the phone.

"*Think*, David, and be *careful!*" yelled Marie in the background. "And don't worry, darling! That lovely street with the row of green trees, my *favorite* tree—"

"*Ting zhi!*" cried the male voice, issuing an order in Chinese. "Take her away! She's giving him information! Quickly. Don't let her speak!"

"You harm her in any way, you'll regret it for the rest of your short life," said Webb icily. "I swear to *Christ* I'll find you."

"There has been no cause for unpleasantness up to this moment," replied the man slowly, his tone sincere. "You heard your wife. She has been treated well. She has no complaints."

"Something's wrong with her! What the hell have you done that she can't *tell* me?"

"It is only the tension, Mr. Bourne. And she *was* telling you something, no doubt in her anxiety trying to describe this location—erroneously, I should add—but even if it were accurate, it would be as useless to you as the telephone number. She is on her way to another apartment, one of millions in Hong Kong. Why would we harm her in any way? It would be counterproductive. A great tai-pan wants to meet with you."

"Yao Ming?"

"Like you, he goes by several names. Perhaps you can reach an accommodation."

"Either we do or he's dead. And so are you."

"I believe what you say, Jason Bourne. You killed a close blood relative of mine who was beyond your reach, in his own island fortress on Lantau. I'm sure you recall."

"I don't keep records. Yao Ming. *When?*"

"Tonight."

"Where?"

"You must understand, he's very recognizable, so it must be a most unusual place."

"Suppose I choose it?"

"Unacceptable, of course. Do not insist. We have your wife."

David tensed; he was losing the control he desperately needed. "Name it," he said.

"The Walled City. We assume you know it."

"*Of* it," corrected Webb, trying to focus what memory he had. "The filthiest slum on the face of the earth, if I remember."

"What else would it be? It is the only legal possession of the People's Republic in all of the colony. Even the detestable Mao Zedong gave permission for our police to purge it. But civil servants are not paid that much. It remains essentially the same."

"What time tonight?"

"After dark, but before the bazaar closes. Between nine-thirty and not later than fifteen minutes to ten."

"How do I find this Yao Ming—who isn't Yao Ming?"

"There is a woman in the first block of the open market who sells snake entrails as aphrodisiacs, predominantly cobra. Go up to her and ask her where a great one is. She will tell you the descending steps to use, which alley to take. You will be met."

"I might never get there. The color of my skin isn't welcome down there."

"No one will harm you. However, I suggest you not wear garish clothing or display expensive jewelry."

"Jewelry?"

"If you own a high-priced watch, do not wear it."

They'd cut your arm off for a watch. Medusa. So be it.

"Thanks for the advice."

"One last thing. Do not think of involving the authorities or your consulate in a reckless attempt to compromise the taipan. If you do, your wife will die."

"That wasn't necessary."

"With Jason Bourne everything is necessary. You will be watched."

"Nine-thirty to nine-forty-five," said Webb, replacing the phone and getting up from the bed. He went to the window and stared out at the harbor. What *was* it? What was Marie trying to tell him?

. . . you know how tired I get sometimes.

No, he did not know that. His wife was a strong Ontario ranch girl who never complained of being tired.

. . . you mustn't worry about me, darling.

A foolish plea, and she must have realized it. Marie did not waste precious moments being foolish. Unless . . . was she rambling incoherently?

. . . It'll be like Paris, David. . . . we both knew where to go . . . that lovely street with the dark green trees.

No, not rambling, only the appearance of rambling; there *was* a message. But what? *What* lovely street with "dark green trees"? Nothing came to him and it was driving him out of his mind! He was failing her. She was sending a signal and it eluded him.

. . . Think, David, and be careful! . . . don't worry, darling! That lovely street with the row of green trees, my favorite tree—

What lovely street? What goddamned row of trees, what *favorite* tree? Nothing made sense to him and it should make sense! He should be able to respond, not stare out a window, his memory blank. Help me, *help me!* he cried silently to no one.

An inner voice told him not to dwell on what he could not understand. There were things to do; he could not willingly walk into the meeting ground of the enemy's choosing without some foreknowledge, some cards of his own to play. . . . *I suggest you do not wear garish clothing.* . . . It would not have been garish in any event, thought Webb, but now it would be something quite opposite— and unexpected.

During the months in which he had peeled away the layers of Jason Bourne one theme kept repeating itself. Change, change, change. Bourne was a practitioner of change; they called him "the chameleon," a man who could melt into different surroundings with ease. Not as a grotesque, a cartoon with fright wigs and nose putty, but as one who could adapt the essentials of his appearance to his immediate environment so that those who had met the "assassin"—rarely, however, in full light or standing close to him—gave widely varying descriptions of the man hunted throughout Asia and Europe. The details were always in conflict: the hair was dark or light; the eyes brown, blue, or speckled; the skin pale, or tanned, or blotched; the clothes well made and subdued if the rendezvous took place in a dimly lit expensive café, or rumpled and ill-fitting if the meeting was held on the waterfront or in the lower depths of a city. Change.

Effortlessly, with the minimum of artifice. David Webb would trust the chameleon within him. Free fall. Go where Jason Bourne directed.

After the harrowing phone call, he went over to the Peninsula Hotel and, with a large, unseen tip, got a room, depositing his attaché case in the hotel vault. He had the presence of mind to register under the name of Cactus's third false passport. If men were looking for him, they would flash the name he used at the Regent; it was all they had.

He again went back across Salisbury Road, used the service elevator, walked rapidly to his room and packed what few clothes he needed in the flight bag. But he did not check out of the Regent. If men were looking for him, he wanted them to look where he was not.

Once settled in the Peninsula, he had time for something to eat, and to forage in several shops until nightfall. By the time darkness came he would be in the Walled City—before nine-thirty. Jason Bourne was giving the commands and David Webb obeyed them.

The Walled City of Kowloon has no visible wall around it, but it is as clearly defined as if there were one made of hard, high steel. It is instantly sensed in the congested open market that runs along the street in front of the row of dark run-down flats—shacks haphazardly perched on top of one another giving the impression that at any moment the entire blighted complex would collapse under its own weight, leaving nothing but rubble where elevated rubble had stood. But there is deceptive strength found as one walks down the short flight of steps into the interior of the sprawling slum. Below ground level, cobblestoned alleyways that are in most cases tunnels traverse beneath the ramshackle structures. In squalid corridors crippled beggars vie with half-dressed prostitutes and drug peddlers in the eerie wash of naked bulbs that hang from exposed wires along the stone walls. A putrid dampness abounds; all is decay and rot, but the strength of time has hardened this decomposition, petrifying it.

Within the foul alleyways in no particular order or balance are narrow, barely lit staircases leading to the vertical series of broken-down flats, the average rising

three stories, two of which are above ground. Inside the
small, dilapidated rooms the widest varieties of narcotics
and sex are sold; all is beyond the reach of the police—
silently agreed to by all parties—for few of the colony's
authorities care to venture into the bowels of the Walled
City. It is its own self-contained hell. Let it be.

Outside in the open market that fills the garbage-
strewn street where no traffic is permitted, soiled tables
piled high with rejected and/or stolen merchandise are
sandwiched between grimy stalls where pockets of vapor
rise from huge vats of boiling oil in which questionable
pieces of meat, fowl, and snake are continuously
plunged, then ladled out and placed on newspapers for
immediate sale. The crowds move under the weak light
of dull streetlamps from one vendor to the next, haggling
in high-pitched voices, shrieking back and forth, buying
and selling. Then there are the curb people, bedraggled
men and women without stalls or tables, whose merchandise is spread out on the pavement. They squat behind
displays of trinkets and cheap jewelry, much of it stolen
from the docks, and woven cages filled with crawling
beetles and fluttering tiny birds.

Near the mouth of the strange, fetid bazaar a lone,
muscular female sat on a low wooden stool, her thick legs
parted, skinning snakes and removing their entrails, her
dark eyes seemingly obsessed with each thrashing ser-
pent in her hands. On either side were writhing burlap
bags, every now and then convulsing as the doomed rep-
tiles struck out in hissing fury at one another, enraged by
their captivity. Clamped under the heavyset woman's
bare right foot was a king cobra, its jet-black body immobile and erect, its head flat, its small eyes steady, hypnotized by the constantly moving crowds. The squalor of
the open market was a fitting barricade for the wall-less
Walled City beyond.

Rounding the corner at the opposite end of the long
bazaar, a disheveled figure turned into the overflowing
avenue. The man was dressed in a cheap, loose-fitting
brown suit, the trousers too bulky, the coat too large, yet
tight around the hunched shoulders. A soft, wide-
brimmed hat, black and unmistakably Oriental, threw a
constant shadow across his face. His gait was slow, as
befitted a man pausing in front of various stalls and tables

examining the merchandise, but only once did he reach tentatively into his pocket to make a single purchase. Then, too, there was a stooped quality in his posture, the frame of a man that had been bent from years of hard labor in the field or on the waterfront, his diet never sufficient for a body from which so much was extracted. There was a sadness as well in this man, a futility born of too little, too late, and too costly for the mind and the body. It was the recognition of impotence, of pride abandoned, for there was nothing to be proud of; the price of survival had been too much. And this man, this stooped figure who haltingly bought a newspaper cone of fried questionable fish, was not unlike many of the males in the marketplace—in fact, one could say he was indistinguishable from them. He approached the muscular woman who was tearing the intestines from a still-writhing snake.

"Where is the great one?" asked Jason Bourne in Chinese, his eyes fixed on the immobile cobra, the grease from the newspaper rolling over his left hand.

"You are early," replied the woman without expression. "It is dark, but you are early."

"I was summoned quickly. Do you question the taipan's instructions?"

"He is fuck-fuck cheap for a taipan!" she spat out in guttural Cantonese. "What do I care? Go down the steps behind me and take the first alleyway to the left. A whore will be standing fifteen, twenty meters down. She waits for the white man and will lead him to the taipan. . . . Are you the white man? I cannot tell in this light and your Chinese is good—but you do not look like a white man, you do not wear a white man's clothes."

"If you were me, would you make a heavenly point of looking like a white man, dressing like a white man, if you were told to come down here?"

"I would make the point of a thousand devils that I was from the Qing Gaoyan!" said the woman, laughing through half-gone teeth. "Especially if you carry money. Do you carry money . . . our *Zhongguo ren?*"

"You flatter me, but no."

"You lie. White people lie with heavenly words about money."

"Very well, I lie. I trust your snake will not attack me for it."

"Fool! He is old and has no fangs, no poison. But he is the heavenly image of a man's organ. He brings me money. Will *you* give me money?"

"For a service, yes."

"*Aiya!* You want this old body, you must have an ax in your trousers! Chop up the whore, not me!"

"No ax, just words," said Bourne, his right hand slipping into his trousers pocket. He withdrew a U.S. $100 bill and palmed it in front of the snake seller's face, keeping it out of sight of the surrounding bargain hunters.

"*Aiya—aiya!*" whispered the woman as Jason pulled it away from her grasping fingers; the dead snake dropped between her thick legs.

"The service," Bourne repeated. "Since you thought I was one of you, I expect others will think so, too. All I want you to do is to tell anyone who asks you that the white man never showed up. Is that fair?"

"*Fair!* Give me the money!"

"The *service?*"

"You bought snakes! Snakes! What do I know of a white man. He never appeared! Here. Here is your snake. Make love!" The woman took the bill, bunched the entrails in her hand and shoved them into a plastic bag on which there was a designer's signature. It read *Christian Dior.*

Remaining stooped, Bourne bowed rapidly twice and backed his way out of the crowd, dropping the snake entrails in the curb far enough away from a streetlight so as not to be noticed. Holding the dripping cone of foul-smelling fish, he repeatedly mimed reaching for mouthfuls as he slowly made his way to the steps and descended into the steaming bowels of the Walled City. He looked at his watch, spilling fish as he did so. It was 9:15; the taipan's patrols would be moving into place.

He had to know the extent of the banker's security. He wanted the lie that he had told a marksman in a deserted office above the harbor walkway to be the truth. Instead of being watched, he wanted to be the one watching. He would memorize each face, each role in the command structure, the rapidity with which each guard made a decision under pressure, the communications equipment, and, above all, discover where the weaknesses were in the taipan's security. David understood that Jason Bourne was taking over; there was a point in what *he* was doing. The banker's note had started with the words: *A wife for a wife . . .* Only one word had to be changed. *A taipan for a wife.*

Bourne turned into the alleyway on his left and walked several hundred feet past sights he scrupulously ignored; a resident of the Walled City would do no less. On a darkened staircase a woman on her knees performed the act for which she was being paid, the man above her holding money in his hand over her head; a young couple, two obvious addicts in near frenzy, were pleading with a man in an expensive black leather jacket; a small boy, smoking a marijuana cigarette, urinated against the stone wall; a beggar without legs clattered on his wheeled board over the cobblestones chanting *"Bong ngo, bong ngo!"*—a plea for alms; and on another dimly lit staircase a well-dressed pimp was threatening one of his whores with facial disfigurement if she did not produce more money. David Webb mused that he was not in Disneyland. Jason Bourne studied the alley as if it were a combat zone behind enemy lines. 9:24. The soldiers would be going to their posts. The outer and the inner man turned around and started back.

The banker's whore was walking into position, her bright red blouse unbuttoned, barely covering her small breasts; the traditional slit in her black skirt reached her thigh. She was a caricature. The "white man" was not to make a mistake. Point one: Accentuate the obvious. Something to remember; subtlety was not a strong suit. Several yards behind her a man spoke into a hand-held radio; he caught up with the woman, shook his head and rushed forward toward the end of the alley and the steps. Bourne stopped, his posture sagging, and turned into the wall. The footsteps were behind him, hurrying, emphatic, the pace quickening. A second Chinese approached and passed him, a small middle-aged man in a dark business suit, tie, and shoes polished to a high gloss. He was no citizen of the Walled City; his expression was a mixture of apprehension and disgust. Ignoring the whore, he glanced at his watch and raced ahead. He had the look and demeanor of an executive ordered to assume duties he found distasteful. A company man, precise, orderly, the bottom line his motive, for the figures did not lie. A banker?

Jason studied the irregular row of staircases; the man had to come from one of them. The sound of the footsteps had been abrupt and recent, and judging by the pace, they had begun no more than sixty or seventy feet away. On the third staircase on the left or the fourth on the right. In one of the flats above either staircase a taipan was waiting for his visitor. Bourne had to find out which and on what level. The taipan had to be surprised, even shocked. He had to understand whom he was dealing with and what his actions would cost him.

Jason started up again, now assuming a drunken walk; the words of an old Mandarin folk tune came to him. *"Me li hua cherng zhang liu yue,"* he sang softly, bouncing gently off the wall as he approached the whore. "I have money," he said pleasantly, his words in Chinese imprecise. "And you, beautiful woman, have what I need. Where do we go?"

"Nowhere, fancy drunk. Get away from here."

"Bong ngo! Cheng bong ngo!" screeched the legless beggar clattering down the alley, careening into the wall as he screamed. *"Cheng bong ngo!"*

"Jau!" yelled the woman. "Get out of here before I kick your useless body off your board, Loo Mi! I've told you not to interfere with business!"

"This cheap drunk is *business?* I'll get you something better!"

"He's not my business, darling. He's an annoyance. I'm waiting for someone."

"Then I'll chop his feet!" shouted the grotesque figure, pulling a cleaver from his board.

"What the hell are you *doing?"* roared Bourne in English, shoving his foot into the beggar's chest, sending the half-man and his board into the opposite wall.

"There are *laws!"* shrieked the beggar. "You attacked a cripple! You are robbing a cripple!"

"Sue me," said Jason, turning to the woman, as the beggar clattered away down the alley.

"You talk . . . English." The whore stared at him.

"So do you," said Bourne.

"You speak Chinese, but you are not Chinese."

"In spirit, perhaps. I've been looking for you."

"You are the *man?*"

"I am."

"I will take you to the taipan."

"No. Just tell me which staircase, which level."

"Those are not my instructions."

"They're new instructions, given by the taipan. Do you question his new instructions?"

"They must be delivered by his head-head man."

"The small *Zhongguo ren* in a dark suit?"

"He tells us everything. He pays us for the taipan."

"Whom does he pay?"

"Ask him yourself."

"The taipan wants to know." Bourne reached into his pocket and pulled out a stack of folded bills. "He told me to give you extra money if you cooperated with me. He thinks his head man may be cheating him."

The woman backed into the wall looking alternately at the money and at Bourne's face. "If you are lying—"

"Why would I lie? The taipan wants to see me, you know that. You're to bring me to him. He told me to dress like this, to behave this way, to find you and watch his men. How would I know about you if he hadn't told me?"

"Up in the market. You are to see someone."

"I haven't been there. I came directly down here." Jason removed several bills. "We're both working for the taipan. Here, he wants you to take this and leave, but you're not to go up in the street." He held out the money.

"The taipan is generous," said the whore, reaching for the bills.

"Which staircase?" asked Bourne, pulling the money back. "Which level? The taipan didn't know."

"Over there," replied the woman, pointing to the far wall. "The third steps, the second level. The money."

"Who's on the head man's payroll? Quickly."

"In the market there is the snake bitch, and the old thief selling bad gold chains from the north, and the wok man with his dirty fish and meat."

"That's all?"

"We talk. That is all."

"The taipan's right, he's being cheated. He'll thank you." Bourne unfolded another bill. "But I want to be fair. Besides the one with the radio, how many others work for the head man?"

"Three others, also with radios," said the whore, her eyes fixed on the money, her hand inching forward.

"Here, take it and leave. Head that way and don't go up on the street."

The woman grabbed the bills and ran down the alley, her high heels clicking, her figure disappearing in the dim light. Bourne watched until she was out of sight, then turned and walked rapidly out of the filthy passageway to the steps. He again assumed a stooped appearance and climbed up into the street. Three guards and a head-head man. He knew what he had to do, and it had to be done quickly. It was 9:36. *A taipan for a wife.*

He found the first guard talking to the fishmonger, talking anxiously with sharp, stabbing gestures. The noise of the crowd was an impediment. The vendor kept shaking his head. Bourne chose a heavyset man near the guard; he rushed forward shoving the unsuspecting onlooker into the guard and sidestepped as the taipan's man recoiled. In the brief melee that erupted, Jason pulled the bewildered guard aside, hammered his knuckles into the base of the man's throat, twisted him as he began to fall, and slashed his rigid hand across the back of the guard's neck at the top of the spine. He dragged the unconscious man across the pavement, apologizing to the crowd in Chinese for his drunken friend. He dropped the guard in the remains of a storefront, took the radio and smashed it.

The taipan's second man required no such tactics. He was off to the side of the crowd by himself, shouting into his radio. Bourne approached, his sorry figure presenting no threat, and he held out his hand, as if he were a beggar. The guard waved him away; it was the last gesture he would remember, for Bourne gripped his wrist, twisted it, and broke the man's arm. Fourteen seconds later the taipan's second guard lay in the shadows of a mound of garbage, his radio thrown into the debris.

The third guard was in conference with the "snake bitch." To Bourne's satisfaction, she, too, kept shaking her head as the fishmonger had done; there was a certain loyalty in the Walled City where bribes were concerned. The man pulled out his radio, but had no chance to use it. Jason ran up to him, grabbed the ancient, toothless cobra and thrust its flat head into the man's face. The horrified gasp, followed by a scream, was all the reaction Jason Bourne needed. The nerves in the throat are a magnificent network of immobilizing, cordlike fibers connecting the body organs to the central nervous system. Bourne played upon them swiftly, and once again dragged his victim through the crowd, apologizing profusely, as he left the unconscious guard on a dark patch of concrete. He held the radio up to his ear; there was nothing on the receiver. It was 9:40. One head-head man remained.

The small, middle-aged Chinese in the expensive suit and polished shoes all but held his nose as he raced from one point to another trying to spot his men, reluctant to make the slightest physical contact with the hordes gathered around the vendors' stalls and tables. His lack of height made it hard for him to see. Bourne watched where he was heading, ran ahead of him, then quickly turned around and sent his fist crashing into the executive's lower abdomen. As the Chinese buckled over, Jason reached around the man's waist with his left arm, picked him up and carried the limp figure to a section of the curb where two men sat, weaving, passing a bottle back and forth. He placed a *Wushu* chop across the banker's neck and dropped him between the two men. Even through their haze the drunken men would make sure their new companion stayed unconscious for a considerable length of time. There were pockets to ransack, clothes and a pair of shoes to be removed. All would bring a price; whatever cash there was would be a bonus for their labors. *9:43.*

Bourne no longer stooped, gone was the chameleon. He rushed across the street overflowing with humanity and raced down the steps and into the alley. He had *done* it! He had removed the Praetorian Guard. *A taipan for a wife!* He reached the staircase—the third staircase in the right wall—and yanked out the remarkable weapon he had purchased from an arms merchant in the Mongkok. As quietly as he could manage, testing each step with a foot, he climbed to the second level. He braced himself outside the door, balanced his weight, lifted his left leg and smashed it into the thin wood.

The door crashed open. He sprang through and crouched, the weapon extended.

Three men faced him, forming a semicircle, each with a gun aimed at his head. Behind them, dressed in a white silk suit, a huge Chinese sat in a chair. The man nodded to his guards.

He had lost. Bourne had miscalculated and David Webb would die. Far more excruciating, he knew Marie's death would soon follow. Let them fire, thought David. Pull the triggers that would mercifully put him out of it! He had killed the only thing that mattered in his life.

"Shoot, goddamn you! *Shoot!*"

11

"Welcome, Mr. Bourne," said the large man in the white silk suit, waving his guards aside. "I assume you see the logic of putting your gun on the floor and pushing it away from you. There's really no alternative, you know."

Webb looked at the three Chinese; the man in the center cracked the hammer back on his automatic. David lowered the gun and shoved it forward. "You expected me, didn't you?" he asked quietly, getting to his feet, as the guard on his right picked up the weapon.

"We didn't know what to expect—except the unexpected. How did you do it? Are my people dead?"

"No. They're bruised and unconscious, not dead."

"Remarkable. You thought I was alone here?"

"I was told you traveled with your head man and three others, not six. I thought it was logical. Any more, it seemed to me, would be conspicuous."

"That's why these men came early to make arrangements and have not left this hole since they arrived. So you thought you could take me, exchange me for your wife."

"It's obvious that she didn't have a damn thing to do

with it. Let her go; she can't hurt you. Kill me but let her go."

"*Pi ge!*" said the banker, ordering two of the guards out of the flat; they bowed and left quickly. "This man will remain," he continued, turning back to Webb. "Outside of the immense loyalty he has for me, he doesn't speak or understand a word of English."

"I see you trust your people."

"I trust no one." The financier gestured at a dilapidated wooden chair across the shabby room, revealing as he did so a gold Rolex on his wrist, diamonds encrusted around its dial, matching his bejeweled gold cuff links. "Sit down," he ordered. "I've gone to great lengths and spent much money to bring about this conference."

"Your head man—I assume it was your head man—" said Bourne aimlessly, studying every detail of the room as he walked over to the chair, "told me not to wear an expensive watch down here. I guess you didn't listen to him."

"I arrived in a soiled, filthy caftan with sleeves wide enough to conceal it. As I look at your clothes, I'm certain the Chameleon understands."

"You're Yao Ming." Webb sat down.

"It is a name I've used, you surely understand that. The Chameleon goes by many shapes and colors."

"I didn't kill your wife—or the man who happened to be with her."

"I know that, Mr. Webb."

"You *what?*" David shot up from the chair and the guard took a rapid step forward, his gun leveled.

"Sit down," repeated the banker. "Don't alarm my devoted friend or we both may regret it, you far more than me."

"You *knew* it wasn't me and still you've *done* this to us!"

"Sit quickly, please."

"I want an *answer!*" said Webb, sitting down.

"Because you are the true Jason Bourne. That is why you are here, why your wife remains in my custody, and will remain so until you accomplish what I ask of you."

"I talked to her."

"I know you did. I permitted it."

"She didn't sound like herself—even considering the

circumstances. She's strong, stronger than I was during those lousy weeks in Switzerland and Paris. Something's *wrong* with her! Is she drugged?''

"Certainly not."

"Is she *hurt?*''

"In spirit, perhaps, but not in any other way. However, she will be hurt and she *will* die, if you refuse me. Can I be clearer?"

"You're dead, taipan."

"The true Bourne speaks. That's very good. It's what I need."

"Spell it out."

"I am being hounded by someone in your name," began the taipan, his voice hard, his intensity mounting. "Far more severely—may the spirits forgive me—than the loss of a young wife. From all sides in all areas, the terrorist, this *new* Jason Bourne, attacks! He kills my people, blows up shipments of valuable merchandise, threatens other taipans with death if they do business with me! His exorbitant fees come from my enemies here in Hong Kong and Macao, and up the Deep Bay water routes, north into the provinces *themselves!*''

"You have a lot of enemies."

"My interests are extensive."

"So, I was told, were those of the man I didn't kill in Macao."

"Oddly enough," said the banker, breathing hard and gripping the arm of his chair in an effort to control himself. "He and I were not enemies. In certain areas our interests converged. It's how he met my wife."

"How convenient. Shared assets, as it were."

"You are offensive."

"They're not my rules," replied Bourne, his eyes cold, leveled at the Oriental. "Get to the point. *My* wife's alive and I want her back without a mark on her or a voice raised against her. If she's harmed in any way whatsoever, you and your *Zhongguo ren* won't be any match for what I'll mount against you."

"You are not in a position to make threats, Mr. Webb."

"Webb isn't," agreed the once most hunted man in Asia and Europe. "Bourne is."

The Oriental looked hard at Jason, then nodded twice as his eyes dropped below Webb's gaze. "Your audacity matches your arrogance. To the point. It's very simple, very clear-cut." The taipan suddenly clenched his right hand into a fist, then raised it and crashed it down on the fragile arm of the decrepit chair. "I want *proof* against my enemies!" he shouted, his angry eyes peering out behind two partially closed walls of swollen flesh. "The only way I'll get it is for you to bring me this all too credible impostor who takes your place! I want him facing me, *watching* me as he feels his life leaving him in agony until he tells me everything I must know. *Bring* him to me, Jason Bourne!" The banker breathed deeply, then added quietly, "Then, and only then, will you be reunited with your wife."

Webb stared at the taipan in silence. "What makes you think I can do it?" he said finally.

"Who better to trap a pretender than the original?"

"Words," said Webb. "Meaningless."

"He's *studied* you! He's analyzed your methods, your techniques. He could not pass himself off as you if he had not. *Find* him! Trap him with the tactics you yourself created."

"Just like that?"

"You'll have help. Several names and descriptions, men I am convinced are involved with this new killer who uses an old name."

"Over in Macao?"

"*Never!* It must *not* be Macao! There's to be no mention, no reference whatsoever to the incident at the Lisboa Hotel. It is closed, finished; you know nothing about it. In no way can my person be associated with what you are doing. You have nothing to do with me! If you surface, you are hunting a man who has assumed your mantle. You are protecting yourself, defending yourself. A perfectly natural thing to do under the circumstances."

"I thought you wanted proof—"

"It will come when you bring me the *impostor!*" shouted the taipan.

"If not Macao, where then?"

"Here in Kowloon. In the Tsim Sha Tsui. Five men were slain in the back room of a cabaret, among them a banker—like myself, a taipan, my associate from time to time and no less influential—as well as three others whose identities were concealed; apparently it was a government decision. I've never found out who they were."

"But you know who the fifth man was," said Bourne.

"He worked for me. He took my place at that meeting. Had I been there myself, your namesake would have killed me. This is where you will start, here in Kowloon, in the Tsim Sha Tsui. I will give you the names of the two known dead and the identities of many men who were the enemies of both, now my enemies. Move quickly. Find the man who kills in your name and bring him to me. And a last warning, Mr. Bourne. Should you try to find out who I am, the order will be swift, the execution swifter. Your wife will die."

"Then so will you. Give me the names."

"They're on this paper," said the man who used the name Yao Ming, reaching into the pocket of his white silk vest. "They were typed by a public stenographer at the Mandarin. There would be no point in trying to trace a specific typewriter."

"A waste of time," said Bourne, taking the sheet of paper. "There must be twenty million typewriters in Hong Kong."

"But not so many taipans of my size and girth, eh?"

"That I'll remember."

"I'm sure you will."

"How do I reach you?"

"You don't. Ever. This meeting never took place."

"Then why *did* it? Why did everything that's happened take place? Say I manage to find and take this cretin who calls himself Bourne—and it's a damn big *if*—what do I do with him? Leave him on the steps outside here in the Walled City?"

"It could be a splendid idea. Drugged, no one would pay the slightest attention beyond rifling his pockets."

"*I'd* pay a lot of attention. A prize for a prize, taipan. I want an ironclad guarantee. I want my wife back."

"What would you consider such a guarantee?"

"First her voice on the phone convincing me she's unharmed, and then I want to see her—say, walking up and down a street under her own power with no one near her."

"Jason Bourne speaks?"

"He speaks."

"Very well. We've developed a high-technology industry here in Hong Kong, ask anyone in the electronics business in your country. On the bottom of that page is a telephone number. When and if—and *only* when and if —the impostor is in your hands, call that number and repeat the words 'snake lady' several times—"

"*Medusa,*" whispered Jason, interrupting. "Airborne."

The taipan arched his brows, his expression noncommittal. "Naturally, I was referring to the woman in the bazaar."

"Like hell you were. Go on."

"As I say, repeat the words several times until you hear a series of clicks—"

"Triggering another number, or numbers," broke in Bourne again.

"Something to do with the sounds of the phrase, I believe," agreed the taipan. "The sibilant *s,* followed by a flat vowel and hard consonants. Ingenious, wouldn't you say?"

"It's called aurally receptive programming, instruments activated by a voice print."

"Since you're not impressed, do let me emphasize the condition under which the call may be made. For your wife's sake, I hope *it* impresses you. The call is to be placed only when you are prepared to deliver the impostor within a matter of minutes. Should you or anyone else use the number and the code words without that guarantee, I'll know a trace is being put out over the lines. In that event, your wife will be killed, and a dead, disfigured white woman without identification dropped into the waters of the out islands. Do I make myself clear?"

Swallowing, suppressing his fury despite the sickening fear, Bourne spoke icily. "The condition is understood. Now you understand mine. When and if I make that call, I'll want to speak to my wife—not within minutes but within seconds. If I don't, whoever's on the line will hear the gunshot and you'll know that your assassin, the prize you say you've got to have, has just had his head blown away. You'll have thirty seconds."

"Your condition is understood and will be met. I'd say the conference is over, Jason Bourne."

"I want my weapon. One of the guards who left has it."

"It will be given to you on your way out."

"He'll take my word for it?"

"He doesn't have to. If you walked out of here, he was to give it to you. A corpse has no need of a gun."

What remain of the stately homes from Hong Kong's extravagant colonial era are high in the hills above the city in an area known as Victoria Peak, named for the island's mountain summit, the crown of all the territory. Here graceful gardens complement rose-bordered paths that lead to gazebos and verandas from which the wealthy observe the splendors of the harbor below and the out islands in the distance. The residences with the most enviable views are subdued versions of the great houses of Jamaica. They are high-ceilinged and intricate; rooms flow into one another at odd angles to take advantage of summer breezes during that long and oppressive season, and everywhere there is polished carved wood surrounding and reinforcing windows made to withstand the winds and the rains of the mountain winter. Strength and comfort are joined in these minor mansions, the designs dictated by climate.

One such house in the Peak district, however, differed from the others. Not in size or strength or elegance, nor in the beauty of its gardens, which were rather more extensive than many of its neighbors', nor in the impressiveness of its front gate and the height of the stone wall bordering the grounds. Part of what made it seem different was the sense of isolation that surrounded it, especially at night when only a few lights burned in the numerous rooms and no sounds came from the windows or the gardens. It was as if the house were barely inhabited; certainly there was no sign of frivolity. But what dramatically set it apart were the men at the gate and others like them who could be seen from the road patrolling the grounds beyond the wall. They were armed and in fatigue uniforms. They were American marines.

The property was leased by the United States Consulate at the direction of the National Security Council. To any inquiries, the consulate was to comment only that during the next month numerous representatives of the American government and American industry would be flying into the colony at various undetermined times, and security as well as the efficacy of accommodations warranted the lease. It was all the consulate knew. However, selected personnel in British MI6, Special Branch, were given somewhat more information, as their cooperation was deemed necessary and had been authorized by London. However, again, it was limited to an immediate-need-to-know basis, also firmly agreed to by London. Those on the highest levels of both governments, including the closest advisers to the President and the Prime Minister, came to the same conclusion: any disclosures regarding the true nature of the property in Victoria Peak could have catastrophic consequences for the Far East and the world. It was a sterile house, the headquarters of a covert operation so sensitive that even the President and the Prime Minister knew few of the details, only the objectives.

A small sedan drove up to the gate. Instantly, powerful floodlights were tripped, blinding the driver, who brought his arm up to shield his eyes. Two marine guards approached on either side of the vehicle, their weapons drawn.

"You should know the car by now, lads," said the large Oriental in the white silk suit squinting through the open window.

"We know the car, Major Lin," replied the lance corporal on the left. "We just have to make sure of the driver."

"Who could impersonate me?" joked the huge major.

"Man Mountain Dean, sir," answered the marine on the right.

"Oh, yes, I recall. An American wrestler."

"My granddad used to talk about him."

"Thank you, son. You might have at least said your father. May I proceed or am I impounded?"

"We'll turn off the lights and open the gate, sir," said the first marine. "By the way, Major, thanks for the name of that restaurant in the Wanchai. It's a class act and doesn't bust the bankroll."

"But, alas, you found no Suzie Wong."

"Who, sir?"

"Never mind. The gate, if you please, lads."

Inside the house, in the library, which had been converted into an office, Undersecretary of State Edward Newington McAllister sat behind a desk, studying the pages of a dossier under the glare of a lamp, making checkmarks in the margins beside certain paragraphs and certain lines. He was consumed, his attention riveted. The intercom buzzed, and he had to force his eyes and his hand to the telephone. "Yes?" He listened and replied. "Send him in, of course." McAllister hung up and returned to the dossier in front of him, the pencil in his hand. On the top of the page he was reading were the words repeated in the same position on each page: *Ultra Maximum Classified. P.R.C. Internal. Sheng Chou Yang.*

The door opened and the immense Major Lin Wenzu of British Intelligence, MI6, Special Branch, Hong Kong, walked in, closed the door, and smiled at McAllister, who remained absorbed in the dossier.

"It's still the same, isn't it, Edward? Buried in the words there's a pattern, a line to follow."

"I wish I could find it," answered the undersecretary of State, reading feverishly.

"You will, my friend. Whatever it is."

"I'll be with you in a moment."

"Take your time," said the major, removing the gold Rolex wristwatch and the cuff links. He placed them on the desk, and spoke quietly. "Such a pity to give these back. They add a certain presence to my presence. You will, however, pay for the suit, Edward. It's not basic to my wardrobe, but as ever in Hong Kong, it was reasonable, even for one of my size."

"Yes, of course," agreed the undersecretary, preoccupied.

Major Lin sat down in the black leather chair in front of the desk, remaining silent for the better part of a minute. It was obvious that he could remain silent no longer. "Is that anything I might help you with, Edward? Or more to the point, is it anything that pertains to the job at hand? Something you can tell me about?"

"I'm afraid it isn't, Lin. On all counts."

"You will have to tell us sooner or later. Our superiors in London will have to tell us. 'Do what he asks,' they say. 'Keep records of all conversations and directives, but follow his orders and advise him.' *Advise* him? There *is* no advice but tactics. A man in an unoccupied office firing four bullets into the wall of the harbor walk, six into the water, and the rest blanks—thank *God* there were no cardiac arrests—and we've created the situation you want. Now, *that* we can understand—"

"I gather everything went very well."

"There was a riot, if that's what you mean by 'very well.' "

"It's what I mean." McAllister leaned back in his chair, the slender fingers of his right hand massaging his temples.

"Score one, my friend. The authentic Jason Bourne was convinced and he made his moves. Incidentally, you will pay for the hospitalization of one man with a broken arm, and two others who claim they are still in shock with extremely painful necks. The fourth is too embarrassed to say anything."

"Bourne's very good at what he does—what he did."

"He's *lethal*, Edward!"

"You handled him, I gather."

"Thinking every second he'd make another move and blow that filthy room apart! I was petrified. The man's a maniac. Incidentally, why is he to stay out of Macao? It's an odd restriction."

"There's nothing he can't do from here. The killings took place here. The impostor's clients are obviously here in Hong Kong, not Macao."

"As usual, that is no answer."

"Let's put it another way, and this much I can tell you. Actually you already know it, since you played the role tonight. The lie about our mythical taipan's young wife and lover having been murdered in Macao. Any thoughts on it?"

"An ingenious device," said Lin, frowning. "Few acts of vengeance are as readily understood as an 'eye for an eye.' In a sense, it's the basis of your strategy—what I know of it."

"What do you think Webb would do if he found out it *was* a lie?"

"He couldn't. You made it clear the killings were covered up."

"You underestimate him. Once in Macao, he'd turn over every piece of garbage to learn who this taipan is. He'd question every bellhop, every maid—probably threaten or bribe a dozen hotel personnel at the Lisboa and most of the police until he learned the truth."

"But we have his wife, and that is not a lie. He will act accordingly."

"Yes, but in a different dimension. Whatever he thinks now—and certainly he must have suspicions—he can't know, know for certain. If he digs in Macao, however, and learns the truth, he will have proof that he's been deceived by his government."

"How, specifically?"

"Because the lie was delivered to him by a senior official of the State Department—namely, me. And by his lights at best, he was betrayed before."

"That much we do know."

"I want a man at all times at immigration in Macao—around the clock. Hire people you can trust, and give them photographs but no information. Offer a bonus for anyone who spots him and calls you."

"It can be done, but he wouldn't risk it. He believes the odds are against him. One informer in the hotel or at police headquarters and his wife dies. He wouldn't take the chance."

"And we can't take *that* chance, however remote. If he found out that he's being used again—betrayed again—he might come unhinged, do things and say things that would have unthinkable consequences for us all. Frankly, if he heads for Macao, he could become a terrible liability rather than the asset we think we've created."

"Termination?" asked the major simply.

"I can't use that word."

"I don't think you'll have to. I was very convincing. I slammed my hand on the chair and raised my voice most effectively. 'Your wife will die!' I yelled. He believed me. I should have trained for the opera."

"You did well."

"It was a performance worthy of Akim Tamiroff."

"Who?"

"Please. I went through this at the gate."

"I beg your pardon?"

"Forget it. In Cambridge they said I'd meet people like you. I had a don in Oriental History who said you can't let go, any of you. You insist on keeping secrets because the *Zhongguo ren* are inferior; they cannot comprehend. Is that the case here, *yang quizi?*"

"Good Lord, no."

"Then what are we *doing?* The obvious I understand. We recruit a man who's in the unique position of hunting a killer because the killer is impersonating him—impersonating the man he was. But to go to such lengths— kidnapping his wife, involving *us,* these elaborate and, frankly, dangerous games we play. Truthfully, Edward, when you gave me the scenario, I myself questioned London. 'Follow orders,' they repeated. 'Above all, keep silent.' Well, as you said a moment ago, it's *not* good enough. We should be told more. Without knowledge, how can Special Branch assume responsibility?"

"For the moment, the responsibility's ours, the decisions ours. London's agreed to that, and they wouldn't have agreed if they weren't convinced it was the best way to go. Everything must be contained; there's no room whatsoever for leakage or miscalculation. Incidentally, those were London's words." McAllister leaned forward, clasping his hands together, his knuckles white from the grip. "I'll tell you this much, Lin. I wish to God it *wasn't* our responsibility, especially with me near the center. Not that I make the final decisions, but I'd rather not make any. I'm not qualified."

"I wouldn't say that, Edward. You're one of the most thorough men I've ever met, you proved that two years ago. You're a brilliant analyst. You don't have to possess the expertise yourself as long as you take your orders from someone who does. All you need is understanding and conviction—and conviction is written all over your troubled face. You will do the right thing if it is given to you to execute."

"Thank you, I guess."

"What you wanted was accomplished tonight, so you'll soon know if your resurrected hunter retains his old skills. During the coming days we can monitor events, but that's all we can do. They're out of our hands. This Bourne begins his dangerous journey."

"He has the names, then?"

"The *authentic* names, Edward. Among the most vicious members of the Hong Kong–Macao underworld—

upper-level soldiers who carry out orders, captains who initiate deals and arrange contracts, violent ones. If there are any in the territory who have knowledge of this impostor-killer, they'll be found on that list."

"We start phase two. Good." McAllister unclasped his hands and looked at his watch. "Good heavens, I had no idea of the time. It's been a long day for you. You certainly didn't have to return the watch and the cuff links tonight."

"I certainly knew that."

"Then why?"

"I don't wish to burden you further, but we may have an unforeseen problem. At least one we hadn't considered, perhaps foolishly."

"What is it?"

"The woman may be ill. Her husband sensed it when he talked with her."

"You mean *seriously?*"

"We can't rule it out—the doctor can't rule it out."

"The *doctor?*"

"There was no point in alarming you. I called in one of our medical staff several days ago—he's completely reliable. She wasn't eating and complained of nausea. The doctor thought it might be anxiety or depression, or even a virus, so he gave her antibiotics and mild tranquilizers. She has not improved. In fact, her condition has rapidly deteriorated. She's become listless; she has trembling seizures and her mind appears to wander. None of this is like that woman, I can assure you."

"It certainly isn't!" said the undersecretary of State as he blinked his eyes rapidly, his lips pursed. "What can we do?"

"The doctor thinks she should be admitted to the hospital immediately for tests."

"She *can't* be! Good *Christ,* it's out of the question!"

The Chinese Intelligence officer rose from the chair and approached the desk slowly. "Edward," he began calmly. "I don't know the ramifications of this operation, but I can obviously piece together several basic objectives, especially one. I'm afraid I must ask you: What happens to David Webb if his wife is seriously ill? What happens to your Jason Bourne if she dies?"

12

"I need her medical history, and I want it just as fast as you can provide it, Major. That's an order, sir, from a former lieutenant in Her Majesty's Medical Corps."

He's the English doctor who examined me. He's very civil, but cold, and, I suspect, a terribly good physician. He's bewildered. That's fine.

"We'll get it for you; there are ways. You say she couldn't tell you the name of her doctor back in the United States?"

That's the huge Chinese who's always polite—unctuous, actually, but rather sincere. He's been nice to me, as his men have been nice to me. He's following orders—they're all following orders—but they don't know why.

"Even in her lucid moments she draws a blank, which is not encouraging. It could be a defense mechanism indicating that she was aware of a progressive illness she wants to block out."

"She's not that sort, Doctor. She's a strong woman."

"Psychological strength is relative, Major. Often the strongest among us are loath to accept mortality. The ego refuses it. Get me her history. I *must* have it."

"A man will call Washington, and people there will make other calls. They know where she lives, her circumstances, and within minutes they'll know her neighbors. Someone will tell us. We'll find her doctor."

"I want everything on a satellite computer printout. We have the equipment."

"Any transmission of information must be received at our offices."

"Then I'll go with you. Give me a few minutes."

"You're frightened, aren't you, Doctor?"

"If it's a neurological disorder, that's always frightening, Major. If your people can work quickly, perhaps I can talk to her doctor myself. That would be optimum."

"You found nothing in your examination?"

"Only possibilities, nothing concrete. There *is* pain here, and there *isn't* pain there. I've ordered a CAT scan in the morning."

"You *are* frightened."

"Shitless, Major."

Oh, you're all doing exactly what I wanted you to do. Good God, I'm hungry! I'll eat for five straight hours when I get out of here —and I will get out! David, did you understand? Did you understand what I was telling you? The dark trees are maple trees; they're so common, darling, so identifiable. The single leaf is Canada. The embassy! Here in Hong Kong it's the consulate! That's what we did in Paris, my darling! It was terrible then, but it won't be terrible here. I'll know someone. Back in Ottawa I instructed so many who were being posted all over the world. Your memory is clouded, my love, but mine isn't. . . . And you must understand, David, that the people I dealt with then are not so different from the people who are holding me now. In some ways, of course, they're robots, but they're also individuals who think and question and wonder why they are asked to do certain things. But they follow a regimen, darling, because if they don't, they get poor service reports, which is tantamount to a fate worse than dismissal —which rarely happens—because it means no advancement, limbo. They've actually been kind to me—gentle, really—as if they're embarrassed by what they've been ordered to do but must carry out their assignments. They think I'm ill and they're concerned for me, genuinely concerned. They're not criminals or killers, my sweet David. They're bureaucrats in search of direction! They're bureaucrats, David! This whole incredible thing has GOVERNMENT written all over it. I know! These are the sort of people I worked with for years. I was one of them!

Marie opened her eyes. The door was closed, the room empty, but she knew a guard was outside—she had heard the Chinese major giving instructions. No one was permitted in her room but the English doctor and two specific nurses the guard had met and who would be on duty until morning. She knew the rules, and with that knowledge she could break them.

She sat up—*Jesus, I'm hungry!*—and was darkly amused at the thought of their neighbors in Maine being questioned about her doctor. She barely knew her neighbors and there *was* no doctor. They had been in the university town less than three months, starting with the late summer session for David's preparations, and with all the problems of renting a house and learning what the new wife of a new associate professor should do, or be, and finding the stores and the laundry and the bedding and the linens—the thousand and ten things a woman does to make a home—there simply had been no time to think about a doctor. Good Lord, they had lived with doctors for eight months, and except for Mo Panov she would have been content never to see another one.

Above all, there was David, fighting his way out of his personal tunnels, as he called them, trying so hard not to show the pain, so grateful when there was light and memory. *God,* how he attacked the books, overjoyed when whole stretches of history came back to him, but the joy was balanced by the anguish of realizing it was only segments of his own life that eluded him. And so often at night she would feel the mattress ripple and know he was getting out of bed to be by himself with his half-thoughts and haunting images. She would wait a few minutes, and then go out into the hallway and sit on the steps, listening. And once in a great while it happened: the quiet sobbing of a strong, proud man in agony. She would go to him and he would turn away; the embarrassment and the hurt were too much. She would say, "You're not fighting this yourself, darling. We're fighting it together. Just as we fought before." He would talk then, reluctantly at first, then expanding, the words coming faster and faster until the floodgates burst and he would find things, discover things. *Trees, David! My favorite tree, the maple tree. The maple leaf, David! The consulate, my darling!* She had work to do. She reached for the cord and pressed the button for the nurse.

Two minutes later the door opened and a Chinese woman in her mid-forties entered, her nurse's uniform starched and immaculate. "What can I do for you, my dear?" she said pleasantly, in pleasantly accented English.

"I'm dreadfully tired, but I'm having a terrible time getting to sleep. May I have a pill that might help me?"

"I'll check with your doctor; he's still here. I'm sure it

will be all right." The nurse left and Marie got out of bed. She went to the door, the ill-fitting hospital gown slipping down over her left shoulder, and with the air conditioning, the slit in the back bringing a chill. She opened the door, startling the muscular young guard who sat in a chair on the right.

"Yes, Mrs. . . . ?" The guard jumped up.

"Shhh!" ordered Marie, her index finger at her lips. "Come in here! *Quickly!"*

Bewildered, the young Chinese followed her into the room. She walked rapidly to the bed and climbed on it but did not pull up the covers. She sloped her right shoulder; the gown slipped off, held barely in place by the swell of her breast.

"Come here!" she whispered. "I don't want anyone to hear me."

"What is it, lady?" asked the guard, his gaze avoiding Marie's exposed flesh and focusing instead on her face and her long auburn hair. He took several steps forward, but still kept his distance. "The door is closed. No one can hear you."

"I want you to—" Her whisper fell below an audible level.

"Even I can't hear you, Mrs. . . ." The man moved closer.

"You're the nicest of my guards. You've been very kind to me."

"There was no reason to be otherwise, lady."

"Do you know why I'm being held?"

"For your own safety," the guard lied, his expression noncommittal.

"I see." Marie heard the footsteps outside drawing nearer. She shifted her body; the gown traveled down, baring her legs. The door opened and the nurse entered.

"Oh?" The Chinese woman was startled. It was obvious that her eyes appraised a distasteful scene. She looked at the embarrassed guard as Marie covered herself. "I wondered why you were not outside."

"The lady asked to speak with me," replied the man, stepping back.

The nurse glanced quickly at Marie. "Yes?"

"If that's what he says."

"This is foolish," said the muscular guard, going to the

door and opening it. "The lady's not well," he added. "Her mind strays. She says foolish things." He went out the door and closed it firmly behind him.

Again the nurse looked at Marie, her eyes now questioning. "Do you feel all right?" she asked.

"My mind does not stray, and I'm not the one who says foolish things. But I do as I'm told." Marie paused, then continued. "When that giant of a major leaves the hospital, please come and see me. I have something to tell you."

"I'm sorry, I cannot do that. You must rest. Here, I have a sedative for you. I see you have water."

"You're a *woman,*" said Marie, staring hard at the nurse.

"Yes," agreed the Oriental flatly. She placed a tiny paper cup with a pill in it on Marie's bedside table and returned to the door. She took a last, questioning look at her patient and left.

Marie got off the bed and walked silently to the door. She put her ear to the metal panel; outside in the corridor she heard the muffled sounds of a rapid exchange, obviously in Chinese. Whatever was said and however the brief, excited conversation was resolved, she had planted the seed. *Work on the visual,* Jason Bourne had emphasized and reemphasized during the hell they had gone through in Europe. *It's more effective than anything else. People will draw the conclusions you want on the basis of what they see far more than from the most convincing lies you can tell them.*

She went to the clothes closet and opened it. They had left the few things they had bought for her in Hong Kong at the apartment, but the slacks, blouse, and shoes she had worn the day they brought her to the hospital were hanging up; it had not occurred to anyone to remove them. Why should they have? They could see for themselves that she was a very sick woman. The trembling and spasms had convinced them; they saw it all. Jason Bourne would understand. She glanced at the small white telephone on the bedside table. It was a flat, self-contained unit, the panel of touch buttons built into the instrument. She wondered, although there was no one she could think of calling. She went to the table and picked it up. It was dead, as she expected it would be. There was the signal for the nurse; it was all she needed and all she was permitted.

She walked to the window and raised the white shade, only to greet the night. The dazzling, colored lights of Hong Kong lit up the sky, and she was closer to the sky than to the ground. As David would say—or rather, Jason: *So be it. The door. The corridor.*

So be it.

She crossed to the washbasin. The hospital-supplied toothbrush and toothpaste were still encased in plastic; the soap was also virginal, wrapped in the manufacturer's jacket, the words guaranteeing purity beyond the breath of angels.

Next there was the bathroom; nothing much different except a dispenser of sanitary napkins and a small sign in four languages explaining what not to do with them. She walked back into the room. What was she looking for? Whatever it was she had not found it.

Study everything. You'll find something you can use. Jason's words, not David's. Then she saw it.

On certain hospital beds—and this was one of them— there is a handle beneath the baseboard that when turned one way or the other raises or lowers the bed. This handle can be removed—and often is—when a patient is being fed intravenously, or if a physician wants him to remain in a given position—for example, in traction. A nurse can unlock and remove this handle by pressing in, turning to the left, and yanking it out as the cog lock is released. This is frequently done during visiting hours, when visitors might succumb to a patient's wishes to change position against the doctor's wishes. Marie knew this bed and she knew this handle. When David was recovering from the wounds he received at Treadstone 71, he was kept alive by intravenous feedings; she had watched the nurses. Her soon-to-be husband's pain was more than she could bear, and the nurses were obviously aware that in her desire to make things easier for him, she might disrupt the medical treatment. She knew how to remove the handle, and once removed, it was nothing less than a wieldy angle iron.

She removed it and climbed back into the bed, the handle beneath the covers. She waited, thinking how different her two men were—in one man. Her lover, Jason, could be so cold and patient, waiting for the moment to spring, to shock, to rely for survival upon violence. And her husband, David, so giving, so willing to listen—the scholar—avoiding violence at all costs because he had been there and he hated the pain and the anxiety—above all, the necessity to eliminate one's feelings to become a mere animal. And now he was called upon to be the man he detested. David, my *David!* Hold on to your *sanity!* I love you so.

Noises in the corridor. Marie looked at the clock on the bedside table. Sixteen minutes had passed. She placed both her hands above the covers as the nurse entered, lowering her eyelids as though she were drowsy.

"All right, my dear," said the woman, taking several steps from the door. "You have touched me, I will not deny that. But I have my orders—very specific instructions about you. The major and your doctor have left. Now, what is it you wanted to tell me?"

"Not . . . now," whispered Marie, her head sinking into her chin, her face more asleep than awake. "I'm so tired. I took . . . the pill."

"Is it the guard outside?"

"He's sick. . . . He never touches me—I don't care. He gets me things. . . . I'm *so* tired."

"What do you mean, 'sick'?"

"He . . . likes to look at women. . . . He doesn't . . . bother me when I'm . . . asleep." Marie's eyes closed.

"*Zang!*" said the nurse under her breath. "Dirty, *dirty!*" She spun on her heels, walked out the door, closed it, and addressed the guard. "The woman is asleep! Do you understand me!"

"That is most heavenly fortunate."

"She says you never touch her!"

"I never even thought about it."

"Don't think about it now!"

"I do not need lectures from you, hag nurse. I have a job to do."

"See that you do it! I will speak to Major Lin Wenzu in the morning!" The woman glared at the man and walked down the corridor, her pace and her posture aggressive.

"You!" The harsh whisper came from Marie's door, which was slightly ajar. She opened it an inch further and spoke. "That *nurse!* Who is she?"

"I thought you were asleep, Mrs. . . . ." said the bewildered guard.

"She told me she was going to tell you that."

"What?"

"She's coming *back* for me! She says there are connecting doors to the other rooms. Who *is* she?"

"She *what?*"

"Don't talk! Don't look at me! She'll *see* you!"

"She went down the hallway to the right."

"You never can tell. Better a devil you know than one you don't! You know what I mean?"

"I do not know what *anybody* means!" pleaded the guard, talking softly, emphatically, to the opposite wall. "I do not know what *she* means and I do not know what *you* mean, lady!"

"Come inside. *Quickly!* I think she's a Communist! From Peking!"

"Beijing?"

"I won't *go* with her!" Marie pulled back the door, then spun behind it.

The guard rushed in as the door slammed shut. The room was dark; only the light in the bathroom was on, its glow diminished by the bathroom door, which was nearly closed. The man could be seen, but he could not see. "Where are you, Mrs. . . . ? Be calm. She will not take you anywhere—"

The guard was not capable of saying anything further. Marie had crashed the iron handle across the base of his skull with the strength of an Ontario ranch girl quite used to the bullwhip in a cattle drive. The guard collapsed; she knelt down and worked quickly.

The Chinese was muscular but not large, not tall. Marie was not large, but she was tall for a woman. With a hitch here and a tuck there, the guard's clothes and shoes fit reasonably well for a fast exit, but her hair was the problem. She looked around the room. *Study everything. You'll find something you can use.* She found it. Hanging from a chrome bar on the bedside table was a hand towel. She pulled it off, piled her hair on top of her head and wrapped the towel around it, tucking the cloth within itself. It undoubtedly looked foolish and could hardly bear close scrutiny, but it *was* a turban of sorts.

Stripped to his undershorts and socks, the guard moaned and began to raise himself, then collapsed back into unconsciousness. Marie ran to the closet, grabbed her own clothes, and went to the door, opening it cautiously, no more than an inch. Two nurses—one Oriental, the other European—were talking quietly in the hallway. The Chinese was not the woman who had returned to hear her complaint about the guard. Another nurse appeared, nodded to the two, and went directly to a door across the hall. It was a linen supply closet. A telephone rang at the floor desk fifty feet down the hallway; before the circular desk was a bisecting corridor. An EXIT sign hung from the ceiling, the arrow pointing to the right. The two conversing nurses turned and started toward the desk; the third left the linen closet carrying a handful of sheets. *The cleanest escape is one done in stages, using whatever confusion there is.*

Marie slipped out of the room and ran across the hall to the linen closet. She went inside and closed the door. Suddenly, a woman's roar of protest filled the hallway, petrifying her. She could hear heavy racing footsteps, coming closer; then more footsteps.

"The guard!" yelled the Chinese nurse in English. "Where is that dirty guard?"

Marie opened the closet door less than an inch. Three excited nurses were in front of her hospital room; they burst inside.

"You! You took off your clothes! *Zangsile* dirty man! Look in the bathroom!"

"You!" yelled the guard unsteadily. "You let her get *away!* I will hold you for my superiors."

"Let me go, filthy man! You lie!"

"You are a *Communist!* From *Beijing!*"

Marie slipped out of the linen closet, a stack of towels over her shoulder, and ran to the bisecting corridor and the EXIT sign.

"Call Major Lin! I've caught a Communist infiltrator!"

"Call the police! He is a pervert!"

Out on the hospital grounds, Marie ran into the parking lot, into the darkest area, and sat breathless in the shadows between two cars. She had to think; she had to appraise the situation. She could not make any mistakes. She dropped the towels and her clothes and began going through the guard's pockets, looking for a wallet or a billfold. She found it, opened it, and counted the money in the dim light. There was slightly more than $600 Hong Kong, which was slightly less than $100 American. It was barely enough for a hotel room; then she saw a credit card issued by a Kowloon bank. *Don't leave home without it.* If she had to, she would present the card—if she had to —and if she could find a hotel room. She removed the money and the plastic card, put the wallet back into the pocket, and began the awkward process of changing clothes while studying the streets beyond the hospital grounds. To her relief, they were crowded, and those crowds were her immediate security.

A car suddenly raced into the parking lot, its tires screeching, as it careened in front of the EMERGENCY door. Marie rose and looked through the automobile windows. The heavyset Chinese major and the cold, precise doctor leaped out of the car and raced toward the entrance. As they disappeared through the doors, Marie ran out of the parking lot and into the street.

She walked for hours, stopping to gorge herself at a fast-food restaurant until she could not stand the sight of another hamburger. She went to the ladies' room and looked at herself in the mirror. She had lost weight and there were dark circles under her eyes, yet withal, she was herself. But the damned *hair!* They would be scouring Hong Kong for her, and the first items of any description would be her height and her hair. She could do little about the former, but she could drastically modify the latter. She stopped at a pharmacy and bought bobby pins and several clasps. Then remembering what Jason had asked her to do in Paris when her photograph appeared in the newspapers, she pulled her hair back, securing it into a bun, and pinned both sides close to her head. The result was a much harsher face, heightened by the loss of weight and no makeup. It was the effect Jason—*David*— had wanted in Paris. . . . No, she reflected, it was not David in Paris. It was Jason Bourne. And it was night, as it had been in Paris.

"Why you do that, miss?" asked a clerk standing near the mirror at the cosmetics counter. "You have such pretty hair, very beautiful."

"Oh? I'm tired of brushing it, that's all."

Marie left the pharmacy, bought flat sandals from a vendor on the street, and an imitation Gucci purse from another—the *G*'s were upside down. She had $45 American left and no idea where she would spend the night. It was both too late and too soon to go to the consulate. A Canadian arriving after midnight asking for a roster of personnel would send out alarms; also she had not had time to figure out how to make the request. Where could she go? She needed sleep. *Don't make your moves when you're tired or exhausted. The margin for error is too great. Rest is a weapon. Don't forget it.*

She passed an arcade that was closing up. A young American couple in blue jeans were bargaining with the owner of a T-shirt stand.

"Hey, come on, man," said the youthful male. "You want to make just *one* more sale tonight, don't you? I mean, so you cut your profit a bit, but it's still a few *dineros* in your pocket, right?"

"No *dineros*," cried the merchant, smiling. "Only dollars, and you offer too few! I have children. You take the precious food from their mouths!"

"He probably owns a restaurant," said the girl.

"You want restaurant? Authentic-real Chinese food?"

"Jesus, you're right, Lacy!"

"My third cousin on my father's side has an exquisite stand two streets from here. Very near, very cheap, very good."

"Forget it," said the boy. "Four bucks, U.S., for the six T's. Take it or leave it."

"I take. Only because you are too strong for me." The merchant grabbed the proffered bills and shoved the T-shirts into a paper bag.

"You're a wonder, Buzz." The girl kissed him on the cheek and laughed. "He's still working on a four hundred percent markup."

"That's the trouble with you business majors! You don't consider the aesthetics. The smell of the hunt, the pleasure of the verbal conflict!"

"If we ever get married, I'll be supporting you for the rest of my miserable life, you great negotiator."

Opportunities will present themselves. Recognize them, act on them. Marie approached the two students.

"Excuse me," she said, speaking primarily to the girl. "I overheard you talking—"

"Wasn't I *terrific?*" broke in the young man.

"Very agile," replied Marie. "But I suspect your friend has a point. Those T-shirts undoubtedly cost him less than twenty-five cents apiece."

"Four hundred percent," said the girl, nodding. "Keystone should be so lucky."

"Key *who?*"

"A jeweler's term," explained Marie. "It's one hundred percent."

"I'm surrounded by philistines!" cried the young man. "I'm an art history major. Someday I'll run the Metropolitan!"

"Just don't try to buy it," said the girl, turning to Marie. "I'm sorry, we're not flakes, we're just having fun. We interrupted you."

"It's most embarrassing, really, but my plane was a day late and I missed my tour into China. The hotel is full and I wondered—"

"You need a place to crash?" interrupted the art history student.

"Yes, I do. Frankly, my funds are adequate but limited. I'm a schoolteacher from Maine—economics, I'm afraid."

"Don't be," said the girl, smiling.

"I'm joining my tour tomorrow, but I'm afraid that's tomorrow, not tonight."

"We can help you, can't we, Lacy?"

"I'm sure we can. Our college has an arrangement with the Chinese University of Hong Kong."

"It's not much on room service but the price is right," said the young man. "Three bucks, U.S., a night. But, holy roller, are they antediluvian!"

"He means there's a certain puritan code over here. The sexes are separated."

" 'Boys and girls together—' " sang the art history major. "Like *hell* they are!" he added.

. . .

Marie sat on the cot in the huge room under a 50-foot ceiling; she assumed it was a gymnasium. All around her young women were asleep and not asleep. Most were silent, but a few snored, others lighted cigarettes, and there were sporadic lurchings toward the bathroom, where the fluorescent lights remained on. She was among children, and she wished she were a child now, free of the terrors that were everywhere. *David, I need you! You think I'm so strong, but, darling, I can't cope! What do I do? How do I do it!*

Study everything, you'll find something you can use.—Jason Bourne.

13

The rain was torrential, pitting the sand, snapping into the floodlights that lit up the grotesque statuary of Repulse Bay—reproductions of enormous Chinese gods, angry myths of the Orient in furious poses, some rising as high as thirty feet. The dark beach was deserted, but there were crowds in the old hotel up by the road and the anachronistic hamburger shop across the way. They were strollers and drop-ins, tourists and islanders alike, who had come down to the bay for a late-night drink or something to eat and to look out at the forbidding statues repelling whatever malign spirits might at any moment emerge from the sea. The sudden downpour had forced the strollers inside; others waited for the storm to let up before heading home.

Drenched, Bourne crouched in the foliage twenty feet from the base of a fierce-looking idol halfway down on the beach. He wiped the rain from his face as he stared at the concrete steps that led to the entrance of the old Colonial Hotel. He was waiting for the third name on the taipan's list.

. . .

The first man had tried to trap him on the Star Ferry, the agreed-upon meeting ground, but Jason, wearing the same clothes he had worn at the Walled City, had spotted the man's two stalking patrols. It was not as easy as looking for men with radios, but it had not been difficult, either. By the third trip across the harbor, Bourne not having appeared at the appointed window on the starboard side, the same two men had passed by his contact twice, each speaking briefly, and each going to opposite positions, their eyes fixed on their superior. Jason had waited until the ferry approached the pier and the passengers started en masse toward the exit ramp in the bow. He had taken out the Chinese on the right with a blow to the kidneys as he passed him in the crowd, then struck the back of the man's head with the heavy brass paperweight; the passengers rushed by in the dim light. Bourne then walked through the emptying benches to the other side; he faced the second man, jammed his gun into the patrol's stomach and marched him to the stern. He arched the man above the railing and shoved him overboard as the ship's whistle blew in the night and the ferry pulled into the Kowloon pier. He then returned to his contact by the deserted window at midship.

"You kept your word," Jason said. "I'm afraid I'm late."

"*You* are the one who called?" The contact's eyes had roamed over Bourne's shabby clothes.

"I'm the one."

"You don't look like a man with the money you spoke of on the telephone."

"You're entitled to that opinion." Bourne withdrew a folded stack of American bills, $1,000 denominations visible when rolled open.

"You are the man." The Chinese had glanced quickly over Jason's shoulders. "What is it that you want?" the man asked anxiously.

"Information about someone for hire who calls himself Jason Bourne."

"You have reached the wrong person."

"I'll pay generously."

"I have nothing to sell."

"I think you do." Bourne had put away the money and

pulled out his weapon, moving closer to the man as the Kowloon passengers streamed on board. "You'll either tell me what I want to know for a fee, or you'll be forced to tell me for your life."

"I know only this," the Chinese had protested. "My people will not *touch* him!"

"Why not?"

"He's not the same man!"

"What did you say?" Jason held his breath, watching the man closely.

"He takes risks he would never have taken before." The Chinese again looked beyond Bourne; sweat broke out on his hairline. "He comes back after two years. Who knows what happened? Drink, narcotics, disease from whores, who knows?"

"What do you mean, 'risks'?"

"That is *what* I mean! He walks into a cabaret in the Tsim Sha Tsui—there was a riot, the police were on their way. Still, he enters and kills five men! He could have been caught, his clients traced! He would not have done such a thing two years ago."

"You may have your sequence backward," said Jason Bourne. "He may have gone in—as one man—and started the riot. He kills *as* that man, and leaves as another, escaping in the confusion."

The Oriental stared briefly into Jason's eyes, suddenly more frightened than before as he again looked at the shabby, ill-fitting clothes in front of him. "Yes, I imagine that is possible," he said tremulously, now whipping his head first to one side, then the other.

"How can this Bourne be reached?"

"I don't know, I swear on the *spirits!* Why do you ask me these questions?"

"*How?*" repeated Jason, leaning into the man, their foreheads touching, the gun shoved into the Oriental's lower abdomen. "If you won't touch him, you know where he *can* be touched, where he can be reached! Now, *where?*"

"Oh, Christian *Jesus.*"

"Goddamn it, not Him! *Bourne!*"

"*Macao!* It is whispered he works out of Macao, that is all I know, I *swear* it!" The man looked in panic to his right and left.

"If you're trying to find your two men, don't bother, I'll tell you," said Jason. "One's in a clump over there, and I hope the other can swim."

"Those men are— Who *are* you?"

"I think you know," Bourne had answered. "Go to the back of the ferry and stay there. If you take one step forward before we dock, you'll never take another."

"Oh, God, you *are*—"

"I wouldn't finish that if I were you."

The second name was accompanied by an unlikely address, a restaurant in Causeway Bay that specialized in classic French food. According to Yao Ming's brief notes, the man acted as the manager, but was actually the owner, and a number of the waiters were as adept with guns as they were with trays. The contact's home address was not known; all his business was done at the restaurant, and it was suspected that he had no permanent residence. Bourne had returned to the Peninsula, discarded his jacket and hat, and walked rapidly through the crowded lobby to the elevator; a well-dressed couple had tried not to show their shock at his appearance. He had smiled and muttered apologetically.

"A company treasure hunt. It's kind of silly, isn't it."

In his room, he had permitted himself a few moments to be David Webb again. It was a mistake; he could not stand the suspension of Bourne's train of thought. *I'm him again. I have to be. He knows what to do. I don't!* . . . He had showered off the filth of the Walled City and the oppressive humidity of the Star Ferry, shaved away the shadow on his face, and dressed for a late French dinner.

I'll find him, Marie! I swear to Christ I'll find him! It was David Webb's promise, but it was Jason Bourne who shouted in fury.

The restaurant looked more like an exquisite rococo dining palace on Paris's Avenue Montaigne than a one-story structure in Hong Kong. Intricate chandeliers hung from the ceiling with the tiny bulbs dimmed; encased candles flickered on tables with the purest linen and the finest silver and crystal.

"I'm afraid we have no tables this evening, monsieur," the maître d' said. He was the only Frenchman in evidence.

"I was told to ask for Jiang Yu and say it was urgent," Bourne had replied, showing a $100 bill, American. "Do you think *he* might find something, if this finds him?"

"*I* will find it, monsieur." The maître d' subtly shook Jason's hand, receiving the money. "Jiang Yu is a fine member of our small community, but it is I who select. *Comprenez-vous?*"

"*Absolument.*"

"*Bien!* You have the face of an attractive, sophisticated man. This way, please, monsieur."

The dinner was not to be had; events occurred too quickly. Within minutes after the arrival of his drink, a slender Chinese in a black suit had appeared at his table. If there was anything odd about him, thought David Webb, it was in the darker color of his skin and the larger slope of his eyes. Malaysian was in his bloodline. *Stop it!* commanded Bourne. *That doesn't do us any good!*

"You asked for me?" said the manager, his eyes searching the face that looked up at him. "How can I be of service?"

"By first sitting down."

"It is most irregular to sit with guests, sir."

"Not really. Not if you own the place. Please. Sit down."

"Is this another tiresome intrusion by the Bureau of Taxation? If so, I hope you enjoy your dinner, which you will pay for. My records are quite clear and quite accurate."

"If you think I'm British, you haven't listened to me. And if by 'tiresome' you mean that half a million dollars is boring, then you can get the hell out of my sight and I'll enjoy my dinner." Bourne leaned back in the booth and sipped his drink with his left hand. His right was hidden.

"Who *sent* you?" asked the Oriental of mixed blood, as he sat down.

"Move away from the edge. I want to talk very quietly."

"Yes, of course." Jiang Yu inched his way directly opposite Bourne. "I must ask. Who sent you?"

"I must ask," said Jason, "do you like American movies? Especially our Westerns?"

"Of course. American films are beautiful, and I admire the movies of your old West most of all. So poetic in retribution, so righteously violent. Am I saying the correct words?"

"Yes, you are. Because right now you're in one."

"I beg your pardon?"

"I have a very special gun under the table. It's aimed between your legs." Within the space of a second, Jason held back the cloth, pulled up the weapon so the barrel could be seen, and immediately shoved the gun back into place. "It has a silencer that reduces the sound of a forty-five to the pop of a champagne cork, but not the impact. *Liao jie ma?*"

"*Liao jie* . . ." said the Oriental, rigid, breathing deeply in fear. "You are with Special Branch?"

"I'm with no one but myself."

"There is no half million dollars, then?"

"There's whatever you consider your life is worth."

"Why *me?*"

"You're on a list," Bourne answered truthfully.

"For *execution?*" whispered the Chinese, gasping, his face contorted.

"That depends on you."

"I must pay you not to *kill* me?"

"In a sense, yes."

"I don't carry half a million dollars in my pockets! Nor here on the premises!"

"Then pay me something else."

"*What?* How *much?* You confuse me!"

"Information instead of money."

"What information?" asked the Chinese as his fear turned into panic. "What information would *I* have? Why come to *me?*"

"Because you've had dealings with a man I want to find. The one for hire who calls himself Jason Bourne."

"*No!* Never did it happen!"

The Oriental's hands began to tremble. The veins in his throat throbbed, and his eyes for the first time strayed from Jason's face. The man had lied.

"You're a liar," said Bourne quietly, pushing his right arm further underneath the table as he leaned forward. "You made the connection in Macao."

"Macao, *yes!* But *no* connection. I swear on the graves of my family for generations!"

"You're very close to losing your stomach and your life. You were sent to Macao to reach him!"

"I was sent, but I did *not* reach him!"

"Prove it to me. How were you to make contact?"

"The *Frenchman*. I was to stand on the top steps of the burned-out Basilica of St. Paul on the Calcada. I was to wear a black kerchief around my neck and when a man came up to me—a Frenchman—and remarked about the beauty of the ruins, I was to say the following words: 'Cain is for Delta.' If he replied, 'And Carlos is for Cain,' I was to accept him as the link to Jason Bourne. But I *swear* to you, he never—"

Bourne did not hear the remainder of the man's protestations. Staccato explosions erupted in his head; his mind was thrown back. Blinding white light filled his eyes, the crashing sounds were unbearable. *Cain is for Delta and Carlos is for Cain. . . . Cain is for Delta! Delta One is Cain! Medusa moves; the snake sheds his skin. Cain is in Paris and Carlos will be his!* They were the words, the codes, the challenges hurled at the Jackal. *I am Cain and I am superior and I am here! Come find me, Jackal! I dare you to find Cain, for he kills better than you do. You'd better find me before I find you, Carlos. You're no match for Cain!*

Good God! Who halfway across the world would know those words—*could* know them? They were locked away in the deepest archives of covert operations! They were a direct connection to *Medusa!*

Bourne had nearly squeezed the trigger of the unseen automatic, so sudden was the shock of this incredible revelation. He removed his index finger, placing it around the trigger housing; he had come close to killing a man for revealing extraordinary information. But how could it have *happened?* Who was the conduit to the new "Jason Bourne" that *knew* such things?

He had to come down, he knew that. His silence was betraying him, betraying his astonishment. The Chinese was staring at him; the man was inching his hand beyond the edge of the booth. "Pull that back, or your balls and your stomach will be blown away."

The Oriental's shoulder yanked up and his hand appeared on the table. "What I have told you is true," the man said. "The Frenchman never came to me. If he had,

I would tell you everything. So would you if you were me. I protect only myself."

"Who sent you to make the contact? Who gave you the words to use?"

"That is honestly beyond me, you must believe that. All is done by telephone through second and third parties who know only the information they carry. The proof of integrity is in the arrival of the funds I am paid."

"How do they arrive? Someone has to give them to you."

"Someone who is a no one, who is hired himself. An unfamiliar host of an expensive dinner party will ask to see the manager. I will accept his compliments and during our conversation an envelope will be slipped to me. I will have ten thousand American dollars for reaching the Frenchman."

"Then what? How do you reach him?"

"One goes to Macao, to the Kam Pek casino in the downtown area. It is mostly for the Chinese, for the games of *fan-tan* and *dai sui*. One goes to Table Five and leaves the telephone number of a Macao hotel—not a private telephone—and a name, any name, not one's own, naturally."

"He calls you at that number?"

"He may or he may not. You stay twenty-four hours in Macao. If he has not called you by then, you have been turned down because the Frenchman has no time for you."

"Those are the rules?"

"Yes. I was turned down twice, and the single time I was accepted he did not appear at the Calcada steps."

"Why do you think you were turned down? Why do you think he didn't show up?"

"I have no idea. Perhaps he has too much business for his master killer. Perhaps I said the wrong things to him on the first two occasions. Perhaps on the third he thought he saw suspicious men on the Calcada, men he believed were with me and meant him no good. There were no such people, naturally, but there is no appeal."

"Table Five. The dealers," said Bourne.

"The croupiers change constantly. His arrangement is with the table. A blanket fee, I imagine. To be divided. And certainly he does not go to the Kam Pek himself—

he undoubtedly hires a whore from the streets. He is very cautious, very professional."

"Do you know anyone else who's tried to reach this Bourne?" asked Bourne. "I'll know if you're lying."

"I think you would. You are obsessed—which is not my business—and you trapped me in my first denial. No, I do not, sir. That is the truth, for I do not care to have my intestines blown away with the sound of a champagne cork."

"You can't get much more basic than that. In the words of another man, I think I believe you."

"*Believe,* sir. I am only a courier—an expensive one, perhaps—but a courier, nevertheless."

"Your waiters are something else, I'm told."

"They have not been noticeably observant."

"You'll still accompany me to the door," he had said.

And now there was the third name, a third man, in the downpour at Repulse Bay.

The contact had responded to the code: *"Écoutez, monsieur. 'Cain is for Delta and Carlos is for Cain.' "*

"We were to meet in Macao!" the man had shrieked over the telephone. "Where *were* you?"

"Busy," said Jason.

"You may be too late. My client has very little time and he is very knowledgeable. He hears that your man moves elsewhere. He is disturbed. You promised him, Frenchman!"

"Where does he think my man is going?"

"On another assignment, of course. He's heard the details!"

"He's wrong. The man is available if the price is met."

"Call me back in several minutes. I will speak to my client and see if matters are to be pursued."

Bourne had called five minutes later. Consent was given, the rendezvous set. Repulse Bay. One hour. The statue of the war god halfway down the beach on the left toward the pier. The contact would wear a black kerchief around his neck; the code was to remain the same.

Jason looked at his watch; it was twelve minutes past the hour. The contact was late, and the rain was not a problem—on the contrary, it was an advantage, a natural cover. Bourne had scouted every foot of the meeting

ground, forty feet in every direction that had a sight line
to the statue of the idol, and he had done so after the
appointed time, using up minutes as he kept his eyes on
the path to the statue. Nothing so far was irregular.
There was no trap in the making.

The *Zhongguo ren* came into view, his shoulders
hunched as he dashed down the steps in the downpour,
as if the shape of his body would ward off the rain. He ran
along the path toward the statue of the war god and
stopped as he approached the huge, snarling idol. He
skirted the wash of the floodlights, but what could briefly
be seen of his face conveyed his anger at finding no one
in sight.

"Frenchman, *Frenchman!*"

Bourne raced back through the foliage toward the
steps, checking once more before rendezvous, reducing
his vulnerability. He edged his way around the thick
stone post that bordered the steps and peered through
the rain at the upper path to the hotel. He saw what he
hoped to God he would *not* see! A man in a raincoat and
hat came out of the run-down Colonial Hotel and broke
into a fast walk. Halfway to the steps he stopped, pulling
something out of his pocket; he turned; there was a slight
glow of light . . . returned instantly by a corresponding
tiny flash at one of the windows of the crowded lobby.
Penlights. Signals. A scout was on his way to a forward
post, as his relay or his backup confirmed communications. Jason spun around and retraced the path he had
made through the drenched foliage.

"*Frenchman,* where *are* you?"

"Over here!"

"Why did you not answer? *Where?*"

"Straight ahead. The bushes in front of you. *Hurry up!*"

The contact approached the foliage; he was an arm's
length away. Bourne sprang up and grabbed him, spinning him around and pushing him further into the wet
bushes, as he did so clamping his left hand over the man's
mouth. "If you want to live, don't make a sound!"

Thirty feet into the shoreline woods, Jason slammed
the contact into the trunk of a tree. "Who's with you?"
he asked harshly, slowly removing his hand from the
man's mouth.

"*With* me? *No* one is with me!"

"Don't *lie!*" Bourne pulled out his gun and placed it against the contact's throat. The Chinese crashed his head back into the tree, his eyes wide, his mouth gaping. "I don't have time for traps!" continued Jason. "I don't have *time!*"

"And there is no one *with* me! My word in these matters is my livelihood! Without it I have no profession!"

Bourne stared at the man. He put the gun back in his belt, gripped the contact's arm and propelled him to the right. "Be quiet. Come with me."

Ninety seconds later Jason and the contact had crawled through the soaking wet underbrush toward an area of the path some twenty-odd feet to the west of the massive idol. The downpour covered whatever noises might have been picked up on a dry night. Suddenly, Bourne grabbed the Oriental's shoulder, stopping him. Up ahead the scout could be seen, crouching, hugging the border of the path, a gun in his hand. For a moment he crossed through a wash of the statue's floodlight before he disappeared; it was only for an instant, but it was enough. Bourne looked at the contact.

The Chinese was stunned. He could not take his eyes off the spot in the light where the scout had crossed through. His thoughts were coming to him rapidly, the terror in him building; it was in his stare. "*Shi,*" he whispered. "*Jiagian!*"

"In short English words," said Jason, speaking through the rain. "That man's an executioner?"

"*Shi!* . . . Yes."

"Tell me, what have you brought me?"

"Everything," answered the contact, still in shock. "The first money, the instructions . . . everything."

"A client doesn't send money if he's going to kill the man he's hiring."

"I know," said the contact softly, nodding his head and closing his eyes. "It is me they want to kill."

His words to Liang on the harbor walk had been prophetic, thought Bourne. "*It's not a trap for me. . . . It's for you. . . . You did your job and they can't allow any traces. . . . They can't afford you any longer.*"

"There's another up at the hotel. I saw them signaling

each other with flashlights. It's why I couldn't answer you
for several minutes."

The Oriental turned and looked at Jason; there was no
self-pity in his eyes. "The risks of my profession," he said
simply. "As my foolish people say, I will join my ancestors, and I hope they are not so foolish. Here." The
contact reached into his inside pocket and withdrew an
envelope. "Here is everything."

"Have you checked it out?"

"Only the money. It's all there. I would not meet with
the Frenchman with less than his demands, and the rest
I do not care to know." Suddenly the man looked hard
at Bourne, blinking his eyes in the downpour. "But you
are *not* the Frenchman!"

"Easy," said Jason. "Things have come pretty fast for
you tonight."

"Who *are* you?"

"Someone who just showed you where you stood. How
much money did you bring?"

"Thirty thousand American dollars."

"If that's the first payment, the target must be someone impressive."

"I assume he is."

"Keep it."

"*What?* What are you *saying?*"

"I'm not the Frenchman, remember?"

"I do not understand."

"I don't even want the instructions. I'm sure someone
of your professional caliber can turn them to your advantage. A man pays well for information that can help him;
he pays a hell of a lot more for his life."

"Why would you *do* this?"

"Because none of it concerns me. I have only one
concern. I want the man who calls himself Bourne and I
can't waste time. You've got what I just offered you plus
a dividend—I'll get you out of here alive if I have to leave
two corpses here in the Bay, I don't care. But you've got
to give me what I asked for on the phone. You said your
client told you the Frenchman's assassin was going someplace else. *Where?* Where is *Bourne?*"

"You talk so rapidly—"

"I told you, I haven't *time!* Tell me! If you refuse, I
leave and your client kills you. Take your choice."

"Shenzen," said the contact, as if frightened at the name.

"China? There's a target in *Shenzen?"*

"One can assume that. My wealthy client has sources in Queen's Road."

"What's that?"

"The consulate of the People's Republic. A very unusual visa was granted. Apparently it was cleared on the highest authority in Beijing. The source did not know why, and when he questioned the decision he was promptly removed from the section. He reported this to my client. For money, of course."

"Why was the visa unusual?"

"Because there was no waiting period and the applicant did not appear at the consulate. Both are unheard of."

"Still, it was just a visa."

"In the People's Republic there is no such thing as 'just a visa.' Especially not for a white male traveling alone under a questionable passport issued in Macao."

"Macao?"

"Yes."

"What's the entry date?"

"Tomorrow. The Lo Wu border."

Jason studied the contact. "You said your client has sources in the consulate. Do you?"

"What you are thinking will cost a great deal of money, for the risk is very great."

Bourne raised his head and looked through the sheets of rain at the floodlit idol beyond. There was movement; the scout was searching for his target. "Wait here," he said.

The early morning train from Kowloon to the Lo Wu border took barely over an hour. The realization that he was in China took less than ten seconds.

Long Live the People's Republic!

There was no need for the exclamation point, the border guards lived it. They were rigid, staring, and abusive, pummeling passports with their rubber stamps with the fury of hostile adolescents. There was, however, an ameliorating support system. Beyond the guards a phalanx of young women in uniform stood smiling behind several long tables stacked with pamphlets extolling the beauty and virtues of their land and its system. If there was hypocrisy in their postures, it did not show.

Bourne had paid the betrayed, marked contact the sum of $7,000 for the visa. It was good for five days. The purpose of the visit was listed as "business investments in the Economic Zone," and was renewable at Shenzen immigration with proof of investment along with the corroborating presence of a Chinese banker through whom the money was to be brokered. In gratitude, and for no additional charge, the contact had given him the name of a Shenzen banker who could easily steer "Mr. Cruett" to investment possibilities, the said Mr. Cruett being still registered at the Regent Hotel in Hong Kong. Finally, there was a bonus from the man whose life he had saved in Repulse Bay: the description of the man traveling under a Macao passport across the Lo Wu border. He was "6′ 1″ tall, 185 lbs., white skin, light brown hair." Jason had stared at the information, unconsciously recalling the data on his own government ID card. It had read: "HT: 6′ 1″ WT: 187 lbs. White Male. Hair: Lt. Brn." An odd sense of fear spread through him. Not the fear of confrontation; he wanted that, above all, for he wanted Marie back above everything. Instead, it was the horror that he was responsible for the creation of a monster. A stalker of death that came from a lethal virus he had perfected in the laboratory of his mind and body.

It had been the first train out of Kowloon, occupied in the main by skilled labor and the executive personnel permitted—enticed—into the Free Economic Zone of Shenzen by the People's Republic in hopes of attracting foreign investments. At each stop on the way to the border, as more and more passengers boarded, Bourne had walked through the cars, his eyes resting for an intense instant on each of the white males, of whom there was a total of only fourteen by the time they reached Lo Wu. None had even vaguely fit the description of the man from Macao—the description of himself. The new "Jason Bourne" would be taking a later train. The original would wait on the other side of the border. He waited now.

During the four hours that passed he explained sixteen times to inquiring border personnel that he was waiting for a business associate; he had obviously misunderstood the schedule and had taken a far too early train. As with people in any foreign country, but especially in the Orient, the fact that a courteous American had gone to the trouble of making himself understood in their language was decidedly beneficial. He was offered four cups of coffee, seven hot teas, and two of the uniformed girls had giggled as they presented him with an overly sweet Chinese ice cream cone. He accepted all—to do otherwise would have been rude, and since most of the Gang of Four had lost not only their faces but their heads, rudeness was out, except for the border guards.

It was 11:10. The passengers emerged through the long, fenced open-air corridor after dealing with immigration—mostly tourists, mostly white, mostly bewildered and awed to be there. The majority were in small tour groups, accompanied by guides—one each from Hong Kong and the People's Republic—who spoke acceptable English, or German, or French and, reluctantly, Japanese for those particularly disliked visitors with more money than Marx or Confucius ever had. Jason studied each white male. The many that were over six feet in height were too young or too old or too portly or too slender or too obvious in their lime-green and lemon-yellow trousers to be the man from Macao.

Wait! Over there! An older man in a tan gabardine suit who appeared to be a medium-sized tourist with a limp was suddenly taller—and the limp was gone! He walked rapidly down the steps through the middle of the crowd and ran into the huge parking lot filled with buses and tour vans and a few taxis, each with a ZHAN—off-duty—posted in the front windows. Bourne raced after the man, dodging between the bodies in front of him, not caring whom he pushed aside. *It was the man—the man from Macao!*

"Hey, are you crazy? Ralph, he shoved me!"

"Shove back. What do you want from me?"

"Do something!"

"He's gone."

The man in the gabardine suit jumped into the open door of a van, a dark green van with tinted windows that according to the Chinese characters belonged to a department called the Chutang Bird Sanctuary. The door slid shut and the vehicle instantly broke away from its parking space and careened around the other vehicles into the exit lane. Bourne was frantic; he could not let him go! An old taxi was on his right, the motor idling. He pulled the door open, to be greeted by a shout.

"*Zhan!*" screamed the driver.

"*Shi ma?*" roared Jason, pulling enough American money from his pocket to insure five years of luxury in the People's Republic.

"*Aiya!*"

"*Zou!*" ordered Bourne, leaping into the front seat and pointing to the van, which had swerved into the semicircle. "Stay with him and you can start your own business in the zone," he said in Cantonese. "I *promise* you!"

Marie, I'm so close! I know it's him! I'll take him! He's mine now! He's our deliverance!

The van sped out of the exit road, heading south at the first intersection, avoiding the large square jammed with tour buses and crowds of sightseers cautiously avoiding the endless stream of bicycles in the streets. The taxi driver picked up the van on a primitive highway paved more with hard clay than asphalt. The dark-windowed vehicle could be seen up ahead entering a long curve in front of an open truck carrying heavy farm machinery. A tour bus waited at the end of the curve, swinging into the road behind the truck.

Bourne looked beyond the van; there were hills up ahead and the road began to rise. Then another tour bus appeared, this one behind them.

"*Shumchun,*" said the driver.

"*Bin do?*" asked Jason.

"The Shumchun water supply," answered the driver in Chinese. "A very beautiful reservoir, one of the finest lakes in all China. It sends its water south to Kowloon and Hong Kong. Very crowded with visitors this time of year. The autumn views are excellent."

Suddenly the van accelerated, climbing the mountain road, pulling away from the truck and the tour bus. "Can't you go faster? Get around the bus, that truck!"

"Many curves ahead."

"Try it!"

The driver pressed his foot to the floor and swerved

around the bus, missing its bulging front by inches as he was forced back in line by an approaching army half-track with two soldiers in the cabin. Both the soldiers and the tour guides yelled at them through open windows. "Sleep with your ugly mothers!" screamed the driver, full of his moment of triumph, only to be faced with the wide truck filled with farm machinery blocking the way.

They were going into a sharp right curve. Bourne gripped the window and leaned out as far as he could for a clearer view. "There's no one coming!" he yelled at the driver through the onrushing wind. "Go ahead! You can get around. *Now!*"

The driver did so, pushing the old taxi to its limits, the tires spinning on a stretch of hard clay, which made the cab sideslip dangerously in front of the truck. Another curve, now sharply to the left, and rising steeper. Ahead the road was straight, ascending a high hill. The van was nowhere to be seen; it had disappeared over the crest of the hill.

"*Kuai!*" shouted Bourne. "Can't you make this damn thing go faster?"

"It has never been this fast! I think the fuck-fuck spirits will explode the motor! Then what will I do? It took me five years to buy this unholy machine, and many unholy bribes to drive in the Zone!"

Jason threw a handful of bills on the floor of the cab by the driver's feet. "There's ten times more if we catch that van! Now, *go.*"

The taxi soared over the top of the hill, descending swiftly into an enormous glen at the edge of a vast lake that seemed to extend for miles. In the distance Bourne could see snow-capped mountains and green islands dotting the blue-green water as far as the eye could see. The taxi came to a halt beside a large red and gold pagoda reached by a long, polished concrete staircase. Its open balconies overlooked the lake. Refreshment stands and curio shops were scattered about on the borders of the parking lot, where four tour buses were standing with the dual guides shouting instructions and pleading with their charges not to get in the wrong vehicles at the end of their walks.

The dark-windowed van was nowhere to be seen.

Bourne shifted his head swiftly, looking in all directions. Where *was* it? "What's that road over there?" he asked the driver.

"Pump stations. No one is permitted down that road, it is patrolled by the army. Around the bend is a high fence and a guardhouse."

"Wait here." Jason climbed out of the cab and started walking toward the prohibited road, wishing he had a camera or a guidebook—something to mark him as a tourist. As it was, the best he could do was to assume the hesitant walk and wide-eyed expression of a sightseer. No object was too insignificant for his inspection. He approached the bend in the badly paved road; he saw the high fence and part of the guardhouse—then all of it. A long metal bar fell across the road, two soldiers were talking, their backs to him, looking the other way—looking at two vehicles parked side by side farther down by a square concrete structure painted brown. One of the vehicles was the dark-windowed van, the other the brown sedan. The van began to move. It was heading back to the gate!

Bourne's thoughts came rapidly. He had no weapon; it was pointless even to consider carrying one across the border. If he tried to stop the van and drag the killer out, the commotion would bring the guards, their rifle fire swift and accurate. Therefore he had to draw the man from Macao out—of *his* own volition. The rest Jason was primed for; he would take the impostor one way or another. Take him back to the border and crossing over—one way or another. No man was a match for him; no eyes, no throat, no groin safe from an assault, swift and agonizing. David Webb had never come to grips with that reality. Bourne lived it.

There *was* a way!

Jason ran back to the beginning of the deserted bend in the road, beyond the view of the gate and the soldiers. He reassumed the pose of the mesmerized sightseer and listened. The van's engine fell to idle; the creaking meant the gate was being lifted. Only moments now. Bourne held his position in the brush by the side of the road. The van rounded the turn as he timed his moves.

He was suddenly there, in front of the large vehicle, his expression terrified, as he spun to the side below the driver's window and slammed the flat of his hand into the door, uttering a cry of pain as if he had been struck, perhaps killed, by the van. He lay supine on the ground as the vehicle came to a stop; the driver leaped out, an innocent about to protest his innocence. He had no chance to do so. Jason's arm was extended; he yanked the man by the ankle, pulling him off his feet, and sending his head crashing back into the side of the van. The driver fell unconscious, and Bourne dragged him back to the rear of the van beneath the clouded windows. He saw a bulge in the man's jacket; it was a gun, predictably, considering his cargo. Jason removed it and waited for the man from Macao.

He did not appear. It was not logical.

Bourne scrambled to the front of the van, gripped the rubberized ledge to the driver's seat, and lunged up, his weapon at the ready, sweeping the rear seats from side to side.

No one. It was empty.

He climbed back out and went to the driver, spat in his face and slapped him into consciousness.

"Nali?" he whispered harshly. "Where is the man who was in here?"

"Back there!" replied the driver, in Cantonese, shaking his head. "In the official car with a man nobody knows. Spare my terrible life! I have seven children!"

"Get up in the seat," said Bourne, pulling the man to his feet and pushing him to the open door. "Drive out of here as fast as you can."

No other advice was necessary. The van shot out of the Shumchun reservoir area, careening around the curve into the main exit at such speed that Jason thought it would go over the bank. *A man nobody knows.* What did that mean? No matter, the man from Macao was trapped. He was in a brown sedan inside the gate on the forbidden road. Bourne raced back to the taxi and climbed into the front seat; the scattered money had been removed from the floor.

"You are satisfied?" said the cabdriver. "I will have ten times what you dropped on my unworthy feet?"

"Cut it, Charlie Chan! A car's going to come out of that road to the pump station and you're going to do exactly what I tell you. Do you understand me?"

"Do you understand ten times the amount you left in my ancient, undistinguished taxi?"

"I understand. It could be fifteen times if you do your job. Come on, *move.* Get over to the edge of the parking lot. I don't know how long we'll have to wait."

"Time is money, sir."

"Oh, shut up!"

The wait was roughly twenty minutes. The brown sedan appeared, and Bourne saw what he had not seen before. The windows were tinted darker than those of the van; whoever was inside was invisible. Then Jason heard the very last words he wanted to hear.

"Take your money back," said the driver quietly. "I will return you to Lo Wu. I have never seen you."

"Why?"

"That is a government car—one of our government's official vehicles—and I will not be the one who follows it."

"Wait a minute! Just—wait a minute. *Twenty* times what I gave you, with a bonus if it all comes out all right! Until I say otherwise you can stay way behind him. I'm just a tourist who wants to look around. No, wait! Here, I'll show you! My visa says I'm investing money. Investors are permitted to look around!"

"Twenty times?" said the driver, staring at Jason. "What guarantee do I have that you will fulfill your promise?"

"I'll put it on the seat between us. You're driving; you could do a lot of things with this car I wouldn't be prepared for. I won't try to take it back."

"Good! But I stay far behind. I know these roads. There are only certain places one can travel."

Thirty-five minutes later, with the brown sedan still in sight but far ahead, the driver spoke again. "They go to the airfield."

"What airfield?"

"It is used by government officials and men with money from the south."

"People investing in factories, industry?"

"This is the Economic Zone."

"I'm an investor," said Bourne. "My visa says so. Hurry up! *Close* in!"

"There are five vehicles between us, and we agreed—I stay far behind."

"Until I said otherwise! It's different now. I have money. I'm investing in China!"

"We will be stopped at the gate. Telephone calls will be made."

"I've got the name of a banker in Shenzen!"

"Does he have your name, sir? And a list of the Chinese firms you are dealing with? If so, you may do the talking at the gate. But if this banker in Shenzen does not know you, you will be detained for giving false information. Your stay in China would be for as long as it took to thoroughly investigate you. Weeks, months."

"I have to reach that car!"

"You approach that car, you will be shot."

"*Goddamn it!*" shouted Jason in English, then instantly reverting to Chinese: "Listen to me. I don't have time to explain, but I've got to *see* him!"

"This is not my business," said the driver coldly, warily.

"Get in line and drive up to the gate," ordered Bourne. "I'm a fare you picked up in Lo Wu, that's all. I'll do the talking."

"You ask too much! I will not be seen with someone like you."

"Just do it," said Jason, pulling the gun from his belt.

The pounding in his chest was unbearable as Bourne stood by a large window looking out on the airfield. The terminal was small and for privileged travelers. The incongruous sight of casual Western businessmen carrying attaché cases and tennis rackets unnerved Jason because of the stark contrast to the uniformed guards, standing about rigidly. Oil and water were apparently compatible.

Speaking English to the interpreter, who translated accurately for the officer of the guard, he had claimed to be a bewildered executive instructed by the consulate on Queen's Road in Hong Kong to come to the airport to meet an official flying in from Beijing. He had misplaced the official's name, but they had met briefly at the State Department in Washington and would recognize each other. He implied that the present meeting was looked

upon with great favor by important men on the Central
Committee. He was given a pass restricting him to the
terminal, and lastly, he asked if the taxi could be permitted to remain in case transportation was needed later.
The request was granted.

"If you want your money, you'll stay," he had said to
the driver in Cantonese as he picked up the folded bills
between them.

"You have a gun and angry eyes. You will kill."

Jason had stared at the driver. "The last thing on earth
I want to do is kill the man in that car. I would only kill
to protect his life."

The brown sedan with the dark, opaque windows was
nowhere in the parking area. Bourne walked as rapidly as
he thought acceptable into the terminal, to the window
where he stood now, his temples exploding with anger
and frustration, for outside on the field he saw the government car. It was parked on the tarmac not fifty feet
away from him, but an impenetrable wall of glass separated him from it—and deliverance. Suddenly the sedan
shot forward toward a medium-sized jet several hundred
yards north on the runway. Bourne strained his eyes,
wishing to Christ he had binoculars! Then he realized
they would have been useless; the car swung around the
tail of the plane and out of sight.

Goddamn it!

Within seconds the jet began rolling to the foot of the
runway as the brown sedan swerved and raced back toward the parking area and the exit.

What could he *do? I can't be left this way! He's there! He's
me and he's there! He's getting away!* Bourne ran to the first
counter and assumed the attitude of a terribly distraught
man.

"The plane that's about to take off! I'm supposed to be
on it! It's going to Shanghai and the people in Beijing
said I was to be *on* it! *Stop* it!"

The clerk behind the counter picked up her telephone.
She dialed quickly, then exhaled through her tight lips in
relief. "That is not your plane, sir," she said. "It flies to
Guangdong."

"Where?"

"The Macao border, sir."

"Never! It must not be Macao!" the taipan had screamed.

. . . *"The order will be swift, the execution swifter! Your wife will die!"*

Macao. Table Five. The Kam Pek casino.

"If he heads for Macao," McAllister had said quietly, *"he could be a terrible liability. . . ."*

"Termination?"

"I can't use that word."

14

"You will *not,* you *cannot* tell me this!" shouted Edward Newington McAllister, leaping out of his chair. "It's *unacceptable!* I can't handle it. I won't *hear* of it!"

"You'd better, Edward," said Major Lin Wenzu. "It happened."

"It's my fault," added the English doctor, standing in front of the desk in the Victoria Peak, facing the American. "Every symptom she exhibited led to a prognosis of rapid, neurological deterioration. Loss of concentration and visual focus; no appetite and a commensurate drop in weight—most significantly, spasms when there was a complete lack of motor controls. I honestly thought the degenerative process had reached a negative crisis—"

"What the hell does *that* mean?"

"That she was dying. Oh, not in a matter of hours or even days or weeks, but that the course was irreversible."

"Could you have been right?"

"I would like nothing better than to conclude that I was, that my diagnosis was at least reasonable, but I can't. Simply put, I was dragooned."

"You were *hit?*"

"Figuratively, yes. Where it hurts the most, Mr. Under-secretary. My professional pride. That bitch fooled me with a carnival act, and she probably doesn't know the difference between a femur and a fever. Everything she did was calculated, from her appeals to the nurse to clubbing and disrobing the guard. All her moves were planned and the only disorder was mine."

"Christ, I've got to reach Havilland!"

"*Ambassador* Havilland?" asked Lin, his eyebrows arched.

McAllister looked at him. "Forget you heard that."

"I will not repeat it, but I can't forget. Things are clearer, London's clearer. You're talking General Staff and Overlord and a large part of Olympus."

"Don't mention that name to anyone, Doctor," said McAllister.

"I've quite forgotten it. I'm not sure I even know who he is."

"What can I say? What are you *doing*?"

"Everything humanly possible," answered the major. "We've divided Hong Kong and Kowloon up into sections. We're questioning every hotel, thoroughly examining their registrations. We've alerted the police and the marine patrols; all personnel have copies of her description and have been instructed that finding her is the territory's priority concern—"

"My God, what did you *say*? How did you explain?"

"I was able to help here," said the doctor. "In light of my stupidity it was the least I could do. I issued a medical alert. By doing so, we were able to enlist the help of paramedic teams who've been sent out from all the hospitals, staying in radio contact for other emergencies, of course. They're scouring the streets."

"What kind of medical alert?" asked McAllister sharply.

"Minimum information, but the sort that creates a stir. The woman was known to have visited an unnamed island in the Luzon Strait that is off limits to international travelers for reasons of a rampant disease transmitted by unclean eating utensils."

"Categorizing it as such," interrupted Lin, "our good doctor removed any hesitation on the part of the teams to approach her and take her into custody. Not that they would, but every basket has its less than perfect fruit and we cannot afford any. I honestly believe we'll find her, Edward. We all know she stands out in a crowd. Tall, attractive, that hair of hers—and over a thousand people looking for her."

"I hope to God you're right. But I worry. She received her first training from a chameleon," said McAllister.

"I beg your pardon?"

"It's nothing, Doctor," said the major. "A technical term in our business."

"Oh?"

"I've got to have the entire file, *all* of it!"

"What, Edward?"

"They were hunted together in Europe. Now they're apart, but still hunted. What did they do then? What will they do now?"

"A thread? A pattern?"

"It's always there," said McAllister, rubbing his right temple. "Excuse me, gentlemen, I must ask you to leave. I have a dreadful call to make."

Marie bartered clothes and paid a few dollars for others. The result was acceptable: with her hair pulled back under a floppy wide-brimmed sun hat, she was a plain-looking woman in a pleated skirt and a nondescript gray blouse that concealed any outline of a figure. The flat sandals lowered her height and the ersatz Gucci purse marked her as a gullible tourist in Hong Kong, exactly what she was not. She called the Canadian consulate and was told how to get there by bus. The offices were in the Asian House, fourteenth floor, Hong Kong. She took the bus from the Chinese University through Kowloon and the tunnel over to the island; she watched the streets carefully and got off at her stop. She rode up in the elevator, satisfied that none of the men riding with her gave her a second glance; that was not the usual reaction. She had learned in Paris—taught by a chameleon—how to use the simple things to change herself. The lessons were coming back to her.

"I realize this will sound ridiculous," she said in a casual, humorously bewildered voice to the receptionist, "but a second cousin of mine on my mother's side is posted here and I promised to look him up."

"That doesn't sound ridiculous to me."

"It will when I tell you I've forgotten his name." Both women laughed. "Of course, we've never met and he'd probably like to keep it that way, but then I'd have to answer to the family back home."

"Do you know what section he's in?"

"Something to do with economics, I believe."

"That would be the Division of Trade most likely." The receptionist opened a drawer and pulled out a narrow white booklet with the Canadian flag embossed on the cover. "Here's our directory. Why don't you sit down and look through it?"

"Thanks very much," said Marie, going to a leather armchair and sitting down. "I have this terrible feeling of inadequacy," she added, opening the directory. "I mean I *should* know his name. I'm sure *you* know the name of your second cousin on your mother's side of the family."

"Honey, I haven't the vaguest." The receptionist's phone rang; she answered it.

Turning the pages, Marie read quickly, scanning down the columns looking for a name that would evoke a face. She found three, but the images were fuzzy, the features not clear. Then on the twelfth page, a face *and* a voice leaped up at her as she read the name. *Catherine Staples.*

"Cool" Catherine, "Ice-cold" Catherine, "Stick" Staples. The nicknames were unfair and did not give an accurate picture or appraisal of the woman. Marie had gotten to know Catherine Staples during her days with the Treasury Board in Ottawa when she and others in her section briefed the diplomatic corps prior to their overseas assignments. Staples had come through twice, once for a refresher course on the European Common Market . . . the second, *of course,* for Hong Kong! It was thirteen or fourteen months ago, and although their friendship could not be called deep—four or five lunches, a dinner that Catherine had prepared, and one reciprocated by Marie—she had learned quite a bit about the woman who did her job better than most men.

To begin with, her rapid advancement at the Department of External Affairs had cost her an early marriage. She had forsworn the marital state for the rest of her life, she declared, as the demands of travel and the insane hours of her job were unacceptable to any man worth having. In her mid-fifties, Staples was a slender, energetic woman of medium height, who dressed fashionably but simply. She was a no-nonsense professional with a sardonic wit that conveyed her dislike of cant, which she saw through swiftly, and self-serving excuses, which she would not tolerate. She could be kind, even gentle, with men and women unqualified for the work they were assigned through no fault of their own, but brutal with those who had issued such assignments, regardless of rank. If there was a phrase that summed up Senior Foreign Service Officer Catherine Staples, it was "tough but fair"; also, she was frequently very amusing in a self-deprecating way. Marie hoped she would be fair in Hong Kong.

"There's nothing here that rings a bell," said Marie, getting out of the chair and bringing the directory back to the receptionist. "I feel so stupid."

"Do you have any idea what he looks like?"

"I never thought to ask."

"I'm sorry."

"I'm sorrier. I'll have to place a very embarrassing call to Vancouver. . . . Oh, I did see one name. It has nothing to do with my cousin, but I think she's a friend of a friend. A woman named Staples."

" 'Catherine the Great'? She's here, all right, although a few of the staff wouldn't mind seeing her promoted to ambassador and sent to Eastern Europe. She makes them nervous. She's topflight."

"Oh, you mean she's here now?"

"Not thirty feet away. You want to give me your friend's name and see if she has time to say hello?"

Marie was tempted, but the onus of officialdom prohibited the shortcut. If things were as Marie thought they were and alarms had been sent out to friendly consulates, Staples might feel compelled to cooperate. She probably would not, but she had the integrity of her office to uphold. Embassies and consulates constantly sought favors from one another. She needed time with Catherine, and not in an official setting. "That's very nice of you," Marie said to the receptionist. "My friend would get a kick out of it. . . . Wait a minute. Did you say *'Catherine'*?"

"Yes. Catherine Staples. Believe me, there's only one."

"I'm sure there is, but my friend's friend is Christine. Oh, Lord, this isn't my day. You've been very kind, so I'll get out of your hair and leave you in peace."

"You've been a pleasure, hon. You should see the ones who come in here thinking they bought a Cartier watch for a hell of a good price until it stops and a jeweler tells them the insides are two rubber bands and a miniature yo-yo." The receptionist's eyes dropped to the Gucci purse with the inverted *G*'s. "Oh, oh," she said softly.

"What?"

"Nothing. Good luck with your phone call."

Marie waited in the lobby of the Asian House for as long as she felt comfortable, then went outside and walked back and forth in front of the entrance for nearly an hour in the crowded street. It was shortly past noon, and she wondered if Catherine even bothered to have lunch—lunch would be a very good idea. Also, there was another possibility, an impossibility perhaps, but one she could pray for, if she still knew how to pray. David might appear, but it would not be as David, it would be as Jason Bourne, and that could be anyone. Her husband in the guises of Bourne would be far more clever; she had seen his inventiveness in Paris and it was from another world, a lethal world where a misstep could cost a person his life. Every move was premeditated in three or four dimensions. What if I . . . ? What if he . . . ? The intellect played a far greater role in the violent world than the nonviolent intellectuals would ever admit—their brains would be blown away in a world they scorned as barbarian because they could not think fast enough or deeply enough. *Cogito ergo* nothing. Why was she thinking these things? She belonged to the latter and so did David! And then the answer was very clear. They had been thrown back; they had to survive and find each other.

There she *was!* Catherine Staples walked—marched—out of the Asian House and turned right. She was roughly forty feet away; Marie started running, pummeling off bodies in her path as she tried to catch up. *Try never to run, it marks you.* I don't care! I must talk to her!

Staples cut across the pavement. There was a consulate car, with the maple-leaf insignia printed on the door, waiting for her at the curb. She was climbing inside.

"No! *Wait!*" shouted Marie, crashing through the crowd, grabbing the door as Catherine was about to close it.

"I *beg* your pardon?" cried Staples, as the chauffeur spun around in his seat, a gun appearing out of nowhere.

"*Please!* It's *me!* Ottawa. The briefings."

"*Marie?* Is that *you?*"

"Yes. I'm in trouble and I need your help."

"Get in," said Catherine Staples, moving over on the seat. "Put that silly thing away," she ordered the driver. "This is a friend of mine."

Canceling her scheduled lunch on the pretext of a summons from the British delegation—a common occurrence during the round-robin conferences with the People's Republic over the 1997 treaty—Foreign Service Officer Staples instructed the driver to drop them off at the beginning of Food Street in Causeway Bay. Food Street encompassed the crushing spectacle of some thirty restaurants within the stretch of two blocks. Traffic was prohibited on the street and even if it was not, there was no way motorized transport could make its way through the mass of humanity in search of some four thousand tables. Catherine led Marie to the service entrance of a restaurant. She rang the bell, and fifteen seconds later the door opened, followed by the wafting odors of a hundred Oriental dishes.

"Miss Staples, how good to see you," said the Chinese dressed in the white apron of a chef—one of many chefs. "Please-please. As always, there is a table for you."

As they walked through the chaos of the large kitchen, Catherine turned to Marie. "Thank God there are a few perks left in this miserably underpaid profession. The owner has relatives in Quebec—damn fine restaurant on St. John Street—and I make sure his visa gets processed, as they say, 'damn-damn quick.' "

Catherine nodded at one of the few empty tables in the rear section; it was near the kitchen door. They were seated, literally concealed by the stream of waiters rushing in and out of the swinging doors, as well as by the continuous bustle taking place at the scores of tables throughout the crowded restaurant.

"Thank you for thinking of a place like this," said Marie.

"My dear," replied Staples in her throaty, adamant voice. "Anyone with your looks who dresses the way you're dressed now, and makes up the way you're made up, doesn't care to draw attention to herself."

"As they say, that's putting it mildly. Will your lunch date accept the British delegation story?"

"Without a thought to the contrary. The mother country is marshaling its most persuasive forces. Beijing buys enormous quantities of much needed wheat from us—but then you know that as well as I do, and probably a lot more in terms of dollars and cents."

"I'm not very current these days."

"Yes, I understand." Staples nodded, looking sternly yet kindly at Marie, her eyes questioning. "I was over here by then, but we heard the rumors and read the European papers. To say we were in shock can't describe the way those of us who knew you felt. In the weeks that followed we all tried to get answers, but we were told to let it alone, drop it—for *your* sake. 'Don't pursue it,' they kept saying. 'It's in her best interests to stay away.' . . . Of course, we finally heard that you were exonerated of all charges—*Christ,* what an insulting phrase after what you were put through! Then you just faded, and no one heard anything more about you."

"They told you the truth, Catherine. It *was* in my interest—our interests—to stay away. For months we were kept hidden, and when we took up our civilized lives again it was in a fairly remote area and under a name few people knew. The guards, however, were still in place."

"We?"

"I married the man you read about in the papers. Of course, he wasn't the man *described* in the papers; he was in deep cover for the American government. He gave up a great deal of his life for that awfully strange commitment."

"And now you're in Hong Kong and you tell me you're in trouble."

"I'm in Hong Kong and I'm in serious trouble."

"May I assume that the events of the past year are related to your current difficulties?"

"I believe they are."

"What can you tell me?"

"Everything I know because I want your help. I have no right to ask it unless you know everything I know."

"I like succinct language. Not only for its clarity but because it usually defines the person delivering it. You're also saying that unless I know everything I probably can't do anything."

"I hadn't thought of it that way, but you're probably right."

"Good. I was testing you. In the *nouvelle diplomatie*, overt simplicity has become both a cover and a tool. It's frequently used to obscure duplicity, as well as to disarm an adversary. I refer you to the recent proclamations of your new country—new as a wife, of course."

"I'm an economist, Catherine, not a diplomat."

"Combine the talents that I know you have, and you could scale the heights in Washington as you would have in Ottawa. But then you wouldn't have the obscurity you so desire in your regained civilized life."

"We *must* have that. It's all that matters. I don't."

"Testing again. You were not without ambition. You love that husband of yours."

"Very much. I want to find him. I want him back."

Staples's head snapped as her eyes blinked. "He's *here?*"

"Somewhere. It's part of the story."

"Is it complicated?"

"Very."

"Can you hold back—and I *mean* that, Marie—until we go someplace where it's quieter?"

"I was taught patience by a man whose life depended on it twenty-four hours a day for three years."

"Good God. Are you hungry?"

"Famished. That's also part of the story. As long as you're here and listening to me, may we order?"

"Avoid the *dim sum*, it's oversteamed and overfried. The duck, however, is the best in Hong Kong. . . . *Can* you wait, Marie? Would you rather leave?"

"I can wait, Catherine. My whole life's on hold. A half hour won't make any difference. And if I don't eat I won't be coherent."

"I know. It's part of the story."

They sat opposite each other in Staples's flat, a coffee table between them, sharing a pot of tea.

"I think," said Catherine, "that I've just heard what amounts to the most blatant misuse of office in thirty years of foreign service—on our side, of course. Unless there's a grave misinterpretation."

"You're saying you don't believe me."

"On the contrary, my dear, you couldn't have made it up. You're quite right. The whole damn thing's full of illogical logic."

"I didn't say that."

"You didn't have to, it's there. Your husband is primed, the possibilities implanted, and then he's shot up like a nuclear rocket. *Why?*"

"I told you. There's a man killing people who claims he's Jason Bourne—the role David played for three years."

"A killer's a killer, no matter the name he assumes, whether it's Genghis Khan or Jack the Ripper, or, if you will, Carlos the Jackal—even the assassin Jason Bourne. Traps for such men are planned with the consent of the trappers."

"I don't understand you, Catherine."

"Then listen to me, my dear. This is an old-time mind speaking. Remember when I went to you for the Common Market refresher with the emphasis on Eastern trade?"

"Yes. We cooked dinners for each other. Yours was better than mine."

"Yes, it was. But I was really there to learn how to convince my contacts in the Eastern block that I could use the fluctuating rates of exchange so that purchases made from us would be infinitely more profitable for them. I did it. Moscow was furious."

"Catherine, what the hell has that got to do with me?"

Staples looked at Marie, her gentle demeanor again underlined with firmness. "Let me be clearer. If you thought about it at all, you had to assume that I'd come to Ottawa to gain a firmer grasp of European economics so as to do my job better. In one sense that was true, but it wasn't the real reason. I was actually there to learn how to use the fluctuating rates of the various currencies and offer contracts of the greatest advantage to our potential clients. When the deutsche mark rose, we sold on the franc or the guilder or whatever. It was built into the contracts."

"That was hardly self-serving."

"We weren't looking for profits, we were opening markets that had been closed to us. The profits would come later. You were very clear about exchange rate speculation. You preached its evils, and I had to learn to be something of a devil—for a good cause, of course."

"All right, you picked what brains I have for a purpose I didn't know about—"

"It had to be kept totally secret, obviously."

"But what's it got to do with anything I've told you?"

"I smell a bad piece of meat, and this nose is experienced. Just as I had an ulterior motive to go to you in Ottawa, whoever is doing this to you has a deeper reason than the capture of your husband's impostor."

"Why do you say that?"

"Your husband said it first. This is primarily and quite properly a police matter, even an international police matter for Interpol's highly respected Intelligence network. They're far more qualified for this sort of thing than State Departments or Foreign Offices, CIA's or MI-Six's. Overseas Intelligence branches don't concern themselves with nonpolitical criminals—everyday murderers—they can't afford to. My God, most of those asses would expose whatever covers they'd managed to build if they interfered with police work."

"McAllister said otherwise. He claimed that the best people in U.S. and U.K. Intelligence were working on it. He said the reason was that if this killer who's posing as my husband—what my husband was in people's eyes— murdered a high political figure on either side, or started an underworld war, Hong Kong's status would be in immediate jeopardy. Peking would move quickly and take over, using the pretext of the '97 treaty. 'The Oriental doesn't tolerate a disobedient child'—those were his words."

"Unacceptable and *unbelievable!*" retorted Catherine Staples. "Either your undersecretary is a liar or he has the IQ of a fern! He gave you *every* reason for our Intelligence services to stay *out* of it, to stay absolutely *clean!* Even a hint of covert action would be disastrous. That *could* fire up the wild boys on the Central Committee. Regardless, I don't believe a word he said. London would never permit it, not even the mention of Special Branch's name."

"Catherine, you're wrong. You weren't listening. The man who flew to Washington for the Treadstone file was British, and he *was* MI-Six. Good Lord, he was murdered for that file."

"I heard you before. I simply don't believe it. Above all else, the Foreign Office would insist that this whole mess remain with the police and *only* the police. They wouldn't let MI-Six in the same restaurant with a detective third grade, even on Food Street. Believe me, my dear, I know what I'm talking about. These are very delicate times and *no* time for hanky-panky, especially the sort that has an official Intelligence organization messing around with an assassin. No, you were brought here and your husband was forced to follow for quite another reason."

"For heaven's sake, *what?*" cried Marie, shooting forward in her chair.

"I don't know. There's someone else perhaps."

"*Who?*"

"It's quite beyond me."

Silence. Two highly intelligent minds were pondering the words each had spoken.

"Catherine," said Marie finally. "I accept the logic of everything you say, but you also said everything was rife with illogical logic. Suppose I'm right, that the men who held me were not killers or criminals, but bureaucrats following orders they didn't understand, that *government* was written all over their faces and in their evasive explanations, even in their concern for my comfort and well-being. I know you think that the McAllister I described to you is a liar or a fool, but suppose he's a liar and not a fool? Assuming these things—and I believe them to be true—we're talking about *two* governments acting in concert during these very delicate times. What then?"

"Then there's a disaster in the making," said Senior Foreign Officer Staples quietly.

"And it revolves around my husband?"

"*If* you're right, yes."

"It's possible, isn't it?"

"I don't even want to think about it."

15

Forty miles southwest of Hong Kong, beyond the out islands in the South China Sea, is the peninsula of Macao, a Portuguese colony in ceremonial name only. Its historical origins are in Portugal, but its modern, freewheeling appeal to the international set, with its annual Grand Prix and its gambling and its yachts, is based on the luxuries and life-styles demanded by the wealthy of Europe. Regardless, make no mistake. It is Chinese. The controls are in Peking.

Never! It must not be Macao! The order will be swift, the execution swifter! Your wife will die!

But the assassin was in Macao, and a chameleon had to enter another jungle.

Scanning the faces and peering into the shadowed corners of the small, packed terminal, Bourne moved with the crowd out onto the pier of the Macao hydrofoil, a trip that took roughly an hour. The passengers were divided into three distinct categories: returning residents of the Portuguese colony—in the main Chinese and silent; professional gamblers—a racial mix talking quietly when they talked at all, continually glancing around to size up their competition; and late-night revelers—boisterous tourists, exclusively white, many of them drunk, in oddly shaped hats and loud tropical shirts.

He had left Shenzen and taken the three o'clock train from Lo Wu to Kowloon. The ride was exhausting, his reasoning stunned, his emotions were drained. The impostor-killer had been so close! If only he could have isolated the man from Macao for less than a minute, he could have gotten him out! There were ways. Both their visas were in order; a man doubled up in pain, his throat damaged to the point of speechlessness, could be passed off as a sick man, a diseased man perhaps, an unwelcome visitor whom they would gladly have let go. But it was not to be, not this time. If only he could have *seen* him!

And then there was the startling discovery that this new assassin, this myth that was no myth but a brutal killer, had a connection in the People's Republic. It was profoundly disturbing, for Chinese officials who acknowledged such a man would do so only to use him. It was a complication David did not want. It had nothing to do with Marie and himself, and the two of them were all he cared about. *All* he cared about! Jason Bourne: *Bring in the man from Macao!*

He had gone back to the Peninsula, stopping at the New World Centre to buy a dark, waist-length nylon jacket and a pair of navy blue sneakers with a heavy tread. David Webb's anxiety was overpowering. Jason Bourne planned without consciously having a plan. He ordered a light meal from room service and picked at it as he sat on the bed staring mindlessly at a television news program. Then David lay back on the pillow, briefly closing his eyes, wondering where the words came from: *Rest is a weapon. Don't forget it.* Bourne woke up fifteen minutes later.

Jason had purchased a ticket for the 8:30 run at a booth in the Mass Transit concourse in the Tsim Sha Tsui during the rush hour. To be certain he was not being followed—and he had to be *absolutely* certain—he had taken three separate taxis to within a quarter of a mile of the Macao Ferry pier an hour before departure and walked the rest of the way. He had then entered upon a ritual he had been trained to perform. The memory of that training was clouded, but not the practice. He had melted into the crowds in front of the terminal, dodging, weaving, going from one pocket to another, then abruptly standing motionless on the sidelines, concentrating on the patterns of movement behind him, looking for someone he had seen moments before, a face or a pair of anxious eyes directed at him. There had been no one. Yet Marie's life depended on the certainty, so he had repeated the ritual twice again, ending up inside the dimly lit terminal filled with benches that fronted the dock and the open water. He kept looking for a frantic face, for a head that kept turning, a person spinning in place, intent on finding someone. Again, there had been no one. He was free to leave for Macao. He was on his way there now.

He sat in a rear seat by the window and watched the lights of Hong Kong and Kowloon fade into a glow in the Asian sky. New lights appeared and disappeared as the hydrofoil gathered speed and passed the out islands, islands belonging to China. He imagined uniformed men peering through infrared telescopes and binoculars, not sure what they were looking for but ordered to observe everything. The mountains of the New Territories rose ominously, the moonlight glancing off their peaks and accentuating their beauty, but also saying: *This is where you stop. Beyond here, we are different.* It was not really so. People hawked their goods in the squares of Shenzen. Artisans prospered; farmers butchered their animals and lived as well as the educated classes in Beijing and Shanghai— usually with better housing. China was changing, not fast enough for the West, and certainly it was still a paranoid giant, but withal, thought David Webb, the distended stomachs of children, so prevalent in the China of years ago, were disappearing. Many at the top of the inscrutable political ladder were fat, but few in the fields were starving. There had been progress, mused David, whether much of the world approved of the methods or not.

The hydrofoil decelerated, its hull lowered into the water. It passed through a space between the boulders of a man-made reef illuminated by floodlights. They were in Macao, and Bourne knew what he had to do. He got up, excused himself past his seat companion, and walked up the aisle where a group of Americans, a few standing, the rest sitting, were huddled around their seats, singing an obviously rehearsed rendition of "Mr. Sandman."

> "Boom boom boom boom . . .
> Mr. Sandman, sing me a song
> Boom boom boom boom
> Oh, Mr. Sandman . . ."

They were high, but not drunk, not obstreperous. Another group of tourists, by the sound of their speech German, encouraged the Americans, and at the end of the song applauded.

"*Gut!*"

"*Sehr gut!*"

"*Wunderbar!*"

"*Danke, meine Herren.*" The American standing nearest Jason bowed to the Germans. A brief, friendly conversation followed, the Germans speaking English and the American replying in German.

"That was a touch of home," said Bourne to the American.

"Hey, a *Landsmann!* That song also dates you, pal. Some of those oldies are goldies, right? Say, are you with the group?"

"Which group is that?"

"Honeywell-Porter," answered the man, naming a New York advertising agency Jason recognized as having branches worldwide.

"No, I'm afraid not."

"I didn't think so. There're only about thirty of us, counting the Aussies, and I thought I pretty much knew everybody. Where are you from? My name's Ted Mather. I'm from H.P.'s L.A. office."

"My name's Howard Cruett. No office, I teach, but I'm from Boston."

"Beanburg! Let me show you *your Landsmann,* or is it *Stadtsmann?* Howard, meet Beantown Bernie." Mather bowed again, this time to a man slumped back in the seat by the window, his mouth open, his eyes closed. He was obviously drunk and wore a Red Sox baseball cap. "Don't bother to speak, he can't hear. Bernard the Brain is from our Boston office. You should have seen him three hours ago. J. Press suit, striped tie, pointer in his hand and a dozen charts only he could understand. But I'll say this for him—he kept us awake. I think that's why we all had a few—him too many. What the hell, it's our last night."

"Heading back tomorrow?"

"Late-evening flight. Gives us time to recover."

"Why Macao?"

"A mass itch for the tables. You, too?"

"I thought I'd give them a whirl. Christ, that cap makes me homesick! The Red Sox may take the pennant, and until this trip I hadn't missed a game!"

"And Bernie won't miss his hat!" The advertising man laughed, leaning over and yanking the baseball cap off

Bernard the Brain's head. "Here, Howard, you wear it. You deserve it!"

The hydrofoil docked. Bourne got off and went through immigration with the boys from Honeywell-Porter as one of them. As they descended the steep cement staircase down into the poster-lined terminal, Jason —with the visor of his Red Sox cap angled down and his walk unsteady—spotted a man by the left wall studying the new arrivals. In the man's hand was a photograph, and Bourne knew the face on the photograph was his. He laughed at one of Ted Mather's remarks as he held on to the weaving Beantown Bernie's arm.

Opportunities will present themselves. Recognize them, act on them.

The streets of Macao are almost as garishly lit as those of Hong Kong; what is lacking is the sense of too much humanity in too little space. And what is different—different and anachronistic—are the many buildings on which are fixed blazing modern signs with pulsating Chinese characters. The architecture of these buildings is very old Spanish—Portuguese, to be accurate—but textbook Spanish, Mediterranean in character. It is as if an initial culture had surrendered to the sweeping incursion of another, but refused to yield its first imprimatur, proclaiming the strength of its stone over the gaudy impermanence of colored tubes of glass. History is purposely denied; the empty churches and the ruins of a burnt-out cathedral exist in a strange harmony with overflowing casinos where the dealers and croupiers speak Cantonese and the descendants of the conquerors are rarely seen. It is all fascinating and not a little ominous. It is Macao.

Jason slipped away from the Honeywell-Porter group and found a taxi whose driver must have been trained by watching the annual Macao Grand Prix. He was taken to the Kam Pek casino—over the driver's objections.

"Lisboa for you, not Kam Pek! Kam Pek for Chinee! *Dai sui! Fan-tan!*"

"Kam Pek, *cheng nei,*" said Bourne, adding the Cantonese *please,* but saying no more.

The casino was dark. The air was humid and foul, and the curling smoke that spiraled around the shaded lights above the tables sweet and full and pungent. There was a bar set back away from the games; he went to it and sat down on a stool, lowering his body to lessen his height. He spoke in Chinese, the baseball cap throwing a shadow across his face, which was probably unnecessary, as he could barely read the labels of the bottles on the counter. He ordered a drink, and when it came he gave the bartender a generous tip in Hong Kong money.

"*Mgoi,*" said the aproned man, thanking him.

"*Hou,*" said Jason, waving his hand.

Establish a benign contact as soon as you can. Especially in an unfamiliar place where there could be hostility. That contact could give you the opportunity or the time you need. Was it Medusa or was it Treadstone? It did not matter that he could not remember.

He turned slowly on the stool and looked at the tables; he found the dangling placard with the Chinese character for "five." He turned back to the bar and took out his notebook and ballpoint pen. He then tore off a page and wrote out the telephone number of a Macao hotel he had memorized from the *Voyager* magazine provided to passengers on the hydrofoil. He printed a name he would recall only if it was necessary and added the following: *No friend of Carlos.*

He lowered his glass below the bar counter, spilled the drink, and held up his hand for another. With its appearance, he was more generous than before.

"*Mgoi saai,*" said the bartender, bowing.

"*Msa,*" said Bourne, again waving his hand, then suddenly holding it steady, a signal for the bartender to remain where he was. "Would you do me a small favor?" he continued in the man's language. "It would take you no more than ten seconds."

"What is it, sir?"

"Give this note to the dealer at Table Five. He's an old friend, and I want him to know I'm here." Jason folded the note and held it up. "I'll pay you for the favor."

"It is my heavenly privilege, sir."

Bourne watched. The dealer took the note, opened it briefly as the bartender walked away, and shoved it beneath the table. The waiting began.

It was interminable, so long that the bartender was relieved for the night. The dealer was moved to another table, and two hours later he was also replaced. And two hours after that still another dealer took over Table Five. The floor beneath him now damp with whisky, Jason logically ordered coffee and settled for tea; it was ten minutes past two in the morning. Another hour and he would go to the hotel whose number he had written down and, if he had to buy shares in its stock, get a room. He was fading.

The fading stopped. It was happening! A Chinese woman in the slit-skirted dress of a prostitute walked up to Table Five. She sidestepped her way around the players to the right corner and spoke quickly to the dealer, who reached under the counter and unobtrusively gave her the folded note. She nodded and left, heading for the door of the casino.

He does not appear himself, of course. He uses whores from the street.

Bourne left the bar and followed the woman. Out in the dark street, which had a number of people in it but was deserted by Hong Kong standards, he stayed roughly fifty feet behind her, stopping every now and then to look into the lighted store windows, then hurrying ahead so as not to lose her.

Don't accept the first relay. They think as well as you do. The first could be an indigent looking for a few dollars and who knows nothing. Even the second or the third. You'll recognize the contact. He'll be different.

A stooped old man approached the whore. Their bodies brushed, and she shrieked at him while passing him the note. Jason feigned drunkenness and turned around, taking up the second relay.

It happened four blocks away, and the man *was* different. He was a small, well-dressed Chinese, his compact body with its broad shoulders and narrow waist exuding strength. The quickness of his gestures as he paid the seedy old man and began walking rapidly across the street was a warning to any adversary. For Bourne it was an irresistible invitation; this was a contact with authority, a link to the Frenchman.

Jason dashed to the other side; he was close to fifty yards behind the man and losing ground. There was no point in being subtle any longer; he broke into a run. Seconds later he was directly behind the contact, the soles of his sneakers having dulled the sound of his racing feet. Up ahead was an alleyway that cut between what looked like two office buildings; the windows were dark. He had to move quickly, but move in such a way that would not cause a commotion, not give the night strollers a reason to shout or call for the police. In this, the odds were with him; most of the people wandering around were more drunk or drugged than sober, the rest weary laborers, having finished their working hours, anxious to get home. The contact approached the opening of the alley. *Now.*

Bourne rushed ahead to the man's right side. "The *Frenchman!*" he said in Chinese. "I have news from the Frenchman! *Hurry!*" He spun into the alley, and the contact, stunned, his eyes bulging, had no choice but to walk like a bewildered zombie into the mouth of the alleyway. *Now!*

Lunging from the shadows, Jason grabbed the man's left ear, yanking it, twisting it, propelling the contact forward, bringing his knee up into the base of the man's spine, his other hand on the man's neck. He threw him down into the bowels of the dark alley, racing with him, crashing his sneaker into the back of the contact's knee; the man fell, spinning in the fall, and stared up at Bourne. "*You!* It is *you!*" Then the contact winced in the dim light. "No," he said, suddenly calm, deliberate. "You are *not* him."

Without a warning move, the Chinese lashed his right leg out, shoving his body off the pavement like a speeding trajectory in reverse. He caught the muscles of Jason's left thigh, following the blow with his left foot, pummeling it into Bourne's abdomen as he leaped to his feet, hands extended and rigid, his muscular body moving fluidly, even gracefully, in a semicircle and in anticipation.

What followed was a battle of animals, two trained executioners, each move made in intense premeditation, each blow lethal if it landed with full impact. One fought for his life, the other for survival and deliverance—and the woman he could not live without, *would* not live without. Finally, height and weight and a motive beyond life itself made the difference, giving victory to one and defeat to the other.

Entwined against the wall, both sweating and bruised,

blood trickling from mouths and eyes, Bourne hammer-locked the contact's neck from behind, his left knee jammed into the small of the man's back, his right leg wrapped around the contact's ankles, clamping them.

"You know what happens next!" he whispered breathlessly, spacing the Chinese words for final emphasis. "One snap and your spine goes. It's not a pleasant way to die. And you don't *have* to die. You can live with more money than the Frenchman would ever pay you. Take my word for it, the Frenchman and his killer won't be around much longer. Take your choice. *Now!*" Jason strained; the veins in the man's throat were distended to the point of bursting.

"*Yes, yes!*" cried the contact. "I live, not die!"

They sat in the dark alleyway, their backs against the wall, smoking cigarettes. It was established that the man spoke English fluently, which he had learned from the nuns in a Portuguese Catholic school.

"You're very good, you know," said Bourne, wiping the blood from his lips.

"I am the champion of Macao. It is why the Frenchman pays me. But you bested me. I am dishonored, no matter what happens."

"No you're not. It's just that I know a few more dirty tricks than you do. They're not taught where you were trained, and they never should be. Besides, no one will ever know."

"But I am young! You are old."

"I wouldn't go that far. Besides, I stay in pretty good shape, thanks to a crazy doctor who tells me what to do. How old do you think I am?"

"You are over *thirty!*"

"Agreed."

"*Old!*"

"Thanks."

"You are also very strong, very heavy—but it is more than that. I am a sane man. You are *not!*"

"Perhaps." Jason crushed out his cigarette on the pavement. "Let's talk sensibly," he said, pulling money from his pocket. "I meant what I said, I'll pay you well. . . . Where's the Frenchman?"

"Everything is not in balance."

"What do you mean?"

"Balance is important."

"I know that, but I don't understand you."

"There is a lack of harmony, and the Frenchman is angry. How much will you pay me?"

"How much can you tell me?"

"Where the Frenchman and his assassin will be tomorrow night."

"Ten thousand American dollars."

"Aiya!"

"But only if you take me there."

"It is across the *border!"*

"I have a visa for Shenzen. It's good for another three days."

"It may help, but it is not legal for the Guangdong border."

"Then you figure it out. Ten thousand dollars, American."

"I will figure it out." The contact paused, his eyes on the money held out by the American. "May I have what I believe you call an installment?"

"Five hundred dollars, that's all."

"Negotiations at the border will cost much more."

"Call me. I'll bring you the money."

"Call you where?"

"Get me a hotel room here in Macao. I'll put my money in its vault."

"The Lisboa."

"No, not the Lisboa. I can't go there. Someplace else."

"There is no problem. Help me to my feet. . . . *No!* It would be better for my dignity if I did not need help."

"So be it," said Jason Bourne.

Catherine Staples sat at her desk, the disconnected telephone still in her hand; absently she looked at it and hung up. The conversation she had just concluded astonished her. As there was no Canadian Intelligence Force currently operating in Hong Kong, foreign service officers cultivated their own sources within the Hong Kong police for those times when accurate information was needed. These occasions were invariably in the interests of Canadian citizens residing in or traveling through the colony. The problems ranged from those arrested to those assaulted, from Canadians who were swindled to those doing the swindling. Then, too, there were deeper concerns, matters of security and espionage, the former covering visits of ranking government officials, the latter involving means of protection against electronic surveillance and the gaining of sensitive information through acts of blackmail against consulate personnel. It was quiet but common knowledge that agents from the Eastern bloc and fanatically religious Middle East regimes used drugs and prostitutes of both sexes for whatever the preferences of both sexes in a never-ending pursuit of a hostile government's classified data. Hong Kong was a needle and meat market. And it was in this area that Staples had done some of her best work in the territory. She had saved the careers of two attachés in her own consulate, as well as an American and three British. Photographs of personnel in compromising acts had been destroyed along with the corresponding negatives, the extortionists banished from the colony with threats not simply of exposure but of physical harm. In one instance, an Iranian consular official, yelling in high dudgeon from his quarters at the Gammon House, accused her of meddling in affairs far above her station. She had listened to the ass for as long as she could tolerate the nasal twang, then terminated the call with a short statement: "Didn't you know? Khomeini likes little boys."

All of this had been made possible through her relationship with a late-middle-aged English widower who had opted for retirement from Scotland Yard to become chief of Crown Colonial Affairs in Hong Kong. At sixty-seven, Ian Ballantyne had accepted the fact that his tenure at the Yard was over, but not the use of his professional skills. He was willingly posted to the Far East, where he shook up the Intelligence division of the colony's police, and in his quiet way shaped an aggressively efficient organization that knew more about Hong Kong's shadow world than did any of the other agencies in the territory, including MI6, Special Branch. Catherine and Ian had met at one of those bureaucratically dull dinners demanded by consular protocol, and after prolonged conversation laced with wit and appraisal of his table partner, Ballantyne had leaned over and said simply, "Do you think we can still do it, old girl?"

"Let's try," she had replied.

They had. They enjoyed it, and Ian became a fixture in Staples's life, no strings or commitments attached. They liked each other; that was enough.

And Ian Ballantyne had just given the lie to everything Undersecretary of State Edward McAllister told Marie Webb and her husband in Maine. There was no taipan in Hong Kong named Yao Ming, and his impeccable sources—read very well paid—in Macao assured him there had been no double murder involving a taipan's wife and a drug runner at the Lisboa Hotel. There had been no such killings since the departure of the Japanese occupation forces in 1945. There had been numerous stabbings and gunshot wounds around the tables in the casino, and quite a few deaths in the rooms attributed to overdoses of narcotics, but no such incident as described by Staples's informer.

"It's a fabric of lies, Cathy old girl," Ian had said. "For what purpose, I can't fathom."

"My source is legitimate, old darling. What do you smell?"

"Rancid odors, my dear. Someone is taking a great risk for a sizable objective. He's covering himself, of course —one can buy anything over here, including silence—but the whole damn thing's fiction. Do you want to tell me more?"

"Suppose I told you it's Washington-oriented, not U.K.?"

"I'd have to contradict you. To go this far London has to be involved."

"It doesn't make sense!"

"From your viewpoint, Cathy. You don't know theirs. And I can tell you this—that maniac, Bourne, has us all in a sticky wicket. One of his victims is a man nobody will talk about. I won't even tell you, my girl."

"Will you if I bring you more information?"

"Probably not, but do try."

Staples sat at her desk filtering the words.

One of his victims is a man nobody will talk about.

What did Ballantyne mean? What was happening? And why was a former Canadian economist in the center of the sudden storm?

Regardless, she was safe.

. . .

Ambassador Havilland, attaché case in hand, strode into the office in Victoria Peak as McAllister bounced out of the chair, prepared to vacate it for his superior.

"Stay where you are, Edward. What news?"

"Nothing, I'm afraid."

"*Christ,* I don't want to hear that!"

"I'm sorry."

"Where's the retarded son of a bitch who let this happen?"

McAllister blanched as Major Lin Wenzu, unseen by Havilland, rose from the couch against the back wall. "I am the retarded son of a bitch, the Chinese who let it happen, Mr. Ambassador."

"I'll not apologize," said Havilland, turning and speaking harshly. "It's your necks we're trying to save, not ours. We'll survive. You won't."

"I'm not privileged to understand you."

"It's not his fault," protested the undersecretary of State.

"Is it *yours*?" shouted the ambassador. "Were you responsible for her custody?"

"I'm responsible for everything here."

"That's very Christian of you, Mr. McAllister, but at the moment we're not reading the Scriptures in Sunday school."

"It was *my* responsibility," broke in Lin. "I accepted the assignment and I failed. Simply put, the woman outsmarted us."

"You're Lin, Special Branch?"

"Yes, Mr. Ambassador."

"I've heard good things about you."

"I'm sure my performance invalidates them."

"I'm told she also outsmarted a very able doctor."

"She did," confirmed McAllister. "One of the best internists in the territory."

"An Englishman," added Lin.

"That wasn't necessary, Major. Any more than your slipping in the word 'Chinese' in reference to yourself. I'm not a racist. The world doesn't know it, but it hasn't time for that crap." Havilland crossed to the desk; he placed the attaché case on top, opened it, and removed a thick manila envelope with black borders. "You asked for the Treadstone file. Here it is. Needless to say, it cannot leave this room and when you're not reading it, lock it in the vault."

"I want to start as soon as possible."

"You think you'll find something there?"

"I don't know where else to look. Incidentally, I've moved to an office down the hall. The vault's in here."

"Feel free to come and go," said the diplomat. "How much have you told the major?"

"Only what I was instructed to tell him." McAllister looked at Lin Wenzu. "He's complained frequently that he should be told more. Perhaps he's right."

"I'm in no position to press my complaint, Edward. London was firm, Mr. Ambassador. Naturally, I accept the conditions."

"I don't want you to 'accept' anything, Major. I want you more frightened than you've ever been in your life. We'll leave Mr. McAllister to his reading and take a stroll. As I was driven in I saw a large attractive garden. Will you join me?"

"It would be a privilege, sir."

"That's questionable, but it *is* necessary. You must thoroughly understand. You've *got* to find that woman!"

Marie stood at the window in Catherine Staples's flat looking down at the activity below. The streets were crowded, as always, and she had an overpowering urge to get out of the apartment and walk anonymously among those crowds, in those streets, walk around the Asian House in hopes of finding David. At least she would be moving, staring, hearing, hoping—not thinking in silence, half going crazy. But she could not leave; she had given her word to Catherine. She had promised to stay inside, admit no one, and answer the phone only if a second, immediate call was preceded by two previous rings. It would be Staples on the line.

Dear Catherine, capable Catherine—frightened Catherine. She tried to hide her fear, but it was in her probing questions, asked too quickly, too intensely, her reactions to answers too astonished, frequently accompanied by a shortness of breath, as her eyes strayed, her thoughts obviously racing. Marie had not understood, but she did understand that Staples's knowledge of the dark world of the Far East was extensive, and when such a knowledgeable person tried to conceal her fear of what she heard, there was far more to the tale than the teller knew.

The telephone. Two rings. Silence. Then a third. Marie ran to the table by the couch and picked up the phone as the third bell began. *"Yes?"*

"Marie, when this liar, McAllister, spoke to you and your husband, he mentioned a cabaret in the Tsim Sha Tsui, if I recall. Am I right?"

"Yes, he did. He said that an Uzi—that's a gun—"

"I know what it is, my dear. The same weapon was supposedly used to kill the taipan's wife and her lover in Macao, wasn't that it?"

"That's it."

"But did he say anything about the men who had been killed in the cabaret over in Kowloon? Anything at all?"

Marie thought back. "No, I don't think so. His point was the weapon."

"You're positive."

"Yes, I am. I'd remember."

"I'm sure you would," agreed Staples.

"I've gone over that conversation a thousand times. Have you learned anything?"

"Yes. No such killing as McAllister described to you ever took place at the Lisboa Hotel in Macao."

"It was covered up. The banker paid."

"Nowhere near what my impeccable source has paid— in more than money. In the coveted, impeccable stamp of his office which can lead to far greater profits for a very long time. In exchange for information, of course."

"Catherine, what are you *saying?*"

"This is either the clumsiest operation I've ever heard of, or a brilliantly conceived plan to involve your husband in ways he would never have considered, certainly never agreed to. I suspect it's the latter."

"Why do you say that?"

"A man flew into Kai-tak Airport this afternoon, a statesman who's always been far more than a diplomat. We all know it but the world doesn't. His arrival was on all our printouts. He demurred when the media tried to interview him, claiming he was strictly on vacation in his beloved Hong Kong."

"And?"

"He's never taken a vacation in his life."

McAllister ran out into the walled garden with its trellises and white wrought-iron furniture and rows of roses and rock-filled ponds. He had put the Treadstone file in the vault, but the words were indelibly printed on his mind. Where *were* they? Where was *he?*

There they were! Sitting on two concrete benches beneath a cherry tree, Lin leaning forward, mesmerized. McAllister could not help it; he broke into a run, out of breath when he reached the tree, staring at the major from Special Branch, MI6.

"Lin! When Webb's wife took the call from her husband—the call you terminated—what *exactly* did she say?"

"She began talking about a street in Paris where there was a row of trees, her favorite trees, I think she said," replied Lin, bewildered. "She was obviously trying to tell him where she was, but she was totally wrong."

"She was totally *right!* When I questioned you, you also said that she told Webb that 'things had been terrible' on that street in Paris, or something like that—"

"That's what she said," interrupted the major.

"But that they'd be better over *here."*

"That is what she said."

"In Paris a man was killed at the embassy, a man who tried to help them both!"

"What are you trying to say, McAllister?" interrupted Havilland.

"The *row* of trees is insignificant, Mr. Ambassador, but not her *favorite* tree. The maple tree, the maple *leaf.* Canada's symbol! There is no Canadian embassy in Hong Kong, but there *is* a consulate. That's their meeting ground. It's the pattern! It's Paris all over again!"

"You didn't alert friendly embassies—consulates?"

"Goddamn it!" exploded the undersecretary of State. "What the hell was I going to say? I'm under an oath of silence, remember, *sir?"*

"You're quite right. The rebuke is deserved."

"You cannot tie all our hands, Mr. Ambassador," said Lin. "You are a person I respect greatly, but a few of us, too, must be given a measure of respect if we are to do our jobs. The same respect you just gave me in your telling me of this most frightening thing. Sheng Chou Yang. *Incredible!*"

"Discretion must be absolute."

"It will be," said the major.

"The Canadian consulate," said Havilland. "Get me the roster of its entire personnel."

16

The call had come at five o'clock in the afternoon and Bourne was ready for it. No names were exchanged.

"It is arranged," said the caller. "We are to be at the border shortly before twenty-one hundred hours, when the guard changes shifts. Your Shenzen visa will be scrutinized and rubber stamps will fly, but none will touch it. Once inside you are on your own, but you did not come through Macao."

"What about getting back out? If what you told me is true and things go right, there'll be someone with me."

"It will not be me. I will see you over and to the location. After that, I leave you."

"That doesn't answer my question."

"It is not so difficult as getting in, unless you are searched and contraband is found."

"There won't be any."

"Then I would suggest drunkenness. It is not uncommon. There is an airfield outside of Shenzen used by special—"

"I know it."

"You were on the wrong airplane, perhaps, that too is not uncommon. The schedules are very bad in China."

"How much for tonight?"

"Four thousand, Hong Kong, and a new watch."

"Agreed."

. . .

Some ten miles north of the village of Gongbei the hills rise, soon becoming a minor range of densely forested small mountains. Jason and his former adversary from the alley in Macao walked along the dirt road. The Chinese stopped and looked up at the hills above.

"Another five or six kilometers and we will reach a field. We will cross it and head up into the second level of woods. We must be careful."

"You're sure they'll be there?"

"I carried the message. If there is a campfire, they will be there."

"What was the message?"

"A conference was demanded."

"Why across the border?"

"It could *only* be across the border. That, too, was part of the message."

"But you don't know why."

"I am only the messenger. Things are not in balance."

"You said that last night. Can't you explain what you mean?"

"I cannot explain it to myself."

"Could it be because the conference had to take place over here? In China?"

"That is part of it, certainly."

"There's more?"

"*Wen ti,*" said the guide. "Questions that arise from feelings."

"I think I understand." And Jason did. He had the same questions, the same feelings, when it had become clear to him that the assassin who called himself Bourne was riding in an official vehicle of the People's Republic.

"You were too generous with the guard. The watch was too expensive."

"I may need him."

"He may not be in the same post."

"I'll find him."

"He'll sell the watch."

"Good. I'll bring him another."

Crouching, they ran through the tall grass of the field one section at a time, Bourne following the guide, his eyes constantly roving over their flanks and up ahead, finding

shadows in the darkness—and yet not total darkness.
Fast, low-flying clouds obscured the moon, filtering the
light, but every now and then shafts streamed down for
brief moments illuminating the landscape. They reached
a rising stretch of tall trees and began making their way
up. The Chinese stopped and turned, both hands raised.

"What is it?" whispered Jason.

"We must go slowly, make no noise."

"Patrols?"

The guide shrugged. "I do not know. There is no
harmony."

They crawled up through the tangled forest, stopping
at every screech of a disturbed bird and the subsequent
flutter of wings, letting the moments pass. The hum of
the woods was pervasive; the crickets clicked their incessant symphony, a lone owl hooted, to be answered by
another, and small ferretlike creatures scampered
through the underbrush. Bourne and his guide came to
the end of the tall trees; there was a second sloping field
of high grass in front of them, and in the distance were
the jagged dark outlines of another climbing forest.

There was also something else. A glow at the top of the
next hill, at the summit of the woods. It was a campfire,
the campfire! Bourne had to hold himself in check, stop
himself from getting up and racing across the field and
plunging into the woods, scrambling up to the fire. Patience was everything now, and he was in the dark environs he knew so well; vague memories told him to trust
himself—told him that he was the best there was. Patience. He would get across the field and silently make his
way to the top of the forest; he would find a spot in the
woods with a clear view of the fire, of the meeting
ground. He would wait, and watch; he would know when
to make his move. He had done it so often before—the
specifics eluded him, but not the pattern. A man would
leave, and like a cat stalking silently through the forest he
would follow that man until the moment came. Again, he
would know that moment, and the man would be his.

Marie, I won't fail us this time. I can move with a kind of
terrible purity now—that sounds crazy, I know, but then it's true.
. . . I can hate with purity—that's where I came from, I think.
Three bleeding bodies floating into a riverbank taught me to hate.
A bloody hand print on a door in Maine taught me to reinforce

*that hate, and never to let it happen again. I don't often disagree
with you, my love, but you were wrong in Geneva, wrong in Paris.
I am a killer.*

"What is *wrong* with you?" whispered the guide, his
head close to Jason's. "You do not follow my signal!"

"I'm sorry. I was thinking."

"So am I, *peng you!* For our lives!"

"You don't have to worry, you can leave now. I see the
fire up there on the hill." Bourne pulled money from his
pocket. "I'd rather go alone. One man has less chance of
being spotted than two."

"Suppose there are other men—patrols? You bested
me in Macao, but I am not unworthy in this regard."

"If there are such men, I intend to find one."

"In the name of Jesus, *why?*"

"I want a gun. I couldn't risk bringing one across the
border."

"*Aiya!*"

Jason handed the guide the money. "It's all there. Nine
thousand five hundred. You want to go back in the woods
and count it? I've got a small flashlight."

"One does not question the man who has bested him.
Dignity would not permit such impropriety."

"Your words are terrific, but don't buy a diamond in
Amsterdam. Go on, get out of here. It's my territory."

"And this is my gun," said the guide, taking a weapon
from his belt and handing it to Bourne as he took the
money. "Use it if you must. The magazine is full—nine
shells. There is no registry, no trace. The Frenchman
taught me."

"You took this across the *border?*"

"You brought the watch, I did not. I might have
dropped it into a garbage bag but then I saw the guard's
face. I will not need it now."

"Thanks. But I should tell you, if you've lied to me, I'll
find you. Count on it."

"Then the lies would not be mine and the money
would be returned."

"You're too much."

"You bested me. I must be honorable in all things."

Bourne crawled slowly, ever so slowly, across the expanse of tall, starched grass filled with nettles, pulling the

needles from his neck and forehead, grateful for the nylon jacket that repelled them. He instinctively knew something his guide did not know, why he did not want the Chinese to come with him. A field with high grass was the most logical place to have patrols; the reeds moved when hidden intruders crawled through them. Therefore one had to observe the swaying grass from the ground and go forward with the prevailing breezes and the sudden mountain winds.

He saw the start of the woods, trees rising at the edge of the grass. He began to raise himself to a crouching position, then suddenly, swiftly, lowered his body and remained motionless. Up ahead to his right, a man stood on the border of the field, a rifle in his hands, watching the grass in the intermittent moonlight, looking for a pattern of reeds that bent against the breezes. A gust of wind swirled down from the mountains. Bourne moved with it, coming to within ten feet of the guard. Half a foot by half a foot he crawled to the edge of the field; he was now parallel with the man whose concentration was focused in front of him, not on his flanks. Jason inched up so he could see through the reeds. The guard looked to his left. *Now!*

Bourne sprang out of the grass and, rushing forward, lunged at the man. In panic, the guard instinctively swung the butt of the rifle to ward off the sudden attack. Jason grabbed the barrel, twisting it over the man's head, and crashed it down on the exposed skull as he rammed his knee into the guard's rib cage. The patrol collapsed. Bourne quickly dragged him into the high grass, out of sight. With as few movements as possible, Jason removed the guard's jacket and ripped the shirt from his back, tearing the cloth into strips. Moments later the man was bound in such a way that with every move he tightened the improvised straps. His mouth was gagged, a torn sleeve wrapped around his head holding the gag in place.

Normally, as in previous times—Bourne instinctively knew it had been the normal course of similar events—he would have lost no time racing out of the field and starting up through the woods toward the fire. Instead, he studied the unconscious figure of the Oriental below; something disturbed him—something not in harmony. For openers, he had expected the guard would be in the

uniform of the Chinese army, for he all too vividly recalled the sight of the government vehicle in Shenzen
and knew who was inside. But it was not simply the absence of a uniform, it was the clothes this man wore. They
were cheap and filthy, rancid with the smell of grease-
laden food. He reached down and twisted the man's face,
opening his mouth; there were few teeth, black with
decay. What kind of guard was this, what kind of patrol?
He was a thug—no doubt experienced—a brute criminal,
contracted in the skid rows of the Orient where life was
cheap and generally meaningless. Yet the men at this
"conference" dealt in tens of thousands of dollars. The
price they paid for a life was very high. Something was
not in balance.

Bourne grabbed the rifle and crawled out of the grass.
Seeing nothing, hearing nothing but the murmurs of the
forest before him, he got to his feet and raced into the
woods. He climbed swiftly, silently, stopping as before
with every screech of a bird, every flutter of wings, each
abrupt cessation of the cricket symphony. He did not
crawl now, he crept on bent legs, holding the barrel of
the rifle, a club if the need arose. There could be no
gunshots unless his life depended on them, no warning
to his quarry. The trap was closing, it was simply a matter
of patience now, patience and the final stalk when the
jaws of the trap would snap shut. He reached the top of
the forest, gliding noiselessly behind a boulder on the
edge of the campsite. Silently he lowered the rifle to the
ground, withdrew from his belt the gun that the guide
had given him and peered around the huge rock.

What he had expected to find below in the field he now
saw. A soldier, standing erect in his uniform, a sidearm
strapped to his waist, was roughly twenty feet to the left
of the fire. It was as if he wanted to be seen but not
identified. Out of balance. The man looked at his watch;
the waiting had begun.

It lasted the better part of an hour. The soldier had
smoked five cigarettes; Jason had remained still, barely
breathing. And then it happened, slowly, subtly, no he-
ralding trumpets, an entrance devoid of drama. A second
figure appeared; he walked casually out of the shadows,
parting the final branches of the forest as he came into
view. And, without warning, bolts of lightning streaked

down from the night sky, burning, searing into David Webb's head, numbing the mind of Jason Bourne.

For as the man came into the light of the fire, Bourne gasped, gripping the barrel of the gun to keep from screaming—or from killing. He was looking at a ghost of himself, a haunting apparition from years ago come back to stalk him, no matter who was the hunter now. The face was at once his face yet not his face—perhaps the face as it might have been before the surgeons altered it for Jason Bourne. Like the lean, taut body, the face was younger—younger than the myth he was imitating—and in that youth was strength, the strength of a Delta from Medusa. It was *incredible.* Even the guarded, catlike walk, the long arms loose at the sides that were so obviously proficient in the deadly arts. It *was* Delta, the Delta he had been told about, the Delta who had become Cain and finally Jason Bourne. He was looking at himself but not himself, yet withal a killer. An assassin.

A crack in the distance intruded upon the sounds of the mountain forest. The assassin stopped, then spun away from the fire and dove to his right as the soldier dropped to the ground. A deafening, echoing, staccato burst of gunfire erupted from the woods; the killer rolled over and over on the campsite grass, bullets ripping up the earth as he reached the darkness of the trees. The Chinese soldier was on one knee, firing wildly in the assassin's direction.

Then the ear-shattering battle escalated, not from one level to the next but in three separate stages. The explosions were immense. A first grenade destroyed the campsite, followed by a second, uprooting trees, the dry, windblown branches catching fire, and finally a third, hurled high in the air, detonating with enormous force in the area of the woods from which the machine gun had been triggered. Suddenly flames were everywhere, and Bourne shielded his eyes, moving around the boulder, weapon in hand. A trap had been set for the killer and he had walked into it! The Chinese soldier was dead, his gun blown away, as well as most of his body. A figure suddenly raced from the left into the inferno that had been the campsite, then whipped around and ran through the flames, turning twice and, seeing Jason, firing at him. The assassin had doubled back in the woods, hoping to trap and kill those who would kill him. Spinning, Bourne leaped first to his right, then to his left, then fell to the ground, his eyes on the running man. He got to his feet and sprang forward. *He could not let him get away!* He raced through the raging fires; the figure ahead of him was weaving through the trees. It was the killer! The impostor who claimed to be the lethal myth that had enraged Asia, using that myth for his own purposes, destroying the original and the wife that man loved. Bourne ran as he had never run before, dodging trees and leaping over the underbrush with an agility that denied the years between Medusa and the present. He was *back* in Medusa! He *was* Medusa! And with every ten yards he closed the gap by five. He knew the forests, and every forest was a jungle and every jungle was his friend. He had survived in the jungles; without thinking—only feeling—he knew their curvatures, their vines, the sudden pits and the abrupt ravines. He was gaining, *gaining!* And then he was *there,* the killer only feet ahead of him!

With what seemed like the last breath in his body, Jason lunged—Bourne against Bourne! His hands were the claws of a mountain cat as he gripped the shoulders of the racing figure in front of him, his fingers digging into the hard flesh and bone as he whipped the killer back, his heels dug into the earth, his right knee crashing up into the man's spine. His rage was such that he consciously had to remind himself not to kill. *Stay alive!* You are my freedom, *our* freedom!

The assassin screamed as the true Jason Bourne hammerlocked his neck, wrenching the head to the right and forcing the pretender down. Both fell to the ground, Bourne's forearm jammed across the man's throat, his left hand clenched, repeatedly pounding the killer's lower abdomen, forcing the air out of the weakening body.

The face? The *face?* Where was the face that belonged to years ago? To an apparition that wanted to take him back into a hell that memory had blocked out. Where was the *face?* This was not *it!*

"*Delta!*" screamed the man beneath him.

"What did you *call me?*" shouted Bourne.

"*Delta!*" shrieked the writhing figure. "Cain is for *Carlos, Delta is for Cain!*"

"Goddamn you! Who—"

"D'Anjou! I am d'Anjou! Medusa! Tam Quan! We have no names, only symbols! For God's sake, Paris! The Louvre! You saved my life in Paris—as you saved so many lives in Medusa! I am d'Anjou! I told you what you had to know in Paris! You are Jason Bourne! The madman who runs from us is but a creation! My creation!"

Webb stared at the contorted face below, at the perfectly groomed gray moustache and the silver hair that swept back over the aging head. The nightmare had returned . . . he was in the steaming infested jungles of Tam Quan with no way out and death all around them. Then suddenly he was in Paris, nearing the steps of the Louvre in the blinding afternoon sunlight. Gunshots. Cars screeching, crowds screaming. He had to save the face beneath him! Save the face from Medusa who could supply the missing pieces of the insane puzzle!

"D'Anjou?" whispered Jason. "You're d'Anjou?"

"If you will give me back my throat," choked the Frenchman, "I will tell you a story. I'm sure you have one to tell me."

Philippe d'Anjou surveyed the wreckage of the campsite, now a smoking ruin. He crossed himself as he searched the pockets of the dead "soldier," removing whatever valuables he found. "We'll free the man below when we leave," he said. "There's no other access to this place. It's why I posted him there."

"And told him to look for what?"

"Like you, I'm from Medusa. Fields of grass—poets and consumers notwithstanding—are both avenues and traps. Guerrillas know that. We knew that."

"You couldn't have anticipated me."

"Hardly. But I could and did anticipate every countermove my creation might consider. He was to arrive alone. The instructions were clear, but who could trust him, least of all me?"

"You're ahead of me."

"It's part of my story. You'll hear it."

They walked down through the woods, the elderly d'Anjou gripping the trunks of trees and saplings to ease the descent. They reached the field, hearing the muted screams of the bound guard as they walked into the tall grass. Bourne cut the cloth straps with his knife and the Frenchman paid him.

"*Zou ba!*" yelled d'Anjou. The man fled into the darkness. "He is garbage. They are all garbage, but they kill willingly for a price and disappear."

"You tried to kill *him* tonight, didn't you? It was a trap."

"Yes. I thought he was wounded in the explosions. It's why I went after him."

"I thought he'd doubled back to take you at the rear."

"Yes, we would have done that in Medusa—"

"It's why I thought you were him." Jason suddenly shouted in fury. "What have you *done?*"

"It's part of the story."

"I want to hear it. *Now!*"

"There's a flat stretch of ground several hundred yards, over there to the left," said the Frenchman, pointing. "It used to be a grazing field, but recently it's been used by helicopters flying in to meet with an assassin. Let's go to the far end and rest—and talk. Just in case what remains of the fire draws anyone from the village."

"It's five miles away."

"Still, this is China."

The clouds had dispersed, blown away with the night winds; the moon was descending, yet was still high enough to wash the distant mountains with its light. The two men of Medusa sat on the ground. Bourne lit a cigarette as d'Anjou spoke. "Do you remember back in Paris, that crowded café where we talked after the madness at the Louvre?"

"Sure. Carlos nearly killed us both that afternoon."

"You nearly trapped the Jackal."

"But I didn't. What about Paris, the café?"

"I told you then I was coming back to Asia. To Singapore or Hong Kong, perhaps the Seychelles, I think I said. France was never good for me—or to me. After Dienbienphu—everything I had was destroyed, blown up by our own troops—the talk of reparations was meaningless. Hollow babbling from hollow men. It's why I joined Medusa. The only possible way to get back my own was with an American victory."

"I remember," said Jason. "What's that got to do with tonight?"

"As is obvious, I came back to Asia. Since the Jackal had seen me, the routing was circuitous, which left me time to think. I had to make a clear appraisal of my circumstances and the possibilities before me. As I was fleeing for my life, my assets were not extensive but neither were they pathetic. I took the risk of returning to the shop in St. Honoré that afternoon and frankly stole every *sou* in and out of sight. I knew the combination of the safe, and fortunately it was well endowed. I could comfortably buy myself across the world, out of Carlos's reach, and live for many weeks without panic. But what was I to do with myself? The funds would run out, and my skills—so apparent in the civilized world—were not such that would permit me to live out the autumn of my life over here in the comfort that was stolen from me. Still, I had not been a snake in the head of Medusa for nothing. God knows I discovered and developed talents I never dreamed were within me—and found, frankly, that morality was not an issue. I had been wronged, and I could wrong others. And nameless, faceless strangers had tried to kill me countless times, so I could assume the responsibility for the death of nameless, faceless other strangers. You see the symmetry, don't you? At once removed, the equations became abstract."

"I hear a lot of horseshit," replied Bourne.

"Then you are not listening, Delta."

"I'm not Delta."

"Very well. Bourne."

"I'm not—go on, perhaps I am."

"Comment?"

"Rien. Go on."

"It struck me that regardless of what happened to you in Paris—whether you won or lost, whether you were killed or spared—Jason Bourne was finished. And by all the holy saints, I knew Washington would never utter a word of acknowledgment or clarification; you would simply disappear. 'Beyond-salvage,' I believe is the term."

"I'm aware of it," said Jason. "So I was finished."

"Naturellement. But there would be no explanations, there could *not* be. *Mon Dieu,* the assassin they invented

had gone mad—he had *killed!* No, there would be nothing. Strategists retreat into the darkest shadows when their plans go—'off the wire,' I think is the phrase."

"I'm aware of that one, too."

"*Bien.* Then you can comprehend the solution I found for myself, for the last days of an older man."

"I'm beginning to."

"*Bien encore.* There was a void here in Asia. Jason Bourne was no longer, but his legend was still alive. And there are men who will pay for the services of such an extraordinary man. Therefore I knew what I had to do. It was simply a matter of finding the right contender—"

"Contender?"

"Very well, *pretender,* if you wish. And train him in the ways of Medusa, in the ways of the most vaunted member of that so unofficial, criminal fraternity. I went to Singapore and searched the caves of the outcasts, often fearing for my life, until I found the man. And I found him quickly, I might add. He was desperate; he had been running for his life for nearly three years, staying, as they say, only steps away from those hunting him. He is an Englishman, a former Royal Commando who got drunk one night and killed seven people in the London streets while in a rage. Because of his outstanding service record he was sent to a psychiatric hospital in Kent, from which he escaped and somehow—God *knows* how—made his way to Singapore. He had all the tools of the trade; they simply needed to be refined and guided."

"He looks like me. Like I used to look."

"Far more now than he did. The basic features were there, also the tall frame and the muscular body; they were assets. It was merely a question of altering a rather prominent nose and rounding a sharper chin than I remembered your having—as Delta, of course. You were different in Paris, but not so radically that I could not recognize you."

"A commando," said Jason quietly. "It fits. Who is he?"

"He's a man without a name but not without a macabre story," replied d'Anjou, gazing at the mountains in the distance.

"No name . . . ?"

"None he ever gave me that he would not contradict

in the next breath—none remotely authentic. He guards that name as if it were the sole extension of his life, its revelation inevitably leading to his death. Of course, he's right; the present circumstances are a case in point. If I had a name, I could forward it through a blind to the British authorities in Hong Kong. Their computers would light up; specialists would be flown from London and a manhunt that I could never mount would be set in motion. They'd never take him alive—he wouldn't permit it and they wouldn't care to—and thus my purpose would be served."

"Why do the British want him terminated?"

"Suffice it to say that Washington had its Mai Lais and its Medusa, while London has a far more recent military unit led by a homicidal psychotic who left hundreds slaughtered in his wake—few distinctions were made between the innocent and the guilty. He holds too many secrets, which, if exposed, could lead to violent eruptions of revenge throughout the Mideast and Africa. Practicality comes first, you know that. Or you should."

"He *led?*" asked Bourne, as stunned as he was bewildered.

"No mere foot soldier he, Delta. He was a captain at twenty-two and a major at twenty-four when rank was next to impossible to obtain due to Whitehall's service economies. No doubt he'd be a brigadier or even a full general by now if his luck had held out."

"That's what he told you?"

"In periodic drunken rages when ugly truths would surface—but never his name. They usually occurred once or twice a month, several days at a time when he'd block out his life in a drunken sea of self-loathing. Yet he was always coherent enough before the outbursts came, telling me to strap him down, confine him, protect him from himself. . . . He would relive horrible events from his past, his voice hoarse, guttural, hollow. As the drink took over he would describe scenes of torture and mutilation, questioning prisoners with knives puncturing their eyes, and their wrists slit, ordering his captives to watch as their lives flowed out of their veins. So far as I could piece the fragments together, he commanded many of the most dangerous and savage raids against the fanatical uprisings of the late seventies and early eighties, from Yemen down to the bloodbaths in East Africa. In one moment of besotted jubilation he spoke of how Idi Amin himself would stop breathing at the mention of his name, so widespread was his reputation for matching—even surpassing—Amin's strategy of brutality." D'Anjou paused, nodding his head slowly and arching his brows in the Gallic acceptance of the inexplicable. "He was subhuman —*is* subhuman—but for all that a highly intelligent so-called officer and a gentleman. A complete paradox, a total contradiction of the civilized man. . . . He'd laugh at the fact that his troops despised him and called him an animal yet none ever dared to raise an official complaint."

"Why not?" asked Jason, stirred and pained at what he was hearing. "Why didn't they report him?"

"Because he always brought them out—most of them out—when the order of battle seemed hopeless."

"I see," said Bourne, letting the remark ride with the mountain breezes. "No, I *don't* see," he cried angrily, as if suddenly, unexpectedly stung. "Command structure is *better* than that. Why did his superiors put up with him? They had to *know!*"

"As I understood his rantings, he got the jobs done when others couldn't—or wouldn't. He learned the secret we in Medusa learned long ago. Play by the enemy's most ruthless conditions. Change the rules according to the culture. After all, human life to others is not what it is to the Judeo-Christian concept. How could it be? For so many, death is a liberation from intolerable human conditions."

"Breathing is *breathing!*" insisted Jason harshly. "Being is *being* and thinking is *thinking!*" added David Webb. "He's a Neanderthal."

"No more than Delta was at certain times. And you got *us* out of how many—"

"Don't *say* that!" protested the man from Medusa, cutting off the Frenchman. "It wasn't the same."

"But certainly a variation," insisted d'Anjou. "Ultimately the motives do not really matter, do they? Only the results. Or don't you care to accept the truth? You lived it once. Does Jason Bourne now live with lies?"

"At the moment I simply live—from day to day, from night to night—until it's over. One way or another."

"You must be clearer."

"When I want to or have to," replied Bourne icily. "He's good, then, isn't he? Your commando—major without a name. Good at what he does."

"As good as Delta—perhaps better. You see, he has no conscience, none whatsoever. You, on the other hand, as violent as you were, showed flashes of compassion. Something inside you demanded it. 'Spare this man,' you would say. 'He is a husband, a father, a brother. Incapacitate him, but let him live, let him function later.' . . . My creation, your impostor, would never do that. He wants always the final solution—death in front of his eyes."

"What happened to him? Why did he kill those people in London? Being drunk's not a good enough reason, not where he's been."

"It is if it's a way of life you can't resign from."

"You keep your weapon in place unless you're threatened. Otherwise you invite the threats."

"He used no weapon. Only his hands that night in London."

"What?"

"He stalked the streets looking for imagined enemies —that's what I gathered from his ravings. 'It was in their eyes!' he'd scream. 'It's always in the eyes! They know who I am, *what* I am.' I tell you, Delta, it was both frightening and tedious, and I never got a name, never a specific reference other than Idi Amin, which any drunken soldier of fortune would use to further himself. To involve the British in Hong Kong would mean involving myself, and, after all, I certainly could not do that. The whole thing's so frustrating, so I went back to the ways of Medusa. Do it yourself. You taught us that, Delta. You constantly told us—ordered us—to use our imagination. That's what I did tonight. And I failed, as an old man might be expected to fail."

"Answer my question," pressed Bourne. "Why did he kill those people in London?"

"For a reason as banal as it was pointless—and entirely too familiar. He'd been rejected, and his ego could not tolerate that rejection. I sincerely doubt that any other emotion was involved. As with all his indulgences, sexual activity is simply an animal release; no affection is involved, for he has no capacity for it. *Mon Dieu,* he was so *right!"*

"Again. What happened?"

"He had returned, wounded, from some particularly brutal duty in Uganda expecting to take up where he left off with a woman in London—someone, I gather, rather highborn, as the English say, a throwback to his earlier days, no doubt. But she refused to see him and hired armed guards to protect her house in Chelsea after he called her. Two of those men were among the seven he killed that night. You see, she claimed his temper was uncontrollable and his bouts of drinking made him murderous, which, of course, they did. But for me he was the perfect contender. In Singapore I followed him outside a disreputable bar and saw him corner two murderous thugs in an alleyway—*contrebandiers* who had made a great deal of money with a narcotics sale in that filthy waterfront cave—and watched as he backed them against the wall, slashing both their throats with a single sweep of his knife and removing the proceeds from their pockets. I knew then that he had it all. I had found my Jason Bourne. I approached him slowly, silently, my hand extended, holding more money than he had extracted from his victims. We talked. It was the beginning."

"So Pygmalion created his Galatea, and the first contract you accepted became Aphrodite and gave it life. Bernard Shaw would love you, and I could kill you."

"To what end? You came to find him tonight. I came to destroy him."

"Which is part of your story," said David Webb, looking away from the Frenchman at the fired mountains, thinking of Maine and the life with Marie that had been so violently disrupted. "You *bastard!"* he suddenly shouted. "I *could* kill you! Have you any idea what you've *done?"*

"That is your story, Delta. Let me finish mine."

"Make it neat. . . . *Echo.* That *was* your name, wasn't it? Echo?" *The memories came back.*

"Yes, it was. You once told Saigon that you would not travel without 'old Echo.' I had to be with your team because I could discern trouble with the tribes and the village chiefs that others could not—which had little to do with my alphabetical symbol. Of course, it was nothing mystic. I had lived in the colonies for ten years. I knew when the *Quan-si* were lying."

"Finish your story," ordered Bourne.

"Betrayal," said d'Anjou, palms outstretched. "Just as you were created, I created my own Jason Bourne. And just as you went mad, my creation did the same. He turned on me; he became the reality that was my invention. Dismiss Galatea, Delta, he became Frankenstein's monster with none of that creature's torment. He broke away from me and began to think for himself, *do* for himself. Once his desperation left him—with my inestimable help and a surgeon's knife—his sense of authority came back to him, as well as his arrogance, his ugliness. He considers me a trifle. That's what he called me, a 'trifle'! An insignificant nonentity who *used* him! *I* who created him!"

"You mean he makes contracts on his own?"

"Perverted contracts, grotesque and extraordinarily dangerous."

"But I traced him through you, through *your* arrangements at the Kam Pek casino. Table Five. The telephone number of a hotel in Macao and a name."

"A method of contact he finds convenient to maintain. And why not? It's virtually security-proof and what can I do? Go to the authorities and say, 'See here, gentleman, there's this fellow I'm somewhat responsible for who insists on using arrangements I created so he can be paid for killing someone.' He even uses my conduit."

"The *Zhongguo ren* with the fast hands and faster feet?"

D'Anjou looked at Jason. "So that's how you did it, how you found this place. Delta hasn't lost his touch, *n'est-ce pas?* Is the man alive?"

"He is, and ten thousand dollars richer."

"He's a money-hungry *cochon.* But I can hardly criticize, I used him myself. I paid him five hundred to pick up and deliver a message."

"That brought your creation here tonight so you could kill him? What made you so sure he'd come?"

"A Medusan's instinct, and skeletal knowledge of an extraordinary liaison he has made, a contact so profitable to him and so dangerous it could have all Hong Kong at war, the entire colony paralyzed."

"I heard that theory before," said Jason, recalling

McAllister's words spoken that early evening in Maine, "and I still don't believe it. When killers kill each other, they're the ones who usually lose. They blow themselves away and informers come out of the woodwork thinking they might be next."

"If the victims are restricted to such a convenient pattern, certainly you are right. But not when they include a powerful political figure from a vast and aggressive nation."

Bourne stared at d'Anjou. *"China?"* he asked softly.

The Frenchman nodded. "Five men were killed in the Tsim Sha Tsui—"

"I know that."

"Four of those corpses were meaningless. Not the fifth. He was the Vice-Premier of the People's Republic."

"Good God!" Jason frowned, the image of a car coming to him. A car with its windows blacked out and an assassin inside. An official government vehicle of the Chinese government.

"My sources tell me that the wires burned between Government House and Beijing, practicality and face winning out—*this* time. After all, what was the Vice-Premier doing in Kowloon, to begin with? Was such an august leader of the Central Committee also one of the corrupted? But, as I say, that is this time. No, Delta, my creation must be destroyed before he accepts another contract that could plunge us all into an abyss."

"Sorry, Echo. Not killed. Taken and brought to someone else."

"That is your story, then?" asked d'Anjou.

"Part of it, yes."

"Tell me."

"Only what you have to know. My wife was kidnapped and brought to Hong Kong. To get her back—and I'll get her back, or every goddamned one of you will die—I have to deliver your son-of-a-bitch creation. And now I'm one step closer because you're going to help me, and I mean *really* help me. If you don't—"

"Threats are unnecessary, Delta," interrupted the former Medusan. "I know what you can do. I've seen you do it. You want him for your reasons and I want him for mine. The order of battle is joined."

17

Catherine Staples insisted that her dinner guest have another vodka martini, demurring for herself, as her glass was still half full.

"It's also half empty," said the thirty-two-year-old American attaché, smiling wanly and nervously, pushing his dark hair away from his forehead. "That's stupid of me, Catherine," he added. "I'm sorry, but I can't forget that you saw the photographs—never mind that you saved my career and probably my life—it's those god-damned photographs."

"No one else saw them except Inspector Ballantyne."

"But *you* saw them."

"I'm old enough to be your mother."

"That compounds it. I look at you and feel so ashamed, so damned dirty."

"My former husband, wherever he is, once said to me that there was absolutely nothing that could or should be considered dirty in sexual encounters. I suspect there was a motive for his making the statement, but I happen to think he was right. Look, John, put them out of your mind. I have."

"I'll do my best." A waiter approached; the drink was ordered by signal. "Since your call this afternoon I've been a basket case. I thought more had surfaced. That was a twenty-four-hour period of pure outer space."

"You were heavily and insidiously drugged. On that level you weren't responsible. And *I'm* sorry, I should have told you it had nothing to do with our previous business."

"If you had, I might have earned my salary for the last five hours."

"It was forgetful and cruel of me. I apologize."

"Accepted. You're a great girl, Catherine."

"I appeal to your infantile regressions."

"Don't bet too much money on that."

"Then don't you have a fifth martini."

"It's only my second."

"A *little* flattery never hurt anyone."

They laughed quietly. The waiter returned with John Nelson's drink; he thanked the man and turned back to Staples. "I have an idea that the prospect of flattery didn't get me a free meal at the Plume. This place is out of my range."

"Mine, too, but not Ottawa's. You'll be listed as a terribly important person. In fact you are."

"That's nice. No one ever told me. I'm in a pretty good job over here because I learned Chinese. I figured that with all those Ivy League recruits, a boy from Upper Iowa College in old Fayette, Big I, ought to have an edge somewhere."

"You have it, Johnny. The consulates like you. Our out-posted 'Embassy Row' thinks very highly of you, and they should."

"If they do, it's thanks to you and Ballantyne. And *only* you two." Nelson paused, sipped his martini, and looked at Staples over the rim of the glass. He lowered his drink and spoke again. "What is it, Catherine? Why am I important?"

"Because I need your help."

"Anything. *Anything* I can do."

"Not so fast, Johnny. It's deep-water time and I could be drowning myself."

"If anyone deserves a lifeline from me, it's you. Outside of minor problems, our two countries live next door to each other and basically like each other—we're on the same side. What is it? How can I help you?"

"Marie St. Jacques . . . Webb," said Catherine, studying the attaché's face.

Nelson blinked, his eyes roving aimlessly in thought. "Nothing," he said. "The name doesn't mean anything to me."

"All right, let's try Raymond Havilland."

"*Oh,* now that's another barrel of pickled herring." The attaché widened his eyes and cocked his head.

"We've *all* been scuttlebutting about *him*. He hasn't come to the consulate, hasn't even called our head honcho, who wants to get his picture in the papers with him. After all, Havilland's a class act—kind of metaphysical in this business. He's been around since the loaves and the fishes, and he probably engineered the whole scam."

"Then you're aware that over the years your aristocratic ambassador has been involved with more than diplomatic negotiations."

"Nobody ever says it, but only the naïve accept his above-the-fray posture."

"You *are* good, Johnny."

"Merely observant. I do earn some of my pay. What's the connection between a name I *do* know and one that I don't?"

"I wish I knew. Do you have any idea why Havilland is over here? Any rumors you've picked up?"

"I've no idea why he's here, but I do know you won't find him at a hotel."

"I assume he has wealthy friends—"

"I'm sure he does, but he's not staying with them, either."

"Oh?"

"The consulate quietly leased a house in Victoria Peak, and a second marine contingent was flown over from Hawaii for guard duty. None of us in the upper-middle ranks knew about it until a few days ago when one of those dumb things happened. Two marines were having dinner in the Wanchai and one of them paid the bill with a temporary check drawn on a Hong Kong bank. Well, you know servicemen and checks; the manager gave this corporal a hard time. The kid said neither he nor his buddy had had time to round up cash and that the check was perfectly good. Why didn't the manager call the consulate and talk to a military attaché?"

"Smart corporal," broke in Staples.

"Unsmart consulate," said Nelson. "The military boys had gone for the day, and our hotshot security personnel in their limitless paranoia about secrecy hadn't rostered the Victoria Peak contingent. The manager said later that the corporal showed a couple of ID's and seemed like a nice kid, so he took a chance."

"That was reasonable of him. He probably wouldn't

have if the corporal had behaved otherwise. Again, smart marine."

"He *did* behave otherwise. The next morning down at the consulate. He read the riot act in all but barracks language in a voice so loud even I heard him, and my office is at the end of the corridor from the reception room. He wanted to know who the hell we civvies thought they were up there on that mountain and how come they weren't rostered, since they'd been there for a week. He was one angry gyrene, let me tell you."

"And suddenly the whole consulate knew there was a sterile house in the colony."

"You said that, Catherine, I didn't. But I'll tell you exactly what the memorandum to all personnel instructed us to say—the memo arrived on our desks an hour after the corporal had left, having spent twenty minutes with some very embarrassed security clowns."

"And what you were instructed to say is not what you believe."

"No comment," said Nelson. "The house in Victoria was leased for the convenience and security of traveling government personnel as well as representatives of U.S. corporations doing business in the territory."

"Hogwash. Especially the latter. Since when does the American taxpayer pick up those kinds of tabs for General Motors and ITT?"

"Washington is actively encouraging an expansion of trade in line with our widening open-door policy with respect to the People's Republic. It's consistent. We want to make things easier, more accessible, and this place is crowded as hell. Try getting a decent reservation on two days' notice."

"You sound like you rehearsed that."

"No comment. I've told you only what I was instructed to tell you should you bring the matter up—which I'm sure you did."

"Of course I did. I have friends in the Peak who think the neighborhood's going to seed, what with all those corporal types hanging around." Staples sipped her drink. "Havilland's up there?" she asked, placing the glass back on the table.

"Almost guaranteed."

"Almost?"

"Our information officer—her office is next to mine— wanted to get some PR mileage out of the ambassador. She asked the CG which hotel he was at, and she was told that he wasn't. Then whose residence? Same answer. 'We'll have to wait until he calls us, if he does,' said our boss. She cried on my shoulder, but the order was firm. No tracking him down."

"He's up in the Peak," concluded Staples quietly. "He's built himself a sterile house and he's mounted an operation."

"Which has something to do with this Webb, this Marie St. Somebody Webb?"

"St. Jacques. Yes."

"Do you want to tell me about it?"

"Not now—for your sake as well as mine. If I'm right and anyone thought you'd been given information, you could be transferred to Reykjavik without a sweater."

"But you said you didn't know what the connection was, that you wished you did."

"In the sense that I can't understand the reasons for it if, indeed, it exists. I only know one side of the story and it's filled with holes. I could be wrong." Catherine again drank a small portion of her whisky. "Look, Johnny," she continued. "Only you can make the decision and if it's negative, I'll understand. I have to know if Havilland's being over here has anything to do with a man named David Webb and his wife, Marie St. Jacques. She was an economist in Ottawa before her marriage."

"She's Canadian?"

"Yes. Let me tell you why I have to know without telling you so much you could get into trouble. If the connection's there, I have to go one way; if it's not, I can turn a hundred and eighty degrees and take another route. If it's the latter, I can go public. I can use the newspapers, radio, television, anything that can spread the word and pull her husband in."

"Which means he's out in the cold," broke in the attaché. "And you know where she is, but others don't."

"As I said before, you're very quick."

"But if it's the former—if there *is* a connection to Havilland, which you believe there is—"

"No comment. If I answered you, I'd be telling you more than you should know."

"I see. It's touchy. Let me think." Nelson picked up his martini, but instead of drinking he put it down. "How about an anonymous phone call that I got?"

"Such as?"

"A distraught Canadian woman looking for information about her missing American husband."

"Why would she have called you? She's experienced in government circles. Why not the consul general himself?"

"He wasn't in. I was."

"I don't want to disabuse you of your dreams of glory, Johnny, but you're not next in line."

"You're right. And anyone could check the switchboard and find out I never got the call."

Staples frowned, then leaned forward. "There is a way if you're willing to lie a bit further. It's based on reality. It happened, and no one could say that it didn't."

"What is it?"

"A woman stopped you in Garden Road when you were leaving the consulate. She didn't tell you very much but enough to alarm you, and she wouldn't go inside because she was frightened. She's the distraught woman looking for her missing American husband. You could even describe her."

"Start with her description," said Nelson.

Sitting in front of McAllister's desk, Lin Wenzu read from his notebook as the undersecretary of State listened. "Although the description differs, the differences are minor and easily achieved. Hair pulled back and covered by a hat, no makeup, flat shoes to reduce her height but not that much—it is she."

"And she claimed not to recognize the name of anyone in the directory who could be her so-called cousin?"

"A second cousin on her mother's side. Just farfetched yet specific enough to be credible. According to the receptionist she was quite awkward, even flustered. She also carried a purse that was so obviously a Gucci imitation that the receptionist took her for a backwoods hick. Pleasant but gullible."

"She recognized someone's name," said McAllister.

"If she did, why didn't she ask to see him? She wouldn't waste time under the circumstances."

"She probably assumed that we'd sent out an alert, that she couldn't take the chance of being recognized, not on the premises."

"I don't think that would concern her, Edward. With what she knows, what she's been through, she could be extremely convincing."

"With what she *thinks* she knows, Lin. She can't be sure of anything. She'll be very cautious, afraid to make a wrong move. That's her husband out there, and take my word for it—I saw them together—she's extremely protective of him. My God, she stole over five million dollars for the simple reason that she thought quite correctly he'd been wronged by his own people. By her lights he deserved it—*they* deserved it—and let Washington go to hell in a basket."

"She did that?"

"Havilland cleared you for everything. She did that and got away with it. Who was going to raise his voice? She had clandestine Washington just the way she wanted it. Frightened and embarrassed, both to the teeth."

"The more I learn, the more I admire her."

"Admire her all you like, just *find* her."

"Speaking of the ambassador, where is he?"

"Having a quiet lunch with the Canadian High Commissioner."

"He's going to tell him everything?"

"No, he's going to ask for blind cooperation with a telephone at his table so he can reach London. London will instruct the commissioner to do whatever Havilland asks him to do. It's all been arranged."

"He moves and shakes, doesn't he?"

"There's no one like him. He should be back any minute now—actually, he's late." The telephone rang and McAllister picked it up. "Yes? . . . No, he's not here. *Who?* . . . Yes, of course, I'll talk to him." The undersecretary covered the mouthpiece and spoke to the major. "It's our consul general. I mean American."

"Something's happened," said Lin, nervously getting out of his chair.

"Yes, Mr. Lewis, this is McAllister. I want you to know how much we appreciate everything, sir. The consulate's been most cooperative."

Suddenly, the door opened and Havilland walked into the room.

"It's the American consul general, Mr. Ambassador," said Lin. "I believe he was asking for you."

"This is no time for one of his damned dinner parties!"

"Just a minute, Mr. Lewis. The ambassador just arrived. I'm sure you want to speak with him." McAllister extended the phone to Havilland, who walked rapidly to the desk.

"Yes, Jonathan, what is it?" His tall, slender body rigid, his eyes fixed on an unseen spot in the garden beyond the large bay window, the ambassador stood in silence, listening. Finally, he spoke. "Thank you, Jonathan, you did the right thing. Say absolutely *nothing* to anyone and I'll take it from here." Havilland hung up and looked alternately at McAllister and Lin. "Our breakthrough, if it is a breakthrough, just came from the wrong direction. Not the Canadian but the *American* consulate."

"It's not consistent," said McAllister. "It's not Paris, not the street with her favorite tree, the maple tree, the maple *leaf*. That's the *Canadian* consulate, *not* the American."

"And with that analysis are we to disregard it?"

"Of course not. What happened?"

"An attaché named Nelson was stopped in Garden Road by a Canadian woman trying to find her American husband. This Nelson offered to help her, to accompany her to the police but she was adamant. She wouldn't go to the police, and neither would she go back with him to his office."

"Did she give any reasons?" asked Lin. "She appeals for help and then refuses it."

"Just that it was personal. Nelson described her as high-strung, overwrought. She identified herself as Marie Webb and said that perhaps her husband had come to the consulate looking for her. Could Nelson ask around and she'd call him back."

"That's *not* what she said before," protested McAllister. "She was clearly referring to what had happened to them in Paris, and that meant reaching an official of her own government, her own country. Canada."

"Why do you persist?" asked Havilland. "That's not a criticism, I simply want to know why."

"I'm not sure. Something's not right. Among other things, the major here established the fact that she did go to the Canadian consulate."

"Oh?" The ambassador looked at the man from Special Branch.

"The receptionist confirmed it. The description was close enough, especially for someone trained by a chameleon. Her story was that she had promised her family she would look up a distant cousin whose last name she had forgotten. The receptionist gave her a directory and she went through it."

"She found someone she knew," interrupted the undersecretary of State. "She made contact."

"Then there's your answer," said Havilland firmly. "She learned that her husband had *not* gone to a street with a row of maple trees, so she took the next best course of action. The American consulate."

"And identifies herself when she has to know people are looking for her all over Hong Kong?"

"Giving a false name would serve no purpose," the ambassador replied.

"They both speak French. She could have used a French word—*toile,* for instance. It means web."

"I know what it means, but I think you're reaching."

"Her husband would have understood. She would have done something less obvious."

"Mr. Ambassador," interrupted Lin Wenzu, slowly taking his eyes off McAllister. "Hearing your words to the American consul general, that he should say absolutely nothing to anyone, and now fully understanding your concerns for secrecy, I assume Mr. Lewis has not been apprised of the situation."

"Correct, Major."

"Then how did he know to call you? People frequently get lost here in Hong Kong. A missing husband or a missing wife is not so uncommon."

For an instant Havilland's expression was creased with self-doubt. "Jonathan Lewis and I go back a long time," he said, his voice lacking its usual authority. "He may be something of a bon vivant, but he's no fool—he wouldn't be here if he were. And the circumstances under which the woman stopped his attaché—well, Lewis knows me and he drew certain conclusions." The diplomat turned to McAllister; when he continued, his authority gradually returned. "Call Lewis back, Edward. Tell him to instruct this Nelson to stand by for a call from you. I'd prefer a less direct approach, but there isn't time. I want you to question him, question him on anything and everything you can think of. I'll be listening on the line in your office."

"You agree, then," said the undersecretary. "Something's wrong."

"Yes," answered Havilland, looking at Lin. "The major saw it and I didn't. I'd phrase it somewhat differently, but it's essentially what disturbs him. The question is not why Lewis called me, it's why an attaché went to *him*. After all, a highly agitated woman says her husband's missing but she won't go to the police, won't enter the consulate. Normally such a person would be dismissed as a crank. Certainly on the surface it's not a matter to bring to the attention of an overworked CG. Call Lewis."

"Of course. But, first, did things go smoothly with the Canadian commissioner? Will he cooperate?"

"The answer to your first question is no, things did not go smoothly. As to the second, he has no choice."

"I don't understand."

Havilland exhaled in weary irritation. "Through Ottawa he'll provide us with a list of everyone on his staff who's had any dealings whatsoever with Marie St. Jacques—reluctantly. That's the cooperation he's been instructed to deliver, but he was damned testy about it. To begin with, he himself went through a two-day seminar with her four years ago, and he ventured that probably a quarter of the consulate had done the same. Not that she'd remember them, but they certainly would remember her. She was 'outstanding,' was the way he put it. She's also a Canadian who was thoroughly messed up by a group of American assholes—mind you, he had no compunction at all using the word—in some kind of mentally deranged black operation—yes, that was the phrase he used, 'mentally deranged'—an *idiotic* operation mounted by these same assholes—indeed, he repeated it —that has never been satisfactorily explained." The ambassador stopped briefly, smiling briefly, as he coughed a short laugh. "It was all very refreshing. He didn't pull a single punch, and I haven't been talked to like that since my dear wife died. I need more of it."

"But you *did* tell him it was for her own good, didn't you? That we've *got* to find her before any harm's done to her."

"I got the distinct impression that our Canadian friend had serious doubts about my mental faculties. Call Lewis. God knows when we'll get that list. Our maple leaf will probably have it sent by train from Ottawa to Vancouver, and then on a slow freighter to Hong Kong, where it'll get lost in the mailroom. In the meantime, we've got an attaché who behaves very strangely. He leaps over fences when no such jumps are required."

"I've met John Nelson, sir," said Lin. "He's a bright lad and speaks a fair Chinese. He's quite popular with the consulate crowd."

"He's also something else, Major."

Nelson hung up the phone. Beads of perspiration had broken out on his forehead; he wiped them off with the back of his hand, satisfied that he had handled himself as well as he did, all things considered. He was especially pleased that he had turned the thrust of McAllister's questions against the questioner, albeit diplomatically.

Why did you feel compelled to go to the consul general?

Your call would seem to answer that, Mr. McAllister. I sensed that something out of the ordinary had happened. I thought the consul should be told.

But the woman refused to go to the police; she even refused to come inside the consulate.

As I said, it was out of the ordinary, sir. She was nervous and tense, but she wasn't a ding-dong.

A what?

She was perfectly lucid, you could even say controlled, in spite of her anxiety.

I see.

I wonder if you do, sir. I have no idea what the consul general told you, but I did suggest to him that what with the house in Victoria Peak, the marine guards, and then the arrival of Ambassador Havilland, he might consider calling someone up there.

You suggested it?

Yes, I did.

Why?

I don't think it would serve any purpose for me to speculate on these matters, Mr. McAllister. They don't concern me.

Yes, of course, you're right. I mean—yes, all right. But we must find that woman, Mr. Nelson. I've been instructed to tell you that if you can help us it would be greatly to your advantage.

I want to help in any event, sir. If she reaches me, I'll try to set up a meeting somewhere and call you. I knew I was right to do what I did, to say what I did.

We'll wait for your call.

Catherine was on target, thought John Nelson, there was one hell of a connection. So much of a connection that he did not dare use his consulate phone to reach Staples. But when he did reach her, he would ask her some very hard questions. He trusted Catherine, but the photographs and their consequences notwithstanding, he was not for sale. He got up from his desk and headed for the door of his office. A suddenly remembered dental appointment would suffice. As he walked down the corridor toward the reception room his thoughts returned to Catherine Staples. Catherine was one of the strongest people he had ever met, but the look in her eyes last night had conveyed not strength, but a kind of desperate fear. It was a Catherine he had never seen before.

"He diverted your questions to his own ends," said Havilland, coming through the door, the immense Lin Wenzu behind him. "Do you agree, Major?"

"Yes, and that means he anticipated the questions. He was primed for them."

"Which means someone primed him!"

"We never should have called him," said McAllister quietly, sitting behind the desk, his nervous fingers once again massaging his right temple. "Nearly everything he brought up was meant to provoke a response from me."

"We had to call him," insisted Havilland, "if only to learn that."

"He stayed in control. I lost it."

"You could not have behaved differently, Edward," said Lin. "To react other than you did would have been to question his motives. In essence, you would have threatened him."

"And at the moment, we don't want him to feel threatened," agreed Havilland. "He's getting information for someone, and we've got to find out who it is."

"And that means Webb's wife *did* reach someone she knew and told that person everything." McAllister leaned forward, his elbows on the desk, his hands tightly clasped.

"You were right, after all," said the ambassador, looking down at the undersecretary of State. "A street with her favorite maple trees. Paris. The inevitable repetition. It's quite clear. Nelson is working for someone in the Canadian consulate—and whoever it is, is in touch with Webb's wife."

McAllister looked up. "Then Nelson's either a damn fool or a bigger damn fool. By his own admission he knows—at least, he assumes—that he's dealing with highly sensitive information involving an adviser to presidents. Dismissal aside, he could be sent to prison for conspiring against the government."

"He's not a fool, I can assure you," said Lin.

"Then either someone is forcing him to do this against his will—blackmail most likely—or he's being paid to find out if there's a connection between Marie St. Jacques and this house in Victoria Peak. It can't be anything else." Frowning, Havilland sat down in the chair in front of the desk.

"Give me a day," continued the major from MI6. "Perhaps I can find out. If I can, we'll pick up whoever it is in the consulate."

"No," said the diplomat whose expertise lay in covert operations. "You have until eight o'clock tonight. We can't afford *that,* but if we can avoid a confrontation and any possible fallout, we must try. Containment is everything. Try, Lin. For God's sake, *try.*"

"And after eight o'clock, Mr. Ambassador? What then?"

"Then, Major, we pull in our clever and evasive attaché and break him. I'd much prefer to use him without his knowing it, without risking alarms, but the woman comes first. Eight o'clock, Major Lin."

"I'll do everything I can."

"And if we're wrong," went on Havilland, as if Lin Wenzu had not spoken, "if this Nelson has been set up as a blind and knows nothing, I want all the rules broken.

I don't care how you do it or how much it costs in bribes or the garbage you have to employ to get it done. I want cameras, telephone taps, electronic surveillance—whatever you can manage—on every single person in that consulate. Someone there knows where she is. Someone there is hiding her."

"Catherine, it's John," said Nelson into the pay phone on Albert Road.

"How good of you to call," answered Staples quickly. "It's been a trying afternoon, but do let's have drinks one of these days. It'll be so good to see you after all these months, and you can tell me about Canberra. But do tell me one thing now. Was I right in what I told *you*?"

"I have to see you, Catherine."

"Not even a hint?"

"I have to see you. Are you free?"

"I have a meeting in forty-five minutes."

"Then later, around five. There's a place called the Monkey Tree in the Wanchai, on Gloucester—"

"I know it. I'll be there."

John Nelson hung up. There was nothing else to do but go back to the office. He could not stay away for three hours, not after his conversation with Undersecretary of State Edward McAllister; appearances precluded such an absence. He had heard about McAllister; the undersecretary had spent seven years in Hong Kong, leaving only months before Nelson had arrived. Why had he returned? Why was there a sterile house in Victoria Peak with Ambassador Havilland suddenly in residence? Above all, why was Catherine Staples so frightened? He owed Catherine his life, but he had to have a few answers. He had a decision to make.

Lin Wenzu had all but exhausted his sources. Only one gave him pause for thought. Inspector Ian Ballantyne, as he usually did, answered questions with other questions, rather than delivering concise answers himself. It was maddening, for one never knew whether or not the vaunted transfer from Scotland Yard knew something about a given subject, in this case an American attaché named John Nelson.

"Met the chap several times," Ballantyne had said. "Bright sort. Speaks your lingo, did you know that?"

"My 'lingo,' Inspector?"

"Well, damn few of us did, even during the Opium War. Interesting period of history, wasn't it, Major?"

"The Opium War? I was talking about the attaché John Nelson."

"Oh, is there a connection?"

"With what, Inspector?"

"The Opium War."

"If there is, he's a hundred and fifty years old and his dossier says thirty-two."

"Really? That young, eh?"

But Ballantyne had employed several pauses too many to satisfy Lin. Regardless, if the old war-horse did know something, he was not going to reveal it. Everyone else —from the Hong Kong and Kowloon police to the "specialists" who worked the American consulate gathering information for payment—gave Nelson as clean a bill of health as was respectable in the territory. If Nelson had a vulnerable side, it was in his extensive and not too discriminating search for sex, but insofar as it was heterosexual, and he was single, it was to be applauded, not condemned. One "specialist" told Lin that he heard Nelson had been warned to have himself medically checked on a fairly regular basis. No crime; the attaché was a cocksman—ask him to dinner.

The telephone rang; Lin grabbed it. "Yes?"

"Our subject walked to the Peak Tram and took a taxi to the Wanchai. He is in a café called the Monkey Tree. I am with him. I can see him."

"It's out of the way and very crowded," said the major. "Has anyone joined him?"

"No, but he asked for a table for two."

"I'll be there as soon as I can. If you have to leave, I'll contact you by radio. You're driving Vehicle Seven, are you not?"

"Vehicle Seven, sir. . . . *Wait!* A woman is walking toward his table. He's getting up."

"Do you recognize her?"

"It's too dark here. No."

"Pay the waiter. Disrupt the service. But not obviously,

only for a few minutes. I'll use our ambulance and the siren until I'm a block away."

"Catherine, I owe you so much, and I want to help you in any way I can, but I have to know more than what you've told me."

"There's a connection, isn't there? Havilland and Marie St. Jacques."

"I won't confirm that—I *can't* confirm it—because I haven't spoken to Havilland. I did, however, speak to another man, a man I've heard a lot about who used to be stationed here—one hell of a brain—and he sounded as desperate as you did last night."

"I seemed that way to you last night?" said Staples, smoothing her gray-streaked hair. "I wasn't aware of it."

"Hey, come on. Not in your words, maybe, but in the way you talked. The stridency was just below the surface. You sounded like *me* when you gave me the photographs. Believe me, I can identify."

"Johnny, believe *me*. We may be dealing with something neither one of us should get near, something way up in the clouds that we—*I*—don't have the knowledge to make a proper decision."

"I have to make a decision, Catherine." Nelson looked up for the waiter. "Where are those goddamned drinks?"

"I'm not panting."

"I am. I owe you everything and I like you and I know you wouldn't use the photographs against me, which makes it all worse—"

"I gave you all there were, and we burned the negatives together."

"So my debt's *real*, don't you see that? *Jesus*, the kid was what—twelve years *old?*"

"You didn't know that. You were drugged."

"My passport to oblivion. No secretary of State in my future, only secretary of kiddie-porn. One hell of a trip!"

"It's over and you're being melodramatic. I just want you to tell me if there's a connection between Havilland and Marie St. Jacques—which I think you can do. Why is that so difficult? I *will* know what to do then."

"Because if I do, I have to tell Havilland that I told you."

"Then give me an hour."

"Why?"

"Because I *do* have several photographs in my vault at the consulate," lied Catherine Staples.

Nelson shot back in his chair, stunned. "Oh, *God.* I don't *believe* this!"

"Try to understand, Johnny. We all play hardball now and then because it's in the best interests of our employers—our individual countries, if you like. Marie St. Jacques was a friend of mine—*is* a friend of mine—and her life became nothing in the eyes of self-important men who ran a covert operation that didn't give a holy damn about her and her husband. They used them both and then tried to *kill* them both! Let me tell you something, Johnny. I detest your Central Intelligence Agency and your State Department's so grandly named Consular Operations. It's not that they're bastards, it's that they're such *stupid* bastards. And if I sense that an operation is being mounted, again using these two people who've been through so much pain, I intend to find out why and act accordingly. But no more blank checks with their lives. I'm experienced and they're not, and I'm angry enough—no, *furious* enough—to demand answers."

"Oh, *Christ*—"

The waiter arrived with their drinks, and as Staples looked up to signify thanks, her eyes were drawn to a man by a telephone booth in the crowded outside corridor watching them. She looked away.

"What's it going to be, Johnny?" she continued. "Confirm or deny?"

"Confirmed," whispered Nelson, reaching for his glass.

"The house in Victoria Peak?"

"Yes."

"Who was the man you spoke with, the one who had been stationed here?"

"McAllister. Undersecretary of State McAllister."

"Good *Lord!*"

There was excessive movement in the outside corridor. Catherine shielded her eyes and turned her head slightly, which widened her peripheral vision. A large man entered and walked toward the telephone against the wall. There was only one man like him in all of Hong Kong. It was *Lin Wenzu*, MI6, Special Branch! The Americans had enlisted the best, but it could be the worst for Marie and her husband.

"You've done nothing wrong, Johnny," said Staples, rising from her chair. "We'll talk further, but right now I'm going to the ladies' room."

"Catherine?"

"What?"

"Hardball?"

"Very hard, my darling."

Staples walked past a shrinking Lin, who turned away. She went into the ladies' room, waited several seconds, then walked out with two other women and broke away, continuing down the corridor and into the Monkey Tree's kitchen. Without saying a word to the startled waiters and cooks, she found the exit and went outside. She ran up the alley into Gloucester Road; she turned left, her stride quickening until she found a phone booth. Inserting a coin, she dialed.

"Hello?"

"*Marie,* get out of the flat! My car's in a garage a block to your right as you leave the building. It's called Ming's; the sign's in red. Get there as quickly as you can! I'll meet you. *Hurry!*"

Catherine Staples hailed a taxi.

"The woman's name is Staples, Catherine *Staples!*" said Lin Wenzu sharply into the phone on the corridor wall of the Monkey Tree, raising his voice to be heard over the din. "Insert the consulate disk and search it through the computer. *Quickly!* I want her address and make damn-damn sure it's current!" The muscles of the major's jaw worked furiously as he waited, listening. The answer was delivered, and he issued another order: "If one of our team's vehicles is in the area, get on the radio and tell him to head over there. If not, dispatch one immediately." Lin paused, again listening. "The American woman," he said quietly into the phone. "They're to watch for her. If she's spotted, close in and take her. We're on our way."

"Vehicle Five, *respond!*" repeated the radio operator, speaking into a microphone, his hand on a switch in the lower right-hand corner of the console in front of him.

The room was white and without windows, the hum of the air conditioning low but constant, the whir of the filtering system even quieter. On three walls there were banks of sophisticated radio and computer equipment above spotless white counters made of the smoothest Formica. There was an antiseptic quality about the room; hardness was everywhere. It might have been an electronics laboratory in a well-endowed medical center, but it was not. It was another kind of center. The communications center of MI6, Special Branch, Hong Kong.

"Vehicle Five *responding!*" shouted an out-of-breath voice over the speaker. "I received your signal, but I was a street away covering the Thai. We were right. Drugs."

"Go on scrambler!" ordered the operator, throwing the switch. There was a whistling sound that stopped as abruptly as it had started. "You're off the Thai," continued the radioman. "You're nearest. Get over to Arbuthnot Road; the Botanical Garden entrance is the quickest way." He gave the address of Catherine Staples's building and ended with a final command. "The American woman. Watch for her. Take her."

"*Aiya,*" whispered the breathless agent from Special Branch.

Marie tried not to panic, imposing a control over herself she did not feel. The situation was ludicrous. It was also deadly serious. She was dressed in Catherine's ill-fitting robe, having taken a long hot bath and, far worse, having washed her clothes in Staples's kitchen sink. They were hanging over the plastic chairs on Catherine's small balcony and were still wet. It had seemed so natural, so logical, to wash away the heat and the dirt of Hong Kong from herself as well as from strangers' clothes. And the cheap sandals had raised blisters on the soles of her feet; she had broken an ugly one with a needle and walking was difficult. But she dared not walk, she had to run.

What had happened? Catherine was not the sort of person to issue peremptory commands. Any more than she herself was, especially with David. People like Catherine avoided the imperative approach because it only clouded a victim's thinking—and her friend Marie St. Jacques was a victim now, not to the degree that poor David was, but a victim nevertheless. *Move!* How often had Jason said that in Zurich and Paris? So frequently she still tensed at the word.

She dressed, the wet clothes clinging to her body, and rummaged through Staples's closet for a pair of slippers. They were uncomfortable but softer than the sandals. She could run; she *had* to run.

Her hair! Oh, *Christ,* the hair! She ran to the bathroom, where Catherine kept a porcelain jar filled with hairpins and clasps. In seconds, she secured her hair on the top of her head, walked rapidly back into the flat's tiny living room, found her foolish hat and jammed it on.

The wait for the elevator was interminable! According to the lighted numbers above the panels, both elevators jogged between floors one, three, and seven, neither venturing above to the ninth floor. Preceding residents going out for the evening had programmed the vertical monsters, delaying her descent.

Avoid elevators whenever you can. They're traps. Jason Bourne. Zurich.

Marie looked up and down the hallway. She saw the fire-exit staircase door and ran to it.

Out of breath, she lunged into the short lobby, composing herself as best she could to deflect the glances directed at her by five or six tenants, some entering, some leaving. She did not count; she could barely see; she had to get out!

My car's in a garage a block to your right as you leave the building. It's called Ming's. Was it to the right? Or was it *left?* Out on the pavement she hesitated. *Right* or *left?* "Right" meant so many things, "left" was more specific. She tried to think. What had Catherine *said?* Right! She had to go right; it was the first thing that came to her mind. She had to trust that.

Your first reflections are the best, the most accurate, because the impressions are stored in your head, like information in a data bank. That's what your head is. Jason Bourne. Paris.

She started running. Her left slipper fell off; she stopped, stooping down to retrieve it. Suddenly a car came careening around the gates of the Botanical Gardens across the wide street, and, like an angry heat-

searching missile, whipped to its left and zeroed in on
her. The automobile swerved in a semicircle, screeching
as it spun in the road. A man leaped out and raced toward
her.

18

There was nothing else to do. She was cornered, trapped.
Marie screamed, and screamed again, and again, as the
Chinese agent approached, her hysteria mounting as the
man politely but firmly took her by the arm. She recognized him—he was one of *them*, one of the bureaucrats!
Her screams reached a crescendo. People stopped and
turned in the street. Women gasped as startled men
stepped hesitantly forward or looked around frantically
for the police, several shouting for them.

"*Please, Mrs. . . . !*" cried the Oriental, trying to keep
his voice controlled. "No harm will come to you. Allow
me to escort you to my vehicle. It is for your own protection."

"*Help me!*" shrieked Marie as the astonished twilight
strollers gathered into a crowd. "This man's a *thief!* He
stole my purse, my money! He's trying to take my jewelry!"

"See here, chap!" shouted an elderly Englishman,
hobbling forward, raising his walking stick. "I've sent a
lad for the police, but until they arrive, by God, I'll *thrash*
you!"

"Please, sir," insisted the man from Special Branch
quietly. "This is a matter for the authorities, and I am
with the authorities. Permit me to show you my identification."

"*Easy, myte!*" roared a voice with an Australian accent
as a man rushed forward, gently pushing the elderly Brit-
isher aside and lowering his cane. "You're a grand fair
dinkum, old man, but don't half bother yourself! These

punks call for a younger type." The strapping Australian stood in front of the Chinese agent. "Tyke yer hands off the lady, punkhead! And I'd be goddamned quick about it, if I were you."

"Please, sir, this is a serious misunderstanding. The lady is in danger and she is wanted for questioning by the authorities."

"I don't see you in no uniform!"

"Permit me to show you my credentials."

"That's what he said an hour ago when he attacked me in Garden Road!" shouted Marie hysterically. "People tried to help me then! He lied to everyone! Then he stole my purse! He's been *following* me!" Marie knew that none of the things she kept screaming made sense. She could only hope for confusion, something that Jason had taught her to use.

"I'm not saying it *agyne,* myte!" yelled the Australian, stepping forward. "Tyke yer bloody hands off the lady!"

"Please, sir. I cannot do that. Other officials are on their way."

"Oh, they are, are they? You punkheads travel in gangs, do you? Well, you'll be a pitiful sight for their eyes when they get here!" The Australian grabbed the Oriental by the shoulder, spinning him to his left. But as the man from Special Branch spun, his right foot—the toe of his leather shoe extended like a knife point—whipped around, crashing up into the Australian's abdomen. The good Samaritan from Down Under doubled over, falling to his knees.

"I'll ask you again not to *interfere,* sir!"

"Do you, now? You slope-eyed *son of a bitch!*" The furious Australian lunged up, hurling his body at the Oriental, his fists pounding the man from Special Branch. The crowd roared its approval, its collective voice filling the street—and Marie's arm was *free!* Then other sounds joined the melee. Sirens, followed by three racing automobiles, among them an ambulance. All three swerved in their sudden turns, as tires screeched and the vehicles came to jolting stops.

Marie plunged through the crowd and reached the inner pavement; she started running toward the red sign a half block away. The slippers had fallen off her feet; the

swollen, shredded blisters burned, sending shafts of pain
up her legs. She could not allow herself to think about
pain. She had to run, *run, get away!* Then the booming
voice surged over and through the noises in the street,
and she pictured a large man roaring. It was the huge
Chinese they called the major.

"Mrs. *Webb!* Mrs. Webb, I *beg you! Stop!* We mean you
no harm! You'll be told *everything!* For God's sake, *stop!*"

Told everything! thought Marie. Told lies and *more lies!*
Suddenly people were rushing toward her. What were
they *doing? Why . . .* ? Then they raced past, mostly men,
but not all men, and she understood. There was a panic
in the street—perhaps an accident, mutilation, death.
Let's go see. Let's watch! From a distance, mind you.

*Opportunities will present themselves. Recognize them, act on
them.*

Marie suddenly whipped around, crouching, lunging
through the still-onrushing crowd to the curb, keeping
her body as low as possible, and ran back to where she
had come so close to recapture. She kept turning her
head to her left—watching, hoping. She *saw* him through
the racing bodies! The huge major ran past in the other
direction; with him was another man, another well-
dressed man, another bureaucrat.

The crowd was cautious, as the ghoulish are always
cautious, inching forward but not so far as to get involved. What they saw was not flattering to the Chinese
onlookers or to those who held the martial arts of the
Orient in mystical esteem. The lithe, strapping Australian, his language magnificently obscene, was pummeling three separate assailants out of his personal
boxing ring. Suddenly, to the astonishment of everyone,
the Australian picked up one of his fallen adversaries and
let out a roar as loud as the immense major's. "Fer *Christ's
syke!* Will you cryzies cut this out? Yer not punkheads,
even I can tell *that!* We was *both* snookered!"

Marie ran across the wide street to the entrance of the
Botanical Gardens. She stood under a tree by the gate
with a direct line of sight to Ming's Parking Palace. The
major had passed the garage, pausing at several alleyways
that intersected Arbuthnot Road, sending his subordinate down several of them, constantly looking around for

his support troops. They were not there; Marie saw that for herself as the crowd dispersed. All three were breathing hard and leaning against the ambulance, led there by the Australian.

A taxi drove up to Ming's. No one, at first, got out, then the driver emerged. He walked into the open garage and spoke to someone behind a glass booth. He bowed in thanks, returned to the cab, and spoke to his passenger. Cautiously his fare opened the door and stepped onto the curb. It was Catherine! She, too, walked into the wide opening, far more rapidly than the driver, and spoke into the glass booth, shaking her head, indicating that she had been told what she did not want to hear.

Suddenly Lin appeared. He was retracing his steps, obviously angered by the men who were supposed to be tracing *his* steps. He was about to cross the open garage; he would see Catherine!

"Carlos!" screamed Marie, assuming the worst, knowing it would tell her everything. *"Delta!"*

The major spun around, his eyes wide in shock. Marie raced into the Botanical Gardens; it was the *key! Cain is for Delta and Carlos will be killed by Cain* ... or whatever the codes were that had been spread through Paris! They *were* using David again! It wasn't a probability anymore, it was the reality! They—*it*— the United States government—was sending her husband out to play the role that had nearly killed him, killed by his own people! What kind of bastards *were* they? ... Or, conversely, what kind of ends justified the means supposedly sane men would use to reach them?

Now more than ever she had to find David, find him before he took risks others should be taking! He had given so much and now they asked for more, demanded more in the cruelest way possible. But to find him she had to reach Catherine, who was no more than a hundred yards away. She had to draw out the enemy and get back across the street without the enemy seeing her. *Jason, what can I do?*

She hid behind a cluster of bushes, inching farther inside, as the major ran through the Garden's gates. The immense Oriental stopped and looked around with his squinting, penetrating gaze, then turned and shouted for his subordinate, who had apparently emerged from an alley on Arbuthnot Road. The second man had difficulty getting across the street; the traffic was heavier and slower because of the stationary ambulance and two additional vehicles blocking the normal flow near the entrance to the Botanical Gardens. The major suddenly grew furious as he saw and understood the reasons for the growing traffic.

"Get those fools to move the cars!" he roared. "And send them over here. . . . *No!* Send one to the gates on Albany Road. The rest of you come back here! *Hurry!*"

The early-evening strollers became more numerous. Men loosened the ties they had worn all day at their offices, while women carried high-heeled shoes in casual bags, supplanting them with sandals. Wives wheeling baby carriages were joined by husbands; lovers embraced and walked arm in arm among the rows of exploding flowers. The laughter of racing children pealed across the Gardens, and the major held his place by the entrance gate. Marie swallowed, the panic in her growing. The ambulance and the two automobiles were being moved; the traffic began to flow normally.

A crash! Near the ambulance an impatient driver had rammed the car in front of him. The major could not help himself; the proximity of the accident so close to his official vehicle forced him to move forward, obviously to ascertain whether or not his men were involved. *Opportunities will present themselves . . . use them.* Now!

Marie raced around the far end of the bushes, then dashed across the grass to join a foursome on the gravel path that led out of the Gardens. She glanced to her right, afraid of what she might see but knowing she had to know. Her worst fears were borne out; the huge major had sensed—or seen—the figure of a woman running behind him. He paused for a moment, uncertain, unsure, then broke into a rapid stride toward the gate.

A horn blew—four short, quick blasts. It was Catherine, waving at her through the open window of a small Japanese car as Marie raced into the street.

"Get in!" shouted Staples.

"He saw me!"

"Hurry!"

Marie jumped into the front seat as Catherine gunned

the small car and swerved out of line, half on the side-
walk, then swung back with a break in the accelerating
traffic. She turned into a side street and drove swiftly
down it to an intersection where there was a sign with a
red arrow pointing right. *Central. Business District.* Staples
turned right.

"Catherine!" shouted Marie. "He *saw* me!"

"Worse," said Staples. "He saw the car."

"A two-door green Mitsubishi!" shouted Lin Wenzu into
his hand-held radio. "The license number is AOR-five,
three, five, zero—the zero could be a six, but I don't think
so. It doesn't matter, the first three letters will be enough.
I want it flashed on all points, emergency status using the
police telephone banks! The driver and the passenger
are to be taken into custody and there are to be no conversations with either party. It is a Government House
matter and no explanations will be given. Get on this!
Now!"

Staples turned into a parking garage on Ice House Street.
The newly lighted, bright red sign of the Mandarin could
be seen barely a block away. "We'll rent a car," said
Catherine as she accepted her ticket from the man in the
booth. "I know several head boys at the hotel."

"*We* park? You park?" The grinning attendant obviously hoped for the former.

"You park," replied Staples, withdrawing several
Hong Kong dollars from her purse. "Let's go," she said,
turning to Marie. "And stay on my right, in the shadows,
close to the buildings. How are your feet?"

"I'd rather not say."

"Then don't. There's no time to do anything about
them now. Bear up, old girl."

"Catherine, stop sounding like C. Aubrey Smith in
drag."

"Who's that?"

"Forget it. I like old movies. Let's go."

Marie hobbling, the two women walked down the
street to a side entrance of the Mandarin. They climbed
the hotel steps and went inside. "There's a ladies' room
to the right, past the line of shops," said Catherine.

"I see the sign.".

"Wait there. I'll be with you as soon as I can make arrangements."

"Is there a drugstore here?"

"I don't want you walking around. There'll be descriptions out everywhere."

"I understand that, but can *you* walk around? Just a bit."

"Bad time of the month?"

"*No, my feet!* Vaseline, skin lotion, sandals—no, *not* sandals. Rubber thongs, perhaps, and peroxide."

"I'll do what I can, but time is everything."

"It's been that way for the past year. A terrible treadmill. Will it stop, Catherine?"

"I'm doing my damnedest to see to it. You're a friend and a countryman, my dear. And I'm a very *angry* woman —and speaking of such—how many women did you encounter in the hallowed halls of the CIA or its bumbling counterpart at the State Department, Consular Operations?"

Marie blinked, trying to remember. "None, actually."

"Then *fuck* 'em!"

"There was a woman in Paris—"

"There always *is,* dear. Go to the ladies' room."

"An automobile is a hindrance in Hong Kong," said Lin, looking at the clock on the wall of his office in the headquarters of MI6, Special Branch. It read 6:34. "Therefore we must assume she intends driving Webb's wife some distance, hiding her, and will not risk taxi records. Our eight o'clock deadline has been rescinded, the chase now takes its place. We must intercept her. Is there anything we haven't considered?"

"Putting the Australian in jail," suggested the short, well-dressed subordinate firmly. "We suffered casualties in the Walled City, but *his* were a public embarrassment. We know where he's staying. We can pick him up."

"On what charge?"

"Obstruction."

"To what end?"

The subordinate shrugged angrily. "Satisfaction, that's all."

"You've just answered your own question. Your pride is inconsequential. Stick to the woman—the women."

"You're right, of course."

"Every garage, the car rental agencies here on the island and in Kowloon all have been reached by the police, correct?"

"Yes, sir. But I must point out that the Staples woman could easily call upon one of her friends—her Canadian friends—and she would have an automobile we could not track."

"We operate on what we can control, not what we can't. Besides, from what I knew before and what I have subsequently learned about Foreign Service Officer Staples, I would say she's acting alone, certainly not under official sanction. She won't involve anyone else for the time being."

"How can you be sure?"

Lin looked at his subordinate; he had to choose his words carefully. "Just a guess."

"Your guesses have a reputation for accuracy."

"An inflated judgment. Common sense is my ally." The telephone rang. The major's hand shot out. "Yes?"

"Police Central Four," droned a male voice.

"We appreciate your cooperation, Central Four."

"A Ming's Parking Palace responded to our inquiry. The Mitsubishi AOR has a space there leased on a monthly basis. The owner's name is Staples. Catherine Staples, a Canadian. The car was taken out roughly thirty-five minutes ago."

"You've been most helpful, Central Four," said Lin. "Thank you." He hung up and looked at his anxious subordinate. "We now have three new pieces of information. The first is that the inquiry we sent out through the police was definitely sent out. The second is that at least one garage wrote down the information, and thirdly, Mrs. Staples leases her parking space by the month."

"It's a start, sir."

"There are three major and perhaps a dozen minor rental agencies, not counting the hotels, which we've covered separately. Those are manageable statistics, but, of course, the garages are not."

"Why not?" questioned the subordinate. "At most there are, perhaps, a hundred. Who cares to build a garage in Hong Kong when he could house a dozen shops

—businesses? At maximum, the police telephone banks are twenty to thirty operators. They can reach them all."

"It's not the numbers, old friend. It's the mentality of the employees, for the jobs are not enviable. Those who can write are too lazy or too hostile to bother, and those who can't, flee from any association with the police."

"One garage responded."

"A true Cantonese. It was the owner."

"The owner should be told!" cried the parking boy in shrill Chinese to the booth attendant at the garage on Ice House Street.

"Why?"

"I explained it to you! I wrote it *down* for you—"

"Because you go to school and write somewhat better than I do does not make you boss-boss here."

"You cannot write at all! You were shit-shit afraid! You called for me when the man on the telephone said it was a police emergency. You illiterates always run from the police. That was the *car,* the green Mitsubishi I parked on Level Two! If you won't call the police, you must call the owner."

"There are things they don't teach you in school, boy with small organ."

"They teach us not to go against the police. It is bad joss."

"I *will* call the police—or, better, you may be their hero."

"Good!"

"*After* the two women return, and I have a short talk with the driver."

"What?"

"She thought she was giving me—us—two dollars, but it was eleven. One of the bills was a ten-dollar note. She was very nervous, very upset. She is frightened. She did not watch her money."

"You said it *was* two dollars!"

"And now I'm being honest. Would I be honest with you if I did not have both our interests in my heart?"

"In what way?"

"I will tell this rich, frightened American—she spoke American—that you and I have not called back the police on *her* behalf. She will reward us on the spot—very, *very* generously—for she will understand that she may not retrieve her car without doing so. You may watch me from inside the garage by the other telephone. After she pays, I will send another boy for her car, which he will have great trouble finding, for I will give him the wrong location, and you will call the police. The police will arrive, we will have done our heavenly duty, and had a night of money like few other nights in this miserable job."

The parking boy squinted, shaking his head. "You're right," he said. "They don't teach such things in school. And I suppose I do not have a choice."

"Oh, but you do," said the attendant, pulling a long knife from his belt. "You can say no, and I will cut out your talk-talk tongue."

Catherine approached the concierge's desk in the Mandarin lobby, annoyed that she did not know either of the two clerks behind the counter. She needed a favor quickly, and in Hong Kong that meant dealing with a person one knew. Then to her relief she spotted the evening shift's Number one concierge. He was in the middle of the lobby trying to mollify an excited guest. She moved to the right and waited, hoping to catch Lee Teng's eye. She had cultivated Teng, sending numerous Canadians to him when problems of convenience had seemed insurmountable. He had always been paid handsomely.

"Yes, may I be of help, Mrs. . . . ?" said the young Chinese clerk, moving in front of Staples.

"I'll wait for Mr. Teng, if you please."

"Mr. Teng is very busy, Mrs. . . . A very bad time for Mr. Teng. You are a guest of the Mandarin, Mrs. . . . ?"

"I'm a resident of the territory and an old friend of Mr. Teng. Where possible I bring my business here so the desk gets the credit."

"*Ohh* . . . ?" The clerk responded to Catherine's nontourist status. He leaned forward, speaking confidentially. "Lee Teng has terrible joss tonight. The lady goes to the grand ball at Government House but her clothes go to Bangkok. She must think Mr. Teng has wings under his jacket and jet engines in his armpits, yes?"

"An interesting concept. The lady just flew in?"

"Yes, Mrs. . . . But she had many pieces of luggage. She did not miss the one she misses now. She blames first her husband and now Lee Teng."

"Where's her husband?"

"In the bar. He offered to take the next plane to Bangkok, but his kindness only made his wife angrier. He will not leave the bar, and he will not get to Government House in a way that will make him pleased with himself in the morning. Bad joss all around. . . . Perhaps I can be of assistance to you while Mr. Teng does his best to calm everybody."

"I want to rent a car and I need one as fast as you can get it for me."

"*Aiya,*" said the clerk. "It is seven o'clock at night, and the rental offices do little leasing in the evening hours. Most are closed."

"I'm sure there are exceptions."

"Perhaps a hotel car with a chauffeur?"

"Only if there's nothing else available. As I mentioned, I'm not a guest here and, frankly, I'm not made of money."

"Who among us'?" asked the clerk enigmatically. "As the good Christian Book says—somewhere, I think."

"Sounds right," agreed Staples. "Please, get on the phone and do your best."

The young man reached beneath the counter and pulled out a plastic-bound list of car rental agencies. He went to a telephone several feet to his right, picked it up, and started dialing. Catherine looked over at Lee Teng; he had steered his irate lady to the wall by a miniature palm in an obvious attempt to keep her from alarming the other guests who sat around the ornate lobby greeting friends and ordering cocktails. He was speaking rapidly, softly, and, by God, thought Staples, he was actually getting her attention. Whatever her legitimate complaints, mused Catherine, the woman was an ass. She wore a chinchilla stole in just about the worst climate on earth for such delicate fur. Not that she, Foreign Service Officer Staples, ever had to consider such a problem. She might have if she had chucked the FSO status and stuck with Owen Staples. The son of a bitch owned at least four banks in Toronto now. Not a bad sort, really, and to add to her sense of guilt, Owen had never remarried. Not *fair*, Owen! She had run across him three years ago, after her stint in Europe, while attending the Brit-organized conference in Toronto. They had had drinks at the Mayfair Club in the King Edward Hotel, not so unlike the Mandarin, actually.

"Come on, Owen. Your looks, your *money*—and you had the looks before your money—why not? There are a thousand beautiful girls within a five-block radius who'd grab you."

"Once was enough, Cathy. You taught me that."

"I don't know, but you make me feel—oh, I don't know—somehow so guilty. I left you, Owen, but not because I wasn't fond of you."

" 'Fond' of me?"

"You know what I mean."

"Yes, I think so." Owen had laughed. "You left me for all the right reasons, and I accepted your leaving without animus for like-minded reasons. If you had waited five minutes longer, I think I would have thrown you out. I'd paid the rent that month."

"You bastard!"

"Not at all, neither of us. You had your ambitions and I had mine. They simply weren't compatible."

"But that doesn't explain why you never remarried."

"I just told you. You taught me, my dear."

"Taught you what? That *all* ambitions are incompatible?"

"Where they existed in our extremes, yes. You see, I learned that I wasn't interested on any permanent basis in anyone who *didn't* have what I suppose you'd call a passionate 'drive,' or an overriding ambition, but I couldn't live with such a person day in and day out. And those without ambition left something wanting in our relationship. No permanency there."

"But what about a family? Children?"

"I have two children," Owen had said quietly. "Of whom I'm immensely—fond. I love them very much, and their very ambitious mothers have been terribly kind. Even *their* subsequent respective husbands have been understanding. While they were growing up I saw my children constantly. So, in a sense, I had three families. Quite civilized, if frequently confusing."

"*You?* The paragon of the community, the banker's *banker!* The man they said took a shower in a Dickens' *nightshirt!* A deacon of the church!"

"I gave *that* up when you left. At any rate, it was simply statecraft on my part. You practice it every day."

"*Owen,* you never *told* me."

"You never asked, Cathy. You had your ambitions and I had mine. But I will tell you my one regret, if you want to hear it."

"I do."

"I'm genuinely sorry that we never had a child together. Judging by the two I have, he or she would have been quite marvelous."

"You bastard, I'm going to cry."

"Please don't. Let's be honest, neither of us has any regrets."

Catherine's reverie was suddenly interrupted. The clerk lurched back from the telephone, his hands triumphantly on the counter. "You have good *joss,* Mrs. . . . !" he cried. "The dispatcher at the Apex agency on Bonham Strand East was still there, and he has cars available but nobody to drive one here."

"I'll take a taxi. Write out the address." Staples looked around for the hotel drugstore. There were too many people in the lobby, too much confusion. "Where can I buy some—skin lotion or Vaseline, sandals or thongs?" she asked, turning to the clerk.

"There is a newspaper stand down the hallway to the right, Mrs. . . . They have many of the items you describe. But, may I please have money, as you must present a receipt to the dispatcher? It is one thousand dollars, Hong Kong, whatever remains to be returned or additional monies to be added—"

"I don't have that much on me. I'll have to use a card."

"So much the better."

Catherine opened her purse and pulled out a credit card from an inside pocket. "I'll be right back," she said, placing it on the counter, as she started for the hallway on the right. For no reason in particular, she glanced over at Lee Teng and his distraught lady. To her brief amusement, the overdressed woman in the foolish fur was nodding appreciatively as Teng pointed to the line of overpriced shops one reached by climbing a staircase above the lobby. Lee Teng was a true diplomat. Without question, he had explained to the overwrought guest that she had an option that would both serve her needs and her nerves and hit her errant husband in his financial solar plexus. This was Hong Kong, and she could purchase the best and the most glittering, and for a price everything would be ready in time for the grand ball at Government House. Staples continued toward the hallway.

"Catherine!" The name was so sharply spoken Staples froze. *"Please,* Mrs. *Catherine!"*

Rigid, Staples turned. It was Lee Teng, who had broken away from his now mollified guest. "What is it?" she asked, frightened as the middle-aged Teng approached, his face lined with concern, sweat evident on his balding skull.

"I saw you only moments ago. I had a problem."

"I know all about it."

"So do you, Catherine."

"I beg your pardon?"

Teng glanced at the counter—oddly enough, not at the young man who had helped her, but at the other clerk, who was at the opposite end of the desk. The man was by himself, with no guests in front of him, and he was looking at his associate. "Damn bad joss!" exclaimed Teng under his breath.

"What are you talking about?" asked Staples.

"Come over here," said the Number one concierge of the night shift as he pulled Catherine to the side, away from the sight of the counter. He reached into his pocket and removed a perforated half-page of paper on which there was a computer printout. "Four copies of this were sent down from upstairs. I managed to obtain three, but the fourth is under the counter."

Emergency. Government control. A Canadian woman by the name of Mrs. Catherine Staples may attempt to lease an automobile for personal use. She is fifty-seven years of age, with partially gray hair, of medium height, and a slender figure. Delay all proceedings and contact Police Central Four."

Lin Wenzu had drawn a conclusion based on an observation, thought Catherine, along with the knowledge that anyone who willingly drove a car in Hong Kong was either crazy or had a peculiar reason for doing so. He was covering his bases quickly and completely. "The young man just got me a car over in Bonham Strand East. He obviously hasn't read this."

"He found you a rental at this hour?"

"He's writing up the credit charge now. Do you think he'll see this?"

"It is not him that I worry about. He is in training and I can tell him anything and he will accept what I say. The other one not so; he wants my job badly. Wait here. Stay out of sight."

Teng walked to the counter as the clerk was anxiously looking around, the layered credit card slips in his hand. Lee Teng took the charges and put them in his pocket. "That won't be necessary," he said. "Our customer has changed her mind. She found a friend in the lobby who will drive her."

"Oh? Then I should tell our associate not to bother. As the amount is over the limit, he is clearing it for me. I am still somewhat unsure and he offered—"

Teng waved him quiet as he crossed to the second clerk on the telephone at the other end of the counter. "You may give me the card and forget the call. There are too many distressed ladies tonight for me! This one has found other means of transportation."

"Certainly, Mr. Teng," said the second clerk obsequiously. He handed over the credit card, apologized quickly to the operator on the line, and hung up the telephone.

"A bad night." Teng shrugged, turning, and heading back into the crowded lobby-lounge. He approached Catherine, pulling out his billfold as he did so. "If you are short of money, I will cover it. Don't use this."

"I'm not short at home or at the bank, but I don't carry so much with me. It's one of the unwritten rules."

"One of the better ones," said Teng, nodding.

Staples took the bills in Teng's hand and looked up at the Chinese. "Do you want an explanation?" she asked.

"It's not required, Catherine. Whatever Central Four says, I know you are a good person, and if you are not and you run away and I never see my money again, I am still many thousands, Hong Kong, to the better."

"I shan't run anywhere, Teng."

"You will not walk, either. One of the chauffeurs owes me a good turn, and he's in the garage now. He will drive you to your car in Bonham Strand. Come, I'll take you down there."

"There's someone else with **me**. I'm taking her out of Hong Kong. She's in the ladies' room."

"I'll wait in the hallway. Do hurry."

"Sometimes I think the time passes more quickly when we are flooded with problems," said the second, somewhat older clerk to his younger associate-in-training as he removed the half-page computer printout from beneath the counter and unobtrusively shoved it into his pocket.

"If you are right, Mr. Teng has barely experienced fifteen minutes since we came on duty two hours ago. He's very good, isn't he?"

"His lack of head hair helps him. People look upon him as having wisdom even when he has no wise words to offer."

"Still, he has a way with people. I wish to be very much like him one day."

"Lose some hair," said the second clerk. "In the meantime, since there is no one bothering us, I have to go to the toilet. By the way, just in case I ever need to know a rental agency open at this hour, it *was* the Apex on Bonham Strand East, wasn't it?"

"Oh, yes."

"That was very diligent of you."

"I simply went by the list. It was near the end."

"Some of us would have stopped before then. You are to be commended."

"You are too kind to an unworthy trainee."

"I want only the best for you," said the older clerk. "Always remember that."

The older man left the counter. He cautiously went past the potted palms until he saw Lee Teng. The night concierge was standing at the foot of the hallway to the right; it was enough. He was waiting for the woman. The clerk turned quickly and walked up the staircase to the line of shops with less dignity than was proper. He was in a hurry and entered the first boutique at the top of the steps.

"Hotel business," he said to the bored saleswoman as he grabbed the phone off the wall behind a glass counter displaying glistening precious stones. He dialed.

"Police Central Four."

"Your directive, sir, regarding the Canadian woman, Mrs. Staples—"

"Do you have information?"

"I believe so, sir, but it is somewhat embarrassing for me to relay it."

"Why is that? This is an emergency, a government matter!"

"Please understand, Officer, I am only a minor employee, and it is quite possible the night concierge did not recall your directive. He is a very busy man."

"What are you trying to say?"

"Well, Officer—sir—the woman I overheard asking for the concierge bore a striking resemblance to the description in the government directive. But it would be most embarrassing for me if it was learned that I called you."

"You will be protected. You may remain anonymous. What is the information?"

"Well, sir, I overheard . . ." With cautious ambivalence, the first assistant clerk did his best for himself and consequently the worst for his superior, Lee Teng. His final statements, however, were concise and without equivocation. "It is the Apex Car Rental Agency in Bonham Strand East. I suggest you hurry, as she is on her way there now."

The early-evening traffic was less dense than the rush hour, but still formidable. It was the reason why Catherine and Marie looked uneasily at each other in the backseat of the Mandarin's limousine; the chauffeur, rather than accelerating into the sudden wide space in front of him, swung the enormous automobile into an empty section of the curb in Bonham Strand East. There was no sign of a rental agency on either side of the street.

"Why are we stopping?" asked Staples sharply.

"Mr. Teng's instructions, Mrs. . . . ." answered the chauffeur turning around in the seat. "I will lock the car with the alarm on. No one will bother you, as the lights flash beneath all four door handles."

"That's very comforting, but I'd like to know why you're not taking us to the car."

"I will bring the car to you, Mrs. . . . ."

"I beg your pardon?"

"Mr. Teng's instructions. He was very firm, and he is making the proper phone call to the Apex garage. It is in the next street, Mrs. . . . I shall be back presently." The chauffeur removed his hat and his jacket, placed both on the seat, switched on the alarm and climbed out.

"What do you make of it?" asked Marie, putting her right leg over her knee and holding tissues she had taken from the ladies' room against the sole of her foot. "Do you trust this Teng?"

"Yes, I do," replied Catherine, her expression bewildered. "I can't understand it. He's obviously being extra cautious—but they're extra risks for himself—and I don't know why. As I told you back at the Mandarin, that computerized missive about me said 'Government Control.' Those two words are not taken lightly in Hong Kong. What in the world is he doing? And why?"

"Obviously, I can't answer you," said Marie. "But I can make an observation."

"What is it?"

"I saw the way he looked at you. I'm not sure you did."

"What?"

"I'd say he's very fond of you."

"Fond . . . of me?"

"It's one way to put it. There are stronger ways, of course."

Staples turned away and looked out the window. "Oh, my *God*," she whispered.

"What's the matter?"

"A little while ago, back at the Mandarin, and for reasons too unreasonable to analyze—it started with a foolish woman in a chinchilla stole—I thought about Owen."

"Owen?"

"My former husband."

"Owen Staples? The *banker*, Owen Staples?"

"That's my name and that's my boy—*was* my boy. In those days one stayed with the acquired name."

"You never told me your husband was Owen Staples."

"You never asked me, my dear."

"You're not making sense, Catherine."

"I suppose not," agreed Staples, shaking her head. "But I was thinking about the time Owen and I met a couple of years ago in Toronto. We had drinks at the Mayfair Club and I learned things about him I never.

would have believed before. I was genuinely happy for him despite the fact that the bastard nearly made me cry."

"Catherine, for heaven's sake what's that got to do with right *now*?"

"It's got to do with Teng. We also had drinks one evening, not at the Mandarin, of course, but at a café on the waterfront in Kowloon. He said it wouldn't be good joss for me to be seen with him here on the island."

"Why not?"

"That's what I said. You see, he was protecting me then just as he's protecting me now. And I may have misunderstood him. I assumed he was simply looking after an additional source of income, but I may have been terribly wrong."

"In what way?"

"He said a strange thing that night. He said he wished things were different, that the differences between people were not so obvious and those differences not so disturbing to other people. Of course, I accepted his banalities as a rather amateurish attempt at . . . at statecraft, as my former husband phrased it. Perhaps it was something else."

Marie laughed quietly as their eyes locked. "Dear, *dear* Catherine. The man's in love with you."

"Christ in *Calgary,* I don't need this!"

Lin Wenzu sat in the front seat of the MI6 Vehicle Two, his patient gaze on the entrance of the Apex agency on Bonham Strand East. Everything was in order; both women would be in his custody within a matter of minutes. One of his men had gone inside and spoken to the dispatcher. The agent had proffered his government identification and was shown the evening's records by the frightened employee. The dispatcher, indeed, *had* a reservation for a Mrs. Catherine Staples but it had been canceled, the car in question assigned to another name, the name of a chauffeur from the hotel. And since Mrs. Catherine Staples was no longer leasing a car, the dispatcher saw no reason to call Police Control Four. What was there to say? And no, certainly not, no one else could pick up the car, as it was reserved by the Mandarin.

Everything was in order, thought Lin. Victoria Peak

would feel an enormous sweep of relief the moment he reached the sterile house with his news. The major knew the exact words he would say: "The women are taken— the *woman* is taken."

Across the street a man in shirt sleeves entered the agency door. He appeared hesitant to Lin and there was something. . . . A taxi suddenly drove up and the major bolted forward, reaching for the door handle—the hesitant man was forgotten.

"Be alert, lads," said Lin into the microphone attached to the dashboard radio. "We must be as quick and as unobtrusive as possible. No Arbuthnot Road can be tolerated here. And no weapons, of course. *Ready,* now!"

But there was nothing to be ready for; the taxi drove away without disgorging anyone.

"Vehicle *Three!*" said the major curtly. "Get that license and call the cab company! I want them in radio contact. Find out exactly what their taxi was doing here! Better yet, follow it and do as I tell you. It could be the women."

"I believe there was only a man in the backseat, sir," said the driver.

"They could have ducked below the seat! Damned eyes. A man, you say?"

"Yes, sir."

"I smell a rotten squid."

"Why, Major?"

"If I knew, the stench would not be so strong."

The waiting continued, and the immense Lin Wenzu began to perspire. The dying sun cast both a blinding orange light through the windshield and pockets of dark shadows along Bonham Strand East.

"It's too long," whispered the major to himself.

Static erupted from the radio. "We have the report from the cab company, sir."

"Go on!"

"The taxi in question is trying to find an import house on Bonham Strand East, but the driver told his fare that the address must be on Bonham Strand *West.* Apparently, his passenger is very angry. He got out and threw money into the window only moments ago."

"Break away and return here," ordered Lin as he watched the garage doors opening across the street at the

Apex agency. A car emerged, turning left, driven by the shirt-sleeved man.

The sweat now rolled down the major's face. Something was *not* in order; another order was being superimposed. What was it that bothered him? What *was* it?"

"Him!" shouted Lin to his startled driver.

"Sir?"

"A wrinkled white shirt, but trousers creased like steel. A uniform! A *chauffeur!* Swing around! *Follow* him!"

The driver held his hand on the horn, breaking the line of traffic, as he made a U-turn while the major issued instructions to the backups, ordering one to stay at the Apex agency, the others to take up the new chase.

"Aiya!" screamed the driver, jamming on his brakes, screeching to a stop, as a huge brown limousine roared out of a side street blocking their way. Only the slightest contact had been made, the government car barely touching the left rear door of the large automobile.

"Feng zi!" yelled the limousine's chauffeur, calling Lin's driver a crazy dog, as he jumped out of his outsized sedan to see if any damage had been done to his vehicle.

"Lai! Lai!" shrieked the major's driver, leaping out, ready for combat.

"Stop it!" roared Wenzu. "Just get him *out* of here!"

"It is *he* who does not move, sir!"

"Tell him he must *do* so! Show him your identification!"

All traffic came to a stop; horns blared, people in automobiles and in the streets yelled angrily. The major closed his eyes and shook his head in frustration. There was nothing he could do but get out of the car.

As another did from the limousine. A middle-aged Chinese with a balding head. "I gather we have a problem," said Lee Teng.

"I *know* you!" shouted Lin. "The Mandarin!"

"Many who have the taste to frequent our fine hotel know me, sir. I'm afraid I cannot reciprocate. Have you been a guest, sir?"

"What are you *doing* here?"

"It is a confidential errand for a gentleman at the Mandarin, and I have no intention of saying anything further."

"Damn-*damn!* A government directive was sent out! A

Canadian woman named Staples! One of your people called us!"

"I have no idea what you're talking about. For the last hour I have been trying to solve a problem for a guest who's attending the ball at Government House tonight. I'd be happy to furnish you with her name—if your position warrants it."

"My position *warrants* it! I repeat! Why have you stopped us?"

"I believe it was your man who sped across the changing light."

"Not *so!*" screamed Lin's driver.

"Then it is a matter for the courts," said Lee Teng. "May we proceed?"

"*Not* yet," replied the major, approaching the Mandarin's concierge. "I repeat again. A government directive was received at your hotel. It stated clearly that a woman named Staples might try to lease a car and you were to report the attempt to Police Central Four."

"Then *I* repeat, sir. I have not been near my desk for well over an hour, nor have I seen any such directive as you describe. However, in cooperation with your unseen credentials, I will tell you that all car rental arrangements would have to be made through my first assistant, a man, quite frankly, I have found quite compromising in many areas."

"But *you* are *here!*"

"How many guests at the Mandarin have late business in Bonham Strand East, sir? Accept the coincidence."

"Your eyes smile at me, *Zhongguo ren.*"

"Without laughter, sir. I will proceed. The damage is minor."

"I don't give a damn if you and your people have to stay there all *night,*" said Ambassador Havilland. "It's the only crack we've *got.* The way you've described it she'll return the car and then pick up her own. *Goddamn* it, there's a Canadian-American strategy conference at four o'clock tomorrow afternoon. She *has* to be back! Stay *with* it! Stay with all the *posts!* Just bring her in to me!"

"She will claim harassment. We will be breaking the laws of international diplomacy."

"Then *break* them! Just get her here, in Cleopatra's

carpet, if you have to! I haven't any time to waste—not a *minute!*"

Held firmly in check by two agents, a furious Catherine Staples was led into the room in the house on Victoria Peak. Lin Wenzu had opened the door; he now closed it as Staples faced Ambassador Raymond Havilland and Undersecretary of State Edward McAllister. It was 11:35 in the morning, the sun streaming through the large bay window overlooking the garden.

"You've gone too far, Havilland," said Catherine, her throaty voice ice-like in its flat delivery.

"I haven't gone far enough where you're concerned, Mrs. Staples. You actively compromised a member of the American legation. You engaged in extortion to the grave disservice of my government."

"You can't prove that because there's no evidence, no photographs—"

"I don't have to prove it. At precisely seven o'clock last night the young man drove up here and told us everything. A sordid little chapter, isn't it?"

"Damn *fool!* He's blameless, but *you're* not! And since you bring up the word 'sordid,' there's nothing he's done that could match the filth of your own actions." Without missing a verbal beat, Catherine looked at the undersecretary of State. "I presume this is the liar called McAllister."

"You're very trying," said the undersecretary.

"And you're an unprincipled lackey who does another man's dirty work. I've heard it all and it's all disgusting! But every thread was woven"—Staples snapped her head toward Havilland—"by an *expert.* Who gave *you* the right to play *God? Any* of you? Do you know what you've done to those two people out there? Do you know what you've *asked* of them?"

"We know," said the ambassador simply. "I know."

"She knows, too, in spite of the fact that I didn't have the heart to give her the final confirmation. *You,* McAllister! When I learned it was you up here, I wasn't sure she could handle it. Not at the moment. But I intend to tell her. You and your lies! A taipan's wife murdered in Macao—oh, the symmetry of it all, what an excuse to take another man's wife! *Lies!* I have my sources and it never *happened!* Well, get this straight. I'm bringing her in to the consulate under the full protection of my government. And if I were you, Havilland, I'd be damned careful about throwing around alleged illegalities. You and your goddamned people have lied to and manipulated a Canadian citizen into a life-threatening operation—whatever the hell it is *this* time. Your arrogance is simply beyond belief! But I assure you it's coming to a stop. Whether my government likes it or not, I'm going to expose you, *all* of you! You're no better than the barbarians in the KGB. Well, the American juggernaut of covert operations is going to be handed a bloody setback! I'm sick of you, the *world* is sick of you!"

"My dear woman!" shouted the ambassador, losing the last vestiges of control in his sudden anger. "Make all the threats you like, but you *will* hear me out! And if after you've heard what I have to say you wish to declare *war,* you go right ahead! As the song says, *my* days are dwindling down, but not millions of others'! I'd like to do what I can to prolong those other lives. But you may disagree, so declare your war, dear lady! And, by Christ, *you* live with the consequences!"

———

19

———

Leaning forward in the chair, Bourne snapped the trigger housing out of its recess and checked the weapon's bore under the light of the floor lamp above him. It was a repetitive, pointless exercise; the bore was spotless. During the past four hours he had cleaned d'Anjou's gun three times, dismantling it three times and each time oiling each mechanism until each part of the dark metal glistened. The process occupied his time. He had studied d'Anjou's arsenal of weapons and explosives, but since most of the equipment was in sealed boxes, conceivably tripped against theft, he let them be and concentrated on the single gun. There was only so much pacing one could

do in the Frenchman's flat on the Rua das Lorchas overlooking Macao's Porto Interior—or Inner Harbor—and
they had agreed he was not to go outside in daylight.
Inside, he was as safe as he could be anywhere in Macao.
D'Anjou, who changed residences at will and whim, had
rented the waterfront apartment less than two weeks ago
using a false name and a lawyer he had never met, who
in turn employed a "rentor" to sign the lease, which the
attorney sent by messenger to his unknown client by way
of the checkroom at the crowded Floating Casino. Such
were the ways of Philippe d'Anjou, formerly Echo of
Medusa.

Jason reassembled the weapon, depressed the shells in
the magazine, and cracked it up through the handle. He
got out of the chair and walked to the window, the gun
in his hand. Across the expanse of water was the People's
Republic, so accessible for anyone who knew the procedures arising from simple human greed. There was nothing new under the sun since the time of the pharaohs
where borders were concerned. They were erected to be
crossed—one way or another.

He looked at his watch. It was close to five o'clock; the
afternoon sun was descending. D'Anjou had called him
from Hong Kong at noon. The Frenchman had gone to
the Peninsula with Bourne's room key, packed his suitcase without checking out, and was taking the one o'clock
jetfoil back to Macao. Where was he? The trip took barely
an hour, and from the Macao pier to the Rua das Lorchas
was no more than ten minutes by cab. But then predicta-
bility was not Echo's strong suit.

Fragments of the Medusa memories came back to
Jason, triggered by the presence of d'Anjou. Although
painful and frightening, certain impressions provided a
certain comfort, again thanks to the Frenchman. Not only
was d'Anjou a consummate liar when it counted most and
an opportunist of the first rank, but he was extraordinarily resourceful. Above all, the Frenchman was a
pragmatist. He had proven that in Paris, and those
memories were clear. If he was delayed, there was a good
reason. If he did not appear, he was dead. And this last
was unacceptable to Bourne. D'Anjou was in a position
to do something Jason wanted above all to do himself but
dared not risk Marie's life in doing it. It was risk enough

that the trail of the impostor-assassin had brought him to Macao in the first place, but as long as he stayed away from the Lisboa Hotel he trusted his instincts. He would remain hidden from those looking for him—looking for someone who even vaguely resembled him in height, or build, or coloring. Someone asking questions in the Lisboa Hotel.

One call from the Lisboa to the taipan in Hong Kong and Marie was dead. The taipan had not merely threatened—threats were too often a meaningless ploy—he had used a far more lethal expedient. After shouting and crashing his large hand on the arm of the fragile chair, he had quietly given his word: Marie would die. It was a promise made by a man who kept his promises, kept his word.

Yet for all that, David Webb sensed something he could not define. There was about the huge taipan something a bit larger than life, too operatic, that had nothing to do with his size. It was if he had used his immense girth to advantage in a way that large men rarely do, preferring to let only their sheer size do the impressing. Who *was* the taipan? The answer was at the Lisboa Hotel, and since he dared not go there himself, d'Anjou's skills could serve him. He had told the Frenchman very little; he would tell him more now. He would describe a brutal double killing, the weapon an Uzi, and say that one of the victims was a powerful taipan's wife. D'Anjou would ask the questions he could not ask, and if there were answers he would take another step toward Marie.

Play the scenario.—Alexander Conklin.

Whose scenario?—David Webb.

You're wasting time!—Jason Bourne. *Find the impostor. Take him!*

Quiet footsteps in the outside hallway. Jason spun away from the window and raced silently to the wall, pressing his back against it, the gun leveled at the door, where the swinging panel would conceal him. A key was cautiously, quietly inserted. The door swung slowly open.

Bourne crashed it back into the intruder, spinning around and grabbing the stunned figure in the frame. He yanked him inside and kicked the door shut, the weapon aimed at the head of the fallen man, who had dropped a suitcase and a very large package. It was d'Anjou.

"That's one way to get your head blown off, Echo!"

"*Sacre-bleu!* It is also the last time I will ever be considerate of you! You don't see yourself, Delta. You look as you did in Tam Quan, without sleep for days. I thought you might be resting."

Another memory, briefly flashed. "In Tam Quan," said Jason, "you told me I had to sleep, didn't you? We hid in the brush and you formed a circle around me and damn near gave me an order to get some rest."

"It was purely a self-serving request. *We* couldn't get ourselves out of there, only *you* could."

"You said something to me then. What was it? I listened."

"I explained that rest was as much a weapon as any blunt instrument or firing mechanism man had ever devised."

"I used a variation later. It became an axiom for me."

"I'm so glad you had the intelligence to listen to your elders. May I please rise? Will you *please* lower that damned gun?"

"Oh, sorry."

"We have no time," said d'Anjou, getting up and leaving the suitcase on the floor. He tore the brown paper off the large package. Inside were pressed khaki clothes, two belted holsters and two visored hats; he threw them all on a chair. "These are uniforms. I have the proper identifications in my pocket. I am afraid I outrank you, Delta, but then age has its privileges."

"They're uniforms of the Hong Kong police."

"Kowloon, to be precise. We may have our *chance*, Delta! It's why I was so long getting back. Kai-tak Airport! The security is enormous, just what the impostor wants in order to show he's better than you ever were! There's no guarantee, of course, but I'd stake my life on it—it's the classic challenge for an obsessed maniac. 'Mount your forces, I'll break through them!' With one kill like that he reestablishes the legend of his utter invincibility. It's him, I'm sure of it!"

"Start from the beginning," ordered Bourne.

"As we dress, yes," agreed the Frenchman, removing

his shirt and unbuckling his trousers. *"Hurry!* I have a motor launch across the road. Four hundred horsepower. We can be in Kowloon in forty-five minutes. Here! This is yours! *Mon Dieu,* the money I've spent makes me want to vomit!"

"The PRC patrols," said Jason, peeling off his clothes and reaching for the uniform. "They'll shoot us out of the water!"

"Idiot, certain known boats are negotiated with by radio in code. There is, after all, honor among us. How do you think we run our merchandise? How do you think we survive? We meet in coves at the Chinese islands of Teh Sa Wei and payments are made. *Hurry!"*

"What about the airport? Why are you so sure it's him?"

"The Crown governor. Assassination."

"What?" shouted Bourne, stunned.

"I walked from the Peninsula to the Star Ferry with your suitcase. It's only a short distance, and the ferry is far quicker than a taxi through the tunnel. As I passed the Kowloon Police Hill on Salisbury Road I saw seven patrol cars drive out at emergency speed, one behind the other, all turning left, which is not to the godown. It struck me as odd—yes, two or three for a local eruption, but *seven?* It was good joss, as these people say. I called my contact on the Hill and he was cooperative—it was also not much of an internal secret any longer. He said if I stayed around I'd see another ten cars, twenty vans, all heading out to Kai-tak within the next two hours. Those I saw were the advance search teams. They had received word through their underground sources that an attempt was to be made on the Crown governor's life."

"Specifics!" commanded Bourne harshly, buckling his trousers and reaching for the long khaki shirt that served as a jacket under the bullet-laden holster belt.

"The governor is flying in from Beijing tonight with his own entourage from the Foreign Office, as well as another Chinese negotiating delegation. There will be newspaper people, television crews, everyone. Both governments want full coverage. There is to be a joint meeting tomorrow between all the negotiators and leaders of the financial sector."

"The '97 treaty?"

"Yet another round in the endless verbosity about the Accords. But, for all our sakes, just pray they keep talking pleasantly."

"The *scenario*," said Jason softly, stopping all movement.

"What scenario?"

"The one you yourself brought up, the scenario that had the wires burning between Peking and Government House. Kill a Crown governor for the murder of a vice-premier? Then perhaps a foreign secretary for a ranking member of the Central Committee—a prime minister for a chairman? How far does it go? How many selected killings before the breaking point is reached? How long before the parent refuses to tolerate a disobedient child and marches into Hong Kong? Christ, it *could* happen. Someone *wants* it to happen!"

D'Anjou stood motionless, holding the wide belt of the holster with its ominous strand of brass-capped shells. "What I suggested was no more than speculation based on the random violence caused by an obsessed killer who accepts his contracts without discrimination. There's enough greed and political corruption on both sides to justify that speculation. But what you're suggesting, Delta, is quite different. You're saying it's a plan, an organized plan to disrupt Hong Kong to the point that the Mainland takes over."

"The scenario," repeated Jason Bourne. "The more complicated it gets, the simpler it appears."

The rooftops of Kai-tak Airport were swarming with police, as were the gates and the tunnels, the immigration counters and the luggage areas. Outside, on the immense field of black tarmac, powerful floodlights were joined by roving, sharper searchlights probing every moving vehicle, every inch of visible ground. Television crews uncoiled cables under watching eyes, while interviewers standing behind sound trucks practiced pronunciation in a dozen languages. Reporters and photographers were kept beyond the gates as airport personnel shouted through the amplifiers that roped-off sections on the field would soon be available for all legitimate journalists with proper passes issued by the Kai-tak management. It was madness. And then the totally unexpected happened as a sudden rainstorm swept over the colony from the darkness of the western horizon. It was yet another autumn deluge.

"The impostor has good luck—good joss—as they say, doesn't he?" said d'Anjou as he and Bourne in their uniforms marched with a phalanx of police through a covered walkway made of corrugated tin to one of the huge repair hangars. The hammering of the rain was deafening.

"Luck had nothing to do with it," replied Jason. "He studied the weather reports from as far away as Sichuan. Every airport has them. He spotted it yesterday, if not two days ago. Weather's a weapon, too, Echo."

"Still, he could not dictate the arrival of the Crown governor on a Chinese aircraft. They are often hours late, *usually* hours late."

"But not days, *not* usually. When did the Kowloon police get word of the attempt?"

"I asked specifically," said the Frenchman. "Around eleven-thirty this morning."

"And the plane from Peking was scheduled to arrive sometime this evening?"

"Yes, I told you that. The newspaper and the television people were ordered to be here by nine o'clock."

"He studied the weather reports. Opportunities present themselves. You grab them."

"And this is what *you* must do, Delta! *Think* like him, *be* him! It is our chance!"

"What do you think I'm doing? . . . When we get to the hangar, I want to break away. Can your ersatz identification make it possible?"

"I am a British Sector commander from the Mongkok Divisional Police."

"What does *that* mean?"

"I really don't know, but it was the best I could do."

"You don't sound British."

"Who would know that out here at Kai-tak, old *chap*?"

"The British."

"I'll avoid them. My Chinese is better than yours. The *Zhongguo ren* will respect it. You'll be free to roam."

"I have to be," said Jason Bourne. "If it's your commando, I want him before anyone else spots him! Here. *Now!*"

. . .

Roped stanchions were moved out of the high-domed hangar by maintenance personnel in glossy yellow rain slickers. Then a truckload of the yellow coats arrived for the police contingents; men caught them as they were thrown out of the rear of the van. Putting them on, the police then formed several groups to receive instructions from their superiors. Order was rapidly emerging from the confusion compounded by the newly arrived, bewildered troops and the problems caused by the sudden downpour. It was the sort of order Bourne distrusted. It was too smooth, too conventional for the job they faced. Ranks of brightly dressed soldiers marching forward were in the wrong place with the wrong tactics when seeking out guerrillas—even one man trained in guerrilla warfare. Each policeman in his yellow slicker was both a warning and a target—and he was also something else. A pawn. Each could be replaced by another dressed the same way, by a killer who knew how to assume the look of his enemy.

Yet the strategy of infiltration for the purpose of a kill was suicidal, and Jason knew there was no such commitment on the part of his impostor. Unless . . . unless the weapon to be used had a sound level so low, the rain would eliminate it . . . but even then the target's reaction could not be instantaneous. A cordon would immediately be erected around the killing ground at the first sign of the Crown governor's collapse, every exit blocked, everyone in the vicinity ordered under guns to remain in place. A delayed reaction? A tiny air dart whose impact was no greater than a pinprick, a minor annoyance to be swatted away like a bothersome fly, as the lethal drop of poison entered the bloodstream to cause death slowly but inevitably, time not a consideration. It was a possibility, but again there were too many obstacles to surmount, too much accuracy demanded beyond the limits of an air-compressed weapon. The Crown governor would undoubtedly be wearing a protective vest, and targeting the face was out. Facial nerves exaggerated pain, and any foreign object making contact so close to the eyes would produce an immediate and dramatic reaction. That left the hands and the throat: the first were too small and conceivably could be moving too fast; the second was simply too limited an area. A high-powered rifle on a rooftop? A rifle of unquestioned accuracy with an infrared telescopic sight? Another possibility—an all too familiar yellow slicker replaced by one worn by an assassin. But again, it was suicidal, for such a weapon would produce an isolated explosion, and to mount a silencer would reduce the accuracy of the rifle to the point where it could not be trusted. The odds were against a killer on a rooftop. The kill would be too obvious.

And the kill was everything. Bourne understood that, especially under the circumstances. D'Anjou was right. All the factors were in place for a spectacular assassination. Carlos the Jackal could not ask for more—nor could Jason Bourne, reflected David Webb. To pull it off in spite of the extraordinary security would crown the new "Bourne" king of his sickening profession. Then *how?* Which option would he *use?* And after the decision was made, what avenue of escape would be most effective, most possible?

One of the television trucks with their complicated equipment was too obvious a means for an escape. The incoming aircraft's maintenance crews were checked and double- and triple-checked; an outsider would be spotted instantly. All the journalists would pass through electronic gates that picked up an excess of ten milligrams of metal. And the rooftops were out. *How,* then?

"You're cleared!" said d'Anjou, suddenly appearing at his side, holding a piece of paper in his hand. "This is signed by the prefect of the Kai-tak police."

"What did you tell him?"

"That you are a Jew trained by the Mossad in antiterrorist activities and posted to us in an exchange program. The word will be spread."

"Good God, I don't speak *Hebrew!*"

"Who here does? Shrug and continue in your tolerable French—which *is* spoken here but very badly. You'll get away with it."

"You're impossible, you know that, don't you?"

"I know that Delta, when he was our leader in Medusa, told Command Saigon that he would not go out in the field without 'old Echo.'"

"I must have been out of my mind."

"You were less in command of it then, I'll grant you that."

"Thanks a lot, Echo. Wish me luck."

"You don't need luck," said the Frenchman. "You are Delta. You will always be Delta."

Removing the bright yellow rain slicker and the visored hat, Bourne walked outside and showed his clearance to the guards by the hangar doors. In the distance, the press was being herded through the electronic gates toward the roped stanchions. Microphones had been placed on the edge of the runway, and police vans were joined by motorcycle patrols forming a tight semicircle around the press conference area. The preparations were about complete, all the security forces in place, the media equipment in working order. The plane from Peking had obviously begun its descent in the downpour. It would land in a matter of minutes, minutes Jason wished could be extended. There were so many things to look for and so little time to search. *Where? What?* Everything was both possible and impossible. Which option would the killer use? What vantage point would he zero in on for the perfect kill? And how would he most logically escape from the killing ground alive?

Bourne had considered every option he could think of and ruled each out. *Think again!* And *again!* Only minutes left. Walk around and start at the beginning . . . the beginning. The premise: the assassination of the Crown governor. Conditions: seemingly airtight, with security police training guns from rooftops, blocking every entrance, every exit, every staircase and escalator, all in radio contact. The odds were overwhelmingly against. Suicide. . . . Yet it was these same heavily negative odds that the impostor-killer found irresistible. D'Anjou had been right again: with one spectacular kill under these conditions an assassin's supremacy would be established —or reestablished. What had the Frenchman said? *With one kill like that he reestablishes the legend of his invincibility.*

Who? Where? How? Think! Look!

The downpour drenched his Kowloon police uniform. He continuously wiped the water from his face as he moved about peering at everyone and everything. *Noth-*

ing! And then the muted roar of the jet engines could be heard in the distance. The jet from Peking was making its final approach at the far end of the runway. It was landing.

Jason studied the crowd standing inside the roped stanchions. An accommodating Hong Kong government, in deference to Peking and in the desire for "full coverage," had supplied ponchos and squares of canvas and cheap pocket raincoats for all who wanted them. The Kai-tak personnel countered the media's demands for an inside conference by stating simply—and wisely without explanation—that it was not in the interests of security. The statements would be short, an aggregate of no more than five or six minutes. Certainly the fine members of the journalistic establishment could tolerate a little rain for such an important event.

The photographers? *Metal!* Cameras were passed through the gates but not all "cameras" took pictures. A relatively simple device could be inserted and locked into a mount, a powerful firing mechanism that released a bullet—or a dart—with the assistance of a telescopic view-finder. Was that the way? Had the assassin taken *that* option, expecting to smash the "camera" under his feet and take another from his pocket as he moved swiftly to the outskirts of the crowd, his credentials as authentic as those of d'Anjou and the "antiterrorist" from the Mossad? It was possible.

The huge jet dropped onto the runway, and Bourne walked quickly into the roped-off area, approaching every photographer he could see, looking—looking for a man who looked like himself. There must have been two dozen men with cameras; he became frantic as the plane from Peking taxied toward the crowd, the flood- and searchlights now centered on the space around the microphones and the television crews. He went from one photographer to the next, rapidly ascertaining that the man could not be the killer, then looking again to see if postures were erect, faces cosmeticized. Again *nothing!* No one! He had to *find* him, *take* him! Before anyone else found him. The assassination was beside the point, it was irrelevant to him! Nothing mattered except Marie!

Go back to the beginning! Target—the Crown governor. Conditions—highly negative for a kill, the target under maximum security, undoubtedly protected by personal armor, the whole security corps orderly, disciplined, the officers in tight command. . . . The *beginning?* Something was missing. Go over it again. The Crown governor—the target, a single kill. Method of the kill: suicide ruled out everything but a delayed-reaction device—an air dart, a pellet—yet the demands of accuracy made such a weapon illogical, and the loud report of a conventional gun would instantly activate the entire security force. *Delay?* Delayed *action,* not *re*action! The beginning, the first assumption, was *wrong!* The target was not just the Crown governor. *Not* a single kill but multiple killings, indiscriminate killings! How much more spectacular! How much more effective for a maniac who wanted to throw Hong Kong into chaos! And the chaos would begin instantly with the security forces. *Dis*order, escape!

Bourne's mind was racing as he roamed through the crowd in the downpour, his eyes darting everywhere. He tried to recall every weapon he had ever known. A weapon that could be fired or released silently, unobtrusively from a restricted, densely populated area, its effect delayed long enough for the killer to reposition himself and make a clean escape. The only device that came to mind was a grenade, but he immediately dismissed it. Then the thought of time-fused dynamite or *plastique* struck him. The latter was far more manageable in terms of delays and concealment. The plastic explosives could be set in time spans of minutes and fractions of minutes rather than a few seconds only; they could be hidden in small boxes or in wrapped packages, even narrow briefcases—or thicker cases supposedly filled with photographic equipment, not necessarily carried by a photographer. He started again, going back into the crowd of reporters and photographers, his eyes scanning the black tarmac below trousers and skirts, looking for an isolated container that remained stationary on the hard asphalt. Logic made him concentrate on the rows of men and women nearest the roped-off runway. In his mind the "package" would be no more than twelve inches in length if it was thick, twenty if it was an attaché case. A smaller charge would not kill the negotiators of both governments. The airfield lights were strong, but they created myriad shadows, darker pockets within the darkness. He wished he had had the sense to carry a flashlight —he had *always* carried one, if only a penlight, for it, too, was a weapon! Why had he *forgotten*? Then to his astonishment he saw flashlight beams crisscrossing the black floor of the airfield, darting between the same trousers and skirts he had been peering beyond. The security police had arrived at the same theory, and why shouldn't they? La Guardia Airport, 1972; Lod Airport, Tel Aviv, 1974; Rue de Bac, Paris, 1975; Harrods, London, 1982. And a half-dozen embassies from Teheran to Beirut, why *shouldn't* they? They were current, he was not. His thinking was slow—and he could not allow that!

Who? Where?

The enormous 747 starship of the People's Republic came into view like a great silver bird, its jet engines roaring through the deluge, whirring down as it was maneuvered into position on alien ground. The doors opened and the parade began. The two leaders of the British and the Chinese delegations emerged together. They waved and walked in unison down the metal staircase, one in the impeccable clothes of Whitehall, the other in the drab, rankless uniform of the People's army. They were followed by two lines of aides and adjutants, Occidentals and Orientals doing their best to appear congenial with one another for the cameras. The leaders approached the microphones, and as the voices droned over the loudspeakers and through the rain the next minutes were a blur for Jason. A part of his mind was on the ceremony that was taking place under the floodlights, the larger part on the final search—for it *would* be final. If the impostor was there, he had to *find* him—*before* the kill, before the *chaos!* But, goddamn it, *where?* Bourne moved out beyond the ropes on the far right to get a better view of the proceedings. A guard objected; Jason showed the man his clearance and remained motionless, studying the television crews, their looks, their eyes, their equipment. If the assassin was among them, which one *was* he?

"We are jointly pleased to announce that further progress has been made with regard to the Accords. We of the United Kingdom . . ."

"We of the People's Republic of China—the only true

China on the face of the earth—express a desire to find a close communion with those who wish . . ."

The speeches were interrupted by each leader giving support to his counterpart, yet letting the world know there was still much to negotiate. There was tension beneath the civility, the verbal placebos, and the plastic smiles. And Jason found nothing he could focus on, *nothing,* so he wiped the rain from his face and nodded to the guard as he ducked under the rope and moved once again back through the crowd behind the stanchions. He threaded his way to the left side of the press conference.

Suddenly, Bourne's eyes were drawn to a series of headlights in the downpour that curved into the runway at the far end of the field and rapidly accelerated toward the stationary aircraft. Then, as if on cue, there was a swelling of applause. The brief ceremony was over, signified by the arrival of the official limousines, each with a motorcycle escort driving up between the delegations and the roped-off crowd of journalists and photographers. Police surrounded the television trucks, ordering all but two preselected cameramen to get inside their vehicles.

It was the moment. If anything was going to happen, it would happen now. If an instrument of death was about to be placed, its charge to be exploded within the time span of a minute or less, it would have to be placed *now!*

Several feet to his left, he saw an officer of a police contingent, a tall man whose eyes were moving as rapidly as his own. Jason leaned toward the man and spoke in Chinese while holding out his clearance, shielding it from the rain with his hand. "I'm the man from the Mossad!" he yelled, trying to be heard through the applause.

"Yes, I know about you!" shouted the officer. "I was told. We're grateful you're here!"

"Do you have a flashlight—a torch?"

"Yes, of course. Do you want it?"

"Very much."

"Here."

"Clear me!" ordered Bourne, lifting the rope, gesturing for the officer to follow. "I haven't time to show papers!"

"Certainly!" The Chinese followed, reaching out and

intercepting a guard who was about to stop Jason—by shooting him if it was necessary. "Let him be! He's one of us! He's trained in this sort of thing!"

"The Jew from the Mossad?"

"It is he."

"We were told. Thank you, sir. . . . But, of course, he can't understand me."

"Oddly enough, he does. He speaks *Guangdong hua.*"

"In Food Street there is what they call a Kosur restaurant that serves our dishes—"

Bourne was now between the row of limousines and the roped stanchions. As he walked down the line of rope, his flashlight directed below on the black tarmac, he gave orders in Chinese and English—shouting yet not shouting; the commands of a reasonable man looking, perhaps, for a lost object. One by one the men and women of the press moved back, explaining to those behind them. He approached the lead limousine; the flags of both Great Britain and the People's Republic were displayed respectively on the right and left, indicating that England was the host, China the guest. The representatives rode together. Jason concentrated on the ground; the exalted passengers were about to enter the elongated vehicle with their most trusted aides amid sustained applause.

It *happened,* but Bourne was not sure what it was! His left shoulder touched another shoulder and the contact was electric. The man he had grazed first lurched forward and then had swung back with such ferocity that Jason was shoved off balance. He turned and looked at the man on the police escort motorcycle, then raised his flashlight to see through the dark plastic oval of the helmet.

Lightning struck, sharp, jagged bolts crashing into his skull, his eyes riveted as he tried to adjust to the incredible. He was staring at *himself*—from only years ago! The dark features behind the opaque bubble were *his!* It was the *commando!* The *impostor!* The *assassin!*

The eyes that stared back at him also showed panic, but they were quicker than Webb's. A flattened, rigid hand lashed out, crashing into Jason's throat, cutting off all speech and thought. Bourne fell back, unable to scream,

grabbing his neck, as the assassin lurched off his motorcycle. He rushed past Jason and ducked under the rope.

Get him! Take him! . . . *Marie!* The words were absent
—only hysterical thoughts screamed silently in Bourne's
mind. He retched, exploding the chop in his throat, and
leaped over the rope, plunging into the crowd, following
the path of fallen-away bodies that had been pummeled
by the killer in his race to escape.

"Stop . . . *him!*" Only the last word emerged from
Jason's throat; it was a hoarse whisper. "Let *me through!*"
Two words were audible, but no one was listening. From
somewhere near the terminal a band was playing in the
downpour.

The path was closed! There were only people, people,
people! Find him! Take him! *Marie!* He's gone! He's *disappeared!* "Let me through!" he screamed, the words now
clear but heeded by no one. He yanked and pulled and
bucked his way to the edge of the crowd, another crowd
facing him behind the glass doors of the terminal.

Nothing! No one! The killer was gone!

Killer? The *kill!*

It was the limousine, the *lead* limousine with the flags
of both countries! *That* was the target! Somewhere in
that car or beneath that car was the timed mechanism that
would blow it to the skies, killing the leaders of both
delegations. Result—the scenario . . . chaos. *Takeover!*

Bourne spun around, frantically looking for someone
in authority. Twenty yards beyond the rope, standing at
attention as the British anthem was being played, was an
officer of the Kowloon police. Clipped to his belt was a
radio. A *chance!* The limousines had started their stately
procession toward an unseen gate in the airfield.

Jason yanked the rope, pulling it up, toppling a stan-
chion, and started running toward the short, erect Chinese officer. *"Xun su!"* he roared.

"Shemma?" replied the startled man, instinctively
reaching for his holstered gun.

"Stop them! The cars, the *limousines!* The one in *front!*"

"What are you talking about? Who are you?"

Bourne nearly struck the man in frustration. *"Mossad!"*
he screamed.

"You are the one from Israel? I've heard—"

"*Listen* to me! Get on that radio and tell them to stop! Get everyone out of that car! It's going to blow! *Now!*"

Through the rain the officer looked up into Jason's eyes, then nodded once and pulled the radio from his belt. "This is an emergency! Clear the channel and patch me to Red Star One. *Immediately.*"

"*All* the cars!" interrupted Bourne. "Tell them to peel away!"

"*Change!*" cried the police officer. "Alert all vehicles. Put me through!" And with his voice tense but controlled, the Chinese spoke clearly, emphasizing each word. "This is Colony Five and we have an emergency. With me is the man from the Mossad and I relay his instructions. They are to be complied with at once. Red Star One is to stop instantly and order everyone out of the vehicle, instructing them to run for cover. All other cars are to turn to the left toward the center of the field, away from Red Star One. Execute *immediately!*"

Stunned, the crowds watched as in the distance the engines roared in unison. Five limousines swung out of position, racing into the outer darkness of the airport. The first car screeched to a stop; the doors opened and men leaped out, running in all directions.

Eight seconds later it happened. The limousine called Red Star One exploded forty feet from an open gate. Flaming metal and shattered glass spiraled up into the downpour as the band music halted in midbreath.

Peking. 11:25 P.M.

Above the northern suburbs of Peking is a vast compound rarely spoken of, and certainly not for public inspection. The major reason is security, but there is also an element of embarrassment in this egalitarian society. For inside this sprawling, forested enclave in the hills are the villas of China's most powerful figures. The compound is shrouded in secrecy, as befits a complex enclosed by a high wall of gray stone, the entrances guarded by seasoned army veterans, the dense woods within continuously patrolled by attack dogs. And if one were to speculate on the social or political relationships cultivated there, it should be noted that no villa can be seen from another, for each structure is surrounded by its own inner wall, and all personal guards are personally selected after years of obedience and trust. The name, when it is spoken, is Jade Tower Mountain, which refers not to a geological mountain, but to an immense hill that rises above the others. At one time or another, with the ebb and flow of political fortunes, such men as Mao Zedong, Liu Shaoqi, Lin Biao, and Zhou Enlai lived here. Among the residents now was a man shaping the economic destiny of the People's Republic. The world press referred to him simply as Sheng, and the name was immediately recognizable. His full name was Sheng Chou Yang.

A brown sedan sped down the road fronting the imposing gray wall. It approached Gate Number Six, and as though preoccupied, the driver suddenly applied the brakes and the car sideslipped into the entrance, stopping inches from the bright orange barrier that reflected the beams of the headlights. A guard approached.

"Who is it you come to see and what is your name? I will need your official identification."

"Minister Sheng," said the driver. "And my name is not important, nor are my papers required. Please inform the minister's residence that his emissary from Kowloon is here."

The soldier shrugged. Such replies were standard at Jade Tower Mountain, and to press further might result in a conceivable transfer from this heavenly duty where the leftover food was beyond one's imagination and even foreign beer was given for obedient and cooperative service. Still, the guard used the telephone. The visitor had to be admitted properly. To do otherwise could bring one to kneel in a field and be shot in the back of the head. The guard returned to the gatehouse and dialed the villa of Sheng Chou Yang.

"Admit him. *Quickly!*"

Without going back to the sedan, the guard pressed a button and the orange bar was raised. The car raced in, far too quickly over the gravel, thought the guard. The emissary was in a great hurry.

"Minister Sheng is in the garden," said the army officer at the door, looking beyond the visitor, his eyes darting about, peering into the darkness. "Go to him."

The emissary rushed through the front room filled with red lacquered furniture to an archway beyond which was a walled garden complete with four connecting lily ponds subtly lit with yellow lights beneath the water. Two intersecting paths of white gravel formed an X between the ponds, and low black wicker chairs and tables were placed at the far end of each path within an oval setting. Seated alone at the end of the eastern leg by the brick wall was a slender man of medium height, with close-cropped, prematurely gray hair and gaunt features. If there was anything about him that might startle someone meeting him for the first time, it was his eyes, for they were the dark eyes of a dead man, the lids never blinking even for an instant. Contrarily, they were also the eyes of a zealot whose blind dedication to a cause was the core of his strength; white heat was in the pupils, lightning in the orbs. These were the eyes of Sheng Chou Yang, and at the moment they were on fire.

"*Tell* me!" he roared, both hands gripping the black arms of the wicker chair. "Who *does* this?"

"It's all a *lie*, Minister! We have checked with our people in Tel Aviv. There is no such man as was described. There is no agent from the Mossad in Kowloon! A *lie!*"

"What action did you take?"

"It is most confusing—"

"What *action?*"

"We are tracing an Englishman in the Mongkok whom no one seems to know about."

"Fools and *idiots!* Idiots and *fools!* Whom have you spoken with?"

"Our key man in the Kowloon police. He is bewildered, and I'm sorry to say I think he is frightened. He made several references to Macao, and I did not like his voice."

"He is dead."

"I will transmit your instructions."

"I'm afraid you cannot." Sheng gestured with his left hand, his right in shadows, reaching beneath the low table. "Come pay your obedience to the Kuomintang," he commanded.

The emissary approached the minister. He bowed low and reached for the great man's left hand. Sheng lifted his right hand. In it was a gun.

An explosion followed, blowing the emissary's head away. Fragments of skull and tissue seared into the lily ponds. The army officer appeared in the archway as the corpse sprang back from the impact with the white gravel.

"Dispose of him," ordered Sheng. "He heard too much, learned too much . . . presumed too much."

"Certainly, Minister."

"And reach the man in Macao. I have instructions for him and they are to be implemented immediately, while the fires in Kowloon still light up the sky. I want him here."

As the officer approached the dead courier, Sheng suddenly rose from the chair, and walked slowly to the edge of the nearest pond, his face illuminated by the lights beneath the water. He spoke once again, his voice flat but filled with purpose.

"Soon all of Hong Kong and the territories," he said, staring at a lily pad. "Soon thereafter, all of China."

"You lead, Minister," said the officer, watching Sheng, his eyes glowing with devotion. "We follow. The march you promised has begun. We return to our Mother and the land will be ours again."

"Yes, it will," agreed Sheng Chou Yang. "We cannot be denied. *I* cannot be denied."

20

By noon of that paralyzing day when Kai-tak was merely an airport and not an assassination field, Ambassador Havilland had described to a stunned Catherine Staples the broad outlines of the Sheng conspiracy with its roots in the Kuomintang. Objective: a consortium of taipans with a central leader, whose son Sheng was, taking over Hong Kong, and turning the colony into the conspirators' own financial empire. Inevitable result: the conspiracy would fail, and the raging giant that was the People's Republic would strike out, marching into Hong Kong, destroying the Accords and throwing the Far East into

chaos. In utter disbelief Catherine had demanded sub-
stantiation, and by 2:15 had twice read the State Department's lengthy and top secret dossier on Sheng Chou
Yang, but she continued to strenuously object, as the
accuracy of authorship could not be verified. At 3:30 she
had been taken to the radio room and by satellite-scram-
bler transmission was presented with an array of "facts"
by a man named Reilly of the National Security Council
in Washington.

"You're only a voice, Mr. Reilly," Staples had said.
"How do I know you're not down at the bottom of the
Peak in the Wanchai?"

There was at that moment a pronounced click on the
line and a voice Catherine and the world knew very well
was speaking to her. "This is the President of the United
States, Mrs. Staples. If you doubt that, I suggest you call
your consulate. Ask them to reach the White House by
diplomatic phone and request a confirmation of our
transmission. I'll hang on. You'll receive it. At the moment I have nothing better to do—*nothing* more vital."

Shaking her head and briefly closing her eyes, Catherine had answered quietly, "I believe you, Mr. President."

"Forget about me, believe what you've heard. It's the
truth."

"It's just so unbelievable—*inconceivable.*"

"I'm no expert, Mrs. Staples, and I never claimed to
be, but then neither was the Trojan Horse very believa-
ble. Now, that may be legend and Menelaus' wife may
have been a figment of a campfire storyteller's imagination, but the concept is valid—it's become a symbol of an
enemy destroying his adversary from within."

"Menelaus . . . ?"

"Don't believe the media, I've read a book or two. But
do believe our people, Mrs. Staples. We need you. I'll call
your Prime Minister if it will help, but, in all honesty, I'd
rather not. He might feel it necessary to confer with others."

"No, Mr. President. Containment *is* everything. I'm
beginning to understand Ambassador Havilland."

"You're one up on me. I don't always understand
him."

"Perhaps it's better that way, sir."

                                    . . . .

At 3:58 there was an emergency call—highest priority—
to the sterile house in Victoria Peak, but it was not for
either the Ambassador or Undersecretary of State McAllister. It was for Major Lin Wenzu, and when it came, a
frightening vigil began that lasted four hours. The scant
information was so electrifying that all concentration was
riveted on the crisis, and Catherine Staples telephoned
her consulate telling the High Commissioner that she
was not well and would not attend the strategy conference with the Americans that afternoon. Her presence in
the sterile house was welcome. Ambassador Havilland
wanted the foreign service officer to see and understand
for herself how close the Far East was to upheaval. How
an inevitable error on either Sheng's or his assassin's part
could bring about an explosion so drastic that troops
from the People's Republic could move into Hong Kong
within hours, bringing not only the colony's world trade
to a halt, but with it widespread human suffering—savage
rioting everywhere, death squads from the left and the
right exploiting resentments going back forty years, racial and provincial factions pitted against one another
and the military. Blood would flow in the streets and the
harbor, and as nations everywhere had to be affected,
global war was a very real possibility. He said these things
to her as Lin worked furiously on the telephone, giving
commands, coordinating his people with the colony's police and the airport's security.

It all had started with the major from MI6 cupping the
phone and speaking in a quiet voice in that Victorian
room in Victoria Peak: "Kai-tak tonight. The Sino-British
delegations. Assassination. The target is the Crown governor. They believe it's Jason Bourne."

"I can't *understand* it!" protested McAllister, leaping
from the couch. "It's premature. Sheng isn't ready! We'd
have gotten an inkling of it if he was—an official statement from his ministry alluding to a proposed commission of some sort. It's *wrong!*"

"Miscalculation?" asked the ambassador coldly.

"Possibly. Or something else. A strategy we haven't
considered."

"Go to work, Major," said Havilland.

After issuing his last orders, Lin received a final order
himself from Havilland before heading for the airport.

"Stay out of sight, Major," said the ambassador. "I mean that."

"Impossible," replied Lin. "With respect, sir, I must be with my men *on* the scene. These are experienced eyes."

"With equal respect," continued Havilland. "I must make it a condition of your getting through the outside gate."

"*Why,* Mr. Ambassador?"

"With your perspicacity, I'm surprised you ask."

"I have to! I don't understand."

"Then perhaps it's my fault, Major. I thought I'd made it clear why we went to such extremes to bring *our* Jason Bourne over here. Accept the fact that he's extraordinary, his record proves it. He has his ears not only to the ground, but they're also locked into the four winds. We must presume, if the medical prognosis is accurate and portions of his memory continue to come back to him, that he has contacts all over this part of the world in nooks and crannies we know nothing about. Suppose— just suppose, Major—that one of those contacts informs him that an emergency alert has been sent out for Kai-tak Airport tonight, that a large security force has been gathered to protect the Crown governor. What do you think he'd do?"

"Be there," answered Lin Wenzu softly, reluctantly. "Somewhere."

"And suppose again that *our* Bourne saw *you*? Forgive me, but you are not easily overlooked. The discipline of his logical mind—logic, discipline, and imagination were always his means of survival—would force him to find out precisely who you are. Need I say more?"

"I don't think so," said the major.

"The connection is made," said Havilland, overriding Lin's words. "There is no taipan with a murdered young wife in Macao. Instead there is a highly regarded field officer of British Intelligence posing as a fictitious taipan, having fed him yet another lie, echoing a previous lie. He will know that once again he has been manipulated by government forces, manipulated in the most brutal fashion possible—the abduction of his wife. The mind, Major, is a delicate instrument, his more delicate than most. There's only so much stress it can take. I don't even want to think about what he might do—what *we* might be forced to do."

"It was always the weakest aspect of the scenario, and yet it was the core," said Lin.

" 'An ingenious device,' " interrupted McAllister, obviously quoting. " 'Few acts of vengeance are as readily understood as an eye for an eye.' Your words, Lin."

"If so, you should *not* have chosen me to play your taipan!" insisted the major. "There's a crisis here in Hong Kong and you've crippled me!"

"It's the same crisis facing all of us," said Havilland gently. "Only this time we have a warning. Also, who else could we have chosen? What other Chinese but the proven chief of Special Branch would have been cleared by London for what you were initially told, to say nothing of what you know now? Set up your command post inside the airport's tower. The glass is dark."

In silence the huge major turned angrily and left the room. "Is it wise to let him go?" asked McAllister as he, the ambassador and Catherine Staples watched Lin leave.

"Certainly," answered the diplomat of covert operations.

"I spent several weeks here with MI-Six," continued the undersecretary rapidly. "He's been known to disobey in the past."

"Only when the orders were given by posturing British officers with less experience than himself. He was never reprimanded; he was right. Just as he knows I'm right."

"How can you be sure?"

"Why do you think he said we've crippled him? He doesn't like it, but he accepts it." Havilland walked behind the desk and turned to Catherine. "Please sit down, Mrs. Staples. And, Edward, I should like to ask a favor of you, and it has nothing to do with confidentiality. You know as much as I do and you're probably more current, and I'll no doubt call for you if I need information. However, I'd like to talk with Mrs. Staples alone."

"By all means," said the undersecretary, gathering up papers on the desk as Catherine sat down in a chair facing the diplomat. "I've a great deal of thinking to do. If this Kai-tak thing isn't a hoax—if it's a direct order from Sheng—then he's conceived of a strategy we really *haven't* considered, and that's dangerous. From every avenue, every direction I've explored, he has to offer up his clearinghouse, his damned economic commission, under *stable* conditions, not *unstable*. He could blow everything apart—but he's not stupid, he's brilliant. What's he *doing?*''

"Consider, if you will," broke in the ambassador, frowning as he sat down, "the reverse of our approach, Edward. Instead of implanting his financial clearinghouse of assorted taipans during a period of stability, he does so in *instability*—but with sympathy—the point being to restore order quickly. No raging giant but rather a protective father, caring for his emotionally disturbed offspring, wanting to calm it down."

"To what advantage?"

"It takes place rapidly, that's all. Who would so closely examine a group of respected financiers from the colony put in place during a crisis? After all, they *represent* stability. It's something to think about."

McAllister held the papers in his hands and looked at Havilland. "It's too much of a gamble for him," he said. "Sheng risks losing control of the expansionists in the Central Committee, the old military revolutionaries who are looking for any excuse to move into the colony. A crisis based on violence would play right into their hands. That's the scenario we gave Webb, and it's a realistic one."

"Unless Sheng's own position is now strong enough to suppress them. As you said yourself, Sheng Chou Yang has made China a great deal of money, and if there ever was a basically capitalistic people, it's the Chinese. They have more than a healthy respect for money, it's an obsession."

"They also have respect for the old men of the Long March, and it, too, is obsessive. Without those early Maoists most of China's younger leadership would be illiterate peasants breaking their backs in the field. They revere those old soldiers. Sheng wouldn't risk a confrontation."

"Then there's an alternative theory that could be a combination of what we're both saying. We did *not* tell Webb that a number of the more vocal leaders of Peking's old guard haven't been heard from in months. And in several instances, when the word was officially released, this one or that one had died of natural causes, or a tragic accident, and in one case was removed in disgrace. Now, if our assumption is right, that at least some of these silenced men are victims of Sheng's hired gun—"

"Then he's solidified his position by elimination," broke in McAllister. "Westerners are all over Peking; the hotels are filled to capacity. What's one more—especially an assassin who could be anyone—an attaché, a business executive . . . a chameleon."

"And who better than the manipulative Sheng to set up secret meetings between *his* Jason Bourne and selected victims? Any number of pretexts would do, but primarily military high-tech espionage. The targets would leap at it."

"If any of this is near the truth, Sheng's much further along than we thought."

"Take your papers. Request anything you need from our Intelligence people and MI-Six. Study everything, but find us a pattern, Edward. If we lose a Crown governor tonight, we may be on our way to losing Hong Kong in a matter of days. For all the wrong reasons."

"He'll be protected," muttered McAllister, heading for the door, his face troubled.

"I'm counting on it," said the ambassador, as the undersecretary left the room. Havilland turned to Catherine Staples. "Are you *really* beginning to understand me?" he asked.

"The words and their implications, yes, but not certain specifics," replied Catherine, looking oddly at the door the undersecretary of State had just closed. "He's a strange man, isn't he?"

"McAllister?"

"Yes."

"Does he bother you?"

"On the contrary. He lends a certain credibility to everything that's been said to me. By you, by that man Reilly—even by your President, I'm afraid." Staples turned back to the ambassador. "I'm being honest."

"I want you to be. And I understand the wavelength you're on. McAllister's one of the best analytical minds in the State Department, a brilliant bureaucrat who will never rise to the level of his own worth."

"Why not?"

"I think you know, but if you don't, you sense it. He's a thoroughly moral man and that morality has stood in the way of his advancement. Had I been cursed with his sense of moral outrage, I never would have become the man I am—and in my defense, I never would have accomplished what I have. But I think you know that too. You said as much when you came in here."

"Now you're the one being honest. I appreciate it."

"I'm glad. I want the air cleared between us because I want your help."

"Marie?"

"And beyond," said Havilland. "What specifics disturb you? What can I clarify?"

"This clearinghouse, this commission of bankers and taipans Sheng will propose to oversee the colony's financial policies—"

"Let me anticipate," interrupted the diplomat. "On the surface they will be disparate in character and position and eminently acceptable. As I said to McAllister when we first met, if we thought the whole insane scheme had a prayer, we'd look the other way and wish them great success, but it doesn't have a chance. All powerful men have enemies; there'll be skeptics here in Hong Kong and in Peking—jealous factions who've been excluded—and they'll dig deeper than Sheng expects. I think you know what they'll find."

"That all roads, above and below ground, lead to Rome. Rome here being this taipan, Sheng's father, whose name your highly selective documents never mention. He's the spider whose webs reach out to every member of that clearinghouse. He controls them. For God's sake, who the hell *is* he?"

"I wish we knew," said Havilland, his voice flat.

"You really *don't?*" asked Catherine Staples, astonished.

"If we did, life would be far simpler, and I would have told you. I'm not playing games with you, we've never learned who he is. How many taipans are there in Hong Kong? How many zealots wanting to strike back at Peking in any way they can in the cause of the Kuomintang? By their lights China was stolen from them. Their motherland, the graves of their ancestors, their possessions—

everything. Many were decent people, Mrs. Staples, but many others were not. The political leaders, the warlords, the landlords, the immensely rich—they were a privileged society that gorged themselves on the sweat and suppression of millions. And if that sounds like a crock of today's Communist propaganda, it was a classic case of yesterday's provocation that gave rise to such bilge. We're dealing with a handful of obsessed expatriates who want their own back. They forget the corruption that led to their own collapse."

"Have you thought of confronting Sheng himself? Privately?"

"Of course, and his reaction is all too predictable. He would feign outrage and tell us bluntly that if we pursue such despicable fantasies in an attempt to discredit him, he'll void the China Accords, claiming duplicity, and move Hong Kong into Peking's economic orbit immediately. He'd claim that many of the old-line Marxists on the Central Committee would applaud such a move, and he'd be right. Then he would look at us and probably say, 'Gentlemen, you have your choice. Good day.' "

"And if you made Sheng's conspiracy public the same thing would happen, and he knows *you know* it," said Staples, frowning. "Peking *would* pull out of the Accords blaming Taiwan and the West for messing around. Their face is beet-red with internal capitalistic corruption, so the territory marches to a Marxist drum—actually they wouldn't have a choice. And what follows is economic collapse."

"That's the way we read it," agreed Havilland.

"The solution?"

"There's only one. Sheng."

Staples nodded her head. "Hardball," she said.

"The most extreme act, if that's what you mean."

"That's obviously what I mean," said Catherine. "And Marie's husband, this Webb, is intrinsic to the solution?"

"Jason Bourne is intrinsic to it, yes."

"Because this impostor, this assassin who calls himself Bourne, can be trapped by the extraordinary man he emulates—as McAllister put it, but not in that context. He takes his place and pulls out Sheng where he can implement the solution, the extreme solution. . . . Hell, he kills him."

"Yes. Somewhere in China, of course."

"In China . . . 'of course'?"

"Yes, making it appear as internal fratricide with no external connections. Peking can't blame anyone but unknown enemies of Sheng within its own hierarchy. Regardless, at that juncture, if it happens, it's probably going to be irrelevant. The world won't officially hear of Sheng's death for weeks, and when the announcement is made, his 'sudden demise' will undoubtedly be attributed to a massive coronary or a cerebral hemorrhage, certainly not to murder. The giant does not parade its aberrations, it conceals them."

"Which is precisely what you want."

"Naturally. The world goes on, the taipans are cut off from their source, Sheng's clearinghouse collapses like a house of cards, and reasonable men go forward honoring the Accords for everyone's benefit. . . . But we're a long way from there, Mrs. Staples. To begin with, there's today, tonight. Kai-tak. It could be the beginning of the end, for we have no immediate countermeasures to put in place. If I appear calm, it's an illusion born of years of concealing tension. My two consolations at this moment are that the colony's security forces are among the best on earth, and second—the tragedy of death notwithstanding—is that Peking has been alerted to the situation. Hong Kong's concealing nothing, nor does it care to. So, in a sense, it becomes both a joint risk and a joint venture to protect the Crown governor."

"How does that help if the worst happens?"

"For what it's worth, psychologically. It may avert the appearance if not the fact of instability, for the emergency has been labeled beforehand as an isolated act of premeditated violence, not symptomatic of the colony's unrest. Above all, it's been shared. Both delegations have their own military escorts; they'll be put to use."

"So on such subtle points of protocol a crisis can be contained?"

"From what I've been told, you don't need any lessons in containing crises, or precipitating them, either. Besides, everything can go off the wire with one development that throws subtleties into the garbage heap. Despite everything I've said, I'm frightened to death. There's so much room for error and miscalculation—

they're our enemies, Mrs. Staples. All we can do is wait, and waiting is the hardest part, the most draining."

"I have other questions," said Catherine.

"By all means, ask as many as you like. Make me think, make me sweat, if you can. It may help us both take our minds off the waiting."

"You just referred to my questionable abilities in the area of containing crises. But you added—I think more confidently—that I could also precipitate them."

"I'm sorry, I couldn't resist. It's a bad habit."

"I assume you meant the attaché, John Nelson."

"Who? . . . Oh, yes, the young man from the consulate. What he lacks in judgment he makes up in courage."

"You're wrong."

"About the judgment?" asked Havilland, his thick eyebrows arched in mild astonishment. "Really?"

"I'm not excusing his weaknesses, but he's one of the finest people you've got. His professional judgment is superior to that of most of your more experienced personnel. Ask anyone in the consulates who's been in conferences with him. He's also one of the few who speak a damn good Cantonese."

"He also compromised what he knew was a highly classified operation," said the diplomat curtly.

"If he hadn't, you wouldn't have found me. You wouldn't have come within arm's reach of Marie St. Jacques, which is where you are now. An arm's reach."

"An 'arm's reach' . . . ?" Havilland leaned forward, his eyes angry, questioning. "Surely, you won't continue to hide her."

"Probably not. I haven't decided."

"My God, woman, after everything you've been told! She's got to be here! Without her we've lost, we've all lost! If Webb found out she wasn't with us, that she'd disappeared, he'd go mad! You've got to deliver her!"

"That's the point. I can deliver her anytime. It doesn't have to be when you say."

"No!" thundered the ambassador. "When and if our Jason Bourne completes his assignment, a series of telephone calls will be placed putting him in direct contact with his wife!"

"I won't give you a telephone number," said Staples matter-of-factly. "I might as well give you an address."

"You don't know what you're doing! What do I have to say to *convince* you?"

"Simple. Reprimand John Nelson verbally. Suggest counseling, if you wish, but keep everything off the record and keep him here in Hong Kong, where his chances for recognition are the best."

"Jesus *Christ!*" exploded Havilland. "He's a drug addict!"

"That's ludicrous but typical of the primitive reaction of an American 'moralist' given a few key words."

"*Please,* Mrs. Staples—"

"He was drugged; he doesn't *take* drugs. His limit is three vodka martinis, and he likes girls. Of course, a few of your male attachés prefer boys, and their limit is nearer six martinis, but who's counting? Frankly, I personally don't give a damn what adults do within the four walls of a bedroom—I don't really believe that whatever it is affects what they do *outside* the bedroom—but Washington has this peculiar preoccupation with—"

"All *right,* Mrs. Staples! Nelson is reprimanded—by me —and the consul general will not be informed and nothing goes into his record. Are you *satisfied?*"

"We're getting there. Call him this afternoon and tell him that. Also tell him to get his extracurricular act together for his own benefit."

"That will be a pleasure. Is there anything *else?*"

"Yes, and I'm afraid I don't know how to put it without insulting you."

"That hasn't fazed you."

"It fazes me now because I know far more than I did three hours ago."

"Then insult me, dear lady."

Catherine paused, and when she spoke her voice was a cry for understanding. It was hollow yet vibrant and filled the room. "*Why?* Why did you *do* it? Wasn't there *another* way?"

"I presume you mean Mrs. Webb."

"Of course I mean Mrs. Webb, and no less her husband! I asked you before, have you any idea what you've *done* to them? It's *barbaric* and I mean that in the full ugliness of the word. You've put both of them on some kind of medieval rack, literally pulling their minds and their bodies apart, making them live with the knowledge that they may never see each other again, each believing that with a wrong decision one can cause the other's death. An American lawyer once asked a question in a Senate hearing, and I'm afraid I must ask it of you. . . . Have you no sense of decency, Mr. Ambassador?"

Havilland looked wearily at Staples. "I have a sense of duty," he said, his voice tired, his face drawn. "I had to develop a situation rapidly that would provoke an immediate response, a total commitment to act instantly. It was based on an incident in Webb's past, a terrible thing that turned a civilized young scholar into—the phrase used to describe him was the 'supreme guerrilla.' I needed that man, that hunter, for all the reasons you've heard. He's here, he's hunting, and I assume his wife is unharmed and we obviously never intended anything else for her."

"The incident in Webb's past. That was his first wife? In Cambodia?"

"You know, then?"

"Marie told me. His wife and two children were killed by a lone jet fighter sweeping down along a river, strafing the water where they were playing."

"He became another man," said Havilland, nodding. "His mind snapped, and it became *his* war despite the fact that he had little or no regard for Saigon. He was venting his outrage in the only way he knew how, fighting an enemy who had stolen his life from him. He would usually take on only the most complex and dangerous assignments where the objectives were major, the targets within the framework of command personnel. One doctor said that in his mental warp Webb was killing the killers who sent out other mindless killers. I suppose it makes sense."

"And by taking his second wife in Maine you raised the specter of his first loss. The incident that turned him into this 'supreme guerrilla,' then later as Jason Bourne, hunter of Carlos the Jackal."

"Yes, Mrs. Staples, *hunter*," interjected the diplomat quietly. "I wanted that hunter on the scene immediately. I couldn't waste any time—not a minute—and I didn't know any other way to get immediate results."

"He's an Oriental *scholar!*" cried Catherine. "He understands the dynamics of the Orient a hell of a lot better than any of us, the so-called experts. Couldn't you have *appealed* to him, appealed to his sense of history, pointing out the consequences of what could *happen?*"

"He may be a scholar, but he's first a man who believes —with certain justification—that he was betrayed by his government. He asked for help and a trap was set to kill him. No appeals of mine would have broken through that barrier."

"You could have *tried!*"

"And risk delay when every hour counted? In a way, I'm sorry you've never been put in my position. Then, perhaps, you might really understand me."

"Question," said Catherine, holding up her hand defiantly. "What makes you think that David Webb will go into China after Sheng if he *does* find and take the impostor? As I understand it, the agreement is for him to deliver the man who calls himself Jason Bourne and Marie is returned to him."

"At that point, if it occurs, it doesn't really matter. *That's* when we'll tell him why we did what we did. That's when we'll appeal to his Far East expertise and the global consequences of Sheng's and the taipans' machinations. If he walks away, we have several experienced field agents who can take his place. They're not men you'd care to bring home to meet your mother, but they're available and they can do it."

"How?"

"Codes, Mrs. Staples. The original Jason Bourne's methods always included codes between himself and his clients. That was the structured myth, and the impostor has studied every aspect of the original. Once this new Bourne is in our hands we'll get the information we need one way or another—confirmed by chemicals, of course. We'll know how to reach Sheng, and that's all we have to know. One meeting in the countryside outside Jade Tower Mountain. One kill and the world goes on. I'm not capable of coming up with any other solution. Are you?"

"No," said Catherine softly, slowly shaking her head. "It's hardball."

"Give us Mrs. Webb."

"Yes, of course, but not tonight. She can't go anywhere, and you've got enough to worry about with Kaitak. I took her to a flat in Tuen Mun in the New Territories. It belongs to a friend of mine. I also brought her to a doctor who bandaged her feet—she bruised them badly running from your Lin Wenzu—and he gave her a sedative. My God, she's a wreck; she hasn't slept in days, and the pills didn't do much for her last night; she was too tense, still too frightened. I stayed with her and she talked until dawn. Let her rest. I'll pick her up in the morning."

"How will you manage it? What will you say?"

"I'm not sure. I'll call her later and try to keep her calm. I'll tell her I'm making progress—more, perhaps, than I thought I would. I just want to give her hope, to ease the tension. I'll tell her to stay near the phone, get as much rest as she can, and I'll drive up in the morning, I think with good news."

"I'd like to send a backup with you," said Havilland. "Including McAllister. He knows her, and I honestly believe his moral suasion will be communicated. It will bolster your case."

"It might," agreed Catherine, nodding. "As you said, I sensed it. All right, but they're to stay away until I've talked to her, and that could take a couple of hours. She has a finely honed distrust of Washington, and I've got a lot of convincing to do. That's her husband out there and she loves him very much. I can't and I won't tell her that I approve of what you did, but I can say that in light of the extraordinary circumstances—not excluding the conceivable economic collapse of Hong Kong—I understand why you did it. What *she* has to understand—if nothing else—is that she's closer to her husband being *with* you than being away from you. Of course, she may try to kill you, but that's your problem. She's a very feminine, good-looking woman, more than attractive, quite striking actually, but remember she's a ranch girl from Calgary. I wouldn't advise being alone with her in a room. I'm sure she's wrestled calves to the ground far stronger than you."

"I'll bring in a squad of marines."

"Don't. She'd turn them against you. She's one of the most persuasive people I've ever met."

"She has to be," replied the ambassador, leaning back in his chair. "She forced a man with no identity, with overwhelming feelings of guilt, to look into himself and walk out of the tunnels of his own confusion. No easy task. . . . Tell me about her—not the dry facts of a dossier, but the *person.*"

Catherine did, telling what she knew from observation and instinct. Time passed; the minutes and the half hours punctuated with repeated phone calls apprising Havilland of the conditions at Kai-tak Airport. The sun descended beyond the walls of the garden outside. A light supper was provided by the staff.

"Would you ask Mr. McAllister to join us?" said Havilland to a steward.

"I asked Mr. McAllister if I could bring him something, sir, and he was pretty firm about it. He told me to get out and leave him alone."

"Then never mind, thank you."

The phone calls kept coming; the subject of Marie St. Jacques was exhausted, and the conversation now turned exclusively on the developments at Kai-tak. Staples watched the diplomat in amazement, for the more intense the crisis became, the slower and more controlled was his speech.

"Tell me about yourself, Mrs. Staples. Only what you care to professionally, of course."

Catherine studied Raymond Havilland and began quietly. "I sprang from an ear of Ontario corn. . . ."

"Yes, of course," said the ambassador with utter sincerity, glancing at the phone.

Staples now understood. This celebrated statesman was carrying on an innocuous conversation while his mind was riveted on an entirely different subject. Kai-tak. His eyes kept straying to the telephone; his wrist turned constantly so that he could look at his watch, and yet he never missed the breaks in their dialogue where he was expected to voice a response.

"My former husband sells shoes—"

Havilland's head snapped up from looking at his watch. He would not have been thought capable of an embarrassed smile, but he showed one at that moment. "You've caught me," he said.

"A long time ago," said Catherine.

"There's a reason. I know Owen Staples quite well."

"It figures. I imagine you move in the same circles."

"I saw him last year at the Queens Plate race in Toronto. I think one of his horses ran respectably well.

He looked quite grand in his cutaway, but then he was one of the Queen Mother's escorts."

"When we were married, he couldn't afford a suit off the rack."

"You know," said Havilland, "when I read up on you and learned about Owen, I had a fleeting temptation to call him. Not to *say* anything, obviously, but to ask him about you. Then I thought, My God, in this age of post-marital civility, suppose they still talk with each other. I'd be tipping my hand."

"We're still talking, and you tipped your hand when you flew into Hong Kong."

"For you, perhaps. But only after Webb's wife reached you. Tell me, what did you think when you first heard I was here?"

"That the U.K. had called you in for consultation on the Accords."

"You flatter me—"

The telephone rang, and Havilland's hand flew out for it. The caller was Lin Wenzu, reporting the progress being made at Kai-tak, or more substantively, as was apparent, the lack of progress.

"Why don't they simply call the whole damn thing off?" asked the ambassador angrily. "Pile them into their cars and get the hell out of there!" Whatever reply the major offered only served to further exasperate Havilland. "That's ridiculous! This isn't a show of gamesmanship, it's a potential assassination! No one's image or honor is involved under the circumstances, and believe me, the world isn't hanging by its collective teeth waiting for that damned press conference. Most of it's asleep, for God's sake!" Again the diplomat listened. Lin's remarks not only astonished him, they infuriated him. "The *Chinese* said that? It's *preposterous!* Peking has no right to make such a demand! It's—" Havilland glanced at Staples. "It's *barbaric!* Someone should tell them it's not their Asian faces that are being saved; it's the Anglo Crown governor's, and *his* face is attached to his head, which could be blown *off!*" Silence; the ambassador's eyes blinked in angry resignation. "I know, I know. The heavenly red star must continue to shine in a heavenly blackout. There's nothing you can do, so do your best, Major. Keep calling. As one of my grandchildren puts it, I'm 'eating bananas,' whatever the hell that means." Havilland hung up and looked over at Catherine. "Orders from Peking. The delegations are not to run in the *face* of Western terrorism. Protect all concerned, but carry on."

"London would probably approve. The 'Carry on' has a familiar ring."

"Orders from Peking . . ." said the diplomat softly, not hearing Staples. "Orders from *Sheng!*"

"Are you quite sure of that?"

"It's *his* ballgame! He calls the shots. My God, he *is* ready!"

The tension grew geometrically with each quarter hour, until the air was filled with electricity. The rains came, pounding the bay window with a relentless tattoo. A television set was rolled in and turned on, the American ambassador-at-large and the Canadian foreign service officer watching in fear and in silence. The huge jet taxied in the downpour to its appointed rendezvous with the crowds of reporters and camera crews. The English and the Chinese honor guards emerged first, simultaneously from both sides of the open door. Their appearance was startling, for instead of a stately processional expected of such military escorts, these squads moved rapidly into flanking positions down the metal steps, elbows bent skyward, sidearms gripped, guns at the ready. The leaders then filed out waving to the onlookers; they started down the staircase followed by two lines of awkwardly grinning subordinates. The strange "press conference" began, and Undersecretary of State Edward McAllister burst into the room, the heavy door crashing into the wall as he flung it open.

"I *have* it!" he cried, a page of paper in his hand. "I'm *sure* I have it!"

"Calm *down,* Edward! Speak sensibly."

"The Chinese delegation!" shouted McAllister out of breath, racing to the diplomat and thrusting the paper at him. "It's headed by a man named Lao Sing! The second in command is a general named Yunshen! They're powerful, and they've opposed Sheng Chou Yang for years, objecting to his policies openly on the Central Committee! Their inclusion in the negotiating teams was Sheng's apparent willingness to have a balance—which made him look fair in the eyes of the old guard."

"For God's sake, what are you trying to *say?*"

"It's *not* the Crown governor! Not *just* him! It's *all* of them! With one action he removes his two strongest opponents in Peking and clears the path for himself. Then, as you put it, he implants his clearinghouse—his taipans —during a period of *instability,* now shared by *both* governments!"

Havilland yanked the telephone out of its cradle. "Get me Lin at Kai-tak," he ordered the switchboard. *"Quickly!* . . . Major Lin, please. At *once!* . . . What do you mean, he's not there? Where *is* he? . . . Who's this? . . . Yes, I know who you are. Listen to me and listen carefully! The target is *not* the Crown governor alone, it's worse. It includes two members of the Chinese delegation. Separate all parties—You *know that?* . . . A man from the *Mossad?* What the hell . . . ? There's no such arrangement, there *couldn't* be! . . . Yes, of course, I'll get off the line." Breathing rapidly, his lined face pale, the diplomat looked at the wall and spoke in a barely audible voice. "They found out, from God knows where, and are taking immediate countermeasures. . . . *Who?* For Christ's sake, who *was* it?"

"*Our* Jason Bourne," said McAllister quietly. "He's there."

On the television screen a distant limousine jolted to a stop while others peeled away into the darkness. Figures fled from the stationary car in panic, and seconds later the screen was filled with a blinding explosion.

"He's there," repeated McAllister, whispering. "He's *there!*"

21

The motor launch pitched violently in the darkness and the torrential rains. The crew of two bailed out the water that continuously swept back over the gunwales as the grizzled Chinese-Portuguese captain, squinting through the cabin's large windows, inched his way forward toward the black outlines of the island. Bourne and d'Anjou flanked the boat's owner; the Frenchman spoke, raising his voice over the downpour. "How far do you judge it to the beach?"

"Two hundred meters, plus or minus ten or twenty," said the captain.

"It's time for the light. Where is it?"

"In the locker beneath you. On the right. Another seventy-five meters and I hold. Any farther, the rocks can be dangerous in this weather."

"We have to get into the beach!" cried the Frenchman. "It's imperative, I *told* you that!"

"Yes, but you forgot to tell me there would be this rain, these swells. Ninety meters, and you can use the little boat. The engine is strong, you'll get there."

"*Merde!*" spat out d'Anjou, opening the locker and pulling out a casement light. "That could leave a hundred-plus meters!"

"In any event it would not be less than fifty, I told *you* that."

"And between the two is deep water!"

"Shall I turn around and head for Macao?"

"And get us blown up by the patrols? You make payment when it is due or you do not make your destination! You *know* that!"

"One hundred meters, no more."

D'Anjou nodded testily while holding the casement light up to his chest. He pressed a button, immediately releasing it, and for a brief moment an eerie, dark blue flash illuminated the pilot's window. Seconds later a corresponding blue signal was seen through the mottled glass from the island's shoreline. "You see, *mon capitaine,* had we not come in for the rendezvous this miserable scow would have been blown out of the water."

"You were fond enough of her this afternoon!" said the helmsman, working furiously at the wheel.

"That was *yesterday* afternoon. It is now one-thirty the next morning and I have come to know your thieving ways." D'Anjou replaced the light in the locker and glanced at Bourne, who was looking at him. Each was doing what he had done many times in the days of

Medusa—checking out a partner's apparel and equipment. Both men had rolled their clothing in canvas bags —trousers, sweaters and thin rubber skullcaps, all black. The only equipment other than Jason's automatic and the Frenchman's small .22 caliber pistol were scabbarded knives—all unseen. "Get in as close as you can," said d'Anjou to the captain. "And remember, you won't receive the final payment if you're not here when we return."

"Suppose they take your money and *kill* you?" cried the pilot, spinning the wheel. "Then I'm *out!*"

"I'm touched," said Bourne.

"Have no fear of that," answered the Frenchman, glaring at the Chinese-Portuguese. "I've dealt with this man many times over many months. Like you, he is the pilot of a fast boat and every bit the thief you are. I line his Marxist pockets so that his mistresses live like concubines of the Central Committee. Also, he suspects I keep records. We are in God's hands, perhaps better."

"Then take the light," muttered the captain grudgingly. "You may need it, and you're no good to me stranded or ripped up on the rocks."

"Your concern overwhelms me," said d'Anjou, retrieving the light and nodding at Jason. "We'll familiarize ourselves with the skiff and its motor."

"The motor's under thick canvas. Don't start it until you're in the water!"

"How do we know it *will* start?" asked Bourne.

"Because I want my money, Silent One."

The ride into the beach drenched them both, both bracing themselves against the panels of the small boat, Jason gripping the sides and d'Anjou the rudder and the stern so as to keep from pitching overboard. They grazed a shoal. Metal ground against the rocks as the Frenchman swerved the rudder to starboard, pushing the throttle to maximum.

The strange, dark blue flash came once again from the beach. They had strayed in the wet darkness; d'Anjou angled the boat toward the signal and within minutes the bow struck sand. The Frenchman swung the stick down, elevating the motor, as Bourne leaped overboard, grabbing the rope and pulling the small craft up on the beach.

He gasped, startled by the figure of a man suddenly next to him, gripping the line in front of him. "Four hands are better than two," shouted the stranger, an Oriental, in perfectly fluent English—English with an American accent.

"You're the *contact?*" yelled Jason, bewildered, wondering if the rain and the waves had distorted his hearing.

"That's such a foolish term!" replied the man, shouting back. "I'm simply a friend!"

Five minutes later, having beached the small boat, the three men walked through the thick, shorefront foliage, which was suddenly replaced by scrubby trees. The "friend" had constructed a primitive lean-to out of a ship's tarpaulin; a small fire faced the dense woods in front, unseen from the sides and the rear, concealed by the tarp. The warmth was welcome; the winds and the drenching rain had chilled Bourne and d'Anjou. They sat cross-legged around the fire and the Frenchman spoke to the uniformed Chinese.

"This was hardly necessary, Gamma—"

"Gamma?" erupted Jason.

"I've implemented certain traditions of our past, Delta. Actually, I could have used *Tango* or *Fox Trot*—it wasn't *all* Greek, you know. The Greek was reserved for the leaders."

"This is a bullshit conversation. I want to know why we're here. Why you haven't paid him and we get the hell out?"

"Man . . . !" said the Chinese, drawing out the word, purposely emphasizing the American idiom. "This cat's uptight! What's his beef?"

"My beef, *man,* is that I want to get back to that boat. I really don't have time for tea!"

"How about Scotch?" said the officer of the People's Republic, reaching behind him, pulling his arm forward, and displaying a bottle of perfectly acceptable whisky. "We'll have to share the cork, as it were, but I don't think we're infectious people. We bathe, we brush our teeth, we sleep with clean whores—at least *my* heavenly government makes sure they're clean."

"Who the hell *are* you?" asked Jason Bourne.

" 'Gamma' will do, Echo's convinced me of that. As to

what I am, I leave that to your imagination. You might try USC—that's the University of Southern California—with graduate studies in Berkeley—all those protests in the sixties, surely you remember them."

"You were a part of that crowd?"

"Certainly not! I was a staunch conservative, a member of the John Birch Society who wanted them all *shot!* Screeching freaks with no regard for their nation's moral commitments."

"This *is* a bullshit conversation."

"My friend Gamma," interrupted d'Anjou, "is the perfect intermediary. He is an educated double or triple or conceiveably a quadruple agent working all sides for the benefit of his own interests. He is the totally amoral man, and I respect him for that."

"You came back to China? To the People's Republic?"

"It's where the money was," admitted the officer. "Any repressive society offers vast opportunities for those willing to take minor risks on behalf of the repressed. Ask the commissars in Moscow and the Eastern bloc. Of course, one must have contacts in the West and possess certain talents that can also serve the regimental leaders. Fortunately, I'm an exceptional sailor, courtesy of friends in the Bay Area who owned yachts and small motor craft. I'll return one day. I really do like San Francisco."

"Don't try to fathom his Swiss accounts," said d'Anjou. "Instead, let's concentrate on why Gamma has made us such a pleasant retreat in the rainstorm." The Frenchman took the bottle and drank.

"It will cost you, Echo," said the Chinese.

"With you, what doesn't? What is it?" D'Anjou passed the bottle to Jason.

"I may speak in front of your companion?"

"Anything."

"You'll want the information. I guarantee it. The price is one thousand American."

"That's it?"

"It should be enough," said the Chinese officer, taking the bottle of Scotch from Bourne. "There are two of you, and my patrol boat is half a mile away in the south cove. My crew thinks I'm holding a secret meeting with our undercover people in the colony."

"I'll 'want the information,' and you'll 'guarantee it.' For those words I'm to produce a thousand dollars without a struggle when it's entirely possible you have a dozen *Zhongguo ren* outside in the bush."

"Some things must be taken on faith."

"Not my money," countered the Frenchman. "You don't get a *sou* until I have an idea what you're selling."

"You are Gallic to the core," said Gamma, shaking his head. "Very well. It concerns your disciple, the one who no longer follows his master, but instead picks up his thirty pieces of silver and a great deal more."

"The *assassin?*"

"*Pay* him!" ordered Bourne, rigid, staring at the Chinese officer.

D'Anjou looked at Jason and the man called Gamma, then pulled up his sweater and unbuckled his soaking wet trousers. He reached below his waist and forced up an oilcloth money belt; he unzipped the center pocket, slipped out the bills one after another with his fingers and held them out for the Chinese officer. "Three thousand for tonight and one for this new information. The rest is counterfeit. I always carry an extra thousand for contingencies, but only a thousand—"

"The *information,*" broke in Jason Bourne.

"He paid for it," replied Gamma. "I shall address him."

"Address whomever the hell you like, just talk."

"Our mutual friend in Guangzhou," began the officer speaking to d'Anjou. "The radioman at Headquarters One."

"We've done business," said the Frenchman guardedly.

"Knowing I'd be meeting you here at this hour, I refueled at the pumps in Zhuhai Shi shortly after ten-thirty. There was a message for me to reach him—we have a safe relay. He told me there was a call rerouted through Beijing with an unidentified Jade Tower priority code. It was for Soo Jiang—"

D'Anjou bolted forward, both hands on the ground. "The *pig!*"

"Who is he?" asked Bourne quickly.

"Supposedly chief of Intelligence for Macao operations," replied the Frenchman, "but he would sell his mother to a brothel if the price was right. At the moment he is the conduit to my once and former disciple. My *Judas!*"

"Who's suddenly been summoned to Beijing," interrupted the man called Gamma.

"You're *sure* of that?" said Jason.

"Our mutual friend is sure," answered the Chinese, still looking at d'Anjou. "An aide to Soo came to Headquarters One and checked all of tomorrow's flights from Kai-tak to Beijing. Under his department's authorization he reserved space—a single space—on every one. In several cases it meant that the original passengers were reduced to stand-by status. When an officer at Headquarters One asked for Soo's personal confirmation, the aide said he had left for Macao on urgent business. Who has business in Macao at midnight? Everything's closed."

"Except the casinos," volunteered Bourne. "Table Five. The Kam Pek. Totally controlled circumstances."

"Which, in light of the reserved space," said the Frenchman, "means that Soo isn't sure when he will reach the assassin."

"But he *is* sure he'll reach him. Whatever message he's carrying is nothing short of an order that has to be complied with." Jason looked at the Chinese officer. "Get us into Beijing," he said. "The airport, the earliest flight. You'll be rich, I guarantee it."

"Delta, you're *mad!*" cried d'Anjou. "Peking is out of the question!"

"Why? No one's looking for us and there are French, English, Italians, Americans—God knows who else—all over the city. We've both got passports that'll get us through."

"Be reasonable!" pleaded Echo. "We'll be in their nets. Knowing what we know, if we're spotted in the vaguest questionable circumstances we'll be killed on the spot! He'll show up again down here, most likely in a matter of days."

"I don't have days," said Bourne coldly. "I've lost your creation twice. I'm not going to lose him a third time."

"You think you can possibly take him in *China?*"

"Where else would he least expect a trap?"

"*Madness!* You *are* mad!"

"Make the arrangements," Jason ordered the Chinese officer. "The first flight out of Kai-tak. When I've got the tickets, I'll hand over fifty thousand dollars American to whoever gives them to me. Send someone you can trust."

"Fifty *thousand* . . . ?" The man called Gamma stared at Bourne.

The skies over Peking were hazy, the dust traveling on the winds from the North China plains creating pockets of vapid yellows and dull browns in the sunlight. The airport, like all other internationals, was immense, the runways a crisscrossing patchwork of black avenues, several over two miles in length. If there was a difference between Peking airport and its Western counterparts, it was in the huge dome-shaped terminal with its adjacent hotel and various freeways leading into the complex. Although contemporary in design, there was an underlying sense of functionalism and an absence of eye-pleasing touches. It was an airport to be used and admired for its efficiency, not for its beauty.

Bourne and d'Anjou went through customs with a minimum of effort, the way eased for them by their fluent Chinese. The guards were actually pleasant, barely glancing at their minimal luggage, more curious about their linguistic ability than their possessions. The chief official accepted without question the story of two Oriental scholars on a holiday where pleasant travels would no doubt find their way into the lecture halls. They converted a thousand dollars each into *renminbi*—literally, the People's Money—and were given nearly two thousand *yuan* apiece in return. And Bourne took off the glasses he had purchased in Washington from his friend Cactus.

"One thing bewilders me," said the Frenchman as they stood in front of an electronic sign showing the next three hours of arrivals and departures. "Why would he be flown in on a commercial plane? Certainly, whoever is paying him has government or military aircraft at his disposal."

"Like ours, those aircraft have to be signed out and accounted for," answered Jason. "And whoever it is has to keep his distance from your assassin. He has to come in as a tourist or a businessman and then the convoluted process of making contact begins. At least that's what I'm counting on."

"*Madness!* Tell me, Delta, if you *do* take him—and I add that it's a significant 'if' because he's extraordinarily capable—have you any idea how to get him out?"

"I've got money, American money, large bills, more than you can imagine. It's in the lining of my jacket."

"That's why we stopped at the Peninsula, isn't it? Why you told me not to check you out yesterday. Your money's there."

"It was. In the hotel safe. I'll get him out."

"On the wings of Pegasus?"

"No, probably a Pan Am flight with the two of us helping a very sick friend. Actually, somewhere along the line I think you gave me the idea."

"Then I am a mental case!"

"Stay by the window," said Bourne. "There's another twelve minutes before the next plane is due from Kai-tak, but then that could mean two minutes or twelve hours. I'm going to buy us both a present."

"Madness," mumbled the Frenchman, too tired to do more than shake his head.

Jason returned, directing d'Anjou into a corner within sight of the immigration doors, which were kept closed except for those passengers emerging from customs. Bourne reached into his inside jacket pocket and pulled out a long, thin, brightly covered box with the sort of gaudy wrapping found in souvenir shops the world over. He removed the top; inside on ersatz felt was a narrow brass letter-opener, with Chinese characters along the handle. The point was obviously honed and sharp. "Take it," said Jason. "Put it in your belt."

"How's the balance?" asked Medusa's Echo as he slid the blade under his trousers.

"Not bad. It's about halfway to the base of the handle and brass gives it weight. The thrust should be decent."

"Yes, I recall," said d'Anjou. "One of the first rules was never to throw a knife, but one evening at dusk you watched a Gurkha take out a scout ten feet away without firing a shot or risking hand-to-hand combat. His carbine bayonet spun through the air like a whirling missile, right

into the scout's chest. The next morning you ordered the
Gurkha to teach us—some did better than others.''

"How did you do?"

"Reasonably well. I was older than all of you, and
whatever defenses I could learn that did not take great
physical exertion I felt drawn to. Also I kept practicing.
You saw me; you commented on it frequently.''

Jason looked at the Frenchman. "It's funny, but I don't
remember any of that.''

"I just naturally thought . . . I'm sorry, Delta.''

"Forget it. I'm learning to trust things I don't understand.''

The vigil continued, reminding Bourne of his wait in
Lo Wu as one trainload after another crossed the border,
no one revealed until a short, elderly man with a limp
became someone else in the distance. The 11:30 plane
was over two hours late. Customs would take an additional fifty minutes.

"*That* one!'' cried d'Anjou, pointing to a figure walking
out of the immigration doors.

"With a cane?'' asked Jason. "With a limp?''

"His shabby clothes cannot conceal his shoulders!''
exclaimed Echo. "The gray hair is too new; he hasn't
brushed it sufficiently, and the dark glasses too wide. Like
us, he is tired. You were right. The summons to Beijing
had to be complied with, and he is careless.''

"Because 'rest is a weapon' and he disregarded it?''

"Yes. Last night Kai-tak had to have taken its toll on
him, but, more important, he had to obey. *Merde!* His fees
must be in the hundreds of thousands!''

"He's heading for the hotel,'' said Bourne. "Stay back
here, I'll follow him—at a distance. If he spotted you,
he'd run and we could lose him.''

"He could spot *you!*''

"Not likely. I invented the game. Also, I'll be behind
him. Stay here. I'll come back for you.''

Carrying his flight bag, his gait showing the weariness
of jet lag, Jason fell in line with the disembarked passengers heading into the hotel, his eyes on the gray-haired
man up ahead. Twice the former British commando
stopped and turned around, and twice, with each brief
movement of the shoulders, Bourne also turned and bent

down, as if brushing an insect from his leg or adjusting the strap of his flight bag, his body and face out of sight. The crowd at the registration counter grew and Jason was eight people behind the killer in the second line, making himself as inconspicuous as possible, continually stooping to kick his flight bag ahead. The commando reached the female clerk; he showed his papers, signed the register, and limped with his cane toward a bank of brown elevators on the right. Six minutes later Bourne faced the same clerk. He spoke in Mandarin.

"Ni neng bang-zhu wo ma?" he began, asking for help. "It was a sudden trip and I've no place to stay. Just for the night."

"You speak our language very well," said the clerk, her almond-shaped eyes wide in appreciation. "You do us honor," she added politely.

"I hope to do much better during my stay here. I'm on a scholarly trip."

"It is the best kind. There are many treasures in Beijing, and elsewhere, of course, but this is the heavenly city. You have no reservation?"

"I'm afraid not. Everything was last-minute, if you know what I mean."

"As I speak both languages, I can tell you that you said it correctly in ours. Everything is rush-rush. I'll see what I can do. It will not be terribly grand, of course."

"I can't afford terribly grand," said Jason shyly. "But I have a roommate—we can share the same bed, if necessary."

"I'm certain it will be on such short notice." The clerk's fingers leafed through the file cards. *"Here,"* she said. "A single back room on the second floor. I think it may fit your economics—"

"We'll take it," agreed Bourne. "By the way, a few minutes ago I saw a man in this line whom I'm sure I know. He's getting on now, but I think he was an old professor of mine when I studied in England. Gray-haired, with a cane . . . I'm certain it's he. I'd like to call him."

"Oh, yes, I remember." The clerk now separated the most recent registration cards in front of her. "The name is Wadsworth, Joseph Wadsworth. He's in three-twenty-

five. But you may be wrong. His occupation is listed as
an off-shore oil consultant from Great Britain."

"You're right, wrong man," said Jason, shaking his
head in embarrassment. He took the key to the room.

"We can take him! *Now!*" Bourne gripped d'Anjou's arm,
pulling the Frenchman away from the deserted corner of
the terminal.

"Now? So easily? So quickly? It is incredible!"

"The opposite," said Jason, leading d'Anjou toward
the crowded row of glass doors that was the entrance to
the hotel. "It's completely credible. Your man's mind is
on a dozen different things right now. He's got to stay out
of sight. He can't place a call through a switchboard, so
he'll remain in his room waiting for a call to *him* giving
him his instructions." They walked through a glass door,
looked around and headed to the left of the long counter.
Bourne continued, speaking rapidly. "Kai-tak didn't
work last night, so he has to consider another possibility.
His own elimination on the basis that whoever discovered the explosives under the car saw him and identified
him—which is the truth. He has to insist that his client be
alone at the arranged rendezvous so he can reach him
one on one. It's his ultimate protection." They found a
staircase and started climbing. "And his clothes," went
on Medusa's Delta, "he'll change them. He can't appear
as he *was* and he can't appear as he *is*. He has to be
someone else." They reached the third floor, and Jason,
his hand on the knob, turned to d'Anjou. "Take my word
for it, Echo, your boy's involved. He's got exercises going
on in his head that would challenge a Russian chess
player."

"Is this the academic speaking or the man they once
called Jason Bourne?"

"Bourne," said David Webb, his eyes cold, his voice
ice. "If it ever was, it's now."

The flight bag strapped over his shoulder, Jason slowly
opened the staircase door, inching his body into the
frame. Two men in dark pin-striped suits walked up the
hallway toward him complaining at the apparent lack of
room service; their speech was British. They opened the
door to their room and went inside. Bourne pulled the

staircase door back and pushed d'Anjou through; they walked down the corridor. The room numbers were in Chinese and English.

341, 339, 337—they were in the right hallway, the room was along the left wall. Three Indian couples suddenly emerged from a brown elevator, the women in their saris, the men in tight-fitting trousers; they passed Jason and d'Anjou chattering, looking for their rooms, the husbands obviously annoyed to be carrying their own luggage.

335, 333, 331—

"This is the *end!*" screamed a female voice as an obese woman in hair curlers strode martially out of a door on the right wearing a bathrobe. The nightgown underneath trailed below, twice snarling her feet. She yanked it up, revealing a pair of legs worthy of a rhinoceros. "The toilet doesn't work and you can *forget* the phone!"

"Isabel, I told you!" shouted a man in red pajamas peering through the open door. "It's the jet lag. Get some sleep and remember this isn't Short Hills! Don't nitpick. Expand yourself!"

"Since I can't use the bathroom, I have no choice! I'll find *some* slant-eyed bastard and yell like hell! Where are the stairs? I wouldn't walk *into* one of those goddamned elevators. If they move at all, it's probably sideways and right through the walls into a seven forty-seven!"

The distraught woman swept by on her way to the staircase exit. Two of the three Indian couples had difficulty with their keys, finally managing to negotiate the locks with loud, well-placed kicks, and the man in the red pajamas slammed the door of his room after shouting to his wife in high dudgeon. "It's like that class reunion at the club! You're so *embarrassing,* Isabel!"

329, 327 . . . 325. The room. The hallway was deserted. They could hear the strains of Oriental music from behind the door. The radio was turned up, the volume loud, to be made louder with the first ring of a telephone bell. Jason pulled d'Anjou back and spoke quietly against the wall. "I don't remember any Gurkhas or any scouts—"

"A part of you did, Delta," interrupted Echo.

"Maybe, but that's beside the point. This is the beginning of the end of the road. We'll leave our bags out here. I'll go for the door and you follow hard. Keep your blade ready. But I want you to understand something, and there *can't* be a mistake—don't throw it unless you absolutely *have* to. If you do, go for his legs. Nothing above the waist."

"You put more faith in an older man's accuracy than I do."

"I'm hoping I won't have to call on it. These doors are made of hollow plywood and your assassin's got a lot on his mind. He's thinking about strategy, not about us. How could we know he's here, and even if we did, how could we get across the border on such short notice? And I *want* him! I'm *taking* him! Ready?"

"As I ever will be," said the Frenchman, lowering his small suitcase and pulling the brass letter-opener from his belt. He held the blade in his hand, his fingers spread, seeking the balance.

Bourne slipped the flight bag off his shoulder to the floor and quietly positioned himself in front of Room 325. He looked at d'Anjou. Echo nodded, and Jason sprang toward the door, his left foot a battering ram, crashing into the space below the lock. The door plunged inward, as though blown apart; wood shattered, hinges were torn from their bolts. Bourne lunged inside, rolling over and over on the floor, his eyes spinning in all directions.

"*Arrêtez!*" roared d'Anjou.

A figure came through an inner doorway—the gray-haired man, the *assassin!* Jason sprang to his feet, hurling himself at his quarry, grabbing the man's hair, yanking him to the left, then to the right, crashing him back into the doorframe. Suddenly the Frenchman screamed as the brass blade of the letter-opener flashed through the air, embedding itself in the wall, the handle quivering. It was off the mark, a warning.

"Delta! *No!*"

Bourne stopped all movement, his quarry pinned, helpless under his weight and grip.

"*Look!*" cried d'Anjou.

Jason slowly moved back, his arms rigid, caging the figure in front of him. He stared into the gaunt, wrinkled face of a very old man with thinning gray hair.

22

Marie lay on the narrow bed staring up at the ceiling. The rays of the noonday sun streamed through the shadeless windows, filling the small room with blinding light and too much heat. Sweat matted her face, and her torn blouse clung to her moist skin. Her feet ached from the midmorning madness that had begun as a walk down an unfinished coastal road to a rocky beach below—a stupid thing to do, but at the time the only thing she *could* do; she had been going out of her mind.

The sounds of the street floated up, a strange cacophony of high-pitched voices, sudden shrieks and bicycle bells and the blaring horns of trucks and public buses. It was as if a crowded, bustling, hustling section of Hong Kong had been ripped out of the island and set down in some faraway place where a wide river and endless fields and distant mountains replaced Victoria Harbor and the countless rows of ascending tall buildings made of glass and stone. In a sense the transplant had happened, she reflected. The miniature city of Tuen Mun was one of those space-oriented phenomena that had sprung up north of Kowloon in the New Territories. One year it had been an arid river plain, the next a rapidly developing metropolis of paved roads and factories, shopping districts, and spreading apartment buildings, all beckoning those from the south with the promise of housing and jobs in the thousands, and those who heeded the call brought with them the unmistakable hysteria of Hong Kong's commerce. Without it they would be filled with innocuous anxieties too placid to contend with; these were the descendants of Guangzhou—the province of Canton—not world-weary Shanghai.

Marie had awakened with the first light, what sleep she

had managed had been wracked with nightmares—and knew that she faced another suspension of time until Catherine called her. Staples had telephoned late last night, dragging her out of a sleep induced by total exhaustion, only to tell her cryptically that several unusual things had happened that could lead to favorable news. She was meeting a man who had taken an interest, a remarkable man who could help. Marie was to stay in the flat by the telephone in case there were new developments. Since Catherine had instructed her not to use names or specifics on the phone, Marie had not questioned the brevity of the call. "I'll phone you first thing in the morning, my dear." Staples had abruptly hung up.

She had not called by 8:30 or by 9:00, and by 9:36 Marie could stand it no longer. She reasoned that names were unnecessary, each knew the other's voice, and Catherine had to understand that David Webb's wife was entitled to *something* "first thing in the morning." Marie had dialed Staples's flat in Hong Kong; there was no answer, so she dialed again to make sure she had spun the correct numbers. Nothing. In frustration and without caring, she had called the consulate.

"Foreign Service Officer Staples, please. I'm a friend from the Treasury Board in Ottawa. I'd like to surprise her."

"The connection's very good, honey."

"I'm not *in* Ottawa, I'm here," said Marie, picturing the face of the talkative receptionist only too well.

"Sorry, hon, Mrs. Staples is off-premises with no instructions. To tell you the truth, the High Commish is looking for her too. Why don't you give me a number—"

Marie lowered the phone into its cradle, panic rising in her. It was nearly 10:00, and Catherine was an early riser. "First thing in the morning" might be anytime between 7:30 and 9:30, most likely splitting the difference, but not ten o'clock, *not* under the circumstances. And then twelve minutes later the phone had rung. It was the beginning of a far less subtle panic.

"Marie?"

"Catherine, are you all *right?"*

"Yes, of course."

"You said 'first thing in the morning'! Why didn't you

call before? I've been going out of my mind! Can you talk?"

"Yes, I'm in a public booth—"

"What's happened? What's *happening?* Who's the man you met with?"

There had been a brief pause on the line from Hong Kong. For an instant it seemed awkward and Marie had not known why. "I want you to stay calm, my dear," said Staples. "I didn't call before because you need all the rest you can get. I may have the answers that you want, that you need. Things are not as terrible as you think, and you *must* stay calm."

"Damn it, I *am* calm, at least I'm reasonably sensible! What the hell are you talking about?"

"I can tell you that your husband's alive."

"And I can tell you that he's very good at what he does —what he *did.* You're not telling me anything!"

"I'm driving out to see you in a few minutes. The traffic's rotten, as usual, made worse by all the security surrounding the Sino-British delegations, tying up the streets and the tunnel, but it shouldn't take me more than an hour and a half, perhaps two."

"Catherine, I want *answers!*"

"I'm bringing them to you, a few at least. Rest, Marie, try to relax. Everything's going to be all right. I'll be there soon."

"This *man,*" asked David Webb's wife, pleading. "Will he be with you?"

"No, I'll be alone, no one with me. I want to talk. You'll see him later."

"All right."

Had it been Staples's tone of voice? Marie had wondered after hanging up. Or that Catherine had literally told her nothing after admitting she could talk freely over a public phone? The Staples she knew would try to allay the fears of a terrified friend if she had concrete facts to offer in comfort, even a single piece of vital information, if the fabric of the whole was too complex. *Something.* David Webb's wife deserved *something!* Instead there had been a diplomat's talk, the allusion to but not the substance of reality. Something was wrong, but it was beyond her understanding. Catherine had protected her, taken enormous risks for her both professionally, in terms of not seeking guidance from her consulate, and personally, in confronting acute physical danger. Marie knew that she should feel gratitude, overwhelming gratitude, but instead she felt a growing sense of doubt. *Say it again, Catherine,* she had screamed inside herself, *say everything will be all right! I can't think anymore. I can't think in here! I've got to get out . . . I've got to have air!*

She had lurched about unsteadily for the clothes they had bought for her when they had reached Tuen Mun last night, clothes purchased after Staples had taken her to a doctor who ministered to her feet, applying cushioned gauze, giving her hospital slippers and prescribing thick-soled sneakers if she had to do any extended walking during the next several days. Actually, Catherine had picked out the clothes while Marie waited in the car, and considering the tension Staples was under, her selections were both functional and attractive. A light green, sheer cotton skirt was complemented by a white cotton blouse and a small white-shell purse. Also a pair of dark green slacks—shorts were inappropriate—and a second, casual blouse. All were successful counterfeits of well-known designers, the labels correctly spelled.

"They're very nice, Catherine. Thank you."

"They go with your hair," Staples had said. "Not that anyone in Tuen Mun will notice—I want you to stay in the flat—but we'll have to leave here sometime. Also, in case I get stuck at the office and you need anything, I've put some money in the purse."

"I thought I wasn't supposed to leave the flat, that we were going to pick up a few things at a market."

"I don't know what's back in Hong Kong any more than you do. Lin could be so furious he might dig up an old colonial law and put me under house arrest. . . . There's a shoe store in Blossom Soon Street. You'll have to go inside and try on the sneakers yourself. I'll come with you, of course."

Several moments had passed and Marie spoke. "Catherine, how do you know so much about this place? I've yet to see another Occidental in the streets. Whose flat is it?"

"A friend's," said Staples without further elaboration. "There's no one using it a great deal of the time, so I come up here to get away from it all." Catherine had said no more; the subject was not to be explored. Even when they had talked for most of the night, no amount of prodding had brought forth any more information from Staples. It was a topic she simply would not discuss.

Marie had put on the slacks and the blouse and struggled with the outsized sneakers. Cautiously she had walked down the stairs and into the busy street, instantly aware of the stares she attracted, wondering whether she should turn around and go back inside. She could not; she was finding a few minutes of freedom from the stifling confines of the small apartment and they were like a tonic. She strolled slowly, painfully, down the pavement, mesmerized by the color and the hectic movement and the unending, staccato chatter all around her. As in Hong Kong, garish signs rose everywhere above the buildings, and everywhere people haggled with one another alongside stands and in storefront doorways. It *was* as if a slice of the colony had been uprooted and set down on a vast frontier.

She had found an unfinished road at the end of a back street, the work apparently abandoned but only temporarily, as leveling machinery—unused and rusting—stood on the borders. Two signs in Chinese were on either side of the road at the top of a slope. Taking each step carefully, she made her way down the steep decline to the deserted shoreline and sat on a cluster of rocks; the minutes of freedom were opening up precious moments of peace. She looked out and watched the boats sailing from the docks of Tuen Mun, as well as those heading in from the People's Republic. From what she could see, the first were fishing craft, nets draped over bows and gunwales, while those from the Chinese Mainland were mostly small cargo ships, their decks bulging with crates of produce. There were also the sleek, gray navy patrol boats flying the colors of the People's Republic. Ominous black guns were mounted on all sides of the various craft, uniformed men standing motionless next to them, peering through binoculars. Every now and then a naval vessel would pull alongside a fishing boat, provoking wildly excited gestures from the fishermen. Stoic responses were the replies as the powerful patrols would slowly spin and slip away. It was all a game, thought Marie. The North was quietly asserting its total control while the

South was left to protest the disturbance of its fishing grounds. The former had the strength of hard steel and a disciplined chain of command, the latter soft nets and perseverance. No one was the victor except those opposing sisters, Boredom and Anxiety.

"*Jing-cha!*" shouted a male voice from behind in the distance.

"*Shei!*" shrieked a second. "*Ni zai zher gan shemma?*"

Marie spun around. Two men up on the road had broken into a run; they were racing down the unfinished access toward her, their screams directed at her, commanding her. Awkwardly she got to her feet, steadying herself on the rocks as they ran up to her. Both men were dressed in some sort of paramilitary clothing, and as she looked at them she realized they were young—late teenagers, twenty at most.

"*Bu xing!*" barked the taller boy, looking back up the hill, and gesturing for his companion to grab her. Whatever it was, it was to be done quickly. The second boy pinned her arms from behind.

"*Stop* this!" cried Marie, struggling. "Who *are* you?"

"Lady speaks English," observed the first young man. "*I* speak English," he added proudly, unctuously. "I worked for a jeweler in Kowloon." Again he glanced up at the unfinished road.

"Then tell your friend to take his hands off me!"

"The lady does not tell me what to do. I tell the lady." The postadolescent came closer, his eyes fixed on the swell of Marie's breasts under the blouse. "This is forbidden road, a forbidden part of the shore. The lady did not see the signs?"

"I don't read Chinese. I'm sorry, I'll leave. Just tell him to let go of me." Suddenly Marie felt the body of the young man behind her pressing against her own. "*Stop* it!" she yelled, hearing quiet laughter in her ear, feeling a warm breath on her neck.

"Is the lady to meet a boat with criminals from the People's Republic? Does she signal men on the water?" The taller Chinese raised both his hands to Marie's blouse, his fingers on the top buttons. "Is she concealing a radio perhaps, a signaling device? It is our duty to learn these things. The police expect it of us."

"*Goddamn you,* take your *hands* off me!" Marie twisted

violently, kicking out in front of her. The man behind pulled her back off her feet as the taller boy grabbed her legs, straddling them with his own and scissoring them. She could not move; her body was stretched taut diagonally up from the rocky beach, held firmly in place. The first Chinese ripped off her blouse and then her brassiere, and cupped her breasts with both hands. She screamed and thrashed and screamed again until she was slapped and two fingers pincered her throat, cutting off all sound but throated coughs. The nightmare of Zurich came back to her—rape and death on the Guisan Quai.

They carried her to a stretch of tall grass, the boy behind clamping his hand over her mouth, then replacing it quickly with his right arm, cutting off air and any screams she might have managed as he yanked her forward. She was thrown to the ground, one of her attackers now covering her face with his bare stomach as the other began pulling off her slacks and thrusting his hands between her legs. It *was* Zurich, and instead of writhing in the cold Swiss darkness there was the wet heat of the Orient; instead of the Limmat, another river, far wider, far more deserted; instead of one animal there were two. She could feel the body of the tall Chinese on top of her, thrusting in his panic, furious that he was not able to enter her, her thrashing repelling his assault. For an instant the boy across her face reached under his trousers to his groin—there was a brief moment of space and for Marie the world went mad! She sank her teeth into the flesh above her, drawing blood, feeling the sickening flesh in her mouth.

Screams followed; her arms were released. She kicked as the young Oriental rolled away clutching his stomach; she crashed her knee up into the exposed organ above her waist, then clawed at the wild-eyed, sweating face of the taller man, now screaming herself—yelling, pleading, shouting as she had never shouted in her life before. Holding his testicles beneath his shorts, the infuriated boy threw himself down on her, but rape was no longer a consideration, he wanted only to keep her quiet. Suffocating, the darkness had begun to close in on Marie—and then she had heard other voices in the distance, excited voices closing that distance, and she knew she had to send up a final cry for help. In a desperate surge, she dug her nails into the contorted face above her, for an instant freeing her mouth from the grip.

"Here! Down *here!* Over *here!"*

Bodies were suddenly swarming around her; she could hear slaps and kicks and furious screams, but none of the madness was directed at her. Then the darkness had come, her last thoughts only partly about herself. *David! David, for God's sake where are you? Stay alive, my dearest! Don't let them take your mind again. Above all, don't allow that! They want mine and I won't give it to them! Why are they doing this to us? Oh, my God, why?*

She had awakened on a cot in a small room with no windows, a young Chinese woman wiping her forehead with a cool, perfumed cloth. *"Where . . . ?"* whispered Marie. "Where is this? Where *am* I?"

The girl smiled sweetly and shrugged, nodding at a man on the other side of the cot, a Chinese Marie judged to be in his thirties, dressed in tropical clothes, a white guayabera instead of a shirt. "Permit me to introduce myself," said the man in accented but clear English. "My name is Jitai, and I am with the Tuen Mun branch of the Hang Chow Bank. You are in the back room of a fabric shop belonging to a friend and client, Mr. Chang. They brought you here and called for me. You were attacked by two hoodlums of the Di-di Jing Cha, which can be translated as the Young People's Auxiliary Police. It is one of those well-meant social programs that have many benefits, but on occasion also have their very rotten apples, as you Americans say."

"Why do you think I'm American?"

"Your speech. While you were unconscious you spoke about a man named David. A dear friend, no doubt. You wish to find him."

"What else did I say?"

"Nothing, really. You were not very coherent."

"I don't know anyone named David," said Marie firmly. "Not in that way. It must have been one of those deliriums that go back to the first grade."

"It is immaterial. It is your well-being that matters. We are filled with shame and sorrow at what happened."

"Where are those two punks, those *bastards?"*

"They are caught and will be punished."

"I hope they spend ten years in jail."

The Chinese frowned. "To bring that about will mean involving the police—a formal complaint, a hearing before a magistrate, so many legalities." Marie stared at the banker. "Now, if you wish, I will accompany you to the police and act as your interpreter, but it was our opinion that we should first hear your desires in this regard. You have been through so much—and you are alone here in Tuen Mun for reasons only you know."

"No, Mr. Jitai," said Marie quietly. "I'd rather not press charges. I'm all right, and vengeance isn't a high priority with me."

"It is with us, madame."

"What do you mean?"

"Your attackers will carry our shame to their wedding beds, where their performances will be less than expected."

"I see. They *are* young—"

"This morning, as we have learned, is not their first offense. They are filth, and lessons must be taught."

"This morning? Oh, my God, what *time* is it? How long have I been here?"

The banker looked at his watch. "Nearly an hour."

"I've got to get back to the apartment—the flat—right away. It's important."

"The ladies wish to mend your clothing. They're excellent seamstresses and it will not take long. However, they believed you should not wake up without your clothes."

"I haven't time. I have to get back now. Oh, Christ! I don't know where it is and I don't have an address!"

"We know the building, madame. A tall, attractive white woman alone in Tuen Mun is noticed. Word spreads. We'll take you there at once." The banker turned and spoke in rapid Chinese, addressing a half-opened door behind him, as Marie sat up. She was suddenly aware of the crowd of people peering inside. She got to her feet—her painful feet—and stood for a moment, weaving but slowly finding her balance, holding the ripped folds of her blouse together.

The door was pulled back and two old women entered, each carrying an article of brightly colored silk. The first was a kimonolike garment, which was gently lowered over her head to cover her torn blouse and much of her soiled green slacks. The second was a long, wide sash, which was wrapped around her waist and tied, also gently. Tense as she was, Marie saw that each article was exquisite.

"Come, madame," said the banker, touching her elbow. "I will escort you." They walked out into the fabric shop, Marie nodding and trying to smile as the crowd of Chinese men and women bowed to her, their dark eyes filled with sadness.

She had returned to the small apartment, removed the beautiful sash and garment, and lay down on the bed trying to make sense where no reason was to be found. She buried her face in the pillow, trying to push the horrible images of the morning out of her head, but the ugliness was beyond purging. Instead, it made the sweat pour out of her, and the tighter she closed her eyes, the more violent the images became, interweaving the terrible memories of Zurich on the Guisan Quai when a man named Jason Bourne had saved her life.

She stifled a scream and leaped off the bed, standing there, trembling. She walked into the tiny kitchen and turned on the faucet, reaching for a glass. The stream of water was weak and thin and she watched vacantly as the glass filled, her mind elsewhere.

There are times when people should put their heads on hold— God knows I do it more than a reasonably respected psychiatrist should. . . . Things overwhelm us . . . we have to get our acts together. Morris Panov, friend to Jason Bourne.

She shut off the faucet, drank the lukewarm water, and went back toward the confining room that served the triple functions of sleeping, sitting, and pacing. She stood in the doorframe and looked around, knowing what she found so grotesque about her sanctuary. It was a cell, as surely as if it were in some remote prison. Worse, it was a very real form of solitary confinement. She was again isolated with her thoughts, with her terrors. She walked to a window as a prisoner might, and peered at the world outside. What she saw was an extension of her cell; she was not free down in that teeming street below either. It was not a world she knew, and it did not welcome her. Quite aside from the obscene madness of the morning on the beach, she was an intruder who could neither understand nor be understood. She was alone, and that loneliness was driving her crazy.

Numbly Marie gazed at the street. The *street?* There she was! Catherine! She was standing with a man by a gray car, their heads turned, watching three *other* men ten yards behind them by a second car. All five were glaringly apparent, for they were like no other people in the street. They were Occidentals in a sea of Chinese, strangers in an unfamiliar place. They were obviously excited, concerned about something, as they kept nodding their heads and looking in all directions, especially across the street. At the apartment house. Three of the men had close-cropped hair—military cuts . . . marines. *American marines!*

Catherine's companion, a civilian to judge by his hair, was talking rapidly, his index finger jabbing the air. . . . Marie *knew* him! It was the man from the State Department, the one who had come to see them in Maine! The undersecretary with the dead eyes, who kept rubbing his temples and barely protested when David told him he did not trust him. It was *McAllister!* He was the man Catherine said she was to meet.

Suddenly, abstract and terrible pieces of the horrible puzzle fell into place as Marie watched the scene below. The two marines by the second car crossed the street and separated. The one standing with Catherine talked briefly with McAllister, then ran to his right, pulling a small hand-held radio from his pocket. Staples spoke to the undersecretary of State and glanced up at the apartment house. Marie spun away from the window.

I'll be alone, no one with me.

All right.

It was a trap! Catherine Staples had been reached. She was not a friend; she was the *enemy!* Marie knew she had to run. *For God's sake, get away!* She grabbed the white-shell purse with the money, and for a split second stared at the silks from the fabric shop. She picked them up and ran out of the flat.

There were two hallways, one running the width of the building along the front with a staircase on the right leading down to the street, the other hallway bisecting the first to form an inverted T, and leading to a door in the rear. It was a second staircase used for carrying garbage to the bins in the back alley. Catherine had casually pointed it out when they arrived, explaining that there

was an ordinance forbidding refuse in the street, which
was the main thoroughfare of Tuen Mun. Marie raced
down the bisecting hall to the rear door and opened it.
She gasped, suddenly confronted by the stooped figure
of an old man with a straw broom in his hand. He
squinted at her for a moment, then shook his head, his
expression one of intense curiosity. She stepped out into
the dark landing as the Chinese went inside; she held the
door slightly open, waiting for the sight of Staples emerging from the front stairs. If Catherine, finding the flat
empty, quickly returned to the staircase so as to rush
down into the street to McAllister and the marine contingent, Marie could slip back into the apartment and pick
up the clothes Staples had bought for her. In her panic
she had only fleetingly thought about them, grabbing the
silks instead, not daring to lose precious moments rummaging through the closet where Catherine had hung
them, stuffed among various other clothing. She thought
about them now. She could not walk, much less run
through the streets in a torn blouse and filthy slacks.
Something was *wrong.* It was the old man! He just stood
there staring at the crack in the doorframe.

"Go *away!*" whispered Marie.

Footsteps. The clacking of high-heeled shoes walking
rapidly up the metal staircase in the front of the building.
If it was Staples, she would pass the bisecting hallway on
her way to the flat.

"*Deng yi deng!*" yelped the old Chinese, still standing
motionless with his broom, still staring at her. Marie
closed the door further, watching through barely a half
inch of space.

Staples came into view, glancing briefly, curiously at
the old man, apparently having heard his sharp, high-
pitched angry voice. Without breaking stride she continued down the hall, intent only on reaching the flat.
Marie waited; the pounding in her chest seemed to echo
throughout the dark stairwell. Then the words came,
pleas shouted in hysteria. "*No! Marie!* Marie, where *are*
you?" The footsteps hammered now, racing on the cement. Catherine rounded the corner and began running
toward the old Chinese and the door—toward *her.*
"Marie, it's not what you *think!* For *God's* sake, *stop!*"

Marie Webb spun and ran down the dark steps. Suddenly, a shaft of bright yellow sunlight spread up the staircase, and just as suddenly was no more. The ground-floor door three stories below had been opened; a figure in a dark suit had entered swiftly, a marine taking up his post. The man raced up the steps; Marie crouched in the corner of the second landing. The marine reached the top step, about to round the turn, steadying himself on the railing. Marie lunged out, her hand—the hand with the bunched silks—crashing into the astonished soldier's face, catching him off balance; she slammed her shoulder into the marine's chest, sending him reeling backwards down the staircase. Marie passed his tumbling body on the steps as she heard the screams from above. "Marie! *Marie!* I know it's you! For Christ's sake, *listen* to me!"

She lurched out into the alley, and another nightmare began its dreadful course, played out in the blinding sunlight of Tuen Mun. Running through the connecting thoroughfare behind the row of apartment buildings, her feet now bleeding inside the sneakers, Marie threw the kimonolike garment over her head and stopped by a row of garbage cans, where she removed her green slacks and threw them inside the nearest one. She then draped the wide sash over her head, covering her hair, and ran into the next alleyway that led to the main street. She reached it and seconds later walked into the mass of humanity that was a slice of Hong Kong in the new frontier of the colony. She crossed the street.

"*There!*" shouted a male voice. "The tall one!"

The chase began again, but abruptly, without any indication, it was different. A man raced down the pavement after her, suddenly stopped by a wheeled stand blocking his way; he tried to shove it aside, only to put his hands into recessed pots of boiling fat. He screamed, overturning the cart, and was now met with shrieks by the proprietor obviously demanding payment, as he and others surrounded the marine, forcing him back into the curb.

"There's the *bitch!*"

As Marie heard the words she was confronted by a phalanx of women shoppers. She spun to her right and ran into another alley off the street, an alley she suddenly discovered was a dead end, ending with the wall of a

Chinese temple. It happened again! Five young men—
teenagers in paramilitary outfits—suddenly appeared
from a doorway and gestured for her to pass.

"Yankee *criminal!* Yankee *thief!*" The shouts were in
the cadence of a rehearsed foreign language. The young
men locked arms and without violence intercepted the
man with close-cropped hair, crowding him against a
wall.

"Get out of my way, you pricks!" shouted the marine.
"Get out of my way or I'll take every one of you brats!"

"You raise your arms . . . or a weapon—" cried a voice
in the background.

"I never said anything about a weapon!" broke in the
soldier from Victoria Peak.

"But if you do either," continued the voice, "they will
release their arms, and five Di-di Jing Cha—so many
trained by our American friends—will certainly contain
one man."

"Goddamn it, *sir!* I'm only trying to do my *job!* It's
none of your business!"

"I'm afraid it is, sir. For reasons you do not know."

"*Shit!*" The marine leaned against the wall, out of
breath, and looked at the smiling young faces in front of
him.

"*Lai!*" said a woman to Marie, pointing to a wide,
oddly shaped door with no visible handle on what appeared to be a thick, impenetrable exterior. "*Xiao xin.*
Kaa-fill."

"*Careful?* I understand." An aproned figure opened
the door and Marie rushed inside, instantly feeling the
harsh blasts of cold air. She was standing in a large walkin refrigerator where carcasses of meat hung eerily on
hooks under the glow of mesh-encased light bulbs. The
man in the apron waited a full minute, his ear at the door.
Marie wrapped the wide silk sash around her neck and
clutched her arms to ward off the sudden, bitter cold
made worse by the contrasting oppressive heat outside.
Finally, the clerk gestured for her to follow him; she did
so, threading her way around the carcasses until they
reached the huge refrigerator's entrance. The Chinese
yanked a metal lever and pushed the heavy door open,
nodding for Marie, who was shivering, to walk through.
She now found herself in a long, narrow deserted butcher

shop, the bamboo blinds on the front windows filtering the intense noonday sunlight. A white-haired man stood behind the counter by the far-right window, peering through the slats at the street outside. He beckoned for Marie to join him quickly. Again she did as she was instructed, and noticed an oddly shaped floral wreath behind the glass of the front door, which appeared to be locked.

The older man indicated that Marie should look through the window. She parted two curved bamboo slats and gasped, astonished at the scene outside. The search was at its frenzied peak. The marine with scalded hands kept waving them in the air as he went from store to store across the street. She saw Catherine Staples and McAllister in a heated conversation with a crowd of Chinese who obviously were objecting to the foreigners disturbing the peaceful if hectic way of life in Tuen Mun. McAllister in his panic apparently had shouted something offensive and was challenged by a man twice his age, an ancient in an Oriental gown, who had to be restrained by younger, cooler heads. The undersecretary of State backed away, his arms raised, pleading innocence, as Staples shouted to no avail in her efforts to extricate them both from the angry mob.

Suddenly, the marine with the wounded hands came crashing out of a doorway across the street; shattered glass flew in all directions as he rolled on the pavement, yelling in pain as his hands touched the cement. He was pursued by a young Chinese dressed in the white tunic, sash, and knee-length trousers of a martial-arts instructor. The marine sprang to his feet, and as his Oriental adversary ran up to him he pounded a low left hook into the young man's kidney, and followed it with a well-aimed right fist into the Oriental face, pummeling his assailant back into the storefront while screaming in agony at the pain both blows caused his scalded hands.

A last marine from Victoria Peak came running down the street, one leg limping, his shoulders sagging as if damaged from a fall—a fall down a flight of stairs, thought Marie, as she watched in amazement. He came to the aid of his anguished comrade and was very effective. The amateurish attempts at combat by the berobed students of the unconscious martial-arts instructor were met by a flurry of slashing legs, crashing chops, and the whirling maneuvers of a judo expert.

Suddenly again, with no warning whatsoever, the cacophonic strains of Oriental music swelled in the street, the cymbals and the primitive wood instruments reaching abrupt crescendos with each stride of the ragtag band that marched down the street, its followers carrying placards mounted with flowers. The fighting stopped as arms were restrained everywhere. Silence spread along the main avenue of commerce of Tuen Mun. The Americans were confused; Catherine Staples choked back her frustration and Edward McAllister threw up his hands in exasperation.

Marie watched, literally hypnotized by the change outside. Everything came to a stop, as if a halt had been ordered by an announcement from some sepulchral presence not to be denied. She shifted her angle of sight between the bamboo blinds and looked at the ragged group approaching. It was led by the banker Jitai! It was heading for the butcher shop!

Her eyes darting, Marie saw Catherine Staples and McAllister race past the odd gathering in front of the shop. Then across the street the two marines once again took up the chase. They all disappeared in the blinding sunlight.

There was a knock on the front door of the butcher shop. The old man with white hair removed the wreath and opened it. The banker, Jitai, walked in and bowed to Marie.

"Did you enjoy the parade, madame?" he asked.

"I wasn't sure what it was."

"A funeral march for the dead. In this instance, no doubt, for the slain animals in Mr. Woo's cold storage."

"*You . . . ? This was all planned?*"

"In a state of readiness, you might say," explained Jitai. "Frequently our cousins from the north manage to get across the border—not the thieves but family members wishing to join their own—and the soldiers want only to capture them and send them back. We must be prepared to protect our own."

"But *me . . . ?* You *knew?*"

"We watched; we waited. You were in hiding, running from someone, that much we did know. You told us that when you said you did not care to go before the magistrate, to 'press charges,' as you put it. You were directed into the alley outside."

"The line of women with the shopping bags—"

"Yes. They crossed the street when you did. We must help you."

Marie glanced at the anxious faces of the crowd beyond the bamboo slats, then looked at the banker. "How do you know I'm not a criminal?"

"It doesn't matter. The outrage against you resulting from two of our people is what matters. Also, madame, you do not look or speak like a fugitive from justice."

"I'm not. And I do need help. I have to get back to Hong Kong, to a hotel where they won't find me, where there's a telephone I can use. I don't really know who, but I have to reach people who can help me . . . help us." Marie paused, her eyes locked with Jitai's. "The man named David is my husband."

"I can understand," said the banker. "But first you have to see a doctor."

"What?"

"Your feet are bleeding."

Marie looked down. Blood had seeped through the bandages, penetrating the canvas of her sneakers. They were a sickening mess. "I guess you're right," she agreed.

"Then there will be clothes, transportation—I myself will find you a hotel under any name you wish. And there is the matter of money. Do you have funds?"

"I don't know," said Marie, putting the silks on the counter and opening the white-shell purse. "That is, I haven't looked. A friend—someone that I thought was a friend—left me money." She pulled out the bills Staples had placed in the purse.

"We are not wealthy here in Tuen Mun, but perhaps we can help. There was talk of taking up a collection."

"I'm not a poor woman, Mr. Jitai," interrupted Marie. "If that is necessary and, frankly, if I'm alive, every cent will be returned with interest far in excess of the prime rate."

"As you wish. I am a banker. But what would such a lovely lady like yourself know of interests and prime rates?" Jitai smiled.

"You're a banker and I'm an economist. What do bankers know about the impacts on floating currencies caused by inflated interests, especially in the prime rates?" Marie smiled for the first time in a very long time.

She had over an hour to think in the countryside quiet as she sat in the taxi that drove her down to Kowloon. It would be another forty-five minutes once they reached the less quiet outskirts, particularly a congested district called Mongkok. The contrite people of Tuen Mun had been not only generous and protective, but inventive as well. The banker, Jitai, apparently had confirmed that the hoodlums' victim was indeed a white woman in hiding and running for her life, and therefore, as she was in the process of reaching people who might help her, perhaps her appearance might be altered. Western clothes were brought from several shops, clothes that struck Marie as odd; they seemed drab and utilitarian, neat but dreary. Not cheap, but the kind of clothes that would be selected by a woman who had either no sense of design or felt herself above it. Then after an hour in the back room of a beauty shop she understood why such a costume had been chosen. The women fussed over her; her hair was washed and blown dry, and when the process was over she had looked in the mirror, barely breathing as she did so. Her face—drawn, pale and tired—was framed by a shell of hair no longer a striking auburn but mouse-gray with subtle tinges of white. She had aged more than a decade; it was an extension of what she had attempted after escaping from the hospital but far bolder, far more complete. She was the Chinese image of the upper-middle-class, serious, no-nonsense tourist—probably a widow—who peremptorily issued instructions, counted her money, and never went anywhere without a guidebook, which she continuously checked off with each site visited on her well-organized itinerary. The people of Tuen Mun knew such tourists well and their portrait was accurate. Jason Bourne would approve.

There were other thoughts, however, that occupied her on the ride to Kowloon, desperate thoughts that she tried to control and keep in perspective, pushing away the panic that could so easily engulf her, causing her to do the wrong thing, make a wrong move that could harm

David—kill David. *Oh, God, where are you? How can I find you? How?*

She searched her memory for anyone who could help her, constantly rejecting every name and every face that came to her because in one way or another each had been a part of that horrible strategy so ominously termed *beyond-salvage*—the death of an individual the only acceptable solution. Except, of course, Morris Panov, but Mo was a pariah in the eyes of the government; he had called the official killers by their rightful names: incompetents and murderers. He would get nowhere, and conceivably bring about a second order for beyond-salvage.

Beyond-salvage . . . A face came to her, a face with tears running down his cheeks, muted cries for mercy in his tremulous voice, a once-close friend of a young foreign service officer and his wife and children in a remote outpost called Phnom Penh. *Conklin!* His name was *Alexander Conklin!* Throughout David's long convalescence he had tried repeatedly to see her husband, but David would not permit it, saying that he would kill the CIA man if he walked through the door. The crippled Conklin had wrongfully, stupidly made accusations against David, not listening to the pleas of an amnesiac, instead assuming treachery and "turning"—to the point where he had tried to kill David himself outside of Paris. And, finally, he had mounted a last attempt on New York's Seventy-first Street, at a sterile house called Treadstone 71, that nearly succeeded. When the truth about David was known, Conklin had been consumed with guilt, shattered by what he had done. She had actually felt sorry for him; his anguish was so genuine, his guilt so devastating to him. She had talked with Alex over coffee on the porch, but David would never see him. He was the only one she could think of that made sense—any sense at *all!*

The hotel was called the Empress, on Chatham Road in Kowloon. It was a small hotel in the crowded Tsim Sha Tsui frequented by a mix of cultures, neither rich nor poor, by and large salesmen from the East and West who had business to do without the largess of executive expense accounts. The banker, Jitai, had done his job; a single room had been reserved for a Mrs. Austin, Penelope Austin. The "Penelope" had been Jitai's idea, for he had read many English novels, and Penelope seemed "so right." *So be it,* as Jason Bourne would have said, thought Marie.

She sat on the edge of the bed and reached for the telephone, unsure of what to say but knowing she had to say it. "I need the number of a person in Washington, D.C., in the United States," she said to the operator. "It's an emergency."

"There is a charge for overseas information—"

"Charge it," broke in Marie. "It's urgent. I'll stay on the line."

"Yes?" said the voice filled with sleep. *"Hello?"*

"Alex, it's Marie Webb."

"Goddamn you, where *are* you? Where are *both* of you? He *found* you!"

"I don't know what you're talking about. I haven't found him and he hasn't found me. You *know* about all this?"

"Who the hell do you think almost broke my *neck* last week when he flew into Washington? *David!* I've got relays on every phone that can reach me! Mo Panov's got the same! Where *are* you?"

"Hong Kong—Kowloon, I guess. The Empress Hotel, under the name of Austin. David *reached* you?"

"And Mo! He and I have turned every trick in the deck to find out what the hell is going on and we've been *stonewalled!* No, I take it back—not stonewalled—no one else knows what's going on either! I'd know if they did! Good *Christ,* Marie, I haven't had a drink since last Thursday!"

"I didn't know you missed it."

"I miss it! What's *happening?"*

Marie told him, including the unmistakable stamp of government bureaucracy on the part of her captors, and her escape, and the help given by Catherine Staples that turned into a trap, engineered by a man named McAllister, whom she had seen on the street with Staples.

"McAllister? You *saw* him?"

"He's here, Alex. He wants to take me back. With me he controls *David,* and he'll *kill* him! They tried before!"

There was a pause on the line, a pause filled with anguish. *"We* tried before," said Conklin softly. "But that was then, not now."

"What can I *do?*"

"Stay where you are," ordered Alex. "I'll be on the earliest plane to Hong Kong. Don't go out of your room. Don't make any more calls. They're searching for you, they have to be."

"David's *out* there, Alex! Whatever they've forced him to do because of me, I'm frightened to death!"

"Delta was the best man ever developed in Medusa. No one better ever walked into that field. I know. I saw."

"That's one aspect, and I've taught myself to live with it. But not the *other,* Alex! His *mind!* What will happen to his *mind?*"

Conklin paused again, and when he spoke his voice was pensive. "I'll bring a friend with me, a friend to all of us. Mo won't refuse. Stay put, Marie. It's time for a show-down. And, by *Christ,* there's going to be one!"

23

"Who *are you?*" screamed Bourne in a frenzy, gripping the old man by the throat and pressing him into the wall.

"Delta, *stop it!*" commanded d'Anjou. "Your voice! People will hear you. They'll think you're killing him. They'll call the desk."

"I *may* kill him and the phones don't work!" Jason released the impostor's impostor, released his throat but gripped the front of his shirt, ripping it as he swung the man down into a chair.

"The *door,*" continued d'Anjou steadily, angrily. "Put it in place as best you can, for God's sake. I want to get out of Beijing alive, and every second with you diminishes my prospects. The *door!*"

Half crazed, Bourne whipped around, picked up the shattered door and shoved it into the frame, adjusting the sides and kicking them into place. The old man massaged his throat and suddenly tried to spring out of the chair.

"*Non, mon ami!*" said the Frenchman, blocking him. "Stay where you are. Do not concern yourself with me, only with him. You see, he really might kill you. In his rage he has no respect for the golden years, but since I'm nearly there, I do."

" 'Rage'? This is an *outrage!*" sputtered the old man, coughing his words. "I fought at El Alamein and, by Christ, I'll fight *now!*" Again the old man struggled out of the chair, and again d'Anjou pushed him back as Jason returned.

"Oh, the stoically heroic British," observed the Frenchman. "At least you had the grace not to say Agincourt."

"Cut the crap!" shouted Bourne, pushing d'Anjou aside and leaning over the chair, his hands on both arms, crowding the old man back into the seat. "You tell me where he is and you tell me quickly, or you may wish you never got out of El Alamein!"

"Where *who* is, you maniac?"

"You're not the man downstairs! You're not Joseph Wadsworth going up to Room three-twenty-five!"

"This *is* Room three-twenty-five and I *am* Joseph Wadsworth! Brigadier, retired, Royal Engineers!"

"When did you check in?"

"Actually, I was spared that drudgery," replied Wadsworth haughtily. "As a professional guest of the government, certain courtesies are extended. I was escorted through customs and brought directly here. I must say the room service is hardly up to snuff—God knows, it's not the Connaught—and the damned telephone's mostly on the fritz."

"I asked you *when!*"

"Last night, but since the plane was six hours late, I suppose I should say this morning."

"What were your instructions?"

"I'm not sure it's any of your business."

Bourne whipped out the brass letter-opener from his belt and held the sharp point against the old man's throat. "It is, if you want to get out of that chair alive."

"Good God, you *are* a maniac."

"You're right, I haven't much time for sanity. In fact, none at all. The *instructions!*"

"They're harmless enough. I was to be picked up

sometime around twelve noon, and as it's now after three, one can assume that the People's government is not run by the clock any more than its airline."

D'Anjou touched Bourne's arm. "The eleven-thirty plane," said the Frenchman quietly. "He's the decoy and knows nothing."

"Then your Judas is here in another room," replied Jason over his shoulder. "He *has* to be!"

"Don't say any more, he'll be questioned." With sudden and unexpected authority, d'Anjou edged Bourne away from the chair and spoke in the impatient tones of a superior officer. "See here, Brigadier, we apologize for the inconvenience, it's a damned nuisance, I know. This is the third room we've broken into—we learned the name of each occupant for the purposes of shock interrogation."

"Shock *what?* I don't understand."

"One of four people on this floor has smuggled in over five million dollars' worth of narcotics. Since it wasn't the three of you, we have our man. I suggest you do as the others are doing. Say your room was broken into by a raging drunk, furious over the accommodations—that's what they're saying. There's a lot of that going around, and it's best not to be put under suspicion, even by mistaken association. The government here often over-reacts."

"Wouldn't want that," sputtered Wadsworth, formerly of the Royal Engineers. "Damned pension's little enough to get by on. This is a bloody feather from the goose's ass."

"The door, Major," ordered d'Anjou, addressing Jason. "Easy, now. Try to keep it upright." The Frenchman turned to the Englishman. "Stand by and hold it, Brigadier. Just lean it back and give us twenty minutes to get our man, then do whatever you like. Remember, a raging drunk. For your own sake."

"Yes, yes, of course. A drunk. Raging."

"Come, Major!"

Out in the hallway they picked up their bags and started rapidly toward the staircase. "Hurry *up!*" said Bourne. "There's still time. He has to make his change —*I'd* have to make it! We'll check the street entrances, the taxi stands, try to pick two logical ones, or, goddamn it, *illogical* ones. We'll each take one and work out signals."

"First there are two doors," broke in d'Anjou breathlessly. "In this hallway. Pick any two you wish, but do it quickly. Kick them in and yell abusive language, slurring your words, of course."

"You were *serious?*"

"Never more so, Delta. As we saw for ourselves, the explanation is entirely plausible, and embarrassment will restrict any formal investigation. The management will no doubt persuade our brigadier to keep his mouth shut. They could lose their comfortable jobs. Quickly now! Take your choice and do the job!"

Jason stopped at the next door on the right. He braced himself, then rushed toward it, crashing his shoulder into the middle of the flimsy upper panel. The door flew open.

"Madad demaa!" screamed a woman in Hindi, half out of her sari, which was draped around her feet.

"Kyaa baat hai?" shrieked a naked man racing out of the bathroom, hastily covering his genitals.

Both stood gaping at the mad intruder, who lurched about with unfocused eyes as he swept articles off the nearest bureau, yelling in a coarse, drunken voice. "Rotten hotel! *Toilets* don't work, phones don't work! Nothing —*Jesus,* this isn't my *room!* Shhorry . . ."

Bourne weaved out, slamming the door shut behind him.

"That was fine!" said d'Anjou. "They had trouble with the lock. *Hurry.* One more. *That* one!" The Frenchman pointed to a door on the left. "I heard laughter inside. Two voices."

Again Jason crashed into a door, smashing it open, roaring his drunken complaints. However, instead of being met by two startled guests, he faced a young couple, both bare to the waist, each drawing on a pinched cigarette, inhaling deeply, their eyes glazed.

"Welcome, neighbor," said the young American male, his voice floating, his diction precise, if at quarter speed. "Don't let things trouble you so. The phones don't work, but our can does. Use it, share it. Don't get so uptight."

"What the *hell* are you doing in my *room?*" yelled Jason even more drunkenly, his slur now obscuring his words.

"If this is your room, macho boy," interrupted the girl, swaying in her chair, "you were privy to private things and we're not like that." She giggled.

"Christ, you're *stoned!*"

"And without taking the Lord's name in vain," countered the young man, "you're very drunk."

"We don't believe in alcohol," added the spaced-out girl. "It produces hostility. It rises to the surface like Lucifer's demons."

"Get yourself detoxified, neighbor," continued the young American liltingly. "Then get healthy with grass. I will lead you into the fields where you will find your soul again—"

Bourne raced out of the room, slamming the door, and grabbed d'Anjou's arm. "Let's *go,*" he said, adding as they approached the staircase, "If that story you gave the brigadier gets around, those two will spend twenty years deballing sheep in Outer Mongolia."

The Chinese proclivity for close observation and intense security dictated that the airport hotel have a single large entrance in the front for guests, and a second for employees at the side of the building. The latter was replete with uniformed guards who scrutinized everyone's working papers and searched all purses and bags and bulging pockets when the employees left for the day. The lack of familiarity between guards and workers suggested that the former were changed frequently, putting space between potential bribes and bribers.

"He won't chance the guards," said Jason as they passed the employees' exit after hastily checking their two suitcases, pleading lateness for a meeting due to the delayed plane. "They look as if they get Brownie points for picking up anyone who steals a chicken wing or a bar of soap."

"They also intensely dislike those who work here," agreed d'Anjou. "But why are you so certain he's still in the hotel? He knows Beijing. He could have taken a taxi to another hotel, another room."

"Not looking the way he did on the plane, I told you that. He wouldn't allow it. *I* wouldn't. He wants the freedom to move around without being spotted or followed. He's got to have it for his own protection."

"If that's the case, they could be watching his room

right now. Same results. They'll know what he looks
like."

"If it were me—and that's all I've got to go on—he's
not there. He's made arrangements for another room."

"You contradict yourself!" objected the Frenchman as
they approached the crowded entrance of the airport
hotel. "You said he'd be receiving his instructions by
phone. Whoever calls will ask for the room they assigned
him, certainly not the decoy's, not Wadsworth's."

"If the phones are working—a condition that's a plus
for your Judas, incidentally—it's a simple matter to have
calls transferred from one room to another. A plug is
inserted in the switchboard if it's primitive, or programmed if it's computerized. It's not a big deal. A business conference, old friends on the plane—read that any
way you like—or no explanation at all, which is probably
best."

"Fallacy!" proclaimed d'Anjou. "His client here in
Beijing will alert the hotel operators. He'll be wired into
the switchboard."

"That's the one thing he won't do," said Bourne, pushing the Frenchman through a revolving door out onto the
pavement, which was crawling with confused tourists and
businessmen trying to arrange transportation. "It's a
gamble he can't afford to take," continued Jason as they
walked past a line of small, shabby buses and well-aged
taxis at the curb. "Your commando's client has to keep
maximum distance between the two of them. There can't
be the slightest possibility that a connection could be
traced, so that means everything's restricted to a very
tight, very elite circle, with no runs on a switchboard, no
calling attention to anyone, especially your commando.
They won't risk wandering around the hotel either.
They'll stay away from him, let him make the moves.
There are too many secret police here; someone in that
elite circle could be recognized."

"The phones, Delta. From all we've heard, they're *not*
working. What does he do then?"

Jason frowned while walking, as if trying to recall the
unremembered. "Time's on his side, that's the plus. He'll
have backup instructions to follow in case he's not
reached within a given period of time after his arrival—

for whatever reasons—and there could be any number considering the precautions they have to take."

"In that event they'd still be watching for him, wouldn't they? They'd wait somewhere outside and try to pick him up, no?"

"Of course, and he knows that. He has to get by them and reach his position without being seen. It's the only way he retains control. It's his first job."

D'Anjou gripped Bourne's elbow. "Then I think I've just spotted one of the spotters."

"What?" Jason turned, looking down at the Frenchman and slowing his pace.

"Keep walking," ordered d'Anjou. "Head over to that truck, the one half out on the street with the man on the extension ladder."

"It follows," said Bourne. "It's the telephone repair service." Remaining anonymous in the crowds, they reached the truck.

"Look up. Look interested. Then look to your left. The van quite far ahead of the first bus. Do you see it?"

Jason did, and instantly he knew the Frenchman was right. The van was white and fairly new and had tinted glass windows. Except for the color it could be the van that had picked up the assassin in Shenzen, at the Lo Wu border. Bourne started to read the Chinese characters on the door panel. *"Niao Jing Shan.* . . . My God, it's the same! The name doesn't matter—it belongs to a *bird sanctuary,* the Jing Shan *Bird* Sanctuary! In Shenzen it was Chutang, here something else. How did you notice it?"

"The man in the open window, the last window on this side. You can't see him too clearly from here, but he's looking back at the entrance. He's also somewhat of a contradiction—for an employee of a bird sanctuary, that is."

"Why?"

"He's an army officer, and by the cut of his tunic and the obviously superior fabric, one of high rank. Is the glorious People's Army now conscripting egrets for its assault troops? Or is he an anxious man waiting for someone he's been ordered to pick up and follow, using a rather acceptable cover flawed by an angle of sight that demands an open window?"

"Can't go anywhere without Echo," said Jason Bourne, once Delta, the scourge of Medusa. "Bird sanctuaries—Christ, it's *beautiful*. What a smoke screen. So removed, so peaceful. It's one *hell* of a cover."

"It's so Chinese, Delta. The righteous mask conceals the unrighteous face. The Confucian parables warn of it."

"That's not what I'm talking about. Back in Shenzen, at Lo Wu, where I missed your boy the first time, he was picked up by a van then—a van with tinted windows—and it also belonged to a government bird sanctuary."

"As you say, an excellent cover."

"It's more than that, Echo. It's some kind of mark or identification."

"Birds have been revered in China for centuries," said d'Anjou, looking at Jason, his expression puzzled. "They've always been depicted in their great art, the great silks. They're considered delicacies for both the eye and the palate."

"In this case they could be a means to something much simpler, much more practical."

"Such as?"

"Bird sanctuaries are large preserves. They're open to the public but subject to government regulations, as they are everywhere."

"Your point, Delta?"

"In a country where any ten people opposed to the official line are afraid to be seen together, what better place than a nature preserve that usually stretches for miles? No offices or houses or apartments being watched, no telephone taps or electronic surveillance. Just innocent bird-watchers in a nation of bird lovers, each holding an official pass that permits him entry when the sanctuary is officially closed—day or night."

"From Shenzen to Peking? You're implying a situation larger than we had considered."

"Whatever it is," said Jason, glancing around. "It doesn't concern us. Only *he* does. . . . We've got to separate but stay in sight. I'll head over—"

"No need!" broke in the Frenchman. "There he is!"

"*Where?*"

"Move back! Closer to the truck. In its shadow."

"Which one *is* he?"

"The priest patting the child, the little girl," answered d'Anjou, his back to the truck, staring into the crowd in front of the hotel's entrance. "A man of the cloth," continued the Frenchman bitterly. "One of the guises I taught him to use. He had a priestly black suit made for him in Hong Kong complete with an Anglican benediction sewn into the collar under the name of a Savile Row tailor. It was the suit I recognized first. I paid for it."

"You come from a wealthy diocese," said Bourne, studying the man he wanted more than his life to race over and take, to subdue and force up into a hotel room and start on the road back to Marie. The assassin's cover was good—more than good—and Jason tried to analyze that judgment. Gray sideburns protruded below the killer's dark hat; thin steel-rimmed glasses were perched low on the nose of his pale, colorless face. His eyes wide and his brows arched, he showed joy and wonder at what he saw in this unfamiliar place. All were God's works and God's children, signified by the act of being drawn to a little Chinese girl and patting her head lovingly, smiling and nodding graciously to the mother. That was it, thought Jason, in grudging respect. The son of a bitch exuded *love*. It was in his every gesture, every hesitant movement, every glance of his gentle eyes. He *was* a compassionate man of the cloth, a shepherd of his flock. And as such, in a crowd he might be glanced at but instantly dismissed by eyes seeking out a killer.

Bourne remembered. *Carlos!* The Jackal had been dressed in the clothes of a priest, his dark Latin features above the starched white collar, walking out of the church in Neuilly-sur-Seine in Paris. Jason had *seen* him! They had seen each other, their eyes locking, each knowing who the other was without words being spoken. *Get Carlos. Trap Carlos. Cain is for Charlie and Carlos is for Cain!* The codes had exploded in his head as he raced after the Jackal in the streets of Paris . . . only to lose him in the traffic, as an old beggar, squatting on the pavement, smiled obscenely.

This was not Paris, thought Bourne. There was no army of dying old men protecting this assassin. He would take this jackal in Peking.

"Be ready to move!" said d'Anjou, breaking into Jason's memories. "He's nearing the bus."

"It's full."

"That's the point. He'll be the last one on. Who refuses a pleading priest in a hurry? One of my lessons, of course."

Again the Frenchman was right. The door of the small, packed shabby bus began to close, stopped by the inserted arm of the priest, who wedged his shoulder inside and obviously begged to be released, as he had been caught. The door snapped open; the killer pressed himself inside and the door closed.

"It's the express to Tian An Men Square," said d'Anjou. "I have the number."

"We have to find a taxi. Come on!"

"It will not be easy, Delta."

"I've perfected a technique," replied Bourne, walking out of the shadow of the telephone truck as the bus passed by, the Frenchman at his heels. They weaved through the crowd in front of the airport hotel and proceeded down the line of taxis until they reached the end. A last cab rounded the circle, about to join the line, when Jason rushed into the street, holding up the palms of his hands unobtrusively. The taxi came to a stop as the driver pushed his head out the window.

"*Shemma?*"

"*Wei!*" cried Bourne, running to the driver and holding up fifty American dollars' worth of unmetered yuan. "*Bi yao bang zhu,*" he said, telling the man he needed help badly and would pay for it.

"*Hao!*" exclaimed the driver as he grabbed the money. "*Bingle ba!*" he added, justifying his action on behalf of a tourist who was suddenly ill.

Jason and d'Anjou climbed in, the driver vocally annoyed that there was a second fare entering the curbside door. Bourne dropped another twenty yuan over the seat, and the man was mollified. He swung his cab around, away from the line of taxis, and retraced his path out of the airport complex.

"Up ahead there is a bus," said d'Anjou, leaning forward in the seat, addressing the driver in an awkward attempt at Mandarin. "Can you understand me?"

"Your tongue is Guangzhou, but I understand."

"It is on the way to Tian An Men Square."

"Which gate?" asked the driver. "Which bridge?"

"I don't know. I know only the number on the front of the bus. It is seven-four-two-one."

"Number one ending," said the driver. "Tian Gate, second bridge. Imperial city entrance."

"Is there a parking section for the buses?"

"There will be a line of many bus-vehicles. All are filled. They are very crowded. Tian An Men is very crowded this angle of the sun."

"We should pass the bus I speak of on the road, which is favorable to us for we wish to be at Tian An Men before it arrives. Can you do this?"

"Without difficulty," answered the driver, grinning. "Bus-vehicles are old and often break down. We may get there several days before it reaches the heavenly north gate."

"I hope you're not serious," interrupted Bourne.

"Oh, no, generous tourist. All the drivers are superior mechanics—when they have the good fortune to locate their engines." The driver laughed contemptuously and pressed his foot on the accelerator.

Three minutes later they passed the "bus-vehicle" carrying the killer. Forty-six minutes after that they reached the sculptured white marble bridge over the flowing waters of a man-made moat that fronted the massive Gate of Heavenly Peace, where the leaders of China displayed themselves on the wide platform above, approving the paraded instruments of war and death. Inside the misnomered gate is one of the most extraordinary human achievements on earth. Tian An Men Square. The electrifying vortex of Beijing.

The majesty of its sheer vastness first catches the visitor's eye, then the architectural immensity of the Great Hall of the People on the right, where reception areas accommodate as many as three thousand people. The single banquet hall seats over five thousand, the major "conference room" ten thousand with space to spare. On the opposite side of the Gate, reaching toward the clouds, is a four-sided shaft of stone, an obelisk mounted on a two-story terrace of balustraded marble, all glistening in the sunlight, while in the shadows below on the huge base of the structure are carved the struggles and triumphs of Mao's revolution. It is the Monument to the People's Heroes, Mao first in the pantheon. There are other buildings, other structures—memorials, museums, gates and libraries—as far as the eye can see. But, above all, the eye is struck by the compelling vastness of open space. Space and people . . . and for the ear something else, totally unexpected. A dozen of the world's great stadiums, all dwarfing Rome's Colosseum, could be placed within Tian An Men Square and not exhaust the acreage; people in the hundreds of thousands can wander about the open areas and still leave room for hundreds of thousands more. But there is an absence of an element whose lack would never have been found in Rome's bloody arena, much less tolerated in the contemporary great stadiums of the world. Sound; it is barely there, only decibels above silence, interrupted by the soft rippling notes of bicycle bells. The quiet is at first peaceful, and then frightening. It is as though an enormous, transparent geodesic dome had been lowered over a hundred acres, as an unspoken, but understood, command from a nether kingdom repeatedly informs those below that they are in a cathedral. It is unnatural, unreal, and yet there is no hostility toward the unheard voice, only acceptance—and that is more frightening. Especially when the children are quiet.

Jason observed these things quickly and dispassionately. He paid the driver the sum based on the odometer reading and shifted his concentration to the purpose and the problems facing him and d'Anjou. For whatever reason, whether a phone call had reached him or whether he had opted for back-up instructions, the commando was on his way to Tian An Men Square. The pavane would begin with his arrival, the slow steps of the cautious dance bringing the killer closer and closer to his client's representative, the assumption being that the client would remain out of sight. But no contact would be made until the impostor was convinced the rendezvous was clean. Therefore the "priest" would mount his own surveillance, circling the appointed coordinates of the meeting ground, searching out whatever armed minions were in place. He would take one, perhaps two, pressing them at the point of a knife or jamming a silenced gun into their ribs to elicit the information he needed; a false look in the eyes would tell him that the conference was a prelude to execution. Finally, if the landscape seemed clear, he would propel a minion under a gun to approach the client's representative and give his ultimatum: the client himself must show up and walk into the net of the assassin's making. Anything else was unacceptable; the central figure, the client, had to be the deadly balance. A second meeting ground would be established. The client would arrive first, and at the first sign of deception he would be blown away. That was the way of Jason Bourne. It would be the commando's if he had half a brain in his head.

Bus number 7421 rolled lethargically into place at the end of the line of vehicles disgorging tourists. The assassin in priestly garb emerged, helping an elderly woman down to the pavement, patting her hand as he nodded his gentle good-byes. He turned away, walked rapidly to the rear of the bus, and disappeared around it.

"Stay a good thirty feet behind and watch me," said Jason. "Do as I do. When I stop, you stop; when I turn, you turn. Be in a crowd; go from one group to another, but make sure there are always people around you."

"Be careful, Delta. He is not an amateur."

"Neither am I." Bourne ran to the end of the bus, stopped, and edged his way around the hot, foul-smelling louvers of the rear engine. His priest was about fifty yards ahead, his black suit a dark beacon in the hazy sunlight. Crowds or no crowds, he was easy to follow. The commando's cover was acceptable, his playing of it even more so, but like most covers there was always the glaring but unrecognized liability. It was in limiting those liabilities that the best distinguished themselves from the merely better. Professionally, Jason approved the clerical status, not the clerical color. A Roman priest might be wedded to black, but not an Anglican vicar; a solid gray was perfectly acceptable under the collar. Gray faded in the sunlight, black did not.

Suddenly, the assassin broke away from the crowd and walked up behind a Chinese soldier taking pictures, the camera at eye level, the soldier's head moving constantly. Bourne understood. This was no insignificant enlisted man on leave in Beijing; he was too mature, his uniform too well tailored—as d'Anjou had remarked about the army officer in the truck. The camera was a transparent device to scan the crowds; the initial meeting ground was not far away. The commando, now playing his role to the fullest, clasped a fatherly right hand on the military man's left shoulder. His left was unseen, but his black coat filled the space between them—a gun had been jammed into the officer's ribs. The soldier froze, his expression stoic even in his panic. He moved with the assassin, the commando now gripping his arm and issuing orders. The soldier abruptly, out of character, bent over, holding his left side, recovering quickly and shaking his head; the weapon had been rammed again into his rib cage. He would follow orders, or he would die in Tian An Men Square. There was no compromise.

Bourne spun around, lowering his body and tying a perfectly firm shoelace, apologizing to those behind him. The assassin had checked his rear flank; the evasive action was demanded. Jason stood up. Where *was* he? Where was the *impostor? There!* Bourne was bewildered; the commando had let the soldier go! *Why?* The army officer was suddenly running through the crowds, screaming, his gestures wildly spastic, then in a frenzy he collapsed, and chattering, excited people gathered around his unconscious body.

Diversion! *Watch* him. Jason raced ahead, feeling the time was right. It had been not a gun but a needle—not jammed but puncturing the soldier's rib cage. The assassin had taken out one protector; he would look for another, and perhaps another after that. The scenario Bourne had predicted was being played out. And as the killer's concentration was solely on his search for his next victim, the time was right! *Now!* Jason knew he could take out anyone on earth with a paralyzing blow to the kidneys, especially a man whose least concern was an attack on himself—for the quarry was attacking and his concentration was absolute. Bourne closed the gap between himself and the impostor. Fifty feet, forty, thirty-five, thirty . . . he broke away from one crowd into another . . . the black-suited "priest" was within reach. He could *take* him! *Marie!*

A soldier. Another soldier! But now, instead of an assault there was communication. The army man nodded and gestured to his left. Jason looked over, bewildered. A short Chinese in civilian clothing and carrying a government briefcase was standing at the foot of a wide

stone staircase that led up to the entrance of an immense
building with granite pillars everywhere supporting twin
sloping pagoda roofs. It was directly behind the Heroes'
Monument, the carved calligraphy over the huge doors
proclaiming it to be the Chairman Mao Memorial Hall.
Two lines were moving up the steps, guards separating
the individual groups. The civilian was between the two
lines, the briefcase a symbol of authority; he was left
alone. Suddenly, without any indication that he would
make such a move, the tall assassin gripped the soldier's
arm, propelling the smaller army man in front of him.
The officer's back arched, his shoulders snapping upright; a weapon had been shoved into his spine, the commands specific.

As the excitement mounted and the crowds and the
police kept running to the collapsed first soldier, the
assassin and his captive walked steadily toward the civilian at the steps of the Mao Memorial. The man was afraid
to move, and again Bourne understood. These men were
known to the killer; they were at the core of the tight, elite
circle that led to the assassin's client, and that client was
nearby. They were no mere minions; once they appeared
the lesser figures took on lesser importance, for these
men rarely exposed themselves. The diversion, which
was now reduced to a mild disturbance as the police
swiftly controlled the crowds and carried the body away,
had given the impostor the seconds he needed to control
the chain that led to the client. The soldier in his grip was
dead if he disobeyed, and with a single shot any reasonably competent marksman could kill the man by the
steps. The meeting was in two stages, and as long as the
assassin controlled the second stage he was perfectly willing to proceed. The client was obviously somewhere inside the vast mausoleum and could not know what was
happening outside, nor would a mere minion dare follow
his superiors up into the conference area.

There was no more time for analyzing, Jason knew. He
had to act. *Quickly.* He had to get inside Mao Zedong's
monument and watch, wait for the meeting to conclude
one way or another—and the repugnant possibility that
he might have to protect the assassin crossed his mind.
Yet it was within the realm of reality and the only plus for
him was the fact that the impostor had followed a sce-

nario he himself might have created. And if the conference was peaceful, it was simply a matter of following the assassin, by then inevitably buoyed by the success of his tactics as well as by whatever the client delivered—and taking an unsuspecting supreme egotist in Tian An Men Square.

Bourne turned, looking for d'Anjou. The Frenchman was on the edge of a controlled tourist group; he nodded, as if he had read Delta's thoughts. He pointed to the ground beneath him, then made a circle with his index finger. It was a silent signal from their days in Medusa. It meant he would remain where he was, but if he had to move he would stay in sight of that specific location. It was enough. Jason crossed behind the assassin and his prisoner, and walked diagonally through the crowd, rapidly negotiating the open space to the line on the right half of the staircase and up to the guard. He spoke pleadingly in polite Mandarin: "High Officer, I'm most embarrassed! I was so taken by the calligraphy on the People's Monument that I lost my group, which passed through here only minutes ago."

"You speak our language very well," said the astonished guard, apparently used to the strange accents of tongues he neither knew nor cared to know. "You are most courteous."

"I'm simply an underpaid teacher from the West who has an enduring love of your great nation, High Officer."

The guard laughed. "I'm not so high, but our nation is great. My daughter wears blue jeans in the street."

"I beg your pardon?"

"It's nothing. Where is your tour-group identification?"

"My what?"

"The name tag to be worn on all outer clothing."

"It kept falling off," said Bourne, shaking his head helplessly. "It wouldn't stay pinned. I must have lost it."

"When you catch up, see your guide and get another. Go ahead. Get in back of the line on the steps. Something is going on. The next group may have to wait. You'll miss your tour."

"Oh? Is there a problem?"

"I don't know. The official with the government briefcase gives us our orders. I believe he counts the yuan that could be made here, thinking this holy place should be like Beijing's underground train."

"You've been most kind."

"Hurry, sir."

Bourne rushed up the steps, bending down behind the crowd, once again tightening a secure shoelace, his head angled to watch the assassin's progress. The imposter talked quietly to the civilian with the soldier still in his grip—but something was odd. The short Chinese in the dark suit nodded, but his eyes were not on the impostor; they were focused beyond the commando. Or were they? Jason's angle of vision was not the best. No matter, the scenario was being followed, the client reached on the assassin's terms.

He walked through the doors into the semidarkness, as awed as everyone in front of him by the sudden appearance of the enormous white marble sculpture of a seated Mao, rising so high and so majestically that one nearly gasped in its presence. Too, theatricality was not omitted. The shafts of light that played on the exquisite, seemingly translucent marble created an ethereal effect that isolated the gigantic sitting figure from the velvet tapestry behind it and the outer darkness around it. The massive statue with its searching eyes seemed alive and aware.

Jason pulled his own eyes away and looked for doorways and corridors. There were none. It *was* a mausoleum, a hall dedicated to a nation's saint. But there were pillars, wide high shafts of marble that provided areas of seclusion. In the shadows behind any one of them could be the meeting ground. He would wait. He would stay in other shadows and watch.

His group entered the second great hall, and it was, if anything, more electrifying than the first. Facing them was a crystal glass coffin encasing the body of Chairman Mao Zedong, draped in the Red flag, the waxen corpse in peaceful repose—the closed eyes, however, any second likely to open wide and glare in fiery disapproval. There were flowers surrounding the raised sarcophagus, and two rows of dark green pine trees in huge ceramic pots lined the opposing walls. Again shafts of light played a dramatic symphony of color, pockets of darkness pierced by intersecting beams that washed over the brilliant yellows and reds and blues of the banks of flowers.

A commotion somewhere in the first hall briefly intruded on the awed silence of the crowd, but was arrested as rapidly as it had begun. As the last tourist in line, Bourne broke away without being noticed by the others. He slipped behind a pillar, concealed in the shadows, and peered around the glistening white marble.

What he saw paralyzed him as a dozen thoughts clashed in his head—above all, the single word *trap!* There was no group following his own! It was the last admitted—*he* was the last *person* admitted—before the heavy doors were closed. That was the sound he had heard—the shutting of the doors and the disappointed groans from those outside waiting to be admitted.

Something is going on. . . . The next group may have to wait. . . . A kindly guard on the steps.

My God, from the beginning it was a *trap!* Every move, every appearance had been calculated! From the *beginning!* The information paid for on a rain-soaked island, the nearly unobtainable airline tickets, the first sight of the assassin at the airport—a professional killer capable of a far better disguise, his hair too obvious, his clothes inadequate to cover his frame. Then the complication with an old man, a retired brigadier from the Royal Engineers—so illogically logical! So right, the scent of deception so accurate, so irresistible! A soldier in a truck's window, not looking for *him* but for *them!* The priestly black suit—a dark beacon in the sunlight, paid for by the impostor's creator—so easily spotted, so easily followed. *Christ,* from the *beginning!* Finally, the scenario played out in the immense square, a scenario that could have been written by Bourne himself—again irresistible to the pursuer. A reverse trap: Catch the hunter as he stalks his quarry!

Frantically Jason looked around. Ahead in the distance was a steady shaft of sunlight. The exit doors were at the other end of the mausoleum; they would be watched, each tourist studied as he left.

Footsteps. Over his right shoulder. Bourne spun to his left, pulling the brass letter-opener from his belt. A figure in a gray Mao suit, the cut military, cautiously passed by the wide pillar in the dim outer light of the pine trees. He was no more than five feet away. In his hand was a gun, the bulging cylinder on the barrel a guarantee that a detonation would be reduced to the sound of a spit. Jason made his lethal calculations in a way David Webb would never understand. The blade had to be inserted in such a way as to cause instant death. No noise could come from his enemy's mouth as the body was pulled back into darkness.

He lunged, the rigid fingers of his left hand clamped vise-like over the man's face as he plunged the letter-opener into the soldier's neck, the blade rushing through sinew and fragile cartilage, severing the windpipe. In one motion, Bourne dropped his left hand, clutching the large weapon still in his enemy's grip, and swung the corpse around, dropping with it under the branches of the row of pine trees lined up along the right wall. He slid the body out of sight into the dark shadows between two large ceramic pots holding the roots of two trees. He crawled over the corpse, the weapon in front of his face, and made his way back against the wall toward the first hall, to where he could see without being seen.

A second uniformed man crossed through the shaft of light that lit up the darkness of the entrance to the second hall. He stood in front of Mao's crystal coffin, awash in the eerie beams, and looked around. He raised a hand-held radio to his face and spoke, listening; five seconds later his expression changed to one of concern. He began walking rapidly to his right, tracing the assigned path of the first man. Jason scrambled back toward the corpse, hands and knees silently pounding the marble floor, and moved out toward the edge of the low-slung branches.

The soldier approached, walking more slowly, studying the last people in the line up ahead. *Now!* Bourne sprang up as the man passed, hammerlocking his neck, choking off all sound as he pulled him back down under the branches, the gun pressed far up in the flesh of the soldier's stomach. He pulled the trigger; the muffled report was like a burst of air, no more. The man expunged a last violent breath and went limp.

He had to get *out!* If he was trapped and killed in the awesome silence of the mausoleum, the assassin would roam free and Marie's death would be assured. His enemies were closing the reverse trap. He had to reverse the reversal and somehow survive! *The cleanest escape is made in stages, using whatever confusion there is or can be created.*

Stages One and Two were accomplished. A certain confusion already existed if other men were whispering into radios. What had to be brought about was a focal point of disruption so violent and unexpected that those hunting him in the shadows would themselves become the subjects of a sudden, hysterical search.

There was only one way and Jason felt no obscure heroic feelings of I-may-die-trying. He *had* to do it! He had to make it work. Survival was everything, for reasons beyond himself. The professional was at his apex, calm and deliberate.

Bourne stood up and walked through branches, crossing the open space to the pillar in front of him. He then ran to the one behind, and then the one behind that, the first pillar in the second hall, thirty feet from the dramatically lit coffin. He edged his body around the marble and waited, his eyes on the entrance door.

It happened. *They* happened. The officer who was the assassin's "captive" emerged with the short civilian carrying his government briefcase. The soldier held a radio at his side; he brought it up to speak and listen, then shook his head, placing the radio in his right-hand pocket and removing the gun from his holster. The civilian nodded once, reached under his jacket and pulled out a short-barreled revolver. Each walked forward toward the glass coffin containing the remains of Mao Zedong, then looked at each other and began to separate, one to the left, one to the right.

Now! Jason raised his weapon, took rapid aim and fired. *Once!* A hair to the right. *Twice!* The spits were like coughs in shadows as both men fell into the sarcophagus. Grabbing the edges of his coat, Bourne gripped the hot cylinder on the barrel of his pistol and spun it off. There were five shells left. He squeezed the trigger in rapid succession. The explosions filled the mausoleum, echoing off the marble walls, shattering the crystal glass of the coffin, the bullets embedding themselves in the spastically jerked corpse of Mao Zedong, one penetrating a bloodless forehead, another blowing out an eye.

Sirens erupted; clamoring bells split the air and deaf-

ened the ear, as soldiers, appearing at once from everywhere, raced in panic toward the scene of the horrible
outrage. The two lines of tourists, feeling trapped in the
eerie light of the house of death, exploded into hysteria.
En masse, the crowds rushed toward the doors and the
sunlight, trampling those in their paths. Jason Bourne
joined them, crashing his way into the center of an inside
column. Reaching the blinding light of Tian An Men
Square, he raced down the steps.

D'Anjou! Jason ran to his right, rounding the stone
corner, and ran down the side of the pillared structure
until he reached the front. Guards were doing their best
to calm the agitated crowds while trying to find out what
had happened. A riot was in the making.

Bourne studied the place where he had last seen d'Anjou, then moved his eyes over a grid area within which the
Frenchman might logically be seen. Nothing, no one
even vaguely resembling him.

Suddenly, there was the screeching of tires far off on
a thoroughfare to Jason's left. He whipped around and
looked. A van with tinted windows had circled the stan-
chioned pavement and was speeding toward the south
gate of Tian An Men Square.

They had taken d'Anjou. Echo was gone.

24

"Qu'est-ce qu'il y a?
"Des coups de feu! Les gardes sont paniqués!"
Bourne heard the shouts and, running, joined the
group of French tourists led by a guide whose concentration was riveted on the chaos taking place on the steps of
the mausoleum. He buttoned his jacket, covering the gun
in his belt, and slipped the perforated silencer into his
pocket. Glancing around, he moved quickly back through
the crowd next to a man taller than himself, a well-
dressed man with a disdainful expression on his face.

Jason was grateful that there were several others of nearly equal height in front of them; with luck and in the excitement he might remain inconspicuous. Above, at the top of the mausoleum's stairs, the doors had been partially opened. Uniformed men were racing back and forth along the stairs. Obviously the leadership was a shambles, and Bourne knew why. It had fled, had simply disappeared, wanting no part of the terrible events. All that concerned Jason now was the assassin. Would he come out? Or had he found d'Anjou, capturing his creator himself and leaving with Echo in the van, convinced that the original Jason Bourne was trapped, a second unlikely corpse in the desecrated mausoleum.

"Qu'est-ce que c'est?" asked Jason, addressing the tall, well-dressed Frenchman beside him.

"Another ungodly delay, no doubt," replied the man in a somewhat effeminate Parisian accent. "This place is a madhouse, and my tolerance is at an end! I'm going back to the hotel."

"Can you do that?" Bourne upgraded his French from middle-class to a decent *université*. It meant so much to a Parisien. "I mean, are we permitted to leave our tour? We hear constantly that we must stay together."

"I'm a businessman, not a tourist. This 'tour,' as you call it, was not part of my agenda. Frankly, I had the afternoon off—these people linger endlessly over decisions—and thought I'd take in a few sights, but there wasn't a French-speaking driver available. The concierge assigned me—mind you, *assigned* me—to this group. The guide, you know, is a student of French literature and speaks as though she had been born in the seventeenth century. I haven't a clue what this so-called tour is all about."

"It's the five-hour excursion," explained Jason accurately, reading the Chinese characters printed on the identification tag affixed to the man's lapel. "After Tian An Men Square we visit the Ming tombs, then drive out to watch the sunset from the Great Wall."

"Now, really, I've *seen* the Great Wall! My God, it was the first place all twelve of those bureaucrats from the Trade Commission took me, prattling incessantly through the interpreter that it was a sign of their permanence. Shit! If the labor wasn't so unbelievably cheap and the profits so extraordinary—"

"I, too, am in business, but for a few days also a tourist. My line is wicker imports. What's yours, if I may ask?"

"Fabrics, what else? Unless you consider electronics, or oil, or coal, or perfume—even wicker." The businessman allowed himself a superior and knowing smile. "I tell you, these people are sitting on the wealth of the world and they haven't the vaguest idea what to *do* with it."

Bourne looked closely at the tall Frenchman. He thought of Medusa's Echo and a Gallic aphorism that proclaimed that the more things changed the more they remained the same. *Opportunities will present themselves. Recognize them, act on them.* "As I said," continued Jason while staring up at the chaos on the staircase, "I, too, am a businessman, who is taking a short sabbatical—courtesy of our government's tax incentives for those of us who plow the foreign fields—but I've traveled a great deal here in China and have learned a good deal of the language."

"Wicker has come up in the world," said the Parisien sardonically.

"Our quality product is a white-enameled staple of the Côte d'Azur, as well as points north and south. The family Grimaldi has been a client for years." Bourne kept his eyes on the staircase.

"I stand corrected, my business friend . . . in the foreign fields." For the first time the Frenchman actually looked at Jason.

"And I can tell you now," said Bourne, "that no more visitors will be permitted into Mao's tomb, and that everyone on every tour in the vicinity will be cordoned off and possibly detained."

"My God, *why?*"

"Apparently something terrible happened inside and the guards are shouting about foreign gangsters. . . . Did you say you were *assigned* to this tour but not really a part of it?"

"Essentially, yes."

"Grounds for at least speculation, no? Detention, almost certainly."

"*Inconceivable!*"

"This is China—"

"It cannot be! Millions upon millions of francs are hanging in the balance! I'm only here on this horrid tour because—"

"I suggest you leave, my business friend. Say you were out for a stroll. Give me your identification tag and I'll get rid of it for you—"

"Is *that* what it is?"

"Your country of origin and passport number are on it. It's how they control your movements while you're on a guided tour."

"I'm *forever* in your debt!" cried the businessman, ripping the plastic tag off his lapel. "If you're ever in Paris—"

"I spend most of the time with the prince and his family in—"

"But of *course!* Again, my thanks!" The Frenchman, so different and yet so much like Echo, left in a hurry, his well-dressed figure conspicuous in the hazy, grayish-yellow sunlight as he headed toward the Heavenly Gate—as obvious as the false quarry who had led a hunter into a trap.

Bourne pinned the plastic tag to his own lapel and now became part of an official tour; it was his way out of the gates of Tian An Men Square. After the group had been hastily diverted from the mausoleum to the Great Hall, the bus passed through the northern gate, and Jason saw through the window the apoplectic French businessman pleading with the Beijing police to let him pass. Fragments of reports of the outrage had been fitted together. The word was spreading. A white foreigner had horribly defiled the coffin and the hallowed body of Chairman Mao. A white terrorist from a tour without the proper identification on his outer clothing. A guard on the steps had reported such a man.

"I do recalleth," said the tour guide in obsolete French. She was standing by the statue of an angry lion on that extraordinary Avenue of Animals, where huge stone replicas of large cats, horses, elephants, and ferocious mythical beasts lined the road, guarding the final way to the tombs of the Ming Dynasty. "But my memory faileth where your usage of our language concerns my immediate reflections. And I do feel without reflected doubt that you just performed that indulgence."

A student of French literature and speaks as though she were in the seventeenth century . . . an indignant businessman, now undoubtedly far more indignant.

"I didn't before," replied Bourne in Mandarin, "because you were with others and I didn't care to stand out. But let's speak your language now."

"You do so very well."

"I thank you. Then you do recall that I was added to your tour at the last minute?"

"The manager of the Beijing Hotel actually spoke to my superior, but, yes, I do recall." The woman smiled and shrugged. "In truth, as it is such a large group, I only recall giving a tall man his tour-group emblem, and it is in front of my face right now. You will have to pay additional yuan on your hotel bill. I am sorry, but then you are not part of the tourist program."

"No, I'm not, because I'm a businessman negotiating with your government."

"May you do well," said the guide with her piquant smile. "Some do, some do not."

"My point is that I may not be able to do *anything*," said Jason, smiling back. "My Chinese speech is far better than my Chinese reading. A few minutes ago several words fell into place for me and I realized I'm to be at the Beijing Hotel in about a half hour from now for a meeting. How can I do that?"

"It is a question of finding transportation. I will write out what you need and you can present it to the guards at the Dahongmen—"

"The Great Red Gate?" interrupted Bourne. "The one with the arches?"

"Yes. There are bus-vehicles that will take you back to Beijing. You may be late, but then it is customary, I understand, for government people to be late also." She took out a notebook from the pocket of her Mao jacket and then a reedlike ballpoint pen.

"I won't be stopped?"

"If you are, ask those who stop you to call the government people," said the guide, writing out instructions in Chinese and tearing off the page.

.   .   .

"This is not your tour group!" barked the operator of the bus in lower-class Mandarin, shaking his head and stabbing his finger at Jason's lapel. The man obviously expected his words to have no effect whatsoever on the tourist, so he compensated with exaggerated gestures and a strident voice. It was also apparent that he hoped that one of his superiors under the arches of the Great Red Gate would take notice of his alertness. One did.

"What's the problem?" asked a well-spoken soldier, walking rapidly up to the door of the bus, parting his way through the tourists behind Bourne.

Opportunities will present themselves. . . .

"There's no problem," said Jason curtly, even arrogantly, in Chinese, as he withdrew the guide's note, thrusting it into the hand of the young officer. "Unless you wish to be responsible for my missing an urgent meeting with a delegation from the Trade Commission, whose military procurements chief is a General Liang-Somebody-or-other."

"You speak the Chinese language." Startled, the soldier pulled his eyes away from the note.

"I'd say that's obvious. So does General Liang."

"I do not understand your anger."

"Perhaps you'll understand General Liang's," interrupted Bourne.

"I do not know a General Liang, sir, but then there are so many generals. You are upset with the tour?"

"I'm upset with the fools who told me it was a three-hour excursion when it turns out to be *five* hours! If I miss this meeting because of incompetence there'll be several *very* upset commissioners, including a powerful general of the People's army who's anxious to conclude certain purchases from France." Jason paused, holding up his hand, then continued quickly in a softer voice. "If, however, I get there on time I'll certainly commend—by name—anyone who might help me."

"*I* will help you, sir!" said the young officer, his eyes bright with dedication. "This sick whale of a bus could take you well over an hour, and that is only if this miserable driver stays on the road. I have at my disposal a much faster vehicle and a fine driver who will escort you. I would do so myself, but it would not be proper to leave my post."

"I'll also mention your commitment to duty to the general."

"It's my natural instinct, sir. My name is—"

"Yes, do let me have your name. Write it on that slip of paper."

Bourne sat in the bustling lobby of the Beijing Hotel's east wing, a half-folded newspaper covering his face, the left edge off-center so he could see the line of doors that was the entrance. He was waiting, watching for the sight of Jean-Louis Ardisson of Paris. It had not been difficult for Jason to learn his name. Twenty minutes ago he had walked up to the guided-tour travel desk and said to the female clerk in his best Mandarin, "I'm sorry to bother you, but I'm first interpreter for all French delegations having business with government industry, and I'm afraid I've lost one of my confused sheep."

"You must be a fine interpreter. You speak excellent Chinese. What happened to your . . . bewildered sheep?" The woman permitted herself a slight giggle at the phrase.

"I'm not sure. We were having coffee in the cafeteria, about to go over his schedule, when he looked at his watch and said he would call me later. He was going on one of the five-hour tours and apparently was late. It was an inconvenience for me, but I know what happens when visitors first arrive in Peking. They're overwhelmed."

"I believe they are," agreed the clerk. "But what can we do for you?"

"I need to know the correct spelling of his name, and whether he has a middle name or what's called a baptismal name—the specifics that must be included on the government papers that I'll fill out for him."

"But how can we help?"

"He left this behind in the cafeteria." Jason held up the French businessman's identification tag. "I don't know how he even got on the tour."

The woman laughed casually as she reached under the counter for the day's tour ledger. "He was told the departure area and the guide understood; each carries a list. Those things fall off all the time, and she no doubt gave him à temporary ticket." The clerk took the tag and began turning pages as she continued, "I tell you, the idiots who make these are not worth the small yuan they are paid. We have all these precise regulations, these strict rules, and we are made to look foolish at the beginning. *Who is who?*" The woman stopped, her finger on an entry in the ledger. "Oh, bad-luck spirits," she said softly, looking up at Bourne. "I do not know if your sheep is bewildered, but I can tell you he bleats a great deal. He believes himself very grand and was himself very disagreeable. When he was told there was no chauffeur who spoke French, he took it as an insult to his nation's honor as well as his own—which was more important to him. Here, you read the name. I cannot pronounce it."

"Thank you so much," said Jason, reading.

He had then gone to a house phone marked "English" and asked the operator for Mr. Ardisson's room.

"You may *dial* it, sir," said the male operator, a note of triumph in his voice—this was high technology. "It is Room one-seven-four-three. Very fine accommodations. Very fine view of the Forbidden City."

"Thank you." Bourne had dialed. There was no answer. Monsieur Ardisson had not yet returned, and under the circumstances he might not return for quite a while. Still, a sheep that was known for bleating a great deal would not stay silent if his dignity was affronted or his business was in jeopardy. Jason decided to wait. The outlines of a plan were coming into focus. It was a desperate strategy based on probabilities, but it was all he had left. He bought a month-old French magazine at the newsstand and sat down, feeling suddenly drained and helpless.

The face of Marie intruded on David Webb's inner screen, and then the sound of her voice filled the close air around him, echoing in his ears, suspending thought and creating a terrible pain at the center of his forehead. Jason Bourne removed the intrusion with the force of a sledgehammer. The screen went dark, its last flickering light rejected by harsh commands spoken by an ice-cold authority: *Stop it! There is no time. Concentrate on what we must think about. Nothing else!*

Jason's eyes strayed intermittently, constantly returning to the entrance. The clientele of the east-wing lobby was international, a mix of languages, of clothing from

Fifth and Madison avenues, Savile Row, St. Honoré, and the Via Condotti, as well as the more somber apparel of both Germanys and the Scandinavian countries. The guests wandered in and out of the brightly lighted shops, amused and intrigued by the pharmacy selling only Chinese medicines, and flocking into the crafts shop next to a large relief map of the world on the wall. Every now and then someone with an entourage came through the doors; also, obsequious interpreters bowing and translating between uniformed government officials trying to appear casual and weary executives from across the globe whose eyes were dazed from jet lag and the need for sleep, to be preceded, perhaps, by whisky. This might be Red China, but negotiations were older than capitalism, and the capitalists, aware of their fatigue, would not discuss business until they could think straight. Bravo Adam Smith and David Hume.

There he was! Jean-Louis Ardisson was being escorted through the doors by no fewer than four Chinese bureaucrats, all of whom were doing their best to mollify him. One rushed ahead to the lobby liquor store as the others detained him by the elevator, chattering continuously through the interpreter. The buyer returned carrying a plastic bag, the bottom stretched and sagging under the weight of several bottles. There were smiles and bows as the elevator doors opened. Jean-Louis Ardisson accepted his booty and walked inside, nodding once as the doors closed.

Bourne remained seated watching the lights as the elevator ascended. *Fifteen, sixteen, seventeen.* It had reached the top floor, Ardisson's floor. Jason got up and walked back to the bank of telephones. He looked at the sweep hand of his watch; he could only guess at the timing, but a man in an agitated state would not stroll slowly to his room once he left the elevator. The room signified a measure of peace, even the relief of solitude after several hours of tension and panic. To be held for questioning by the police in a foreign country was frightening for anyone, but it became terrifying when an incomprehensible language and radically different faces were added to the knowledge that the prisoner was in a country where people frequently disappeared without explanation. After such an ordeal a man would enter his room and in no particular order would collapse, trembling in fear and exhaustion; light one cigarette after another, forgetting where he left the last one; take several strong drinks, swallowing rapidly for a faster effect; and grab the telephone to share his dreadful experience, unconsciously hoping to minimize the aftereffects of his terror by sharing them. Bourne could allow Ardisson's collapsing, and as much wine or liquor as the man could handle, but he could not permit the telephone. There could be no sharing, no lessening of the terror. Rather, Ardisson's terror had to be extended, amplified to the point where he would be paralyzed, fearing for his life if he left his room. Forty-seven seconds had elapsed; it was time to call.

"Allo?" The voice was strained, breathless.

"I'll speak quickly," said Jason quietly in French. "Stay where you are and do not use the telephone. In precisely eight minutes I'll knock on your door, twice rapidly, then once. Admit me, but no one else before me. Especially a maid or a housekeeper."

"Who *are* you?"

"A countryman who must speak to you. For your own safety. Eight minutes." Bourne hung up and returned to the chair, counting off the minutes and calculating the time it took an elevator with the usual number of passengers to go from one floor to the next. Once on a specific floor, thirty seconds were enough to reach any room. Six minutes went by, and Jason walked to an elevator where the lighted numbers indicated it would be the next to reach the lobby. Eight minutes were ideal for priming a subject; five were too few, not long enough for the right degree of tension. Six were better but passed too quickly. Eight, however, while still within an urgent time span, provided those additional moments of anxiety that wore down a subject's resistance. The plan was not yet clear in Bourne's mind. The objective, however, was crystallized, absolute. It was all he had left, and every instinct in his Medusan body told him to go after it. Delta One knew the Oriental mind. In one respect it had not varied for centuries. Secrecy was worth ten thousand tigers, if not a kingdom.

He stood outside the door of 1743, looking at his watch. Eight minutes precisely. He knocked twice, paused, then knocked once again. The door opened and a shocked Ardisson stared at him.

"*C'est vous!*" cried the businessman, bringing his hand to his lips.

"*Soyez tranquille,*" said Jason, stepping inside and closing the door. "We have to talk," he continued in French. "I must know what happened."

"*You!* You were next to me in that horrid place. We *spoke.* You took my *identification!* You were the cause of *everything!*"

"Did you mention me?"

"I didn't *dare.* It would have looked as if I had done something illegal—giving my pass to someone else. Who *are* you? Why are you here? You've caused me enough trouble for one day! I think you should leave, monsieur."

"Not until you tell me exactly what happened." Bourne walked across the room and sat down in a chair next to a red lacquered table. "It's urgent that I know."

"Well, it's not urgent that I tell you. You have no right to walk in here, make yourself comfortable, and give me orders."

"I'm afraid I do have that right. Ours was a private tour and you intruded."

"I was *assigned* to that damn tour!"

"On whose orders?"

"The concierge, or whatever you call that idiot downstairs."

"Not him. Above him. Who was it?"

"How would *I* know? I haven't the vaguest idea what you're talking about."

"You left."

"My God, it was *you* who *told* me to leave!"

"I was testing you."

"Testing . . . ? This is unbelievable!"

"Believe," said Jason. "If you're telling the truth, no harm will come to you."

"*Harm?*"

"We do not kill the innocent, only the enemy."

"*Kill* . . . the *enemy?*"

Bourne reached under his jacket, took the gun from his belt, and placed it on the table. "Now, convince me you're not the enemy. What happened after you left us?"

Stunned, Ardisson staggered back into the wall, his wide, frightened eyes riveted on the weapon. "I swear by all the saints you are talking to the wrong man," he whispered.

"Convince me."

"Of *what?*"

"Your innocence. What happened?"

"I . . . Down in the square," began the terrified businessman, "I thought about the things *you* said, that something terrible had happened inside Mao's tomb, and that the Chinese guards were shouting about foreign gangsters, and how people were going to be cordoned off and detained—especially someone like me who was not really part of the tour group. . . . So I started to run—my God, I couldn't *possibly* be placed in such a situation! Millions of francs are involved, half the cost of Singapore, profits on a scale unheard of in the high-fashion industry! I'm no mere bargainer, I represent a *consortium!*"

"So you began running and they stopped you," interrupted Jason, anxious to get the nonessentials out of the way.

"*Yes!* They spoke so rapidly I didn't understand a word anyone was saying, and it was an hour before they found an official who spoke French!"

"Why didn't you simply tell them the truth? That you were with our tour."

"Because I was running away from that damned tour and I had given *you* my damned identification card! How would *that* look to these barbarians who see a fascist *criminal* in every white face?"

"The Chinese people are not barbarians, monsieur," said Bourne gently. Then suddenly he shouted. "It is only their government's political philosophy that's *barbaric!* Without the grace of *Almighty God,* with only *Satan's* benediction!"

"I beg your pardon?"

"Later, perhaps," replied Jason, his voice abruptly calm again. "So an official who spoke French arrived. What happened then?"

"I told him I was out for a stroll—*your* suggestion, monsieur. And that I suddenly remembered I was expecting a call from Paris and was hurrying back to the hotel, which accounted for my running."

"Quite plausible."

"Not for the official, monsieur. He began abusing me, making the most insulting remarks and insinuating the most dreadful things. I wonder what in the name of God happened in that tomb?"

"It was a beautiful piece of work, monsieur," answered Bourne, his eyes wide.

"I beg your pardon?"

"Later perhaps. So the official was abusive?"

"Entirely! But he went too far when he attacked Paris fashions as a decadent bourgeois industry! I mean, after all, we *are* paying money for their damned fabrics—they certainly don't have to know the margins, of course."

"So what did you do?"

"I carry a list of the names with whom I'm negotiating—some are rather important, I understand, as they should be, considering the money. I insisted the official contact them, and I refused—and I *did* refuse—to answer any more questions until at least several of them arrived. Well, after another *two* hours they did, and let me tell you, *that* changed things! I was brought back here in a Chinese version of a limousine—damned cramped for a man of my size—and four escorts. And far worse, they told me that our final conference is postponed yet again. It will not take place tomorrow morning but instead in the evening. What kind of hour is that to do *business?*" Ardisson pushed himself away from the wall, breathing hard, his eyes now pleading. "That's all there is to tell you, monsieur. You really *do* have the wrong man. I am not involved in anything over here but my consortium."

"You *should* be!" cried Jason accusingly, raising his voice again. "To do business with the godless is to debase the work of the *Lord!*"

"I beg your pardon?"

"You have satisfied me," said the chameleon. "You are simply a mistake."

"A what?"

"I will *tell* you what happened inside the tomb of Mao Zedong. *We* did it. We shot up the crystal coffin as well as the body of the infamous unbeliever!"

"You *what?*"

"And we will continue to destroy the enemies of Christ

wherever we find them! We will bring His message of love back into the world if we have to kill every diseased animal who thinks otherwise! It will be a *Christian* globe or no globe at *all!*"

"Surely there is room for negotiation. Think of the money, the *contributions.*"

"Not from Satan!" Bourne rose from the chair, picked up the gun and shoved it under his belt, then buttoned his jacket and tugged at the cloth as though it were a military tunic. He approached the distraught businessman. "You are not the enemy, but you're close, monsieur. Your billfold, please, and your trade papers, including the names of those with whom you negotiate."

"Money . . . ?"

"We do not accept contributions. We have no need of them."

"Then *why?*"

"For your protection as well as ours. Our cells here must check out individuals to see whether or not you're being used as a dupe. There is evidence we may have been infiltrated. Everything will be returned to you tomorrow."

"I really must protest—"

"Don't," broke in the chameleon, reaching under his jacket, his hand remaining there. "You asked who I was, no? Suffice it to say that as our enemies employ the services of such as the P.L.O. and the Red Armies, the Ayatollah's fanatics and Baader-Meinhof, we have mounted our own brigades. We neither seek nor offer any quarter. It is a struggle unto death."

"My God!"

"We fight in His name. Do not leave this room. Order your meals from room service. Do not call your colleagues or your counterparts here in Beijing. In other words, stay out of sight and pray for the best. In truth, I must tell you that if I myself was followed and it is known that I came to your room, you will simply disappear."

"*Unbelievable* . . . !" His eyes suddenly unfocused, Ardisson's whole body began to tremble.

"Your billfold and your papers, please."

. . .

Showing the full array of Ardisson's papers, including the Frenchman's list of government negotiators, Jason hired a car under the name of Ardisson's consortium. He made it plain to a relieved dispatcher at the China International Travel Service on Chaoyangmen Street that he both read and spoke Mandarin, and as the rented car would be driven by one of the Chinese officials, no driver was required. The dispatcher told him the car would be at the hotel by 7:00 P.M. If everything fell into place, he would have twenty-four hours to move as freely as a Westerner could in Beijing. The first ten of those hours would tell him whether or not a strategy conceived in desperation would lead him out of the darkness or plunge both Marie and David Webb into an abyss. But Delta One knew the Oriental mind. For a score of centuries it had not varied in one respect. Secrecy was worth ten thousand tigers, if not a kingdom.

Bourne walked back to the hotel, stopping in the crowded shopping district of Wang Fu Jing, around the corner of the hotel's east wing. At number 255 was the Main Department Store, where he made the necessary purchases of clothing and hardware. At number 261 he found a shop named Tuzhang Menshibu, translated as the Seal Engraving Store, where he selected the most official-looking stationery he could find. (To his amazement and delight, Ardisson's list included not one but two generals, and why not? The French produced the Exocet, and although hardly high-fashion, it was high on the list of high-tech military.) Finally, at the Arts Store, numbered 265 on the Wang Fu Jing, he bought a calligraphy pen and a map of Beijing and its environs, as well as a second map showing the roads leading from Beijing to the southern cities.

Carrying his purchases back to the hotel, he went to a desk in the lobby and began his preparations. First, he wrote a note in Chinese relieving the driver of the rented car of all responsibility in turning the automobile over to the foreigner. It was signed by a general and amounted to an order. Second, he spread out the map and circled a small green area on the outskirts of northwest Beijing.

The Jing Shan Bird Sanctuary.

Secrecy was worth ten thousand tigers, if not a kingdom.

25

Marie leaped out of the chair at the shrill, jangling bell of the telephone. She ran, limping and wincing, across the room and picked it up. "Yes?"

"Mrs. Austin, I presume."

"*Mo?* . . . Mo Panov! Thank *God.*" Marie closed her eyes in gratitude and relief. It had been nearly thirty hours since she had spoken to Alexander Conklin, and the waiting and the tension—above all, the helplessness—had driven her to the edge of panic. "Alex said he was going to ask you to come with him. He thought you would."

"Thought? Was there a doubt? How are you feeling, Marie? And I don't expect an answer from Pollyanna."

"Going mad, Mo. I'm trying not to, but I'm going *mad!*"

"As long as you haven't completed the journey I'd say you were remarkable, and the fact that you're fighting every step of the way even more so. But then you don't need any chicken-soup psychology from me. I just wanted an excuse to hear your voice again."

"To find out whether I was a babbling wreck," said Marie gently, making a statement.

"We've been through too much together for such a third-rate subterfuge—I'd never get away with it with you. Which I just didn't."

"Where's Alex?"

"Talking into the pay phone next to me; he asked me to call you. Apparently he wants to speak with you while whoever it is he's talking to is still on the line. . . . Wait a second. He's nodding. The next voice you hear, et cetera, et cetera."

"Marie?"

"*Alex?* Thank you. *Thank* you for coming—"

"As your husband would say, 'No time for that.' What were you wearing when they last saw you?"

"Wearing?"

"When you got away from them."

"I got away twice. The second time was in Tuen Mun."

"Not then," interrupted Conklin. "The contingent was small and there was too much confusion—if I remember what you told me. A couple of marines actually saw you but nobody else did. *Here.* Here in Hong Kong. That'd be the description they'd start with, the one that would stick in their minds. What were you wearing then?"

"Let me think. At the hospital—"

"Later," broke in Alex. "You said something to me about swapping clothes and buying a few things. The Canadian consulate, Staples's apartment. Can you remember?"

"Good Lord, how can *you* remember?"

"No mystery, I make notes. It's one of the by-products of alcohol. Hurry, Marie. Just generally, what were you wearing?"

"A pleated skirt—yes, a gray pleated skirt, that was it. And a kind of bluish blouse with a high collar—"

"You'd probably change that."

"What?"

"Never mind. What else?"

"Oh, a hat, a fairly wide-brimmed hat to cover my face."

"*Good!*"

"And a fake Gucci purse I bought in the street. Oh, and sandals to make me shorter."

"I want the height. We'll stick to heels. That's fine, that's all I need."

"For *what,* Alex? What are you doing?"

"Playing Simon Says. I know perfectly well the State Department passport computers picked me up, and with my smooth, athletic walk even State's warthogs could spot me in customs. They won't know a damn thing, but someone's giving them orders and I want to know who else shows up."

"I'm not sure I understand."

"I'll explain later. Stay where you are. We'll get there as soon as we can make a clean break. But it has to be *very* clean—sterile, in fact—so it may take an hour or so."

"What about Mo?"

"He has to stay with me. If we separate now, at the least they'll follow him, at worst they'll take him in."

"What about you?"

"They won't touch me beyond a tight surveillance."

"You're confident."

"I'm angry. They can't know what I've left behind or with whom or what my instructions are if there's a break in any prearranged phone calls. For them, right now I'm a walking—limping—megabomb that could blow apart their entire operation, whatever the *hell* it is."

"I know you say there's no time, Alex, but I've got to tell you something. I'm not sure why, but I have to. I think one of the things about you that so hurt and enraged David was the fact that he thought you were the best at what you did. Every once in a while, when he'd have a few drinks or his mind wandered—opening a door or two for him—he'd shake his head sadly or pound his fist furiously and ask himself, *Why?* 'Why?' he'd say. 'He was better than that . . . he was the best.' "

"I was no match for Delta. No one was. Ever."

"You sound awfully good to me."

"Because I'm not coming in from the cold, I'm going out. With a better reason than I've ever had in my life before."

"Be careful, Alex."

"Tell *them* to be careful." Conklin hung up the phone, and Marie felt the tears rolling slowly down her cheeks.

Morris Panov and Alex left the gift shop in the Kowloon railroad station and headed for the escalator that led to the lower level, Tracks 5 and 6. Mo, the friend, was perfectly willing to follow his former patient's instructions. But, Panov, the psychiatrist, could not resist offering his professional opinion.

"No wonder you people are all fucked up," he said, carrying a stuffed panda under his arm and a brightly colored magazine in his hand. "Let me get this straight. When we go downstairs, I walk to the right, which is Track six, and then proceed to my left toward the rear of the train, which we assume will arrive within minutes. Correct, so far?"

"Correct," answered Conklin, beads of sweat on his forehead as he limped beside the doctor.

"I then wait by the last pillar, holding this foul-smelling stuffed animal under my arm while glancing through the pages of this extremely pornographic magazine, until a woman approaches me."

"Correct again," said Alex as they stepped down into the escalator. "The panda's a perfectly normal gift; it's a favorite with Westerners. Think of it as a present to her kid. The porno magazine simply completes the recognition signal. Pandas and dirty pictures with naked women don't usually go together."

"On the contrary, the combination could be positively Freudian."

"Score one for the funny farm. Just do as I say."

"Say? You never told me *what* I was to say to the woman."

"Try 'Nice to meet you,' or 'How's the kid?' It doesn't matter. Give her the panda and get back to this escalator as fast as you can without running." They reached the lower platform, and Conklin touched Panov's elbow, angling the doctor to the right. "You'll do fine, Coach. Just do as I say and come back here. Everything's going to be all right."

"That's easier said from where I usually sit."

Panov walked down to the end of the platform as the train from Lo Wu thundered into the station. He stood by the last pillar, and as passengers by the hundreds poured out the doors the doctor awkwardly held the black-and-white panda under his arm and raised the magazine in front of his face. And when it happened, he nearly collapsed.

"You must be Harold!" exclaimed the loud falsetto voice as a tall figure, heavily made up under a soft, wide-brimmed hat and dressed in a gray pleated skirt, slapped his shoulder. "I'd know you *anywhere,* darling!"

"Nice to meet you. How's the kid?" Morris could barely speak.

"How's *Alex?*" countered the suddenly bass male voice quietly. "I owe him and I pay my debts, but this is crazy! Has he still got both his oars in the water?"

"I'm not sure any of you do," said the astonished psychiatrist.

"Quickly," said the strange figure. "They're closing in. Give me the panda, and when I start running, fade into the crowd and get out of here! *Give* it to me!"

Panov did as he was told, aware that several men were breaking through the straggling groups of passengers and converging on them. Suddenly, the heavily rouged man in women's clothes ran behind the thick pillar and emerged on the other side. He kicked off his high heels, circled the pillar again, and like a broken-field football back raced into the crowd nearest the train, passing a Chinese who tried to grab him, dodging through pummeled bodies and startled faces. Behind him other men took up the chase, thwarted by the increasingly hostile passengers who began using suitcases and knapsacks to ward off the bewildering assaults. Somehow in the near riot the panda was put in the hands of a tall Occidental female who was also holding an unfolded train schedule. The woman was grabbed by two well-dressed Chinese; she screamed; they looked at her, yelled at each other, and plunged ahead.

Morris Panov again did as he had been instructed to do: he quickly mingled with the departing crowd on the opposite side of the platform and walked rapidly along the edge of Track 5 back to the escalator, where a line had formed. There was a line but no Alex Conklin! Suppressing his panic, Mo slowed his pace but kept walking, looking around, scanning the crowds, as well as those riding up on the escalator. What had *happened?* Where was the CIA man?

"Mo!"

Panov spun to his left, the brief shout both a relief and a warning. Conklin had edged his way partially around a pillar thirty feet beyond the escalator. From his quick, rapid gestures he made it clear that he had to stay where he was, and for Mo to reach him, but slowly, cautiously. Panov assumed the air of a man annoyed with the line, a man who would wait for the crowd to thin out before attempting to get on the escalator. He wished he smoked or at least had not thrown the pornographic magazine down onto the tracks; either would have given him something to do. Instead, he clasped his hands behind his back and strolled casually along the deserted area of the platform, glancing around twice, frowning at the line. He reached the pillar, slid behind it, and gasped.

At Conklin's feet lay a stunned, middle-aged man in a raincoat, with Conklin's clubbed foot in the center of his back. "I'd like you to meet Matthew Richards, Doctor. Matt's an old Far East hand going back to the early Saigon days when we first knew each other. Of course, he was younger then and a lot more agile. But then, again, weren't we all."

"For Christ's sake, Alex, let me up!" pleaded the man named Richards, shaking his head as best he could in his supine position. "My head hurts like hell! What did you hit me with, a *crowbar?*"

"No, Matt. The shoe belonging to my nonexistent foot. Heavy, isn't it? But then it has to take a lot of abuse. As to letting you up, you know I can't do that until you answer my questions."

"Goddamn it, I *have* answered them! I'm a lousy case officer, not the station chief. We picked you up from a D.C. directive that said to put you under surveillance. Then State moved in with another 'direct,' which I *didn't* see!"

"I told you, I find that hard to believe. You've got a tight unit here; everybody sees everything. Be reasonable, Matt, we go back a long time. What did the State directive say?"

"I don't *know.* It was eyes-only for the SC!"

"That's 'station chief,' Doctor," said Conklin, looking over at Panov. "It's the oldest cop-out we have. We use it all the time when we get in rhubarbs with other government agencies. 'What do *I* know? Ask the SC.' That way our noses are clean because no one wants to hassle a station chief. You see, SC's have a direct line to Langley, and depending on the Oval Yo-Yo, Langley has a direct line to the White House. It's very politicized, let me tell you, and has very little to do with gathering intelligence."

"Very enlightening," said Panov, staring at the supine man, not knowing what else to say, grateful that the platform was now practically deserted, and the pillar at the rear was in shadows.

"*No* cop-out!" yelled Richards, struggling under the pressing weight of Conklin's heavy boot. "*Jesus,* I'm telling you the truth! I get out next February! Why would I want any trouble from you or anybody *else* at headquarters?"

"Oh, Matt, poor Matt, you never were the best or the brightest. You just answered your own question. You can taste that pension just like me, and you don't want any waves. I'm listed as a pickup, a tight surveillance, and you don't want to louse up a directive where you're concerned. Okay, pal, I'll wire back an evaluation report that'll get you transferred to Central American demolitions until your time's up—if you last that long."

"Cut it out!"

"Imagine, being skunk-trapped behind a pillar in a crowded train station by a lousy cripple. They'll probably let you mine a few harbors all by yourself."

"I don't *know* anything!"

"Who are the Chinese?"

"I don't—"

"They're not the police, so who *are* they?"

"Government."

"What branch? They had to tell you that—the SC had to tell you. He couldn't expect you to work blind."

"That's just it, we *are!* The only thing he told us was that they were cleared by D.C. on the top floors. He swore that was all *he* knew! What the hell were we supposed to do? Ask to see their driver's licenses?"

"So no one's accountable because no one knows anything. It'd turn out nice if they were Chin-Comms picking up a defector, wouldn't it?"

"The SC's accountable. We lay it on *him.*"

"Oh, the higher morality of it all. 'We just follow orders, *Herr General.*'" Conklin employed the hard German *G* for the rank. "And, naturally, *Herr General* doesn't know anything either because he's following *his* orders." Alex paused, squinting. "There was one man, a big fellow who looked like a Chinese Paul Bunyan." Conklin stopped. Richards's head suddenly twitched, as did his body. "Who is he, Matt?"

"I don't know . . . for sure."

"*Who?*"

"I've seen him, that's all. He's hard to miss."

"That isn't all. Because he is hard to miss *and* considering the places where you've seen him, you asked questions. What did you learn?"

"Come on, Alex! It's just gossip, nothing set in concrete."

"I love gossip. Tattle, Matt, or this ugly, heavy thing on my leg may just have to pound your face. You see, I can't control it; it's got a mind of its own and it doesn't like you. It can be very hostile, even to me." With effort, Conklin suddenly raised his club foot and pounded it down between Richards's shoulder blades.

"*Christ!* You're breaking my back!"

"No, I think it wants to break your face. Who *is* he, Matt?" Again, grimacing, Alex raised his false foot and lowered it now on the base of the CIA man's skull.

"All *right!* As I said, it's not gospel, but I've heard he's high up in Crown CI."

"Crown CI," explained Conklin to Morris Panov, "means British Counter Intelligence here in Hong Kong, which means a branch of MI-Six, which means they take their orders from London."

"Very enlightening," said the psychiatrist, as bewildered as he was appalled.

"*Very,*" agreed Alex. "May I have your necktie, Doctor?" asked Conklin as he began removing his own. "I'll replace it out of contingency funds because we now have a new wrinkle. I'm officially at work. Langley is apparently funding—by way of Matthew's salary and time—something involving an ally's Intelligence operation. As a civil servant under a like classification I should put my shoulder to the wheel. I need your necktie, too, Matt."

Two minutes later, Case Officer Richards lay behind the pillar, his feet and hands tied and his mouth drawn taut, all accomplished with three neckties.

"We're sterile," said Alex, studying what remained of the crowd beyond the pillar. "They've all gone after our decoy, who's probably halfway to Malaysia by now."

"Who was she—*he*? I mean, he certainly wasn't a woman."

"No sexism intended, but a woman probably couldn't have made it out of here. He did, taking the others with him—after him. He jumped over the escalator railing and worked his way up. Let's go. We're clear."

"But who *is* he?" pressed Panov, as they walked around the pillar toward the escalator and the few stragglers forming a short line.

"We've used him occasionally over here, mainly as a pair of eyes for out-of-the-way border installations, which he knows something about, since he has to get past them with his merchandise."

"Narcotics?"

"He wouldn't touch them; he's a top-notch jock. He runs stolen gold and jewels, operating between Hong Kong, Macao, and Singapore. I think it has something to do with what happened to him a number of years ago. They took away his medals for conduct unbecoming just about everything. He posed for some raunchy photographs when he was in college and needed the money. Later, through the good offices of a sleazy publisher with the ethics of an alley cat, they surfaced and he was crucified, ruined."

"That magazine I carried!" exclaimed Mo as they both stepped onto the escalator.

"Something like it, I guess."

"What medals?"

"1976 Olympics. Track and field. The high hurdles were his specialty."

Speechless, Panov stared at Alexander Conklin as they rose on the escalator, nearing the entrance to the terminal. A platoon of sweepers carrying wide brooms over their shoulders appeared on the opposite escalator heading down to the platform. Alex jerked his head toward them, snapped the fingers of his right hand, and with the thumb extended, jabbed the air in the direction of the terminal's exit doors above. The message was clear. Within moments a bound CIA agent would be found behind a pillar.

"That'd be the one they call the major," said Marie, sitting in a chair opposite Conklin while Morris Panov knelt beside her, examining her left foot. *"Ouch!"* she cried, pulling back her crossed leg. "I'm sorry, Mo."

"Don't be," said the doctor. "It's a nasty bruise spread over the second and third metatarsals. You must have taken quite a spill."

"Several. You know about feet?"

"Right now I feel more secure with podiatry than psychiatry. You people live in a world that would drive my profession back to the Middle Ages—not that most of us aren't still there; the words are just cuter." Panov looked up at Marie, his eyes straying to her severely styled gray-streaked hair. "You had fine medical treatment, dark-redhead-that-was. Except the hair. It's atrocious."

"It's brilliant," corrected Conklin.

"What do you know? You were a patient of mine." Mo returned to the foot. "They're both healing nicely—the cuts and the blisters, that is—the bruise will take longer. I'll pick up some things later and change the dressings." Panov got up and pulled a straight-backed chair away from the small writing table.

"You're staying here then?" asked Marie.

"Down the hall," said Alex. "I couldn't get either of the rooms next door."

"How did you even manage that?"

"Money. This is Hong Kong, and reservations are always getting lost by somebody who isn't around. . . . Back to the major."

"His name is Lin Wenzu. Catherine Staples told me he was with British Intelligence, speaks English with a U.K. accent."

"She was *sure?*"

"Very. She said he was considered the best Intelligence officer in Hong Kong, and that included everyone from the KGB to the CIA."

"It's not hard to understand. His name is Wenzu, not Ivanovitch or Joe Smith. A talented native is sent to England, educated and trained, and brought back to assume a responsible position in government. Standard colonial policy, especially in the area of law enforcement and territorial security."

"Certainly from a psychological viewpoint," added Panov, sitting down. "There are fewer resentments that way, and another bridge is built to the governed foreign community."

"I understand that," said Alex, nodding, "but something's missing; the pieces don't fit. It's one thing for London to give a green light for an undercover D.C. operation—which everything we've learned tells us this is, only more bizarre than most—but it's another for MI-

Six to lend us their local people in a colony the U.K. is still running."

"Why?" asked Panov.

"Several reasons. First, they don't trust us—oh, not that they mistrust our intentions, just our brains. In some ways they're right, in others they're dead wrong, but that's their judgment. Second, why risk exposing their personnel for the sake of decisions made by an American bureaucrat with no expertise in on-the-scene deep-cover administration? That's the sticking point, and London would reject it out of hand."

"I assume you're referring to McAllister," said Marie.

"Till the cows come home from a field of new alfalfa." Conklin shook his head, exhaling as he did so. "I've done my research, and I can tell you he's either the strongest or the weakest factor in this whole damned scenario. I suspect the latter. He's pure, cold brains, like McNamara before his conversion to doubt."

"Knock off the bullshit," said Mo Panov. "What do you mean in straight talk, not chicken soup? Leave that to me."

"I mean, *Doctor,* that Edward Newington McAllister is a rabbit. His ears spring up at the first sign of conflict or off-the-wire lapses, and he scampers off. He's an analyst and one of the best, but he is *not* qualified to be a case officer, to say nothing of a station chief, and don't even consider his being the strategist behind a major covert operation. He'd be laughed off the scene, believe me."

"He was terribly convincing with David and me," broke in Marie.

"He was given that script. 'Prime the subject,' he was told. Stick to the convoluted narrative that would become clearer to the subject in stages once he made his first moves, which he had to make because you were gone."

"Who wrote the script?" asked Panov.

"I wish I knew. No one I reached in Washington knows, and that includes a number of people who should know. They weren't lying; after all these years I can spot a swallow in a voice. It's so damn deep and filled with so many contradictions it makes Treadstone Seventy-one look like an amateur effort—which it wasn't."

"Catherine said something to me," interrupted Marie. "I don't know whether it will help or not, but it stuck in my mind. She said a man flew into Hong Kong, a 'states-man,' she called him, someone who was 'far more than a diplomat,' or something like that. She thought there might be a connection with everything that's happened."

"What was his name?"

"She never told me. Later, when I saw McAllister down in the street with her, I assumed it was he. But maybe not. The analyst you just described and the nervous man who spoke to David and me is hardly a diplomat, much less a statesman. It had to be someone else."

"When did she say this to you?" asked Conklin.

"Three days ago, when she was hiding me in her apartment in Hong Kong."

"*Before* she drove you up to Tuen Mun?" Alex leaned forward in the chair.

"Yes."

"She never mentioned him again?"

"No, and when I asked her, she said there was no point in either of us getting our hopes up. She had more digging to do, was the way she put it."

"You *settled* for that?"

"Yes, I did, because at the time I thought I understood. I had no reason to question her then. She was taking a personal and professional risk helping me—accepting my word on her own without asking for consular advice, which others might have done simply to protect them-selves. You mentioned the word 'bizarre,' Alex. Well, let's face it, what I told her was so bizarre it was outra-geous—including a fabric of lies from the U.S. State De-partment, vanishing guards from the Central Intelligence Agency, suspicions that led to the higher levels of your government. A lesser person might have backed away and covered herself."

"Gratitude notwithstanding," said Conklin gently, "she was withholding information you had a right to know. *Christ,* after everything you and David have been through—"

"You're wrong, Alex," interrupted Marie softly. "I told you I thought I understood her, but I didn't finish. The cruelest thing you can do to a person who's living every hour in panic is to offer him or her a hope that turns out false. When the crash comes it's intolerable. Believe me, I've spent over a year with a man desperately looking for answers. He's found quite a few, but those he followed only to find them wrong nearly broke him. Dashed hopes are no fun for the one hoping."

"She's right," said Panov, nodding his head and looking at Conklin. "And I think you know it, don't you?"

"It happened," replied Alex, shrugging and looking at his watch. "At any rate, it's time for Catherine Staples."

"She'll be watched, *guarded!*" It was Marie who now sat forward in her chair, her expression concerned, her eyes questioning. "They'll assume you both came over here because of me, and that you reached me and I told you about her. They'll expect you to go after her. They'll be waiting for you. If they could do what they've done so far, they could kill you!"

"No, they couldn't," said Conklin, getting up and limping toward the bedside telephone. "They're not good enough," he added simply.

"You're a goddamned basket case!" whispered Matthew Richards from behind the wheel of the small car parked across the street from Catherine Staples's apartment.

"You're not very grateful, Matt," said Alex, sitting in the shadows next to the CIA man. "Not only did I not send in that evaluation report, but I also let you get me back under surveillance. Thank me, don't insult me."

"Shit!"

"What did you tell them back at the office?"

"What else? I was mugged, for Christ's sake."

"By how many?"

"At least five teenaged punks. *Zhongguo ren.*"

"And if you fought back, making a lot of ruckus, I might have spotted you."

"That's the story board," agreed Richards quietly.

"And when I called you, naturally it was one of the street people you've cultivated who saw a white man with a limp."

"Bingo."

"You might even get a promotion."

"I just want to get out."

"You'll make it."

"Not this way."

"So it was old Havilland himself who blew into town."

"You didn't get that from me! It was in the papers."

"The sterile house in Victoria Peak wasn't in the papers, Matt."

"Hey, come *on,* that was a trade-off! You're nice to me, I'm nice to you. No lousy report about me getting clobbered by a shoe with no foot in it and you get an address. Anyway, I'd deny it. You got it from Garden Road. It's all over the consulate, thanks to a pissed-off marine."

"Havilland," mused Alex out loud. "It fits. He's tightass with the British, even talks like them. . . . My God, I should have recognized the voice!"

"The voice?" asked a perplexed Richards.

"Over the phone. Another page in the scenario. It was *Havilland!* He wouldn't let anyone else do it! 'We've *lost* her.' Oh, *Jesus,* and I was sucked right in!"

"Into what?"

"Forget it."

"Gladly."

An automobile slowed down and stopped across the street in front of Staples's apartment house. A woman got out of the rear curbside door, and seeing her in the wash of the streetlights, Conklin knew who it was. Catherine Staples. She nodded to the driver, turned around and walked across the pavement to the thick glass doors of the entrance.

Suddenly, an engine roaring at high pitch filled the quiet street by the park. A long black sedan swerved out of a space somewhere behind them and screeched to a stop beside Staples's car. Staccato explosions thundered from the second vehicle. Glass was shattered both in the street and across the pavement as the windows of the parked automobile were blown away, along with the driver's head, and the doors of the apartment house riddled, collapsing in bloody fragments, as the body of Catherine Staples was nailed into the frame under the fusillade of bullets.

Tires spinning, the black sedan raced away in the dark street, leaving the carnage behind, blood and torn flesh everywhere.

"Jesus *Christ!*" roared the CIA man.

"Get out of here," ordered Conklin.

"Where? For Christ's sake, where?"

"Victoria Peak."

"Are you out of your *mind?*"

"No, but somebody else is. One blue-blooded son of a bitch has been taken. He's been *had*. And he's going to hear it first from me. *Move!*"

26

Bourne stopped the black Shanghai sedan on the dark, tree-lined, deserted stretch of road. According to the map, he had passed the Eastern Gate of the Summer Palace—actually once a series of ancient royal villas set down on acres of sculptured countryside dominated by a lake known as Kunming. He had followed the shoreline north until the colored lights of the vast pleasure ground of emperors past faded, giving way to the darkness of the country road. He extinguished the headlights, got out, and carried his purchases, now in a waterproof knapsack, to the wall of trees lining the road, and dug his heel into the ground. The earth was soft, making his task easier, for the possibility that his rented car might be searched was real. He reached inside the knapsack, pulled out a pair of workman's gloves and a long-bladed hunting knife. He knelt down and dug a hole deep enough to conceal the sack; he left the top of it open, picked up the knife and cut a notch in the trunk of the nearest tree to expose the white wood beneath the bark. He replaced the knife and gloves in the knapsack, pressed it down into the earth and covered it with dirt. He returned to the car, checked the odometer, and started the engine. If the map was as accurate about distances as it was in detailing those areas in and around Beijing where it was prohibited to drive, the entrance to the Jing Shan Sanctuary was no more than three-quarters of a mile away around a long curve up ahead.

The map was accurate. Two floodlights converged on the high green metal gate beneath huge panels depicting brightly colored birds; the gate was closed. In a small glass-enclosed structure on the right sat a single guard.

At the sight of Jason's approaching headlights he sprang up and ran out. It was difficult to tell whether the man's jacket and trousers were a uniform or not; there was no evidence of a weapon.

Bourne drove the sedan up to within feet of the gate, climbed out, and approached the Chinese behind it, surprised to see that the man was in his late fifties or early sixties.

"*Bei tong, bei tong!*" began Jason before the guard could speak, apologizing for disturbing him. "I've had a terrible time," he continued rapidly, pulling out the list of the French-assigned negotiators from his inside pocket. "I was to be here three and a half *hours* ago, but the car didn't arrive and I couldn't reach Minister—" He picked out the name of a textile minister from the list. "—Wang Xu, and I'm sure he's as upset as I am!"

"You speak our language," said the bewildered guard. "You have a car with no driver."

"The minister cleared it. I've been to Beijing many, many times. We were going to have dinner together."

"We are closed, and there is no restaurant here."

"Did he leave a note for me, perhaps?"

"No one leaves anything here but lost articles. I have very nice Japanese binoculars I could sell you cheap."

It happened. Beyond the gate, about thirty yards down the dirt road, Bourne saw a man in the shadows of a tall tree, a man wearing a long tunic—four buttons—an *officer.* Around his waist was a thick holster belt. A weapon.

"I'm sorry, I have no use for binoculars."

"A present, perhaps?"

"I have few friends and my children are thieves."

"You are a sad man. There is nothing but children and friends—and the spirits, of course."

"Now, really, I simply want to find the *minister.* We are discussing *renminbi* in the millions!"

"The binoculars are but a few yuan."

"All *right!* How much?"

"Fifty."

"Get them for me," said the chameleon impatiently, reaching into his pocket, his gaze casually straying beyond the green fence as the guard rushed back to the gatehouse. The Chinese officer had retreated farther into

the shadows but was still watching the gate. The pounding in Jason's chest once again felt like kettledrums—as
it so often had in the days of Medusa. He had turned a
trick, exposed a strategy. Delta knew the Oriental mind.
Secrecy. The lone figure did not, of course, confirm it, but
he did not deny it, either.

"Look how grand they are!" cried the guard, running
back to the fence and holding out the binoculars. "One
hundred yuan."

"You said fifty!"

"I didn't notice the lenses. Far superior. Give me the
money and I'll throw them over the gate."

"Very well," said Bourne, about to push the money
through the crisscrossing mesh of the fence. "But under
one condition, *thief.* If by any chance you are questioned
about me, I choose not to be embarrassed."

"Questioned? That's foolish. There's no one here but
me."

Delta was right.

"But in case you are, I insist you tell the truth! I am a
French businessman urgently seeking this minister of
textiles because my car was unpardonably delayed. I will
not be embarrassed!"

"As you wish. The money, please."

Jason shoved the yuan bills through the fence; the
guard clutched them and threw the binoculars over the
gate. Bourne caught them and looked pleadingly at the
Chinese. "Have you any idea where the minister might
have gone?"

"Yes, and I was about to tell you without additional
money. Men so grand as you and he would no doubt go
to the dining house named Ting Li Guan. It is a favorite
of rich foreigners and powerful men of our heavenly
government."

"Where is it?"

"In the Summer Palace. You passed it on this road. Go
back fifteen, twenty kilometers, and you will see the great
Dong An Men gate. Enter it, and the guides will direct
you, but show your papers, sir. You travel in a very
unusual way."

"Thank you!" yelled Jason, running to the car. *"Vive la
France!"*

"How beautiful," said the guard, shrugging, heading back to his post and counting his money.

The officer walked quietly up to the gatehouse and tapped on the glass. Astonished, the night watchman leaped out of his chair and opened the door.

"Oh, sir, you startled me! I see you were locked inside. Perhaps you fell asleep in one of our beautiful resting places. How unfortunate. I will open the gate at once!"

"Who was that man?" asked the officer calmly.

"A foreigner, sir. A French businessman who has had much misfortune. As I understood him, he was to meet the minister of textiles here hours ago and then proceed to dinner, but his automobile was delayed. He's very upset. He does not wish to be embarrassed."

"What minister of textiles?"

"Minister Wang Xu, I believe he said."

"Wait outside, please."

"Certainly, sir. The gate?"

"In a few minutes." The soldier picked up the telephone on the small counter and dialed. Seconds later he spoke again. "May I have the number of a minister of textiles named Wang Xu? . . . Thank you." The officer pressed down the center bar, released it, and dialed again. "Minister Wang Xu, please?"

"I am he," said a somewhat disagreeable voice at the other end of the line. "Who is this?"

"A clerk at the Trade Council Office, sir. We're doing a routine check on a French businessman who has you listed as a reference—"

"Great Christian *Jesus,* not that idiot *Ardisson!* What's he done now?"

"You know him, sir?"

"I wish I didn't! Special this, special that! He thinks that when he defecates, the odor of lilacs fills the stalls."

"Were you to have dinner with him tonight, sir?"

"Dinner? I might have said *anything* to keep him quiet this afternoon! Of course, he hears only what he wants to hear and his Chinese is terrible. On the other hand, it's perfectly possible that he would use my name to obtain a reservation when he didn't have one. I told you, special this, special that! Give him whatever he wants. He's a lunatic but harmless enough. We'd send him back to Paris on the next plane if the fools he represents weren't paying so much for such third-rate material. He's cleared for the best illegal whores in Beijing! Just don't bother me, I'm entertaining." The minister abruptly hung up.

His mind at ease, the army officer replaced the phone and walked outside to the night watchman. "You were accurate," he said.

"The foreigner was most agitated, sir. And very confused."

"I'm told both conditions are normal for him." The army man paused for a moment, then added, "You may open the gate now."

"Certainly, sir." The guard reached into his pocket and pulled out a ring of keys. He stopped, looking over at the officer. "I see no automobile, sir. It is many kilometers to any transportation. The Summer Palace would be the first—"

"I've telephoned for a car. It should be here in ten or fifteen minutes."

"I'm afraid *I* will not be here then, sir. I can see the light of my relief's bicycle down the road now. I am off duty in five minutes."

"Perhaps I'll wait here," said the officer, dismissing the watchman's words. "There are clouds drifting down from the north. If they bring rain, I could use the gatehouse for shelter until my car arrives."

"I see no clouds, sir."

"Your eyes are not what they once were."

"Too true." The repeated ringing of a bicycle bell broke the outer silence. The relief guard approached the fence as the watchman started to unlock the gate. "These young ones announce themselves as though they were descending spirits from heaven."

"I should like to say something to you," said the officer sharply, stopping the watchman in his tracks. "Like the foreigner, I, too, do not wish to be embarrassed for catching an hour of much needed sleep in a beautiful resting place. Do you like your job?"

"Very much, sir."

"And the opportunity to sell such things as Japanese binoculars turned over to you for safekeeping?"

"Sir?"

"My hearing's acute and your shrill voice is loud."

"*Sir?*"

"Say nothing about me and I will say nothing about your unethical activities, which would undoubtedly send you into a field with a pistol put to your head. Your behavior is reprehensible."

"I have never *seen* you, sir! I swear on the spirits in my soul!"

"We in the party reject such thoughts."

"Then on anything you *like!*"

"Open the gate and get out of here."

"First my bicycle, sir!" The watchman ran to the far edge of the fence, wheeled out his bicycle and unlocked the gate. He swung it back, nodding with relief as he literally threw the new man the ring of keys. Mounting the saddle of his bicycle, he sped off down the road.

The second guard walked casually through the gate holding his bicycle by the handlebars. "Can you imagine?" he said to the officer. "The son of a Kuomintang warlord taking the place of a feeble-minded peasant who would have served us in the kitchens."

Bourne spotted the white notch in the tree trunk and drove the sedan off the road between two pine trees. He turned off the lights and got out. Rapidly he broke numerous branches to camouflage the car in the darkness. Instinctively, he worked quickly—he would have done so in any event—but to his alarm, within seconds after he finished concealing the sedan, headlights appeared far down on the road to Beijing. He bent down, kneeling in the underbrush and watched the automobile pass by, fascinated by the sight of a bicycle strapped to its roof, then concerned when moments later the noise of the engine was abruptly cut off; the car had stopped around the bend up ahead. Wary that some part of his own car had been seen by an experienced field man who would park out of sight and return on foot, Jason raced across the road into the tangled brush beyond the trees. He ran in spurts to his right, from pine to pine, to the midpoint of the curve where again he knelt in the shadowed greenery, waiting, studying every foot of the thoroughfare's borders, listening for any sound that did not belong to the hum of the deserted country road.

Nothing. Then finally something, and when he saw what it was, it simply did not make sense. Or did it? The man on the bicycle with a friction light on the front fender was pedaling up the road as if his life depended on a speed he could not possibly attain. As he drew closer Bourne saw that it was the watchman . . . on a bicycle . . . and a bicycle had been strapped to the roof of the car that had stopped around the bend. Had it been for the watchman? Of course not; the car would have proceeded to the gate. . . . A second bicycle? A second watchman— arriving on a bicycle? *Of course.* If what he believed was true, the guard at the gate would be changed, a conspirator put in his place.

Jason waited until the watchman's light was barely a speck in the distant darkness, then ran in the road back to his car and the tree with the notch in the bark. He now dug up the knapsack and began sorting out the articles of his trade. He removed his jacket and white shirt and put on a black turtleneck sweater; he secured the sheath of the hunting knife to the belt of his dark trousers and shoved the automatic with a single shell in it on the other side. He picked up two spools connected by a three-foot strand of thin wire, and thought that the lethal instrument was far better than the one he had fashioned in Hong Kong. Why not? He was much closer to his objective, if anything he had learned in that distant Medusa had any value. He rolled the wire into both spools equally, and carefully pushed them down inside his trousers' right back pocket, then picked up a small penlight and clipped it to the lower edge of his right front pocket. He placed a long, double strand of outsized Chinese firecrackers, which was folded and held in place by an elastic band, in his left front pocket along with three books of matches and a small wax candle. The most awkward item was a hand-held medium-gauge wire cutter, the size of a pair of pliers. He inserted it head down into his left back pocket, then sprang the release so that the two short handles were pressed against the cloth, thus locking the instrument in its shell. Finally, he reached for a wrapped pile of clothing that was coiled so tight its dimensions were no more than that of a rolling pin. He centered it on his spine, pulled the elastic band around his waist, and snapped the clips into place. He might never use the clothes but then he could leave nothing to chance—he was too close!

I'll take him, Marie! I swear I'll take him and we'll have our life again. It's David and I love you so! I need you so!

Stop it! There are no people, only objectives. No emotions, only targets and kills and men to be eliminated who stand in the way. I have no use for you, Webb. You're soft and I despise you. Listen to Delta—listen to Jason Bourne!

The killer who was a killer by necessity buried the knapsack with his white shirt and tweed jacket and stood up between the pine trees. His lungs swelled at the thought of what was before him, one part of him frightened and uncertain, the other furious, ice-cold.

Jason started walking north into the curve, going from tree to tree as he had done before. He reached the car that had passed him with the bicycle strapped to its roof; parked on the side of the road, it had a large sign taped under the front window. He edged closer and read the Chinese characters, smiling to himself as he did so:

This is a disabled official vehicle of the government. Tampering with any part of the mechanism is a serious crime. Theft of this vehicle will result in the swift execution of the offender.

In the lower left-hand corner there was a column in small print:

People's Printing Plant Number 72. Shanghai.

Bourne wondered how many hundreds of thousands of such signs had been made by Printing Plant 72. Perhaps they took the place of a warranty, two with each vehicle.

He backed into the shadows and continued around the bend until he reached the open space in front of the floodlit gate. His eyes followed the line of the green fence. On the left it disappeared into the forest darkness. On the right it extended perhaps two hundred feet beyond the gatehouse, running the length of a parking lot with numbered areas for tour buses and taxis, where it angled sharply south. As he expected, a bird sanctuary in China would be enclosed, a deterrent for poachers. As d'Anjou had phrased it: "Birds have been revered in China for centuries. They're considered delicacies for the eyes and the palate." Echo. Echo was gone. He wondered if d'Anjou had suffered . . . *No time.*

Voices! Bourne snapped his head back toward the gate as he lurched into the nearest foliage. The Chinese army officer and a new, much younger watchman—no, now definitely a guard—walked out from behind the gatehouse. The guard was wheeling a bicycle while the officer held a small radio to his ear.

"They'll start arriving shortly after nine o'clock," said the army man, lowering the radio and shoving down the antenna. "Seven vehicles each three minutes apart."

"The truck?"

"It will be the last."

The guard looked at his watch. "Perhaps you should get the car, then. If there's a telephone check, I know the routine."

"A good thought," agreed the officer, clamping the radio to his belt and taking the bicycle's right handlebar. "I have no patience with those bureaucratic females who bark like chows."

"But you must have," insisted the guard, laughing. "And you must take out the lonely ones, the ugly ones, and perform at your best between their legs. Suppose you received a poor report? You could lose this heavenly job."

"You mean that feeble-minded peasant you relieved—"

"No, no," broke in the guard, releasing the bicycle. "They seek out the younger ones, the handsome ones, like me. From our photographs, of course. He's different; he pays them yuan from his sales of lost items. I sometimes wonder if he makes a profit."

"I have trouble understanding you civilians."

"Correction, if I may, Colonel. In the true China I am a captain in the Kuomintang."

Jason was stunned by the younger man's remark. What he had heard was incredible! *In the true China I am a captain in the Kuomintang.* The *true* China? *Taiwan?* Good God, had it *started?* The war of the two Chinas? Was that what these men were about? *Madness!* Wholesale slaughter! The Far East would be blown off the face of the earth! Christ! In his hunt for an assassin had he stumbled on the *unthinkable?*

It was too much to absorb, too frightening, too cataclysmic. He had to move quickly, putting all thought on hold, concentrating only on movement. He read the radium dial of his watch. It was 8:54, and he had very little time to do what had to be done. He waited until the army officer bicycled past, then made his way cautiously, silently through the foliage until he saw the fence. He approached it, taking out the penlight from his pocket, flashing it twice to judge the dimensions. They were extraordinary. Its height was no less than twelve feet, and the top angled outward like the inner barricade of a prison fence with coils of barbed wire strung along the parallel strands of steel. He reached into his back pocket, squeezed the handles together and removed the wire cutter. He then probed with his left hand in the darkness, and when he found the crisscrossing wires closest to the ground, he placed the head of the cutter to the lowest.

Had David Webb not been desperate, and Jason Bourne not furious, the job would not have been accomplished. The fence was no ordinary fence. The gauge of the metal was far, far stronger than that of any barricade enclosing the most violent criminals on earth. Each strand took all the strength Jason had as he manipulated the cutter back and forth until the metal snapped free. And each snap came, but only with the passing of precious minutes.

Again Bourne looked at the glowing dial of his watch. 9:06. Using his shoulder, his feet digging into the ground, he bent the barely two-foot vertical rectangle inward through the fence. He crawled inside, sweat drenching his body everywhere, and lay on the ground breathing heavily. *No time. 9:08.*

He rose unsteadily to his knees, shook his head to clear it and started to his right, holding the fence for support until he came to the corner that fronted the parking area. The floodlit gate was two hundred feet to his left.

Suddenly, the first vehicle arrived. It was a Russian Zia limousine, vintage late sixties. It circled into the parking lot and took the first position on the right beside the gatehouse. Six men got out and walked in martial unison toward what was apparently the main path of the bird sanctuary. They disappeared in the dark, the beams of flashlights illuminating their way. Jason watched closely; he would be taking that path.

Three minutes later, precisely on schedule, a second car drove through the gate and parked alongside the Zia. Three men got out of the back while the driver and the front-seat passenger talked. Seconds later the two men emerged, and it was all Bourne could do to control himself when his stare centered in on the passenger, the tall, slender passenger who moved like a cat as he walked to the rear of the automobile to join the driver. It was the assassin! The chaos at Kai-tak Airport had demanded the elaborate trap in Beijing. Whoever was stalking this assassin had to be caught quickly and silenced. Information had to be leaked, reaching the assassin's creator—for who else knew the hired killer's tactics better than the one who had taught them to him? Who else wanted revenge more than the Frenchman? Who else was capable of unearthing the other Jason Bourne? D'Anjou was the key, and the impostor's client knew it.

And Jason Bourne's instincts—born of the gradually, painfully remembered Medusa—were accurate. When the trap had so disastrously collapsed inside Mao's tomb, a desecration that would shake the republic, the elite circle of conspirators had to regroup swiftly, secretly, beyond the scrutiny of their peers. An unparalleled crisis faced them; there was no time to lose in determining their next moves.

Paramount, however, was secrecy. Wherever they met, secrecy was their most crucial weapon. *In the true China I am a captain in the Kuomintang.* Christ! Was it *possible?*

Secrecy. For a lost kingdom? Where better could it be found than in the wild acreages of idyllic government bird sanctuaries, official parks controlled by powerful moles from the Kuomintang in Taiwan? A strategy that came out of desperation had led Bourne to the core of an incredible revelation. *No time! It's not your business! Only he is!*

Eighteen minutes later the six automobiles were in place, the passengers dispersed, joining their colleagues somewhere within the dark forest of the sanctuary. Finally, twenty-one minutes after the arrival of the Russian limousine, a canvas-covered truck lumbered through the

gate, making a wide circle and parking next to the last
entry, no more than thirty feet from Jason. Shocked, he
watched as bound and gagged men and women with gaping mouths held in place by strands of cloth were pushed
out of the van; without exception they fell, rolling on the
ground, moaning in protest and in pain. Then just within
the covered opening a man was struggling, twisting his
short, thin body and kicking at the two guards, who held
him off and finally threw him down on the graveled parking lot. It was a white man. . . . Bourne *froze.* It was
d'Anjou! In the glow of the distant floodlights he could
see that Echo's face was battered, his eyes swollen. When
the Frenchman pulled himself to his feet, his left leg kept
bending and collapsing, yet he would not give in to his
captors' taunting; he remained defiantly on his feet.

Move! Do something! What? *Medusa—we had signals.*
What were they? Oh God, what *were* they? Stones, sticks,
rocks . . . *gravel!* Throw something to make a sound, a
small distracting sound that could be anything—away
from an area, ahead, as *far* ahead as possible! Then follow it up quickly. *Quickly!*

Jason dropped to his knees in the shadows of the right-
angled fence. He reached down and grabbed a small
handful of gravel and threw it in the air over the heads
of prisoners struggling to their feet. The brief clatter on
the roofs of several cars was by and large lost amid the
stifled cries of the bound captives. Bourne repeated the
action, now with a few more stones. The guard standing
next to d'Anjou glanced over in the direction of the splat-
tering gravel, then dismissed the sound when his attention was suddenly drawn to a woman who had gotten to
her feet and had started to run toward the gate. He raced
over, grabbed her by the hair, and threw her back into the
group. Again Jason reached for more stones.

He stopped all movement. D'Anjou had fallen to the
ground, his weight on his right knee, his bound hands
supporting him on the gravel. He watched the distracted
guard, then slowly he turned in Bourne's direction.
Medusa was never far away from Echo—*he had remembered.*
Swiftly, Jason shoved the palm of his hand out, once,
twice. The dim reflected light off his flesh was enough; the
Frenchman's gaze was drawn to it. Bourne moved his

head forward in the shadows. Echo saw him! Their eyes made contact. D'Anjou nodded, then turned away, and awkwardly, painfully rose to his feet as the guard returned.

Jason counted the prisoners. There were two women and five men, including Echo. They were herded by the guards, both of whom had removed heavy night sticks from their belts and used them as prods, driving the group toward the path outside the parking lot. D'Anjou fell. He collapsed on his left leg, twisting his body as he dropped to the ground. Bourne watched closely; there was something strange about the fall. Then he understood. The fingers of the Frenchman's hands, which were tied together in front, were spread apart. Covering the movement with his body, Echo scooped up two fistfuls of gravel, and as a guard approached, pulling him to his feet, d'Anjou again stared briefly in Jason's direction. It was a signal. Echo would drop the tiny stones as long as they lasted so that his fellow Medusan would have a path to follow.

The prisoners were directed to the right, out of the graveled area, as the young guard, the "captain in the Kuomintang," locked the gate. Jason ran out of the shadows of the fence into the shadows of the truck, pulling the hunting knife from its sheath as he crouched by the hood, looking at the gatehouse. The guard was just outside the door, speaking into the hand-held radio that connected him to the meeting ground. The radio would have to be taken out. So would the man.

Tie him up. Use his clothes to gag him.

Kill him! There can't be any additional risks. Listen to me!

Bourne dropped to the ground, plunging the hunting knife into the truck's left front tire, and as it deflated he ran to the rear and did the same. Rounding the back of the truck, he raced into the space between it and the adjacent automobile. Pivoting back and forth as he moved forward, he slashed the remaining tires of the truck and those on the left side of the car. He repeated the tactic down the line of vehicles until he had slashed all the tires except those of the Russian Zia, only ten-odd yards away from the gatehouse. It was time for the guard.

Tie him—

Kill him! Each step has to be covered, and each step leads back to your wife!

Silently, Jason opened the door of the Russian automobile, reached inside and released the hand brake. Closing the door as quietly as he had opened it, he judged the distance from the hood to the fence; it was approximately eight feet. Gripping the window frame, he pressed his full weight forward, grimacing as the huge car began to roll. Giving the vehicle a final, surging shove, he dashed in front of the car next to the Zia as the limousine crashed into the fence. He lowered himself out of sight and reached into his right back pocket.

Hearing the crash, the startled guard ran around the gatehouse and into the parking lot, shifting his eyes in all directions, then staring at the stationary Zia. He shook his head, as if accepting a vehicle's unexplained malfunction, and walked over to the door.

Bourne sprang out of the darkness, the spools in both hands, the wire arcing over the guard's head. It was over in less than three seconds, no sound emitted other than a sickening expulsion of air. The garrote was lethal; the captain from the Kuomintang was dead.

Removing the radio from the man's belt, Jason searched the clothes. There was always the possibility that something might be found, something of value. There was—*were!* The first was a weapon—not surprisingly, an automatic. The same caliber as the one he had taken from another conspirator in Mao's tomb. Special guns for special people, another recognition factor, the armaments consistent. Instead of one shell, he now had the full complement of nine, in addition to a silencer that precluded disturbing the revered dead in a revered mausoleum. The second was a billfold that contained money and an official document proclaiming the bearer to be a member of the People's Security Forces. The conspirators had colleagues in high places. Bourne rolled the corpse under the limousine, slashed the left tires and raced around the car, plunging his hunting knife into those on the right. The huge automobile settled into the ground. The captain from the Kuomintang was provided a secure, concealed resting place.

Jason ran to the gatehouse, debating whether or not to

shoot out the floodlights, and he decided against it. If he survived he would need the illumination of the landmark. If—*if*? He *had* to survive! *Marie!* He went inside and, kneeling below the window, removed the shells from the guard's automatic, inserting them into his own. He then looked around for schedules or instructions; there was a roster tacked to the wall next to the ring of keys hanging on a nail. He grabbed the keys.

A telephone rang! The earsplitting bell reverberated off the glass walls of the small gatehouse. *If there's a telephone check, I know the routine. A captain from the Kuomintang.* Bourne rose, picked up the phone from the counter and crouched again, spreading his fingers over the mouthpiece.

"*Jing Shan,*" he said hoarsely. "Yes?"

"Hello, my thrusting butterfly," answered a female voice in what Jason determined to be decidedly uncultured Mandarin. "How are all your birds tonight?"

"They're fine but I'm not."

"You don't sound like yourself. This is Wo, isn't it?"

"With a terrible cold and vomiting and running back to the stalls every two minutes. Nothing stays down or inside."

"Will you be all right in the morning? I don't wish to be contaminated."

Take out the lonely ones, the ugly ones. . . .

"I wouldn't want to miss our date—"

"You'll be too weak. I'll call you tomorrow night."

"My heart withers like the dying flower."

"Cow dung!" The woman hung up.

As he talked Jason's eyes strayed to a pile of heavy coiled chain in the corner of the gatehouse, and he understood. In China, where so many mechanical things failed, the chain was a backup should the lock in the center of the gate refuse to close. On top of the coiled chain was an ordinary steel padlock. One of the keys on the ring should fit it, he thought, as he inserted several until the lock sprang open. He gathered up the chain and started outside, then stopped, turned around, and ripped the telephone out of the wall. One more piece of malfunctioning equipment.

At the gate he uncoiled the chain and wound the entire

length around the midpoint of the two center posts until
there was a bulging mass of coiled steel. He pressed four
links of the chain together so that the open spaces were
clear, inserted the curved bar, and secured the lock. Everything was stretched taut, and contrary to generally
accepted belief, firing a bullet into the mass of hard metal
would not blow it apart, only heighten the possibility that
a deflected bullet might kill the one firing and endanger
the lives of anyone else in the area. He turned and started
down the center path, once more staying in the shadows
of the border.

The path was dark. The glow from the floodlit gate was
blocked by the dense woods of the bird sanctuary, but the
light was still visible in the sky. Cupping his penlight in
the palm of his left hand, his arm stretched downward
toward the ground, he could see every six or seven feet
a small piece of gravel. Once he saw the first two or three
he knew what to look for: tiny discolorations on the dark
earth, the distance relatively consistent between them.
D'Anjou had squeezed up each stone, probably between
his thumb and forefinger, rubbing it as hard as he could
to remove the grime of the parking lot and impart the oils
of his flesh so that each might stand out. The battered
Echo had not lost his presence of mind.

Suddenly, there were two stones, not one, and only
inches apart. Jason looked up, squinting in the tiny glow
of the concealed penlight. The two stones were no accident, but another signal. The main path continued
straight ahead, but the one taken by the herded prisoners
veered sharply to the right. Two stones meant a turn.

Then, abruptly, there was a change in the relative distances between the pebbles. They were farther and farther apart, and just when Bourne thought there were no
more, he saw another. Suddenly, there were two on the
ground, marking another intersecting path. D'Anjou
knew he was running out of stones and so had begun a
second strategy, a tactic that quickly became clear to
Jason. As long as the prisoners remained on a single
path, there would be no stones, but when they turned
into other paths, two pieces of gravel indicated the direction.

He skirted the edges of marshes, and went deep into

fields and out of them, everywhere hearing the sudden fluttering of wings and the screeches of disturbed birds as they winged off into the moonlit sky. Finally there was only one narrow path and it led down into a glen of sorts—

He stopped, instantly extinguishing the cupped penlight. Below, about a hundred feet down the narrow path he saw the glow of a cigarette. It moved slowly, casually up and down, an unconcerned man smoking, but still a man placed where he was for a reason. Then Jason studied the darkness beyond—because it was a different darkness; specks of light flickered now and then through the dense woods of the descending glen. Torches, perhaps, for there was nothing constant about the barely discernible light. Of course, torches. He had reached it. Below in the distant glen, beyond the guard with his cigarette, was the meeting ground.

Bourne lurched into the tangled brush on the right side of the path. He started down only to find that the serpentine reeds were like fishnets, stalks woven together by years of erratic winds. To rip them apart or to break them would create noise inconsistent with the normal sounds of the sanctuary. Snaps and zipperlike scratchings were not the sudden fluttering of wings or the screeches of disturbed inhabitants. They were man-made and signified a different intrusion. He reached for his knife, wishing the blade were longer, and began a journey that had he remained on the path would have taken him no more than thirty seconds. It took him now nearly twenty minutes to slice his way silently to within sight of the guard.

"My *God!*" Jason held his breath, suppressing the cry in his throat. He had slipped; the slithering, hissing creature beneath his left foot was at least a yard and a half in length. It coiled around his leg, and in panic he clutched a part of the body, pulling it away from his flesh, and severing it in midair with his knife. The snake thrashed violently about for several seconds, then the spasms stopped; it was dead, uncoiled at his foot. He closed his eyes and shivered, letting the moment pass. Again he crouched and crept closer to the guard, who was now lighting another cigarette or trying to light it with one match after another that failed to ignite. The guard seemed furious with his government-subsidized book of matches.

"*Ma de shizi, shizi!*" he said under his breath, the cigarette in his mouth.

Bourne crawled forward, slicing the last few reeds of thick grass until he was six feet from the man. He sheathed the hunting knife, and again reached into his right back pocket for the garrote. There could be no misplaced blade that permitted a scream; there could only be utter silence broken by an unheard expulsion of air.

He's a human being! A son, a brother, a father!

He is the enemy. He's our target. That's all we have to know. Marie is yours, not theirs.

Jason Bourne lunged out of the grass as the guard inhaled his first draft of tobacco. The smoke exploded from his gaping mouth. The garrote was arced in place, the trachea severed as the patrol fell back in the underbrush, his body limp, his life over.

Whipping out the bloody wire, Jason shook it in the grass, then rolled the spools together and shoved them back into his pocket. He pulled the corpse deeper into the foliage, away from the path, and began searching the pockets. He first found what felt like a thick wad of folded toilet tissue, not at all uncommon in China where such paper was continuously in short supply. He unsnapped his penlight, cupped it and looked at his find, astonished. The paper was folded and soft but it was not tissue. It was *renminbi,* thousands of yuan, more than several years' income for most Chinese. The guard at the gate, the "captain of the Kuomintang," had money—somewhat more than Jason thought usual—but nowhere near this amount. A billfold was next. There were photographs of children, which Bourne quickly replaced, a driving permit, a housing allocation certificate, and an official document proclaiming the bearer to be . . . a member of the *People's Security Forces!* Jason pulled out the paper he had taken from the first guard's billfold and placed both side by side on the ground. They were identical. He folded both and put them into his pocket. A last item was as puzzling as it was interesting. It was a pass allowing the bearer access to Friendship Stores, those shops that serve foreign travelers and are all but prohibited to the Chi-

nese except for the highest government officials. Whoever the men were below, thought Bourne, they were a
strange and rarefied group. Subordinate guards carried
enormous sums of money, enjoyed official privileges
light years beyond their positions, and bore documents
identifying themselves as members of the government's
secret police. If they *were* conspirators—and everything
he had seen and heard from Shenzen to Tian An Men
Square to this wildlife preserve would seem to confirm it
—the conspiracy reached into the hierarchy of Beijing.
No time! It's not your concern!

The weapon strapped to the man's waist was, as he
expected, similar to the one in his belt, as well as the gun
he had thrown into the woods at the Jing Shan gate. It
was a superior weapon, and weapons were symbols. A
sophisticated weapon was no less a mark of status than
an expensive watch, which might have many imitators,
but those who had a schooled eye for the merchandise
would know the genuine article. One might merely show
it to confirm one's status, or deny it as government issue
from an army that bought its weapons from every available source in the world. It was a subtle point of recognition—only one superior kind allocated to one elite circle.
No time! It's no concern of yours! Move!

Jason extracted the shells, put them in his pocket, and
threw the gun into the forest. He crawled out to the path
and started slowly, silently, down toward the flickering
light beyond the wall of high trees below.

It was more than a glen, it was a huge well dug out of
prehistoric earth, a rupture dating from the Ice Age that
had not healed. Birds flapped above, in fear and curiosity; owls hooted in angry dissonance. Bourne stood at the
edge of the precipice looking down through the trees at
the gathering below. A pulsating circle of torches illuminated the meeting ground. David Webb gasped,
wanting to vomit, but the ice-cold command dictated
otherwise: *Stop it. Watch. Know what we're dealing with.*

Suspended from the limb of a tree by a rope attached
to his bound wrists, his arms stretched out above him, his
feet barely inches off the ground, a male prisoner writhed
in panic, muted cries coming from his throat, his eyes
wild and pleading above his gagged mouth.

A slender, middle-aged man dressed in a Mao jacket and trousers stood in front of the violently twisting body. His right hand was extended, clasping the jeweled hilt of an upended sword, its blade long and thin, its point resting in the earth. David Webb recognized the weapon—weapon and not a weapon. It was a ceremonial sword of a fourteenth-century warlord belonging to a ruthless class of militarists who destroyed villages and towns and whole countrysides, and were even suspected of opposing the will of the Yuan emperors—Mongols who left nothing but fire and death and the screams of children in their wake. The sword was also used for ceremonies far less symbolic, far more brutal than rites performed at the dynasty's courts. David felt a wave of nausea and apprehension gripping him as he watched the scene below.

"Listen to me!" shouted the slender man in front of the prisoner as he turned to address his audience. His voice was high-pitched but deliberate, instructive. Bourne did not know him, but his was a face that would be hard to forget. The close-cropped gray hair, the gaunt, pale features—above all, the stare. Jason could not see the eyes clearly, but it was enough that the fires of the torches danced off them. They, too, were on fire.

"The nights of the great blade *begin!*" screamed the slender man suddenly. "And they will continue *night* after *night* until all those who would betray us are sent to *hell!* Each of these poisonous insects have committed crimes against our holy cause, crimes we are aware of, all of which could lead to the great crime demanding the great blade." The speaker turned to the suspended prisoner. *"You!* Indicate the truth and *only* the truth! Do you know the Occidental?"

The prisoner shook his head, throated moans accompanying the wild movement.

"Liar!" shrieked a voice from the crowd. "He was in the Tian An Men this afternoon!"

Again the prisoner shook his head spastically in panic.

"He spoke against the true China!" shouted another. "I heard him in the Hua Gong Park among the young people!"

"And in the coffee house on the Xidan Bei!"

The prisoner convulsed, his wide, stunned eyes fixed

in shock on the crowd. Bourne began to understand. The man was hearing lies and he did not know why, but Jason knew. The star-chamber inquisition was in session; a troublemaker, or a man with doubts, was being eliminated in the name of a greater crime. And on the outside possibility that he might have committed it. *The nights of the great blade begin—night after night!* It was a reign of terror inside a small, bloody kingdom within a vast land where centuries of bloodstained warlords had prevailed.

"He did these things?" shouted the gaunt-faced orator. "He *said* these things?"

A frenzied chorus of affirmatives filled the glen.

"In the Tian An Men. . . . !"

"He talked to the Occidental. . . . !"

"He betrayed us all. . . . !"

"He caused the trouble at the hated Mao's tomb. . . . !"

"He would see us dead, our cause lost. . . . !"

"He speaks against our leaders and wants them killed. . . . !"

"To oppose our leaders," said the orator, his voice calm but rising, "is to *vilify* them, and, by so doing, to remove the care one must accord the precious gift called life. When these things occur, the gift must be taken away."

The suspended man writhed more furiously, his cries growing louder and matching the moans of the other prisoners who were forced to kneel in front of the speaker in full view of the imminent execution. Only one kept refusing, continuously trying to rise in disobedience and disrespect, and continuously beaten down by the guard nearest him. It was Philippe d'Anjou. Echo was sending another message to Delta, but Jason Bourne could not understand it.

". . . this diseased, ungrateful hypocrite, this teacher of the young, who was welcomed like a brother into our dedicated ranks because we believed the words he spoke —so courageously, we thought—in opposition to our motherland's tormentors, is no more than a *traitor*. His words are *hollow*. He is a sworn companion of the treacherous winds and they would take him to our enemies, the tormentors of Mother China! In his death may he find purification!" The now shrill-voiced orator pulled the sword out of the ground. He raised it above his head.

And so that his seed may not be spread, recited the scholar David Webb to himself, recalling the words of the ancient incantation and wanting to close his eyes, but unable to, ordered by his other self not to. *We destroy the well from which the seed springs, praying to the spirits to destroy all it has entered here on earth.*

The sword arced vertically down, hacking into the groin and genitalia of the screaming, twisting body.

And so that his thoughts may not be spread, diseasing the innocent and the weak, we pray to the spirits to destroy them wherever they may be, as we here destroy the well from which they spring.

The sword was now swung horizontally, slashing through the prisoner's neck. The writhing body fell to the ground under a shower of blood from the severed head, which the slender man with the eyes of fire continued to abuse with the blade until there was no recognition of a human face.

The rest of the terrified prisoners filled the glen with wails of horror as they groveled on the ground, soiling themselves, begging for mercy. Except one. D'Anjou rose to his feet and stared in silence at the messianic man with the sword. The guard approached. Hearing him, the Frenchman turned and spat in his face. The guard, mesmerized, perhaps sickened by what he had seen, backed away. What was Echo *doing? What was his message?*

Bourne then looked over at the executioner with the gaunt face and the close-cropped gray hair. He was wiping the long blade of the sword with a white silk scarf as aides removed the body and what was left of the prisoner's skull. He pointed to a striking, attractive woman who was being dragged by the two guards over to the rope. Her posture was erect, defiant. Delta studied the executioner's face. Beneath the maniacal eyes, the man's thin mouth was stretched into a slit. He was smiling.

He was dead. Sometime. Somewhere. Perhaps tonight. A butcher, a bloodstained, blind fanatic who would plunge the Far East into an unthinkable war—China against China, the rest of the world to follow.

Tonight!

27

"This woman is a courier, one of those to whom we gave our *trust*," went on the orator, gradually escalating his voice like a fundamentalist minister, preaching the gospel of love while his eye is on the work of the devil. "The trust was not earned but given in *faith*, for she is the wife of one of our own, a brave soldier, a first son of an illustrious family of the true China. A man who as I speak now risks his life infiltrating our enemies in the south. He, too, gave her his trust . . . and she *betrayed* that trust, she *betrayed* that gallant husband, she betrayed us *all!* She is no more than a *whore* who sleeps with the *enemy!* And while her lust is satiated how many secrets has she revealed, how much *deeper* is her betrayal? Is she the Occidental's contact here in Beijing? Is she the one who informs on us, who tells our enemies what to look for, what to expect? How else could this terrible day have happened? Our most experienced, dedicated men set a trap for our enemies that would have cut them down, ridding ourselves of Western criminals who see only riches by groveling in front of China's tormentors. It is related that she was at the airport this morning. The *airport!* Where the trap was in *progress!* Did she give her wanton body to a dedicated man, drugging him, perhaps? Did her lover tell her what to do, what to say to our *enemies?* What has this harlot *done?*"

The scene was set, thought Bourne. A case so flagrantly leapfrogging over facts and "related" facts that even a court in Moscow would send a puppet prosecutor back to the drawing board. The reign of terror within the warlord tribe continued. *Weed out the misfits among the misfits. Find the traitor. Kill anyone who might be he or she.*

A subdued but angry chorus of "Whore!" and "Traitor!" came from the audience, as the bound woman struggled with the two guards. The orator held up his hands for silence. It was immediate.

"Her lover was a despicable journalist for the Xinhua News Agency, that lying, discredited organ of the despicable regime. I say 'was,' for as of an hour ago the loathsome creature is dead, shot through the head, his throat cut, for all to know that he, too, was a traitor! I have spoken myself to this whore's husband, for I accord him honor. He instructed me to do as our ancestral spirits demand. He wants nothing further to do with her—"

"*Aiyaaa!*" With extraordinary strength and fury the woman ripped the tightly bound cloth from her mouth. "*Liar!*" she screamed. "Killer of *killers!* You killed a decent man and I have betrayed *no one!* It is *I* who have been betrayed! I was not at the airport, and you know it! I have never seen this Occidental and you know that, too! I knew nothing of this trap for Western criminals and you can see the truth in my face! How *could* I?"

"By whoring with a dedicated servant of the cause and corrupting him, *drugging* him! By offering him your breasts and misused tunnel-of-corruption, withholding, withdrawing, until the herbs make him *mad!*"

"*You're* mad! You say these things, these *lies,* because you sent my husband south and came to me for many days, first with promises and then with threats. I was to *service* you. It was my duty, you said! You lay with me and I learned things—"

"Woman, you are *contemptible!* I came to you pleading with you to leave honor to your husband, to the cause! To abandon your lover and seek forgiveness."

"A *lie!* Men came to you, taipans from the south sent by my husband, men who could not be seen near your high offices. They came secretly to the shops below my flat, the flat of a so-called honorable widow—another lie you left for me and my child!"

"*Whore!*" shrieked the wild-eyed man with the sword.

"Liar to the depths of the northern lakes!" shouted the woman in reply. "Like you, my husband has many women and cares nothing for me! He beats me and you tell me it is his right, for he is a great son of the true China! I carry messages from one city to another, which if found on me would bring me torture and death, and I receive only scorn, never paid for my railroad fares, or the yuan withheld from my place of work, for you tell me it is my *duty!* How is my girl child to eat? The child your great son of China barely recognizes, for he wanted only sons!"

"The spirits would not grant you sons, for they would be *women,* disgracing a great house of China! *You* are the traitor! You went to the airport and reached our enemies permitting a great criminal to escape! You would enslave us for a thousand years—"

"You would make us your cattle for *ten* thousand!"

"You don't know what freedom is, woman."

"*Freedom?* From your mouth? You tell me—you tell *us* —you will give us back the freedoms our elders had in the true China but *what* freedoms, *liar?* The freedom that demands blind obedience, that takes the rice from my child, a child dismissed by a father who believes only in *lords*—war*lords,* land*lords,* lords of the earth! *Aiya!*" The woman turned to the crowd, rushing forward, away from the orator. "*You!*" she cried. "*All* of you! I have not betrayed you, nor our cause, but I have learned many things. All was not as this great liar says! There *is* much pain and restriction, which we all know, but there was pain *before, restriction* before! . . . My lover was no evil man, no blind follower of the regime, but a literate man, a gentle man, and a believer in *eternal* China! He wanted the things *we* want! He asked only for time to correct the evils that had infected the old men in the committees that lead us. There will be changes, he told me. Some are showing the way. *Now!* . . . Do not permit the liar to do this to me! Do not permit him to do it to *you!*"

"*Whore! Traitor!*" The blade came slashing through the air, decapitating the woman. Her headless body lurched to the left, her head to the right, both spouting geysers of blood. The messianic orator then swung the sword down, slicing into her remains, but the silence that had fallen on the crowd was heavy, awesome. He stopped; he had lost the moment. He regained it swiftly. "May the sacred ancestral spirits grant her peace and purification!" he shouted, his eyes roving, stopping, staring at each member of his congregation. "For it is not in hatred that I end her life, but in compassion for her weakness. She will find peace and forgiveness. The spirits will under-stand—but *we* must understand here in the *motherland!*

We cannot deviate from our *cause*—we must be *strong!* We must—"

Bourne had had enough of this maniac. He was hatred incarnate. And he was dead. Sometime. Somewhere. Perhaps tonight—if possible, *tonight!*

Delta unsheathed his knife and started to his right, crawling through the dense Medusan woods, his pulse strangely quiet, a furious core of certainty growing within him—David Webb had vanished. There were so many things he could not remember from those clouded, faraway days, but there was much, too, that came back to him. The specifics were unclear but not his instincts. Impulses directed him, and he was at one with the darkness of the forest. The jungle was not an adversary; instead it was his ally, for it had protected him before, saved him before in those distant, disordered memories. The trees and the vines and the underbrush were his friends; he moved through and around them like a wild cat, surefooted and silent.

He turned to his left above the ancient glen and began his descent while focusing on the tree where the assassin stood so casually. The orator had once again altered his strategy in dealing with his congregation. He was cutting his losses in place of cutting up another woman—a sight the sons of mothers found borderline madness, regardless of any earthly cause. The impassioned pleas of a dead, mutilated female prisoner had to be put out of mind. A master of his craft—his art—the orator knew when to revert to the gospel of love, momentarily omitting Lucifer. Aides had swiftly removed the evidence of violent death, and the remaining woman was summoned with a gesture of the ceremonial sword. She was no more than eighteen, if that, and a pretty girl, weeping and vomiting, as she was dragged forward.

"Your tears and your illness are not called for, child," said the orator in his most paternal voice. "It was always our intent to spare you, for you were asked to perform duties beyond your competence at your age, privileged to learn secrets beyond your understanding. Youth frequently speaks when it should be silent. . . . You were seen in the company of two Hong Kong brothers—but not *our* brothers. Men who work for the disgraced English Crown, that enfeebled, decadent government that

sold out the motherland to our tormentors. They gave
you trinkets, pretty jewelry and lip rouge and French
perfume from Kowloon. Now, child, what did you give
them?''

The young girl, hysterically coughing vomit through
her gag, shook her head furiously, the tears streaming
down her face.

"Her hand was beneath a table, between a man's legs,
in a café on the Guangquem!" shouted an accuser.

"It was one of the pigs who work for the British!"
added another.

"*Youth* is subject to arousal," said the orator, looking
up at those who had spoken, his eyes glaring, as if commanding silence. "There is forgiveness in our hearts for
such young exuberance—as long as betrayal is no part of
that arousal, that exuberance."

"She was at the Qian Men Gate. . . . !"

"She was *not* in the Tian An Men. I, *myself*, have determined it!" shouted the man with the sword. "Your information is wrong. The only question that remains is a
simple one. *Child!* Did you *speak* of us? Could your words
have been conveyed to our enemies here or in the
south?"

The girl writhed on the ground, her whole body swaying frantically back and forth, denying the implied accusation.

"I accept your innocence, as a father would, but not
your foolishness, child. You are too free with your as-
sociations, your love of trinkets. When these do not serve
us, they can be dangerous."

The young woman was put in the custody of a smug,
obese middle-aged member of the chorus for "instruc-
tion and reflective meditation." From the expression on
the man's face it was clear that his mandate would be far
more inclusive than that prescribed by the orator. And
when he was finished with her, a child-siren who had
elicited secrets from the Beijing hierarchy that demanded
young girls—believing that such liaisons, as Mao had
decreed, extended their life spans—would disappear.

Two of the three remaining Chinese men were literally
put on trial. The initial charge was trafficking in drugs,
their network the Shanghai-Beijing axis. Their crime,
however, was not distributing narcotics, but constantly

skimming off the profits, depositing huge sums of money into personal accounts in numerous Hong Kong banks. Several in the audience stepped forward to corroborate the damning evidence, stating that as subordinate distributors they had given the two "bosses" great sums of cash never recorded in the organization's secret books. That was the initial charge, but not the major one. It came with the high-pitched singsong voice of the orator. "You travel south to Kowloon. Once, twice, often *three* times a month. The Kai-tak Airport. . . .*You!*" screamed the zealot with the sword, pointing to the prisoner on his left. "You flew back this afternoon. You were in Kowloon last night. Last *night!* The Kai-tak! We were *betrayed* last night at the *Kai-tak!*" The orator walked ominously out of the light of the torches to the two petrified men kneeling in front. "Your devotion to money transcends your devotion to our cause," he intoned like a sorrowful but angry patriarch. "Brothers in blood and brothers in thievery. We've known for many weeks now, known because there was so much anxiety in your greed. Your money had to multiply like rodents in putrid sewers, so you went to the criminal triads in Hong Kong. How enterprising, industrious, and how grossly stupid! You think certain triads are unknown to us or we to them? You think there are not areas where our interests might converge? You think they have less *loathing* for traitors than *we* do?"

The two bound brothers groveled in the dirt, rising to their knees in supplication, shaking their heads in denial. Their muted cries were pleas to be heard, to be allowed to speak. The orator approached the prisoner on his left and yanked the gag downward, the rope scraping the man's flesh.

"We betrayed *no one,* great sir!" he shrieked. "*I* betrayed no one! I was at the Kai-tak, *yes,* but only in the crowds. To *observe,* sir! To be filled with joy!"

"To whom did you speak?"

"No one, great sir! Oh, yes, the clerk. To confirm my flight for the next morning, sir, that was all, I swear on the spirits of our ancestors. My young brother's and mine, sir."

"The money. What about the money you *stole?*"

"Not stole, great sir. I *swear* it! We believed in our

proud hearts—hearts made proud by our cause—that we could use the money to advantage for the true China! Every yuan of profit was to be returned to the *cause!*"

The crowd thundered its response. Derisive catcalls were hurled at the prisoners; dual thematic fugues of treachery and theft filled the glen. The orator raised his arms for silence. The voices trailed off.

"Let the word be spread," he said slowly with gathering force. "Those of our growing band who might harbor thoughts of betrayal be *warned.* There is no mercy in us, for none was shown us. Our cause is righteous and pure and even thoughts of treachery are an abomination. Spread the word. You don't know who we are or where we are—whether a bureaucrat in a ministry or a member of the security police. We are nowhere and we are everywhere. Those who waver and doubt are dead. . . . The trial of these poisonous dogs is over. It's up to you, my children."

The verdict was swift and unanimous: guilty on the first count, probable on the second. The sentence: one brother would die, the other would live, to be escorted south to Hong Kong, where the money would be retrieved. The choice was to be decided by the age-old ritual of *yi zang li,* literally "one funeral." Each man was given an identical knife with blades that were serrated and razor-sharp. The area of combat was a circle, the diameter ten paces. The two brothers faced each other and the savage ritual began as one made a desperate lunge and the other sidestepped away from the attack, his blade lacerating the attacker's face.

The duel within the deadly circle, as well as the audience's primitive reactions to it, covered whatever noise Bourne made in his decision to move quickly. He raced down through the underbrush, snapping branches and slashing away the webbed reeds of high grass, until he was twenty feet behind the tree where the assassin was standing. He would return and move closer, but first there was d'Anjou. Echo had to know he was *there.*

The Frenchman and the last male Chinese prisoner were off to the right of the circle, the guards flanking them. Jason crept forward as the crowd roared insults and encouragement at the gladiators. One of the combatants, both now covered with blood, had delivered a near-fatal blow with his knife, but the life he wanted to end would not surrender. Bourne was no more than eight or nine feet from d'Anjou; he felt around the ground and picked up a fallen branch. With another roar from the crazed audience he snapped it twice. From the three sections he held in his hand he stripped the foliage and reduced the bits of wood into manageable sticks. He took aim and hurled the first end over end, keeping the trajectory low. It fell short of the Frenchman's legs. He threw the second; it struck the back of Echo's knees! D'Anjou nodded his head twice to acknowledge Delta's presence. Then the Frenchman did a strange thing. He began moving his head slowly back and forth. Echo was trying to tell him something. Suddenly, d'Anjou's left leg collapsed and he fell to the ground. He was yanked up harshly by the guard on his right, but the man's concentration was on the bloody battle taking place within the one-funeral circle.

Again Echo shook his head slowly, deliberately, finally holding it steady and staring to his left, his gaze on the assassin who had moved away from the tree to watch the deadly combat. And then he turned his head once more, now directing his stare at the maniac with the sword.

D'Anjou collapsed again, this time struggling to his feet before the guard could touch him. As he rose he moved his thin shoulders back and forth. And breathing deeply, Bourne closed his eyes in the only brief moment of grief he could permit himself. The message was clear. Echo was taking himself out, telling Delta to go after the assassin—and while doing so, to kill the evangelical butcher. D'Anjou knew he was too battered, too weak to be any part of an escape. He would only be an impediment, and the impostor came first . . . Marie came first. Echo's life was over. But he would have his bonus in the maniacal butcher's death, the zealot who would surely take his life.

A deafening scream filled the glen; the crowd was abruptly silent. Bourne snapped his head to the left, where he could see beyond the edge of the row of onlookers. What he saw was as sickening as what he had seen during the past violent minutes. The messianic orator had sunk his ceremonial sword in the neck of a combatant; he pulled it out as the bloodied corpse rattled in death and sprawled on the ground. The minister of killing raised his head and spoke. *"Surgeon!"*

"Yes, sir?" said a voice from the crowd.

"Tend to the survivor. Mend him as best you can for his imminent journey south. If I'd let this continue, both would be dead and our money gone. These close-knit families bring years of hostility to the *yi zang li.* Take his brother away and throw him into the swamps with the others. All will be sweet carrion for the more aggressive birds."

"Yes, sir." A man with a black medicine bag stepped forward into the dirt-ringed circle as the dead body was hauled away and a stretcher appeared out of the darkness from the far end of the crowd. Everything had been planned, everything considered. The doctor administered a hypodermic into the arm of the moaning, blood-covered brother, who was carried out of the circle of brotherly death. Wiping his sword with a fresh silk cloth, the orator nodded his head in the direction of the two remaining prisoners.

Stunned, Bourne watched as the Chinese beside d'Anjou calmly undid his bound wrists and reached up to the back of his neck, untying the supposedly strangling strip of cloth and rope that supposedly kept his gaping mouth incapable of any sound but throated moans. The man walked over to the orator and spoke in a raised voice, addressing both his leader and the crowd of followers. "He says nothing and he reveals nothing, yet his Chinese is fluent and he had every opportunity to speak to me before we boarded the truck and the gags were in place. Even then I communicated with him by loosening my own, offering to do the same for him. He refused. He is obstinate and corruptly brave, but I am sure he knows what he will not tell us."

"Tong ku, tong ku!" Wild shouts came from the crowd, demanding torture. To these were added instructions narrowing the area for pain to be inflicted to the testicles of the Occidental.

"He is old and frail and will collapse into unconsciousness, as he has done before," insisted the false prisoner. "Therefore I suggest the following, with our leader's permission."

"If there's a chance of success, whatever you wish," said the orator.

"We have offered him his freedom in exchange for the information, but he does not trust us. He's been dealing with the Marxists too long. I propose taking our reluctant ally to the Beijing airport and using my position to secure him passage on the next plane to Kai-tak. I will clear him through immigration, and all he must do before boarding with his ticket is give me the information. Where is there a greater show of trust? We will be in the midst of our enemies, and if his conscience is so offended, all he has to do is raise his voice. He has seen and heard more than any person who ever walked away from us alive. We might in time become true allies, but first there must be trust."

The orator studied the provocateur's face, then shifted his gaze to d'Anjou, who stood erect, peering out of his swollen eyes, listening without expression. Then the man with the bloodstained sword turned and addressed the assassin by the tree, suddenly speaking in English. "We have offered to spare this insignificant manipulator if he tells us where his comrade can be found. Do you agree?"

"The Frenchman will lie to you!" said the killer in a clipped British accent, stepping forward.

"To what purpose?" asked the orator. "He has his life, his freedom. He has little or no regard for others, his entire dossier is proof of that."

"I'm not sure," said the Englishman. "They worked together in an outfit called Medusa. He talked about it all the time. There were rules—codes, you might call them. He'll lie."

"The infamous Medusa was made up of human refuse, men who would kill their brothers in the field if it could save their own lives."

The assassin shrugged. "You asked for my opinion," he said. "That's it."

"Let us ask the one to whom we are prepared to offer mercy." The orator reverted to Mandarin, issuing orders, as the assassin returned to the tree and lit a cigarette. D'Anjou was brought forward. "Untie his hands; he's not going anywhere. And remove the rope from his mouth. Let him be heard. Show him we can extend . . . trust, as well as less attractive aspects of our nature."

D'Anjou shook his hands at his sides, then raised his right and massaged his mouth. "Your trust is as compassionate and convincing as your treatment of prisoners," he said in English.

"I forgot." The orator raised his eyebrows. "You understand us, don't you?"

"Somewhat more than you think," replied Echo.

"Good. I prefer speaking English. In a sense, this is between us, isn't it?"

"There's nothing between us. I try never to deal with madmen, they're so unpredictable." D'Anjou glanced over at the assassin by the tree. "I've made mistakes, of course. But somehow I think one will be rectified."

"You can live," said the orator.

"For how long?"

"Longer than tonight. The remainder is up to you, your health and your abilities."

"No, it's not. It's all ended when I walk off that plane in Kai-tak. You won't miss as you did last evening. There'll be no security forces, no bulletproof limousines, just one man walking in or out of the terminal, and another with a silenced pistol or a knife. As your rather unconvincing fellow 'prisoner' of mine put it, I've been here tonight. I've seen, I've heard, and what I've seen and heard marks me for death. . . . Incidentally, if he wonders why I didn't confide in him, tell him he was far too obvious, too anxious. And that suddenly loosened mouthpiece. Really! He could never become a pupil of mine. Like you, he has unctuous words, but he's fundamentally stupid."

"Like *me?*"

"Yes, and there's no excuse for you. You're a well-educated man, a world traveler—it's in your speech. Where did you matriculate? Was it Oxford? Cambridge?"

"The London School of Economics," said Sheng Chou Yang, unable to stop himself.

"Well put—the old school tie, as the English say. Yet for all of that you're hollow. A clown. You're not a scholar, not even a student, only a zealot with no sense of reality. You're a fool."

"You *dare* say this to me?"

"*Fengzi,*" said Echo, turning to the crowd. "*Shenjing*

bing!" he added, laughing, explaining that he was conversing with a crazy corkscrew.

"*Stop* that!"

"*Wei shemme?*" continued the enfeebled Frenchman, asking *Why?*—including the crowd as he spoke in Chinese. "You're taking these people to their oblivion because of your lunatic theories of changing lead into gold! Piss into wine! But as that unfortunate woman said—*whose* gold, *whose* *wine? Yours* or *theirs?*" D'Anjou swept his hand toward the crowd.

"I *warn* you!" cried Sheng in English.

"You *see!*" shouted Echo hoarsely, weakly in Mandarin. "He will not talk with me in your language! He *hides* from you! This spindly-legged little man with the big sword—is it to make up for what he lacks elsewhere? Does he hack women with his blade because he has no other equipment and can do nothing else with them? And look at that balloon head with the foolish flat top—"

"*Enough!*"

"—and the eyes of a screeching, disobedient, *ugly* child! As I say, he's nothing more than a crazy corkscrew. Why give him your time? He'll give you only piss in return, no wine at all!"

"I'd stop it if I were you," said Sheng, stepping forward with his sword. "They'll kill you before I do."

"Somehow I doubt that," answered d'Anjou in English. "Your anger clouds your hearing, Monsieur Windbag. Did you not detect a snicker or two? I did."

"*Gou le!*" roared Sheng Chou Yang, ordering Echo to be silent. "You will give us the information we must have," he continued, his shrill Chinese the bark of a man accustomed to being obeyed. "The games are finished and we will not tolerate you any longer! Where is the killer you brought from Macao?"

"Over there," said d'Anjou casually, gesturing his head toward the assassin.

"Not *him!* The one who came *before.* This madman you called back from the grave to avenge you! Where is your rendezvous? Where do you meet? Your base here in Beijing, where *is* it?"

"There is no rendezvous," answered Echo, reverting to English. "No base of operations, no plans to meet."

"There *were* plans! You people always concern yourselves with contingencies, *emergencies*. It's how you survive!''

"Survived. Past tense, I fear me."

Sheng raised his sword. "You tell us or you die—unpleasantly, monsieur."

"I'll tell you this much. If he could hear my voice, I would explain to him that *you* are the one he must kill. For you are the man who will bring all Asia to its knees with millions drowning in oceans of their brothers' blood. He must tend to his own business, I understand that, but I would tell him with my last breath that *you* must be *part* of that business! I would tell him to *move. Quickly!*''

Mesmerized by d'Anjou's performance, Bourne winced as if struck. Echo was sending a final signal! *Move! Now!* Jason reached into his left front pocket and pulled out the contents as he crawled swiftly through the woods beyond the staging area of the savage rituals. He found a large rock rising several feet out of the ground. The air was still behind it and its size more than enough to conceal his work. As he started he could hear d'Anjou's voice; it was weak and tremulous, but nevertheless defiant. Echo was finding resources within himself not only to face his final moments but also to buy Delta the precious few he needed.

". . . Don't be hasty, *mon général* Genghis Khan, or whoever you are. I am an old man and your minions have done their work. As you observed, I'm not going anywhere. On the other hand, I'm not sure I care for where you intend to send me. . . . We were not clever enough to perceive the trap you set for us. If we had been, we would never have walked into it, so why do you think we were clever enough to agree on a rendezvous?"

"Because you *did* walk into it," said Sheng Chou Yang calmly. "You followed—*he* followed—the man from Macao into the mausoleum. The madman expected to come out. Your contingencies would include both chaos and a rendezvous."

"On the surface your logic might appear unassailable—"

"*Where?*" shouted Sheng.

"My inducement?"

"Your *life!*''

"Oh, yes, you mentioned that."

"Your time runs short."

"I shall *know* my time, monsieur!" *A last message. Delta understood.*

Bourne struck a match, cupping the flame, and lit the thin wax candle, the fuse embedded an eighth of an inch below the top. He quickly crawled deeper into the woods, unraveling the string attached to the succeeding double rolls of fireworks. He reached the end and started back toward the tree.

". . . What guarantee do I have for my life?" persisted Echo, perversely enjoying himself, a master of chess plotting his own inevitable death.

"The truth," replied Sheng. "It's all you need."

"But my former pupil tells you that I'll lie—as you have lied so consistently this evening." D'Anjou paused and repeated his statement in Mandarin. *"Liao jie?"* he said to the onlookers, asking if they understood.

"Stop that!"

"You repeat yourself incessantly. You really must learn to control it. It's such a tiresome habit."

"And my patience is at an end! *Where* is your *madman?"*

"In your line of work, *mon général,* patience is not only a virtue but a necessity."

"Hold it!" shouted the assassin, springing away from the tree, astonishing everyone. "He's stalling you! He's *playing* with you. I *know* him!"

"For what reason?" asked Sheng, his sword poised.

"I don't know," said the British commando. "I just don't like it, and that's reason enough for me!"

Ten feet behind the tree, Delta looked at the radium dial of his watch, concentrating on the second hand. He had timed the burning candle in the car, and the time was now. Closing his eyes, pleading with something he could not understand, he grabbed a handful of earth and hurled it high to the right of the tree, arcing it farther to the right of d'Anjou. When he heard the first drops of the shower, Echo raised his voice to the loudest roar he could command.

"Deal with you?" he screamed. "I would as soon deal with the archangel of *darkness!* I may yet have to, but then again I may not, for a merciful God will know that you have committed sins beyond any I have approached, and

I leave this earth wanting only to take you *with* me! Your obscene brutality aside, *mon général*, you are a fatuous, hollow *bore*, a cruel joke on your people! Come *die* with me, General *Dung!*"

With his final words, d'Anjou flung himself at Sheng Chou Yang, clawing at his face, spitting into the wide, astonished eyes. Sheng leaped back, swinging the cere-monial sword, slashing the blade into the Frenchman's head. Mercifully quick, it was over for Echo.

It *began!* A staccato burst of fireworks filled the glen, resounding through the woods, swelling in intensity as the stunned crowd reacted in shock. Men threw them-selves to the ground, others scrambled behind trees and into the underbrush, yelling in panic, frightened for their lives.

The assassin lurched behind the tree trunk, crouching, a weapon in his hand. Bourne, with the silencer affixed to his gun, strode up to the killer and stood over him. He took aim and fired, blowing the weapon out of the assas-sin's hand, the flesh between the commando's thumb and forefinger erupting in blood. The killer spun around, his eyes wide, his mouth gaping in shock. Jason fired again, now creasing the assassin's cheekbone.

"Turn around!" ordered Bourne, shoving the barrel of his gun into the commando's left eye. "Now, grab the tree! *Grab* it! Both arms, tight, *tighter!*" Jason rammed the weapon into the back of the killer's neck as he peered around the trunk. Several of the torches that were stuck in the ground had been ripped up, their flames extin-guished.

Another series of explosions came from deeper within the woods. Panicked men began to fire their guns in the direction of sounds. The assassin's leg moved! Then his right hand! Bourne fired two shots directly into the tree; the bullets seared the wood, shattering the bark less than an inch from the commando's skull. He gripped the trunk, his body still, rigid.

"Keep your head to the left!" said Jason harshly. "You move once more and it's blown away!" *Where was he? Where was the killer maniac with the sword? Delta owed that much to Echo. Where . . . there!* The man with the fanatical eyes was rising from the ground, looking everywhere at once, shouting orders to those near him and demanding a weapon. Jason stepped away from the tree and raised his gun. The zealot's head stopped moving. Their eyes met. Bourne fired just as Sheng pulled a guard in front of him. The soldier arched backward, his neck snapping under the impact of the bullets. Sheng held on to the body, using it as a shield, as Jason fired twice more, jolting the guard's corpse. He could not do it! Whoever the maniac was, he was covered by a dead soldier's body! Delta could not do what Echo had told him to do! General *Dung* would survive! I'm *sorry*, Echo! *No time! Move! Echo was gone.* . . . *Marie!*

The assassin shifted his head, trying to see. Bourne squeezed the trigger. Bark exploded in the killer's face and he whipped his hands up to his eyes, then shook his head, blinking to regain his vision.

"Get up!" ordered Jason, gripping the assassin's throat and pivoting the commando toward the path he had broken through the underbrush as he raced down into the glen. "You're coming with me!"

A third series of fireworks, deeper still in the woods, exploded in rapid, overlapping bursts. Sheng Chou Yang screamed hysterically, commanding his followers to go in two directions—toward the vicinity of the tree and after the detonating sounds. The explosions stopped as Bourne propelled his prisoner into the brush, ordering the killer to lie prone, Jason's foot on the back of his neck. Bourne crouched, feeling the ground; he picked up three rocks and threw them in the air one after another past the men searching the area around the tree, each rock thrown farther away. The diversion had its effect.

"*Nali!*"

"*Shu ner!*"

"*Bu! Caodi ner!*"

They began moving forward, weapons at the ready. Several rushed ahead, plunging into the overgrowth. Others joined them as the fourth and last cannonade of fireworks burst forth. In spite of the distance the reports were as loud or louder than the previous explosions. It was the final stage, the climax of the display, longer and more booming than the explosions preceding it.

Delta knew that time was now measured in minutes, and if ever a forest was a friend, this one had to be now. In moments, perhaps seconds, men would find the hol-

low shells of exploded fireworks strewn on the ground
and the tactical distraction would be exposed. A massive,
hysterical race for the gate would follow.

"*Move!*" ordered Bourne, grabbing the assassin's hair,
pulling him to his feet, and shoving him forward. "Remember, you *bastard*, there isn't a trick you've learned I
haven't perfected, and that makes up for a certain difference in our ages! You *look* the wrong way, you've got two
bullet holes for eye sockets. Move *out!*"

As they raced up the broken path through the wooded
glen, Bourne reached into his pocket and pulled out a
handful of shells. While the assassin ran in front of him,
breathlessly rubbing his eyes and wiping away the blood
from his cheek, Jason removed the clip from his automatic, replaced his full complement of bullets, and
cracked the magazine back into place. Hearing the sound
of a weapon being dismantled, the commando whipped
his head around but realized he was too late; the gun was
already reassembled. Bourne fired, grazing the killer's
ear. "I warned you," he said, breathing loud but steadily.
"Where do you want it? In the center of your forehead?"
He leveled the automatic in front of him.

"Good *Christ*, that butcher was right!" cried the British
commando holding his ear. "You *are* a madman!"

"And you're dead unless you move. *Faster!*"

They reached the corpse of the guard who had been
posted on the narrow path leading down to the deep
glen. "Go to the right!" ordered Jason.

"*Where*, for Christ's sake? I can't *see!*"

"There's a path. You'll feel the space. *Move!*"

Once on the bird sanctuary's series of dirt thoroughfares, Bourne kept jamming his automatic into the assassin's spine, forcing the killer to run faster, *faster!* For a
moment David Webb returned, and a grateful Delta acknowledged him. Webb was a runner, a ferocious runner,
for reasons that went back in time and tortured memories
past Jason Bourne to the infamous Medusa. Racing feet
and sweat and the wind against his face made living each
day easier for David, and at the moment Jason Bourne
was breathing hard but nowhere near as breathlessly as
the younger, stronger assassin.

Delta saw the glow of light in the sky—the gate was at
the end of a field and past three dark, twisting paths. No

more than half a mile! He fired a shot between the commando's churning legs. "I want you to run *faster!*" he said, imposing control on his voice, making it seem that the strenuous movement had minor effect on him.

"*Jesus,* I *can't!* I've got no *wind* left!"

"Find it," commanded Jason.

Suddenly, in the distance behind them they heard the hysterical shouts of men ordered by their maniacal leader back to the gate, told to find and kill an intruder so dangerous that their very lives and fortunes were hanging in the balance. The jagged, paper remnants of fireworks had been found; a radio had been activated with no response from a gatehouse. *Find him! Stop him! Kill him!*

"If you have any ideas, Major, forget them!" yelled Bourne.

"*Major?*" said the commando, barely able to speak, as he kept running.

"You're an open book to me, and what I've read makes me sick! You watched d'Anjou die like a slaughtered pig. You grinned, you *bastard.*"

"He *wanted* to die! He wanted to *kill* me!"

"*I'll* kill you if you stop running. But before I do, I'll slice you up from your balls to your throat so slowly you'll wish you'd gone with the man who created you."

"Where's my choice? You'll kill me anyway!"

"Maybe I won't. Ponder it. Maybe I'm saving your life. Think about it!"

The assassin ran faster. They raced through the final dark path, running into the open space of the floodlit gate.

"The parking lot!" shouted Jason. "The far right end!" Bourne stopped. "*Hold it!*" The bewildered assassin stood still in his tracks. Jason took out his penlight, then aimed his automatic. As he walked up to the killer's back he fired five shots, missing with one. The floodlights exploded; the gate fell into darkness and Bourne rammed the gun into the base of the commando's skull. He turned on the penlight, shining it into the side of the assassin's face. "The situation is in hand, Major," he said. "The operation proceeds. *Move,* you son of a *bitch!*"

Racing across the darkened parking lot, the killer stumbled, sprawling prone on the gravel. Jason fired twice in the glow of the penlight; the bullets ricocheted

away from the commando's head. He got to his feet and
continued running past the cars and the truck to the end
of the lot.

"The fence!" cried Bourne in a loud whisper. "Head
over to it." At the edge of the gravel he gave another
order. "Get on your hands and knees—look *straight
ahead!* You turn around, I'm the last thing you'll see.
Now, crawl!" The assassin reached the broken opening
in the fence. "Start through it," said Jason, once more
reaching into his pocket for shells and quietly removing
the automatic's magazine. "*Stop!*" he whispered when
the psychotic former commando was halfway through.
He replaced the expended bullets in the darkness and
cracked the magazine into its chamber. "Just in case you
were counting," he said. "Now get through there and
crawl two lengths away from the fence. *Hurry up!*"

As the assassin scrambled under the bent wire, Bourne
crouched and surged through the opening inches behind
him. Expecting otherwise, the commando whipped
around, rising to his knees. He was met by the beam of
the penlight, the glow illuminating the weapon leveled at
his head. "I'd have done the same," said Jason, getting
to his feet. "I'd have thought the same. Now go back to
the fence, reach under, and yank that section back into
place. *Quickly!*"

The killer did as he was told, straining as he pulled the
thick wire mesh down. At the three-quarter mark Bourne
spoke. "That's enough. Get up and walk past me with
your hands behind your back. Go straight ahead, shoul-
dering your way through the branches. My light's on your
hands. If you unclasp them I'll kill you. Am I clear?"

"You think I'd snap a limb back in your face?"

"*I* would."

"You're clear."

They reached the road in front of the eerily dark gate.
The distant shouts were clearer now, the advance party
was nearer. "Down the road," said Jason. "*Run!*" Three
minutes later he snapped on the penlight. "*Stop!*" he
shouted. "That pile of green over there, can you see it?"

"Where?" asked the breathless assassin.

"My beam's on it."

"They're branches, parts of the pine trees."

"Pull them away. *Hurry up!*"

The commando began throwing the branches aside, in moments revealing the black Shanghai sedan. It was time for the knapsack. Bourne spoke. "Follow my light, to the left of the hood."

"To what?"

"The tree with the white notch on the trunk. See it?"

"Yes."

"Under it, about eighteen inches in front, there's loose dirt. Beneath there's a knapsack. Dig it out for me."

"Fucking technician, aren't you."

"Aren't *you?*"

Without replying, the sullen killer dug through the dirt and pulled the knapsack out of the ground. With the straps in his right hand, he stepped forward as if to hand the bag to his captor. Then suddenly he swung the knapsack, sweeping it diagonally up toward Jason's weapon and the penlight as he lunged forward, the fingers of his hands spread like the extended claws of a furious cat.

Bourne was prepared. It was the precise moment *he* would have used to gain the advantage, however transient, for it would have given him the seconds he needed to race away into the darkness. He stepped back, smashing the automatic into the assassin's head as the lunging figure passed him.

He crashed his knee down into the back of the splayed-out commando, grabbing the assassin's right arm while clenching the penlight between his teeth.

"I *warned* you," said Jason, yanking the killer up by his right arm. "But I also *need* you. So instead of your life, we'll do a little bullet surgery." He put the barrel of his automatic laterally against the flesh of the assassin's arm muscle and pulled the trigger.

"*Jesus!*" screamed the killer as the spit echoed and blood erupted.

"No bone was broken," said Delta. "Only muscle tissue, and now you can forget about using your arm. You're fortunate that I'm a merciful man. In that knapsack is gauze and tape and disinfectant. You can repair yourself, Major. Then you're going to drive. You'll be my chauffeur in the People's Republic. You see, I'll be in the backseat with my gun at your head, and I have a map. If I were you, I wouldn't make a wrong turn."

· · ·

Twelve of Sheng Chou Yang's men raced to the gate, with only four flashlights among them.

"*Wei shemme? Cuo wu!*"

"*Mafan! Feng Kuang!*"

"*You mao bing!*"

"*Wei fan!*"

A dozen screaming voices were raised against the unlit floodlights, blaming everything and everyone from inefficiency to treachery. The gatehouse was checked; the electric switches and the telephone were found to be inoperative, the guard was nowhere in evidence. Several studied the coiled chain around the gate's lock and issued orders to the others. Since none could get out, they reasoned, the offenders had to be inside the sanctuary.

"*Biao!*" shouted the infiltrator who had been d'Anjou's false prisoner. "*Quan bu zai zheli!*" he shrieked, telling the others to share the lights and search the parking lot, the surrounding woods, and the swamps beyond. The hunters spread out with guns extended, racing across the parking area in different directions. Seven additional men arrived, only one carrying a flashlight. The false prisoner demanded it and proceeded to explain the situation so as to form another search party. He was countered by objections that one light among them was insufficient for the darkness. In frustration the organizer roared a series of profanities, ascribing incredible stupidity to everyone but himself.

The dancing flames of torches grew brighter as the last of the conspirators arrived from the glen, led by the striding figure of Sheng Chou Yang, the ceremonial sword swinging at his side in its belted scabbard. He was shown the coiled chain and apprised of the circumstances by the infiltrator.

"You're not thinking correctly," said Sheng, exasperated. "Your approach is wrong! That chain was not placed there by one of our people to keep the criminal or criminals inside. Instead, it was put there by the offender or the offenders to delay us, to keep *us* inside!"

"But there are too many obstacles—"

"Studied and considered!" shouted Sheng Chou Yang. "Must I repeat myself? These people are survivors. They stayed alive in that criminal battalion called Medusa because they considered everything! They *climbed* out!"

"Impossible," protested the younger man. "The top pipe and the extended panel of barbed wire are electrified, sir. Any weight in excess of thirty pounds activates them. That way the birds and animals are not electrocuted."

"Then they found the source of the current and shut it off!"

"The switches are *inside,* and at least seventy-five meters from the gate concealed in the ground. Even I'm not sure where they are."

"Send someone up," ordered Sheng.

The subordinate looked around. Twenty feet away two men were talking quietly, rapidly, to each other, and it was doubtful either had heard the heated conversation. "You!" said the young leader, pointing to the man on the left.

"Sir?"

"Scale the fence!"

"Yes, sir!" The lesser subordinate ran to the fence and leaped up, his hands gripping the open, crisscrossing squares of wire mesh, as his feet worked furiously below. He reached the top pipe and started over the angled panel of coiled barbed wire. *"Aiyaaa!"*

A shattering cascade of static was accompanied by blinding, blue-white bolts of fired electricity. His body rigid, his hair and eyebrows singed to their roots, the climber fell backward, hitting the earth with the impact of a heavy flat rock. Flashlight beams converged. The man was dead.

"The *truck!*" screamed Sheng. "This is *idiocy!* Bring out the truck and break through! Do as I say! *Instantly!*"

Two men raced into the parking lot and within seconds the roar of the truck's powerful engine filled the night. The gears whined as the reverse was found. The heavy truck lurched backward, its whole chassis shaking violently until it came to a sudden, leaden stop. The deflated tires spun, smoke curling up from the burning rubber. Sheng Chou Yang stared in growing apprehension and fury.

"The *others!*" he shrieked. "Start the others! *All* of them!"

One by one the vehicles were started, and one after another each lurched in reverse only to rattle and groan, sinking into the gravel, unable to move. In a frenzy, Sheng ran up to the gate, pulled out a gun, and fired twice into the coiled chain. A man on his right screamed, holding his bleeding forehead, as he fell to the ground. Sheng raised his face to the dark sky and screamed a primeval roar of protest. He yanked out his ceremonial sword and began crashing it repeatedly down on the chained lock of the gate. It was an exercise in futility.

The blade broke.

28

"There's the house, the one with the high stone wall," said CIA Case Officer Matthew Richards as he drove the car up the hill in Victoria Peak. "According to our information, there are marines all over the place, and it won't do me any goddamned good being seen with *you*."

"I gather you want to owe me a few more dollars," said Alex Conklin, leaning forward and peering through the windshield. "It's negotiable."

"I just don't want to be *involved*, for Christ's sake! And dollars I haven't got."

"Poor Matt, sad Matt. You take things too literally."

"I don't know what you're talking about."

"I'm not sure I do, either, but drive by the house as if you were going to somebody else's place. I'll tell you when to stop and let me out."

"You will?"

"Under conditions. Those are the dollars."

"Oh, shit."

"They're not hard to take and I may not even call them in. The way I see it now, I'll want to stay on ice and out of sight. In other words, I want a man inside. I'll call you several times a day asking you if our lunch or dinner dates are still on, or whether I'll see you at the Happy Valley Race—"

"Not *there*," interrupted Richards.

"All right, the Wax Museum—anything that comes to mind, except the track. If you say 'No, I'm busy,' I'll know I'm not being closed in on. If you say 'Yes,' I'll get out."

"I don't even know where the hell you're staying! You told me to pick you up on the corner of Granville and Carnarvon."

"My guess is that your unit will be called in to keep the lines straight and the responsibility where it belongs. The British will insist on it. They're not going to take a solo fall if D.C. blows it. These are touchy times for the Brits over here, so they'll cover their colonial asses."

They passed the gate. Conklin shifted his gaze and studied the large Victorian entrance.

"I swear, Alex, I don't know what you're talking about."

"That's better yet. Do you agree? Are you my guru inside?"

"Hell, yes. I can do without the marines."

"Fine. Stop here. I'll get out and walk back. As far as anyone's concerned I took the tram to the Peak, got a cab to the wrong house, and made my way to the right address only a couple of hundred feet down the road. Are you happy, Matt?"

"Ecstatic," said the case officer, scowling, as he braked the car.

"Get a good night's sleep. It's been a long time since Saigon, and we all need more rest as we get older."

"I heard you were a lush. It's not true, is it?"

"You heard what we wanted you to hear," replied Conklin flatly. This time, however, he was able to cross the fingers of both hands before he climbed awkwardly out of the car.

A brief knock and the door was flung open. Startled, Havilland looked up as Edward McAllister, his face ashen, walked rapidly into the room. "Conklin's at the gate," said the undersecretary. "He's demanding to see you and says he'll stay there all night if he has to. He also says if it gets chilly, he'll build a fire in the road to keep warm."

"Crippled or not, he hasn't lost his panache," said the ambassador.

"This is totally unexpected," continued McAllister,

massaging his right temple. "We're not prepared for a confrontation."

"It seems we haven't a choice. That's a public road out there, and it's the province of the colony's Fire Department in the event our neighbors become alarmed."

"Surely, he wouldn't—"

"Surely, he would," broke in Havilland. "Let him in. This isn't only unexpected, it's extraordinary. He hasn't had time to assemble his facts or organize an attack that would give him leverage. He's openly exposing his involvement, and given his background in covert to black operations, he wouldn't do that lightly. It's far too dangerous. He, himself, once gave the order for beyond-salvage."

"We can presume he's in touch with the *woman*," protested the undersecretary, heading for the telephone on the ambassador's desk. "That gives him all the facts he needs!"

"No, it doesn't. She hasn't got them."

"And you," said McAllister, his hand on the phone. "How does he know to come to *you?*"

Havilland smiled grimly. "All he'd have to hear is that I'm in Hong Kong. Besides, we spoke, and I'm sure he's put it all together."

"But this *house?*"

"He'll never tell us. Conklin's an old Far East hand, Mr. Undersecretary, and he has contacts we can't presume to know about. And we won't know what brings him here unless he's admitted, will we?"

"No, we won't." McAllister picked up the phone; he dialed three digits. "Officer of the Guard? . . . Let Mr. Conklin through the gate, search him for a weapon, and escort him yourself to the East Wing office. . . . He *what?* . . . Admit him quickly and put the damn thing out!"

"What happened?" asked Havilland as the undersecretary hung up the phone.

"He started a fire on the other side of the road."

Alexander Conklin limped into the ornate Victorian room as the marine officer closed the door. Havilland rose from the chair and came around the desk, his hand extended.

"Mr. Conklin?"

"Keep your hand, Mr. Ambassador. I don't want to get infected."

"I see. Anger precludes civility?"

"No, I really don't want to catch anything. As they say over here, you're rotten joss. You're carrying something. A disease, I think."

"And what might that be?"

"Death."

"So melodramatic? Come, Mr. Conklin, you can do better than that."

"No, I mean it. Less than twenty minutes ago I saw someone killed, cut down in the street with forty or fifty bullets in her. She was blown into the glass doors of her apartment house, her driver shot up in the car. I tell you the place is a mess, blood and glass all over the pavement—"

Havilland's eyes were wide with shock, but it was the hysterical voice of McAllister that stopped the CIA man. "Her? *She?* Was it the *woman?*"

"*A* woman," said Conklin, turning to the undersecretary, whose presence he had not yet acknowledged. "You McAllister?"

"Yes."

"I don't want to shake your hand either. She was involved with both of you."

"Webb's wife is *dead?*" yelled the undersecretary, his whole body paralyzed.

"No, but thanks for the confirmation."

"Good God!" cried the long-standing ambassador of the State Department's clandestine activities. "It was Staples. Catherine *Staples!*"

"Give the man an exploding cigar. And thanks again for the second confirmation. Are you planning to have dinner with the Canadian consulate's High Commissioner soon? I'd love to be there—just to watch the renowned Ambassador Havilland at work. Gosh and golly, I betcha us low-level types could learn an awful lot."

"*Shut up, you goddamned fool!*" shouted Havilland, crossing behind the desk and plummeting into his chair; he leaned back, his eyes closed.

"That's the one thing I'm *not* going to do," said Conklin, stepping forward, his clubbed foot pounding the floor. "You are *accountable . . . sir!*" The CIA man leaned over, gripping the edge of the desk. "Just as you're accountable for what's happened to David and Marie Webb! Who the *fuck* do you think you are? And if my language offends you, *sir,* look up the derivation of the offending word. It comes from a term in the Middle Ages meaning to plant a seed in the ground, and in a way that's your specialty! Only in your case they're rotten seeds—you dig in clean dirt and turn it into filth. Your seeds are lies and deception. They grow inside of *people,* turning them into angry and frightened puppets, dancing on *your* strings to *your* goddamned scenarios! I repeat, you aristocratic son of a bitch, who the fuck do you think you are?"

Havilland half opened his lidded eyes and leaned forward. His expression was that of an old man willing to die, if only to remove the pain. But those same eyes were alive with a cold fury that saw things others could not see. "Would it serve your argument if I said to you that Catherine Staples said essentially the same thing to me?"

"Serves it and completes it!"

"Yet she was killed because she joined forces with us. She didn't like doing that, but in her judgment there was no alternative."

"Another *puppet?*"

"No. A human being with a first-rate mind and a wealth of experience who understood what faced us. I mourn her loss—and the manner of her death—more than you can imagine."

"Is it her loss, *sir* or is it the fact that your holy operation was *penetrated?*"

"How *dare* you?" Havilland, his voice low and cold, rose from the chair and stared at the CIA man. "It's a little late for you to be moralizing, Mr. Conklin. Your lapses have been all too apparent in the areas of deception and ethics. If you'd had your way, there'd be no David Webb, no Jason Bourne. *You* put him beyond-salvage, no one else did. You planned his execution and nearly succeeded."

"I've paid for that lapse. *Christ,* how I've paid for it!"

"And I suspect you're still paying for it, or you wouldn't be in Hong Kong now," said the ambassador, nodding his head slowly, the coldness leaving his voice. "Lower your cannons, Mr. Conklin, and I'll do the same.

Catherine Staples really *did* understand, and if there's any meaning in her death, let's try to find it."

"I haven't the vaguest idea where to start looking."

"You'll be given chapter and verse . . . just as Staples was."

"Maybe I shouldn't hear it."

"I have no choice but to insist that you do."

"I guess you weren't listening. You've been penetrated! The Staples woman was killed because it was assumed she had information that called for her to be taken out. In short, the mole who's bored his way in here saw her in a meeting or meetings with both of you. The Canadian connection was made, the order given, and you let her walk around without protection!"

"Are you afraid for your life?" asked the ambassador.

"Constantly," replied the CIA man. "And right now I'm also concerned with someone else's."

"Webb's?"

Conklin paused, studying the old diplomat's face. "If what I believe is true," he said quietly. "There's nothing I can do for Delta that he can't do better for himself. But if he doesn't make it, I know what he'd ask me to do. Protect Marie. And I can do that best by fighting you, not listening to you."

"And how do you propose fighting me?"

"The only way I know how. Down and very dirty. I'll spread the word in all those dark corners in Washington that this time you've gone too far, you've lost your grip, maybe at your age even looney. I've got Marie's story, Mo Panov's—"

"*Morris* Panov?" interrupted Havilland cautiously. "Webb's psychiatrist?"

"You get another cigar. And, last of all, my own contribution. Incidentally, to jog your memory, I'm the only one who talked to David before he came over here. All together, including the slaughter of a Canadian foreign service officer, they'd make interesting reading—as affidavits, carefully circulated, of course."

"By so doing you'd jeopardize *everything.*"

"Your problem, not mine."

"Then, again, I'd have no choice," said the ambassador, ice once more in his eyes and in his voice. "As you issued an order for beyond-salvage, I'd be forced to do the same. You wouldn't leave here alive."

"*Oh, my God!*" whispered McAllister from across the room.

"That'd be the dumbest thing you could do," said Conklin, his eyes locked with Havilland's. "You don't know what I've left behind or with whom. Or what's released if I don't make contact by a certain time with certain people and so on. Don't underestimate me."

"We thought you might resort to that kind of tactic," said the diplomat, walking away from the CIA man as if dismissing him, and returning to his chair. "You also left something else behind, Mr. Conklin. To put it kindly, perhaps accurately, you were known to have a chronic illness called alcoholism. In anticipation of your imminent retirement, and in recognition of your long-past accomplishments, no disciplinary measures were taken, but neither were you given any responsibility. You were merely tolerated, a useless relic about to go to pasture, a drunk whose paranoid outbursts were the talk and concern of your colleagues. Whatever might surface from whatever source would be categorized and substantiated as the incoherent ramblings of a crippled, psychopathic alcoholic." The ambassador leaned back in the chair, his elbow resting on the arm, the long fingers of his right hand touching his chin. "You are to be pitied, Mr. Conklin, not censured. The dovetailing of events might be dramatized by your suicide—"

"*Havilland!*" cried McAllister, stunned.

"Rest easy, Mr. Undersecretary," said the diplomat. "Mr. Conklin and I know where we're coming from. We've both been there before."

"There's a difference," objected Conklin, his gaze never wavering from Havilland's eyes. "I never took any pleasure from the game."

"You think *I* do?" The telephone rang. Havilland shot forward, grabbing it. "Yes?" The ambassador listened, frowning, staring at the darkened bay window. "If I don't sound shocked, Major, it's because the news reached me a few minutes ago. . . . No, not the police but a man I want you to meet tonight. Say, in two hours, is that convenient? . . . Yes, he's one of us now." Havilland raised his eyes to Conklin. "There are those who say he's better

than most of us, and I daresay his past service record
might bear that out. . . . Yes, it's he. . . . Yes, I'll tell him.
. . . What? *What* did you say?" The diplomat again looked
at the bay window, the frown returning. "They covered
themselves quickly, didn't they? Two hours, Major."
Havilland hung up the phone, both elbows on the table,
his hands clasped. He took a deep breath, an exhausted
old man gathering his thoughts, about to speak.

"His name is Lin Wenzu," said Conklin, startling both
Havilland and McAllister. "He's Crown CI which means
MI-Six-oriented, probably Special Branch. He's Chinese
and U.K.-educated and considered about the best Intelligence officer in the territory. Only his size works against
him. He's easily spotted."

"*Where—?*" McAllister took a step toward the CIA
man.

"A little bird, Cock Robin," said Conklin.

"A redheaded cardinal, I presume," said the diplomat.

"Actually, not anymore," replied Alex.

"I see." Havilland unclasped his hands, lowering his
arms on the desk. "He knows who you are, too."

"He should. He was part of the detail at the Kowloon
station."

"He told me to congratulate you, to tell you that your
Olympian outraced them. He got away."

"He's sharp."

"He knows where to find him but won't waste the
time."

"Sharper still. Waste is waste. He told you something
else, too, and since I overheard your flattering assessment of my past, would you care to tell me what it was?"

"Then you'll listen to me?"

"Or be carried out in a box? Or boxes? Where's the
option?"

"Yes, quite true," said the diplomat. "I'd have to go
through with it, you know."

"I know *you* know, *Herr General.*"

"That's offensive."

"So are you. What did the major tell you?"

"A terrorist tong from Macao telephoned the South
China News Agency claiming responsibility for the killings. Only, they said the woman was incidental, the driver
was the target. As a native member of the hated British

secret security arm, he had shot to death one of their leaders on the Wanchai waterfront two weeks ago. The information was correct. He was the protection we assigned to Catherine Staples."

"It's a lie!" shouted Conklin. "*She* was the target!"

"Lin says it's a waste of time to pursue a false source."

"Then he knows?"

"That we've been penetrated?"

"What the hell *else?*" said the exasperated CIA man.

"He's a proud *Zhongguo ren* and has a brilliant mind. He doesn't like failure in any form, especially now. I suspect he's started his hunt. . . . Sit down, Mr. Conklin. We have things to talk about."

"I don't *believe* this!" cried McAllister in a deeply emotional whisper. "You talk of *killings*, of *targets*, of 'beyond -salvage' . . . of a mocked-up *suicide*—the victim *here*, talking about his own *death*—as if you were discussing the Dow-Jones or a restaurant menu! What kind of people *are* you?"

"I've told you, Mr. Undersecretary," said Havilland gently. "Men who do what others won't, or can't, or shouldn't. There's no mystique, no diabolical universities where we were trained, no driving compulsion to destroy. We drifted into these areas because there were voids to fill and the candidates were few. It's all rather accidental, I suppose. And with repetition you find that either you do or you don't have the stomach for it— because somebody has to. Would you agree, Mr. Conklin?"

"This is a waste of time."

"No, it's not," corrected the diplomat. "Explain to Mr. McAllister. Believe me, he's valuable and we need him. He has to understand us."

Conklin looked at the undersecretary of State, his expression without charity. "He doesn't need any explanations from me, he's an analyst. He sees it all as clearly as we do, if not clearer. He knows what the hell is going on down in the tunnels, he just doesn't want to admit it, and the easiest way to remove himself is to pretend to be shocked. Beware the sanctimonious intellect in any phase of this business. What he gives in brains he takes away with phony recriminations. He's the deacon in a whorehouse gathering material for a sermon he'll write when he goes home and plays with himself."

"You were right before," said McAllister, turning toward the door. "This is a waste of time."

"Edward?" Havilland, clearly angry with the crippled CIA man, called out sympathetically to the undersecretary. "We can't always choose the people we deal with, which is obviously the case now."

"I understand," said McAllister coldly.

"Study everyone on Lin's staff," went on the ambassador. "There can't be more than ten or twelve who know anything about us. Help him. He's your friend."

"Yes, he is," said the undersecretary, going out the door.

"Was that *necessary?*" snapped Havilland when he and Conklin were alone.

"Yes, it was. If you can convince me that what you've done was the only route you could take—which I doubt —or if I can't come up with an option that'll get Marie and David out with their lives, if not their sanity, then I'll have to work with you. The alternative of beyond-salvage is unacceptable on several grounds, basically personal, but also because I owe the Webbs. Do we agree so far?"

"We work together, one way or another. Checkmate."

"Given the reality, I want that son of a bitch, McAllister, that *rabbit,* to know where *I'm* coming from. He's in as deep as any of us, and that intellect of his had better go down into the filth and come up with every plausibility and every possibility. I want to know whom we should kill —even those marginally important—to cut our losses and get the Webbs out. I want him to know that the only way he can save his soul is to bury it with accomplishment. If we fail, *he* fails, and he can't go back teaching Sunday school anymore."

"You're too harsh on him. He's an analyst, not an executioner."

"Where do you think the executioners get their input? Where do *we* get our input? From whom? The paladins of congressional oversight?"

"Checkmate, again. You're as good as they say you were. He's come up with the breakthroughs. It's why he's here."

"Talk to me, *sir,*" said Conklin, sitting in the chair, his back straight, his club foot awkwardly at an angle. "I want to hear your story."

"First the woman. Webb's wife. She's all right? She's safe?"

"The answer to your first question is so obvious I wonder how you can ask it. No, she's not all right. Her husband's missing and she doesn't know whether he's alive or dead. As to the second, yes, she's safe. With me, not with you. I can move us around and I know my way around. You have to stay here."

"We're *desperate,*" pleaded the diplomat. "We need her!"

"You've also been penetrated, that doesn't seem to sink in. I won't expose her to that."

"This house is a fortress!"

"All it takes is one rotten cook in the kitchen. One lunatic on a staircase."

"Conklin, *listen* to me! We picked up a passport check —everything fits. It's him, we know it. Webb's in Peking. *Now!* He wouldn't have gone in if he wasn't after the target—the *only* target. If somehow, God knows how, your Delta comes out with the merchandise and his wife isn't in place, he'll kill the one connection we *must have!* Without it we're lost. We're all lost."

"So that was the scenario from the beginning. *Reductio ad absurdum.* Jason Bourne hunts Jason Bourne."

"Yes. Painfully simple, but without the escalating complications he never would have agreed. He'd still be in that old house in Maine, poring over his scholarly papers. We wouldn't have our hunter."

"You really *are* a bastard," said Conklin slowly, softly, a certain admiration in his voice. "And you were convinced he could still do it? Still handle this kind of Asia the way he did years ago as Delta?"

"He has physical checkups every three months, it's part of the government protection program. He's in superb condition—something to do with his obsessive running, I understand."

"Start at the beginning." The CIA man settled into the chair. "I want to hear it step by step because I think the rumors are true. I'm in the presence of a master bastard."

"Hardly, Mr. Conklin," said Havilland. "We're all groping. I'll want your comments, of course."

"You'll get them. Go ahead."

"All right. I'll begin with a name I'm sure you'll recognize. Sheng Chou Yang. Any comment?"

"He's a tough negotiator, and I suspect that underneath his benevolent exterior there's a ramrod. Still, he's one of the most reasonable men in Peking. There should be a thousand like him."

"If there were, the chances of a Far East holocaust would be a thousand times greater."

Lin Wenzu slammed his fist down on the desk, jarring the nine photographs in front of him and making the attached summaries of their dossiers leap off the surface. *Which?* Which *one?* Each had been certified through London, each background checked and rechecked and triple-checked; there was no room for error. These were not simply well-schooled *Zhongguo ren* selected by bureaucratic elimination but the products of an intensive search for the brightest minds in government—and in several cases outside of government—who might be recruited into this most sensitive of services. It had been Lin's contention that the writing was on the wall—the Great Wall, perhaps—and that a superior special Intelligence force manned by the colony's own could well be its first line of defense prior to 1997, and, in the event of a takeover, its first line of cohesive resistance afterwards. The British *had* to relinquish leadership in the area of secret Intelligence operations for reasons that were as clear as they were unpalatable to London: the Occidental could never fully understand the peculiar subtleties of the Oriental mind, and these were not the times to render misleading or poorly evaluated information. London had to know—the West had to know—exactly where things stood . . . for Hong Kong's sake, for the sake of the entire Far East.

Not that Lin believed that his growing task force of Intelligence gatherers was pivotal to policy decisions; he did not. But he believed thoroughly, intensely, that if the colony was to have a Special Branch it should be staffed and run by those who could do the job best, and that did not include veterans, however brilliant, of the European-oriented British secret services. For starters, they all looked alike and were not compatible with either the environment or the language. And after years of work and proven worth, Lin Wenzu had been summoned to London and for three days grilled by unsmiling Far East Intelligence specialists. On the morning of the fourth day, however, the smiles had appeared along with the recommendation that the major be given command of the Hong Kong branch with wide powers of authority. And for a number of years thereafter he had lived up to the commission's confidence, he knew that. He also knew that now, in the single most vital operation of his professional and personal life, he had failed. There were thirty-eight Special Branch officers in his command, and he had selected nine—hand-picked *nine*—to be part of this extraordinary, *insane* operation. Insane until he had heard the ambassador's extraordinary explanation. The nine were the most exceptional of the thirty-eight-man task force, each capable of assuming command if their leader was taken out; he had written as much in their evaluation reports. And he had failed. One of the hand-picked nine was a traitor.

It was pointless to restudy the dossiers. Whatever inconsistencies he might find would take too long to unearth, for they—or *it*—had eluded his own experienced eyes as well as London's. There was no time for intricate analyses, the painfully slow exploration of nine individual lives. He had only one choice. A frontal assault on each man, and the word "front" was intrinsic to his plan. If he could play the role of a taipan, he could play the part of a traitor. He realized that his plan was not without risk—a risk neither London nor the American, Havilland, would tolerate, but it had to be taken. If he failed, Sheng Chou Yang would be alerted to the secret war against him and his countermoves could be disastrous, but Lin Wenzu did not intend to fail. If failure was written on the northern winds, nothing else would matter, least of all his life.

The major reached for his telephone. He pushed the button on his console for the radio operator in the computerized communication center of MI6, Special Branch.

"Yes, sir?" said the voice from the white, sterile room.

"Who in Dragonfly is still on duty?" asked Lin, naming the elite unit of nine who reported in but never gave explanations.

"Two, sir. In vehicles three and seven, but I can reach the rest in a few minutes. Five have checked in—they're at home—and the remaining two have left numbers. One is at the Pagoda Cinema until eleven-thirty, when he'll return to his flat, but he can be reached by beeper until then. The other is at the Yacht Club in Aberdeen with his wife and her family. She's English, you know."

Lin laughed softly. "No doubt charging the British family's bill to our woefully inadequate budget from London."

"Is that possible, Major? If so, would you consider me for Dragonfly, whatever it is?"

"Don't be impertinent."

"I'm sorry, sir—"

"I'm joking, young man. Next week I'll take you to a fine dinner myself. You do excellent work and I rely on you."

"Thank you, sir!"

"The thanks are mine."

"Shall I contact Dragonfly and put out an alert?"

"You may contact each and every one, but quite the opposite of an alert. They've all been overworked, without a clean day off in several weeks. Tell each that, of course, I want any changes of locations to be reported, but unless informed otherwise we're secure for the next twenty-four hours, and the men in vehicles three and seven may drive them home but not up into the Territories for drinks. Tell them I said they should all get a good night's sleep, or however they wish to pass the time."

"Yes, sir. They'll appreciate that, sir."

"I myself will be wandering around in vehicle four. You may hear from me. Stay awake."

"Of course, Major."

"You've got a dinner coming, young man."

"If I may, sir," said the enthusiastic radio operator, "and I know I speak for all of us. We wouldn't care to work for anyone but you."

"Perhaps two dinners."

. . .

Parked in front of an apartment house on Yun Ping Road, Lin lifted the microphone out of its cradle below the dashboard. "Radio, it's Dragonfly Zero."

"Yes, sir?"

"Switch me to a direct telephone line with a scrambler. I'll know we're on scrambler when I hear the echo on my part of the call, won't I?"

"Naturally, sir."

The faint echo pulsated over the line, with the dial tone. The major punched in the numbers; the ringing began and a female voice answered.

"Yes?"

"Mr. Zhou. *Kuai!*" said Lin, his words rushed, telling the woman to hurry.

"Certainly," she replied in Cantonese.

"Zhou here," said the man.

"*Xun su! Xiao Xi!*" Lin spoke in a throated whisper; it was the sound of a desperate man pleading to be heard. "Sheng! Contact instantly! Sapphire is gone!"

"*What?* Who *is* this?"

The major pressed down the bar and pushed a button to the right of the microphone. The radio operator spoke instantly.

"Yes, Dragonfly?"

"Patch into my private line, also on scrambler, and reroute all calls here. Right *away!* This will be standard procedure until I instruct otherwise. *Understood?*"

"Yes, sir," said a subdued radioman.

The mobile phone buzzed and Lin picked it up, speaking casually. "Yes?" he answered, feigning a yawn.

"Major, this is Zhou! I just had a very strange call. A man phoned me—he sounded badly hurt—and told me to contact someone named Sheng. I was to say that Sapphire was *gone.*"

"*Sapphire?*" said the major, suddenly alert. "Say nothing to anyone, Zhou! Damned computers—I don't know how it happened, but that call was meant for me. This is beyond Dragonfly. I repeat, say nothing to anyone!"

"Understood, sir."

Lin started the car and drove several blocks west to Tanlung Street. He repeated the exercise, and again the call came over his private line.

"*Major?*"

"Yes?"

"I just got off the phone with someone who sounded like he was *dying!* He wanted me to . . ."

The explanation was the same: a dangerous error had been made, beyond the purview of Dragonfly. Nothing was to be repeated. The order was understood.

Lin called three more numbers, each time from in front of each recipient's apartment or boardinghouse. All were negative; each man reached him within moments after a call with his startling news and none had raced outside to a random sterile pay phone. The major knew only one thing for certain. Whoever the infiltrator was, he would not use his home phone to make contact. Telephone bills recorded all numbers dialed, and all bills were submitted for departmental audit. It was a routine containment procedure that was welcomed by the agents. Excess charges were picked up by Special Branch as if they were related to business.

The two men in vehicles three and seven, having been relieved of duty, had checked in with headquarters by the fifth telephone call. One was at a girlfriend's house and made it plain that he had no intention of leaving for the next twenty-four hours. He pleaded with the radioman to take all "emergency calls from clients," telling everyone who tried to reach him that his superiors had sent him to the Antarctic. *Negative. It was not the way of a double agent, including the humor. He neither cut himself off nor revealed the whereabouts or the identity of a drop.* The second man was, if possible, more negative. He informed headquarters-communications that he was available for any and all problems, major or minor, related or unrelated to Dragonfly, even to answering the phones. His wife had recently given birth to triplets, and he confided in a voice that bordered on panic—according to the radioman—he got more rest on the job than at home. *Negative.*

Seven down and seven negative. That left one man at the Pagoda Cinema for another forty minutes, and the other at the Yacht Club in Aberdeen.

His mobile phone hummed—emphatically, it seemed, or was it his own anxiety? "Yes?"

"I just received a message for you, sir," said the radio operator. " 'Eagle to Dragonfly Zero. Urgent. Respond.' "

"Thank you." Lin looked at the clock in the center of the dashboard. He was thirty-five minutes late for his appointment with Havilland and the legendary crippled agent from years past, Alexander Conklin. "Young man?" said the major, bringing the microphone back to his lips.

"Yes, sir?"

"I have no time for the anxious if somewhat irrelevant 'Eagle,' but I don't wish to offend him. He'll call again when I don't respond, and I want you to explain that you've been unable to reach me. Of course, when you do, you'll give me the message immediately."

"It will be a delight, Major."

"I beg your pardon?"

"The 'Eagle' who called was very disagreeable. He shouted about appointments that should be kept when they were confirmed and that . . ."

Lin listened to the secondhand diatribe and made a mental note that if he survived the night he would talk to Edward McAllister about telephone etiquette, especially during emergencies. Sugar brought gentle expressions, salt only grimaces. "Yes, yes, I understand, young man. As our ancestors might say, 'May the eagle's beak be caught in its elimination canal.' Just do as I say, and in the meantime—in fifteen minutes from now—raise our man at the Pagoda Cinema. When he calls in, give him my unlisted fourth-level number and patch it into this frequency, scrambler continuing, of course."

"Of course, sir."

Lin sped east on Hennessy Road past Southorn Park to Fleming, where he turned south into Johnston and east again on Burrows Street and the Pagoda Cinema. He swerved into the parking lot, taking the spot reserved for the assistant manager. He stuck a police card in the front window, got out, and ran up to the entrance. There were only a few people at the window for the midnight showing of *Lust in the Orient,* an odd choice for the agent inside. Nevertheless, to avoid calling attention to himself, since he had six minutes to go, he stood behind three men who were waiting in front of the booth. Ninety seconds later he had paid for and received his ticket. He went inside, gave it to the taker, and adjusted his eyes to the darkness and to the pornographic motion picture on the distant screen. It *was* an odd choice of entertainment for the man he was testing, but he had vowed to himself he would permit no prejudgments, no balancing of one suspect against another.

It was admittedly difficult in this case, however. Not that he particularly liked the man who was somewhere in that darkened theater, watching along with the feverishly attentive audience the sexual gymnastics of the wooden "actors." In truth he did *not* like the man; he simply recognized the fact that he was among the best in his command. The agent was arrogant and unpleasant, but he was also a brave soul whose defection from Beijing was eighteen months in the making, his every hour in the Communist capital a threat to his life. He had been a high-ranking officer in the Security Forces, with access to invaluable Intelligence information. And in a heartrending gesture of sacrifice he had left behind a beloved wife and girl child when he escaped south, protecting them with a charred, bullet-ridden corpse that he made sure was identified as himself—a hero of China shot and then burned by a roving band of hoodlums in the recent crime wave that had swept through the Mainland. Mother and daughter were secure, pensioned by the government, and like all high-level defectors, he was subjected to the most rigorous examinations designed to trap potential infiltrators. Here his arrogance had actually helped him. He had made no attempt to ingratiate himself; he was what he was and he had done what he had done for the good of Mother China. Either the authorities could accept him with all he had to offer or he would look elsewhere. Everything checked, except the well-being of his wife and child. They were not being taken care of in the manner the defector had expected. Therefore money was filtered through to her place of work without explanation. She could be told nothing; if there was the slightest suspicion that her husband was alive, she could be tortured for information she did not possess. The in-depth profile of such a man was not the profile of a double agent, regardless of his taste in films.

That left the man in Aberdeen, and he was something of a puzzle to Lin. The agent was older than the others, a small man who always dressed impeccably, a logician and former accountant who professed such loyalty that once Lin had almost made him a confidant, but had pulled himself up short when he was close to revealing things he should not reveal. Perhaps because the man was nearer his own age he felt a stronger kinship. . . . On the other hand, what an extraordinary cover for a mole from Beijing. Married to an Englishwoman, and a member of the rich and social Yacht Club by way of marriage. Everything was in place for him; he was respectability itself. It seemed incredible to Lin that his closest colleague, the man who had imposed such order on his personal life but still wanted to arrest an Australian brawler for causing Dragonfly to lose face, could have been reached by Sheng Chou Yang and corrupted. . . . No, *impossible!* Perhaps, thought the major, he should go back and examine further a comical off-duty agent who wanted all clients to be told he was in the Antarctic, or the overworked father of triplets who was willing to answer phones to escape his domestic chores.

These speculations were not in order! Lin Wenzu shook his head as if ridding his mind of such thoughts. *Now. Here. Concentrate!* His sudden decision to move came from the sight of a stairway. He walked over to it and climbed the steps to the balcony; the projection room was directly in front of him. He knocked once on the door and went inside, the weight of his body breaking the cheap, thin bolt on the door.

"Ting zhi!" yelled the projectionist; a woman was on his lap, his hand under her skirt. The young woman leaped away from her perch and turned to the wall.

"Crown Police," said the major, showing his identification. "And I mean no harm to either of you, please believe that."

"You shouldn't!" replied the projectionist. "This isn't exactly a place of worship."

"That might be disputed, but it certainly isn't a church."

"We operate with a fully paid license—"

"You have no argument from me, sir," interrupted Lin. "The Crown simply needs a favor, and it could hardly be against your interests to provide it."

"What is it?" asked the man, getting up, angrily watching the woman slip through the door.

"Stop the film for, say, thirty seconds and turn up the

lights. Announce to the audience that there was a break and that it will be repaired quickly."

The projectionist winced. "It's almost over! There'll be screaming!"

"As long as there are lights. *Do it!*"

The projector ground down with a whir; the lights came up, and the announcement was made over the loudspeaker. The projectionist was right. Catcalls echoed throughout the motion picture house, accompanied by waving arms and numerous extended third fingers. Lin's eyes scanned the audience—back and forth, row by row.

There was his man. . . . *Two* men—the agent was leaning forward talking to someone Lin Wenzu had never seen before. The major looked at his watch, then turned to the projectionist. "Is there a public phone downstairs?"

"When it works, there is. When it isn't broken."

"Is it working now?"

"I don't know."

"Where is it?"

"Below the staircase."

"Thank you. Start the film again in sixty seconds."

"You said thirty!"

"I've changed my mind. And you do enjoy the privileges of a good job because of a license, don't you?"

"They're *animals* down there!"

"Put a chair against the door," said Lin, going outside. "The lock's broken."

In the lobby beneath the staircase the major passed the exposed pay phone. Barely pausing, he yanked the spiral cord out of the box, and proceeded outside to his car, stopping at the sight of a phone booth across the road. He raced over and read the number, instantly memorizing it, and ran back to the car. He climbed into the seat and looked at his watch; he backed up the automobile, drove out into the street, and double-parked several hundred feet beyond the theater's marquee. He turned his headlights off and watched the entrance.

A minute and fifteen seconds later the defector from Beijing emerged, looking first to his right, then to his left, obviously agitated. He then looked straight ahead, seeing what he wanted to see, what Lin expected him to see, since the telephone in the theater was not working. It was the phone booth on the other side of the road. Lin dialed as his subordinate ran over to it, spinning into the plastic shell that faced the street. It rang before the man could insert his coins.

"*Xun su! Xiao Xi!*" Lin coughed as he whispered. "I knew you would find the phone! *Sheng!* Contact instantly! Sapphire is *gone!*" He replaced the microphone, but left his hand on the instrument, expecting to remove it with the agent's incoming call on his private line.

It did not come. He turned in his seat and looked back at the open, plastic shell of the pay phone across the road. The agent had dialed another number, but the defector was not speaking to him. There was no need to drive to Aberdeen.

The major silently got out of the car, walked across the street into the shadows of the far pavement, and started toward the pay phone. He stayed in the relative darkness, moving slowly, calling as little attention to his bulk as he could, cursing, as he often did, the genes that had produced his outsized figure. Remaining well back in the shadows, he approached the phone. The defector was eight feet away, his back to Lin, talking excitedly, exasperation in every sentence.

"Who is *Sapphire?* Why this *telephone?* Why would he reach *me?* . . . No, I *told* you, he used the leader's name! . . . Yes, that's right, his *name!* No code, no symbol! It was *insane!*"

Lin Wenzu heard all he had to hear. He pulled out his service automatic and walked rapidly out of the darkness.

"The film broke and they turned up the lights! My contact and I were—"

"Hang up the phone!" ordered the major.

The defector spun around. "*You!*" he screamed.

Lin rushed the man, his immense body crushing the double agent into the plastic shell as he grabbed the phone, smashing it into the metal box. "*Enough!*" he roared.

Suddenly, he felt the blade slicing with ice-cold heat into his abdomen. The defector crouched, the knife in his left hand, and Lin squeezed the trigger. The sound of the explosion filled the quiet street as the traitor dropped to the pavement, his throat ripped open by the bullet, blood streaming down his clothes, staining the concrete below.

"*Ni made!*" screamed a voice on the major's left, cursing him. It was the second man, the contact who had been inside the theater talking with the defector. He raised a gun and fired as the major lunged, and Lin's huge bleeding torso fell into the man like a wall. Flesh blew apart in Lin's upper right chest, but the killer's balance was shaken. The major fired his automatic; the man fell clutching his right eye. He was dead.

Across the street, the pornographic film had ended and the crowd began to emerge on the street, sullen, angry, ungratified. And with what remained of his enormous strength, the badly wounded Lin picked up the bodies of the two dead conspirators and half dragged, half carried them back to his car. A number of people from the Pagoda's audience watched him with glazed or disinterested stares. What they saw was a reality they could not contend with or comprehend. It was beyond the narrow confines of their fantasies.

Alex Conklin rose from the chair and limped awkwardly, noisily to the darkened bay window. "What the *hell* do you want me to say?" he asked, turning and looking at the ambassador.

"That given the circumstances I took the only road open to me, the only one that would have recruited Jason Bourne." Havilland held up his hand. "Before you answer, I should tell you in all fairness that Catherine Staples did not agree with me. She felt I should have appealed to David Webb directly. He was, after all, a Far East scholar, an expert who would understand stakes, the tragedy that could follow."

"She was nuts," said Alex. "He would have told you to shove it."

"Thank you for that." The diplomat nodded his head.

"Just hold it," Conklin broke in. "He would have said that to you not because he thought you were wrong, but because he didn't think he could *do* it. What you did—by taking Marie away from him—was to make him go back and be someone he wanted to forget."

"Oh?"

"You really *are* one son of a bitch, you son of a bitch."

Sirens suddenly erupted, ringing throughout the enormous house and the grounds, as searchlights began spinning through the windows. Gunfire accompanied the sound of smashing metal as tires screeched outside. The ambassador and the CIA man lurched to the floor; in seconds it was all over. Both men got to their feet as the door was crashed open. His chest and stomach drenched in blood, Lin Wenzu staggered in, carrying two dead bodies under his arms.

"Here is your traitor, sir," said the major, dropping both corpses. "And a colleague. With these two, I believe we've cut off Dragonfly from Sheng—" Wenzu's eyes rolled upward until the sockets were white. He gasped and fell to the floor.

"Call an *ambulance!*" shouted Havilland to the people who had gathered at the door.

"Get gauze, tape, towels, antiseptic—for Christ's sake, anything you can *find!*" yelled Conklin, limping, racing over to the fallen Chinese. "Stop the goddamned *bleeding!*"

29

Bourne sat in the racing shadows of the backseat, the intermittent moonlight bright, creating brief explosions of light and dark inside the automobile. At sudden, irregular, unexpected moments he leaned forward and pressed the barrel of his gun into the back of his prisoner's neck. "Try crashing off the road and there's a bullet in your head. Do you understand me?"

And always there was the same reply, or a variation of it, spoken in a clipped British accent. "I'm not a fool. You're behind me and you've got a weapon and I can't see you."

Jason had ripped the rearview mirror from its bracket, the bolt having cracked easily in his hand. "Then I'm your eyes back here, remember that. I'm also the end of your life."

"Understood," the former officer in the Royal Commandos repeated without expression.

The government road map spread out on his lap, the penlight cupped in his left hand, the automatic in his right, Bourne studied the roads heading south. As each half hour passed and landmarks were spotted, Jason understood that time was his enemy. Although the assassin's right arm was effectively immobilized, Bourne knew he was no match for the younger, stronger man in sheer stamina. The concentrated violence of the last three days had taken its toll physically, mentally, and—whether he cared to acknowledge it or not—emotionally, and while Jason Bourne did not have to acknowledge it, David Webb proclaimed it with every fiber of his emotional being. The scholar had to be kept at bay, deep down inside, his voice stilled.

Leave me alone! You're worthless to me!

Every now and then Jason felt the dead weight of his lids closing over his eyes. He would snap them open and abuse some part of his body, pinching hard the soft sensitive flesh of his inner thigh or digging his nails into his lips, to create instant pain so as to dispel the exhaustion. He recognized his condition—only a suicidal fool would not—and there was no time or place to remedy it with an axiom he had stolen from Medusa's Echo. *Rest is a weapon, never forget it.* Forget it, Echo . . . brave Echo . . . there's no time for rest, no place to find it.

And while he accepted his own assessment of himself, he also had to accept his evaluation of his prisoner. The killer was totally alert; his sharpness was in his skill at the wheel, for Jason demanded speed over the strange, unfamiliar roads. It was in his constantly moving head, and it was in his eyes whenever Bourne saw them, and he saw them frequently whenever he directed the assassin to slow down and watch for an off-shooting road on the right or the left. The imposter would turn in the seat—the sight of his so-familiar features always a shock to Jason—and ask whether the road ahead was the one his *"eyes"* wanted. The questions were superfluous; the former commando was continuously making his own assessment of his captor's physical and mental condition. He was a trained killer, a lethal machine who knew that survival depended on gaining the advantage over his enemy. He was waiting, watching, anticipating the moment when his adversary's eyelids might close for that brief instant or when the weapon might suddenly drop to the floor, or his enemy's head might recline for a second into the comfort of the backseat. These were the signs he was waiting for, the lapses he could capitalize on to violently alter the circumstances. Bourne's defense, therefore, depended upon his mind, in doing the unexpected so that the psychological balance remained in his favor. How long could it last—could *he* last?

Time was his enemy, the assassin in front of him a secondary problem. In his past—that vaguely remembered past—he had handled killers before, manipulated them before, because they were human beings subject to the wiles of his imagination. *Christ,* it came down to that! So simple, so logical—and he was so tired. . . . His *mind.* There was nothing else left! He had to keep thinking, had to keep prodding his imagination and make it do its work. Balance, *balance!* He had to keep it on *his* side! *Think. Act.* Do the *unexpected!*

He removed the silencer from his weapon, leveled the gun at the closed right-front window, and pulled the trigger. The explosion was ear-shattering, reverberating throughout the enclosed car, as the glass splintered, blowing out into the rushing night air.

"What the hell was *that* for?" screamed the impostor-assassin, clutching the wheel, holding an involuntary swerve in control.

"To teach you about balance," answered Jason. "You should understand that I'm unbalanced. The next shot could blow your head away."

"You're a fucking *lunatic,* that's what you are!"

"I'm glad you understand."

The map. One of the more civilized things about a PRC road map—and consistent with the quality of its vehicles—was the starred indicators of garages which were open twenty-four hours a day along the major routes. One had only to think of the confusion that might result from military and official transports breaking down to understand the necessity; it was heaven-sent for Bourne.

"There's a gas station about four miles down this road," he said to the assassin—to *Jason Bourne,* he reflected. "Stop and refill and don't say a word—which would be foolish if you tried, because you obviously can't speak the language. You must memorize the few pathetic words you need."

"You *do* speak it?"

"It's why I'm the original and you're the fake."

"You can bloody well *have* it, Mr. *Original!*"

Jason fired the gun again, blowing the rest of the window away. "The *fake!*" he yelled, raising his voice over the sound of the wind. "Remember that."

Time was the enemy.

He took a mental inventory of what he had, and it was not much. Money was his primary ammunition; he had more than a hundred Chinese could make in a hundred lifetimes, but money in itself was not the answer. Only time was the answer. If he had a prayer to get out of the vast land of China, it had to be by air, not on the ground. He would not last that long. Again, he studied the map. It would take thirteen to fifteen hours to reach Shanghai —*if* the car held up and if *he* held up, and if *they* could get by the provincial checkpoints where he knew there would be alarms out for a Westerner, or two Westerners, attempting to pass through. He would be taken—*they* would be taken. And even if they reached Shanghai, with its relatively lax airport, how many complications might arise?

There was an option—there were always options. It was crazy and outrageous, but it was the only thing left.

Time was the enemy. Do it. There is no other choice.

He circled a small symbol on the outskirts of the city of Jinan. An airport.

Dawn. Wetness everywhere. The ground, the tall grass, and the metal fence glistened with morning dew. The single runway beyond was a shining black shaft cutting across the close-cropped field, half green with today's moisture, half dullish brown from the pounding of yesterday's broiling sun. The Shanghai sedan was far off the airport road, as far off as the assassin could drive it, again concealed by foliage. The impostor was once more immobilized, now by the thumbs. Pressing the gun into his right temple, Jason had ordered the assassin to wind the spools of wire into double slipknots around each thumb, and then he had snapped the spools away with his cutter, run the wire back and coiled the two remaining strands tightly around the killer's wrists. As the commando discovered, with any slight pressure, such as twisting or separating his hands, the wire dug deeper into his flesh.

"If I were you," said Bourne, "I'd be careful. Can you imagine what it would be like having no thumbs? Or if your wrists were cut?"

"Fucking technician!"

"Believe it."

Across the airfield a light was turned on in a one-story building with a row of small windows along the side. It was a barracks of sorts, simple in design and functional. Then there were other lights—naked bulbs, the glows more like glares. A barracks. Jason reached for the coiled roll of clothing he had removed from the small of his back; he undid the straps, unfurled the garments over the grass and separated them. There was a large Mao jacket, a pair of rumpled outsized trousers, and a visored cloth hat that was standard for the clothes. He put on the hat and the jacket, buttoning the latter over his dark sweater, then stood up and pulled the large trousers over his own. A webbed cloth belt held them in place. He smoothed the drab, bulky jacket over the trousers, and turned to the assassin, who was watching him with astonishment and curiosity.

"Get over to the fence," said Jason, bending down and digging into his knapsack. "Get on your knees and lean into it," he continued, pulling out a five-foot length of thin nylon rope. "Press your face into the links. Eyes front! Hurry *up!*"

The killer did as he was told, his bound hands awkwardly, painfully in front of him between his body and the fence, his head pressed into the wire mesh. Bourne walked rapidly over and quickly threaded the rope through the fence on the right side of the assassin's neck, and with his fingers reaching through the open squares he swung the line across the commando's face and pulled the rope back through. He yanked it taut and knotted it at the base of the assassin's skull. He had worked so swiftly and so unexpectedly that the former officer could barely get out the words before he realized what had happened. "What the *hell* are you—oh, *Christ!*"

"As that maniac remarked about d'Anjou before he

hacked into his head, you're not going anywhere, Major."

"You're going to *leave* me here?" asked the killer, stunned.

"Don't be foolish. We're on the buddy system. Where I go, you go. Actually, you're going first."

"Where?"

"Through the fence," said Jason, taking the wire cutter from the knapsack. He began cutting a pattern around the assassin's torso, relieved that the wire links were nowhere near as thick as those at the bird sanctuary. The outline complete, Bourne stepped back and raised his right foot, placing it between the impostor's shoulder blades. He shoved his leg forward. Killer and fence fell collapsing onto the grass on the other side.

"Jesus!" cried the commando in pain. "Pretty fucking funny, aren't you?"

"I don't feel remotely amusing," replied Jason. "Every move I make is very unfunny, very serious. Get up and keep your voice down."

"For Christ's sake, I'm tied to the damn fence!"

"It's free. Get up and turn around." Awkwardly the assassin staggered to his feet. Bourne surveyed his work; the sight of the outline of wire mesh attached to the killer's upper body, as though held in place by a protruding nose, *was* funny. But the reason for its being there was not funny at all. Only with the assassin secure in front of his eyes was all risk eliminated. Jason could not control what he could not see, and what he could not see could cost him his life. . . . Far more important, the life of David Webb's wife—even David Webb. *Stay away from me! Don't interfere! We're too close!*

Bourne reached over and yanked the bowknot free, holding on to one end of the line. The fence fell away, and before the assassin could adjust, Jason whipped the rope around the commando's head, raising it so that the line was caught in the killer's mouth. He pulled it tight, *tighter*, stretching the assassin's jaw open until it was a gaping dark hole surrounded by a border of white teeth, the flesh creased in place, unintelligible sounds emerging from the commando's throat.

"I can't take credit for this, Major," said Bourne, knotting the thin nylon rope, the remaining thirty-odd inches hanging loose. "I watched d'Anjou and the others. They couldn't talk, they could only gag on their own vomit. You saw them, too, and you grinned. How does it feel, Major? . . . Oh, I forgot, you can't answer, can you?" He shoved the assassin forward, then gripped his shoulder, sending him to the left. "We'll skirt the end of the runway," he said. *"Move!"*

As they rounded the airfield grass, staying in the darkness of the borders, Jason studied the relatively primitive airport. Beyond the barracks was a small circular building with a profusion of glass but no lights shining except a single glare in a small square structure set in the center of the roof. The building was Jinan's terminal, he thought, the barely lit square on top the control tower. To the left of the barracks, at least two hundred feet to the west, was a dark, open, high-ceilinged maintenance hangar with huge wheeled ladders near the wide doors reflecting the early light. It was apparently deserted, with the crews still in their quarters. Down in the southern perimeter of the field, on both sides of the runway and barely discernible, were five aircraft, all props and none imposing. The Jinan Airport was a secondary, even tertiary, landing field, undoubtedly being upgraded, as were so many airports in China in the cause of foreign investment, but it was a long way from international status. Then, again, the air corridors were channels in the sky and not subject to the cosmetic or technological whims of airports. One simply had to enter those channels and stay on course. The sky acknowledged no borders; only earthbound men and machines did. Combined, they were another problem.

"We're going into the hangar," whispered Jason, jabbing the commando's back. "Remember, if you make any noise, I won't have to kill you—they will. And I'll have my chance to get away because you'll be giving it to me. Don't doubt it. Get *down!"*

Thirty yards away a guard walked out of the cavernous structure, a rifle slung over his shoulder, his arms stretching as his chest swelled with a yawn. Bourne knew it was the moment to act; a better one might not present itself. The assassin was prone, his wire-bound hands beneath him, his gaping mouth pressed into the earth. Grabbing the loose nylon rope, Jason gripped the killer's hair, yanking up his head, and looped the line twice around the commando's neck. "You move, you *choke*," whispered Bourne, getting to his feet.

He ran silently to the hangar's wall, then quickly walked to the corner and peered around the edge. The guard had barely moved. Then Jason understood—the man was urinating. Perfectly natural and perfectly perfect. Bourne stepped away from the building, dug his right foot into the grass and rushed forward, his weapon a rigid right hand preceded by an arcing left foot striking the base of the guard's spine. The man collapsed, unconscious. Jason dragged him back to the corner of the hangar, then across the grass to where the assassin lay immobile, afraid to move.

"You're learning, Major," said Bourne, again grabbing the commando's hair and pulling the nylon rope from around his neck. The fact that the looped rope would not have choked the impostor, any more than a loose clothesline wound around a person's neck would, told Delta something. His prisoner could not think geometrically; stresses were not a strong point in the killer's imagination, only the spoken threat of death. It was something to bear in mind. "Get up," ordered Jason. The assassin did so, his gaping mouth swallowing air, his eyes full of hatred. "Think about Echo," said Bourne, his own eyes returning the killer's loathing. "Excuse me, I mean d'Anjou. The man who gave you your life back—*a* life, at any rate, and one you apparently took to. Your Pygmalion, *old chap!* . . . Now, hear me, and hear me well. Would you like the rope removed?"

"*Auggh!*" grunted the assassin, nodding his head, his eyes reduced from hatred to pleading.

"And your thumbs released?"

"*Auggh, auggh!*"

"You're not a guerrilla, you're a gorilla," said Jason, pulling the automatic from his belt. "But as we used to say in the old days—before your time, *chap*—there are 'conditions.' You see, either we both get out of here alive, or we disappear, our mortal remains consigned to a Chinese fire, no past, no present—certainly no retrospective regarding our subzero contributions to society. . . . I see I'm boring you. Sorry, I'll forget the whole thing."

"*Auggh!*"

"Okay, if you insist. Naturally, I won't give you a

weapon, and if I see you trying to grab one, you're dead. But if you behave, we might—just *might*—get away. What I'm really saying to you, Mr. *Bourne,* is that whoever your client is over here can't allow you to live any more than he can *me.* Understand? Dig? *Capisce?*"

"*Auggh!*"

"One thing more," added Jason, tugging at the rope that fell over the commando's shoulder. "This is nylon, or polyurethane, or whatever the hell they call it. When it's burned, it just swells up like a marshmallow; there's no way you can untie it. It'll be attached to both your ankles, both knots curled up into cement. You'll have a step-span of approximately five feet—only because I'm a technician. Do I make myself clear?"

The assassin nodded, and as he did so Bourne sprang to his right, kicking the back of the commando's knees, sending the impostor to the ground, his bound thumbs bleeding. Jason knelt down, the gun in his left hand pressed into the killer's mouth, the fingers of his right undoing the bowknot behind the commando's head.

"Christ *Almighty!*" cried the assassin as the rope fell away.

"I'm glad you're of a religious persuasion," said Bourne, dropping the weapon and rapidly lashing the rope around the commando's ankles, forming a square knot on each; he ignited his lighter and fired the ends. "You may need it." He picked up the gun, held it against the killer's forehead, and uncoiled the wire around his prisoner's wrists. "Take off the rest," he ordered. "Be careful with the thumbs, they're damaged."

"My right arm's no piece of cake, either!" said the Englishman, struggling to remove the slipknots. His hands freed, the assassin shook them, then sucked the blood from his wounds. "You got your magic box, Mr. *Bourne?*" he asked.

"Always an arm's length away, Mr. Bourne," replied Jason. "What do you need?"

"Tape. Fingers bleed. It's called gravity."

"You're well schooled." Bourne reached behind him for the knapsack and pulled it forward, dropping it in front of the commando, his gun leveled at the killer's head. "Feel around. It's a spool near the top."

"Got it," said the assassin, removing the tape and rapidly winding it around his thumbs. "This is one rotten fucking thing to do to anybody," he added when he had finished.

"Think of d'Anjou," said Jason flatly.

"He *wanted* to die, for Christ's sake! What the hell was *I* supposed to do?"

"Nothing. Because you are nothing."

"Well then, that kind of puts me on *your* level, doesn't it, sport? He made me into *you!*"

"You don't have the talent," said Jason Bourne. "You're lacking. You can't think geometrically."

"What does *that* mean?"

"Ponder it." Delta rose to his feet. "Get up," he commanded.

"Tell me," said the assassin, pushing himself off the ground and staring at the weapon aimed at his head. "Why *me?* Why did you ever get out of the business?"

"Because I was never in it."

Suddenly, floodlights—one after another—began to wash over the field, and with a single brilliant illumination, yellow marker lights appeared along the entire length of the runway. Men ran out of the barracks, a number toward the hangar, others behind their quarters where the engines of unseen vehicles abruptly roared. The lights of the terminal were turned on; activity was at once everywhere.

"Take his jacket off and the hat," ordered Bourne, pointing the gun at the unconscious guard. "Put them on."

"They won't fit!"

"You can have them altered in Savile Row. *Move!*"

The impostor did as he was told, his right arm so much a problem that Jason had to hold the sleeve for him. With Bourne prodding the commando with the gun, both men ran to the wall of the hangar, then moved cautiously toward the end of the building.

"Do we agree?" asked Bourne, whispering, looking at the face that was so like his own years ago. "We get out or we die?"

"Understood," answered the commando. "That screaming bastard with his bloody fancy sword is a fucking lunatic. I want out!"

"That reaction wasn't on your face."

"If it had been, the maniac might have turned on me!"

"Who is he?"

"Never got a name. Only a series of connections to reach him. The first was a man at the Guangdong garrison named Soo Jiang—"

"I've heard the name. They call him the Pig."

"It's probably accurate, I don't know."

"Then what?"

"A number is left at Table Five at the casino in—"

"The Kam Pek, Macao," interrupted Jason. "What then?"

"I call the number and speak French. This Soo Jiang is one of the few slants who speak the language. He sets the time of the meet; it's always the same place. I go across the border to a field up in the hills where a chopper comes in and someone gives me the name of the target. And half the money for the kill. . . . *Look!* Here it comes! He's circling into his approach."

"My gun's at your head."

"Understood."

"Did your training include flying one of those things?"

"No. Only jumping out of them."

"That won't do us any good."

The incoming plane, its red lights blinking on the wings, swept down, out of the brightening sky toward the runway. The jet landed smoothly. It taxied to the end of the asphalt, swung to the right, and headed back to the terminal.

"Kai guan qi you!" shouted a voice from in front of the hangar, the man pointing at three fuel trucks off to the side, explaining which one was to be used.

"They're gassing up," said Jason. "The plane's taking off again. Let's get on it."

The assassin turned, his face—that *face*—pleading. "For Christ's sake, give me a knife, *something!*"

"Nothing."

"I can *help!*"

"This is my show, Major, not yours. With a knife you'd slice my stomach apart. No way, *chap.*"

"Da long xia!" cried the same voice from in front of the hangar, describing government officials in terms of large crayfish. *"Fang song,"* he continued, telling everyone to

relax, that the plane would taxi away from the terminal and the first of the three fuel trucks should be driven out to meet it.

The officials disembarked; the plane circled in place and began charging back over the runway while the tower instructed the pilot where he would refuel. The truck raced out; men leaped from the carriage and began pulling the hoses from their recesses.

"It'll take about ten minutes," said the assassin. "It's a Chinese version of an upgraded DC-Three."

The aircraft came to a stop, the engines cut, as rolling ladders were pushed to the wings and men scaled them. The fuel tanks were opened, the nozzles inserted amid constant chatter between the maintenance crews. Suddenly the hatch door in the center of the fuselage was reopened, the metal steps slapping down to the ground. Two men in uniform walked out.

"The pilot and his flight officer," said Bourne, "and they're not stretching their legs. They're checking every damn thing those people are doing. We'll time this very carefully, Major, and when I say 'Move,' you *move.*"

"Straight to the hatch," agreed the assassin. "When the second bloke hits the first step."

"That's about it."

"Diversion?"

"In what way?"

"You had a pretty fancy one last night. You had your own Yank Fourth of July, you did."

"Wrong way. Besides, I used them all up. . . . Wait a minute. The fuel truck."

"You blow it, there goes the plane. Also, you couldn't time it to the blokes getting back on board."

"Not *that* truck," said Jason, shaking his head and staring beyond the commando. "The one over there." Bourne gestured at the nearer of the two red trucks directly in front of them, about a hundred feet away. "If it went up, the first order of business would be to get the plane out of there."

"And we'd be a lot closer than we are now. Let's do it."

"No," corrected Jason. "You'll do it. Exactly the way I tell you with my gun inches from your head. *Move!*"

The assassin in front, they raced out to the truck, covered by the dim light and the commotion around the plane. The pilot and his flight officer were shining flashlights over the engines and barking impatient orders to the maintenance crews. Bourne ordered the commando to crouch down in front of him as he knelt over the open knapsack and withdrew the roll of gauze. He removed the hunting knife from his belt, pulled a coiled hose off its rack, dropping it to the ground, and slid his left hand to the base where it entered the tank.

"*Check* them," he told the commando. "How much longer? And move slowly, Major. I'm watching you."

"I said I wanted *out*. I'm not going to screw up!"

"Sure, you want out, but I've got a hunch you'd rather go it alone."

"The thought never occurred to me."

"Then you're not my man."

"Thanks a lot."

"No, I meant it. The thought would have occurred to *me*. . . . How much longer?"

"Between two and three minutes, as I judge."

"How good is your judgment?"

"Twenty-odd missions in Oman, Yemen, and points south. Aircraft similar in structure and mechanism. I know it all, sport. It's old hat. Two to three minutes, no more than that."

"Good. Get back here." Jason pricked the hose with his knife and made a small incision, enough to permit a steady stream of gasoline to flow out, but little enough so that the pump barely operated. He rose to his feet, covering the assassin with his gun as he handed him the roll of gauze. "Pull out about six feet and drench it with the fuel that's leaking down there." The killer knelt down and followed Bourne's instructions. "Now," continued Jason, "stuff the end into the slit where I've cut the hose. Farther—*farther*. Use your thumb!"

"My arm's not what it used to be!"

"Your left hand is! Press *harder!*" Bourne looked quickly over at the refueling—refueled—aircraft. The commando's judgment had been accurate. Men were climbing off the wings and winding the hoses back into the fuel truck. Suddenly, the pilot and the flight officer were making their final check. They would head for the hatch door in less than a minute! Jason reached into his pocket for matches and threw them down in front of the assassin, his weapon leveled at the killer's head. "Light it. *Now!*"

"It'll go up like a goddamned stick of nitro! It'll blow us both into the sky, especially *me!*"

"Not if you do it right! Lay the gauze on the grass, it's wet—"

"Retarding the fire—?"

"Hurry up! *Do* it!"

"*Done!*" The flame leaped up from the end of the cloth strip, then instantly fell back and began its gradual march up the gauze. "Bloody technician," said the commando under his breath as he rose to his feet.

"Get in front of me," ordered Bourne as he strung the knapsack to his belt. "Start walking straight forward. Lower your height and shrink your shoulders like you did in Lo Wu."

"Jesus Christ! *You* were—?"

"*Move!*"

The fuel truck began backing away from the plane, then circled forward, swinging around the rolling ladders, heading to its left beyond where the first red truck was parked . . . and circling again, now to the right behind *both* stationary trucks to take up its position next to the one with the lighted gauze heading into its fuel tank. Jason whipped his head around, his eyes riveted on the fired tape. It had burst into its final flame! One spark entering the leaking petcock and the exploding tank would send hot metal into its sister trucks' vulnerable shells. Any second!

The pilot gestured to his flight officer. They marched together toward the hatch door.

"*Faster!*" yelled Bourne. "Be ready to run!"

"*When?*"

"You'll know. Keep your shoulders low! Bend your spine, goddamn it!" They turned right toward the plane, passing through an oncoming crowd of maintenance personnel heading back to the hangar. "*Gongju ne?*" cried Jason, admonishing a colleague for having left behind a valuable set of tools by the aircraft.

"*Gong ju?*" shouted a man at the end of the crowd,

grabbing Bourne's arm and holding up a toolbox. Their eyes met and the crewman was stunned, his face contorted in shock. *"Tian a!"* he screamed.

It happened. The fuel truck exploded, sending erratic pillows of fire pulsating into the sky as deadly shards of twisted metal pierced the space above and to the sides of the flaming vehicle. The crews screamed en masse; men raced in all directions, most to the protection of the hangar.

"Run!" shouted Jason. The assassin did not have to be told; both men raced to the plane and the hatch door, where the pilot, who had climbed inside, was peering out in astonishment while the flight officer remained frozen on the ladder. *"Kuai!"* yelled Bourne, keeping his face in the shadows and forcing the commando's head down on the metal steps. *"Jiu feiji . . . !"* he added, screaming, telling the pilot to get out of the fire zone for the safety of the plane—that he was maintenance and would secure the hatchway.

A second truck blew up, the opposing walls of explosives forming a volcanic eruption of fire and spewing metal.

"You're right!" shouted the pilot in Chinese, grabbing his officer co-pilot by the shirt and pulling him inside; both raced up the short aisle to the flight deck.

It was the moment, thought Jason. *He wondered.* "Get in!" he ordered the commando as the third fuel truck blasted over the field and into the early light.

"Right!" yelled the assassin, raising his head and straightening his body for the leap up the steps. Then suddenly, as another deafening explosion took place and the plane's engines roared, the killer spun around on the ladder, his right foot plunging toward Bourne's groin, his hand lashing out to deflect the weapon.

Jason was ready. He crashed the barrel of his gun into the commando's ankle, then swung it up, smashing it across the assassin's temple; blood flowed as the killer fell back into the fuselage. Bourne leaped up the steps, kicking the unconscious body of the impostor back across the metal floor. He yanked the hatchway into place, slamming the latches down and securing the door. The plane began to taxi, instantly swerving to the left away from the flaming center of danger. Jason ripped the knapsack from

his belt, pulled out a second length of nylon rope and tied
the assassin's wrists to two widely separated seat clamps.
There was no way the commando could free himself—
none that Bourne could think of—but just in case he was
mistaken, Jason cut the rope attached to the assassin's
ankles, separated his legs and tied each foot to the opposite clamps across the aisle.

He got up and started toward the flight deck. The
aircraft was now on the runway, racing down the black-
top; suddenly the engines were cut. The plane was stopping in front of the terminal, where the group of
government officials was gathered, watching the ever-
growing conflagrations taking place less than a quarter of
a mile away to the north.

"*Kai ba!*" said Bourne, placing the barrel of his automatic against the back of the pilot's head. The co-pilot
whirled around in his seat. Jason spoke in clear Mandarin
as he shifted his arm. "Watch your dials, and prepare for
takeoff, then give me your maps."

"They will not clear us!" yelled the pilot. "We are to
pick up five outgoing commissioners!"

"To where?"

"Baoding."

"That's north," said Bourne.

"Northwest," insisted the co-pilot.

"Good. Head south."

"It will not be permitted!" shouted the pilot.

"Your first duty is to save the aircraft. You don't know
what's going on out there. It could be sabotage, a revolt,
an uprising. Do as I tell you, or you're both dead. I really
don't care."

The pilot snapped his head around and looked at
Jason. "You are a Westerner! You speak Chinese but you
are a *Westerner!* What are you *doing?*"

"Commandeering this aircraft. You've got plenty of
runway left. *Take off! South!* And give me the maps."

The memories came back. Distant sounds, distant sights,
distant thunder.

*"Snake Lady, Snake Lady! Respond! What are your sector
coordinates?"*

*They were heading into Tam Quan and Delta would not break
silence.* He *knew where they were and that was all that mattered.*

Command Saigon could go to hell, he wasn't about to give the North Viet monitoring posts an inkling as to where they were going.

"If you won't or can't respond, Snake Lady, stay below six hundred feet! This is a friend talking, you assholes! You don't have many down here! Their radar will pick you up over six-fifty."

I know that, Saigon, and my pilot knows it, even if he doesn't like it, and I still won't break silence.

"Snake Lady, we've completely lost you! Can any retard on that mission read an air map?"

Yes, I can read one very well, Saigon. Do you think I'd go up with my team trusting any of you? Goddamnit, that's my brother down there! I'm not important to you but he is!

"You're crazy, Western man!" yelled the pilot. "In the name of the spirits, this is a heavy aircraft and we're barely over the treetops!"

"Keep your nose up," said Bourne, studying a map. "Dip and grab altitude, that's all."

"That is also foolishness!" shouted the co-pilot. "One downdraft at this level and we are into the forests! We are gone!"

"The weather reports on your radio say there's no turbulence anticipated—"

"That is *above*," screamed the pilot. "You don't understand the risks! Not down *here!*"

"What was the last report out of Jinan?" asked Jason, knowing full well what it was.

"They have been trying to track this flight to Baoding," said the officer. "They have been unable to do so for the past three hours. They are now searching the Hengshui mountains. . . . Great spirits, why am I telling *you*? You heard the reports yourself! You speak better than my parents, and they were educated!"

"Two points for the Republic's Air Force. . . . Okay, take a hundred-and-sixty-degree turn in two and a half minutes and climb to an altitude of a thousand feet. We'll be over water."

"We'll be in range of the Japanese! They'll shoot us *down!*"

"Put out a white flag—or better still, I'll get on the radio. I'll think of something. They may even escort us to Kowloon."

"Kowloon!" shrieked the flight officer. "We'll be *shot!"*

"Entirely possible," agreed Bourne. "But not by me," he added. "You see, in the final analysis, I have to get there without you. As a matter of fact, you can't even be a part of my scene. I can't allow that."

"You're making positively *no* sense!" said the exasperated pilot.

"You just make a hundred-and-sixty-degree turn when I tell you." Jason studied the airspeed, calibrating the knots on the map, and calculated the estimated distance he wanted. Below, through the window, he saw the coast of China fall behind them. He looked at his watch; ninety seconds had passed. "Make your turn, Captain," he said.

"I would have made it anyway!" cried the pilot. "I am not of the divine wind of the Kamikaze. I do not fly into my own death."

"Not even for your heavenly government?"

"Least of all."

"Times change," said Bourne, his concentration once more on the air map. "Things change."

"Snake Lady, Snake Lady! Abort! If you can hear me, get out of there and return to base camp. It's a no-win! Do you read me? Abort!"

"What do you want to do, Delta?"

"Keep flying, mister. In three more minutes you can get out of here."

"That's me. What about you and your people?"

"We'll make it."

"You're suicidal, Delta."

"Tell me about it. . . . All right, everyone check your chutes and prepare for cast-off. Someone help Echo, put his hand on the cord."

"Déraisonnable!"

The airspeed held steady at close to 370 miles per hour. The route Jason chose, flying at low altitude through the Formosa Strait—past Longhai and Shantou on the Chinese coast, and Hsinchu and Fengshan on Taiwan—was something over 1,435 miles. Therefore the estimate of four hours, plus or minus minutes, was reasonable. The out islands north of Hong Kong would be visible in less than half an hour.

Twice during the flight they had been challenged by

radio, once from the Nationalist garrison on Quemoy, the other from a patrol plane out of Raoping. Each time Bourne took over communications, explaining in the first instance that they were on a search mission for a disabled ship bringing Taiwanese goods into the Mainland, for the second a somewhat more ominous declaration that as part of the People's Security Forces they were scouting the coast for contraband vessels that had undoubtedly eluded the Raoping patrols. For this last communication, he not only was unpleasantly arrogant but also used the name and the official—highly classified—identification number of a dead conspirator who lay underneath a Russian limousine in the Jing Shan Bird Sanctuary. Whether either interrogator believed him or not was, as he expected, irrelevant. Neither cared to disturb the *status quo ante*. Life was complicated enough. *Let things be, let them go. Where was the threat?*

"Where's your equipment?" asked Jason, addressing the pilot.

"I'm *flying* it!" replied the man, studying his instruments, visibly shaking at each eruption of static from the radio, each reporting communication from commercial aircraft. "As you may or may not know, I have no flight plan. We could be on a collision course with a dozen different planes!"

"We're too low," said Bourne, "and the visibility's fine. I'll trust your eyes not to bump into anybody."

"You're *insane!*" shouted the co-pilot.

"On the contrary. I'm about to walk back into sanity. Where's your emergency equipment? The way you people build things, I can't imagine that you don't have any."

"Such as?" asked the pilot.

"Life rafts, signaling devices—parachutes."

"Great *spirits!*"

"Where?"

"The compartment in the rear of the plane, the door to the right of the galley."

"It's all for the officials," added the co-pilot dourly. "If there are problems, *they* are supplied."

"That's reasonable," said Bourne. "How else would you attend to business?"

"Madness."

"I'm going aft, gentlemen, but my gun will be pointed

right back here. Keep on course, Captain. I'm very experienced and very sensitive. I can feel the slightest variation in the air, and if I do, we're all dead. Understood?"

"Maniac!"

"Tell me about it." Jason got up from the deck and walked back through the fuselage, stepping over his roped-up, splayed-out prisoner, who had given up the struggle to free himself, the layers of dried blood covering the wound at his left temple. "How are things, Major?"

"I made a mistake. What else do you want?"

"Your warm body in Kowloon, that's what I want."

"So some son of a bitch can put me in front of a firing squad?"

"That's up to you. Since I'm beginning to put things together, some son of a bitch might even give you a medal if you play your cards the way you should play them."

"You're very big with the cryptics, Bourne. What does *that* mean?"

"With luck, you'll find out."

"Thanks a lot!" shouted the Englishman.

"No thanks to me. You gave me the idea, *sport.* I asked you if, in your training, you'd learned how to fly one of these things. Do you remember what you told me?"

"What?"

"You said you only knew how to jump out of them."

"Holy shit!"

The commando, the parachute securely strapped to his back, was bound upright between two seats, legs and hands tied together, his right hand lashed to the release cord.

"You look crucified, Major, except that the arms should be extended."

"For God's sake, will you make *sense?*"

"Forgive me. My other self keeps trying to express himself. Don't do anything stupid, you bastard, because you're going out that hatch! Hear me? *Understood?*"

"Understood."

Jason walked to the flight deck, sat on the deck, picked up the map, and spoke to the flight officer. "What's the check?" he asked.

"Hong Kong in six minutes if we don't 'bump into anybody.' "

"I have every confidence in you, but defection notwithstanding, we can't land at Kai-tak. Head north into the New Territories."

"Aiya!" screamed the pilot. "We cross radar! The mad Gurkhas will fire on anything remotely Mainland!"

"Not if they don't pick you up, Captain. Stay below six hundred feet up to the border, then climb over the mountains at Lo Wu. You can make radio contact with Shenzen."

"And what in the name of the spirits do I say?"

"You were hijacked, that's all. You see, I can't allow you to be a part of me. We can't land in the colony. You'd draw attention to a very shy man—and his companion."

The parachutes snapped open above them, the sixty-foot rope connecting them by their waists stretched in the winds, as the aircraft sped north toward Shenzen.

They landed in the waters of a fish hatchery south of Lok Ma Chau. Bourne hauled in the rope, pulling the bound assassin toward him, as the owners of the hatchery screamed on the banks of their squared-off pond. Jason held up money—more money than the husband and wife could earn in a year.

"We are defectors!" he cried. "Rich defectors! Who cares?"

No one cared, least of all the owners of the hatchery. "Mgoi! Mgoissaai!" they kept repeating, thanking the strange pink creatures who fell from the sky, as Bourne dragged the assassin out of the water.

The Chinese garments discarded and the commando's wrists lashed behind his back, Bourne and his captive reached the road that headed south into Kowloon. Their drenched clothes were drying rapidly under the heat of the sun, but their appearance would not attract what few vehicles there were on the road and the fewer still that might be willing to pick up hitchhikers. It was a problem that had to be solved. Solved quickly, accurately. Jason was exhausted; he could barely walk and his concentration was fading. One misstep and he could lose—but he could *not* lose! Not *now!*

Peasants, mainly old women, trudged along the borders of the pavement, their outsized, wide-brimmed black hats shielding withered faces from the sun, yokes spread across ancient shoulders supporting baskets of produce. A few looked curiously at the disheveled Westerners, but only briefly; their world did not invite surprises. It was enough to survive; their memories were strong.

Memories. *Study everything. You'll find something you can use.*

"Get down," said Bourne to the assassin. "On the side of the road."

"What? *Why?*"

"Because if you don't, you won't see three more seconds of daylight."

"I thought you wanted my warm body in Kowloon!"

"I'll take a cold body if I have to. *Down!* On your *back!* Incidentally, you can shout as loud as you want, no one will understand you. You might even be helping me."

"Christ, *how?*"

"You're in trauma."

"*What?*"

"Down! *Now!*"

The killer lowered himself to the pavement, rolled over on his back, and stared into the bright sunlight, his chest heaving with awkward gulps of breath. "I heard the pilot," he said. "You *are* a fucking maniac!"

"To each his own interpretation, Major." Suddenly, Jason turned in the road and began shouting to the peasant women. *"Jiu ming!"* he screamed. *"Qing bangmang!"* He pleaded with the ancient survivors to help his hurt companion, who had either a broken back or crushed ribs. He reached into his knapsack and pulled out money, explaining that every minute counted, that medical help was required as soon as possible. If they could give assistance, he would pay a great deal for their kindness.

As one, the peasants rushed forward, their eyes not on the patient but on the money, their hats flying in the wind, their yokes forgotten.

"Na gunzi lai!" yelled Bourne, asking for splints or sticks of wood that would hold the damaged man rigid.

The women ran into the fields, returning with long bamboo stalks, slicing away the fibers that would give the poor man in pain a measure of relief when he was strapped in place. And having done so amid much vociferous expressions of sympathy and in spite of the patient's protestations in English, they accepted Bourne's money and went on their way.

Except one. She spotted a truck coming down from the north.

"*Duo shao qian?*" she said, leaning into Jason's ear, asking him how much he would pay.

"*Ni shuo ne,*" answered Bourne, telling her to name a price.

She did and Delta accepted. With her arms outstretched, the woman walked out onto the road, and the truck stopped. A second negotiation was made with the driver, and the assassin was loaded onto the van, supine, strapped to the bamboo. Jason climbed on behind him.

"How are you doing, Major?"

"This thing is filled with lousy, fucking ducks!" screamed the commando, staring around at the banks of wooden cages on all sides, the odor overpowering, sickening.

A particular fowl, in its infinite wisdom, chose the moment to squirt a stream of excrement into the assassin's face.

"Next stop, Kowloon," said Jason Bourne, closing his eyes.

30

The telephone rang. Marie spun around in the chair—stopped by Mo Panov's raised hand. The doctor walked across the hotel room, picked up the bedside phone and spoke. "Yes?" he said quietly. He frowned as he listened, then as if he realized that his expression might alarm the patient, he looked over at Marie and shook his head, his hand now dismissing whatever urgency she might have attached to the call. "All right," he continued after nearly a minute. "We'll stay put until we hear from you, but I have to ask you, Alex, and forgive my directness. Did anyone feed you drinks?" Panov winced as he pulled the phone briefly away from his ear. "My only response is that I'm entirely too kind and experienced to speculate on *your* antecedents. Talk to you later." He hung up.

"What's *happened?*" asked Marie, half out of the chair.

"Far more than he could go into, but it was enough." The psychiatrist paused, looking down at Marie. "Catherine Staples is dead. She was shot down in front of her apartment house several hours ago—"

"Oh, my *God*," whispered Marie.

"That huge Intelligence officer," continued Panov. "The one we saw in the Kowloon station whom you called the major and Staples identified as a man named Lin Wenzu—"

"What about him?"

"He's severely wounded and in critical condition at the hospital. That's where Conklin called from, a pay phone in the hospital."

Marie studied Panov's face. "There's a connection between Catherine's death and Lin Wenzu, isn't there?"

"Yes. When Staples was killed, it was apparent that the operation had been penetrated—"

"What operation? By *whom?"*

"Alex said that'll all come later. In any event, things are coming to a boil and this Lin may have given his life to rip out the penetration—'neutralizing it,' was the way Conklin put it."

"Oh, God," cried Marie, her eyes wide, her voice on the edge of hysteria. *"Operations! Penetrations . . . neutralizing,* Lin, even *Catherine*—a friend who turned on me—I don't *care* about those things! What about *David?"*

"They say he went into China."

"Good Christ, they've *killed* him!" screamed Marie, leaping out of the chair.

Panov rushed forward and grabbed her by the shoulders. He gripped her harder, forcing her spastically shaking head to stop its movement, insisting in silence that

she look at him. "Let me tell you what Alex said to me.
. . . *Listen* to me!"

Slowly, breathlessly, as if trying to find a moment of
clarity in her confusion and exhaustion, Marie stood still,
staring at her friend. "What?" she whispered.

"He said that in a way he was glad David was up there
—or out there—because in his judgment he had a better
chance to survive."

"You *believe* that?" screamed David Webb's wife, tears
filling her eyes.

"Perhaps," said Panov, nodding, and speaking softly.
"Conklin pointed out that here in Hong Kong David
could be shot or stabbed in a crowded street—crowds, he
said, were both an enemy and a friend. Don't ask me
where these people find their metaphors, I don't know."

"What the *hell* are you trying to tell me?"

"What Alex told me. He said they made him go back,
made him be someone he wanted to forget. Then he said
there never was anyone like 'Delta.' 'Delta' was the best
there ever was. . . . David Webb *was* 'Delta,' Marie. No
matter what he wanted to put out of his mind, he *was*
'Delta,' Jason Bourne was an afterthought, an extension
of the pain he had to inflict on himself, but his skills were
honed as *'Delta.'* . . . In some respects I know your husband as well as you do."

"In those respects, far better, I'm sure," said Marie,
resting her head against the comforting chest of Morris
Panov. "There were so many things he wouldn't talk
about. He was too frightened, or too ashamed. . . . Oh,
God, Mo! Will he come *back* to me?"

"Alex thinks 'Delta' will come back."

Marie leaned away from the psychiatrist and looked
into his eyes; through the tears her stare was rigid. "What
about *David?*" she asked in a plaintive whisper. "Will *he*
come back?"

"I can't answer that. I wish I could, but I can't."

"I see." Marie released Panov and walked to a window,
and looked down at the crowds below in the congested,
garishly lighted streets. "You asked Alex if he'd been
drinking. Why did you do that, Mo?"

"The moment the words came out I regretted them."

"Because you offended him?" asked Marie, turning
back to the psychiatrist.

"No. Because I knew you'd heard them and you'd want an explanation. I couldn't refuse you that."

"Well?"

"It was the last thing he said to me—two things, actually. He said you were wrong about Staples—"

"*Wrong?* I was *there*. I *saw*. I heard her *lies!*"

"She was trying to protect you without sending you into panic."

"*More* lies! What was the other?"

Panov held his place and spoke simply, his eyes locked with Marie's. "Alex said that as crazy as things seemed, they weren't really so crazy, after all."

"My God, they've turned *him!*"

"Not all the way. He won't tell them where you are—where we are. He told me we should be ready to move within minutes after his next call. He can't take the chance of coming back here. He's afraid he'll be followed."

"So we're running again—with nowhere to go but back into hiding. And all of a sudden there's a rotten growth in our collective armor. Our crippled St. George who slays dragons now wants to lie with them."

"That's not fair, Marie. That's not what he said, not what I said."

"*Bullshit,* Doctor! That's my husband out there, or *up* there! They're using him, *killing* him, without telling us why! Oh, he may—just *may*—survive because he's so terribly good at what he does—*did*—which was everything he despised, but what's going to be left of the man and his *mind*? You're the expert, *Doctor!* What's going to be left when all the memories come back? And they damn well better come back, or he *won't* survive!"

"I told you, I can't answer that."

"Oh, you're *terrific,* Mo! All you've got is carefully qualified positions and no *answers,* not even well-couched projections. You're *hiding!* You should have been an economist! You missed your calling!"

"I miss a lot of things. Almost including the plane to Hong Kong."

Marie stood motionless, as if struck. She burst into a new wave of tears as she ran to Panov, embracing him. "Oh, God, I'm sorry, Mo! Forgive me, *forgive* me!"

"I'm the one who should apologize," said the psychiatrist. "It was a cheap shot." He tilted her head back, gently stroking the gray hair streaked with white. "Lord, I can't stand that wig."

"It's not a wig, Doctor."

"My degrees, by way of Sears Roebuck, never included cosmetology."

"Only taking care of feet."

"They're easier than heads, take my word for it."

The telephone rang. Marie gasped and Panov stopped breathing. He slowly turned his head toward the hateful ringing.

"You try that again or anything like it and you're *dead!*" roared Bourne, gripping the back of his hand where the flesh was darkening from the force of the blow. The assassin, his wrists tied in front of him beneath the sleeves of his jacket, had lunged against the door of the cheap hotel, jamming Jason's left hand into the door-frame.

"What the hell do you *expect* me to do?" the former British commando yelled. "Walk gently into that good night smiling at my own firing squad?"

"So you're a closet reader, too," said Bourne, watching the killer clutch his rib cage, where Jason's right foot had landed an agonizing blow. "Maybe it's time I asked you why you're in the business I was never actually a part of. *Why,* Major?"

"Are you really interested, Mr. Original?" grunted the assassin, falling into a worn-out armchair against the wall. "Then it's my turn to ask why."

"Perhaps because I never understood myself," said David Webb. "I'm quite rational about that."

"Oh, I know all about *you!* It was part of the French-man's training. The great Delta was bonkers! His wife and kiddies were blown up in the water in a place called Phnom Penh by a stray jet. This oh-so-civilized *scholar* went crazy, and it's a fact nobody could control him and nobody gave a damn because he and the teams he led did more damage than most of the search-and-destroys put together. Saigon said you were suicidal, and from its point of view, the more so the better. They wanted you and the garbage you commanded to buy it. They never *wanted* you back. You were an embarrassment!"

Snake Lady, Snake Lady . . . this is a friend talking, you assholes. You don't have many down here. . . . Abort! It's a no-win!

"I know, or I think I know that part of it," said Webb. "I asked about you."

The assassin's eyes grew wide as he stared at his bound wrists. When he spoke, it was barely above a whisper, the voice that emerged an echo of itself, and unreal. "Because I'm *psycho,* you son of a *bitch!* I've known it since I was a kid. The nasty dark thoughts, the knives into animals just to watch their eyes and their mouths. Raping a neighbor's daughter, a vicar's kid, because I knew she couldn't say anything, and then catching up with her on the street afterwards and walking her to school. I was eleven years old. And later, at Oxford, during club hazing, holding a lad under water, just below the surface, until he drowned—to watch *his* eyes, *his* mouth. Then going back to classes and excelling in that nonsense any damn fool could do who had the wits to get out of a thundershower. *There* I was the right sort of fellow, as befitted the son of the father."

"You never sought help?"

"*Help?* With a name like Allcott-Price?"

"*Allcott*—?" Stunned, Bourne stared at his prisoner. "*General* Allcott-Price? Montgomery's boy genius in World War Two? 'Slaughter Allcott,' the man who led the flank attack on Tobruk, and later barreled through Italy and Germany? England's *Patton?*"

"I wasn't alive then, for Christ's sake! I was a product of his third wife—perhaps his fourth, for all I know. He was very large in that department—women, I mean."

"D'Anjou said you never told him your real name."

"He was bloody well right! The *general,* swilling his brandy in his oh-so-superior club in St. James's, has passed the word. '*Kill* him! Kill the rotten *seed* and never let the name out. He's no *part* of me, the woman was a whore!' But I *am* part of him and he knows it. He knows where I get my kicks from, the sadistic bastard, and we both have a slew of citations for doing what we like doing best."

"He knew, then? About your sickness?"

"He knew . . . he knows. He kept me out of Sandhurst —our West Point, in case you don't know—because he didn't want me anywhere near his precious army. He figured they'd find me out and it'd dim his precious image. He damn near had apoplexy when I joined up. He won't have a decent night's sleep until he's told quietly that I'm out—dead out with all the traces buried."

"Why are you telling *me* who you are?"

"Simple," replied the former commando, his eyes boring into Jason's. "The way I read it, whichever way it goes, only one of us is going to make it through. I'll do my damnedest to see that it's me, I told you that. But it may not be—you're no slouch—and if it isn't, you'll have a name you can shock the goddamn world with, probably make a bloody fortune in the bargain, what with literary and cinema rights, that sort of thing."

"Then the general will spend the rest of his life sleeping peacefully."

"*Sleep?* He'll probably blow his brains out! You weren't listening. I said he'd be told quietly, all the traces buried, no name surfacing. But this way *nothing's* buried. It's all hanging out like Maggie's drawers, the whole sick sordid mess with no apologies on my part, chap. I *know* what I am, I accept it. Some of us are just plain different. Let's say we're antisocial, to put it one way; hard-core violent is another; rotten, still another. The only difference with my being different is that I'm bright enough to know it."

"And accept it," said Bourne quietly.

"Wallow in it! Positively intoxicated by the highs! And let's look at it this way. If I lose and the story blows, how many practicing antisocials might be fired up by it? How many other *different* men are out there who'd be only too happy to take my place, as I took yours? This bloody world is crawling with Jason Bournes. Give them direction, give them an idea, and they'll flock to the source and be off and running. That was the Frenchman's essential genius, can't you see?"

"I see garbage, that's all I see."

"Your eyesight's not too shabby. That's what the general will see—a reflection of himself—and he'll have to live with the exposure, choke with it."

"If he wouldn't help you, you should have helped yourself, committed yourself. You're bright enough to know that."

"And cut off all the fun, all the highs? Unthinkable,

sport! You go your way and find the most expendable outfit in the service, hoping the accident will happen that will put an end to it before they peg you for what you are. I found the outfit, but the accident never happened. Unfortunately, competition brings out the best in all of us, doesn't it? We survive because somebody else doesn't want us to. . . . And then, of course, there's drink. It gives us confidence, even the courage to do the things we're not sure we can do."

"Not when you're working."

"Of course not, but the memories are there. The whisky bravado that tells you you *can* do it."

"False," said Jason Bourne.

"Not entirely," countered the assassin. "You draw strength from what you can."

"There are two people," said Jason. "One you know, the other you don't—or you don't want to."

"False!" repeated the commando. "He wouldn't *be* there unless I wanted my kicks, don't kid yourself. And don't delude yourself, either, Mr. Original. You'd be better off putting a bullet in my head, because I'll take you if I can. I'll kill you if I can."

"You're asking me to destroy what you can't live with."

"*Cut* the crap, Bourne! I don't know about you, but I *get* my kicks! I *want* them! I don't want to live *without* them!"

"You just asked me again."

"*Stow* it, you fucker!"

"And again."

"*Stop* it!" The assassin lurched out of the chair. Jason took two steps forward, his right foot again lashing out, again pounding the killer's ribs, sending him back into the chair. Allcott-Price screamed in pain.

"I won't kill you, Major," said Bourne quietly. "But I'll make you wish you were dead."

"Grant me a last wish," coughed the killer, holding his chest with his bound hands. "Even I've done that for targets. . . . I can take the unexpected bullet, but I can't take the Hong Kong garrison. They'd hang me late at night when no one's around, just to make it official, according to the regs. They'd put a thick rope around my neck and make me stand on a platform. I *can't take that!*"

Delta knew when to switch gears. "I told you before,"

he said calmly. "That may not be in store for you. I'm not dealing with the British in Hong Kong."

"You're not *what?*"

"You assumed it, but I never said it."

"You're *lying!*"

"Then you're less talented than I thought, which wasn't much to begin with."

"I *know.* I can't think *geometrically!*"

"You certainly can't."

"Then you're a premium man—what you Americans call a bounty hunter—but you're working privately."

"In a sense, yes. And I have an idea that the man who sent me after you may want to hire you, not kill you."

"Jesus *Christ*—"

"And my price was heavy. Very heavy."

"Then you are in the business."

"Only this once. I couldn't refuse the reward. Lie down on the bed."

"What?"

"You heard me."

"I have to go to the loo."

"Be my guest," replied Jason, walking to the bathroom door and opening it. "It's not one of my favorite sports, but I'll be watching you." The assassin relieved himself with Bourne's gun trained on him. Finished, he walked out into the small, shabby room in the cheap hotel south of the Mongkok. "The bed," said Bourne again, gesturing with his weapon. "Get prone and spread your legs."

"That fairy behind the desk downstairs would love to hear *this* conversation."

"You can phone him later on your own time. Down. *Quickly!*"

"You're always in a hurry—"

"More than you'll ever understand." Jason lifted his knapsack from the floor and put it on the bed, pulling out the nylon cords, as the deranged killer crawled on top of the soiled spread. Ninety seconds later the commando's ankles were lashed to the bed's rear metal springs, his neck circled with the thin white line, the rope stretched and knotted to the springs in front. Finally, Bourne slipped off the pillowcase and tied it around the major's head, covering his eyes and ears, leaving his mouth free to breathe. His wrists bound beneath him, the assassin was again immobilized. But now his head began to twitch in sudden jerks and his mouth stretched with each spasm. Extreme anxiety had overcome former Major Allcott-Price. Jason recognized the signs dispassionately.

The squalid hotel he had managed to find had no such conveniences as a telephone. The only communication with the outside world was a knock on the door, which meant either the police or a wary desk clerk informing the guest that if the room was to be occupied another hour, an additional day's rent was required. Bourne crossed to the door, slipped silently out into the dingy corridor, and headed for the pay phone he had been told was at the far end of the hallway.

He had committed the telephone number to memory, waiting—praying, if it were possible—for the moment when he would dial it. He inserted a coin and did so now, his breath short, the blood racing to his head. *"Snake Lady!"* he said into the phone, drawing out the two words in harsh, flat emphasis. *"Snake Lady,* Snake—!"

"Qing, qing," broke in an impersonal voice over the line, speaking rapidly in Chinese. "We are experiencing a temporary disruption of service for many telephones on this exchange. Service should be resumed shortly. This is a recording. . . . *Qing, qing*—"

Jason replaced the phone; a thousand fragmented thoughts, like broken mirrors, collided in his mind. He walked rapidly back down the dimly lit corridor, passing a whore in a doorway counting money. She smiled at him, raising her hands to her blouse; he shook his head and ran to the room. He waited fifteen minutes, standing quietly by the window, hearing the guttural sounds that emerged from his prisoner's throat. He returned to the door and once more stepped outside noiselessly. He walked to the phone, again inserted money and dialed.

"Qing—" He slammed the telephone down, his hands trembling, the muscles of his jaw working furiously, as he thought about the prostrate "merchandise" he had brought back to exchange for his wife. He picked up the phone for a third time and, using his last coin, dialed *O.* "Operator," he began in Chinese, "this is an emergency! It's most urgent I reach the following number." He gave

it to her, his voice rising in barely controlled panic. "A recording explained that there was difficulty on the line, but this *is* an *emergency*—"

"One minute, please. I will attempt to be of assistance." Silence followed, every second filled with a growing echo in his chest, reverberating like an accelerating kettledrum. His temples throbbed; his mouth was dry, his throat parched—burning, as a new fever spread through him.

"The line is temporarily in disuse, sir," said a second female voice.

"The *line? That line?*"

"Yes, sir."

"Not 'many telephones' on the exchange?"

"You asked the operator about a specific number, sir. I would not know about other numbers. If you have them, I will gladly check for you."

"The recording specifically said *many* telephones, yet you're saying *one line!* Are you telling me you can't confirm a . . . a multiple malfunction?"

"A what?"

"Whether a whole lot of phones aren't *working!* You've got computers. They spell out trouble spots. I told the other operator this is an *emergency!*"

"If it is medical, I will gladly summon an ambulance. If you will give me your address—"

"I want to know whether a lot of phones are out or whether it's just *one!* I *have* to *know* that!"

"It will take me some time to gather such information, sir. It's past nine o'clock in the evening and the repair stations are on reduced crews—"

"But they can tell you if there's an area problem, *goddamn* it!"

"Please, sir, I am not paid to be abused."

"Sorry, I'm *sorry!* . . . Address? Yes, the address! What's the address of the number I gave you?"

"It is unpublished, sir."

"But you *have* it!"

"Actually, I do not, sir. The laws of confidentiality are most strict in Hong Kong. My screen shows only the word 'unpublished.'"

"I repeat! This really *is* a matter of life and death!"

"Then let me reach a hospital. . . . Oh, sir, please wait.

You were correct, sir. My screen now shows that the last three digits of the number you gave me are electronically crossing over into one another, so the repair station is attempting to correct the problem."

"What's the geographical location?"

"The prefix is 'five,' therefore it is on the island of Hong Kong."

"*Narrower!* Whereabouts on the island?"

"Digits on telephone numbers have nothing to do with specific streets or locations. I'm afraid I cannot help you any further, sir. Unless you care to give me your address so that I might send an ambulance."

"My address . . . ?" said Jason bewildered, exhausted, on the edge of panic. "No," he continued, "I don't think I'll do that."

Edward Newington McAllister bent over the desk as the woman replaced the phone. She was visibly shaken, her Oriental face pale from the strain of the call. The undersecretary of State hung up a separate phone on the other side of the desk, a pencil in his right hand, an address on a notepad before him. "You were absolutely wonderful," he said, patting the woman's arm. "We have it. We've *got* him. You kept him on long enough—longer than he would have permitted in the old days—the trace is confirmed. At least the building, and that's enough. A hotel."

"He speaks very fine Chinese. The dialect is rather Northern, but he adjusts to *Guangdong hua.* He also did not trust me."

"It doesn't matter. We'll put people around the hotel. Every entrance and exit. It's on a street called Shek Lung."

"Below the Mongkok, in the Yau Ma Ti, actually," said the woman interpreter. "There's probably only one entrance, through which the garbage is taken every morning, no doubt."

"I have to reach Havilland at the hospital. He shouldn't have *gone* there!"

"He appeared to be most anxious," offered the interpreter.

"Last statements," said McAllister, dialing. "Vital information from a dying man. It's permitted."

"I don't understand any of you." The woman got up from the desk as the undersecretary moved around and sat in the chair. "I can follow instructions, but I don't understand you."

"Good Lord, I forgot. You have to leave now. What I'm discussing is highly classified. . . . We're extremely appreciative and I can assure you you have our gratitude and, I'm quite certain, a bonus, but I'm afraid I must ask you to leave."

"Gladly, sir," said the interpreter. "And you may forget the gratitude, but please include the bonus. I learned that much in Economics Eight at the University of Arizona." The woman left.

"*Emergency,* police facilities!" McAllister fairly shouted into the phone. "The ambassador, please. It's urgent! No, no names are required, thank you, and bring him to a telephone where we can talk privately." The undersecretary massaged his left temple, digging deeper and deeper into his scalp until Havilland got on the line.

"Yes, Edward?"

"He *called.* It *worked.* We know where he *is!* A hotel in the Yau Ma Ti."

"Surround it, but don't make any moves! Conklin has got to understand. If he smells what he thinks is rotten bait, he'll pull back. And if we don't have the wife, we don't have our assassin. For God's sake, don't *blow* this, Edward! Everything must be tight—and very, *very* delicate! Beyond-salvage could well be the next order of business."

"Those aren't words I'm used to, Mr. Ambassador."

There was a pause on the line; when Havilland spoke his voice was cold. "Oh, yes, they are, Edward. You protest too much. Conklin was right about that. You could have said no at the beginning, at Sangre de Cristo in Colorado. You could have walked away but you didn't, you couldn't. In some ways you're like me—without my accidental advantages, of course. We think and outthink; we take sustenance from our manipulations. We swell with pride with every progressive move in the human chess game—where every move can have terrible consequences for someone—because we believe in something. It all becomes a narcotic, and the sirens' songs are really an appeal to our egos. We have our minor powers be-

cause of our major intellects. Admit it, Edward—I have.
And if it makes you feel any better, I'll say what I said
before. Someone has to do it."

"Nor do I care for out-of-context lectures," said McAllister.

"You'll receive no more from me. Just do as I tell you.
Cover all the exits at that hotel, but inform every man
that no overt moves are to be made. If Bourne goes
anywhere, he's to be discreetly followed, not touched
under any circumstances. We *must* have the woman before contact is made."

Morris Panov picked up the phone. "Yes?"

"Something's happened." Conklin spoke rapidly, quietly. "Havilland left the waiting room to take an emergency call. Is anything going on over there?"

"No, nothing. We've just been talking."

"I'm worried. Havilland's men could have found you."

"Good Lord, *how?*"

"Checking every hotel in the colony for a white man
with a limp, that's how."

"You paid the clerk not to say anything to anyone. You
said it was a confidential business conference—perfectly
normal."

"They can pay, too, and say it's a confidential government matter that brings generous rewards or equally
generous harassment. Guess who takes precedence?"

"I think you're overreacting," protested the psychiatrist.

"I don't care what you think, Doctor, just get out of
there. Now. Forget Marie's luggage—if she has any.
Leave as quickly as you can."

"Where should we go?"

"Where it's crowded, but where I can find you."

"A restaurant?"

"It's been too many years and they change names
every twenty minutes over here. Hotels are out; they're
too easily covered."

"If you're right, Alex, you're taking too much
time—"

"I'm *thinking!* . . . All right. Take a cab to the foot of
Nathan Road at Salisbury—have you got that? *Nathan*
and *Salisbury.* You'll see the Peninsula Hotel, but don't go

inside. The strip heading north is called the Golden Mile. Walk up and down on the right side, the *east* side, but stay within the first four blocks. I'll find you, as soon as I can."

"All right," said Panov. "Nathan and Salisbury, the first four blocks north on the right. . . . Alex, you're quite certain you're right, aren't you?"

"On two counts," answered Conklin. "For starters, Havilland didn't ask me to go with him to find out what the 'emergency' was—that's not our arrangement. And if the emergency isn't you and Marie, it means Webb's made contact. If that's the case, I'm not trading away my only bargaining chip, which is Marie. Not without on-sight guarantees. Not with Ambassador Raymond Havilland. Now, get *out* of there!"

Something was wrong! What was it? Bourne had returned to the filthy hotel room and stood at the foot of the bed watching his prisoner, whose twitch was more pronounced now, his stretched body spastically reacting to each nervous movement. What *was* it? Why did the conversation with the Hong Kong operator bother him so? She was courteous and helpful; she even tolerated his abuse. Then what *was* it? . . . Suddenly, words from a long-forgotten past came to him. Words spoken years ago to an unknown operator without a face, with only an irritable voice.

I asked you for the number of the Iranian consulate.

It is in the telephone book. Our switchboards are full and we have no time for such inquiries. Click. Line dead.

That was *it!* The operators in Hong Kong—with justification—were among the most peremptory in the world. They wasted no time, no matter how persistent the customer. The workload in this congested, frenetic financial megalopolis would not permit it. Yet the second operator had been the soul of tolerance. . . . *I would not know about other numbers. If you have them, I will gladly check for you. . . . If you will give me your address. . . . Unless you care to give me your address. . . .* The address! And without really considering the question, he had instinctively answered. *No, I don't think I'll do that.* From deep within him an alarm had gone off.

A *trace!* They had bounced him around, keeping him on the line long enough to put an electronic trace on his call! Pay phones were the most difficult to track down. The vicinity was determined first; next the location or premises, and finally the specific instrument, but it was only a matter of minutes or fractions of minutes between the first step and the last. Had he stayed on long enough? And if so, to what degree of progress? The vicinity? The hotel? The pay phone itself? Jason tried to reconstruct his conversation with the operator—the second operator —when the trace would have begun. Maddeningly, frantically, but with all the precision he could summon, he tried to recapture the rhythm of their words, their voices, realizing that when he had accelerated she had slowed down. *It will take me some time. . . . Actually, I do not, sir. The laws of confidentiality are most strict in Hong Kong*—a lecture! *Oh, sir, please wait. You were correct . . . my screen now shows* —a mollifying explanation, taking up time. *Time!* How could he have *allowed* it? How *long . . . ?*

Ninety seconds—two minutes at the outside. Timing was an instinct for him, rhythms remembered. Say two minutes. Enough to determine a vicinity, conceivably to pinpoint a location, but, given the hundreds of thousands of miles of trunk lines, probably inadequate to pick up a specific phone. For some elusive reason images of Paris came to him, then the blurred outlines of telephone booths as he and Marie raced from one to another through the blinding Paris streets, making blind, untraceable calls, hoping to unravel the enigma that was Jason Bourne. *Four minutes. It takes that long, but we have to get out of the area! They've got that by now!*

The taipan's men—if there *was* a huge, obese taipan, to begin with—might have traced the hotel, but it was unlikely they would have tracked the pay phone or the floor. And there was another time span to be considered, one that could work for him if he in turn worked quickly. If the trace had been made and the hotel unearthed, it would take the hunters some time to reach the southern Mongkok, presuming they were in Hong Kong, which the telephone prefix indicated. The key at the moment was speed. *Quickly.*

"The blindfold stays, Major, but you're moving," he said to the assassin as he swiftly undid the gag and the knots on the mattress springs, coiling the three nylon ropes and stuffing them into the commando's jacket.

"What? What did you say?"

Bourne raised his voice. "Get up. We're going for a walk." Jason grabbed his knapsack, opened the door and checked the hallway. A drunk staggered into a room on the left and slammed the door. The right corridor was clear, all the way up to the pay phone and the fire exit beyond it. *"Move,"* ordered Bourne, shoving his prisoner.

The fire escape would have been rejected by underwriters at a glance. The metal was corroded and the railings bent under pressure. If one was escaping a fire, a smoke-filled staircase might have been preferable. Still, if it descended in the darkness without collapsing, that was all that mattered. Jason grabbed the commando's lapel, leading him down the creaking metal steps until they reached the first landing. Beneath there was a broken ladder extended in its track halfway to the alley below. The drop to the pavement was no more than six or seven feet, easily negotiated going down and—more important—coming back up.

"Sleep well," said Bourne, taking aim in the dim light and crashing his knuckles into the base of the commando's skull. The assassin collapsed on the staircase as Bourne whipped out the cords and secured the killer to the steps and the railing, at the last yanking down the pillowcase, covering the impostor's mouth and tying the cloth tighter. The nocturnal sounds of Hong Kong's Yau Ma Ti and the nearby Mongkok would easily cover whatever cries Allcott-Price might manage—if he awoke before Jason awakened him, which was doubtful.

Bourne climbed down the ladder, dropping into the narrow alleyway only seconds before three young men appeared, running around the corner from the busy street. Out of breath, they huddled in the shadows of a doorway as Jason remained on his knees—he hoped out of sight. Beyond the alley's entrance another group of youths raced by in pursuit, shouting angrily. The three young men lurched from the darkened doorway and ran out, heading in the opposite direction, away from their pursuers. Bourne got up and walked quickly to the mouth of the alley, looking back up at the fire escape. The assassin could not be seen.

He collided simultaneously with two running bodies. Bouncing off them and into the wall, he could only assume that the young men were part of the crowd chasing the previous three who had hidden in the doorway. One of these, however, held a knife menacingly in his hand. Jason did not *need* this confrontation, he could not permit it! Before the youth realized what had happened, Bourne lashed out and gripped the young man's wrist, twisting it clockwise until the blade fell from the youngster's hand while he screamed in pain.

"Get *out* of here!" shouted Jason in harsh Cantonese. "Your gang is no match for your elders and betters! If we see any of you around here, your mothers will get corpses for their labors. Get out!"

"*Aiya!*"

"We look for thieves! For eye-eyes from the north! They steal, they—"

"*Out!*"

The young men fled from the alleyway, disappearing into the semicrowded street in the Yau Ma Ti. Bourne shook his hand, the hand the assassin had tried to crush in the hotel doorframe. In his anxiety he had forgotten about the pain; it was the best way to tolerate it.

He looked up at the sound—*sounds.* Two dark sedans came racing down Shek Lung Street and stopped in front of the hotel. Both vehicles had *official* written all over them. Jason watched in anguish as men climbed out of each car, two from the first, three from the one behind it.

Oh, God, Marie! We're going to lose! I've killed us—oh, Christ, I've killed us!

He fully expected the five men to rush into the hotel, question the desk clerk, take up positions and make their moves. They would learn that the occupants of Room 301 had not been seen leaving the premises; therefore presumably they were still upstairs. The room would be broken into in less than a minute, the fire escape discovered seconds later! Could he *do* it? Could he climb back up, cut loose the killer, get him down into the alley and *escape?* He *had* to! He took a last look before racing back to the ladder.

Then he stopped. Something was wrong—something

unexpected, *totally* unexpected. The first man from the lead car had removed his suit coat—his official dress coat —and loosened his tie. He ran his hand through his hair, disheveling it, and walked—unsteadily?—toward the entrance of the run-down hotel. His four companions were spreading out away from the cars, looking up at the windows, two over to the right, two to the left, toward the alleyway—toward *him*. What was *happening*? These men were not acting *officially*. They were behaving like criminals, like mafiosi closing in on a kill they could not be associated with—a trap laid for others, not themselves. Good God, had Alex Conklin been *wrong* back at Dulles Airport in Washington?

Play the scenario. It's deep down and it's there. Play it out. You can do it, Delta!

No time. There was no time to think any longer. There were no precious instants to lose thinking about the existence or the nonexistence of a huge, obese taipan, too operatic to be real. The two men heading toward him had spotted the alleyway. They began running—toward the alley, toward the "merchandise," toward the destruction and death of everything Jason held dear in this rotten world he would gladly leave but for Marie.

The seconds were ticked off in milliseconds of premeditated violence, at once accepted and at once reviled. David Webb was silenced as Jason Bourne again assumed complete command. *Get away from me! This is all we've got left!*

The first man fell, his rib cage shattered, his voice stilled by the force of a blow to his throat. The second man was accorded preferential treatment. It was vital that he be cognizant, even alert, for what followed. He dragged both men into the deepest shadows of the alley, ripping their clothes with his knife, binding their feet, their arms and their mouths with strips of their own clothing.

His arms pinned beneath Jason's knees, the blade of the knife breaking the flesh around the socket of his left eye, Bourne gave his ultimatum to the second man. "My *wife!* Where *is* she? Tell me *now!* Or lose your eye, then the other one! I'll carve you up, *Zhongguo ren,* believe me!" He ripped the gag from the man's mouth.

"We are not your enemy, *Zhangfu!*" cried the Oriental

in English, using the Cantonese word for husband. "We have been trying to find her! We hunt everywhere!"

Jason stared down at the man, the knife trembling in his hand, his temples throbbing, his personal galaxy about to explode, the heavens to rain down fire and pain beyond his imagination. *"Marie!"* he screamed in agony. "What have you done with her? I was given a *guarantee!* I bring out the merchandise and my wife is returned to me! I was to hear her voice on the phone but the phone doesn't *work!* Instead, a trace is put on me and suddenly *you're* here but my wife *isn't!* Where *is* she?"

"If we knew, she would be here with us."

"Liar!" cried Bourne, drawing out the word.

"I'm not lying to you, sir, nor should I be killed for not lying to you. She escaped from the hospital—"

"The *hospital?"*

"She was ill. The doctor insisted. I was *there,* outside her room, watching over her! She was weak, but she got away—"

"Oh, Christ! Sick? *Weak?* Alone in *Hong Kong?* My God, you've killed her."

"No, sir! Our orders were to see to her comforts—"

"Your orders," said Jason Bourne, his voice flat and cold. "But not your taipan's. He followed other orders, orders given before in Zurich and Paris and on Seventy-first Street in New York. I've been there—*we've* been there. And now you've killed her. You used me, as you used me before, and when you thought it was over, you took her away from me. What's the 'death of one more daughter'? Silence is everything." Jason suddenly gripped the man's face with his left hand, the knife poised in his right. "Who's the fat man? Tell me, or the blade goes in! Who's the *taipan?"*

"He's not a taipan! He is British-schooled and trained, an officer much respected in the territory. He works with your countrymen, the Americans. He's with the Intelligence Service."

"I'm sure he is. . . . From the beginning it was the same. Only this time it wasn't the Jackal but *me.* I was moved around the chessboard until I had no choice but to hunt myself—an extension of myself, a man called Bourne. When he brings him in, kill him. Kill her. They know too much."

"No!" cried the Oriental, perspiring, his eyes wide, staring at the blade pressing into his flesh. "We are told very little, but I have heard *nothing* like that!"

"What are you doing here, then?" asked Jason harshly.

"Surveillance, I *swear* it! That's all!"

"Until the *guns* move in?" said Bourne icily. "So your three-piece suits can stay clean, no blood on your shirts, no traces back to those nameless, faceless people you work for."

"You're *wrong!* We are *not* like that, our superiors are not like that!"

"I told you, I've been there. You're like that, believe me. . . . Now you're going to tell *me* something. Whatever this is, it's down and dirty and totally secure. Nobody runs an operation like that without a camouflaged base. Where is it?"

"I don't understand you."

"Headquarters or Base Camp One, or a sterile house, or a coded Command Center—whatever the hell you want to call it. Where *is* it?"

"Please, I cannot—"

"You *can.* You *will.* If you don't, you're blind, your eyes cut out of your head. *Now!*"

"I have a wife, *children!*"

"So did I. Both counts. I'm losing patience." Jason stopped, only slightly reducing the pressure of the blade. "Besides, if you're so sure you're right—that your superiors aren't what I say they are, where's the harm? Accommodations can be reached."

"Yes!" yelled the frightened man. "Accommodations! They are good men. They won't harm you!"

"They won't have a chance," whispered Bourne.

"What, sir?"

"Nothing. Where *is* it? Where's this oh-so-quiet headquarters? *Now!*"

"Victoria Peak!" said the petrified Intelligence subordinate. "The twelfth house down on the right, with high walls . . ."

Bourne listened to the description of a sterile house, a quiet, patrolled estate among other estates in a wealthy district. He heard what he had to hear; there was nothing else he needed. He smashed the heavy bone handle of the knife into the man's skull, replaced the gag, and rose to his feet. He looked up at the fire escape, at the barely discernible outline of the assassin's body.

They wanted Jason Bourne and were willing to kill for him. They would get two Jason Bournes and die for their lies.

31

Ambassador Havilland confronted Conklin in the hospital corridor outside the police emergency room. The diplomat's decision to speak with the CIA man in the busy white-walled hallway was predicated on the fact that it *was* busy—nurses and attendants, doctors and interns, roamed the halls conferring and answering phones that seemed to ring continuously. Under the circumstances Conklin would be unlikely to indulge in a loud, heated argument. Their discussion might be charged, but it would be quiet; the ambassador could make his case better under those conditions.

"Bourne's made contact," said Havilland.

"Let's go outside," said Conklin.

"We can't," replied the diplomat. "Lin may be about to die any minute or we may be able to see him any minute. We can't miss that opportunity and the doctor knows we're here."

"Then let's go back inside."

"There are five other people in the emergency room. You don't want them overhearing us any more than I do."

"*Christ,* you cover your ass, don't you?"

"I have to think of all of us. Not one or two or three of us, but *all* of us."

"What do you want from me?"

"The woman, of course. You know that."

"I know that—of course. What are you prepared to offer?"

"My God, *Jason Bourne!*"

"I want David Webb. I want Marie's husband. I want to know that he's alive and well in Hong Kong. I want to see him with my own eyes."

"That's impossible."

"Then you'd better tell me why."

"Before he shows himself he expects to speak with his wife within thirty seconds of contact. That's the agreement."

"But you just said he *made* contact!"

"He did. We didn't. We couldn't afford to without having Marie Webb near the phone."

"You've lost me!" said Conklin angrily.

"He had his own conditions, not unlike yours, which is certainly understandable. You were both—"

"What *were* they?" broke in the CIA man.

"If he made the call, it meant that he had the impostor—it was the bilateral agreement."

"Jesus! *'Bilateral'*?"

"Both sides agreed to it."

"I know what it *means!* You just send me into space, that's all."

"Keep your voice down. . . . *His* condition was that if we did not produce his wife within thirty seconds, whoever was on the phone would hear a gunshot, meaning that the assassin was dead, that Bourne had killed him."

"Good old Delta." Conklin's lips formed a thin half-smile. "He never missed a trick. And I suspect he had a follow-up, right?"

"Yes," said Havilland grimly. "A point of exchange is to be mutually agreed upon—"

"Not bilaterally?"

"Shut up! . . . He'll be able to see his wife walking alone, under her own power. When he's satisfied, he'll come out with his prisoner—under a gun, we presume—and the exchange will be made. From the initial contact to the switch, everything is to take place in a matter of minutes, certainly no more than half an hour."

"Double time with no one orchestrating any extraneous moves." Conklin nodded. "But if you didn't respond, how do you know he made contact?"

"Lin put a flag on the telephone number with a second relay to Victoria Peak. Bourne was told that the line was temporarily out of service, and when he tried to get a verification—which under the circumstances he had to do —he was relayed to the Peak. We kept him on the line long enough to trace the location of the pay phone he was using. We know where he is. Our people are on the way there now with orders to stay out of sight. If he smells or sees anything, he'll kill our man."

"A trace?" Alex studied the diplomat's face, not kindly. "He let you keep him talking long enough for *that?*"

"He's in a state of extreme anxiety, we counted on it."

"Webb, maybe," said Conklin. "Not Delta. Not when he thinks about it."

"He'll keep calling," insisted Havilland. "He has no choice."

"Maybe, maybe not. How long has it been since his last call?"

"Twelve minutes," answered the ambassador, looking at his watch.

"And the first one?"

"About a half hour."

"And every time he calls you know about it?"

"Yes. The information's relayed to McAllister."

"Phone him and see if Bourne's tried again."

"Why?"

"Because, as you put it, he's in a state of extreme anxiety and will keep calling. He can't help himself."

"What are you trying to say?"

"That you may have made a mistake."

"Where? How?"

"I don't know, but I *do* know Delta."

"What could he do without reaching us?"

"Kill," said Alex simply.

Havilland turned, looked down the busy hallway, and started walking toward the floor's reception desk. He spoke briefly to a nurse; she nodded and he picked up a telephone. He talked for a moment and hung up. Frowning, he returned to Conklin. "It's odd," he remarked. "McAllister feels the way you do. Edward expected Bourne to call every five minutes, if he waited *that* long."

"Oh?"

"He was led to believe that telephone service might be restored at any moment." The ambassador shook his head, as if dismissing the improbable. "We're all too tense. There could be a number of explanations starting with coins for a pay phone to unsettled bowels."

The emergency-room door opened and the British doctor appeared. "Mr. Ambassador?"

"Lin?"

"A remarkable man. What he's been through would kill a horse, but then they're about the same size and a horse can't manifest a will to live."

"Can we see him?"

"There'd be no point, he's still unconscious—stirring now and then but nowhere near coherent. Every minute he rests without a reversal is encouraging."

"You understand how urgent it is that we talk to him, don't you?"

"Yes, Mr. Havilland, I do. Perhaps more than you realize. You know that I was the one responsible for the woman's escape—"

"I do know," said the diplomat. "I was also told that if she could fool you she could probably fool the best internist at the Mayo Clinic."

"That's dubious, but I like to think I'm competent. Instead, I feel like an idiot. I'll do everything in my power to help you and my good friend Major Lin. The judgment was medical and mine, the error mine, not his. If he makes it through the next hour or so, I believe he has a chance to live. If that happens, I'll bring him to and you can question him as long as you keep your questions brief and simple. If I think a reversal is too severe and that he's slipping away, I'll also call you."

"That's fair, Doctor. Thank you."

"I could do no less. It's what Lin would want. I'll go back to him now."

The waiting began. Havilland and Alex Conklin reached their own bilateral agreement. When Bourne next tried to reach the number for Snake Lady, he was to be told that the line would be clear in twenty minutes. During that time Conklin would be driven to the sterile house on Victoria Peak, prepared to take the call. He would set up the exchange, telling David that Marie was safe and with Morris Panov. The two men returned to the police emergency room and sat in opposite chairs, each silent minute compounding the strain.

The minutes, however, stretched into quarter hours

and these into over an hour. Three times the ambassador called the Peak to ask if there was any word from Jason Bourne. There was none. Twice the English doctor came out to report on Lin's condition. It was unchanged, a fact that allowed for hope rather than diminishing it. Once the emergency-room telephone rang and both Havilland and Conklin snapped their heads toward it, their eyes riveted on the nurse who calmly answered. The call was not for the ambassador. The tension mounted between the two men as every now and then they would look at each other with the same message in their eyes. *Something was wrong. Something had gone off the wire.* A Chinese doctor came out and approached two people in the back of the room, a young woman and a priest; he spoke quietly. The woman screamed, then sobbed and fell into the enveloping arms of the priest. A new police widow had been created. She was led away to say a last good-bye to her husband.

Silence.

The telephone rang again, and again the diplomat and the CIA man stared at the counter.

"Mr. Ambassador," said the nurse, "it's for you. The gentleman says it's most urgent." Havilland got up and hurried to the desk, nodding his thanks, as he took the phone.

Whatever it was, it had happened. Conklin watched, never thinking he would see what he saw now. The consummate diplomat's face became suddenly ashen; his thin, usually tight lips were now parted, his dark brows arched, his eyes wide and hollow. He turned and spoke to Alex, his voice barely audible; it was the whisper of fear.

"Bourne's gone. The impostor's gone. Two of the men were found bound and severely injured." He returned to the phone, his eyes narrowing as he listened. "Oh, my *God!*" he cried, turning back to Conklin.

The CIA man was not there.

David Webb had disappeared, only Jason Bourne remained. Yet he was both more and less than the hunter of Carlos the Jackal. He was Delta the predator, the animal wanting only vengeance for a priceless part of his life that had been taken from him once again. And as an avenging predator, he went through the motions—the instinctive logistics—in a trancelike state, each decision precise, each movement deadly. His eye was on the kill, and his human brain had become animal.

He wandered the squalid streets of the Yau Ma Ti, his prisoner in tow, wrists still in traction, finding what he wanted to find, paying thousands of dollars for items worth a fraction of the amounts paid. Word spread up into the Mongkok about the strange man and his even stranger silent companion, who was bound and feared for his life. Other doors were opened to him, doors reserved for the runners of contraband—drugs, exported whores, jewels, gold, and materials of destruction, deception, death—and exaggerated warnings accompanied the word about this obsessed man carrying thousands on his person.

He is a maniac and he is white and he will kill quickly. It is said two throats were slit by those dishonest to him. It is heard that a Zhongguo ren was shot to death because he cheated on a delivery. He is mad. Give him what he wants. He pays hard cash. Who cares? It is not our problem. Let him come. Let him go. Just take his money.

By midnight Delta had the tools of his lethal trade. And success was uppermost in the Medusan's mind. He *had* to succeed. The kill was everything.

Where was Echo? He needed Echo. Old Echo was his good luck charm!

Echo was dead, slain by a madman with a ceremonial sword in a peaceful forest of birds. Memories.

Echo.

Marie.

I'll kill them for what they did to you!

He stopped a dilapidated taxi in the Mongkok and, showing money, asked the driver to step outside.

"Yes, what is, sir?" asked the man in broken English.

"What's your car worth?" said Delta.

"I do not understand."

"How *much? Money?* For your *car!*"

"You *feng kuang!*"

"*Bu!*" shouted Delta, telling the driver he was not unbalanced. "How much will you take for your car?" he continued in Chinese. "Tomorrow morning you can say it was stolen. The police will find it."

"It's my only source of livelihood and I have a large family! You are crazy!"

"How's four thousand, American?"

"*Aiya.* Take it!"

"*Kuai!*" said Jason, telling the man to hurry. "Help me with this diseased one. He has the shaking sickness and must be tied down so he can't hurt himself."

The owner of the taxi, his eyes on the large bills in Bourne's hand, helped Jason throw the assassin into the back seat, holding the killer down as the man from Medusa whipped the nylon ropes around the commando's ankles, knees and elbows, once again gagging and blindfolding him with the strips of cloth ripped from the cheap hotel's pillowcase. Unable to understand what was being said—shouted in Chinese—the prisoner could only passively resist. It was not merely the punishment inflicted on his wrists with each protesting movement, it was something he saw as he stared at his captor. There was a change in the original Jason Bourne; he had gone into another world, a far darker world. The kill was in the Medusan's extended periods of silence. It was in his eyes.

As he drove through the congested tunnel from Kowloon to the island of Hong Kong, Delta primed himself for the assault, imagining the obstacles that would face him, conjuring up the countermeasures he would employ. All were overdrawn and excessive, thus preparing himself for the worst.

He had done the same in the jungles of Tam Quan. There was nothing he had not considered, and he had brought them out—all but one. A piece of garbage, a man who had no soul but the want for gold, a traitor who would sell the lives of his comrades for small advantage. It was where it had all begun. In the jungles of Tam Quan. Delta had executed the piece of garbage, blown his temple out with a bullet, as this garbage was on a radio relaying their position to the Cong. The garbage was a man from Medusa named Jason Bourne, left to rot in the jungles of Tam Quan. He was the beginning of the madness. Yet Delta had brought out all the others, including a brother he could not remember. He had brought them out through two hundred miles of enemy territory because he had studied the probabilities and imagined the improbabilities—the latter far more important to their escape, for they had happened, and his mind was prepared for the unexpected. It was the same now. There was nothing a sterile house in Victoria Peak could mount that he could not surmount. Death would be answered with death.

He saw the high walls of the estate and drove casually past them—slowly, as a guest or a tourist might, unsure of his way down the stately road. He spotted the glass of the concealed searchlights, noted the barbed wire coiled above the wall. He zeroed in on the two guards in back of the enormous gate. They were in shadows, but the cloth of their marine field jackets reflected what light there was—a mistake, the cloth should have been dulled or replaced by less military apparel. The high wall ended in front; it was the corner; the stone stretched to the right as far as the eye could see. The sterile house was obvious to the trained eye. To the innocent it was clearly the residence of an important diplomat, an ambassador, perhaps, who required protection because of the dangerous times. Terrorism was everywhere; hostages were prized, deterrents the order of the day. Cocktails were served at sundown amid the quiet laughter of the elite who moved governments, but outside the guns were ready, cocked with the darkness, ready to fire. Delta understood. It was why he carried his bulging knapsack.

He drove the battered car off the side of the road. There was no need to conceal it; he would not be coming back. He did not care to come back. Marie was gone and it was over. Whatever lives he had led were finished. David Webb. Delta. Jason Bourne. They were the past. He wanted only peace. The pain had exceeded the limits of his endurance. Peace. But first he must kill. His enemies, Marie's enemies, all the enemies of the men and women everywhere who were driven by the nameless, faceless manipulators would be taught a lesson. A minor lesson, of course, for sanitized explanations would come from the experts, made plausible by complicated words and distorted half-truths. Lies. *Stave off doubts, eliminate the questions, be as outraged as the people themselves and march to the drums of consensus. The objective is everything, the insignificant players nothing but necessary digits in the deadly equations. Use them, drain them, kill them if you must, just get the jobs done because we say so. We see things others cannot see. Do not question us. You have no access to our knowledge.*

Jason climbed out of the car, opened the rear door, and with his knife sliced the ropes away from the assassin's ankles and knees. He then removed the blindfold, keeping the gag in place. He grabbed his prisoner by the shoulder and—

The blow was paralyzing! The killer spun in place, crashing his right knee up into Bourne's left kidney, swinging his clasped bound hands up into Jason's throat as Delta buckled over. A second knee caught Bourne's rib cage; he fell to the ground as the commando raced into the road. *No. It can't happen! I need his gun, his firepower. It's part of the strategy!*

Delta rose to his feet, his chest and side bursting with pain, and plunged after the running figure in the road. In seconds the killer would be enveloped in darkness! The man from Medusa ran faster, the pain forgotten, concentrating only on the assassin in the part of his mind that still functioned. Faster, *faster!* Suddenly headlights shot up from the bottom of the hill, catching the assassin in their beams. The commando lurched to the side of the road to avoid the light. Bourne stayed on the right side of the pavement until the last instant, knowing he was gaining precious yards as the car raced past. His arms useless, the killer stumbled on the soft shoulder of the road; he crawled quickly, awkwardly back to the asphalt, and, getting to his feet, began to run again. It was too late. Delta hurled his shoulder into the base of his prisoner's spine; both men went down. The commando's guttural roars were the sounds of an animal in fury. Jason turned the assassin over and jammed his knee brutally into his prisoner's stomach.

"You listen to me, *scum!*" he said breathlessly, the sweat rolling down his face. "Whether you die or not makes no difference to me. A few minutes from now you won't concern me any longer, but until then you're part of the plan, *my* plan! And whether or not you die then will be up to you, *not* me. I'm giving you a chance, which is more than you ever did for a target. Now, *get* up! Do everything I tell you or your one chance will be blown away with your head—which is exactly what I promised them."

They stopped back at the car. Delta picked up his knapsack and, removing a gun he had taken in Beijing, showed it to the commando. "You begged me for a weapon at the airport in Jinan, remember?" The assassin nodded, his eyes wide, his mouth stretched under the tension of the cloth gag. "It's yours," continued Jason Bourne, his voice flat, without emotion. "Once we're over that wall up there —you in front of me—I'll hand it to you." The killer frowned, his eyes narrowing. "I forgot," said Delta. "You couldn't see it. There's a sterile house about five hundred feet up the road. We're going in. I'm staying, taking out everyone I can. You? You've got nine shells and I'll give you a bonus. One 'bubble.' " The Medusan lifted a packet of *plastique* from the Mongkok out of the knapsack and showed it to his prisoner. "As I read it, you'd never get back over the wall; they'd cut you down. So your only way out is through the gate; it'll be somewhere diagonally to the right. To get there you'll have to kill your way through. The timer on the plastic can be set as low as ten seconds. Handle it any way you like, I don't care. *Capisce?*"

The assassin raised his bound hands, then gestured at the gag. The sounds from his throat indicated that Jason should free his arms and remove the cloth.

"At the wall," said Delta. "When I'm ready, I'll cut the ropes. But when I do, if you try to take the gag off before I tell you, there goes your chance." The killer stared at him and nodded once.

Jason Bourne and the lethal pretender walked up the road on Victoria Peak toward the sterile house.

Conklin limped down the hospital steps as rapidly as he could, holding on to the center rail, looking frantically for a taxi in the drive below. There was none; instead a uniformed nurse stood alone reading the *South China Times* in the glow of the outdoor lights. Every now and then she glanced up toward the parking-lot entrance.

"*Excuse* me, miss," said Alex, out of breath. "Do you speak English?"

"A little," replied the woman, obviously noticing his limp and his agitated voice. "You are with difficulty?"

"Much difficulty. I have to find a taxi. I have to reach someone right away and I can't do it by phone."

"They will call one for you at the desk. They call for me every night when I leave."

"You're waiting . . . ?"

"Here it comes," said the woman as approaching head-lights shone through the parking-lot entrance.

"Miss!" cried Conklin. "This is urgent. A man is dying and another may die if I don't reach him! *Please.* May I—"

"Bie zhaoji," exclaimed the nurse, telling him to calm down. "You have urgency, I have none. Take my taxi. I will ask for another."

"Thank you," said Alex as the cab pulled up to the curb. *"Thank* you!" he added, opening the door and climbing inside. The woman nodded pleasantly and shrugged as she turned and started back up the steps. The glass doors above crashed open and Conklin watched through the rear window as the nurse nearly collided into two of Lin's men. One stopped her and spoke; the other reached the curb and squinted, peering out of the light into the receding darkness beyond. "Hurry!" said Alex to the driver as they passed through the gate. *"Kuai diar,* if that's right."

"It will do," answered the driver wearily in fluent English. " 'Hurry' is better, however."

The base of Nathan Road was the galactic entrance to the luminescent world of the Golden Mile. The blazing colored lights, the dancing, flickering, shimmering lights, were the walls of this congested, urban valley of humanity where seekers sought and sellers shrieked for attention. It was the bazaar of bazaars, a dozen tongues and dialects vying for the ears and the eyes of the ever-shifting crowds. It was here, in this gauntlet of freewheeling commercial chaos, that Alex Conklin got out of the cab. Walking painfully, his limp pronounced, the veins of his footless leg swelling, he hurried up the east side of the street, his eyes roving like those of an angry wildcat seeking its young in the territory of hyenas.

He reached the end of the fourth block, the *last* block. Where were they? Where was the slender, compact Panov and the tall, striking, auburn-haired Marie? His instructions had been clear, *absolute.* The first four blocks north on the right side, the *east* side. Mo Panov had recited them back to him. . . . Oh, *Christ!* He had been looking for two people, one whose physical appearance could belong to hundreds of men in those four crowded blocks. But his *eyes* had been searching for the tall, dark-redheaded woman—which she was *no longer!* Her hair had been dyed *gray* with streaks of *white!* Alex started back down toward Salisbury Road, his eyes now attuned to what he should look for, not what his painful memories told him he would find.

There they *were!* On the outskirts of a crowd surrounding a street vendor whose cart was piled high with silks of all descriptions and labels—the silks relatively genuine, the labels as ersatz as the distorted signatures.

"Come on with me!" said Conklin, his hands on both their elbows.

"Alex!" cried Marie.

"Are you all right?" asked Panov.

"No," said the CIA man. "None of us is."

"It's *David,* isn't it?" Marie grabbed Conklin's arm, gripping it.

"Not now. Hurry up. We have to get out of here."

"They're *here?"* Marie gasped, her gray-haired head turning right and left, fear in her eyes.

"Who?"

"I don't *know!"* she shouted over the din of the crowds.

"No, *they're* not here," said Conklin. "Come on. I've got a taxi holding down by the Pen."

"What pen?" asked Panov.

"I told you. The Peninsula Hotel."

"Oh, yes, I forgot." All three started walking down Nathan Road, Alex—as was obvious to Marie and Morris Panov—with difficulty. "We can slow down, can't we?" asked the psychiatrist.

"No, we *can't!"*

"You're in pain," said Marie.

"Knock it off! *Both* of you. I don't need your horse-shit."

"Then tell us what's *happened!"* yelled Marie as they crossed a street filled with carts they had to dodge, and buyers and sellers and tourist-voyeurs who made for the exotic congestion of the Golden Mile.

"There's the taxi," said Conklin as they approached Salisbury Road. "Hurry up. The driver knows where to go."

Inside the cab, Panov between Marie and Alex, she once again reached out, clutching Conklin's arm. "It *is* David, isn't it?"

"Yes. He's back. He's here in Hong Kong."

"Thank *God!"*

"You hope. We hope."

"What does that mean?" asked the psychiatrist sharply.

"Something's gone wrong. The scenario's off the wire."

"For Christ's sake!" exploded Panov. "Will you speak *English!*"

"He means," said Marie, staring at the CIA man, "that David either did something he wasn't supposed to do, or *didn't* do something he was expected to do."

"That's about it." Conklin's eyes drifted toward the lights of Victoria Harbor and the island of Hong Kong beyond. "I used to be able to read Delta's moves, usually before he made them. Then later, when he was Bourne, I was able to track him when others couldn't, because I understood his options and knew which ones he would take. That is, until things happened to him, and no one could predict anything because he'd lost touch with the Delta inside him. But Delta's back now, and as happened so often so long ago, his enemies have underestimated him. I hope I'm wrong—*Jesus,* I hope I'm *wrong!*"

His gun against the back of the assassin's neck, Delta moved silently through the underbrush in front of the high wall of the sterile house. The killer balked; they were within ten feet of the darkened entrance. Delta jammed the weapon into the commando's flesh and whispered, "There aren't any trip lights in the wall or on the ground. They'd be set off by tree rats every thirty seconds. Keep going! I'll tell you when to stop."

The order came four feet from the gate. Delta grabbed his prisoner by the collar and swung him around, the barrel of the gun still touching the assassin's neck. The man from Medusa then reached into his pocket, pulled out a globule of *plastique* and stretched his arm out as far as he could toward the gate. He pressed the adhesive side of the packet against the wall; he had pre-set the small digital timer in the soft center of the explosive for seven minutes, the number chosen both for luck and to give him time to get the killer and himself in place several hundred feet away. *"Move!"* he whispered.

They rounded the corner of the wall and proceeded along the side to the midpoint, from where the end of the stone was visible in the moonlight. "Wait here," said Delta, reaching into his knapsack, which was strapped across his chest like a bandolier, the bag on his right side. He pulled out a square black box, five inches wide, three high, and two deep. At its side was a coiled forty-foot line of thin, black plastic tubing. It was a battery-amplified speaker; he placed it on top of the wall and snapped a switch in the back; a red light glowed. He uncoiled the thin tubing as he shoved the killer forward. "Another twenty or thirty feet," he said. They reached the spot acceptable to the Medusan. The branches of a cascading willow tree were spread out above the wall, arcing downward. Concealment. "Here!" he whispered harshly, and stopped the commando by gripping his shoulder. He removed the wire cutters from the knapsack and pushed the assassin against the wall; they faced each other. "I'm cutting you loose now, but not free. Do you understand that?" The commando nodded, and Delta snipped the ropes between his prisoner's wrists and elbows while leveling his gun at the assassin's head. He stepped back and bent his right leg forward in front of the killer as he handed him the wire cutters. "Stand on my leg and cut the coils. You can reach them if you jump a bit and slide your hand under for a grip. Don't try anything. You haven't got a gun yet, but I have, and as I'm sure you've gathered, I don't care anymore."

The prisoner did as he was told. The leap from Delta's leg was minimal; the assassin's left arm expertly slithered between the coils, his hand gripping the opposite side of the top of the wall. He severed the coiled wire noiselessly, holding the cutters against the metal on one side to reduce the sound of snapping tension. The open space above was now five feet wide. "Climb up there," said Delta.

The killer did so, and as his left leg swung over the wall, Delta leaped up to grab the assassin's trousers and pulled himself up against the stone, swinging his own left leg over the top. He straddled the wall simultaneously with the commando.

"Nicely done, Major Allcott-Price," he said, a small circular microphone in his hand, his weapon again aimed at the assassin's head. "Not much longer now. If I were you, I'd study the grounds."

. . .

Under Conklin's urgent pleas to the driver, the taxi sped up the road in Victoria Peak. They passed a broken-down car off the side of the road; it seemed out of place in the elegant surroundings, and Alex swallowed as he saw it, wondering in dread if it was really disabled. "There's the house!" cried the CIA man. "For God's sake, *hurry!* Go up to the—"

He did not—could not—finish. Up ahead a shattering explosion filled the road and the night. Fire and stone flew in all directions, as first a large part of the wall collapsed and then the huge iron gates fell forward in eerie slow motion beyond the flames.

"Oh, my God, I was right," said Alexander Conklin softly to himself. "Delta's come back. He wants to die. He *will* die."

32

"*Not yet!*" roared Jason Bourne as the wall blew apart beyond the stately gardens filled with rows of lilacs and roses. "I'll tell you when," he added quietly, holding the small circular microphone in his free hand.

The assassin grunted, his instincts roused to their primeval limits, his desire to kill equal to his desire to survive, the one dependent upon the other. He was on the edge of madness; only the barrel of Delta's gun stopped him from an insane assault. He was still human, and it was better to try to live than to accept death through default. But when, *when?* The nervous tic returned to Allcott-Price's face; his lower lip twitched as screams and shouts and the sound of men running in panic filled the gardens. The killer's hands trembled as he stared at Delta in the dim, pulsating light of the distant flames.

"Don't even think about it," said the man from Medusa. "You're dead if you make a move. You've studied me, so you know there's no reprieve. You make it, you make it on your own. Swing your leg over the wall and be ready to jump when I tell you. Not before." Without warning, Bourne suddenly brought the microphone to his lips and snapped a switch. When he spoke, his amplified words echoed eerily throughout the grounds, a haunting, reverberating sound that matched the thunder of the explosion, made more ominous by its calm simplicity, its frigidity.

"You *marines.* Take cover and stay out of this. It's not your fight. Don't die for the men who brought you here. To them you're garbage. You're expendable—as I was expendable. There's no legitimacy here, no territory to be defended, no honor of your country in question. You're here for the sole purpose of protecting killers. The only difference between you and me is the fact that they used me, too, but now they want to kill me because I know what they've done. Don't die for these men, they're not worth it. I give you my word I won't fire on you unless you shoot at me, and then I'll have no choice. But there's another man here who isn't going to make any deals—"

A fusillade of gunfire erupted, shattering the source of the sound, blasting the unseen speaker randomly off the wall. Delta was ready; it was bound to happen. One of the faceless, nameless manipulators had given an order and it was carried out. He reached into the knapsack, removing a fifteen-inch pre-set tear gas launcher, the canister in place. It could smash heavy glass at fifty yards; he aimed and pulled the trigger. A hundred feet away a bay window was shattered and the fog of gas billowed throughout the room inside. He could see figures running beyond the fragmented glass. Lamps and chandeliers were extinguished, supplanted by a startling array of floodlights positioned in the eaves of the great house and the trunks of the surrounding trees. Suddenly the grounds were awash with blinding white light. The branches of the overhanging tree would be a magnet for darting eyes and leveled weapons, and he understood that no appeal of his would countermand the orders. He had delivered that appeal both as an honest warning and as a salve for what conscience remained to a barely thinking, barely feeling robot avenger. In the shadows of the mind he had left he did not want to take the lives of youngsters called to serve the paranoid egos of manipulators—he had seen too much of that in Saigon years ago. He wanted only the lives of those inside the sterile house, and he intended to have them. Jason Bourne would not be denied. They had taken everything from him, and his personal account was now going to be settled. For the man from Medusa the decision was made —he was a puppet on the strings of his own rage, and apart from that rage his life was over.

"*Jump!*" whispered Delta, swinging his right leg over the wall, pummeling the assassin down to the ground. He followed while the commando was in midair and grabbed the assassin's shoulder as the startled killer—arms extended on his knees—righted himself on the grass. Bourne dragged him out of sight into a latticed arbor with a profusion of bougainvillaea that reached nearly six feet high. "Here's your gun, Major," said the original Jason Bourne. "Mine's on *you,* and don't you forget it."

The assassin simultaneously grabbed the weapon and tore the cloth from his mouth, coughing and spitting out saliva, as a savage burst of gunfire tore leaves and branches all along the wall. "Your little lecture didn't do much fucking good, *did* it?"

"I didn't expect it to. The truth of the matter is that they want you, not me. You see, I'm *really* expendable now. That was their plan from the beginning. I bring you out and I'm dead. My wife's dead. We know too much. She because she learned who they were—she had to, she was the bait—me because they knew I'd put some figures together in Peking. You're messed up with a bloodbath, Major. A megabomb that can blow the whole Far East apart, and will if saner heads in Taiwan don't isolate and rip out those lunatic clients of yours. Only, I don't give a shit anymore. Play your goddamned games and blow yourselves up. I just want to get inside that house."

A squad of marines assaulted the wall, running alongside the stone, rifles poised, ready to fire. Delta pulled a second *plastique* from his knapsack, set the miniaturized digital timer for ten seconds, and threw the packet as far as he could toward the rear garden wall, away from the guards. "Come on!" he ordered the commando, ramming his weapon into the killer's spine. "You in front! Down this path. Nearer the house."

"Give me one of those! Give me a plastic!"

"I don't think so."

"Christ, you gave me your word!"

"Then either I lied or I changed my mind."

"Why? What do *you* care?"

"I care. I didn't know there were so many kids. Too many kids. You could take out ten of them with one of these, maim a lot more."

"It's a little late for you to become such a fucking Christian!"

"The club's not that exclusive; it never was. I know who I want and who I don't want and I don't want kids in pressed GI pajamas. I want the men inside that—"

The explosion came some forty yards away at the rear of the grounds. Trees and dirt, bushes and whole beds of flowers flamed into the air—a panorama of greens and browns and speckled dots of color within the billowing gray smoke illuminated by the hot, white floodlights. *"Move!"* whispered Delta. "To the end of the row. It's about sixty feet from the house and there's a pair of doors —" Bourne closed his eyes in angry futility as a series of seemingly unending spurts of rifle fire filled the rear gardens. *They were children. They fired blindly out of fear, killing imaginary demons but no targets. And they would not listen.*

Another group of marines, these obviously led by an experienced officer, took up equidistant positions in front of the great house and circled it, legs bent, feet dug in for recoils, weapons angled forward. The manipulators had called for their Praetorian guard. So be it. Delta again reached into his knapsack, felt around his arsenal, and removed one of the two manual firebombs he had purchased in the Mongkok. It was similar to a grenade at the top—circular but covered with a shield of heavy plastic. The base, however, was a handle, five inches long, so that the thrower could hurl the explosive farther and with greater accuracy. The trick was in the throwing, the accuracy, and the timing. For once the plastic was removed, the shell of the bomb itself would adhere to any surface by an instant steel-like adhesive activated by air, and with the explosion of a chemical would shoot out in all directions, prolonging the flames, embedding itself in all porous surfaces, seeping and burning. From the removal of the plastic covering to the explosion took fifteen seconds.

The sides of the great house, the sterile house, were the standard Victorian clapboard above an imposing lower border of stone. Delta shoved the assassin into a cluster of roses, stripped off the plastic, and heaved the firebomb into the clapboard far above and to the left of the French doors thirty-odd feet away. It stuck to the wood, the rest was waiting for the seconds to pass while the rifle fire—hesitant now, diminishing—ceased altogether.

The wall of the house blew apart. A gaping hole revealed a formal Victorian bedroom, complete with a canopied bed and delicate English furniture. The flames spread instantly, shooting spokes of fire from a central hub, spewing along the clapboard and spitting inside the house.

An order was given, and again there was an eruption of rifle fire, bullets spraying the flower beds away from the rear garden wall and the contingent of marines who had raced in the direction of the previous explosion. Commands and countercommands were shouted in anger and frustration as two officers appeared, sidearms in their hands. One rounded the circle of protecting guards, checking their positions and their weapons, peering in front of each. The other headed for the side wall and began retracing the route of the first squad, his eyes constantly shifting to his inner flanks, to the succeeding rows of flowers. He stopped beneath the willow tree and studied the wall, then the grass. He raised his head and looked over at the arbor of bougainvillaea. With his weapon, now steadied by both hands, he started toward the arbor.

Delta watched the soldier through the bushes, his own gun still pressed into the commando's back. He removed another *plastique,* set the timer, and threw it over the bushes far forward toward the side wall. "Go through there!" ordered Bourne, pivoting the assassin by the shoulder and sending him into the row of bushes on the left. Jason plunged through after the commando, cracking the barrel of his automatic into the killer's head, stopping him as he lurched for the knapsack. "Just a few more minutes, Major, then you're on your own."

The fourth explosion tore away six feet of the side wall, and as though they expected enemy troops to pour through, the marine guards opened fire on the collapsing stone. In the distance, on the roads of Victoria Peak, two-note sirens wailed in counterpoint to the sounds of carnage taking place within the grounds of the sterile house. Delta pulled out his next to last plastic packet, set the timer for ninety seconds, and heaved it toward the corner of the rear wall where the grounds were deserted. It was the beginning of his final diversion, the rest would be cold mathematics. He removed the tear gas launcher, inserted a canister, and spoke to the commando. "Turn around." The assassin did so, the barrel of Bourne's gun in front of his eyes. "Take this," said Delta. "You can hold it with one hand. When I tell you, fire it into the stone to the right of the French doors. The gas will spread, blinding most of those kids. They won't be able to shoot, so don't waste bullets, you haven't got that many."

The killer did not at first reply. Instead, he raised his weapon level with Bourne's and aimed it at Jason's head. "Now we're one-on-one, Mr. Original," said the commando. "I told you I could take a bullet in the head, I've been waiting for it for years. But somehow I don't think you can take the idea of not getting inside that house." There was a sudden roar of voices and yet another fusillade of gunfire as a squad of marines rushed the collapsed side wall. Delta watched, waiting for the instant when the assassin's concentration would break for that split second. The instant did not come. Instead the commando continued quietly, his voice tense but controlled, as he stared at Jason Bourne. "They must be expecting an invasion, the silly geese. When in doubt attack, as long as your flanks are covered, isn't that right, Mr. Original? . . . Empty your bag of tricks, Delta. It *was* 'Delta,' wasn't it?"

"There's nothing left." Bourne cocked the hammer of his automatic. The assassin did the same.

"Then let's have a feel around," said the commando, his left hand slowly reaching out, softly touching the knapsack strapped on Delta's right hip, their eyes locked. The killer felt the canvas, squeezing the harsh cloth in several places. Again slowly, he withdrew his hand. "With all the shalt-nots in the bloody big Book, none ever mentions a lie, does it? Except false witness, of course, which isn't the same. I guess you took the lapse to heart, sport. There's a shell-framed automatic repeater in there and two or three clips, I judge by the curves, holding at least fifty rounds apiece."

"Forty, to be exact."

"That's a lot of firepower. That little beast could get me out of here. *Give!* Or one of us goes right here. Right now."

The fifth *plastique* explosion shook the ground; the startled assassin blinked. It was enough. Bourne's hand shot up, deflecting the killer's gun, crashing his heavy automatic into the commando's left temple with the force of a hammer.

"Son of a *bitch!*" cried the assassin hoarsely as he fell to his left, Jason's knee on his wrist, the killer's gun wrenched free.

"You keep begging for a quick demise, Major," said Bourne as pandemonium reached its height within the grounds of the Victorian sterile house. The squad of marines that had charged the collapsed side wall were ordered to assault the rear of the gardens. "You really don't like yourself, do you? But you've got a good idea. I will empty my bag of tricks. It's almost time now."

Bourne removed the straps and upturned his open knapsack. The contents fell on the grass, the flames from the ever-expanding fire on the second floor of the sterile house illuminating them. There was one firebomb and one *plastique* left, and, as was accurately described by the assassin, a hand-held repeating MAC-10 machine pistol that needed only its stock frame and a clip to be inserted in order to fire. He inserted the frame of the lethal weapon, cracked in one of the four clips, and shoved the remaining three into his belt. He then released the spring of the launcher, put the canister in place, and reset the mechanism. It was ready to go—*to save the lives of children, children called to die by the aging egos of manipulators.* The firebomb remained. He knew where to direct it. He lifted it up, tore off the shield, and threw it with all his strength toward the A-framed apex above the French doors. It clung to the wood. It was the moment. He pulled the trigger of the launcher, sending the canister of gas into the stone to the right of the French doors. It exploded, bouncing off the wall to the ground; the vapors spread instantly, clouds of gas swirling, choking men within its billowing periphery. Weapons were clung to, but free hands rubbed swollen, watery eyes and covered inflamed nostrils.

The second firebomb exploded, tearing away the elegant Victorian façade above the French doors, shattering the panes of glass, whole sections of the upper wall plummeting down into the tiled foyer beyond. Flames spread upward toward the eaves and inside, firing drapes and upholstery. The marine guards scrambled away from the thunderous explosion and the flames into the clouds of tear gas. A number now dropped their rifles, as all lurched in every direction, colliding with one another, trying to get away from the fumes, gagging, coughing, seeking relief.

Delta rose to a crouch, the machine pistol in his hand, yanking the assassin up beside him. It was time; the chaos was complete. The swirling gas in front of the shattered French doors was being sucked in by the heat of the flames; it would dissipate sufficiently for him to make headway. Once inside, his search would be quick, over in moments. The directors of a covert operation that required a sterile house in foreign territory would stay within the protective confines of the house itself for two reasons. The first was that the size and disposition of the attacking force could not be accurately estimated and the risk of capture or death outside was too great. The second was more practical: papers had to be destroyed, burned, not shredded, as they had learned in Teheran. Directives, dossiers, operational progress reports, background materials, all had to go. The sirens in Victoria Peak were growing louder, nearer; the frantic race up the steep roads was nearly over.

"It's the countdown," said Bourne, setting the timer on the last *plastique* explosive. "I'm not giving this to you, but I'll use it to advantage—both yours and mine. Thirty seconds, Major Allcott-Price." Jason arced the packet as far as he could toward the right front wall.

"My *weapon!* For Christ's sake, give me the gun!"

"It's on the ground. Under my foot."

The assassin lurched down. "Let go of it!"

"When I want to—and I *will* want to. But if you try to take it, the next thing you'll see is a cell in the Hong Kong garrison, and—according to you—a scaffold, a thick rope, and a hangman in your immediate future."

The killer looked up in panic. "You goddamned *liar!* You *lied!*"

"Frequently. Don't you?"

"You *said—*"

"I know what I said. I also know why you're here, and why instead of nine shells you have three."

"What?"

"You're my diversion, Major. When I let you free with the gun, you'll head for the gate or a blown-out section of the wall—whichever, it's your choice. They'll try to stop you. You'll fire back, naturally, and while they concentrate on you, I'll get inside."

"You *bastard!*"

"My feelings are hurt, but then I don't have feelings any longer, so it doesn't matter. I simply have to get inside—"

The last explosion blew up a sculptured tree, its roots smashing into a weakened section of the wall, stones falling out of place, the wall itself half crumbling, splitting rocks forming a V at the center of secondary impact. Marines from the gate contingent rushed forward.

"Now!" roared Delta, rising to his full height.

"Give me the *gun!* Let *go* of it!"

Jason Bourne suddenly froze. He could not move— except that by some instinct or other he crashed his knee up into the killer's throat, sending the assassin over on his side. A man had appeared beyond the shattered glass doors of the burning foyer. A handkerchief covered his face, but it could not cover his limp. His *limp!* With his clubbed foot the silhouetted figure kicked down the left frame of the French doors and awkwardly walked down the three steps to the short flagstone patio fronting the once stately gardens. He dragged himself forward and yelled as loud as he could, ordering the guards who could hear him to hold their fire. The figure did not have to lower his handkerchief, Delta knew the face. It was the face of his *enemy. It was Paris, a cemetery outside of Paris. Alexander Conklin had come to kill him. Beyond-salvage was the order from on high.*

"*David!* It's Alex! Don't do what you're *doing!* Stop it! It's *me*, David! I'm here to help you!"

"You're here to *kill* me! You came to kill me in Paris, you tried again in New York! *Treadstone Seventy-one!* You've got a short memory, you bastard!"

"You don't have *any* memory, *goddamn* you! You became *Delta,* that's what they wanted! I know the whole story, David. I flew over here because we put it together! Marie, Mo Panov, and I! We're all here. Marie's safe!"

"*Lies! Tricks!* All of you, you *killed* her! You would have killed her in Paris, but I wouldn't let you near her! I kept her *away* from you!"

"She's not dead, David! She's *alive!* I can bring her to you! *Now!*"

"More *lies!*" Delta crouched and pulled the trigger, spraying the patio, the bullets ricocheting up into the burning foyer, but for reasons unknown to him they did not cut down the man himself. "You want to pull me out so you can give the order and I'm dead. Beyond-salvage carried out! *No* way, *executioner!* I'm going inside! I want the silent, secret men behind you! They're *there!* I *know* they're there!" Bourne grabbed the fallen assassin and pulled him to his feet, handing him the gun. "You wanted a Jason Bourne, he's *yours!* I'm setting him loose among the roses. Kill him while I kill *you!*"

Half madman, half survivor, the commando lunged through the flowering bushes away from Bourne. He raced first down the path, then instantly returned, seeing that the marine guards were at the north and south areas of the wall. If he showed himself on the east border of the garden, he was caught between both contingents. He was dead if he moved.

"I haven't any more *time,* Conklin!" yelled Bourne. *Why couldn't he kill the man who had betrayed him? Squeeze the trigger! Kill the last of Treadstone Seventy-one! Kill. Kill! What stopped him?*

The assassin threw himself over the row of flowers, clutching the warm barrel of Bourne's machine gun, wrenching it downward, leveling and firing his own gun at Jason. The bullet grazed Bourne's forehead, and in fury, Jason yanked back the trigger of the repeating weapon. Bullets thundered into the ground, the vibrations within their small, deadly arena earth-shattering. He grabbed the Englishman's gun, twisting it counterclockwise. The assassin's mutilated right arm was no match for the man from Medusa. The gun exploded as Bourne wrenched it free. The impostor fell back on the grass, his eyes glazed, within them the knowledge that he had lost.

"*David!* For God's sake, listen to me! You *have* to—"

"There is no *David* here!" screamed Jason, his knee rammed into the assassin's chest. "My rightful name is *Bourne,* sprung from *Delta,* spawned by Medusa! The *Snake Lady! Remember?*"

"We have to talk!"

"We have to die! *You* have to die! The secret men inside are my contract with myself, with *Marie! They* have to die!" Bourne gripped the lapel of the assassin's jacket, pulling him up on his feet. "I repeat! Here's your Jason Bourne! He's all yours!"

"Don't *shoot!* Hold your fire!" roared Conklin as bewildered segments of the three marine contingents began to close in and the deafening sirens of the Hong Kong police roared to a stop at the demolished gate.

The man from Medusa slammed his shoulder into the commando's back, propelling the killer out into the light of the roaring flames and the floodlights. "There he *is!* That's the prize you *wanted!*"

There was a burst of rifle fire as the assassin reeled out, then dove to the ground, rolling over and over to avoid the bullets.

"Stop it! Not *him!* For Christ's sake, hold your fire. Don't *kill* him!" screamed Conklin.

"Not *him?*" roared Jason Bourne. *"Not him?* Only *me!* Isn't that right, you son of a bitch? Now, you *do* die! For *Marie,* for *Echo,* for *all* of us!"

He squeezed the trigger of the machine gun, but still the bullets would not hit their mark! He swung around and, swinging back and forth, aimed his deadly weapon at both converging squads of marines. Again, he fired several prolonged bursts, crouching, ducking, moving from place to place behind the roses. *Yet he angled the barrel above their heads! Why? The children could not stop him. But then the children in their pressed GI issue should not die for the manipulators.* He had to get inside the sterile house. Now! No moments were left. It was now!

"*David!*" A woman's voice. Oh Christ, a *woman's* voice! "David, David, *David!*" A figure in a flowing skirt ran out of the sterile house. She grabbed Alexander Conklin and pushed him away. She stood alone on the patio. "It's *me*, David! I'm *here!* I'm *safe!* Everything's all *right*, my darling!"

Another trick, another lie. It was an old woman with gray hair, white hair! "Get out of my way, lady, or I'll kill you. You're just another lie, another *trick!*"

"David, it's *me!* Can't you *hear* me—"

"I can *see* you! A *trick!*"

"*No,* David!"

"My name's not *David.* I told your scum friend, there's no David here!"

"*Don't!*" screamed Marie, desperately shaking her head and running in front of several marines who had crawled out on the grass, away from the swirling, vanishing clouds of gas. They were on their knees with a clear view of Bourne, getting their bearings, leveling their rifles unsteadily at him. Marie positioned herself between the recovering guards and their target. "Haven't you done *enough* to him? For God's sake, somebody *stop* them!"

"And get blown away by some son of a bitch *terrorist?*" yelled a youthful voice from the ranks by the front wall.

"He's not what you *think!* Whatever he is, the people inside *made* him that way! You heard him. He won't fire on you if you don't shoot!"

"He's already *fired,*" roared an officer.

"You're still *standing!*" yelled back Alex Conklin from the edge of the patio. "And he's a better marksman with more weapons than any man here! Account for it! *I* can!"

"I don't *need* you!" thundered Jason Bourne, once again triggering a burst of machine-gun fire into the burning wall of the sterile house.

Suddenly the assassin was on his feet, crouching, then lunging for the marine nearest him, a hatless youngster still coughing from the gas. The killer grabbed the guard's rifle, kicking him in the head, and fired the weapon into the next nearest marine, who lurched backward grabbing his stomach. The killer spun around; he spotted an officer with a machine pistol not unlike Bourne's; he shot him in the neck, and grabbed the weapon from the falling body. He paused for only a split second evaluating his chances, then whipped the machine pistol up under his left arm. Delta watched, instinctively knowing what the commando would do, knowing, too, that his diversion was about to take place.

The assassin did it. He fired again, one round after another, into the closed ranks of the young, inexperienced marines by the front wall, racing, dodging his way across the short stretch of grass into the shoulder-high row of flowers on Bourne's left. It was his only escape route, the least illuminated—the collapsed right rear wall.

"*Stop* him!" shouted Conklin, limping frantically across the patio. "But don't *shoot!* Don't kill him! For Christ's sake, don't *kill* him!"

"*Bullshit!*" came the reply from someone in the squad of marines by the left rear wall. The assassin, twisting, turning, crouching, his rifle on repeat fire, quickly worked his way toward the broken wall, pinning the guards down by his rapid bursts. The rifle chamber ran out of shells; he threw the weapon down, swinging the murderous machine pistol into place, and started his last race toward the broken wall, spraying the prone contingent of marines. He was there! The darkness beyond was his escape!

"You *motherfucker!*" It was a teenager's cry, the voice immature, in torment, but nevertheless lethal. "You killed my *buddy!* You blew his fucking face off! You're going to *buy* it, you *shithead!*"

A young black marine leaped away from his dead white companion and raced toward the wall as the assassin swung around, vaulting over the stone. Another burst from the killer caught the marine in the shoulder; he lunged to the ground, rolled over twice to his left, and fired four rounds of ammunition.

They were followed by an agonizing, hysterical scream of defiance. It was the scream of death; the assassin, his eyes wide in hatred, fell into the jagged rocks. Major Allcott-Price, formerly of the Royal Commandos, was gone.

Bourne started forward, his weapon raised. Marie ran to the border of the patio, the distance between them no more than a few feet. "Don't *do* it, David!"

"I'm not *David,* lady! Ask your scum-ball friend, we go back a long time. Get out of my way!" *Why couldn't he kill her? One burst, and he was free to do what he had to do! Why?*

"All right!" screamed Marie, holding her place. "There is no David, *all right?* You're Jason Bourne! You're *Delta!* You're anything you want to be, but you're also *mine!* You're my *husband!*" The revelation had the impact of a sudden bolt of lightning on the guards who heard it. The officers, their elbows bent, held up their hands—the universal command to hold fire—as they and the men stared in astonishment.

"I don't *know* you!"

"My voice is my own. You know it, Jason."

"A *trick!* An actress, a *mimic!* A *lie!* It's been done before."

"And if I look different, it's because of you, *Jason Bourne!*"

"Get out of my way or get *killed!*"

"You taught me in *Paris!* On the rue de Rivoli, the Hotel Meurice, the newsstand on the corner. Can you remember? The newspapers with the story out of Zurich, my photograph on all the front pages! And the small hotel in the Montparnasse when we were checking out, the concierge reading the paper, my picture in front of his face! You were so frightened you told me to run outside. . . . The *taxi!* Do you remember the taxi? On the way to Issy-les-Moulineaux—I'll never forget that impossible name. 'Change your hair,' you said. 'Pull it up or push it back!' You said you didn't care what I did so long as I *changed* it! You asked me if I had an eyebrow pencil —you told me to thicken my brows, make them longer! *Your* words, *Jason!* We were running for our lives and you wanted me to look *different,* to remove any likeness to the photograph that was all over *Europe!* I had to become a chameleon because Jason Bourne was a chameleon. He had to teach his lover, his *wife!* That's all I've *done,* Jason!"

"*No!*" cried Delta, drawing the word out into a scream, the mists of confusion enveloping him, sending his mind into the outer regions of panic. The images were there! Rue de Rivoli, the Montparnasse, the taxi. *Listen to me. I am a chameleon called Cain and I can teach you many things I do not care to teach you but I must. I can change my color to accommodate the forest, I can shift with the wind by smelling it. I can find my way through natural and man-made jungles. Alpha,*

Bravo, Charlie, Delta. . . . Delta is for Charlie and Charlie is for Cain. I am Cain. I am death. And I must tell you who I am and lose you.

"You *do* remember!" shouted David Webb's wife.

"A trick! The chemicals—I said the words. They *gave* you the words! They have to *stop* me!"

"They gave me nothing! I want *nothing* from them. I only want my husband! I'm *Marie!*"

"You're a lie! They *killed* her!" Delta squeezed the trigger and the fusillade of bullets exploded the earth at Marie's feet. Rifles were quickly brought up to firing positions.

"Don't *do* it!" screamed Marie, whipping her head over at the marine guards, her eyes glaring, her voice a command. "All right, Jason. If you don't know me, I don't want to live. I can't be plainer than that, my darling. It's why I understand what you're doing. You're throwing your life away because a part of you that's taken over thinks I'm gone and you don't want to live without me. I understand that very well because I don't want to live without you." Marie took several steps across the grass and stood motionless.

Delta raised the machine gun, the snub-nosed sight on the barrel centering on the gray hair streaked with white. His index finger closed around the trigger. Suddenly, involuntarily, his right hand began to tremble, then his left. The murderous weapon began to waver, at first slowly, back and forth, then faster—in circles—as Bourne's head swayed in fitful jerks; the trembling spread; his neck began to lose control.

There was a commotion within the gathering crowd at the smoldering ruins of the gate and the guardhouse several hundred feet away. A man struggled; he was held by two marines. "Let me go, you goddamned fools! I'm a doctor, *his* doctor!" With a surge of strength, Morris Panov broke away and raced across the lawn into the glare of the floodlights. He stopped twenty feet from Bourne.

Delta began to moan; the sound and the rhythm was barbaric. Jason Bourne dropped the weapon . . . and David Webb fell to his knees weeping. Marie started toward him.

"*No!*" commanded Panov, his voice quietly emphatic,

stopping Webb's wife. "He has to come to you. He must."

"He *needs* me!"

"Not that way. He has to recognize you. *David* has to recognize you and tell his other self to let him free. You can't do that for him. He has to do it for himself."

Silence. Floodlights. Fire.

And like a cringing, beaten child, David Webb raised his head, the tears streaming down his cheeks. Slowly, painfully, he rose to his feet and ran into the arms of his wife.

33

They were in the sterile house, in the white-walled communications center—in an antiseptic cell belonging to some futuristic laboratory complex. White-faced computers rose above the white counters on the left, dozens of thin, dark rectangular mouths sporadically indented, their teeth digital readouts forming luminescent green numbers that constantly changed with inviolate frequency alterations and less sophisticated, less secure means of sending and receiving information. On the right was a large white conference table above the white-tiled floor, the only deviation from color conformity and asepsis being several black ashtrays. The players were in place around the table. The technicians had been dismissed, all systems put on hold, only the ominous Red-Alert, a three-by ten-inch panel in the central computer remained active; an operator was outside the closed door should the alarming red lights appear. Beyond this sacrosanct, isolated room the Hong Kong fire fighters were hosing down the last of the smoldering embers as the Hong Kong police were calming the panicked residents from the nearby estates on Victoria Peak—many of whom were convinced that Armageddon had arrived in the form of a Mainland onslaught—telling everyone that the terrible events were the work of a deranged criminal killed by government emergency units. The skeptical Peakers were not satisfied. The times were not on their side; their world was not as it should be and they wanted proof. So the corpse of the dead assassin was paraded on a stretcher past the curious onlookers, the punctured, blood-drenched body partially uncovered for all to see. The stately residents returned to their stately homes, having by this time contemplated all manner of insurance claims.

The players sat in white plastic chairs, living, breathing robots waiting for a signal to commence, none really possessing the courage or the energy to open the proceedings. Exhaustion, mingled with the fear of violent death, marked their faces—marked all but one face. His possessed the deep lines and dark shadows of extreme fatigue, but there was no hollow fear in his eyes, only passive, bewildered acceptance of things still beyond his understanding. Minutes ago death had held no fear for him; it was preferable to living. Now, in his confusion, with his wife gripping his hand, he could feel the swelling of distant anger, distant in the sense that it was far back in the recesses of his mind, relentlessly pushing forward like the faraway thunder over a lake in an approaching summer storm.

"Who did this to us?" said David Webb, his voice barely above a whisper.

"I did," answered Havilland, at the end of the rectangular white table. The ambassador leaned slowly forward, returning Webb's deathlike stare. "If I were in a court of law seeking mercy for an ignominious act, I would have to plead extenuating circumstances."

"Which were?" asked David in a monotone.

"First, there is the crisis," said the diplomat. "Second, there was yourself."

"Explain that," interrupted Alex Conklin at the other end of the table, facing Havilland. Webb and Marie were on his left in front of the white wall, Morris Panov and Edward McAllister opposite them. "And don't leave anything out," added the rogue Intelligence officer.

"I don't intend to," said the ambassador, his eyes remaining on David. "The crisis is real, the catastrophe imminent. A cabal has been formed deep in Peking by a group of zealots led by a man so deeply entrenched in the

hierarchy of his government, so revered as a philosopher-prince that he cannot be exposed. No one would
believe it. Anyone who attempted to expose him would
become a pariah. Worse, any attempt at exposure would
risk a backlash so severe that Peking would cry insult and
outrage, and revert to suspicion and intransigence. But
if the conspiracy is not aborted, it will destroy the Hong
Kong Accords and blow the colony apart. The result will
be the immediate occupation by the People's Republic.
I don't have to tell you what that would mean—economic
chaos, violence, bloodshed and undoubtedly war in the
Far East. How long could such hostilities be contained
before other nations are forced to choose sides? The risk
is unthinkable."

Silence. Eyes locked with eyes.

"Fanatics from the Kuomintang," said David, his voice
flat and cold. "China against China. It's been the war cry
of maniacs for the past forty years."

"But only a cry, Mr. Webb. Words, talk, but no movement, no strikes, no ultimate strategy." Havilland cupped
his hands on the table, breathing deeply. "There is now.
The strategy's in place, a strategy so oblique and devious,
so long in the making, they believe it can't fail. But of
course it will, and when it does, the world will be faced
with a crisis of intolerable proportions. It could well lead
to the final crisis, the one we can't survive. Certainly the
Far East won't."

"You're not telling me anything I haven't seen for
myself. They've gone down deep in high places, and
they're probably spreading, but they're still fanatics, a
lunatic fringe. And if the maniac I saw who was running
the show is anything like the others, they'd all be hanged
in Tian An Men Square. It'd be televised and approved
by every group opposed to capital punishment. He was
—is—a messianic sadist, a butcher. Butchers aren't
statesmen. They're not taken seriously."

"Herr Hitler was in 1933," observed Havilland. "The
Ayatollah Khomeini only a few years ago. But then you
obviously don't know who their true leader is. He'd never
show himself under any circumstances where you might
even remotely see *him*. However, I can assure you he's a
statesman and taken very seriously. However, again, his
objective is not Peking. It's Hong Kong."

"I saw what I saw and heard what I heard, and it'll all be with me for a long time. . . . You don't need me, you never *did! Isolate* them, spread the word in the Central Committee, call in Taiwan to disown them—they *will!* Times change. They don't want that war any more than Peking does."

The ambassador studied the Medusan, obviously evaluating David's information, realizing that Webb had seen enough in Peking to draw conclusions of his own, but not enough to understand the essence of the Hong Kong conspiracy. "It's too late," said the diplomat. "The forces have been set in motion. Treachery at the highest levels of China's government, treachery by the hands of the despised Nationalists, assumed to be in collusion with Western financial interests. Even the devoted followers of Deng Xiaoping could not accept that blow to Peking's pride, that loss of international face—the role of the duped cuckold. Neither would we if it was learned that General Motors, IBM, and the New York Stock Exchange were being run by American traitors, trained in the Soviet, diverting billions to projects not in our nation's interests."

"The analogy is accurate," broke in McAllister, his fingers at his right temple. "Cumulatively, that's what Hong Kong will be to the People's Republic—that and a hundred thousand times more. But there's another element, and it's as alarming as anything else we've learned. I should like to bring it up now—in my position as an analyst, as someone who's supposed to calculate the reactions of adversaries and potential adversaries—"

"Make it short," interrupted Webb. "You talk too much and you keep rubbing your head too much and I don't like your eyes. They belong on a dead fish. You talked too much in Maine. You're a liar."

"Yes. Yes, I understand what you're saying and why you're saying it. But I'm a decent man, Mr. Webb. I believe in decency."

"I don't. Not any longer. Go on. This is all very enlightening, and I don't understand a goddamned thing because nobody's said a goddamned thing that makes sense. What's your contribution, liar?"

"The organized crime factor." McAllister swallowed at David's repeated insult, but still delivered the statement as if he expected everyone to understand. When faced with blank looks, he added. "The *triads!*"

"Mafia-structured groups, Oriental style," said Marie, her eyes on the undersecretary of State. "Criminal brotherhoods."

McAllister nodded. "Narcotics, illegal immigration, gambling, prostitution, loan-sharking—all the usual pursuits."

"And some not so usual," added Marie. "They're deep into their own form of economics. They own banks—indirectly, of course—throughout California, Oregon, the State of Washington, and up into my country, in British Columbia. They launder money in the millions every day by way of international transfers."

"Which only serves to compound the crisis," said McAllister emphatically.

"Why?" asked David. "What's your point?"

"*Crime,* Mr. Webb. The leaders of the People's Republic are obsessed with crime. Reports indicate that over a hundred thousand executions have taken place during the last three years with little distinction made between misdemeanors and felonies. It's consistent with the regime—the origins of the regime. All revolutions believe they are conceived in purity; the purity of the cause is everything. Peking will make ideological adjustments to benefit from the West's marketplace, but there'll be no accommodation for even the hint of organized crime."

"You make them sound like a collection of paranoids," interjected Panov.

"They are. They can't afford to be anything else."

"Ideologically?" asked the psychiatrist skeptically.

"Sheer numbers, Doctor. The purity of the revolution is the cover, but it's the numbers that frighten them. A huge, immensely populated country with vast resources —my God, if organized crime moved in, and with a billion people inside its borders, don't think for a minute the overlords aren't champing at the bit—it could become a *nation* of triads. Villages, towns, whole cities could be divided into 'family' terrains, all profiting from the influx of Western capital and technology. There'd be an explosion of illegal exports flooding the contraband markets across the world. Narcotics from uncountable hills and fields that could not possibly be patrolled, weapons from subsidiary factories set up through graft, textiles from hundreds of underground plants using stolen machinery and peasant labor crippling those industries in the West. *Crime.*"

"That's a 'great leap forward' no one over here's been able to accomplish in the last forty years," said Conklin.

"Who would dare try?" asked McAllister. "If a person can be executed for stealing fifty yuan, who's going to go for a hundred thousand? It takes protection, organization, people in high places. This is what Peking fears, why it's paranoid. The leaders are terrified of corrupters in high places. The political infrastructure could be eroded. The leaders would lose control, and *that* they will not risk. Again, their fears *are* paranoid, but for them they're terribly real. Any hint that powerful criminal factions are in league with internal conspirators, all infiltrating their economy, would be enough for them to disown the Accords and send their troops down into Hong Kong."

"Your conclusion's obvious," said Marie. "But where's the logic? How could it happen?"

"It's happening, Mrs. Webb," answered Ambassador Havilland. "It's why we needed Jason Bourne."

"Somebody had better start at the beginning," said David.

The diplomat did. "It began over thirty years ago when a brilliant young man was sent from Taiwan back to the land of his father's birth and given a new name, a new family. It was a long-range plan; its roots were in zealotry and revenge . . ."

Webb listened as the incredible story of Sheng Chou Yang unfolded, each block in place, each fact convincingly the truth, for there was no reason any longer for lies. Twenty-seven minutes later, when he had finished, Havilland picked up a black-bordered file folder. He lifted the cover, revealing a clasped sheaf of some seventy-odd pages, closed it, and reached over, placing it in front of David. "This is everything we know, everything we've learned—the detailed specifics of everything I've told you. It can't leave this house except as ashes, but you're welcome to read it. If you have any doubts or questions, I swear to you I'll move every source in the United States government—from the Oval Office to the National Security Council—to satisfy you. I could do no less." The diplomat paused, his eyes fixed on Webb's. "Perhaps we have no right to ask it, but we need your help. We need all the information you can give us."

"So you can send someone in to take out this Sheng Chou Yang."

"Essentially, yes. But it's far more complex than that. Our hand must be invisible. It can't be seen or even remotely suspected. Sheng's covered himself brilliantly. Peking looks upon him as a visionary, a great patriot who works slavishly for Mother China—you might say, a saint. His security is absolute. The people around him, his aides, his guards, they're his protective shock troops, their allegiance is solely to him."

"Which is why you wanted the impostor," interrupted Marie. "He was your link to Sheng."

"We knew he had accepted contracts from him. Sheng had to—*has* to—eliminate his opposition, both those who oppose him ideologically and those he intends to exclude from his operations."

"In this latter group," McAllister broke in, "are the leaders of rival triads that Sheng doesn't trust, that the fanatics of the Kuomintang don't trust. He knows that if they're around to see that they're being squeezed out, a destabilizing gangland war would erupt, which Sheng couldn't tolerate any more than the British can with Peking up the street. Within the past two months seven triad overlords have been killed, their organizations crippled."

"The new Jason Bourne was Sheng's perfect solution," continued the ambassador. "The hired assassin with no political or national ties, for, above all, the killings could never be traced back to China."

"But he went to *Peking*," objected Webb. "It's where I tracked him. Even if it started out as a trap for me, which it was—"

"A trap for *you?*" exclaimed Havilland. "They *knew* about you?"

"I came face-to-face with my successor two nights ago at the airport. We each knew who the other was—it was impossible not to know. He wasn't going to keep it a secret and take the fall for a failed contract."

"It *was* you," interrupted McAllister. "I *knew* it!"

"So did Sheng and his people. I was the new gun in

town and had to be stopped, killed on a priority-one basis. They couldn't risk what I'd pieced together. The trap was conceived that night, set that night."

"*Jesus!*" cried Conklin. "I read about Kai-tak in Washington. The papers said it was assumed to be right-wing lunatics. Keep the Commies out of capitalism. Instead, it was *you?*"

"Both governments had to come up with something for the world press," added the undersecretary. "Just as we have to say something about tonight—"

"My *point* is," said David, ignoring McAllister. "This Sheng called for the commando, used him to mount a trap for me, and by doing so made him part of the inner circle. That's no way for a concealed client to keep his distance from a hired killer."

"It is if he didn't expect him to walk out of that circle alive," replied Havilland, glancing at the undersecretary of State. "It's Edward's theory, and one to which I subscribe, that when the final contract was carried out, *or* when it was deemed that he knew too much and was therefore a liability, the impostor was to be killed collecting a payment—believing, of course, that he was being given another assignment. Everything untraceable, the slate clean. The events at Kai-tak no doubt sealed his death warrant."

"He wasn't smart enough to see it," said Jason Bourne. "He couldn't think geometrically."

"I beg your pardon?" asked the ambassador.

"Nothing," answered Webb, again staring at the diplomat. "So everything you told me was part truth, part lie. Hong Kong could blow apart, but not for the reasons you gave me."

"The truth was our credibility; you had to accept that, accept our deep, frightening concerns. The lies were to recruit you." Havilland leaned back in his chair. "And I can't be any more honest than that."

"*Bastards,*" said Webb, his voice low, ice-like.

"I'll grant you that," agreed Havilland. "But as I mentioned before, there were extenuating circumstances, specifically two. The crisis and yourself."

"And?" said Marie.

"Let me ask you, Mr. Webb . . . Mrs. Webb. If we had come to you and stated our case, would you have joined forces with us? Would you willingly have become Jason Bourne again?"

Silence. All eyes were on David as his own strayed blankly over the surface of the table, then rested on the file folder. "No," he said softly. "I don't trust you."

"We knew that," agreed Havilland, again nodding his head. "But from our point of view we *had* to recruit you. You were able to do what no one else could do, and insofar as you did it, I submit that that judgment was correct. The cost was terrible, no one underestimates it, but we felt—I felt—that there was no other choice. Time and the consequences were against us—*are* against us."

"As much as before," said Webb. "The commando's dead."

"The commando?" McAllister leaned forward.

"Your assassin. The impostor. What you did to us was all for nothing."

"Not necessarily," objected Havilland. "It will depend on what you can tell us. News of *a* death up here will be in tomorrow's headlines, we can't stop it, but Sheng can't know *whose* death. No photographs were taken, no press was here at the time, and those who've arrived since have been cordoned off several hundred yards away by the police. We can control the information by simply providing it."

"What about the body?" asked Panov. "There are medical procedures—"

"Overruled by MI-Six," said the ambassador. "This is still British territory, and communications between London, Washington, and Government House were swift. The impostor's face was too shattered for anyone who saw it to give a description, and his remains are in custody, beyond scrutiny. It was Edward's thinking, and he was damn quick about it."

"There's still David and Marie," persisted the psychiatrist. "Too many people saw them, heard them."

"Only several squads of marine guards were close enough to see and hear clearly," said McAllister. "The entire contingent is being flown back to Hawaii in an hour, including two dead and seven wounded. They've left the premises and are sequestered at the airport. There was a great deal of confusion and panic. The police and the firemen were occupied elsewhere; none were in the gardens. We can say anything we like."

"That seems to be a habit with you," commented Webb.

"You heard the ambassador," said the undersecretary, avoiding David's gaze. "We didn't feel we had a choice."

"Be fair to yourself, Edward." Again Havilland looked at Webb while addressing the undersecretary. "*I* didn't feel we had a choice. You strenuously objected."

"I was *wrong*," said McAllister firmly as the diplomat snapped his eyes over at him. "But that's irrelevant," continued the undersecretary quickly. "We've got to decide what we're going to say. The consulate's been swamped by calls from the press—"

"The *consulate*?" broke in Conklin. "Some sterile house!"

"There wasn't time for a proper leasing cover," said the ambassador. "It was kept as quiet as possible and we prepared a plausible story. So far as we know, there were no questions, but the police report had to list the owner and the lessee. How's Garden Road handling it, Edward?"

"Simply that the situation hasn't been clarified. They're waiting for us, but they can't stall much longer. It's better that we prepare something than leave the circumstances to speculation."

"Infinitely," agreed Havilland. "I suspect that means you have something in mind."

"It's stop-gap, but it could serve, if I heard Mr. Webb correctly."

"About what?"

"You've used the word 'commando' several times, I assume not as a figure of speech. The assassin was a commando?"

"Former. An officer and a mental case. Homicidal, to be accurate."

"Did you get an identity, learn his name?"

David looked hard at the analyst, recalling Allcott-Price's words, spoken in a warped sense of sick triumph. *. . . If I lose and the story blows, how many practicing antisocials will be fired up by it? How many other 'different' men are out there who'd be only too happy to take my place, as I took yours? This* *bloody world is crawling with Jason Bournes. Give them direction, an idea—and they'll be off and running. . . .* "I never found out who he was," said Webb simply.

"But nevertheless he *was* a commando."

"That's right."

"Not a Ranger or a Green Beret or Special Forces—"

"No."

"I assume therefore that you mean he was British."

"Yes."

"Then we'll put out a story that implicitly denies those specifics. Not an Englishman, no military record—go in the opposite direction."

"A white male American," said Conklin quietly, with even a measure of respect, as he looked at the under-secretary of State. "Give him a name and a history from a dead file. Preferably fourth-rate garbage, a psychopath with a hang-up so heavy he goes after someone up here."

"Something like that, but perhaps not entirely," said McAllister, awkwardly shifting his position in the chair, as if he did not care to disagree with the experienced CIA man. Or something else. "White male, yes. American, yes. Certainly a man with an obsession so compelling that he's driven to wholesale slaughter, his fury directed at a target—as you say—up here."

"Who?" asked David.

"Me," replied McAllister, his eyes locked with Webb's.

"Which means *me,*" said David. "I'm that *man,* that *obsessed* man."

"Your name would not be used," continued the under-secretary calmly, coldly. "We could invent an American expatriate who several years ago was hunted by the authorities throughout the Far East for crimes ranging from multiple murders to running narcotics. We'll say I cooperated with the police in Hong Kong, Macao, Singapore, Japan, Malaysia, Sumatra, and the Philippines. Through my efforts his operations were effectively shut down and he lost millions. He learns I've returned and am posted here on Victoria Peak. He comes after me, the man who ruined him." McAllister paused, turning to David. "Since I spent a number of years here in Hong Kong, I can't imagine that Peking overlooked me. I'm sure there's an extensive dossier on an analyst who made a number of enemies during his tour of duty here. I *did* make enemies,

Mr. Webb. It was my job. We were trying to increase our influence in this part of the world, and wherever Americans were involved in criminal activities, I did my level best to help the authorities apprehend them, or, at the least, force them out of Asia. It was the best way to show our good intentions, going after our own. It was also the reason State recalled me to Washington. And by using my name we lend a certain authenticity for Sheng Chou Yang. You see, we knew each other. He'll speculate on a dozen possibilities—I hope the right one, but none remotely connected to a British commando."

"The right speculation," interrupted Conklin quietly, "being the fact that no one over here has heard from the first Jason Bourne in a couple of years."

"Exactly."

"So *I'm* the corpse that's in custody," said Webb, "beyond scrutiny."

"You could be, yes," said McAllister. "You see, we don't know what Sheng knows, how deep his penetration went. The only thing we want to establish is that the dead man is *not* his assassin."

"Leaving the way open for another impostor to go back up and draw Sheng out for the kill," added Conklin, respectfully. "You're something, Mr. Analyst. A son of a bitch, but something."

"You'd be exposing yourself, Edward," said Havilland, his gaze leveled at the undersecretary. "I never asked that of you. You *do* have enemies."

"I want to do it this way, Mr. Ambassador. You employ me to render the best judgments that I can, and in my judgment this is the most productive course. There's got to be a convincing smoke screen. My name can provide it—for Sheng. The rest can be couched in ambiguous language, language that everyone we want to reach will understand."

"So be it," said Webb, suddenly closing his eyes, hearing the words Jason Bourne had spoken so often.

"David—" Marie touched his face.

"Sorry." Webb fingered the file folder in front of him, then opened it. On the first page was a photograph with a name printed underneath. It was identified as the face of Sheng Chou Yang, but it was far more than that. It was *the face.* It was the face of the *butcher!* The madman who

hacked women and men to death with his jeweled ceremonial sword, who forced brothers to fight with razor-
sharp knives until one killed the other, who took a brave,
tortured Echo's life with a slash to the head. Bourne
stopped breathing, enraged by the unimaginable cruelty,
as bloody images overcame him. As he stared at the photograph the sight of Echo, throwing his life away to save
Delta, brought him back to that clearing in the forest.
Delta knew that it was Echo's death that had made the
assassin's capture possible. Echo had died defiantly, accepting his unbearably painful execution, so that a fellow
Medusan could not only make good his escape, but obey
a final gesture telling him that the madman with the
sword must be killed!

"*This,*" whispered Jason Bourne, "is the son of your
unknown taipan?"

"Yes," said Havilland.

"Your *revered* philosopher-prince? The Chinese saint
no one can expose?"

"Again, yes."

"You were *wrong!* He showed himself! *Christ,* did he
show himself!"

Stunned, the ambassador shot forward. "You're certain?"

"There's no way I could be more certain."

"The circumstances must have been extraordinary,"
said the astonished McAllister. "And it certainly confirms
that the impostor never would have gotten out of there
alive. Still, the circumstances must have been *earth-shak-
ing* for him!"

"Considering the fact that no one outside of China
ever learned about them, they were. Mao's tomb became
a shooting gallery. It was part of the trap, and they lost.
Echo lost."

"Who?" asked Marie, still gripping his hand.

"A friend."

"Mao's *tomb?*" repeated Havilland. "Extraordinary!"

"Not at all," said Bourne. "How bright. The last place
in China a target would expect an attack. He goes in
thinking he's the pursuer following his quarry, expecting
to pick him up outside, on the other side. The lights are
dim, his guard down. And all the while *he's* the quarry,
hunted, isolated, set up for the kill. Very bright."

"Very *dangerous* for the hunters," said the ambassador. "For Sheng's people. One misstep and they could have been taken. *Insanity!*"

"No missteps were possible. They would have killed their own if I hadn't killed them. I understand that now. When everything went off the wire, they simply disappeared. With Echo."

"Back to Sheng, *please,* Mr. Webb." Havilland was himself obsessed, his eyes pleading. "Tell us what you saw, what you know."

"He's a monster," said Jason quietly, his eyes glazed, staring at the photograph. "He comes from hell, a Savonarola who tortures and kills—men, women, kids— with a smile on his face. He gives sermons like a prophet talking to children, but underneath he's a maniac who rules his gang of misfits by sheer terror. Those shock troops you mentioned aren't troops, they're goons, sadistic thugs who've learned their craft from a master. He's Auschwitz, Dachau, and Bergen-Belsen all rolled into one. God help us all if he runs anything over here."

"He can, Mr. Webb," said Havilland quietly, his terrified gaze fixed on Jason Bourne. "He will. You've just described a Sheng Chou Yang the world has never seen, and at this moment he is the most powerful man in China. As Adolf Hitler marched victoriously into the Reichstag, so Sheng will march into the Central Committee, making it his puppet. What you've told us is far more catastrophic than anything we've conceived of—China against China. . . . Armageddon to follow. Oh, my God!"

"He's an animal," whispered Jason hoarsely. "He has to kill like a predator, but his only hunger is for killing —not for food but for the kill."

"You're talking in *generalities.*" McAllister's interruption was cold but intense. "We have to know more—*I* have to know more!"

"He called a conference." Bourne spoke dreamily, his head swaying, his eyes again riveted on the photograph. "It was the start of—the nights of the great blade, he said. There was a traitor, he said. The conference was something only a madman could create, torches everywhere, held in the countryside, an hour out of Peking, in a bird sanctuary—can you believe it? A *bird* sanctuary—and he really did what I say he did. He killed a man suspended

by ropes, hacking his sword into the screaming body.
Then a woman who tried to argue her innocence, cutting
her head off—her *head!* In front of everyone! And then
two brothers—"

"A *traitor?*" whispered McAllister, ever the analyst.
"Did he *find* one? Did anyone confess? Is there any kind
of counterinsurgency?"

"*Stop* it!" cried Marie.

"*No,* Mrs. Webb! He's going back. He's reliving it.
Look at him. Can't you see? He's *there.*"

"I'm afraid our irritating colleague is right, Marie,"
said Panov softly, watching Webb. "He's in and out, trying to find his own reality. It's okay. Let him ride it. It
could save us all a lot of time."

"*Bullshit!*"

"Forever accurate, my dear, and forever debatable.
Shut up."

". . . There was no traitor, no one who spoke, only the
woman with doubts. He killed her and there was silence,
an awful silence. He was warning everyone, telling everyone that they, the true China, were everywhere and at the
same time they were invisible. In the ministries, in the
security police, everywhere. . . . And then he killed Echo,
but Echo knew he had to die. He wanted to die quickly
because he couldn't live much longer anyway. After they
tortured him, he was in awful shape. Still, if he could give
me time—"

"Who is Echo, David?" asked Morris Panov. "Tell us,
please."

"Alpha, Bravo, Charlie, Delta, Echo . . . Foxtrot—"

"Medusa," said the psychiatrist. "It's Medusa, isn't it?
Echo was in Medusa."

"He was in Paris. The Louvre. He tried to save my life,
but I saved his. That was okay, it was right. He saved mine
before, years ago. 'Rest is a weapon,' he said. He put the
others around me and made me sleep. And then we got
out of the jungle."

" 'Rest is a weapon' . . . ." Marie spoke quietly and
closed her eyes, pressing her husband's hand, the tears
falling down her cheeks. "Oh, *Christ!*"

". . . Echo saw me in the woods. We used the old
signals we used before, years ago. He hadn't forgotten.
None of us ever forget."

"Are we in the countryside, in the bird sanctuary, David?" asked Panov, gripping McAllister's shoulder to stop him from intruding.

"Yes," replied Jason Bourne, his eyes now floating, unfocused. "We both know. He's going to die. So simple, so clear. Die. Death. No more. Just buy time, precious minutes. Then maybe I can do it."

"Do what—*Delta?*" Panov drew out the name in quiet emphasis.

"Take out the son of a bitch. Take out the butcher. He doesn't deserve to live, he has no *right* to live! He kills too easily—with a smile on his face. Echo saw it. I saw it. Now it's *happening*—everything's happening at once. The explosions in the forest, everybody running, shouting. I can *do* it now! He's a clean kill. . . . He *sees* me! He's *staring* at me! He knows I'm his enemy! I *am* your enemy, *butcher!* I'm the last face you'll *see!* . . . What's wrong? Something's *wrong!* He's shielding himself! He's pulling someone in front of him. I have to get out! I can't *do* it!"

"*Can't* or *won't?*" asked Panov, leaning forward. "Are you Jason Bourne or are you David Webb? Who *are* you?"

"*Delta!*" screamed the victim, stunning everyone at the table by his outburst. "I am *Delta!* I am *Bourne!* Cain is for *Delta* and Carlos is for *Cain!*" The victim, whoever he was, collapsed back in the chair, his head snapped down into his chest. He was silent. No one spoke.

It took several minutes—none knew how long, none counted—until the man who was unable to establish an identity for himself raised his head. His eyes were now half free, half prisoner of the agony he was experiencing. "I'm sorry," said David Webb. "I don't know what happened to me. I'm sorry."

"No apologies, David," said Panov. "You went back. It's understandable. It's okay."

"Yes, I went back. Screwy, isn't it?"

"Not at all," said the psychiatrist. "It's perfectly natural."

"I *have* to go back, that's understandable, too, isn't it, Mo?"

"*David!*" screamed Marie, reaching for him.

"I *have* to," said Jason Bourne, gently holding her

wrists. "No one else can do it, it's as simple as that. I know the codes. I know the way. . . . Echo traded in his life for mine, believing I'd do it, that I'd kill the butcher. I failed then. I won't fail now."

"What about *us?*" Marie clutched him, her voice reverberating off the white walls. "Don't *we* matter?"

"I'll come back, I promise you," said David, removing her arms and looking into her eyes. "But I have to go back, can't you understand?"

"For *these* people? These *liars!*"

"No, not for them. For someone who wanted to live— above everything. You didn't know him; he was a survivor. But he knew when his life wasn't worth the price of my death. I had to live and do what I had to do. I had to live and come back to you, he knew that, too. He faced the equation and made his decision. Somewhere along the line we all have to make that decision." Bourne turned to McAllister. "Is there anyone here who can take a picture of a corpse?"

"Whose?" asked the undersecretary of State.

"Mine," said Jason Bourne.

34

The grisly photograph was taken on the white conference table by a sterile house technician under the reluctant supervision of Morris Panov. A bloodstained white sheet covered Webb's body; it was angled across his throat revealing a blood-streaked face, the eyes wide, the features clear.

"Develop the roll as fast as you can and bring me the contacts," instructed Conklin.

"Twenty minutes," said the technician, heading for the door, as McAllister entered the room.

"What's happening?" asked David, sitting up on the table. Marie, wincing, wiped his face with a warm, wet towel.

"The consulate press people called the media," replied the undersecretary. "They said they'd issue a statement in an hour or so, as soon as all the facts were in place. They're mocking one up now. I gave them the scenario with a go-ahead to use my name. They'll work it out with embassy obfuscation and read it to us before issuing it."

"Any word on Lin?" asked the CIA man.

"A message from the doctor. He's still critical but holding on."

"What about the press down the road?" asked Havilland. "We've got to let them in here sooner or later. The longer we wait, the more they'll think it's a cover-up. We can't afford that, either."

"We've still got some rope in that area," said McAllister. "I sent word that the police—at great risk to themselves—were sweeping the grounds for undetonated explosives. Reporters can be very patient under those conditions. Incidentally, in the scenario I gave the press people, I told them to stress the fact that the man who attacked the house was obviously an expert with demolitions."

Jason Bourne, one of the most proficient demolitions men to come out of Medusa, looked at McAllister. The undersecretary looked away. "I've got to get out of here," Jason said. "I've got to get to Macao as quickly as possible."

"*David,* for God's sake!" Marie stood in front of her husband, staring at him, her voice low and intense.

"I wish it didn't have to be this way," said Webb, getting off the table. "I wish it didn't," he repeated softly, "but it *does.* I have to be in place. I have to start the sequence to reach Sheng before the story breaks in the morning papers, before that photograph appears confirming the message I'm sending through channels he's convinced no one knows about. He's got to believe I'm his assassin, the man he was going to kill, not the Jason Bourne from Medusa who tried to kill him in that forest glen. He has to get word from me—from who he thinks I am—before he's given any other information. Because the information I'm sending him is the last thing he wants to hear. Everything else will seem insignificant."

"The bait," said Alex Conklin. "Feed him the critical

information first and the cover falls in place because he's stunned, preoccupied, and accepts the printed official version, in particular the photograph in the newspapers."

"What are you going to tell him?" asked the ambassador, his voice conveying the fact that he disliked the prospect of losing control of this blackest of operations.

"What you told me. Part truth, part lie."

"Spell it out, Mr. Webb," said Havilland firmly. "We owe you a great deal but—"

"You *owe* me what you can't *pay* me!" snapped Jason Bourne, interrupting. "Unless you blow your brains out right here in front of me."

"I understand your anger, but still I must insist. You'll do nothing to jeopardize the lives of five million people, or the vital interests of the United States government."

"I'm glad you got the sequence right—for once. All right, Mr. *Ambassador*, I'll tell you. It's what I would have told you before, if you'd had the decency, the *decency*, to come to me and 'state your case.' I'm surprised it never occurred to you—no, not surprised, shocked—but I guess I shouldn't be. You believe in your rarefied manipulations, in the trappings of your quiet power . . . you probably think you deserve it all because of your great intellect, or something like that. You're all the same. You relish complexity—and *your* explanations of it —so that you can't see when the simple route is a hell of a lot more effective."

"I'm waiting to be instructed," said Havilland coldly.

"So be it," said Bourne. "I listened very carefully during your ponderous explanation. You took pains to *explain* why no one could officially approach Sheng and tell him what you knew. You were right, too. He'd have laughed in your face, or spit in your eye, or told you to pound sand—whatever you like. Sure, he would've. He's got the leverage. You pursue your 'outrageous' accusations, he pulls Peking out of the Hong Kong Accords. You lose. You try to go over his head, good luck. You lose again. You have no proof but the words of several dead men who've had their throats cut, members of the Kuomintang who'd say anything to discredit party officials in the People's Republic. He smiles and, without saying it, lets you know that you'd better go along with him. You

figure you can't go along because the risks are too great
—if the whistle blows on Sheng, the Far East blows. You
were right about that, too—more for the reasons 'Edward'
gave us than you did. Peking might possibly overlook a
corrupt commission as one of those temporary concessions to greed, but it won't permit a spreading Chinese
Mafia to infiltrate its industry or its labor forces or its
government. As 'Edward' said, they could lose their
jobs—"

"I'm still waiting, Mr. Webb," said the diplomat.

"Okay. You recruited me, but you forgot the lesson of
Treadstone Seventy-one. Send out an assassin to catch
an assassin."

"That's the *one* thing we did not forget," broke in the
diplomat, now astonished. "We based *everything* on it."

"For the wrong reasons," said Bourne sharply. "There
was a better way to reach Sheng and draw him out for the
kill. *I* wasn't necessary. My *wife* wasn't necessary! But you
couldn't see it. Your superior brain had to complicate
everything."

"What was it I couldn't see, Mr. Webb?"

"Send in a conspirator to catch a conspirator. *Un*officially. . . . It's too late for that now, but it's what I would
have told you."

"I'm not sure you've told me anything."

"Part truth, part lie—your own strategy. A courier is
sent to Sheng, preferably a half-senile old man who's
been paid by a blind and fed the information over the
phone. No traceable source. He carries a verbal message,
ears only, Sheng's only, nothing on paper. The message
contains enough of the truth to paralyze Sheng. Let's say
that the man sending it is someone in Hong Kong who
stands to lose millions if Sheng's scheme falls apart, a
man smart enough and frightened enough not to use his
name. The message could allude to leaks, or traitors in
the boardrooms, or excluded triads banding together
because they've been cut out—all the things you're certain will happen. The truth. Sheng has to follow up, he
can't afford not to. Contacts are made and a meeting is
arranged. The Hong Kong conspirator is every bit as
anxious to protect himself as Sheng, and every bit as
leery, demanding a neutral meeting ground. It's set. It's
the trap." Bourne paused, glancing at McAllister. "Even

a third-rate demolitions grunt could show you how to carry it off."

"Very quick and very professional," said the ambassador. "And with a glaring flaw. Where do we find such a conspirator in Hong Kong?"

Jason Bourne studied the elder statesman, his expression bordering on contempt. "You make him up," he said. "That's the lie."

Havilland and Alex Conklin were alone in the white-walled room, each at either end of the conference table facing the other. McAllister and Morris Panov had gone to the undersecretary's office to listen on separate telephones to a mocked-up profile of an American killer created by the consulate for the benefit of the press. Panov had agreed to provide the appropriate psychiatric terminology with the correct Washington overtones. David Webb had asked to be alone with his wife until it was time to leave. They had been taken to a room upstairs; the fact that it was a bedroom had not occurred to anyone. It was merely a door to an empty room at the south side of the old Victorian house, away from the water-soaked men and ruins on the north side. Webb's departure had been estimated by McAllister to be in fifteen minutes or less. A car would drive Jason Bourne and the undersecretary to Kai-tak Airport. In the interests of speed and because the hydrofoils stopped running at 2100 hours, a medical helicopter would fly them to Macao, where all immigration permits would be cleared for the delivery of emergency supplies to the Kiang Wu Hospital on the Rua Coelho do Amaral.

"It wouldn't have worked, you know," said Havilland, looking over at Conklin.

"What wouldn't have?" asked the man from Langley, his own thoughts broken off by the diplomat's statement. "What David told you?"

"Sheng never would have agreed to a meeting with someone he didn't know, with someone who didn't identify himself."

"It'd depend on how it was presented. That kind of thing always does. If the critical information is mind-blowing and the facts authentic, the subject doesn't have much of a choice. He can't question the messenger—he doesn't know anything—so he has to go after the source. As Webb put it, he can't afford not to."

"Webb?" asked the ambassador flatly, his brows arched.

"Bourne, Delta. Who the hell knows? The strategy's sound."

"There are too many possible miscalculations, too many chances for a misstep when one side invents a mythical party."

"Tell that to Jason Bourne."

"Different circumstances. Treadstone had a willing agent provocateur to go after the Jackal. An obsessed man who chose extreme risk because he was trained for it and had lived with violence too long to let go. He didn't want to let go. There was no place else for him."

"It's academic," said Conklin, "but I don't think you're in a position to argue with him. You sent him out with all the odds against him and he comes back with the assassin in tow—and he finds *you*. If he said it could be done another way, he's probably right, and you can't say he isn't."

"I can say, however," said Havilland, resting his forearms on the table and fixing his eyes on the CIA man, "that what we did really *did* work. We lost the assassin, but we gained a willing, even obsessed *provocateur*. From the beginning he was the optimum choice, but we never for a minute thought that he could be recruited to do the final job willingly by himself. Now he won't let anybody else do it; he's going back in, demanding his right to do it. So in the end we were right—I was right. One sets the forces in motion, on a collision course, always watching, ready to abort, to kill, if one has to, but knowing that as the complications mount and the closer they come to each other's throat, the nearer the solution is. Ultimately —in their hatreds, their suspicions, their passions—they create their own violence, and the job is done. You may lose your own people, but one has to weigh that loss against what it's worth to disrupt the enemy, to expose him."

"You also risk exposing your own hand, the hand you insisted has to be kept out of sight."

"How so?"

"Because it's not the end yet. Say Webb doesn't make

it. Say he's caught, and you can bet your elegant ass the order will be to take him alive. When a man like Sheng sees that a trap is set to kill him, he'll want to know who's behind it. If pulling out a fingernail or ten doesn't do it —and it probably wouldn't—they'll needle him full of juice and find out where he comes from. He's heard everything you've told him—"

"Even down to the point where the United States government cannot be involved," interrupted the diplomat.

"That's right, and he won't be able to help himself. The chemicals will bring it all out. Your hand's revealed. Washington *is* involved."

"By whom?"

"By Webb, for Christ's sake! By Jason Bourne, if you like."

"By a man with a history of mental illness, with a record of random aggression and self-deception? A paranoid schizophrenic whose logged telephone calls show a man disintegrating into dementia, making insane accusations, wild threats aimed at those trying to help him?" Havilland paused, then added quietly, "Come now, Mr. Conklin, such a man does not speak for the United States government. How could he? We've been searching for him everywhere. He's an irrational, fantasizing time bomb who finds conspiracies wherever his sick, tortured mind takes him. We want him back in therapy. We also suspect that because of his past activities he left the country with an illegal passport—"

"Therapy . . . ?" Alex broke in, stunned by the old man's words. "Past *activities?*"

"Of course, Mr. Conklin. If it's necessary, especially over a hot line—Sheng's hot line—we're willing to admit that he once worked for the government and was severely damaged by that work. But in no way is it possible he would have any official standing. Again, how could he? This tragic, violent man may have been responsible for the death of a wife he claims disappeared."

"*Marie?* You'd use *Marie?*"

"We'd have to. She's in the logs, in the affidavits volunteered by men who knew Webb as a mental patient, who tried to help him."

"Oh, *Jesus!*" whispered Alex, mesmerized by the cold,

precise elder statesman of covert operations. "You told him everything because you had your own backups. Even if he was taken, you could cover your ass with official logs, psychiatric evaluation—you could disassociate yourself! Oh, God, you *bastard.*"

"I told him the truth because he would have known it if I tried to lie to him again. McAllister, of course, went further, emphasizing the organized crime factor which is all too true but a sensitive issue I'd prefer not to bring up. Nobody does. But then I didn't tell Edward everything. He hasn't yet put enough distance between his ethics and the demands of his job. When he does, he may join me on the heights, but I don't think he's capable."

"You told David everything in case he *was* taken," went on Conklin, not listening to Havilland. "If the kill doesn't happen, you *want* him taken. You're *counting* on the amphetamines and the scopolamine. The *drugs!* Then Sheng will get the message that his conspiracy's known to us and he'll get it *unofficially,* not from us but from an unsanctioned mental case. *Jesus!* It's a variation of what Webb *told* you!"

"Unofficially," agreed the diplomat. "So much is achieved that way. No confrontations, very smooth. Very cheap. No cost at all, really."

"Except a man's *life!*" shouted Alex. "He'll be *killed.* He *has* to be killed from everyone's point of view."

"The price, Mr. Conklin, if it must be paid."

Alex waited, as if he expected Havilland to finish his statement. Nothing was forthcoming, only the strong, sad eyes gazing into his. "That's all you've got to say? It's the price—if it has to be paid?"

"The stakes are far higher than we imagined—far higher. You know that as well as I do, so don't look so shocked." The ambassador leaned back in his chair somewhat stiffly. "You've made such decisions before, such calculations."

"Not like this. *Never* like this! You send in your own and you know the risks, but you don't set up a field man sealing off his escape route! He was better off believing —*believing*—he was bringing in the assassin to get his wife back!"

"The objective is different. Infinitely more vital."

"I *know* that. Then you don't *send* him! You get the codes and send someone *else!* Someone who isn't half dead from exhaustion!"

"Exhausted or not, he's the best man for the job and he insists on doing it."

"Because he doesn't know what you've *done!* How you've boxed him in, made him the messenger who has to be killed!"

"I had no choice. As you say, he found me. I had to tell him the truth."

"Then, I repeat, send in someone *else!* A hit team recruited on the outside by a blind, no connection to us, just payment for a professional kill, the target Sheng. Webb knows how to reach Sheng, he told you that. I'll convince him to give you the codes or the sequence or whatever the hell it is, and you buy a *hit* team!"

"You'd put us on a level with the Qaddafis of this world?"

"That's so puerile I can't find words to—"

"Forget it," broke in Havilland. "If it was ever traced back to us—and it *could* be—we'd have to launch against China before they dropped something on us. Unthinkable."

"What you're *doing* here is unthinkable!"

"There are more important priorities than the survival of a single individual, Mr. Conklin, and again you know that as well as I do. It's been your life's work—if you'll forgive me—but the present case is on a higher level than anything you ever experienced. Let's call it a geopolitical level."

"Son of a bitch!"

"Your own guilt is showing now, Alex—if I may call you Alex—since you call in question my immediate family line. *I* never put Jason Bourne beyond-salvage. My most fervent hope is that he'll succeed, that the kill will take place. If that happens, he's free; the Far East is rid of a monster and the world will be spared an Oriental Sarajevo. That's *my* job, Alex."

"At least *tell* him! *Warn* him!"

"I can't. Any more than you would in my position. You don't tell a *tueur à gages*—"

"Come again, elegant ass?"

"A man sent in to kill must have the confidence of his

convictions. He can't, for a second, reflect on his motives or his reasons. He must have no doubts at all. None. The obsession must be intact. It's his only chance to succeed."

"Suppose he doesn't succeed? Suppose he's killed?"

"Then we start again as quickly as possible putting someone else in his place. McAllister will be with him in Macao and learn the sequence codes to reach Sheng. Bourne's agreed to that. If the worst happens, we might even try his conspirator-for-a-conspirator theory. He says it's too late, but he could be wrong. You see, I'm not above learning, Alex."

"You're not above *anything*," Conklin said angrily, getting out of the chair. "But you forgot something—you forgot what you said to David. There's a glaring flaw."

"What's that?"

"I won't let you get away with it." Alex limped toward the door. "You can ask so much of a man, but there comes a point when you don't ask any more. You're *out*, elegant ass. Webb's going to be told the truth. The *whole* truth."

Conklin opened the door. He faced the back of a tall marine, who, upon hearing the sound of the door opening, did a precise about-face, his rifle at port arms.

"Get out of my way, soldier," said Alex.

"*Sorry,* sir!" barked the marine, his eyes distant, staring straight ahead.

Conklin turned back to the diplomat seated behind the desk. Havilland shrugged. "Procedures," he said.

"I thought these people were out of here. I thought they were sequestered at the airport."

"The ones you saw are. These are a squad from the consulate contingent. Thanks to Downing Street's bending a few rules, this is officially U.S. territory now. We are entitled to a military presence."

"I want to see Webb!"

"You can't. He's leaving."

"Who the *hell* do you think you are?"

"My name is Raymond Oliver Havilland. I am ambassador-at-large for the government of the United States of America. My decisions are to be carried out without debate during periods of crisis. This is a period of crisis. Fuck off, Alex."

Conklin closed the door and walked awkwardly back to his chair. "What's next, Mr. *Ambassador?* Do the three of us get bullets in our heads or are we given lobotomies?"

"I'm sure we can all come to a mutual understanding."

They held each other, Marie knowing that he was only partly there, only partly himself. It was Paris all over again, when she knew a desperate man named Jason Bourne, who was trying to stay alive, but not sure he would, or even should, his self-doubts in some ways as lethal to him as those who wanted him killed. But it was not Paris. There were no self-doubts now, no tactics feverishly improvised to elude pursuers, no race to trap the hunters. What reminded her of Paris was the distance she felt between them. David was trying to reach her—generous David, compassionate David—but Jason Bourne would not let him go. Jason was now the hunter, not the hunted, and this strengthened his will. It was summed up in a word he used with staccato regularity: *Move!*

"Why, David? *Why?*"

"I told you. Because I can. Because I have to. Because it has to be done."

"That's not an answer, my darling."

"All right." Webb gently released his wife and held her by the shoulders, looking into her eyes. "For us, then."

"Us?"

"Yes. I'd see those images for the rest of my life. They'd keep coming back and they'd tear me apart because I'd know what I left behind and I wouldn't be able to handle it. I'd go into tailspins and take you with me because for all your brains you haven't the sense to bail out."

"I'd rather go into senseless tailspins with you than without you. Read that as seeing you alive."

"That's not an argument."

"I think it's considerable."

"I'll be calling the moves, not making them."

"What the hell does that mean?"

"I want Sheng taken out, I mean that. He doesn't deserve to live, but I won't be doing the taking—"

"The *God* image doesn't suit you!" interrupted Marie sharply. "Let others make that decision. Walk away from it. Stay safe."

"You're not listening to me. I was there and I saw him —heard him. He *doesn't* deserve to live. In one of his diatribes he called life a precious gift. That may be debatable, depending on the life, but life doesn't mean a thing to him. He wants to kill—maybe he has to, I don't know, ask Panov—it's in his eyes. He's Hitler and Mengele and Genghis Khan . . . the chain-saw killer—whatever—but he has to go. And I have to make sure he goes."

"But *why?*" pleaded Marie. "You haven't *answered* me!"

"I did, but you didn't hear me. One way or another I'd see him every day, hear that voice. I'd be watching him toy with terrified people before killing them, *butchering* them. Try to understand. *I've* tried and I'm no expert, but I've learned a few things about myself. Only an idiot wouldn't. It's the images, Marie, the goddamned *pictures* that keep coming back, opening doors—memories I don't want to know about, but have to. The clearest and simplest way I can put it is that I can't take any more. I can't add to that collection of bad surprises. You see, I want to get better—not entirely cured, I can accept that, live with it—but I can't slide back, either. I *won't* slide back. For both our sakes."

"And you think by engineering a man's death you'll get rid of those images?"

"I think it'll help, yes. Everything's relative, and I wouldn't be here if Echo hadn't thrown his life away so I could live. It's not always fashionable to say it, but like most people I have a conscience. Or maybe it's guilt because I survived. I simply have to do it because I can."

"You've convinced yourself?"

"Yes, I have. I'm best equipped."

"And you say you're calling the moves, not making them?"

"I wouldn't have it any other way. I'm coming back because I want a long life with you, lady."

"What's my guarantee? Who's going to *make* the moves?"

"The whore who got us into this."

"Havilland?"

"No, he's the pimp. McAllister's the whore, he always was. The man who believes in decency, who wears it on his sleeve until the power boys ask him to put out. He'll probably call in the pimp and that's fine. Between them they can do it."

"But *how?*"

"There are men—and women—who will kill if the price is high enough. They may not have the egos of the mythical Jason Bourne or the very real Carlos the Jackal, but they're everywhere in that goddamned filthy shadow world. Edward, the whore, told us he made enemies throughout the Far East, from Hong Kong to the Philippines, from Singapore to Tokyo, all in the name of Washington, who wanted influence over here. If you make enemies, you know who they are, know the signals to send out to reach them. That's what the whore and the pimp are going to do. I'll set up the kill, but someone else will do the killing, and I don't care how many millions it costs them. I'll watch from a distance to make sure that the butcher's killed, that Echo gets what's coming to him, that the Far East is rid of a monster who can plunge it into a terrible war—but that's all I'll do. Watch. McAllister doesn't know it, but he's coming with me. We're extracting our pound of flesh."

"Who's talking now?" asked Marie. "David or Jason?"

The husband paused, his silent thoughts deep. "Bourne," he said finally. "It has to be Bourne until I'm back."

"You *know* that?"

"I accept it. I don't have a choice."

There was a soft, rapid knocking at the bedroom door. "Mr. Webb. It's McAllister. It's time to leave."

35

The Emergency Medical Service helicopter roared across Victoria Harbor past the out islands of the South China Sea toward Macao. The patrol boats of the People's Republic had been apprised by way of the naval station in Gongbei; there would be no firing at the low-flying aircraft on an errand of mercy. As McAllister's luck would have it, a visiting party official from Peking had been admitted to the Kiang Wu Hospital with a bleeding duodenal ulcer. He required RH-negative blood, which was continuously in short supply. *Let them come, let them go. If the official were a peasant from the hills of Zhuhai, he'd be given the blood of a goat and let him hope for the best.*

Bourne and the undersecretary of State wore the white, belted coveralls and caps of the Royal Medical Corps, with no rank of substance indicated on their sleeves; they were merely grousing subordinates ordered to carry blood to a *Zhongguo ren* belonging to a regime that was in the process of further dismantling the Empire. Everything was being done properly and efficiently in the new spirit of cooperation between the colony and its soon-to-be new masters. *Let them come, let them go. It's all a lifetime away and for us without meaning. We will not benefit. We never benefit. Not from them, not from those above.*

The hospital's rear parking area had been cleared of vehicles. Four searchlights outlined the threshold. The pilot shuttered the aircraft into vertical-hold, then began his descent, clammering down toward the concrete landing zone. The sight of the lights and the sound of the roaring helicopter had drawn crowds on the street beyond the hospital's gates on the Rua Coelho do Amaral. That was all to the good, thought Bourne, looking down from the open hatchway. He trusted that even more onlookers would be attracted for the chopper's departure in roughly five minutes as the slapping blades continued to rotate at slow speed, the searchlights remained on, and the cordon of police stayed in place—all signs of this most unusual activity. Crowds were the best that he and McAllister could hope for; in the confusion they could become part of the curious onlookers as two other men in the white coveralls of the Royal paramedics took their places by rushing to the aircraft, their bodies bent beneath the rotors, for the return trip to Hong Kong.

Grudgingly, Jason had to admire McAllister's ability to move his chess pieces. The analyst had the convictions of his connivance. He knew which buttons to press to shift his pawns. In the current crisis the pawn was a doctor at the Kiang Wu Hospital who several years ago had diverted IMF medical funds to his own clinic on the Al-

mirante Sergio. Since Washington was a sponsor of the
International Monetary Fund, and since McAllister had
caught the doctor with his hands in the till, he was in a
position to expose him and had threatened to do so. Yet
the doctor had prevailed. The physician had asked McAllister how he expected to replace him—there was a
dearth of competent doctors in Macao. Would it not be
better for the American to overlook his indiscretion if his
clinic serviced the indigent? With records of such service? The choirboy in McAllister had capitulated, but not
without remembering the doctor's indiscretion—and his
debt. It was being paid tonight.

"Come on!" yelled Bourne, rising and gripping one of
the two canisters of blood. *"Move!"*

McAllister clung to a wall bar on the opposite side of
the aircraft as the helicopter thump-crashed onto the
cement. He was pale, his face frozen into a mask of itself.
"These things are an *abomination*," he mumbled. "Please
wait till we're settled."

"We're settled. It's your schedule, analyst. *Move.*"

Directed by the police, they raced across the parking
area to a pair of double doors held open by two nurses.
Inside, a white-jacketed Oriental doctor, the inevitable
stethoscope hanging from a pocket, grabbed McAllister's
arm.

"Good to see you again, sir," he said in fluent but
heavily accented English. "Although it is under curious
circumstances—"

"So were *yours* three years ago," broke in the analyst
sharply, breathlessly, peremptorily cutting off the once-
errant doctor. "Where do we go?"

"Follow me to the blood laboratory. It is at the end of
the corridor. The head nurse will check the seals and sign
the receipts, after which you will also follow me into
another room where the two men who will take your
places are waiting. Give them the receipts, change
clothes, and they will leave."

"Who are they?" asked Bourne. "Where did you find
them?"

"Portuguese interns," replied the doctor. "Unmonied
young doctors sent from Pedroso to complete their resi-
dencies out here."

"Explanations?" pressed Jason as they started down the hallway.

"None, actually," answered the Macaoan. "What you call in English, 'a trade.' Perfectly legitimate. Two British medics who wish to spend a night over here and two overworked interns who deserve a night in Hong Kong. They will return on the hydrofoil in the morning. They'll know nothing, they'll suspect nothing. They will simply be pleased that an older doctor recognized their needs and deserts."

"You found the right man, analyst."

"He's a thief."

"You're a whore."

"I beg your pardon?"

"Nothing. Let's go."

Once the canisters were delivered, the seals inspected, and the receipts signed, Bourne and McAllister followed the doctor into a locked adjacent office that held drug supplies and had its own door to the corridor, also locked. The two Portuguese interns were waiting in front of the glass cabinets; one was taller than the other and both were smiling. There were no introductions, just nods and a short statement by the doctor, addressing the undersecretary of State.

"On the basis of your descriptions—not that I needed yours—I'd say their sizes are about right, wouldn't you?"

"They'll do," replied McAllister as he and Jason began removing the white coveralls. "These are outsized. If they run fast enough and keep their heads down, they'll be okay. Tell them to leave the garments and the receipts with the pilot. He's to sign us in once he gets to Hong Kong." Bourne and the analyst changed into dark, rumpled trousers and loose-fitting jackets. Each handed his counterpart his coveralls and cap. McAllister said, "Tell them to hurry. Departure's scheduled for less than two minutes."

The doctor spoke in broken Portuguese, then turned back to the undersecretary. "The pilot can't go anywhere without them, sir."

"Everything's timed and officially cleared down to the minute," the analyst snapped, fear now in his voice.

"There's no room for someone to become any more curious than necessary. Everything has to be clockwork. *Hurry!*"

The interns dressed; the caps were low and in place and the receipts for the canisters of blood were in their pockets. The doctor issued his last instructions to the Americans as he handed them two orange hospital passes. "We'll go out together; the door locks automatically. I will immediately escort our young doctors, thanking them loudly and profusely past the police ranks until they can dash to the aircraft. You head to the right, then left into the front lobby and the entrance. I hope—I really do hope—that our association, as pleasant as it has been, is now finished."

"What are these for?" asked McAllister, holding up his hospital pass.

"Probably—hopefully—nothing. But in case you are stopped they explain your presence and you will not be questioned."

"Why? What do they say?" There was no fact, no fragment of data, that the analyst could leave unexplained.

"Quite simply," said the doctor, looking calmly at McAllister, "they describe you as indigent expatriates, totally without funds, whom I generously treat at my clinic without charge. For gonorrhea, to be precise. Naturally, there are the usual identifying features—height, approximate weight, hair and eye coloring, nationality. Yours are more complete, I'm afraid, as I had not met your friend. Naturally, again, there are duplicates in my files, and no one could mistake it was you, sir."

"What?"

"Once you are out on the streets I believe my long-ago debt is canceled. Wouldn't you agree?"

"*Gonorrhea?*"

"Please, sir, as you say, we must hurry. Everything clockwork." The doctor opened the door, ushered out the four men and instantly headed to the left with the two interns toward the side entrance and the medical helicopter.

"Let's go," whispered Bourne, touching McAllister's arm and starting to the right.

"Did you *hear* that man?"

"You said he was a thief."

"He was. *Is!*"

"There are times when a person shouldn't take that bromide about stealing from a thief too literally."

"What does *that* mean?"

"Simply this," said Jason Bourne, looking down at the analyst at his side. "He's got you on several counts. Collusion, corrupt practices, *and* gonorrhea."

"Oh, my God."

They stood at the rear of the crowds by the high fence watching the helicopter roar up from the landing zone and then soar off into the night sky. One by one the searchlights were turned off, and the parking lot was once again lit by its dim lamps. Most of the police climbed into a van; those remaining walked casually back to their previous posts while several of them lighted cigarettes, as if to announce the excitement was over. The crowds began to disperse amid questions hurled at anyone and everyone. *Who was it? Someone very important, no? What do you think happened? Do you think we'll ever be told? Who cares? We had our show, so let's have a drink, yes? Will you look at that woman? A first-class whore, I think, don't you agree? She's my first cousin, you bastard!*

The excitement was over.

"Let's go," said Jason. "We have to move."

"You know, Mr. Webb, you have two commands you use with irritating frequency. 'Move' and 'Let's go.' "

"They work." Both men started across the Amaral.

"I'm as aware as you are that we must move quickly, only you haven't explained where we're going."

"I know I haven't," said Bourne.

"I think it's time you did." They kept walking, with Bourne setting the pace. "You called me a whore," continued the undersecretary.

"You are."

"Because I agreed to do what I thought was right, what had to be done?"

"Because they used you. The boys in power used you and they'll throw you away without thinking twice. You saw limousines and high-level conferences in your future and you couldn't resist. You were willing to throw away my life without looking for an alternative—which is what you're paid to do. You were willing to risk the life of my

wife because the pull was too great. Dinners with the
Forty Committee, perhaps even becoming a member;
quiet, confidential meetings in the Oval Office with the
celebrated Ambassador Havilland. To me that's being a
whore. Only, I repeat, they'll throw you out without a
second thought."

Silence. For nearly a long Macao block. "You think I
don't know that, Mr. Bourne?"

"What?"

"That they'll throw me out."

Again Jason looked down at the meticulous bureaucrat
at his side. "You know that?"

"Of course I do. I'm not in their league and they don't
want me in it. Oh, I've got the credentials and the mind,
but I don't have that extraordinary sense of performance
that they have. I'm not prepossessing. I'd freeze in front
of a television camera—although I watch idiots who do
perform consistently make the most ridiculous errors.
So, you see, I recognize my limitations. And since I can't
do what these men can do, I have to do what's best for
them and for the country. I have to think for them."

"You thought for *Havilland*? You came to us in Maine
and took my *wife* from me! There weren't any other options in that swollen brain of yours?"

"None that I could come up with. None that covered
everything as thoroughly as Havilland's strategy. The
assassin was the untraceable link to Sheng. If you could
hunt him down and bring him in, it was the shortcut we
needed to draw Sheng out."

"You had a hell of a lot more confidence in me than
I did."

"We had confidence in Jason Bourne. In Cain—in the
man from Medusa called Delta. You had the strongest
motive possible: to get your wife back, the wife you love
very much. And there would be no connection whatsoever to our government—"

"We smelled a covert scenario from the beginning!"
exploded Bourne. "*I* smelled it, and so did Conklin."

"Smelling isn't tasting," protested the analyst, as they
rushed down a dark cobblestoned alley. "You knew
nothing concrete that you could have divulged, no intermediary who pointed to Washington. You were ob-

sessed with finding a killer who was posing as you so
that an enraged taipan would return your wife to you—
a man whose own wife had supposedly been murdered
by the assassin who called himself Jason Bourne. At first
I thought it was madness, but then I saw the serpentine
logic of it all. Havilland was right. If there was one man
alive who could bring in the assassin, and in that way
neutralize Sheng, it was you. But you couldn't have any
connection to Washington. Therefore you had to be
maneuvered within the framework of an extraordinary
lie. Anything less, and you might have reacted more
normally. You might have gone to the police, or to government authorities, people you knew in the past—what
you could remember of the past, which was also to our
advantage."

"I did go to people I knew before."

"And learned nothing except that the more you threatened to break silence, the more likely the government
would put you back in therapy. After all, you came from
Medusa and had a history of amnesia, even schizophre-
nia."

"Conklin went to others—"

"And was initially told only enough for us to find out
what he knew, what he'd pieced together. I gather he was
once one of the best we had."

"He was. He still is."

"He put you beyond-salvage."

"History. Under the circumstances, I might have done
the same. He learned a lot more than I did in Washington."

"He was led to believe exactly what he wanted to believe. It was one of Havilland's really more brilliant
strokes and done at a moment's notice. Remember, Alexander Conklin is a burned-out, bitter man. He has no
love for the world he spent his adult life in, nor for the
people with whom he shared that life. He was told that
a *possible* black operation *may* have gone off the wire, that
the scenario *may* have been taken over by hostile elements." McAllister paused as they emerged from the
alley and rounded a corner in the late-night Macao
crowds; colored lights were flashing everywhere. "It was
back to the square-one lie, don't you see?" continued the

analyst. "Conklin was convinced that someone else *had* moved in, that your situation was hopeless and so was your wife's unless you followed the *new* scenario run by the hostile elements that had taken over."

"That's what he told me," said Jason, frowning, remembering the lounge at Dulles Airport and the tears that had come to his eyes. "He told me to play out the scenario."

"He had no choice." McAllister suddenly gripped Bourne's arm, nodding toward a darkened storefront up ahead on the right. "We have to talk."

"We *are* talking," said the man from Medusa sharply. "I know where we're going and there's no time to lose."

"You have to *take* the time," insisted the analyst. The desperation in his voice forced Bourne to stop and look at him, and then to follow him into the recessed storefront. "Before you do *anything,* you have to understand."

"What do I have to understand? The lies?"

"No, the truth."

"You don't know what the truth is," said Jason.

"I know, perhaps better than *you* do. As you said, it's my job. Havilland's strategy would have proved sound had it not been for your wife. She escaped; she got away. She caused the strategy to fall apart."

"I'm aware of that."

"Then surely you're aware of the fact that whether or not he's identified her, Sheng knows about her and understands her importance."

"I hadn't thought about it one way or the other."

"Think about it now. Lin Wenzu's unit was penetrated when it and all of Hong Kong were searching for her. Catherine Staples was killed because she was linked to your wife and it was correctly perceived that through this mystery woman she either had learned too much or was closing in on some devastating truths. Sheng's orders obviously are to eliminate all opposition, even potential opposition. As you saw in Peking, he's a fanatic and sees substance where there are only shadows—enemies in every dark corner."

"What's your point?" asked Bourne impatiently.

"He's also brilliant and his people are all over the colony."

"So?"

"When the story breaks in the morning papers and on television, he'll make certain assumptions and have the house in Victoria Peak as well as MI-Six scrutinized every minute of every hour, even if he has to hold hostage the estate next door and once again infiltrate British Intelligence."

"Goddamn it, what are you *driving* at?"

"He'll find Havilland and then he'll find your wife."

"And?"

"Suppose you fail? Suppose you're killed? Sheng won't rest until he learns everything there is to learn. The key is undoubtedly the woman with Havilland, the tall woman everyone was looking for. She *has* to be because she's the enigma at the center of the mystery and is connected to the ambassador. If anything happens to you, Havilland will be forced to let her go, and Sheng will have her picked up—at Kai-tak, or Honolulu or Los Angeles or New York. Believe me, Mr. Webb, he won't stop until he's caught her. He has to know what's been mounted against him, and she *is* the key. There's no one else."

"Again, your point?"

"Everything could happen all over again with far more horrible results."

"The *scenario?*" asked Jason, bloody images of the glen in the bird sanctuary assaulting him.

"Yes," said the analyst firmly. "Only, this time your wife is taken for real, not simply as part of the strategy to recruit you. Sheng would make certain of it."

"Not if he's dead!"

"Probably not. However, there's the very real risk of failure—that he'll remain alive."

"You're trying to say something but you're not *saying* it!"

"All right, I'll say it now. As the assassin, you're the link to Sheng, the one to reach him, but I'm the one who can draw him out."

"You?"

"It was the reason I told the embassy to use my name in the press release. You see, Sheng knows me, and I listened carefully when you outlined your conspirator-for-a-conspirator theory to Havilland. He didn't buy it and, frankly, I didn't either. Sheng wouldn't accept a conference with an unknown person, but he will with someone he knows."

"Why with you?"

"Part truth, part lie," said the analyst, repeating Bourne's words.

"Thanks for listening so carefully. Now, explain that."

"The truth first, Mr. Webb, or Bourne, or whatever you want to be called. Sheng is aware both of my contributions to my government and of my obvious lack of progress. I'm a bright but unseen, unknown bureaucrat who's been passed over because I lack those qualities that could elevate me, lead me to a degree of prominence, and to lucrative jobs in the private sector. In a way, I'm like Alexander Conklin without his drinking problem, but not without a degree of his bitterness. I was as good as Sheng and he knew it, but he made it and I didn't."

"A touching confessional," said Jason, impatiently again. "But why would he meet with you? How could you draw him out—for a kill, Mr. Analyst, and I trust you know what that means?"

"Because I want a piece of that Hong Kong pie of his. I was nearly killed last night. It was the final indignity, and now after all these years I want something for myself, for my family. That's the lie."

"You're on tenth base. I can't find you."

"Because you're not listening between the lines. That's what I'm paid to do, remember? . . . I've had it. I'm at the end of my professional rope. I was sent over here to trace down and analyze a rumor out of Taiwan. This rumor about an economic conspiracy in Peking seemed to me to have substance, and if it was true, there could be only one source in Peking: my old counterpart from the Sino-American trade conferences, the power behind China's new trade policies. Nothing like this could be done without him, not even contemplated. So I assumed there was at best enough substance for me to contact him, *not* to blow the whistle but officially to *dispose* of the rumor for a price. I could even go so far as to say I see nothing against my government's interests, and certainly not against mine. The main point is that he'd *have* to meet with me."

"Then what?"

"Then you'd tell me what to do. You said a demolitions 'grunt' could do it, so why can't I? Except not with explosives, I couldn't handle that. A weapon, instead."

"You'd get killed."

"I'll accept the risk."

"Why?"

"Because it has to be done, Havilland's right about that. And the instant Sheng sees you're not the impostor, that you're the original assassin, the one who tried to kill him in that bird sanctuary, his guards would cut you down."

"I never intended for him to see me," said Bourne quietly. "You were going to take care of that, but not this way."

In the shadows of the dark storefront, McAllister stared at the Medusan. "You're taking me with you, aren't you?" asked the analyst finally. "Force me, if you have to."

"Yes."

"I thought so. You wouldn't have agreed so readily to my coming with you to Macao. You could have told me how to reach Sheng back at the airport and demanded that we give you a certain amount of time before we acted. We wouldn't have violated it; we're too frightened. Regardless, you can see now that you don't have to force me. I even brought along my diplomatic passport." McAllister paused for a single beat, then added, "And a second one that I removed from the technicians' file—it belongs to that tall fellow who took the picture of you on the table."

"You *what?*"

"All State Department technical personnel dealing in classified matters must surrender their passports. It's a security measure and for their own protection—"

"I have *three* passports," interrupted Jason. "How the hell do you think I got around?"

"We knew you had at least two based on the Bourne records. You used one of the previous names flying into Peking, the one that said you had brown eyes, not hazel. How did you manage that?"

"I wore glasses—clear glass. By way of a friend who uses an odd name and is better than anyone you've got."

"Oh, yes. A black photographer and ID specialist who

calls himself Cactus. Actually, he worked secretly for Treadstone, but then you obviously remembered that, or the fact that he used to come and visit you in Virginia. According to the records, he had to be let go because he deals with criminal elements."

"If you touch him, I'll blow you out of the bureaucratic waters."

"There's no intention of doing so. Right now, however, we'll simply transfer one of the three photographs that best suits the features described in the technician's passport."

"It's a waste of time."

"Not at all. Diplomatic passports have considerable advantages, especially over here. They eliminate the time-consuming process of a temporary visa, and although I'm sure you have sources to buy one, this is easier. China wants our money, Mr. Bourne, *and* our technology. We'll be passed through quickly and Sheng will be able to check immigration and ascertain that I am who I say I am. We'll also be provided with priority transportation if we want it, and that might be important, depending upon our sequential telephone conversations with Sheng and his aides."

"Our sequential *what?*"

"You'll talk with his subordinates in whatever sequence is required. I'll tell you what to say, but when the final clearance is given, *I'll* speak with Sheng Chou Yang."

"You're a *flake!*" yelled Jason, as much into the dark glass of the storefront as at McAllister. "You're an *amateur* in this kind of thing!"

"In what you do, I am, indeed. But not in what I do."

"Why didn't you tell Havilland about this grand plan of yours?"

"Because he wouldn't have permitted it. He would have placed me under house arrest because he thinks I'm inadequate. He'll always think so. I'm not a performer. I don't have those glib answers that ring with sincerity but are also woefully uninformed. This, however, is different, and the performers see it so clearly because it's all part of their global, macho theatrics. Economics aside, this is a conspiracy to undermine the leadership of a suspicious, authoritarian regime. And who's at the core of this conspiracy that *has* to fail? Who are these infiltrators whom Peking trusts as its own? China's most deeply committed enemies—their own brothers from the Kuomintang on Taiwan. Again, to use the vernacular, when the shit hits the fan—as it surely will—the performers on all sides will step up to the podiums and scream their screams of treason and righteous 'internal revolt' because there's nothing else the performers can *do*. The embarrassment's total, complete, and on the world's stage, massive embarrassment leads to massive violence."

It was Bourne's turn to stare at the analyst. As he did, Marie's words came to him, from a different context but not irrelevant in the present case. "That's not an answer," he said. "It's a point of view, but it's not an answer. Why *you*? I hope it's not to prove your decency. That would be very foolish. Very dangerous."

"Oddly enough," said McAllister, frowning, briefly looking at the ground. "Where you and your wife are concerned, I suppose that's part of it—a minor part." The undersecretary of State raised his eyes and continued calmly, "But the basic reason, Mr. Bourne, is that I'm rather tired of being Edward Newington McAllister, maybe a brilliant but surely an inconsequential analyst. I'm the mind in the back room that's brought out when things get too complicated, and then sent back after he's rendered a judgment. You might say I'd like that chance for a moment in the sun—out of the back room, as it were."

Jason studied the undersecretary in the shadows. "A couple of moments ago you said there was the risk of my failing, and I'm experienced. You're not. Have you considered the consequences if *you* fail?"

"I don't think I will."

"You don't think you will," repeated Bourne flatly. "May I ask why?"

"I've thought it out."

"That's nice."

"No, I mean it," protested McAllister. "The strategy is fundamentally simple: to get Sheng alone with me. I can do that but you can't do it for me. And you certainly can't get him alone with you. All I need is a few seconds—and a weapon."

"If I allowed it, I don't know which would frighten me

more. Your succeeding or your failing. May I remind you that you're an undersecretary of State for the United States government? Suppose you're caught? It's good-bye, Charlie, for everyone."

"I've considered that since the day I arrived back in Hong Kong."

"You *what?*"

"For weeks I've thought that this might be the solution, that *I* might be the solution. The government's covered. It's all written down in my papers back on Victoria Peak, with a copy for Havilland and another set to be delivered to the Chinese consulate in Hong Kong in seventy-two hours. The ambassador may even have found his set by now. So, you see, there's no turning back."

"What the hell have you *done!*"

"Described what amounts to a blood feud between Sheng and myself. Given my record and the time I spent over here, as well as Sheng's well-known penchant for secrecy, it's actually quite plausible. Certainly his enemies in the Central Committee will leap at it. If I'm killed or captured, so much attention will be focused on Sheng, so many questions regardless of his denials, he won't dare move—if he survives."

"Good Christ, *save* me," said Bourne, stunned.

"It's not necessary for you to know the particulars, but you'll recognize the main point of your conspirator-for-a-conspirator theory. In essence I accuse him of going back on his word, of cutting me out of his Hong Kong manipulations after I spent years secretly helping him develop the structure. He's cutting me out because he doesn't need me any longer and he knows I can't possibly say anything because I'd be ruined. I wrote that I was even frightened for my life."

"*Forget* it!" shouted Jason. "Forget the whole god-damned thing! It's *crazy!*"

"You're assuming I'll fail. Or be captured. I'm assuming neither—with your help, of course."

Bourne took a deep breath and lowered his voice. "I admire your courage, even your latent sense of decency, but there's a better way and you can provide it. You'll have your moment in the sun, Mr. Analyst, but not this way."

"What way, then?" asked the undersecretary of State, now bewildered.

"I've seen you operate, and Conklin was right. You may be a son of a bitch but you're *something*. You reach into the Foreign Office in London and know who can change the rules. You spent six years over here digging around the dirty-tricks business, tracking killers and thieves and the pimps of the Far East in the name of neighborly government policy. You know which button to press and where the bodies are buried. You even remembered a squirrely doctor here in Macao who owed you a favor and you made him pay."

"That's all second nature. One doesn't easily forget such people."

"Find me others. Find me killers for a price. Between you and Havilland the two of you can do it. You're going to get on the phone to him and tell him these are my demands. He's to transfer a million—five million if he has to—over here to Macao in the morning, and by midafternoon I want a killer unit here ready to go up into China. I'll make the arrangements. I know a rendezvous that's been used before in the hills of Guangdong; there are fields that can easily be reached by helicopter, where Sheng or his lieutenants used to meet with the commando. Once he gets my message he'll make the trip, take my word for it. You just do your part. Dig around that head of yours and come up with three or four experienced scumbags. Tell them the risk is minimal and the price high. That's your moment in the sun, Mr. Analyst. It should be irresistible. You'll have something on Havilland for the rest of his life. He'll make you his chief aide, probably Secretary of State, if you want it. He can't afford not to."

"Impossible," said McAllister quietly, his eyes locked with Jason's.

"Well, maybe Secretary of State's a bit much—"

"What you have just suggested is impossible," broke in the undersecretary.

"Are you telling me there aren't such men, because if you are, you're lying again."

"I'm sure there are. I might even know of several and I'm sure others are on that list of names Lin gave you when he was playing the role of the white-suited taipan in the Walled City. But I wouldn't touch them. Even if Havilland ordered me to, I'd refuse."

"Then you don't want Sheng! Everything you said was just another lie. Liar!"

"You're wrong, I *do* want Sheng. But to use your words, not this way."

"Why not?"

"Because I won't put my government, my country, in that kind of compromised position. Actually, I think Havilland would agree with me. Hiring killers is too traceable, the transferring of money too traceable. Someone gets angry or boastful or drunk; he talks and an assassination is laid at Washington's feet. I couldn't be a part of that. I refer you to the Kennedys' attempts on Castro's life using the Mafia. Insanity. . . . No, Mr. Bourne, I'm afraid you're stuck with me."

"I'm not stuck with anyone! I can reach Sheng; you *can't!*"

"Complicated issues can usually be reduced to simple equations if certain facts are remembered."

"What does that mean?"

"It means I insist we do things my way."

"Why?"

"Because Havilland has your wife."

"She's with *Conklin!* With Mo Panov! He wouldn't *dare*—"

"You don't know him," McAllister interrupted. "You insult him but you don't know him. He's like Sheng Chou Yang. He'll stop at nothing. If I'm right—and I'm sure I am—Mrs. Webb, Mr. Conklin, and Dr. Panov are guests at the house in Victoria Peak for the duration."

"Guests?"

"That house arrest I mentioned a few minutes ago."

"Son of a *bitch!*" whispered Jason, the muscles in his face pulsating.

"Now, how do we reach Peking?"

With his eyes closed, Bourne answered. "A man at the Guangdong garrison named Soo Jiang. I speak to him in French and he leaves a message for us here in Macao. At a table in a casino."

"*Move!*" said McAllister.

36

The telephone rang, startling the naked woman who quickly sat up in the bed. The man lying next to her was suddenly wide awake; he was wary of any intrusion, especially one in the middle of the night, or, more accurately, the early hours of the morning. The expression on his soft, round Oriental face, however, showed that such intrusions were not infrequent, only unnerving. He reached for the phone on the bedside table.

"Wei?" he said softly.

"Macao lai dianhua," replied the switchboard operator at headquarters, Guangdong garrison.

"Connect me on scrambler and remove all recording devices."

"It is done, Colonel Soo."

"I will conduct my own study of that," said Soo Jiang, sitting up and reaching for a small, flat, rectangular object with a raised circle at one end.

"It's not necessary, sir."

"I would hope not for your sake." Soo placed the circle over the mouthpiece and pressed a button. Had there been an intercept on the line, the piercing whistle that suddenly erupted for one second would have continued pulsating until the listening device was removed or a listener's eardrum was punctured. There was only silence, magnified by the moonlight streaming through the window. "Go ahead, Macao," said the colonel.

"Bon soir, mon ami," said the voice from Macao, the French instantly accepted as being spoken by the impostor. *"Comment ça va?"*

"Vous?" gasped Soo Jiang, stunned, swinging his short fat legs from under the sheet and planting them on the

floor. *"Attendez!"* The colonel turned to the woman. "You. Out. Get out of here," he ordered in Cantonese. "Take your clothes and put them on in the front room. Keep the door open so I can see you leave."

"You owe me money!" whispered the woman stridently. "For two times you owe me money, and double for what I did for you below!"

"Your payment is in the fact that I may not have your husband fired. Now get out! You have thirty seconds or you have a penniless husband."

"They call you the Pig," said the woman, grabbing her clothes and rushing to the bedroom door, where she turned, glaring at Soo. *"Pig!"*

"Out."

Seconds later Soo returned to the phone, continuing in French. "What *happened?* The reports from Beijing are incredible! No less so the news from the airfield in Shenzen. He took you prisoner!"

"He's dead," said the voice from Macao.

"Dead?"

"Shot by his own people, at least fifty bullets in his body."

"And *you?"*

"They accepted my story. I was an innocent hostage picked up in the streets and used as a shield as well as a decoy. They treated me well and, in fact, kept me from the press at my insistence. Of course, they're trying to minimize everything, but they won't have much success. The newspaper and television people were all over the place, so you'll read about it in the morning papers."

"My God, where did it *happen?"*

"An estate on Victoria Peak. It's part of the consulate and damned secret. That's why I have to reach your leader-one. I learned things that he should know about."

"Tell *me."*

The "assassin" laughed derisively. "I sell this kind of information, I don't give it away—especially not to pigs."

"You'll be well taken care of," insisted Soo.

"Too well in my book."

"What do you mean by 'leader-one'?" asked the colonel dismissing the remark.

"Your head man, the chief, the big rooster—whatever

you want to call him. He was the man in that forest preserve who did all the talking, wasn't he? The one who used his sword with such efficiency, the wild-eyed corkscrew with the short hair, the one I tried to warn about the Frenchman's delaying tactics—"

"You *dare* . . . ? You did that?"

"*Ask* him. I told him something was wrong, that the Frenchman was stalling him. Christ, I paid for his not listening to me! He should have hacked that French bastard when I told him to! Now you tell him I want to talk to him!"

"Even I do not talk to him," said the colonel. "I reach only subordinates by their code names. I don't know their real ones—"

"You mean the men who fly down to the hills in Guangdong to meet me and deliver the assignments?" interrupted Bourne.

"Yes."

"I won't talk to any of them!" exploded Jason, now posing as his own impostor. "I want to talk to the *man.* And he'd better want to talk to me."

"You will speak with others first, but still, even for them, there must be very strong reasons. They do the summoning, others do not. You should know that by now."

"All right, you can be the courier. I was with the Americans for almost three hours, mounting the best cover I ever mounted in my life. They questioned me at length and I answered them openly—I don't have to tell you that I have backups all over the territory, men and women who'll swear I'm a business associate, or that I was with them at a specific time, no matter who calls—"

"You don't have to tell me that," Soo broke in. "Please, just give me the message I'm to convey. You talked with the Americans. Then what?"

"I listened, too. The colonials have a stupid habit of talking too freely among themselves in the presence of strangers."

"I hear a British voice now. The voice of superiority. We've all heard it before."

"You're damned right. The wogs don't do that, and God knows you slants don't either."

"Please, sir, continue."

"The one who took me prisoner, the man who was killed by the Americans, was an American himself."

"So?"

"I leave a signature with my kills. The name has a long history. It's Jason Bourne."

"We know that. And?"

"He was the *original!* He was an American, and they've been hunting him for nearly two years."

"*And?*"

"They think Beijing found him and hired him. *Someone* in Beijing who needed the most important kill of his life, who needed to kill a man in that house. Bourne's for sale to anybody, an equal-opportunity employee, as the Americans might say."

"Your language is elusive. Please be clearer!"

"There were several others in that room with the Americans. Chinese from Taiwan who said outright that they oppose most of the leaders of the secret societies in the Kuomintang. They were angry. Frightened, too, I think." Bourne stopped. Silence.

"Yes?" pressed the colonel apprehensively.

"They said a number of other things. They also kept mentioning the name of someone called Sheng."

"*Aiya!*"

"That's the message you'll convey and I'll expect a response at the casino within three hours. I'll send someone to pick it up and don't try anything foolish. I have people there who can start a riot as easily as they can roll a seven. Any interference and your men are dead."

"We remember the Tsim Sha Tsui a few weeks ago," said Soo Jiang. "Five of our enemies killed in a back room while a cabaret erupts in violence. There'll be no interference; we're not fools where you are concerned. We often wondered if the original Jason Bourne was as proficient as his successor."

"He wasn't." *Bring up the possibility of a riot at the casino in case Sheng's people try to trap you. Say their men will be killed. You don't have to elaborate. They'll understand. . . . The analyst knew whereof he spoke.* "A question," said Jason, genuinely interested. "When did you and the others decide I wasn't the original?"

"At first sight," replied the colonel. "The years leave

their marks, don't they? The body may remain agile, even improve with care, but the face reflects time; it is inescapable. Your face could not possibly be the face of the man from Medusa. That was over fifteen years ago and you are, at best, a man in your early thirties. The Medusa did not recruit children. You were the reincarnation of the Frenchman."

"The code word is *'crisis'* and you have *three hours,*" said Bourne, hanging up the phone.

"This is *crazy!*" Jason stepped out of the open glass booth in the all-night telephone complex and looked angrily at McAllister.

"You did it very well," said the analyst, writing on a small notepad. "I'll pay the bill." The undersecretary started toward the raised platform where the operators accepted payments for international calls.

"You're missing the point," continued Bourne at McAllister's side, his voice low, harsh. "It can't work. It's too unorthodox, too obvious for anyone to buy it."

"If you were demanding a meeting I'd agree with you, but you're not. You're only asking for a telephone conversation."

"I'm asking him to acknowledge the core of his whole goddamned scam! That he *is* the core!"

"To quote you again," said the analyst, picking up the bill on the counter and holding out money, "he can't afford not to respond. He *has* to."

"With preconditions that'll throw you out of the box."

"I'll want your input in such matters, of course." McAllister took his change, nodding thanks to the weary female operator, and started for the door, Jason beside him.

"I may not have any input to give."

"Under the circumstances, you mean," said the analyst, as they stepped out onto the crowded pavement.

"What?"

"It's not the strategy that upsets you, Mr. Bourne, because it's basically *your* strategy. What makes you furious is that I'm the one implementing it, not you. Like Havilland, you don't think I'm capable."

"I don't think this is the time or the occasion for you to prove you're Machine Gun *Kelly!* If you fail, your life's the last thing that concerns me. Somehow the Far East comes first, the world comes first."

"There's no way I can fail. I told you, even if I fail, I don't. Sheng loses no matter whether he lives or not. In seventy-two hours the consulate in Hong Kong will make sure of it."

"Premeditated self-sacrifice isn't something I approve of," said Jason, as they started up the street. "Self-deluding heroics always get in the way and screw things up. Besides, your so-called strategy reeks of a trap. They'll smell it!"

"They would if *you* negotiated with Sheng and not me. You tell me it's unorthodox, too obvious, the movements of an amateur. That's fine. When Sheng hears me on the phone, everything will fall into place for him. I *am* the embittered amateur, the man who's never been in the field, the first-rate bureaucrat who's been passed over by the system he's served so well. I know what I'm doing, Mr. Bourne. You just get me a weapon."

The request was not difficult to fulfill. Over in Macao's Porto Interior, on the Rua das Lorchas, was d'Anjou's flat, which was a minor arsenal of weapons, the tools of the Frenchman's trade. It was simply a matter of getting inside and selecting those arms most easily dismantled so as to cross the relatively lax border at Guangdong with diplomatic passports. But it took something over two hours, the process of selection being the most time-consuming as Jason put gun after gun in McAllister's hand, with Jason watching the analyst's grip and the expression on his face. The weapon finally chosen was the smallest, lowest calibrated pistol in d'Anjou's arsenal, a Charter Arms .22 with a silencer.

"Aim for the head, at least three bullets in the skull. Anything else would be a beesting."

McAllister swallowed, staring at the gun, as Jason studied the weapons, deciding which had the greatest firepower in the smallest package. He chose for himself three Interdynamic KG-9 machine pistols that used outsized clips holding thirty rounds of ammunition.

With their weapons concealed beneath their jackets, they entered the half-filled Kam Pek casino at 3:35 in the morn-

ing and walked to the end of the long mahogany bar.
Bourne went to the seat he had occupied previously. The
undersecretary sat four stools away. The bartender recognized the generous customer who had given him close to a
week's salary less than a week ago. He greeted him like a
patron with a long history of dispensing largesse.

"*Nei hou a!*"

"*Mchoh La. Mgoi,*" said Bourne, saying that he was fine,
in good health.

"The English whisky, isn't it?" asked the bartender,
sure of his memory, hoping it would produce a reward.

"I told friends at the casino in the Lisboa that they
should talk to you. I think you're the best man behind a
bar in Macao."

"The *Lisboa*? That's where the true money is! I thank
you, sir." The bartender rushed to pour Jason a drink
that would have crippled Caesar's legions. Bourne nodded without comment, and the man turned reluctantly to
McAllister four chairs away. Jason noted that the analyst
ordered white wine, paid with precision, and wrote the
amount in his notebook. The bartender shrugged, performed the unpleasant service, and walked to the center
of the sparsely occupied bar, keeping his eyes on his
favored customer.

Step one.

He was *there!* The well-dressed Chinese in the tailored
dark suit, the martial-arts veteran who did not know
enough dirty moves, the man he had fought in an alley
and who had led him up into the hills of Guangdong.
Colonel Soo Jiang was taking no risks under the circumstances. He wanted only the most proven conduits working tonight. No impoverished old men, no whores.

The man walked slowly past several tables, as if studying the action, appraising the dealers and the players,
trying to determine where he should test his luck. He
arrived at Table Five and, after observing the play of the
cards for nearly three minutes, casually sat down and
withdrew a roll of bills from his pocket. Among them,
thought Jason, was a message marked *Crisis.*

Twenty minutes later the impeccably dressed Chinese
shook his head, put his money back in his pocket, and got
up from the table. He was the *shortcut* to Sheng! He knew

his way around both Macao and the border at Guang-dong, and Bourne knew he had to reach this man, and reach him quickly! He glanced first at the bartender, who had gone to the end of the bar to prepare drinks for a waiter who was serving the tables, then over at McAllister.

"*Analyst!*" he whispered sharply. "*Stay* here!"

"What are you doing?"

"Saying hello to my mother, for Christ's sake!" Jason got off the stool and started for the door after the conduit. Passing the bartender, he said in Cantonese. "I'll be right back."

"It's no problem, sir."

Out on the pavement, Bourne followed the well-dressed man for several blocks until he turned into a narrow, dimly lit side street and approached an empty parked car. He was meeting no one; he had delivered the message and was getting out of the area. Jason rushed forward, and as the conduit opened the car door he touched the man's shoulder. The conduit spun around, crouching, his experienced left foot lashing out viciously. Bourne jumped back, raising his hands in a gesture of peace.

"Let's not go through *this* again," he said in English, for he remembered the man spoke English, taught him by Portuguese nuns. "I still hurt from the beating you gave me a week ago."

"*Aiya! You!*" The conduit raised his hands in a like gesture of noncombat. "You do me honor when I do not deserve it. You bested me that night, and for that reason I have practiced six hours a day to improve myself. . . . You bested me, *then.* But not now."

"Considering your age and then considering mine, take my word for it, you weren't bested. My bones ached far more than yours did, and I'm not about to check out your new training schedule. I'll pay you a lot of money, but I won't fight you. The word for it is cowardice."

"Not you, sir," said the Oriental, lowering his hands and grinning. "You are very good."

"Yes, *me*, sir," replied Jason. "You scare the hell out of me. And you did me a great favor."

"You paid me well. Very well."

"I'll pay you better now."

"The message was for *you?*"

"Yes."

"Then you have taken the Frenchman's place?"

"He's dead. Killed by the people who sent the message."

The conduit looked bewildered, perhaps even sad. "Why?" he asked. "He serviced them well and he was an old man, older than you."

"Thanks a lot."

"Did he betray those he serviced?"

"No, he was betrayed."

"The Communists?"

"Kuomintang," said Bourne, shaking his head.

"*Dong wu!* They are no better than the Communists. What do you want from me?"

"If everything goes right, pretty much what you did before, but this time I want you to stay around. I want to hire a pair of eyes."

"You go up into the hills in Guangdong?"

"Yes."

"You need assistance crossing the border, then?"

"Not if you can find me someone who can shift a photograph from one passport to another."

"It is done every day. The children can do it."

"Good. Then we're down to my hiring your eyes. There's a degree of risk, but not much. There's also twenty thousand dollars, American. Last time I paid you ten, this time it's twenty."

"*Aiya,* a *fortune!*" The conduit paused, studying Bourne's face. "The risk must be great."

"If there's trouble, I'll expect you to get out. We'll leave the money here in Macao, accessible only to you. Do you want the job, or do I look elsewhere?"

"These are the eyes of the hawk bird. Look no further."

"Come back with me to the casino. Wait outside, down the street, and I'll have the message picked up."

The bartender was only too pleased to do as Jason requested. He was confused by the odd word "crisis" that was to be used until Bourne explained that it was the name of a race horse. He carried a "special" drink to a bewildered player at Table Five and returned with the sealed envelope under his tray. Jason had scanned the nearby tables looking for turning heads and shifting eyes amid the spiraling clouds of smoke; he saw none. The sight of the maroon-jacketed bartender among the maroon-jacketed waiters was too common to draw attention. As instructed, the tray was placed between Bourne and McAllister. Jason shook a cigarette out of his pack and shoved a book of matches down the bar toward the nonsmoking analyst. Before the perplexed undersecretary could understand, Bourne got off his stool and walked over to him. "Have you got a light, mister?"

McAllister looked at the matches, quickly picked them up, tore one out and struck it, holding the flame up for the cigarette. When Jason returned to his seat, the sealed envelope was in his hand. He opened it, removed the paper inside and read the typewritten English script: *Telephone Macao—32-61-443.*

He looked around for a pay phone and then realized that he had never used one in Macao, and even if there were instructions, he was not familiar with the Portuguese colony's coins. It was always the little things that loused up the bigger things. He signaled the bartender, who reached him before his hand was back on the bar.

"Yes, sir? Another whisky, sir?"

"Not for a week," said Bourne, placing Hong Kong money in front of him. "I have to make a phone call to someone here in Macao. Tell me where a pay phone is and let me have the proper coins, will you, please?"

"I could not permit so fine a gentleman as yourself to use a common telephone, sir. Between us, I believe many of the customers here may be diseased." The bartender smiled. "Allow me, sir. I have a telephone on my counter —for very special people."

Before Jason could protest or give thanks, a telephone was put in front of him. He dialed as McAllister stared at him.

"Wei?" said a female voice.

"I was instructed to call this number," replied Bourne in English. The dead impostor had not known Chinese.

"We will meet."

"We *won't* meet."

"We insist."

"Then *de*sist. You know me better than that, or you should. I want to talk to the man, and only the *man*."

"You are presumptuous."

"You're less than an idiot. So's the skinny preacher with the big sword unless he talks to me."

"You *dare*—"

"I've heard that once before tonight," interrupted Jason sharply. "The answer is yes, I *do* dare. He's got a hell of a lot more to lose than I do. He's only one client, and my list is growing. I don't need him, but right now I think he needs me."

"Give me a reason that can be confirmed."

"I don't give reasons to corporals. I was once a major, or didn't you know that?"

"There's no need for insults."

"There's no need for this conversation. I'll call you back in thirty minutes. Offer me something better, offer me the *man*. And I'll know if it's himself because I'll ask a question or two that only he can answer. *Ciao,* lady." Bourne hung up.

"What are you *doing?*" whispered an agitated McAllister four chairs away.

"Arranging your day in the sun, and I hope you've got some lotion. We're getting out of here. Give me five minutes, then follow me. Turn right out the door and keep walking. We'll pick you up."

"*We?*"

"There's someone I want you to meet. An old friend —young friend—whom I think you'll approve of. He dresses like you do."

"Someone *else?* Are you *insane?*"

"Don't blow your cool, analyst, we're not supposed to know each other. No, I'm not insane. I just hired a backup in case I'm outthought. Remember, you wanted my input in such matters."

The introductions were short and no names were used, but it was evident that McAllister was impressed by the stocky, broad-shouldered, well-dressed Chinese.

"Are you an executive with one of the firms over

here?" asked the analyst as they walked toward the side street where the conduit's car was parked.

"In a manner of speaking, yes, sir. My own firm, however. I run a courier service for very important people."

"But how did *he* find you?"

"I'm sorry, sir, but I'm sure you can understand. Such information is confidential."

"Good Lord," muttered McAllister, glancing at the man from Medusa.

"Get me to a phone in twenty minutes," said Jason in the front seat. The bewildered undersecretary sat in the back.

"They are using a relay, then?" asked the conduit. "They did so many times with the Frenchman."

"How did he handle them?" asked Bourne.

"With delays. He would say, 'Let them sweat.' May I suggest an hour?"

"You're on. Is there a restaurant open around here?"

"Over in the Rua Mercadores."

"We need food, and the Frenchman was right—he was always right. Let them sweat."

"He was a decent man to me," said the conduit.

"At the end he was some kind of eloquent if perverted saint."

"I do not understand, sir."

"It's not necessary that you do. But I'm alive and he's not because he made a decision."

"What kind of decision, sir?"

"That he should die so that I could live."

"Like the Christian Scriptures. The nuns taught them to us."

"Hardly," said Jason, amused at the thought. "If there'd been another way out we would have taken it. There wasn't. He simply accepted the fact that his death was *my* way out."

"I liked him," said the conduit.

"Take us to the restaurant."

It was all Edward McAllister could do to contain himself. What he did not know and what Bourne would not discuss at the table was choking him with frustration. Twice he tried to broach the subject of relays and the current situation and twice Jason cut him off, admonishing the undersecretary with a stare, as the conduit, in gratitude, looked away. There were certain facts the Chinese knew about and there were other facts he did not care to know about for his own safety.

"Rest and food," mused Bourne, finishing the last of his *tian-suan rou.* "The Frenchman said they were weapons. He was right, of course."

"I suggest he needed the first more than you did, sir," said the conduit.

"Perhaps. Anyway, he was a student of military history. He claimed more battles were lost from fatigue than from inferior firepower."

"This is all *very* interesting," McAllister interrupted sharply, "but we've been here for some time and I'm sure there are things we should be doing."

"We will, Edward. If you're uptight, think what they're going through. The Frenchman also used to say that the enemy's exposed nerves were our best allies."

"I'm becoming rather tired of your Frenchman," said McAllister testily.

Jason looked at the analyst and spoke quietly. "Don't ever say that to me again. You weren't there." Bourne checked his watch. "It's over an hour. Let's find a phone." He turned to the conduit. "I'll need your help," he added. "You just put in the money. I'll dial."

"You said you'd call back in *thirty minutes!*" spat out the woman at the other end of the line.

"I had business to take care of. I have other clients and I'm not too crazy about your attitude. If this is going to be a waste of time, I've got other things to do and you can answer to the *man* when the typhoon comes."

"How could that happen?"

"Come *on,* lady! Give me a trunk filled with more money than you've ever thought about and I might tell you. On the other hand, I probably wouldn't. I like to be owed favors by men in high places. You've got ten seconds and I hang up."

"*Please.* You will meet a man who will take you to a house on the Guia Hill where there is highly sophisticated communications equipment—"

"And where a half-dozen of your goons will crack my skull and throw me into a room where a doctor fills me

with juice and you get it all for *nothing!*" Bourne's anger
was only partly feigned; Sheng's troops were the ones
behaving like amateurs. "I'll tell you about another piece
of sophisticated equipment. It's called a telephone and I
don't think there'd be *communications* from Macao to the
Guangdong garrison if you didn't have scramblers. Of
course, you bought them in Tokyo because if you made
them yourselves they probably wouldn't work! *Use* one.
I'm calling you just once more, lady. Have a number for
me. The *man's* number." Jason hung up.

"That's interesting," said McAllister several feet away
from the pay phone, glancing briefly at the Chinese conduit who had returned to the table. "You used the stick
when I would have used the carrot."

"Used the what?"

"I would have emphasized what extraordinary information I had to reveal. Instead, you threatened, as if you
were dismissing whoever it was."

"Spare me," answered Bourne, lighting a cigarette,
grateful that his hand was not shaking. "For your edifica-
tion I did both. The threat emphasizes the revelation and
the dismissal reinforces both."

"Your input is showing," said the undersecretary of
State, a hint of a smile on his face. "Thank you."

The man from Medusa looked hard at the man from
Washington. "If this damn thing works, can you do it,
analyst? Can you whip out the gun and pull the trigger?
Because if you can't, we're both dead."

"I can do it," said McAllister calmly. "For the Far East.
For the world."

"And for your day in the sun." Jason started toward the
table. "Let's get out of here. I don't want to use this
phone again."

The serenity of Jade Tower Mountain was belied by the
frantic activity inside the villa of Sheng Chou Yang. The
turmoil was caused not by the number of people, for
there were only five, but by the intensity of the players.
The minister listened as his aides came and went from
the garden bringing news of the latest developments and
timidly offered advice, which was instantly withdrawn at
the first sign of displeasure.

"Our people have confirmed the story, sir!" cried a uniformed middle-aged man rushing from the house. "They've talked to the journalists. Everything was as the assassin described and a photograph of the dead man was distributed to the newspapers."

"*Get* it," ordered Sheng. "Have it wired here at once. This whole thing is incredible."

"It's being done," said the soldier. "The consulate sent an attaché to the *South China News*. It should be arriving within minutes."

"Incredible," repeated Sheng softly, his eyes straying to the lily pads in the nearest of the four man-made ponds. "The symmetry is too perfect, the timing too perfect, and that means something is imperfect. Someone has imposed order."

"The assassin?" asked another aide.

"For what purpose? He has no idea that he would have been a corpse before the night was over in the sanctuary. He thought he was privileged, but we were only using him to trap his predecessor, unearthed by our man in Special Branch."

"Then who?" questioned another.

"That's the dilemma. *Who?* Everything is at once tempting yet clumsy. It's all too apparent, fraught with unprofessional ego. The assassin, if he's telling the truth, has to believe he has nothing to fear from me, but still he threatens, conceivably throwing over a most profitable client. Professionals don't do that, and that's what bothers me."

"You are suggesting a third party, Minister?" asked the third aide.

"If so," said Sheng, his eyes now riveted on a single lily pad, "someone with no experience or with the intelligence of an ox. It's a dilemma."

"It's *here*, sir!" shouted a young man, racing into the garden, holding a teletyped photograph.

"Give it to me. *Quickly!*" Sheng grabbed the paper and angled it into the glare of a floodlight. "It is *he!* I'll never forget that face as long as I *breathe!* Clear everything! Tell the woman in Macao to give our assassin the number and electronically sweep all conceivable interceptions. Failure is *death.*"

"Instantly, Minister!" The operator ran back to the house.

"My wife and my children," said Sheng Chou Yang reflectively. "They may be upset by all this disturbance. Will one of you please go inside and explain that affairs of state keep me from their beloved presence?"

"It is my honor, sir," said an aide.

"They suffer so from the demands of my work. They are all angels. One day they will be rewarded."

Bourne touched the conduit's shoulder, then pointed to the lighted marquee of a hotel on the right side of the street. "We'll check in here, then head for a phone booth on the other side of the city. Okay?"

"It's wise," said the Chinese. "They are all over the telephone company."

"And we've got to get some sleep. The Frenchman never stopped telling me that rest was also a weapon. Christ, why do I keep *repeating* myself?"

"Because you're obsessed," said McAllister from the backseat.

"Tell me about it. No, don't."

Jason dialed the number in Macao that tripped a relay in China into a swept telephone in Jade Tower Mountain. As he did so he looked at the analyst. "Does Sheng speak French?" he asked quickly.

"Of course," said the undersecretary. "He deals with the Quai d'Orsay and speaks the language of everyone he negotiates with. It's one of his strengths. But why not use Mandarin? You know it."

"The commando didn't, and if I speak English he might wonder where the British accent went. French'll cover it, as it did with Soo Jiang, and I'll also know whether or not it's Sheng." Bourne stretched a handkerchief across the mouthpiece as he heard a second, echoing ring fifteen hundred miles away. The scramblers were in place.

"*Wei?*"

"*Comme le colonel, je préfère le français.*"

"*Shemma?*" cried the voice, bewildered.

"*Fawen,*" said Jason, the Mandarin for French.

"Fawen? Wo buhui!" replied the man excitedly, stating that he did not speak French. The call was expected. Another voice intruded; it was in the background and too low to be heard. And then it was there on the line.

"Pourquoi vous parlez français?" It was Sheng! No matter the language, Bourne would never forget the orator's singsong delivery. It was the zealous minister of an unmerciful God seducing an audience before assaulting it with fire and brimstone.

"Let's say I feel more comfortable."

"Very well. What is this incredible story you bring? This madness during which a name was mentioned?"

"I was also told you speak French," interrupted Jason.

There was a pause in which only Sheng's steady breathing could be heard. "You know who I am?"

"I know a name that doesn't mean anything to me. It does to someone else, though. Someone you knew years ago. He wants to talk to you."

"What?" screamed Sheng. *"Betrayal!"*

"Nothing of the sort, and if I were you, I'd listen to him. He saw right through everything I told them. The others didn't, but he did." Bourne glanced at McAllister beside him; the analyst nodded his head, as if to say that Jason was convincingly using the words the undersecretary had given him. "He took one look at me and put the figures together. But then the Frenchman's original boy was pretty well shot up; his head was a bloody cauliflower."

"What have you *done?*"

"Probably the biggest favor you ever got, and I expect to be paid for it. Here's your friend. He'll use English." Bourne handed the phone to the analyst, who spoke instantly.

"It's Edward McAllister, Sheng."

"Edward . . . ?" The stunned Sheng Chou Yang could not complete the name.

"This conversation is off the record, with no official sanction. My whereabouts are unlogged and unknown. I'm speaking solely for my own benefit—and yours."

"You . . . astonish me, my old friend," said the minister slowly, fearfully collecting himself.

"You'll read about it in the morning papers and it's

undoubtedly on all the newscasts from Hawaii already. The consulate wanted me to disappear for a few days—the fewer questions the better—and I knew just whom I wanted to go with."

"What happened, and *how* did you—"

"The similarity in their appearance was too obvious to be coincidental," broke in the undersecretary of State. "I suppose d'Anjou wanted to trade on the legend as totally as possible, and that included the physical characteristics for those who had seen Jason Bourne in the past. An unnecessary fillip, in my opinion, but it was effective. In the panic on Victoria Peak—and from the nearly unrecognizable face—no one else noticed that striking resemblance. But then none of the others knew Bourne. I did."

"You?"

"I drove him out of Asia. I'm the one he came to kill, and consistent with his perverse sense of irony and revenge, he decided to do it by leaving the corpse of your assassin on Victoria Peak. Fortunately for me, his ego didn't permit him to evaluate your man's abilities correctly. Once the firing started, our now mutual associate overpowered him and threw him into the guns."

"Edward, the information is coming too fast, I cannot assimilate it. Who brought Jason Bourne back?"

"Obviously the Frenchman. His pupil and immensely successful meal ticket had defected from him. He wanted revenge and knew where to find the one man who could give him that. His colleague from Medusa, the original Jason Bourne."

"Medusa!" whispered Sheng with loathing.

"Despite their reputation, in certain units there were intense loyalties. You save a man's life, he doesn't forget."

"What led you to the *preposterous* conclusion that I have anything to do with the man you call an assassin—"

"Please, Sheng," interrupted the analyst. "It's too late for protestations. We're *talking*. But I'll answer your question. It was in the pattern of several killings. It started with a vice-premier of China in the Tsim Sha Tsui and four other men. They all were your enemies. And at Kai-tak the other night, two of your most vocal critics in the Peking delegation—targets of a bomb. There were also rumors; there always are in the underworld. The whispers spoke of messages between Macao and Guangdong, of powerful men in Beijing—of *one* man with immense power. And finally there was the file. . . . The figures added up. *You.*"

"The *file?* What is this, Edward?" asked Sheng, feigning strength. "Why is this an unofficial, unreported communication between us?"

"I think you know."

"You're a brilliant man. You know I would not ask if I did. We're above such pavanes."

"A brilliant bureaucrat kept in the back room, wouldn't you also say?"

"In truth, I expected better things for you. You provided most of the words and the moves for your so-called negotiators during the trade conferences. And everyone knows you did exemplary work in Hong Kong. By the time you left, Washington had every major influence in the territory in its orbit."

"I've decided to retire, Sheng. I've given twenty years of my life to my government, but I won't give it my death. I won't be ambushed and shot at or truck-bombed. I won't become a target for terrorists, whether it's here or in Iran or Beirut. It's time I got something for myself, for my family. Times change, people change, and living's expensive. My pension and my prospects are far less than I deserve."

"I agree with you completely, Edward, but what has it got to do with *me?* We were compromisers together—adversaries, to be sure, as in a courtroom, but certainly not enemies in the arena of violence. And what in the name of heaven is this foolishness about my name being mentioned by jackals of the Kuomintang?"

"Spare me." The analyst glanced over at Bourne. "Whatever was said by our mutual associate, the words were provided by me; they weren't his. Your name was never mentioned in Victoria Peak, and there were no Taiwanese in our interrogation of your man. I gave him those words because there's a certain validity in them for you. As to your name, it's for a restricted few, their eyes only. It's in the file I mentioned, a file locked in my office

in Hong Kong. It's marked 'Ultra Maximum Security.'
There is only one copy of this file, and it's buried in a
vault in Washington to be released or destroyed only by
me. However, should the unexpected happen—say, a
plane crash, or if I disappeared, or was killed—the file
would be turned over to the National Security Council.
The information in this file, in the wrong hands, could
prove catastrophic for the entire Far East."

"I am intrigued, Edward, by your candid, if incomplete, information."

"Meet with me, Sheng. And bring money, a great deal
of money—American money. Our mutual associate tells
me there are hills in Guangdong where your people flew
down to see him. Meet me there tomorrow, between ten
o'clock and midnight."

"I must protest, my adversarial friend. You have not
provided me with an incentive."

"I can destroy both copies of that file. I was sent over
here to track down a story out of Taiwan, a story so
detrimental to all our interests that a hint of its contents
could start a chain of events that terrifies everyone. I
believe there's considerable substance to the story, and
if I'm right, it can be traced directly to my old counterpart
during the Sino-American conferences. It couldn't be
happening without him. . . . It's my last assignment,
Sheng, and a few words from me can remove that file
from the face of the earth. I simply determine the information to be totally false and dangerously inflammatory,
compiled by your enemies in Taiwan. The few who know
about it want to believe that, take my word for it. The file
is then sent to the shredder. So is the copy in Washington."

"You still have not told me why I should *listen* to
you!"

"The son of a Kuomintang taipan would know. The
leader of a cabal in Beijing would know. A man who could
be disgraced and decapitated tomorrow morning *certainly*
would know."

The pause was long, the breathing erratic over the line.
Finally, Sheng spoke.

"The hills in Guangdong. *He* knows where."

"Only one helicopter," said McAllister. "You and the
pilot, no one else."

37

Darkness. The figure dressed in the uniform of a United States marine dropped down from the top of the wall at the rear of the grounds in the house on Victoria Peak. He crept to his left, passing a sheet of interwoven strands of barbed wire that filled a space where a section of the wall had been blown away, and proceeded around the edge of the property. Staying in the shadows, he raced across the lawn to the corner of the house. He peered around at the demolished bay windows of what had been a large Victorian study. In front of the shattered glass and the profusion of broken frames stood a marine guard, an M-16 rifle planted casually on the grass, the end of the barrel in his hand, a .45 automatic strapped to his belt. The addition of a rifle to the smaller weapon was a sign of max-alert —the intruder understood this, and smiled to see that the guard did not think it necessary to hold the M-16 in his hands. Marines and poised weapons were not welcome. The stock of a rifle would crash into a man's head before he knew it was into its whip. The intruder waited for the opportune moment; it came when the guard's chest swelled with a long yawn and his eyes briefly closed as he inhaled deeply. The intruder raced around the corner, springing off his feet, the wire of a garrote looping over the guard's head. It was over in seconds. There was barely a sound.

The killer left the body where it lay, as it was far darker in this area of the grounds than elsewhere. Many of the rear floodlights had been shattered by the explosions. He got to his feet and edged his way to the next corner, where he took out a cigarette, lighting it with the cupped flame from a butane lighter. He then stepped out into the glare of the floodlights and walked casually around the

corner toward the huge, charred French doors where a
second marine was at his post on the brick steps. The
intruder held the cigarette in his left hand, which covered
his face as he drew on it.

"Out for a smoke?" asked the guard.

"Yeah, I couldn't sleep," said the man, with an American accent that was a product of the Southwest.

"Those fuckin' cots weren't made for sleeping. Just sit
on one and you know it. . . . Hey, *wait* a minute! Who the
hell are *you?*"

The marine had no chance to level his rifle. The intruder lunged, thrusting his knife straight into the
guard's throat with deadly accuracy, cutting off all sound,
all life. The killer quickly dragged the corpse around the
corner of the building and left it in the shadows. He
wiped the blade off on the dead man's uniform, rein-
serted it beneath his tunic, and returned to the French
doors. He entered the house.

He walked down the long, dimly lit corridor at the end
of which stood a third marine in front of a wide, sculptured door. The guard angled his rifle downward and
looked at his watch. "You're early," he said. "I'm not due
to be relieved for another hour and twenty minutes."

"I'm not with this unit, buddy."

"You with the Oahu group?"

"Yeah."

"I thought they got you jokers out of here pronto and
back to Hawaii. That's the scuttlebutt."

"A few of us were ordered to stay behind. We're down
at the consulate now. That guy, what's-his-name, McAllister, has been taking our testimonies all night."

"I tell you, pal, this whole goddamned thing is *weird!*"

"You got it, triple weird. By the way, where's that fruit-
cake's office? He sent me up here to bring him back his
special pipe tobacco."

"It figures. Mix some grass in it."

"Which office?"

"Earlier I saw him and the doctor go in that first door
on the right. Then later, before he left, he went in here."
The guard tilted his head to indicate the door behind
him.

"Whose place is that?"

"I don't know his name, but he's the top banana. They call him the ambassador."

The killer's eyes narrowed. "The ambassador?"

"Yeah. The room's fractured. Half of it's blown apart by that fucking maniac, but the safe's intact, which is why I'm here and another guy outside in the tulips. Must be a couple of million in there for extracurricular activities."

"Or something else," said the intruder softly. "The first door on the right, huh?" he added, turning and reaching under his tunic.

"*Hold* it," said the marine. "Why didn't the gate send word in here?" He reached for the hand-held radio strapped to his belt. "Sorry, but I've got to check you out, buddy. It's standard—"

The killer threw his knife. As it plunged into the guard's chest he hurled himself on the marine, his thumbs centering in on the man's throat. Thirty seconds later he opened the door of Havilland's office and dragged the dead man inside.

They crossed the border in full darkness, business suits and regimental ties replacing the rumpled, nondescript clothes they had worn previously. Added to their attire were two proper attaché cases strapped with *diplomatique* tape, indicating government documents beyond the scrutiny of immigration points. In truth, the cases held their weapons, as well as several additional items Bourne had picked up in d'Anjou's flat after McAllister produced the sacrosanct plastic tape that was respected even by the People's Republic—respected as long as China wanted the same courtesy extended to its own foreign service personnel. The conduit from Macao whose name was Wong—at least that was the name he offered—was impressed by the diplomatic passports, but for safety's sake, as well as for the $20,000 American for which he said he felt a moral obligation, decided to prepare the border-crossing his way.

"It's not as difficult as perhaps I led you to believe before, sir," explained Wong. "Two of the guards are cousins on my blessed mother's side—may she rest with the holy Jesus—and we help each other. I do more for them than they do for me, but then I am in a better position. Their stomachs are fuller than most in the city of Zhuhai Shi and both have television sets."

"If they're cousins," said Jason, "why did you object to the watch I gave one of them before? You said it was too expensive."

"Because he'll sell it, sir, and I don't care to see him spoiled. He'll expect too much from me."

On such considerations, thought Bourne, were the tightest borders in the world patrolled. Regardless, they were directed by Wong to enter the last gate on the right at precisely 8:55; he would cross separately a few minutes later. Their red-striped passports were studied, sent to an inside office, and amid many abrupt smiles on the part of a cousin, the honored diplomats were rapidly passed through. They were instantly welcomed to China by the prefect of the Zhuhai Shi–Guangdong Province Control who returned their passports. She was a short, broad-shouldered, muscular woman. Her English was obscured by a thick accent but was understandable.

"You have government business in Zhuhai Shi?" she asked, her smile belied by her clouded, vaguely hostile eyes. "The Guangdong garrison, perhaps? I can arrange auto transport, please?"

"*Bu xiexie,*" said the undersecretary of State, declining, and then for courtesy's sake reverting to English to show respect for his host's diligence in learning it. "It's a minor conference, lasting for only a few hours, and we'll return to Macao later tonight. We'll be contacted here, so we'll have some coffee and wait."

"In my office, please?"

"Thank you, but I think not. Your people will be looking for us in the . . . *kafie dian*—the café."

"Over on the left-right, sir. On the street. Welcome again to the People's Republic."

"Your courtesy will not be forgotten," said McAllister, bowing.

"You are with thanks," replied the heavyset woman, nodding and striding away.

"To use your words, analyst," said Bourne, "you did that very well. But I should tell you she's not on our side."

"Of course not," agreed the undersecretary. "She's

been instructed to call someone either here at the garrison or in Beijing confirming that we've crossed over. That someone will reach Sheng, and he'll know it's me—and you. No one else."

"He's airborne," said Jason as they walked slowly toward the dimly lit coffee shop at the end of a dingy concrete walkway that emerged on the street. "He's on his way here. Incidentally, we'll be followed, you know that, don't you?"

"No, I don't know that," replied McAllister, looking briefly at Bourne. "Sheng will be cautious. I've given him enough information to alarm him. If he thought there was only one file—which happens to be the truth—he might take chances, thinking he could buy it from me and kill me. But he thinks, or has to assume, that there's a copy in Washington. That's the one he wants destroyed. He won't do anything to upset me or to make me panic and run. Remember, I'm the amateur and I frighten easily. I know him. He's putting it all together now and is probably carrying more money to me than I've ever dreamed of. Of course, he expects to get it back once the files are destroyed and he *does* kill me. So, you see, I have a very strong reason not to fail—or not to succeed by failing."

The man from Medusa again stared at the man from Washington. "You've really thought this out, haven't you?"

"Thoroughly," answered McAllister, looking straight ahead. "For weeks. Every detail. Frankly, I didn't think you'd be a part of it because I thought you'd be dead, but I knew I could reach Sheng. Somehow—unofficially, of course. Any other way, including a confidential conference, would entail protocol, and even if I got him alone, without his aides, I couldn't touch him. It would look like a government-sanctioned assassination. I considered reaching him directly, for old times' sake, and using words that would trigger a response—pretty much what I did last night. As you said to Havilland, the simplest ways are usually the best. We tend to complicate things."

"In your defense, you frequently have to. You can't be caught with a smoking gun."

"That's such a trite expression," said the analyst with a derisive laugh. "What does it mean? That you were led or misled into an error of inconsequential consequence? Policy doesn't revolve around a single man's embarrassment, or it shouldn't. I'm constantly appalled by the people's cries for righteousness when they have no idea, no concept, of how we have to deal."

"Maybe the people every now and then want a straight answer."

"They can't *have* one," said McAllister as they approached the door of the coffee shop, "because they couldn't understand."

Bourne stood in front of the door without opening it. "You're blind," he said, his eyes locked with the undersecretary's. "I wasn't given a straight answer, either, much less an explanation. You've been in Washington too long. You should try a couple of weeks in Cleveland or Bangor, Maine. It might broaden that perspective of yours."

"Don't lecture me, Mr. Bourne. Less than forty-six percent of our population care enough to cast a ballot—which determines the directions we take. It's all left to us —the performers and the professional bureaucrats. We're all you've got. . . . May we go inside, please? Your friend Mr. Wong said we were to spend only a few minutes being seen having coffee and then go out on the street. He said he'd meet us there in exactly twenty-five minutes, and twelve have already elapsed."

"Twelve? Not ten or fifteen, but twelve?"

"Precisely."

"What do we do if he's two minutes late? Shoot him?"

"Very funny," said the analyst, pushing the door open.

They walked out of the coffee shop and into the dark, bruised pavement of the run-down square fronting the Guangdong checkpoint. As it was a slow time at the gates, there were no more than a dozen people crossing the thoroughfare, disappearing into the darkness. Of the three streetlights in the immediate vicinity, only one was working, dimly. Visibility was poor. The twenty-five-minute mark passed, and was stretched to thirty, then approached thirty-eight. Bourne spoke.

"Something's wrong. He should have made contact by now."

"Two minutes and we shoot him?" said McAllister,

instantly disliking his own attempt at humor. "I mean, I gathered that staying calm was everything."

"For two minutes, not close to fifteen," replied Jason. "It's not normal," he added softly, as if to himself. "On the other hand, it could be normally *abnormal*. He wants us to make contact with *him*."

"I don't understand—"

"You don't have to. Just walk alongside me, as if we were strolling, passing the time until we're met. If she sees us, the lady wrestler won't be surprised. Chinese officials are notoriously late for conferences; they feel it gives them the advantage."

" 'Let them sweat'?"

"Exactly. Only that's not who we're meeting now. Come on, let's go to the left; it's darker, away from the light. Be casual; talk about the weather, anything. Nod your head, shake it, shrug—just keep up steady, low-keyed movements."

They walked for about fifty feet when it happened. *"Kam Pek!"* The name of the casino in Macao was whispered, shot out of the shadows beyond a deserted newsstand.

"Wong?"

"Stay where you are and make a show of conversation, but listen to me!"

"What's happened?"

"You're being followed."

"Two points for a brilliant bureaucrat," said Jason. "Any comment, Mr. Undersecretary?"

"It's unexpected but not illogical," answered McAllister. "A safeguard, perhaps. False passports abound over here, as we happen to know."

"Queen Kong checked us out. Strike one."

"Then, perhaps, to make sure we don't link up with the kind of people you suggested last night," whispered the analyst, his words too low to be heard by the Chinese conduit.

"That's possible." Bourne raised his voice slightly so that the conduit could hear him, his eyes on the border gate's entrance. There was no one. "Who's following us?"

"The Pig."

"Soo Jiang?"

"Ever so, sir. It is why I must stay out of sight."

"Anyone else?"

"No one that I could see, but I don't know who is on the road to the hills."

"I'll take him out," said the man from Medusa called Delta.

"*No!*" objected McAllister. "His orders from Sheng may include confirming that we *remain* alone, that we don't meet others. You just agreed it was possible."

"The only way he could do that is to reach others himself. He can't do that—if he can't do that. And your old *friend* wouldn't permit a radio transmission while he's in a plane or a chopper. It could be picked up."

"Suppose there are specific signals—a flare or a powerful flashlight beamed up, telling the pilot everything's clear?"

Jason looked at the analyst. "You *do* think things out."

"There is a way," said Wong from the shadows, "and it is a privilege I should like to reserve for myself, no additional charge."

"What privilege?"

"I will kill the Pig. It will be done in such a way that cannot be compromised."

"*What?*" Astonished, Bourne started to turn his head.

"*Please,* sir! Look straight ahead."

"Sorry. But *why?*"

"He fornicates indiscriminately, threatening the women he favors with loss of employment for themselves and their husbands, even brothers and cousins. Over the past four years he has brought shame to many families, including mine on my blessed mother's side."

"Why hasn't he been killed before now?"

"He travels with armed guards, even in Macao. Yet in spite of this, several attempts have been made by enraged men. They resulted in reprisals."

"Reprisals?" asked McAllister quietly.

"People were chosen, again indiscriminately, and charged with stealing supplies and equipment from the garrison. The punishment for such crimes is death in the fields."

"*Jesus,*" muttered Bourne. "I won't ask questions. You've got reason enough. But how tonight?"

"His guards are not with him now. They may be waiting for him on the road to the hills, but they are not with him *now*. You start out, and if he follows you I will follow him. If he does not follow you, I will know that your journey will not be interrupted and I will catch up with you."

"Catch up with us?" Bourne frowned.

"After I kill the Pig and leave his pig body in its proper and, for him, disgraceful place. The female toilet."

"And if he *does* follow us?" asked Jason.

"My opportunity will come, even as I serve as your eyes. I will see his guards, but they will not see me. No matter what he does, the moment will be there when he separates himself, if only by a few feet in the darkness. It will be enough, and it will be assumed he has brought shame to one of his own men."

"We'll get started."

"You know the way, sir."

"As if I had a road map."

"I will meet you at the base of the first hill beyond the high grass. Do you remember it?"

"It'd be hard to forget. I nearly bought a grave in China there."

"After seven kilometers, head into forest toward the fields."

"I intend to, you taught me. Have a good hunt, Wong."

"I will, sir. I have reason enough."

The two Americans walked across the ravaged old square, away from the dim light into complete darkness. An obese figure in civilian clothes watched them from the shadows of the concrete walkway. He looked at his watch and nodded, half smiling to himself in satisfaction. Colonel Soo Jiang then turned and walked back through the man-made tunnel into the stark immigration complex with iron gates and wooden booths and barbed wire in the distance, all bathed in dull gray light. He was greeted by the prefect of the Zhuhai Shi–Guangdong Province Control, who strode purposefully, martially, enthusiastically, toward him.

"They must be very important men, Colonel," said the prefect, her eyes not at all hostile, but instead with a look that bordered on blind worship. And fear.

"Oh, they are, they are," agreed the colonel.

"Surely they have to be for such an illustrious officer as yourself to make sure of their requirements. I made the telephone call to the man in Guangzhou, as you requested, and he thanked me, but he did not get my name—"

"I will make sure he has it," Soo broke in wearily.

"And I will keep only my best people on the gates to greet them when they return later tonight to Macao."

Soo looked at the woman. "That won't be necessary. They will be taken to Beijing for strictly confidential, highest-level conferences. My orders are to remove all records of their having crossed the Guangdong border."

"That confidential?"

"Ever so, Madame Comrade. These are secret affairs of state and must be kept as such even from your most intimate associates. Your office, please."

"At once," said the broad-shouldered woman, turning with military precision. "I have tea or coffee, and even the British whisky from Hong Kong."

"Ah, yes, the British whisky. May I escort you, comrade? My work is finished."

The two somewhat grotesquely Wagnerian figures marched in waddling lockstep toward the streaked glass door of the prefect's office.

"Cigarettes!" whispered Bourne, gripping McAllister's shoulder.

"Where?"

"Up ahead, off the road on the left. In the woods!"

"I didn't see them."

"You weren't looking for them. They're being cupped but they're there. The barks of the trees get a touch of light one moment, then they're dark the next. No rhythm, just erratic. Men smoking. Sometimes I think the Far East likes cigarettes more than sex."

"What do we do?"

"Exactly what we're doing, only louder."

"What?"

"Keep walking and say whatever comes to mind. They won't understand. I'm sure you know 'Hiawatha' or 'Horatio on the Bridge,' or in your wild college days maybe *Aura Lee*. Don't sing, just say the words; it'll keep your mind off things."

"But *why*?"

"Because this is what you predicted. Sheng is making sure that we don't link up with anyone who could be a threat to him. Let's give him that reassurance, okay?"

"Oh, my God! Suppose one of them speaks English?"

"It's highly unlikely, but if you'd rather, we'll just improvise a conversation."

"No, I'm not good at that. I hate parties and dinners, I never know what to say."

"That's why I suggested the doggerel. I'll interrupt whenever you pause. Go ahead now, speak casually but rapidly. This is no place for Chinese scholars who speak fast English. . . . The cigarettes are out. They've spotted us! Go *on!*"

"Oh, Lord . . . very well. Ah, ah . . . 'Sitting on O'Reilly's porch, telling tales of blood and slaughter—' "

"That's very appropriate!" said Jason, glaring at his pupil.

" 'Suddenly it came to me, why not shag O'Reilly's daughter—' "

"Why, Edward, you constantly surprise me."

"It's an old fraternity song," whispered the analyst.

"*What?* I can't hear you, Edward. Speak up."

" 'Fiddilly-eye-*eee*, fiddilly-eye-*ohh*, fiddilly-eye-eee to the one ball Reilly—' "

"That's terrific!" interrupted Bourne as they passed the section of the woods where only seconds ago concealed men had been smoking. "I think your friend will appreciate your point of view. Any further thoughts?"

"I forgot the words."

"Your thoughts, you mean. I'm sure they'll come to you."

"Something about 'old man Reilly.' . . . Oh, yes, I remember. First there was 'Shag, shag and shag some more, shag until the fun was over,' and *then* came old Reilly. . . . 'Two horse pistols by his side, looking for the dog who shagged his daughter.' I *did* remember."

"You belong in a museum, if Ripley owns one. . . . But look at it this way, you can research the entire project back in Macao."

"What project? . . . There was another that was always great fun. 'A hundred bottles of beer on the wall, a hundred bottles of beer; one fell down'—Oh, Lord, it's been so long. It was repetitious reduction—'ninety-nine bottles of beer on the wall—' "

"Forget it, they're out of earshot."

"Oh? Earshot? Thank God!"

"You sounded fine. If any of those clowns understood a word of English, they're even more confused than I am. Well done, analyst. Come on, let's walk faster."

McAllister looked at Jason. "You did that on purpose, didn't you? You prodded me into remembering something—anything—knowing I'd concentrate and not panic."

Bourne did not answer; he simply made a statement. "Another hundred feet and you keep going by yourself."

"*What?* You're *leaving* me?"

"For about ten, maybe fifteen, minutes. Here, keep walking and angle your arm up so I can put my briefcase on it and open the damn thing."

"Where are you going?" asked the undersecretary as the attaché case rested awkwardly on his left arm. Jason opened it, took out a long-bladed knife, and closed the case. "You can't leave me alone!"

"You'll be all right, nobody wants to stop you—us. If they did, it would have been done."

"You mean that could have been an *ambush?*"

"I was counting on your analytical mind that it wasn't. Take the case."

"But what are you—"

"I have to see what's back there. Keep walking."

The man from Medusa spun off to his left and entered the woods at a turn in the road. Running rapidly, silently, instinctively avoiding the tangled underbrush at the first touch of resistance, he moved to his right in a wide semicircle. Minutes later he saw the glow of cigarettes, and, moving like a forest cat, crept closer and closer until he was within ten feet of the group of men. The intermittent moonlight, filtered through the massive trees, provided enough illumination for him to count the number. There were six, each armed with a lightweight machine gun strapped over his shoulders. . . . And there was something else, something that was strikingly inconsistent.

Each of the men wore the four-buttoned, tailored uniforms of high officers in the army of the People's Republic. And from the snatches of conversation he could hear, it was clear that they spoke Mandarin, not Cantonese, which was the normal dialect for soldiers, even officers, of the Guangdong garrison. These men were not from Guangdong. Sheng had flown in his own elite guard.

Suddenly, one of the officers snapped his lighter and looked at his watch. Bourne studied the face above the flame. He knew it, and seeing it confirmed his judgment. It was the face of the man who had tried to trap Echo by posing as a prisoner on the truck that terrible night, the officer Sheng treated with a degree of deference. A thinking killer with a soft voice.

"*Xian zai,*" said the man, stating that the moment had come. He picked up a hand-held radio and spoke. "*Da li shi, da li shi!*" he barked, raising his party by the code name Marble. "They are alone, there is no one else. We will proceed as instructed. Prepare for the signal."

The six officers rose in unison, adjusted their weapons, and extinguished their cigarettes by grinding them under their boots. They started rapidly for the back country road.

Bourne scrambled around on his hands and knees, got to his feet and raced through the woods. He had to reach McAllister before Sheng's contingent closed in on him and saw through the sporadic moonlight that the analyst was alone. Should the guards become alarmed they might send a different "signal": *Conference aborted.* He reached the turn in the road and ran faster, jumping over fallen branches other men would not see, slithering through vines and linked foliage others would not anticipate. In less than two minutes he sprang silently out of the woods at McAllister's side.

"Good *God!*" gasped the undersecretary of State.

"Be quiet!"

"You're a maniac!"

"Tell me about it."

"It would take hours." With trembling hands, McAllister handed Jason his attaché case. "At least, this didn't explode."

"I should have told you not to drop it or jar it too much."

"Oh, Jesus! . . . Isn't it time to get off the road? Wong said—"

"Forget it. We're staying in plain view until we reach the field on the second hill, then you'll be more in view than me. Hurry up. Some kind of signal's going to be given, which means you were right again. A pilot's going to get clearance to land—no radio communication, just a light."

"We're to meet Wong somewhere. At the base of the first hill, I think he said."

"We'll give him a couple of minutes, but I think we can forget him, too. He'll see what I saw, and if it were me, I'd head back to Macao and twenty thousand, American, and say I lost my way."

"What *did* you see?"

"Six men armed with enough firepower to defoliate one of the hills here."

"Oh, my God, we'll never get *out!*"

"Don't give up yet. That's one of the things *I've* been thinking about." Bourne turned to McAllister as he quickened their pace. "On the other hand," he added, his voice deadly serious. "The risk was always there—doing things your way."

"Yes, I know. I won't panic. I will *not* panic." The woods were suddenly gone; the dirt road now cut a path through fields of tall grass. "What do you think those men are here for?" asked the analyst.

"Backups in case of a trap, which any low life in this business would think it was. I told you that, and you didn't want to believe me. But if something you said is accurate, and I think it is, they'll stay far out of sight—to make sure you won't panic and run. If that's the case, it'll be our way out."

"How?"

"Head to the right, through the field," replied Jason without answering the question. "I'll give Wong five minutes, unless we spot a signal somewhere or hear a plane, but no more. And that long only because I really want the pair of eyes I paid for."

"Could he get around those men without being seen?"

"He can if he's not on his way back to Macao."

They reached the end of the field of high grass and the base of the first hill where trees rose out of the ascending ground. Bourne looked at his watch, then at McAllister. "Let's get up there, out of sight," he said, gesturing at the trees above them. "I'll stay here; you go up farther, but don't walk out on that field, don't expose yourself, stay at the edge. If you see any lights or hear a plane, whistle. You *can* whistle, can't you?"

"Actually, not very well. When the children were younger and we had a dog, a golden retriever—"

"Oh, for Christ's sake! Throw rocks down through the trees, I'll hear them. Go *on!*"

"Yes, I understand. *Move.*"

Delta—for he *was* Delta now—began his vigil. The moonlight was constantly intercepted by the drifting, low-flying clouds and he kept straining his eyes, scanning the field of tall grass, looking for a break in the monotonous pattern, for bent reeds moving toward the base of the hill, toward *him.* Three minutes passed, and he had nearly decided it was a waste of time when a man suddenly lurched out of the grass on his right and plunged into the foliage. Bourne lowered his attaché case and pulled the long knife from his belt.

"Kam Pek!" whispered the man.

"Wong?"

"Yes, sir," said the conduit, walking around the trunks of trees, approaching Jason. "I am greeted with a knife?"

"There are a few other people back there, and frankly, I didn't think you'd show up. I told you you could get out if the risks looked too great. I didn't think it'd happen so early on, but I would have accepted it. Those are impressive weapons they're carrying."

"I might have taken advantage of the situation, but, added to the money, you afforded me an act of immense gratification. For many others as well. More people than you can imagine will give thanks."

"Soo the Pig?"

"Yes, sir."

"Wait a minute," said Bourne, alarmed. "Why are you so sure they'll think one of those men did it?"

"What men?"

"That patrol of machine guns back there! They're not from Guangdong, not from the garrison. They're from *Beijing!*"

"The act took place in Zhuhai Shi. At the gate."

"*Goddamn* you! You've blown *everything!* They were *waiting* for him!"

"If they were, sir, he never would have arrived."

"What?"

"He was getting drunk with the prefect of the gate. He went to relieve himself, which was where I confronted him. He is now next door, lying in a soiled female commode, his throat slit, his genitals removed."

"Good *God* . . . Then he didn't follow us?"

"Nor did he show any indication of doing so."

"I see—no, I don't see. He was cut out of tonight. It's strictly a Beijing operation. Yet he was the primary contact down here—"

"I would know nothing of such matters," broke in Wong defensively.

"Oh, sorry. No, you wouldn't."

"Here are the eyes you hired, sir. Where do you wish me to look and what do you want me to do?"

"Did you have any trouble getting by that patrol in the road?"

"None. I saw them, they did not see me. They are now sitting in the woods at the edge of the field. If it would be of help to you, the man with the radio instructed the one he reached to leave once the 'signal' was given. I don't know what that means, but I presume it concerns a helicopter."

"You presume?"

"The Frenchman and I followed the English major here one night. It's how I knew where to take you before. A helicopter landed and men came out to meet the Englishman."

"That's what he told me."

"*Told* you, sir?"

"Never mind. Stay here. If that patrol across the field starts coming over, I want to know about it. I'll be up in the field before the second hill, on the right. The same field where you and Echo saw the helicopter."

"Echo?"

"The Frenchman." Delta paused, thinking quickly. "You can't light a match, you can't draw attention to yourself—" Suddenly, there were the sharp if muted sounds of objects striking other objects. *Trees! Rocks!* McAllister was signaling him!

"Grab stones, pieces of wood or rocks, and keep throwing them into the woods on the right. I'll hear them."

"I will fill my pockets with some now."

"I have no right to ask you this," said Delta, picking up the attaché case, "but do you have a weapon?"

"A three-fifty-seven-caliber magnum with a beltful of ammunition, courtesy of my cousin on my mother's side, may she rest with the holy Jesus."

"I hope I don't see you, and if I don't, good-bye, Wong. Another part of me may not approve of you, but you're a hell of a man. And believe me, you really did beat me last time."

"No, sir, you bested me. But I would like to try again."

"*Forget* it!" cried the man from Medusa, racing up the hill.

Like a giant, monstrous bird, its lower body pulsating with blinding light, the helicopter descended onto the field. As arranged, McAllister stood in full view, and, as expected, the chopper's searchlight zeroed in on him. Also, as arranged, Jason Bourne was forty-odd yards away, in the shadows of the woods—visible, but not clearly. The rotors wound down to a grinding, abrasive halt. The silence was emphatic. The door opened, the stairs sprang out, and the slender, gray-haired Sheng Chou Yang walked down the steps, carrying a briefcase.

"So good to see you after all these years, Edward," called out a taipan's first son. "Would you care to inspect the aircraft? As you requested, there is no one but myself and my most trusted pilot."

"No, Sheng, you can do it for me!" yelled McAllister, several hundred feet away, pulling a canister from inside his jacket and throwing it toward the helicopter. "Tell the pilot to step outside for a few minutes and spray the cabin. If there's anyone inside, he—or they—will come out quickly."

"This is so unlike you, Edward. Men like us know when to trust one another. We're not fools."

"*Do* it, Sheng!"

"Of course I will." Under orders, the pilot stepped out of the aircraft. Sheng Chou Yang picked up the canister and sprayed the immobilizing fog into the helicopter. Several minutes elapsed; no one came out. "Are you satisfied, or should I blow the damn thing up, which would serve neither of us. Come, my friend, we're beyond these games. We always were."

"But you became what you are. I remained what I was."

"We can correct that, Edward! I can demand your presence at all our conferences. I can elevate you to a position of prominence. You'll be a star in the foreign service firmament."

"It's true, then, isn't it? Everything in the file. You're back. The Kuomintang is back in China—"

"Let's talk quietly together, Edward." Sheng glanced at the presumed assassin in the shadows, then gestured to his right. "This is a private matter."

Bourne moved quickly; he raced to the aircraft while the two negotiators were standing with their backs to him. As the pilot climbed into the chopper and reached his seat, the man from Medusa was behind him.

"An jing!" whispered Jason, ordering the man to keep silent, his KG-9 machine pistol reinforcing the command. Before the stunned pilot could react, Bourne whipped a strip of heavy cloth over the man's head, bridling it across the shocked, open mouth and yanked it taut. Then, pulling a long, thin nylon cord from his pocket, Jason lashed the man to the seat, pinning his arms. There would be no sudden lift-off.

Returning his weapon to the belt under his jacket, Bourne crawled out of the helicopter. The huge machine blocked his view of McAllister and Sheng Chou Yang, which meant that it blocked theirs of him. He walked rapidly back to his previous position, constantly turning his head, prepared to change direction if the two men emerged on either side of the aircraft; the chopper was his visual shield. He stopped; he was near enough; it was time to appear casual. He took out a cigarette and struck a match, lighting it. He then strolled aimlessly, to his left, to where he could just barely see the two figures on the other side of the helicopter. He wondered what was being said between the two enemies. He wondered what McAllister was waiting for.

Do it, analyst. Do it now! It's your maximum opportunity.

Every moment you delay you give away time, and time holds complications! Goddamn it, do it!

Bourne froze. He heard the sound of a stone hitting a tree close to where he had walked out on the field. Then another much nearer and another quickly following. It was Wong's warning! Sheng's patrol was crossing the field below!

Analyst, you'll get us killed! If I run over and shoot, the sound will bring six men rushing us with more firepower than we can handle! For Christ's sake, do it!

The man from Medusa stared at Sheng and McAllister, his self-hatred rising, close to exploding. He never should have let it happen this way. Death by the hands of an amateur, an embittered bureaucrat who wanted his moment in the sun.

"*Kam Pek!*" It was Wong! He had crossed through the woods on the second level and was behind him, concealed in the trees.

"Yes? I heard the stones."

"You will not like what you hear now, sir."

"What is it?"

"The patrol crawls up the hill."

"It's a protective action," said Jason, his eyes riveted on the two figures in the field. "We may still be all right. They can't see a hell of a lot."

"I am not sure that matters, sir. They prepare themselves. I heard them—they've locked their weapons into firing positions."

Bourne swallowed, a sense of futility spreading over him. For reasons he could not fathom, it was a reverse trap. "You'd better get out of here, Wong."

"May I ask? Are these the people who killed the Frenchman?"

"Yes."

"And for whom the Pig, Soo Jiang, has worked so obscenely these past four years?"

"Yes."

"I believe I will stay, sir."

Without saying a word, the man from Medusa walked back to his attaché case. He picked it up and threw it into the woods. "Open it," he said. "If we get out of this, you can spend your days at the casino without picking up messages."

"I do not gamble."

"You're gambling now, Wong."

"Did you really think that we, the great warlords of the most ancient and cultured empire the world has ever known, would leave it to unwashed peasants and their ill-born offspring, schooled in the discredited theories of egalitarianism?" Sheng stood in front of McAllister; he held his briefcase across his chest with both hands. "They should be our slaves, not our rulers."

"It was that kind of thinking that lost you the country —you, the leaders, not the people. They weren't consulted. If they were, there might have been accommodations, compromises, and you would still have it."

"One does not compromise with Marxist animals—or with liars. As I will not compromise with you, Edward."

"What was that?"

With his left hand Sheng snapped his briefcase open and pulled out the file stolen from Victoria Peak. "Do you recognize it?" he asked calmly.

"I don't *believe* it!"

"Believe, my old adversary. A little ingenuity can produce anything."

"It's *impossible!*"

"It's here. In my hand. And the opening page clearly states that there is only one copy, to be sent by military escort under Ultra Maximum Security wherever it goes. Quite correctly, in my judgment, for your appraisal was accurate when we spoke over the telephone. The contents would inflame the Far East—make war unavoidable. The right-wingers in Beijing would march on Hong Kong —right-wingers there, you'd call them left on your side of the world. Foolish, isn't it?"

"I had a copy made and sent to Washington," broke in the undersecretary, quickly, quietly, firmly.

"I don't believe that," said Sheng. "All diplomatic transmissions, by telephone-computer or by pouch, must be cleared by the highest superior officer. The notorious Ambassador Havilland wouldn't permit it, and the consulate wouldn't touch it without his authorization."

"I sent a copy to the *Chinese* consulate!" shouted McAllister. "You're *finished,* Sheng!"

"Really? Who do you think receives *all* communications from *all* outside sources at our consulate in Hong Kong? Don't bother to answer, I'll do it for you. One of our people." Sheng paused, his messianic eyes suddenly on fire. "We are *everywhere*, Edward! We will not be *denied!* We will have our nation back, our *empire!*"

"You're *insane*. It can't work. You'll start a war!"

"Then it will be a *just* war! Governments across the world will have to choose. Individual rule or state rule. Freedom or tyranny!"

"Too few of you gave freedom and too many of you were tyrants."

"We will prevail—one way or the other."

"My God, that's what you *want!* You want to push the world to the brink, force it to choose between annihilation and survival! That's how you think you'll get what you want, that the choice of survival will win out! This economic commission, your whole Hong Kong strategy, is just a *beginning!* You want to spread your poison to the whole Far East! You're a zealot, you're *blind!* Can't you see the tragic consequences—"

"Our nation was *stolen* from us and we will have it *back!* We cannot be *stopped!* We *march!*"

"You *can* be stopped," said McAllister quietly, his right hand edging to the fold in his jacket. *"I'll* stop you."

Suddenly, Sheng dropped his briefcase, revealing a gun. He fired as McAllister instinctively recoiled in terror, grabbing his shoulder.

"Dive!" roared Bourne, racing in front of the aircraft in the wash of its lights, releasing a burst of gunfire from his machine pistol. "Roll, *roll!* If you can move, roll *away!"*

"You!" Sheng screamed, firing two rapid shots down into the fallen undersecretary of State, then raising his weapon and repeatedly pulling the trigger, aiming at the zigzagging man from Medusa running toward him.

"For *Echo!"* shouted Bourne at the top of his lungs. "For the people you hacked to death! For the teacher on a rope you butchered! For the woman that you couldn't stop—oh, *Christ!* For those two brothers, but mainly for *Echo,* you *bastard!"* A short burst exploded from the machine pistol—then no *more,* and no amount of pressure on the trigger could activate it! It was jammed! *Jammed!* Sheng knew it; he leveled his weapon carefully as Jason threw the gun down, pounding toward the killer. Sheng fired; Delta instinctively pivoted to his right, spinning in midair as he pulled his knife from his belt, then planted his foot on the ground, reversing direction, and abruptly lunged toward Sheng. The knife found its mark and the man from Medusa ripped open the fanatic's chest. The actual killer of hundreds and would-be killer of millions was dead.

His hearing had been suspended; it wasn't now. The patrol had raced out of the woods, bursts from machine guns filling the night and the field. . . . Other bursts came from beyond the helicopter—Wong had opened the attaché case and found what he needed. Two soldiers of the patrol fell; the remaining four dropped to the ground; one crawled back into the woods—he was shouting. The *radio!* He was reaching other men, other backups! How far away were they? How *near?*

Priorities! Bourne raced behind the aircraft and over to Wong, who was crouched by a tree at the edge of the woods. "There's another one of those in there!" he whispered. *"Give* it to me!"

"Conserve your ammunition," said Wong. "There's not much more."

"I know that. Stay here and pin them down as best you can but keep your fire low to the ground."

"Where are you going, sir?"

"Circling back through the trees."

"That's what the Frenchman would have ordered me to do."

"He was right. He was always right." Jason dashed deeper into the woods with the bloody knife in his belt; his lungs were bursting, his legs straining, his eyes peering into the forest darkness. He threaded his way through the dense foliage as fast as he could, making as little noise as he could.

Two *snaps!* Thick twigs on the ground broken by having been stepped on! He saw the shrouded silhouette of a figure coming toward him and spun around the trunk of a tree. He knew who it was—the officer with the radio, the thoughtful, soft-spoken killer from the Beijing sanctuary, an experienced combat soldier: Take to the flanks and outflank. What he lacked was guerrilla training, and that lack would cost him his life. One did not step on thick objects in the forest.

The officer walked by, crouching. Jason sprang, his left arm encircling the man's neck, the gun in his hand slammed against the soldier's head, the knife once again doing its work. Bourne knelt down over the corpse, put his weapon in his belt, and took the officer's powerful machine gun. He found two additional clips of ammunition; the odds were better now. It was even possible they would get out alive. Was McAllister alive? Or had a frustrated bureaucrat's moment in the sun ended in perpetual darkness. *Priorities!*

He circled the field's curving border to the point where he had entered it. Wong's sporadic gunfire was keeping the three remaining men of Sheng's elite patrol where they were, afraid to move. Suddenly, something made him turn around—a hum in the distance, a bright fleck in his eye. It was *both!* The sound was that of a racing engine, the fleck a moving searchlight scanning the dark sky. Above the descending trees he could make out a vehicle—a truck—with a searchlight mounted on its van, operated by an experienced hand. The truck sped off the road, obscured now by the high grass; only the bright searchlight was visible, moving faster and faster toward the base of the hill barely two hundred yards below. Priorities. Move!

"Hold fire!" Bourne roared, lurching away from his position. The three officers spun around in place on the ground, their machine guns erupting, bullets spraying the space from which the voice had come.

The man from Medusa stepped out. It was over in seconds as the powerful weapon blew up the earth and those killers who would have killed him.

"Wong!" he shouted, running into the field. "Come *on!* With *me!"* Seconds later he reached the bodies of McAllister and Sheng—one still alive, one a corpse. Jason bent over the analyst, who was moving both arms, his right hand stretched out, trying desperately to reach something. "Mac, can you *hear* me?"

"The *file!"* whispered the undersecretary of State. "Get the *file!"*

"What—?" Bourne looked over at the body of Sheng

Chou Yang, and, in the dim wash of the moonlight, saw the last thing in the world he thought he would see. It was Sheng's black-bordered dossier, one of the most secret, most explosive documents on earth. "Jesus *Christ!*" said Jason softly, reaching for it. "Listen to me, analyst!" Bourne raised his voice as Wong joined them. "We have to move you, and it may hurt, but we haven't a choice!" He glanced up at Wong and continued, "There's another patrol on its way here and it's closing in. An emergency backup, and by my estimate they'll be here in less than two minutes. Grit your teeth, Mr. Undersecretary. We *move!*"

Together Jason and Wong carried McAllister toward the helicopter. Suddenly, Bourne cried out. "Christ, *wait* a minute! . . . *No*, go on—*you* carry him," he shouted to the conduit. "I have to go back!"

"*Why?*" whispered the undersecretary, in agony.

"What are you *doing*, sir?" cried Wong.

"Food for revisionist thought," shouted Jason enigmatically as he raced back to the body of Sheng Chou Yang. When he reached it, he bent down and shoved a flat object under the dead man's tunic. He rose and ran back to the aircraft as Wong was carefully, gently, placing McAllister across two of the backseats. Bourne leaped in the front, took out his knife and slashed the nylon cord that bound the pilot, then cut the cloth that gagged him. The pilot had a spasm of coughing and gasping; even before it subsided, Jason gave his orders.

"*Kai feiji ba!*" he shouted.

"You may speak English," the pilot gasped. "I am fluent. It was a requirement."

"*Airborne*, you son of a bitch! *Now!*"

The pilot snapped the switches and started the rotors as a swarm of soldiers, clearly visible in the helicopter's lights, broke into the field. The new patrol instantly saw the five dead men of Sheng's elite guard. The entire squad began firing at the slowly ascending aircraft.

"Get the hell *out* of here!" roared Jason.

"The armor on this equipment is Sheng's armor," said the pilot calmly. "Even the glass will withstand heavy fire. Where do we go?"

"Hong Kong!" shouted Bourne, astonished to see that

the pilot, now ascending rapidly, powerfully, turned to him, smiling.

"Surely, the generous Americans or the benevolent British will grant me asylum, sir? It is a dream from the spirits!"

"I'll be goddamned," said the man from Medusa as they reached the first layer of low-flying clouds.

"This was a most efficient idea, sir," said Wong from the shadows at the rear of the helicopter. "How did it occur to you?"

"It worked once before," said Jason, lighting a cigarette. "History—even recent history—usually repeats itself."

"Mr. Webb?" whispered McAllister.

"What is it, analyst? How are you feeling?"

"Never mind that. Why did you go back—back to Sheng?"

"To give him a farewell present. A bankbook. A confidential account in the Cayman Islands."

"*What?*"

"It won't do anybody any good. The names and the account numbers have been scissored out. But it'll be interesting to see how Peking reacts to its existence, won't it?"

38

Edward Newington McAllister, on crutches, limped into the once impressive study of the old house on Victoria Peak, its huge bay windows now covered with heavy plastic, the carnage all too apparent. Ambassador Raymond Havilland watched as the undersecretary of State threw the Sheng file on his desk.

"I believe this is something you lost," said the analyst, angling his crutches and settling down in the chair with difficulty.

"The doctors tell me that your wounds aren't critical," said the diplomat. "I'm pleased."

"You're *pleased?* Who the hell are *you* to be so royally pleased?"

"It's a manner of speaking—sounds arrogant, if you like—but I mean it. What you did was extraordinary, beyond anything I would have imagined."

"I'm sure of that." The undersecretary shifted his position, easing his wounded shoulder into the back of the chair. "Actually, I didn't do it. *He* did."

"You made it possible, Edward."

"I was out of my element—my territory, as it were. These people do things the rest of us only dream about, or fantasize, or watch on a screen, disbelieving every moment because it's so outrageously implausible."

"We wouldn't have such dreams, or fantasize, or stay mesmerized by invention, if the fundamentals weren't in the human experience. They do what they do best just as we do what we do best. To each his own territory, Mr. Undersecretary."

McAllister stared at Havilland, his look uncompromising. "How did it happen? How did they get the *file?*"

"Another kind of territory. A professional. Three young men were killed, quite horribly. An impenetrable safe was penetrated."

"Inexcusable!"

"Agreed," said Havilland, leaning forward, suddenly raising his voice. "Just as *your* actions were inexcusable! Who in God's name do you think you *are* to have done what you did? What *right* had you to take matters in your own hands—*inexperienced* hands? You've violated every oath you've ever taken in the service of your government! Dismissal is *inadequate!* Thirty years in prison would more suitably fit your crimes! Have you any idea what might have *happened?* A war that could plunge the Far East—the *world*—into *hell!*"

"I did what I did because I could do it. That's a lesson I learned from Jason Bourne, our Jason Bourne. Regardless, you have my resignation, Mr. Ambassador. Effective immediately—unless you're pressing charges."

"And let you *loose?*" Havilland collapsed back in his chair. "Don't be ridiculous. I've talked with the President and he agrees. You're going to be chairman of the National Security Council."

"Chairman—? I can't *handle* it!"

"With your own limousine and all kinds of other crap."

"I won't know what to say!"

"You know how to *think,* and I'll be at your side."

"Oh, my *God!*"

"Relax. Just evaluate. And tell those of us who speak what to say. That's where the real power is, you know. Not those who speak, but those who think."

"It's all so sudden, so—"

"So *deserved,* Mr. Undersecretary," interrupted the diplomat. "The mind is a marvelous thing. Let's never underestimate it. Incidentally, the doctor tells me Lin Wenzu will pull through. He's lost the use of his left arm, but he'll live. I'm sure you'll have a recommendation to forward to MI-Six, London. They'll respect it."

"Mr. and Mrs. Webb? Where are they?"

"In Hawaii, by now. With Dr. Panov and Mr. Conklin, of course. They don't think much of me, I'm afraid."

"Mr. Ambassador, you didn't give them much reason to."

"Perhaps not, but then that's not my job."

"I think I understand. Now."

"I hope your God has compassion for men like you and me, Edward. I should not care to meet Him if He doesn't."

"There's always forgiveness."

"Really? Then I should not care to know Him. He'd turn out to be a fraud."

"Why?"

"Because He unleashed upon the world a race of unthinking, bloodthirsty wolves who care not one whit about the tribe's survival, only their own. That's hardly a perfect God, is it?"

"He *is* perfect. We're the imperfect ones."

"Then it's only a game for Him. He puts His creations in place, and for His own amusement watches them blow themselves up. He watches us blow ourselves up."

"They're *our* explosives, Mr. Ambassador. We have free will."

"According to the Scriptures, however, it's all *His* will, isn't that so? Let *His* will be done."

"It's a gray area."

"Perfect! One day you might really be Secretary of State."

"I don't think so."

"Nor do I," agreed Havilland. "But in the meantime we do our jobs—keep the pieces in place, stop the world from destroying itself. Thank the spirits, as they say here in the East, for people like you and me, and Jason Bourne *and* David Webb. We push the hour of Armageddon always a day away. What happens when we're not here?"

Her long auburn hair fell over his face, her body pressed against his, her lips next to his lips. David opened his eyes and smiled. It was as though there had been no nightmare that had jarringly interrupted their lives, no outrage inflicted upon them that had brought them to the edge of an abyss that held horror and death. They were together, and the splendid comfort of that reality filled him with profound gratitude. It *was*, and that was enough— more than he ever thought possible.

He began to reconstruct the events of the past twenty-four hours and his smile widened, a brief laugh escaping from his throat. Things were never as they should be, never as one expected. He and Mo Panov had had far too much to drink on the flight from Hong Kong to Hawaii, while Alex Conklin had stayed with iced tea or club soda or whatever newly reformed drunks want others to know they're staying with—no lectures, just quiet martyrdom. Marie had held the eminent Dr. Panov's head while the noted psychiatrist threw up in the British military aircraft's suffocatingly small toilet, and had covered Mo with a blanket when he fell into a dead sleep. She had then gently but firmly rejected her husband's amorous advances, but had made up for those rejections when she and a sobered mate reached the hotel in Kahala. A splendid, delirious night of making love that adolescents dream of, washing away the terrors of the nightmare.

Alex? Yes, he remembered. Conklin had taken the first commercial flight out of Oahu to Los Angeles and Washington. "There are heads to break" was the way he had phrased it. "And I intend to break them." Alexander Conklin had a new mission in his fragmented life. It was called accountability.

Mo? Morris Panov? Scourge of the chicken-soup psychologists and the charlatans of his profession? He was next door in the adjoining room, no doubt nursing the most massive hangover of his life.

"You laughed," whispered Marie, her eyes closed, nestling her face into his throat. "What the hell is so funny?"

"You, me, us—everything."

"Your sense of humor positively *escapes* me. On the other hand, I think I hear a man named David."

"That's all you'll ever hear from now on."

There was a knock on the door, not the door to the hallway but the one to the adjoining room. Panov. Webb got out of bed, walked rapidly to the bathroom and grabbed a towel, whipping it around his naked waist. "Just a second, Mo!" he called out, going to the door.

Morris Panov, his face pale but composed, stood there with a suitcase in his hand. "May I enter the Temple of Eros?"

"You're there, friend."

"I should hope so. . . . Good afternoon, my dear," said the psychiatrist, addressing Marie in the bed, as he went to a chair by the glass door that led to the balcony overlooking the Hawaiian beach. "Don't fuss, don't prepare a meal, and if you get out of bed, don't worry. I'm a doctor. I think."

"How are you, Mo?" Marie sat up, pulling the sheet over her.

"Far better than I was three hours ago, but you wouldn't know anything about that. You're maddeningly sane."

"You were stretched, you had to let loose."

"If you charge a hundred dollars an hour, lovely lady, I'll mortgage my house and sign up for five years of therapy."

"I'd like that defined," said David, smiling and sitting down opposite Panov. "Why the suitcase?"

"I'm leaving. I have patients back in Washington and I like to think they may need me."

The silence was moving, as David and Marie looked at Morris Panov. "What do we say, Mo?" asked Webb. "How do we say it?"

"You don't say anything, I'll do the talking. Marie has been hurt, pained beyond normal endurance. But then her endurance is beyond normality and she can handle it. Perhaps outrageously, we expect as much from certain people. It's unfair, but that's the way it is."

"I had to survive, Mo," said Marie, looking at her husband. "I had to get him back. That's the way it *was.*"

"You, David. You've gone through a traumatizing experience, one that only you can deal with and you don't need any chicken-soup crap from me to face it. You are *you* now, not anybody else. Jason Bourne is gone. He can't come back. Build your life as David Webb—concentrate on Marie and David—that's all there is and all there should be. And if at any moment the anxieties come back —they probably won't, but I'd appreciate your manufacturing a few—call me and I'll take the next plane up to Maine. I love you both, and Marie's beef stew is outstanding."

Sundown, the brilliant orange circle settling on top of the western horizon, slowly disappearing into the Pacific. They walked along the beach, their hands gripped fiercely, their bodies touching—so natural, so right.

"What do you do when there's a part of you that you hate?" said Webb.

"Accept it," answered Marie. "We all have a dark side, David. We wish we could deny it, but we can't. It's there. Perhaps we can't exist without it. Yours is a legend called Jason Bourne, but that's all it is."

"I loathe him."

"He brought you back to me. That's all that matters."

ABOUT THE AUTHOR

ROBERT LUDLUM is the author of seventeen novels published in nineteen languages and twenty-three countries with worldwide sales in excess of one hundred sixty million copies. His works include *The Scarlatti Inheritance, The Osterman Weekend, The Matlock Paper, The Rhinemann Exchange, The Gemini Contenders, The Chancellor Manuscript, The Road to Gandolfo, The Holcroft Covenant, The Matarese Circle, The Bourne Identity, The Parsifal Mosaic, The Aquitaine Progression, The Bourne Supremacy, The Icarus Agenda, Trevayne, The Bourne Ultimatum*, and *The Road to Omaha*. He lives with his wife, Mary, in Florida.